One Thread Pulled

The Dance with Mr. Darcy

DIANA J. OAKS

ISBN: 1475149611
ISBN-13: 978-1475149616

Published by Createspace, an Amazon.com company
www.createspace.com

I dedicate this book to my angel of a mother,
who always told me that I should be a writer.
I wish I had listened sooner.

CONTENTS

ACKNOWLEDGMENTS

I begin with a deep curtsy in the general direction and in honor of that great lady, Jane Austen. Her work is the foundation upon which I built this story. These are her brilliant characters—I just took them from off the shelf and borrowed them for a bit.

I acknowledge, too, the support of my husband, who has agreed to dance the first set with me (though he rarely dances), and was the source of more than one line for Colonel Fitzwilliam in this tale.

Deepest gratitude goes also to the fine writers and gentle Janeites at DarcyandLizzy.com, who have encouraged, advised, and helped me navigate the waters of my first publication. Brenda, Katie, Stephanie, *et al.*—I am in your debt.

Chapter One

THE ASSEMBLY BALL

Ten thousand a year. The words hung in the air of the assembly room like ripe fruit on a low branch. Every eligible young lady at the ball appeared to share the notion that Mr. Bingley's tall, reserved friend was the most desirable man she had ever beheld—every young lady, that is, except Elizabeth Bennet.

Elizabeth had astutely observed a decidedly bored expression on the man's face when her family was introduced to Mr. Darcy. It seemed to Elizabeth that his look was an overt rejection of the friendly smiles bestowed upon him by all the women of her family. His pride was evident to Elizabeth from that moment, although it took the other occupants of the room half the night to realize that Mr. Darcy would not deign to dance with any of the local ladies, only with those from his own party, and even then with some reluctance.

Elizabeth found some amusement in observing the other young ladies discreetly pinching their cheeks and biting lips to bring color to their faces whenever they approached proximity to either Mr. Darcy or Mr. Bingley. The color in her own face came merely from dancing, as she was a popular partner. Elizabeth was, after several merry dances, obliged to sit down for two dances, due to the scarcity of gentlemen at the ball, although she politely claimed that it was to catch her breath.

It was during this time that she overheard a conversation between Mr. Bingley and Mr. Darcy. Mr. Bingley, who had been dancing nonstop, left the floor to persuade his friend to join him.

"Darcy," said Mr. Bingley, "I must have you dance. I hate to see you standing about by yourself in this stupid manner. You had much better dance."

"I certainly shall not. You know how I detest it, unless I am particularly acquainted with my partner. At such an assembly as this, it would be insupportable. Your sisters are engaged, and there is not another woman in the room whom it would not be a punishment to me to stand up with."

"I would not be so fastidious as you are," cried Bingley, "for a kingdom! Upon my honor, I never met with so many pleasant girls in my life, as I have this evening; and there are several of them, you see, uncommonly pretty. My partner, Miss Jane Bennet is an angel, and I am most insistent that you select a partner for the next dance."

Taking a side-glance at the men, Elizabeth saw Mr. Bingley looking at her, which caused her some alarm. She had no desire to be engaged in the next dance with the arrogant Mr. Darcy, particularly not under compulsion. It was evident that Bingley was going to suggest it to his friend. She abruptly rose from her seat and crossed the room to join her friend Charlotte Lucas who was standing near the refreshments. She acquired a drink from the table and turned to speak to Charlotte.

"Well, Lizzy," said Charlotte, "I believe you may have lost your opportunity to dance with the illustrious Mr. Darcy. He watched you cross the room just now most attentively, as did Mr. Bingley."

"I was thirsty." Elizabeth replied. "And you are quite mistaken. Mr. Darcy detests dancing. I heard him say so himself. He shall not be prevailed upon, that is certain."

"Lizzy, they are speaking of you still. I am sure of it." Charlotte murmured as she glanced away from the handsome figures lest the gentlemen assume the same of the two friends.

Elizabeth was less discrete as she looked back from whence she came, laughing. "If they are as you say, dear Charlotte, it cannot be a pleasant conversation. See how cross Mr. Darcy is. And Mr. Bingley, his face is the color of a beet. No, I think they must be speaking of hunting or livestock or similar vexations, for I have done nothing to inspire such aggravation as they reveal." As she spoke, her eyes met with those of Mr. Darcy, and she could not withhold a winsome smile at his expense, although she turned to speak to Charlotte as it lit upon her lips, leaving him to ponder on the source of her amusement.

The rest of the evening was pleasant enough for Elizabeth, who was once again called upon as a partner by Mr. Bingley. She remained on the floor for the rest of the evening and did not spare one more thought to the wealthy but pompous Mr. Darcy.

Mrs. Bennet's wrap was still upon her shoulders in the entryway when she began to regale the events of the evening to Mr. Bennet. The music, the refreshments, the dances, the finery, the lace, she carried on, working herself into near hysteria over every detail.

"Oh! and Mr. Bingley!" she exclaimed, just as Mr. Bennet thought she had finished. "I have saved the best part for last, Mr. Bennet, for Mr. Bingley was quite taken with Jane, as were all the young men. Mr. Bingley danced two dances with Jane, a great compliment I am sure. He has five-thousand a year, you know." A contented sigh escaped her lips, as though she had herself been the belle. "Lizzy danced too, although not nearly so much as Jane!"

Elizabeth smiled at her father, appreciative of the indulgence he gave his wife in listening to her carry on, for it seemed to sooth her mother's pent-up emotions to pour them out upon her husband, and there would be no rest for anyone until she had done so.

"Oh!" Mrs. Bennet exclaimed, once again curtailing a false finish. "I almost forgot to mention that horrible Mr. Darcy, who is hardly worth mentioning, but I must for convention's sake."

"Mr. Darcy?" Mr. Bennet's interest was piqued merely by his wife's lack of enthusiasm for the man.

"Mr. Darcy is a proud, disagreeable man, who refused to stand up with any of your daughters and wandered about the room looking for all the world as the lord of a kingdom. He may have ten-thousand a year, but such an odious temperament could not be borne. No, Mr. Bingley may call him friend, but he is not worthy of our attention." Mrs. Bennet sniffed loudly, as if to punctuate her declaration.

"Oh, but he is handsome," Lydia proclaimed, "although not nearly so handsome nor jolly as the officers in their regimentals!"

"Nor so handsome as Mr. Bingley, I daresay!" Mrs. Bennet added. "He is all that is happy and engaging in a young man. I do hope we shall entertain him very soon at Longbourn."

Jane, who had been listening with care, graced her mother with an encouraging smile; in this, Jane harbored the same hope as her mother.

Chapter Two

REFLECTIONS ON THE BALL

"Oh, Lizzy!" Jane exclaimed with a sigh when the two sisters were finally alone in their bedchamber that night. "Mr. Bingley is all I could ever hope for in a man. He is amiable, to be sure, and handsome, and his manners were very pleasing, do you not think?"

"Why yes," Elizabeth smiled at her sister, "most pleasing, indeed, especially when he bestowed the honor of a second dance on my sister."

"I cannot think of why he would pay such attention to me, Lizzy."

"Jane, he was taken with you. You, of all the ladies in the room captured his favor the moment he set eyes on you."

"His friend Mr. Darcy seemed to favor no one." Jane frowned. "Perhaps he was ill."

Elizabeth laughed with great delight at her sister's comment. "Perhaps he saw nothing in the room that pleased him is more like it. He detests dancing and will only do it with those he is already acquainted with. It is odd, do you not think, to be so reserved at a ball? Why would a man attend if he does not enjoy it?"

"Perhaps he enjoys the music or conversation." Jane offered.

"The music, perhaps, but his conversation with anyone but his friends was practically non-existent. It may be that he enjoys eavesdropping on the conversation of others." Elizabeth giggled.

"Lizzy! You do not know the man," censured Jane. "Perhaps he is shy."

"Shy? I daresay that is not it. Indeed, it was conceit that placed us all beneath his notice."

"But, Lizzy, you did capture his notice—when you were in conversation with Charlotte. Had the ball lasted but a bit longer, or had you offered any encouragement, he may well have engaged you for a dance. You must not think so meanly of him, for he is Mr. Bingley's friend, and I will not be able to bear it if you dislike him."

"I will be as polite as I can, for your sake, should we ever encounter the gentleman again. However, I think it is unlikely that we *shall* ever see him. Mr. Darcy's distaste for the assembly was so complete that I imagine he will quit the county before daybreak!"

The next morning, as she was always wont to do after a ball, Mrs. Bennet's friend Lady Lucas and all her children arrived at Longbourn, eager to discuss the events of the prior evening with Mrs. Bennet.

"Charlotte, you began the evening well, did you not? I recall that you were Mr. Bingley's first partner of the evening." Mrs. Bennet smiled charmingly at her friend's eldest daughter, who, having been deemed by the town a spinster at the age of seven and twenty, was no threat to her girls.

"It is true," began Charlotte, "but I believe that his second partner captivated him the rest of the evening."

"His second ... oh, you mean Jane!" Mrs. Bennet took the opening. "He did dance twice with her, and I heard of a conversation he had with Mr. Robinson where Mr. Bingley described my Jane as the most beautiful girl in the room. He did her great honor in making such a declaration, to be sure."

"Yes," nodded Mrs. Lucas, "to be so singled out by a man of such distinction does credit to your Jane. He also danced once with your Eliza, I believe."

Mrs. Bennet beamed, nodding and fanning herself with a handkerchief.

"I would have liked to see Eliza dance with Mr. Darcy." Charlotte interjected. "Had she not walked away from him at an inopportune moment, I am sure he would have engaged her."

"Mr. Darcy!" Mrs. Bennet fumed. "Well then, for once, my Lizzy had some sense. I am glad to hear it. A man such as that should be set down from time to time to check his pride, if nothing else. If he ever does ask you to dance, Lizzy, you have my leave to set him down again."

"It is unlikely that he will ever ask me to dance, Mama. His pride will not permit it." Elizabeth winked at Charlotte with a smile.

"His pride," said Charlotte, "does not offend me because there is an excuse for it. It is not surprising that so very fine a young man, with family, fortune, everything in his favor, should think highly of himself. I say that he has a right to be proud."

"That is very true." Elizabeth stopped to consider. "His prideful behavior served only to isolate his own person from the gaiety of the ball, and so it is only he who suffered for it. It is not as if any of us sustained an injury to our own pride merely by proximity to his, for we laughed at his ridiculous manner all evening. His pride gave us great sport, so one cannot hold it entirely against him."

"Well, when you say it that way, Lizzy, it would hardly be civil to forbear." Mrs. Bennet sniffed resentfully. "Let us forgive him and be done with it." She waved her handkerchief dismissively and, much to Lydia's joy, turned the conversation to talk of the officers,

Conversation at another house in the neighborhood also turned upon the assembly, for the ladies of Netherfield were eager to share their criticisms with the household. The music was poorly executed, the refreshments not fit for consumption. The assembly room was not ventilated and was too small for proper dancing anyway. Worst of all was the sad group of country folk who had not a farthing's worth of fashion or social grace among them.

Mr. Darcy inexplicably enjoyed the complaining of Miss Bingley and Mrs. Hurst. He was in a foul mood, and the two sisters were skillfully airing his own observations, which amused him.

"Sir William Lucas! Did you hear that the bumbling fool has achieved knighthood? I cannot believe they actually allow one such as him entrance at court." Caroline simpered.

"Perhaps he is the jester." Mrs. Hurst added with a smirk.

"He was a gracious host...," Mr. Bingley attempted to interject.

"And the Bennets. How tedious they were." Caroline rolled her eyes dramatically. "With a mother such as they have, it is a wonder those girls can dress themselves."

"Oh Caroline, be realistic." Mrs. Hurst laughed, "They must have a servant to dress them!"

"The Bennet ladies looked lovely!" Bingley insisted. "And I have never met with pleasanter persons or prettier girls in all my life!"

"Miss Jane Bennet is, I grant you, a sweet girl," Caroline conceded, "and I would not object to knowing her better."

"And what of Eliza Bennet?" Mrs. Hurst queried. "Mr. Darcy, what is your opinion? Was she as pleasant and pretty as our brother claims?"

"Do not ask him such a question, Louisa," said Charles impatiently. "He found her barely tolerable. She was not handsome enough even to tempt him to dance, although had I not met her sister Jane first, I may have had an eye for Eliza myself."

"Barely tolerable?" Caroline raised a brow. "I too was surprised to hear her called a beauty, but when in the country, I suppose, there is none to compare. Were there any ladies you found pleasing?"

"Besides the two of you, Miss Jane Bennet was the only beautiful girl in the room," Darcy declared, "although I did not find Miss Elizabeth Bennet to be exactly plain. Were her features more symmetrical or finer in form, she would be pretty enough, but as they are not, I daresay she is tolerable to look at. As for whether she is pleasant, I am not one to say, although she did appear to have many friends at the ball."

"She is charming, Darcy. You must have seen it," Bingley said eagerly. "What do you say to our calling upon the Bennet house this very day?"

"Not today, Bingley," Darcy stalled. "Definitely not today."

Chapter Three

OH LITTLE TOWN OF MERYTON

The ladies of Longbourn soon waited upon those of Netherfield. The visit was returned in due form. Jane Bennet's gentle nature and pleasing manners quickly won the approval of Miss Bingley and Mrs. Hurst, and they found Elizabeth's quick wit entertaining enough. Having expressed a desire to get to know the eldest Bennet girls better, they made it clear with little subtlety that only the two of them were welcome. A series of calls ensued.

Their reception pleased Jane immensely, for it increased the occasions when she could see their brother without appearing too forward. Jane was the model of decorum, and although she felt herself to be rapidly falling in love with Mr. Bingley, she exercised demure restraint in the outward demonstration of her feelings for him, lest she seem presumptuous to Mr. Bingley before she was certain of his affections.

Elizabeth was less impressed with Miss Bingley and Mrs. Hurst. The looks shared between them when they thought no one was looking were forgivable; but their probing questions designed to bait Jane into revealing information they obviously considered an embarrassment goaded Elizabeth to no end. Elizabeth tried to warn her sister, who would hear none of it. "I am sure that is not what they meant, Lizzy," said Jane. "They are just making conversation."

"But, Jane," Lizzy replied, "what is the purpose of inquiring after the number of cows in our barn or asking which of the Meryton shops we patronize when, indeed, they would not lower themselves to cross the threshold of any establishment in our little town! What could they mean by it?"

"They are used to London, Lizzy, where the shops are very fine. Their curiosity does them credit," Jane replied.

"Their questions are impertinent!" Lizzy exclaimed, "Upon my word, you cannot be insensible of it."

"But, Lizzy," Jane blushed, "they are Mr. Bingley's sisters. They must see my regard for their brother and wish to prove it. It is not so very bad, and I am sure they mean well."

"Oh yes, it is all to do with their brother." Lizzy smiled, her eyes twinkling with delight. "When Mr. Bingley and Mr. Darcy joined us in the drawing room at Netherfield yesterday, you became indifferent to anything or anyone else, I daresay."

"Was I that obvious, Lizzy?" Jane paled.

"Only to your sister." Lizzy assured her. "I diverted the ladies' attention away from you as best I could with the story of Sarah Plimpton and that unfortunate incident with the gooseberry jam."

"That must have been hard on poor Mr. Darcy to be so left out of the conversation."

"Oh, but he was not left out, Jane. He may have been gazing out the window, looking as bored as a lord in Parliament, but he heard the conversation well enough; for I detected a hint of a smile as I concluded the story, and he made reference to it a few minutes later when he suggested gooseberry tarts for tea."

"Let us hope Mr. Darcy is still smiling tonight, then, at Lucas Lodge. I believe it distresses Mr. Bingley a great deal when his friend is in a temper." Jane sighed.

"Then I will tell amusing stories to all of our friends tonight, and Mr. Darcy may eavesdrop and be entertained if he likes." Lizzy laughed at the idea. "Then Mr. Bingley will be content, and you will be satisfied."

That night at Lucas Lodge, Elizabeth was so occupied in observing Mr. Bingley's attentions to her sister that she forgot her promise to capture Mr. Darcy's attention altogether. The joy she felt to see her sister with such a companion as Mr. Bingley could not be restrained, which lit her own countenance in such an animated way that even her friends noticed it, as did Mr. Darcy—for he found her demeanor curiously appealing. He wandered, not aimlessly, about the large room. He edged, nonchalantly, close to where Elizabeth was standing to remain within earshot of her exchanges.

Her voice, he decided, was pleasant to hear, and her laugh, even more so. The astuteness of her opinions struck him, and the witty banter she so readily called up was refreshing and lively. After trailing Elizabeth around the room for over an hour this way, Mr. Darcy ventured to look more directly at her and immediately wondered that he had not previously noticed the intelligence in her dark eyes or the way that they sparkled as she spoke.

On the other side of the room, Mary Bennet began to play a jig, and a number of enthusiastic partners, including Jane and Mr. Bingley, lined up to dance. One of the officers from the militia invited Elizabeth to join him on the floor, which she gladly agreed to do. Mr. Darcy watched her walk away, choosing to observe her dance from where he stood contemplating the sight. Her steps were sprightly as she danced effortlessly and perfectly. Her figure, he noted, was not so ordinary as he had first thought, for it was light and pleasing to the eye. Barely a flicker of emotion crossed his face when the first pang of jealousy struck, but feel it he did, with some astonishment. When the dance had ended, Elizabeth took a seat in the corner next to her friend Charlotte, eager to discuss the events of the evening so far.

"See how happy Jane is!" Elizabeth beamed. "When they have not been dancing, she and Mr. Bingley have been conversing. Jane would be mortified if she realized how *very* unsocial they have been. We must not tell her, for she is very near to being in love with Mr. Bingley."

"She is in love?" Charlotte puzzled. "It is clear that she prefers Mr. Bingley to the others, but she is hardly as demonstrative as one who is in love. If love is engraved in her heart, then she must make her claim quickly; for Mr. Bingley is an eligible man and sure to have many admirers. She should show him more affection, and quickly, before he becomes discouraged!"

"Make her claim!" Elizabeth laughed. "Her regard for him is evident, and it is for Mr. Bingley to make an offer to her, not Jane to make an offering of herself. No, Jane is too proper to declare herself before she is assured of Mr. Bingley's intentions."

"Only a fool, a blackguard or a selfishly conceited man would make a proposal not knowing if the love is requited, Lizzy. Mr. Bingley is none of those things." Charlotte glanced across the room.

"Speaking of conceited men, there is Mr. Darcy, looking at you again. He looks at you a great deal, Lizzy."

"I think perhaps he is playing at a game that I have not heard of." Elizabeth laughed, looking directly at him. "Mr. Darcy thinks that he is very clever, sidling up behind me to listen to my conversations and staring at me from across the room. I think that his object is to intimidate me, but that is not easily done when I am resolved against it. No, he had better go and play his game elsewhere, for he has met his match with me!"

"He is a man of great consequence, my dear Eliza," Charlotte lectured. "You should not take his attentions lightly."

"He is also a man of grave seriousness, Charlotte; since, knowing how much I dearly love to laugh, my only defense is to take his so-called attentions lightly. Shall I say something scandalous the next time he stands near?"

"Hush, Lizzy, he is close by," Charlotte whispered with a wave of her finger indicating his position.

Elizabeth, who had chosen the corner thinking it safe, had failed to account for the camouflage of a nearby pillar and realized with a start that Mr. Darcy had repositioned himself at some point in their conversation. As the two women stopped talking, he turned and addressed Elizabeth, who rose from her seat on his approach.

"Miss Bennet." He bowed slightly.

"Mr. Darcy." Elizabeth responded with a decidedly not-intimidated smile.

"I would speak to you ... in private." Mr. Darcy's tone left no option but for Elizabeth to agree. She indicated her consent with a nod of her head, and he motioned toward a small alcove off the main room, still in plain sight of all, although affording a degree of privacy.

Chapter Four

A CONVERSATION IN PRIVATE

Although Mr. Darcy's manner in approaching her had defied refusal, walking across the room at his side, Elizabeth thought of a half-dozen reasons that she should have declined. She slowed her footsteps, delaying the inevitable. What purpose could he have in seeking a private audience? She snuck a furtive glance upward in hopes of discerning his frame of mind. In this, she was unsuccessful, for his face was as stone. She glanced back at Charlotte, who shrugged helplessly. She spotted Jane and Mr. Bingley in another direction, deep in conversation and unaware of anyone else in the room. Her mother, she saw, was clearly aware that her daughter appeared to be in confidence with the eligible Mr. Darcy, and Elizabeth winced at the shrill voice that pierced the din of conversation and music with the obvious reference to "ten-thousand a year" echoing in the large room.

Reaching the alcove, Elizabeth discreetly moved to the side of the recess with the clearest view of the room, standing where there would be no question of any impropriety in their meeting. She turned to Mr. Darcy expectantly, for although she held no aspirations to such a conversation, her curiosity was nonetheless provoked by his invitation.

Mr. Darcy stood facing the room, watching the small group dancing, as though he had moved merely to gain a better vantage point. His stance was regal and erect as he observed the room for a full minute before he spoke to Elizabeth, and when he did, he did not face her, but spoke straight ahead.

"You are well tonight, Miss Bennet?" He asked coolly.

"Yes, thank you." Elizabeth replied graciously, as she also turned to face the room.

"I see that your family is all in attendance tonight except your father. Is Mr. Bennet well?" His tone was warmer.

"Yes, quite well." Elizabeth smiled as she answered, although he could not see it.

"Your sister—the youngest one—may I inquire as to her age?" Mr. Darcy nodded to where Lydia was dancing.

Elizabeth reddened and sighed, "Lydia is not yet sixteen."

Mr. Darcy looked at Elizabeth, and noting the sudden color in her face found secret delight in it. A smile tugged at the corner of his mouth, which he quickly suppressed. "I have a sister about that same age."

At this disclosure, Elizabeth looked at him with some surprise, having imagined him an only child. "Oh." She pictured Mr. Darcy coping with similar vexations to those Lydia had imposed on her family, an idea she found peculiarly amusing. "Is she out in company?"

"No." Darcy stiffened slightly. "Miss Bennet, I seek your counsel on a matter regarding my sister." He hesitated, waiting for her response, but when none ensued, he proceeded. "It is my custom to acquire a keepsake for Georgiana from each location I visit. This task was simple when she was young. A wooden toy or china doll pleased her then. Would you have a suggestion on a gift, fit for a young lady, which may be found in Hertfordshire?"

Elizabeth frowned slightly with consternation. The fineness of his waistcoat, the fancy silk cravat he wore, indeed everything about him signaled his high standards of quality and taste. "There is nothing, sir, so fine as may be found in London...."

"To make my purchase in London would defeat the purpose of our tradition. Have you nothing to recommend?" Darcy pressed.

Elizabeth thought for a moment. "There is a fan maker who resides in Meryton. He is a member of the guild, and his best fans are usually sold in the London shops. Perhaps a lovely, ornate fan would suit your sister's tastes." Elizabeth offered, adding, "There is also a widow who lives in a small cottage on the road to Meryton. She makes exquisitely embroidered shawls to provide an income for herself. Her workmanship is very fine indeed."

Mr. Darcy nodded. "And which of these gifts would most suit your own sister?"

"The fan," Elizabeth said, glancing at Lydia, whose flirtations with the officers were so overt as to be an embarrassment, "although I would give her the shawl."

Darcy's brow furrowed. "Why would you choose the one least suited?"

The truth, in fact, was that a shawl is rarely used as a flirtation device, while the art of fan beguilement was one her sister was already practicing in the mirror with an everyday fan at home. Elizabeth could not reveal this to Mr. Darcy, however. "The days are colder now, Mr. Darcy. A shawl, she could use today. A fan would not serve until next summer." Elizabeth hesitated, bothered by the question hovering in her mind. "May I inquire as to the reason our discussion required privacy?"

Elizabeth was not the only one who was to conceal the truth now, for although Mr. Darcy prided himself on being honest to a fault, he would not admit, even to himself, that his motivation was, in fact, simply to interact with Elizabeth, unfettered by demands on her attention outside himself. He pretended no design on her. She was too poor, of too mean a position in society to warrant such a consideration, yet his curiosity about her had overpowered his reserve and driven him to seek her out in conversation.

After listening to her converse with her numerous friends in the course of the evening, he concluded that they all regarded her articulate opinions highly, and she shared them freely. He found her knowledgeable and surprisingly practical for a female. With this information, he carefully selected a topic that could not offend.

"The reason?" Mr. Darcy stammered, for he had not expected such a challenge. "Surely it is obvious."

"No, Mr. Darcy, indeed it is not. Should we have held this conversation publicly, the suggestions of my friends would have resulted in more excellent options for your pursuit. I fear you have selected your consultant poorly and limited your alternatives in so doing." The last sentence she said gaily, with a laugh.

"Miss Bennet, I am perfectly satisfied with the alternatives you have presented. I did not wish for Miss Bingley or her sister to be party to, or indeed to hear any word of our conversation, for they would insist upon injecting themselves into my acquisition, and I prefer to make the selection myself. I hope my questions have not been an imposition...."

"Oh, no." Elizabeth assured him, inwardly flattered that in spite of his obvious pride and preference for quality society, it was *her* opinion he had sought. "It just seemed odd, that is all. I will not disclose the details of your errand to anyone. You may count upon my discretion. I do hope your sister appreciates your gift."

At this, Mr. Darcy was emboldened and turned to look directly into Elizabeth's sparkling, dark eyes. They smiled back at him with a warmth and intelligence such as he had never seen and for several seconds his mind simply stopped working, so lost was he in the spell of those eyes, thickly fringed in long, lush lashes, twinkling with the reflected candlelight of the room. After a moment, she flushed and averted her eyes away, unsure as to what was happening between them.

"I am certain that she will, Miss Bennet." He finally muttered. "Thank you for your advice." He placed his hand gently beneath her elbow and guided her back into the room, bringing her within a few steps of Charlotte Lucas before he disengaged and walked away.

Elizabeth joined her friend, who immediately asked, "What did the elegant Mr. Darcy want of you, Eliza? You look quite out of sorts."

Elizabeth shook her head. "It was nothing really, a trifle." She watched his back as the man gracefully walked toward Jane and Mr. Bingley. "There really is nothing to tell." Elizabeth shivered, which brought her out of the dazed state that had overtaken her.

"Lizzy, I saw the way he looked at you just now ... and you at him. Is he to call on you? Are you to dance?" Charlotte was too observant to let the moment pass unchallenged.

"I really cannot discuss it." Elizabeth replied. "I gave him my word."

"You will have to discuss it, I fear, for your mother also witnessed your little tête-à-tête with great interest, and you know her too well to doubt that she will press you." Charlotte warned.

"Oh, I can manage my mama, Charlotte. I will just divert her attention back to Jane and Mr. Bingley, and we shall not hear the end of that subject for an hour." Elizabeth laughed, glancing at where Jane was now engaged in conversation with Caroline Bingley.

Shortly afterward, Mr. Bingley and his sisters, along with Mr. Darcy said goodnight and left the party at Lucas Lodge.

Elizabeth joined Jane, who gushed with excitement. "I have been invited by Caroline to join her and Louisa to dine at Netherfield tomorrow. She expressed a wish to know me better."

Elizabeth, who had always joined her sister in their excursions to Netherfield, did not say anything about her exclusion from the invitation. "Then you shall see Mr. Bingley tomorrow as well?"

"No, Caroline said that the men were to go hunting tomorrow." Jane responded.

Mrs. Bennet, standing a few feet away exclaimed, "What? That will not do!"

"It must do, Mother, for I am certain to dine again at Netherfield." Jane smiled reassuringly at her mother. "If Caroline and Louisa wish to know me better, it is a great compliment."

"Oh, yes, that it is!" Mrs. Bennet crowed. "It is a compliment to your beauty, your social grace and manners. You should learn from your sister, Lizzy, for if you were more like her, you would be invited as well, but your impertinent ways have caught up with you now, can you not see?"

"Yes, Mama, but do not despair. I shall survive the humiliation." Elizabeth smiled at Jane. "A compliment to my sister is all I need to be happy."

Chapter Five

YOU MUST TAKE A HORSE

"Jane!" The cry came moments past dawn. Mrs. Bennet was usually still abed as the sun found its place in the sky, but today, her spot in the bed was already cold. "Jane! You must be about dear girl, quickly, quickly!"

Jane, still in her dressing gown, with the creases in her cheek not yet faded, located her mother on the stairs. "What is it, Mama?"

"Jane dearest, you are to go to Netherfield today!" Mrs. Bennet cried.

"Yes, Mama, I know." Jane blushed prettily. "But that is not until much later in the day. They have invited me to dine, and it would not do for me to appear while their breakfast is still upon the sideboard."

"Of course not. That is pure nonsense." Mrs. Bennet huffed. "But you must take extra care today to look especially nice and as beautiful as you are, it will take the better part of the morning to mark an improvement."

"But why, Mama? I am to dine with Caroline and Louisa, for they are alone today in the house, and begged me to come and let them entertain so they would not be in danger of hating each other. I cannot see how improving my appearance will have any bearing on it."

"But the men, they are hunting today, are they not?"

"Yes." Jane nodded.

"Well, can you not see it is going to rain? That will drive them back to the house, to be sure, but you must be there when they return.

Then you will thank me for the extra care that went into your appearance! Mr. Bingley will see an angel in his drawing room when he arrives. Ooooooh!" With her last syllable, Mrs. Bennet's eyes glazed over slightly, as if the vision of Jane at Netherfield was appearing before her very eyes.

"Can I take the carriage, Papa?" Jane asked as her father crossed the hallway at the bottom of the stairs.

"Jane, no!" Mrs. Bennet interrupted. "You will take the horse. It must be upon horseback that you go, for the carriage will not do."

"But you said it was to rain...." Jane looked at her mother strangely.

"If it were not for me, you girls would never marry!" Mrs. Bennet declared. "You must go on horseback to increase your chance of encountering the hunting party on your way. They will be nowhere near the road, so you must take the shorter route through the woods. I daresay Mr. Bingley will see what a fine figure you are upon the horse and quit the hunt altogether."

"Mama, I do not think that plan is safe." Elizabeth, who stood upon the landing interjected. "They could accidentally shoot Jane."

"Nonsense!" Mrs. Bennet shrieked. "They are shooting at birds, not at women on horseback. You know nothing, Lizzy, and it is nothing to do with you."

"If I take the horse, how am I to return if it is raining?" Jane asked softly.

"You are beginning to see my plan, you clever girl!" Mrs. Bennet said. "They will be forced to keep you for the night, and then you shall break your fast with Mr. Bingley in the morning!"

"The Bingleys have a carriage, Mama." Elizabeth could not hold her tongue. "What makes you suppose they would not transport Jane home themselves?"

"Because," Mrs. Bennet looked at Elizabeth as if she were stupid, "Mr. Bingley will see the opportunity to keep her there, and how can he resist this temptation, when such beauty is before him?"

Jane looked mortified. "Will not Mr. Bingley see this plotting as treacherous?"

"Treacherous!" Mrs. Bennet snorted. "Miss Bingley invited *you*. There can be no deceit in accepting her kind offer. If they ask why you did not come in the carriage, you must tell them that only one horse could be spared from the fields. It is a matter easily explained. Treachery indeed! Now go and make ready, Jane."

"Mama, this is folly." Elizabeth tried to reason.

"Hush, child, I will hear nothing more of the matter. It is settled." Mrs. Bennet sniffed indignantly at her daughter. "I know what is best here, for I am your elder by many a year. I daresay when you are my age, you will do the same for your own daughters. Until then, you can have nothing more to say."

ᘐ

Elizabeth watched from the window as Jane rode away. She had to acknowledge to herself that even though the mount was merely a farm horse, Jane's seat upon it was so elegant and graceful that she was indeed a lovely vision.

Jane's thoughts as she rode along were full of Mr. Bingley. Although it was only his sisters she was to see, anything connected with Charles (as she permitted herself to think of him) was a pleasure worth seeking. Since she hoped to someday be related to Miss Bingley and Mrs. Hurst, this visit alone with them was a welcome opportunity to cement the friendship.

She noted, with unease, the gathering storm clouds in the distance but calculated that she would arrive at Netherfield before they were overhead; so she permitted herself to daydream, only guiding the horse in the general direction of the Netherfield estate.

She was within half a mile of the house and able to see the chimneys above the trees when, suddenly, a brace of pheasants rose noisily from a small pond ahead of her, followed within seconds by several loud gunshots. She saw no birds fall, for the sudden thunderous sound spooked the mare and she found her full attentions focused on her efforts to stay in the saddle. She clung to the reins, with insufficient leverage to pull on them. Finally losing her seat, she found herself upon the ground, the sound of the horse's hoofs fading in the distance.

Mr. Darcy saw the riderless beast first, barreling past the group. He whistled loudly, and the horse slowed to a stop as the hunting group all turned together to see what was the commotion. "Bingley!" he shouted. "It has a side-saddle!" Darcy raced to where the horse stood, its sides heaving and its eyes wide with alarm. "Settle down, girl." He whispered as he approached. He was comfortable with horses, so they were generally responsive to him as well, and the sweet white mare was no exception. "Who was your rider?" he asked, and as if in answer, the horse looked in the direction she had come from, shaking her head as she took one step in that direction. Darcy stopped to get his bearings and said to Mr. Bingley, "This horse has come from Longbourn."

Mr. Bingley paled and began to run down the path toward the Bennet estate. He did not go far before he found Jane. She was still on the ground, although she was attempting to sit up, a trickle of blood trailing down her forehead. "Miss Bennet!" He looked at her desperately then fell to the ground on his knees beside her. "Do not move! Are you well? What has happened?"

Jane looked at Mr. Bingley as if in a trance. "My horse...," she began, "... there were pheasants ... I think I have fallen." She peered at him. "Mr. Bingley, do you have a brother?"

Charles, taken aback by the question looked mystified as he shook his head and denied it with a simple "No."

"But there are two of you, and each is as handsome as the other." Jane looked back and forth in agitated confusion. "I fear I am not well. The ground here is in constant motion, and if it does not stop its wretched spinning, I am going to be ill." She closed her eyes and abruptly lay back down in the grass.

"Bingley." Charles turned at the sound of Darcy's voice to find Mr. Darcy and the rest of the hunting party gathered in a half-circle behind him. "We must get Miss Bennet to the house immediately, before the rain strikes. We must take care, since we do not know the extent of her injuries." Darcy removed his coat, and instructing the stable hands who had accompanied them to go and find some long branches, they constructed a makeshift stretcher for Jane while Mr. Bingley tended to Jane's forehead with his handkerchief. Mr. Darcy, Mr. Bingley, Mr. Hurst and one of the hands carried her while the other hands ran ahead to alert the house.

Chapter Six

SUMMONED TO NETHERFIELD

The Bennet family, but for Jane, had all gathered for tea when the sound of horse hoofs pounding down the drive caused them to suspend their conversation in order to listen more carefully. The steady rain that was falling muffled the sound, but there was no mistaking the neigh of the horse as the rider reined to an abrupt halt. The pounding at the door roused them from their momentary trance, and they collectively jumped up to make their way to the door, which Mrs. Hill had opened to reveal a rain-soaked man in a black cape. Mr. Bennet worked his way past his wife and daughters to accept the letter and invited the man to wait for a response.

He opened the letter, raising it high; the shadows of the women who had gathered around him blocked his light. With a loud "Ahem," he began reading the missive silently. He turned to the messenger and said, "Tell them we will come at once." With a silent nod, the man was gone. The door slammed behind him, the sound of the hooves fading quickly as the man sped away.

Fear filled the eyes of Mrs. Bennet as she cried out. "What? What has happened? Is it my sister?"

Mr. Bennet called for Mr. Hill, ordering the carriage to be brought to the front of the house with haste. He then turned to his wife. "Fanny, please sit down." He took her by the hand and guided her to her chair, and when she was properly settled, he began, his countenance grave. "Jane," he began slowly, "has suffered a fall."

Mrs. Bennet began to wail. "My Jane! Oh no, my Jane! What is to be done, oh, what is to be done?"

"She was taken to Netherfield," Mr. Bennet continued, "and is in the care of Mr. Jones, the apothecary."

Mrs. Bennet was suddenly silent, and with a sniffle, she asked softly, "Is it very bad?"

Mr. Bennet considered his words carefully, for he knew that should he phrase the answer badly, his wife's nervous maladies would create havoc at Longbourn. This would most certainly not be conducive to Jane's recovery. "It is serious. She lives, although she cannot be moved."

"I must go to her!" Mrs. Bennet cried out, beginning to weep.

"You must not go to her." Mr. Bennet was stern. "Longbourn requires its mistress. Lizzy will come with me to Netherfield, to assist with Jane's care. You and your nerves will remain at Longbourn."

"But I am Jane's mother!" Mrs. Bennet protested weakly. "Lizzy will not know what to do for her. I *must* go, for no one else will do."

Mr. Bennet frowned. "I am resolved, Mrs. Bennet. Lizzy, go and get a few things. We will send more to you tomorrow. You may be at Netherfield for some time."

Elizabeth did not look at her mother. "Yes, Papa." She pushed past her sisters and ran to her room, hastily packing a day's worth of clothing in a bundle. Racing back down the stairs, she heard the familiar clatter of the carriage outside as it was brought to the front of the house.

❧

Their arrival at Netherfield was marked by end of the storm, with enormous rays of light breaking through the clouds in all directions as if to defy that anything in the world could be amiss. Elizabeth would normally relish such a sight, but her heart was heavy, and she was anxious to be with her sister.

Mr. Bennet and Elizabeth were taken immediately to the bedchamber where Jane was resting. Mr. Jones invited Mr. Bennet to speak privately in the outer hall, as Elizabeth ran to her sister's bedside. Caroline Bingley was sitting in a chair near the window of the room and addressed Elizabeth quietly. "I am sorry, Eliza, for dear, sweet Jane. She is not herself, and we are all most distressed."

"Not herself?" Elizabeth asked with alarm, for Jane, who had not yet said anything to her sister, appeared reasonably well. Elizabeth scanned Jane again, who had several visible scratches and a large swelling on her head, but was otherwise unmarked by the accident.

"You will see," Caroline replied as she stood to leave. "I will have your dinner sent to the room, so you may stay with your sister."

"Thank you." Elizabeth said as Caroline quit the room. "You are most kind."

Mr. Bennet entered the room as soon as Caroline left it, and standing at the foot of the bed, addressed his eldest daughter. "Jane, I see that you are awake. How are you feeling, my dear? You have given us all quite a scare."

"I am sorry to have caused so much trouble, Papa. I fear that I suffer from dizzy spells, and my head aches most exceedingly, but other than that there is nothing much," Jane spoke softly but clearly. "I hope this has not distressed Mama too much. Tell me, will our Easter preparations be delayed?"

"Lizzy, I would speak to you in the corridor for a moment." Mr. Bennet said as Elizabeth's jaw dropped in dismay at Jane's question. "Jane, we shall return in a moment."

Mr. Bennet related to Elizabeth that which Mr. Jones had said to him about Jane's condition. Upon arrival at Netherfield, she had suffered from an attack of some kind, convulsing and vomiting profusely. She had been in a state of confusion from the moment of her fall, which is not uncommon with a blow to the head according to the apothecary; it was important that she be humored in order to keep her quiet.

She should be awakened every few hours, and plied with as much tea and broth as they could persuade her to take. She was to remain in bed and not be moved until she was recovered. As the swelling on her head lessened, her condition should improve, unless a fever set in. If this occurred, she should send word to Longbourn immediately. The apothecary had brought some preparations to administer for pain, but there was nothing to be done for her other symptoms. When his recitation was complete, Mr. Bennet returned to the room, bid his goodbyes to Jane, and departed, leaving Elizabeth alone with her sister.

Elizabeth sat by Jane's bedside and tenderly took Jane's hand. "Lizzy," Jane said, "where am I? This room is most strange."

"You are at Netherfield." Elizabeth said.

"Oh, then I am at home." Jane sighed happily. "Send my husband to see me, for I would be in far more comfort if he were here."

"Jane, you are not married." Elizabeth said, frowning.

"What has become of Charles?" Jane asked drowsily with a childlike pout.

Charles, Elizabeth knew, was frantically pacing the hallway outside, as agitated and worried as she had ever seen any man; he had hovered close when her father had spoken to her. She had seen the look in his eyes, a look of desperation and regret, and he followed her with a look of longing when Elizabeth had re-entered the room. He had given away much in his vulnerable state. Elizabeth was convinced in those short moments that Charles Bingley had formed a deep attachment to her sister.

"He is near." Elizabeth soothed. "He cannot come to you now, but he is near."

"Then I shall see him?" Jane closed her eyes. "Tell me when he comes home, Lizzy. A husband needs a proper greeting from his wife." Jane relaxed and dozed off.

Elizabeth watched her sister sleep, wondering what Jane had said to Caroline, or to Charles. She set about to tidy up the room when the incessant sound of footsteps in the hallway stopped. She went to the door and opened it a crack. She saw Charles leaning up against the wall, his head against one of his forearms as his shoulders shook. She considered retreating inside the room, pretending she had not seen it, but, overtaken by compassion, she stepped into the hallway.

"Mr. Bingley," she spoke softly. "Jane will be well. You shall see."

Charles stood up with a start and turned slowly to face Elizabeth. "Miss Bennet." The cheer that usually graced his features was gone, replaced with melancholy. "I did not know." His head sagged.

Elizabeth mentally rehearsed what Jane had said to her and wondered what Jane had said before she arrived. Had Jane revealed her feelings in her confused state? Elizabeth pressed her lips together as she shook her head subtly. He continued speaking, "I knew, of course, that she was to dine at Netherfield today with my sisters," Charles explained, "but had I known that she was to come on horseback...." He looked past Elizabeth at the door to the bedchamber, and repeated. "I regret that I did not know."

"Mr. Bingley," Elizabeth reassured him again, "Jane shall be well, and you must know that you are not to blame. This is *not* your fault!"

Charles nodded. "It is nearly time for dinner. I will check again on Miss Bennet later." Elizabeth nodded her assent and turned to go back into Jane's room.

"Miss Bennet." Mr. Bingley said, as if another thought just occurred to him. "Do you know what your sister wants to name her first child?"

Elizabeth turned slowly. "Mr. Bingley? Why do you ask such a question?"

"Do not be alarmed, Miss Bennet, I mean no offense. Your sister said something to me as we carried her to the house after her fall that I have not been able to set aside. I thought perhaps you could help me reconcile it."

"I fear that I cannot help you, Mr. Bingley, for I do not know the answer. You will have to ask Jane when she is better." Elizabeth opened the door and returned to her sister.

৯

The night was long for Elizabeth. Although Jane slept fitfully, Elizabeth slept not at all. She dutifully roused Jane several times to make her sip some tea and provided tender comfort when Jane muttered and moaned.

When morning came, Elizabeth went to the adjacent room for just a few moments to wash and change before returning to be with Jane. When she entered the room, she saw that a breakfast tray had been brought but did not at first notice the man standing near the window, for he had pressed himself backwards into the draperies when she had entered the room.

"Good morning, Jane." Elizabeth said cheerily as she sat on the side of the bed right next to Jane. "Open your eyes, my dear, for it is time I had a proper look at you." She combed Jane's hair lightly with her fingers as Jane made a feeble protest to awakening. "You are not nearly so frightful as you could have been—your beautiful face is barely scratched and will heal soon enough, although I can see some bruising today as well. You will undoubtedly make the peacock colors of a bruise look so appealing on a person that all the ladies of the neighborhood will wish that they could be injured too." Elizabeth's teasing tone disguised her concern, for the swelling on Jane's head had not improved.

"Lizzy," Jane said softly, "I have such a headache. Close the curtains, I pray you, for I cannot open my eyes in this light."

"Of course." Elizabeth had herself opened the curtains at dawn, knowing how much Jane preferred rooms filled with sunlight. She felt foolish for not realizing that Jane's injuries might cause her to be sensitive to it, and she hastened to amend her error. It was at that point that the figure of a man stepped forward from within the curtains.

Chapter Seven

MANAGING MR. BINGLEY

Elizabeth jumped at the sight of him, startled to see Mr. Bingley in Jane's room, but fortunately she caught herself before she made any sound; although she stared in shock for several seconds before proceeding to hastily close the curtains.

He stood before her, smiling shamelessly. He looked over at Jane, clearly quite as pleased with himself as a child caught sneaking a spoonful of jam too late to be stopped. Elizabeth put her hand up to her mouth, signaling him to be silent, and quickly crossed to the doorway, hoping to send him away unnoticed by the household. She peered into the hallway and beckoned him to come. He nodded and tiptoed halfway across the room when Jane's eyes fluttered open and she weakly said, "Charles? Charles, you are here at last. Will you not sit with me now that you have come?"

He stopped walking but looked beseechingly at Elizabeth. Elizabeth shook her head and motioned toward the door, indicating that he should hurry. He hesitated only for a moment before moving to Jane's bedside where he sat in the chair that her sister had previously occupied. He tenderly clasped Jane's hand and, looking earnestly into her eyes, said, "I am here."

Jane smiled and closed her eyes again with a sigh of contentment. "Your hands are so warm, dearest. They are very comforting. Do tell cook to start the hot-cross buns."

Elizabeth took a deep breath before charging over to the bed where she gently pulled the covers higher in an attempt to preserve her sister's modesty. "Jane, Mr. Bingley must go and tend to business now. He cannot stay."

Jane pouted prettily at Mr. Bingley. "Are you going to buy a pony for little Charles now? If that is your errand, go, but do hurry back to me. I cannot rest when you are away."

Elizabeth looked in great frustration at the pair of them. "Mr. Bingley, I would speak with you." She spoke firmly, and Charles stood with some reluctance, holding Jane's hand as long as he could before releasing it and following Elizabeth.

Once in the hallway, Elizabeth smiled warmly. "You are such a gracious host, Mr. Bingley. We are greatly indebted to you for your kindness. You do know, however, that for propriety sake, we must speak of this to no one; and you must not return to my sister's bedchamber, for it will not do."

"She was calling for me, Miss Bennet...," he trailed off. "I wanted to see her," he admitted candidly. "I think that it does her good to see me, or she seems to think so, and she also seems to be rather confused about ... well, she seems to be confused about what time of year it is. It is not yet winter, yet she asked me when we were to paint the eggs for Easter and whether we would travel to Longbourn to visit her parents after church."

"Yes, her injury does seem to have muddled a few things in Jane's mind." Elizabeth acknowledged. "We must not give weight to the ramblings of one who has suffered a blow to the head. She will be right in a few days."

"You heard her speak of 'little Charles' a moment ago, did you not?" Mr. Bingley chuckled when Elizabeth nodded cautiously. "Two nights ago at Lucas Lodge, I told her that, someday, my children would all have ponies, so they could learn to ride while they are young." Charles spoke quickly, as if he feared that his powers of deduction would evaporate before he solved it. "And when we were carrying her to the house, she declared that I must make 'little Charles' stop teasing his sisters, for the eldest must be the model of good behavior to the younger.'" Mr. Bingley's eyes became round with excitement as the final pieces fit together. "She thinks we are married! She thinks we have children! She thinks it is Easter!"

"Mr. Bingley, I fear my sister is not herself." Elizabeth warned. "What she thinks at the moment is fantasy."

"True," he nodded, "but Mr. Jones did say that we should humor her until her symptoms subside. I am, I believe, the object of her fantasy, and I want you to know that I do not object to it ... if it will help Jane. I do wish to help, and will most willingly return to comfort her if you wish it."

"Mr. Bingley, your offer is most generous, but I fear that when Jane does recover in a few days, she would suffer tremendous mortification if she knew of it. My sister will have enough embarrassment over the fall and the imposition of her stay here. Do not add to it by insisting that we indulge in a lie."

Mr. Bingley looked crestfallen. "I see that you are right Miss Bennet. I will not interfere with your sister's convalescence again."

"Bingley!" Mr. Darcy said loudly, although he was just a few feet away, behind them. Both Elizabeth and Mr. Bingley jumped at the sound, for neither had heard him approach. Elizabeth, not knowing how long he had been there, tried to rehearse the content of their conversation in her mind, wondering how much Mr. Darcy had overheard. "Bingley, the carriage has been waiting for some time now. We must be off."

Mr. Bingley nodded, and walked briskly to the stairs. Mr. Darcy however, stayed. He stood, looking at Elizabeth as though he had something to say, so she did not turn immediately to return to Jane's room, but paused, to hear him. Finally, after a time too long for comfort, he asked, "How is your sister today?"

"It is too early to ascertain her condition, for she has just awakened. I must tend to her." Elizabeth's hand reached for the doorknob.

Darcy spoke abruptly. "Her head—is it much swollen?"

Elizabeth nodded. "I fear it is more so today, sir."

"You must reduce the swelling." Darcy said.

"How am I to do it?" Elizabeth challenged. "The apothecary left nothing for swelling, only for pain."

Darcy rolled his eyes and asked, "Is there an ice house nearby?"

"There is one in Meryton." Elizabeth responded, wondering at the question.

"I will send for some ice and clean rags. Wrap pieces of ice in a cloth and apply it to the swollen area—use enough to make it cold. Do not stop doing this even if your sister complains. You must insist upon her cooperation. It may take time, but the swelling will subside with this treatment."

"Thank you, Mr. Darcy. I will do as you say." Elizabeth curtsied.

"You look tired," Darcy commented. "You must also rest."

"A woman always loves to hear that she looks tired, Mr. Darcy. Thank you."

"I did not mean...," Darcy sputtered.

"It is of no import what you meant." Elizabeth replied serenely. "Indeed, it can hardly be expected that a person who has stayed up all night would look rested, so I did not expect to appear so. Your mentioning it has only strengthened my resolve to remain by my sister's side rather than to descend to the lower floors where I may be expected to appear rejuvenated, when in fact, I am not."

"You cannot mean to stay with her all day." Darcy objected. "Let a servant tend her when she sleeps."

"I mean to stay with her until she is well," Elizabeth replied. "No servant can have half the affection and care for her that I do. She is in a most vulnerable state, and I will not allow another to tend to her until she is out of danger."

"You appear to be determined, Miss Bennet." Darcy nodded his acceptance. "I will have a chaise brought to your sister's room so that you may have an opportunity to recline when your sister sleeps. This will, I hope, be an acceptable compromise?"

"Thank you. Yes, Mr. Darcy." Elizabeth nodded gratefully. "That would suit me very well."

"I am happy to oblige." Darcy bowed. "Good day, Miss Bennet." He stood back up to his full posture, and suddenly Elizabeth realized how very tall he was. She looked at him, up and down several times, a slight frown on her face as she recognized a glimmer of attraction to his powerful physique. She shuddered casting the thought away as soon as it registered, and quickly re-entered Jane's room.

Her look was not lost on Mr. Darcy.

Chapter Eight

RUMINATIONS

Mr. Darcy watched Elizabeth retreat to Jane's room, standing for a brief moment to simply stare at the door that separated them before he turned to join Mr. Bingley in the carriage although not before he had left instructions with the staff regarding the promises he had made to Miss Bennet. Mr. Darcy and Mr. Bingley were to dine with the officers today, and Darcy found himself relieved that the ride was not to be lengthy. Charles seemed to be indulging in some sort of private reverie, forcing Darcy to engage in reveries of his own.

His thoughts, usually on business, horses, fencing and the like, continually turned upon his several encounters with Elizabeth Bennet. The last conversation, brief and tense as it was, had immediately put him into a state of restlessness and pleasant agitation over the encounter. Never before had any woman, particularly one of such brief acquaintance, had such a profound effect on his person. He perceived no mercenary tendency in her, which fact alone set her apart from the masses of ladies who vied for his attention wherever he went. Upon reflection, he realized that it was her apparent apathy toward him that first engaged his notice. Then, he had been compelled to watch her.

Elizabeth's face, which he had originally considered rather ordinary, had quickly become a point of fascination for him. It was a canvas of expression, so open and animated that to watch her converse was as engaging as watching a gem sparkle in the sunlight. It had not taken long for him to change his opinion of her beauty, for he knew that the word ordinary could never be ascribed to Elizabeth Bennet.

Her conversations with people who were not her intellectual equals were rendered interesting by the injection of wit she added to them. Her opinions, which she stated with confidence, were usually solid, although he *had* heard her playfully recite opinions back to people, paraphrased to make them think she was agreeing with them, when in fact, the opinion did not match her own. It was so respectfully, yet cleverly, done that he hoped someday she would do this to him, so that he might hear her impression of his opinions.

In their own brief conversations, he had the distinct impression that she was toying with him, verbally challenging him to a duel that she was certain to win, for she established the rules and kept them a secret from him. As perplexing as this was, he found her game engaging, and he inexplicably wanted more of it.

It was a perverse trick of the universe, he decided, that such a delightful creature should be born to a situation such as hers; for with no fortune, no connections and a most disagreeable mother, she was bound to a lower place in society than she deserved.

These ponderings left him discomfited. His attraction toward Miss Bennet could not be acknowledged openly, lest his attentions be mistaken as intentions. Yet he could not ignore his feelings either, for he increasingly craved her company and, with each interaction, found more in her character and her person to admire. He knew it was imperative that he should quit Hertfordshire, not because he found it wanting, but because he liked it too well. He knew just as certainly that he could not bring himself to leave just yet.

Elizabeth set about eating some of the breakfast which had been brought to the room, although it was barely warm, so long had she been delayed. She had managed to get Jane to eat a little bit as well before her sister had dozed again. Mr. Jones had warned that the pain tonic would make Jane drowsy, so it was no surprise to find herself with no occupation. She would request a book from the library at the first opportunity, but for lack of company, needlework or literature, Elizabeth found herself alone with nothing but her thoughts to entertain.

She thought about Jane and the strange turn of her mental state, as well as of Mr. Bingley's response to it. She thought of her mother and hoped that she was feeling some guilt for denying Jane access to the carriage, and had thereby learned a lesson. She thought of her father, who had allowed her mother's foolishness in the first place, and of his subsequent resolve to bar his wife when they had been called to Netherfield. She thought of Caroline Bingley and what she had said upon Elizabeth's arrival yesterday. Finally, when all other thoughts were exhausted, she allowed herself to think about the seeming contradictions of Mr. Darcy.

Was it pride, as she had supposed, that had prevented him from dancing at the Assembly Ball, or was it as Jane had suggested, that he was reserved? He had seemed to be in attendance nearly under duress, so reluctant he had been to stand up with anyone. Although he had not paid her the compliment of singling her out to dance, neither had he slighted her, for he had danced with none of the local ladies, not even Jane.

He had been present at several of their calls to Netherfield to visit Caroline and Louisa, but it was only Mr. Bingley who had shown eagerness to know them. Mr. Darcy had kept his distance, writing letters or standing at the window with his back to the group. It had to be pride, as she had originally thought. Elizabeth reached her conclusion with a slight frown, recalling the way she had laughed about it at the ball and again the next day, excusing his pride because his behavior had amused her.

On the other hand, had he not sought her opinion? A man caught up with pride would surely not have done so. There were others he could have asked, yet he had approached her—and slighted Miss Bingley in so doing. Elizabeth smiled. This alone made her like him a little better, as did the surprising knowledge that Mr. Darcy had a sister. She did not know why this warmed her heart so, perhaps because the gesture of a gift proved he was capable of feeling or that it established at least one thing they had in common.

The mental image of him which she had taken just this morning flashed in her mind, and she blushed, although there was no one to see it; for in that brief instant she had acknowledged to herself that she found the athletic lines of his bearing pleasing to the eye. She had allowed him to be handsome from the first, but this was something more. It had sent a shiver through her body, a reaction she neither desired nor would nurture, for she told herself that such a raw, physical response had nothing to do with his character or amiability and, therefore, could have no place in her opinion of him.

That opinion of him was, at the moment, in flux. His kindness in procuring ice for Jane's head and his concern for her own well-being had come as a surprise. He had taken liberties in commanding the Netherfield servants to do his bidding, yet she had to acknowledge that his manner was so authoritative that it would be a rare servant, indeed, who would decline simply because he was not master of the house.

It was while she was thus engaged in thought that the ice and the chaise were delivered to the room. Elizabeth prepared the ice as Mr. Darcy had instructed and carefully placed it on Jane's head. As predicted, Jane complained, and Elizabeth spent the next hour coaxing Jane to leave it in place. Eventually, however, Jane acquiesced and allowed it, soon declaring that her headache was beginning to subside as well. Once she got Jane settled in with the ice, Elizabeth laid down on the chaise and slept lightly, getting up to refresh the pack frequently so that it would not melt too much and soak the pillows.

Within a few hours, Elizabeth could see that the swelling had visibly reduced, and more importantly, Jane's mind began to clear. Although she still suffered a degree of confusion, particularly about the event of the accident itself, her mind was returned to the present with sufficient clarity that Elizabeth no longer feared that Jane would give away any more of the secret longings of her heart.

Chapter Nine

A BOOK FROM THE LIBRARY

When the sun was low in the sky, Elizabeth opened the curtains again to gaze on the countryside before her. She yearned to leave the room that had held her captive for a day, but it would not do to leave Jane yet. Although her sister was much improved, Jane could sit up for only a moment before she was overcome with dizziness; and she could not yet tolerate solid food, becoming nauseated with even a crust of bread. Jane's headache was still severe, so Elizabeth did not even have the pleasure of sisterly conversation to pass the time, for it pained Jane to speak.

The passage of time seemed suspended as Elizabeth stood in the window, an amber glow enveloping her as the sun sank towards the horizon. The rattling of the coach returning home caught her notice, and she looked down through the glass as Mr. Bingley and Mr. Darcy emerged from the carriage. She smiled at the recollection of Mr. Bingley offering to comfort Jane by posing as her husband. Although it had been scandalously improper, it had also been so genuinely sweet that Elizabeth could not consider it a fault in him. Jane could do worse than to marry such a man, for he clearly adored her, Elizabeth decided, and mentally endorsed Mr. Bingley as a worthy candidate for Jane's heart.

A soft tapping on the door was followed by the maid's entrance. She brought a dinner tray and set it on the small table in the room. She stirred and fed the fire, then went about the room lighting the candles.

When she had finished, she asked, "Is there anything else I can get for you, miss?"

"Perhaps there is." Elizabeth answered. "I would very much like to have something to read to help pass the time while my sister is resting. Would you ask Mr. Bingley if I might borrow a book from his library?"

"Yes, miss." The maid bobbed a curtsy and quit the room as Elizabeth sat down to eat. She had plied Jane with broth all day, but had eaten little herself and realized that she was famished. She was nearly finished with the bowl of soup when there was another knock at the door. Assuming it was the maid, she stated loudly enough to be heard, "Come."

The door swung open to reveal Mr. Darcy nearly filling the threshold, although he did not cross it.

"Have you lost your way, Mr. Darcy?" Elizabeth put down her spoon and dabbed at the corners of her mouth with a napkin. "I am afraid I cannot help you, for I have not left this room all day and do not know my way about the house. Shall I call the maid to guide you?"

Something akin to a smile flickered across his lips, and he stepped into the room—although not far enough to have a view of Jane.

"How is your sister? Has her condition improved?" He shifted into a relaxed stance that appeared as though he had planted himself for a lengthy conversation.

"Why, yes." Elizabeth responded sincerely. "Thank you for your kindness in sending the ice for Jane today. I believe, sir, that it made a difference in the swelling, and she is resting comfortably now." Her eyes met with his for an instant, and she found herself intimidated by the intensity of his gaze. She turned away, gesturing at his other offering. "The chaise is very comfortable."

"I thought you looked more rested," Darcy said, nodding. "I am glad you made use of it."

Elizabeth bristled slightly. "Rest was not my aim today, Mr. Darcy. I believe that when my sister has recovered sufficiently, I will have ample opportunity for respite. Until then, my own rest is but a distraction."

"Your affection for your sister does you credit, but you must not make yourself ill in tending to her." Darcy chided her softly, again stepping closer as he spoke.

"I am perfectly fine," Elizabeth retorted. "I have had rest enough indeed; it is only want of exercise that affects me, for I have not dared to leave Jane. She has been in such a state...."

"A state of *wedlock* as I understand it—your sister has likely never been as happy and content as these past hours have afforded." Darcy said drily. "You need not fear that Bingley gave it away. I confess that I overheard your conversation this morning. Were it not for the seriousness of her injury, it would be a most diverting anecdote."

"Jane could not help it," Elizabeth cried, "and her confusion was of short duration. I assure you that she suffers no such delusions at present, only a headache and dizziness."

"Have you not left the room at all today, Miss Bennet?" Darcy turned the conversation back to Elizabeth.

"Well, I ... well, no." Elizabeth admitted.

A sound in the doorway caused them both to look there, only to see the maid timidly waiting for a break in the conversation. "Begging your pardon, miss, but Master Bingley says that you are most welcome to fetch a book from his library, as soon as you would like."

"You will remain here with the eldest Miss Bennet," Darcy said to the maid, "I will escort Miss Elizabeth to the library." Darcy looked at her, motioned toward the door, picked up a candle and said, "As they say, there is no time like the present."

With a gulp, Elizabeth realized that in truth, she did not know where the library was. It irked her that she needed to be shown the way; but being determined not to spend another day in the room without a book, she nodded and followed him through the doorway.

She walked at his side through the dimly lit hallways, conscious of the length of his enormous strides as she attempted to keep up. He touched her only once, when he turned down a corridor and Elizabeth, unfamiliar with the route, missed it. She felt a light touch on her back as he silently guided her into the turn, and glancing up at him, she found a kindly face looking back at her. *It is the shadows that make him look that way*, Elizabeth told herself, *for had he been a truly kind man, he would not have been so rude about Jane.*

Darcy began to slow down, but Elizabeth increased her pace, recognizing that the doorway ahead must be the haven of the library. She reached for the doorknob excitedly, only to find that Mr. Darcy's hand was already upon it. She drew back at the unexpected contact, inhaling loudly.

"I am informed, Miss Bennet," Mr. Darcy swung the door open as he spoke, "that patience is a virtue."

Elizabeth crossed through the doorway and turned, extracting the candle from Mr. Darcy's hand as she did so. "I beg you to forgive my enthusiasm on reaching our destination, Mr. Darcy. I was, indeed, impatient. Patience, I fear, is not a virtue I own in abundance. I require privacy and time to make my selection. I thank you for showing me the way." She dismissed him with finality, "I will close the door behind me when I am done here and am perfectly capable of finding my way back to Jane." She entered the room, holding the candle high in order to illuminate the shelves, and then approached the nearest collection to peruse more closely.

Mr. Darcy stepped back with a slight bow. He fully intended to leave then, yet there was something in her attitude that unsettled him. He stayed just beyond the doorway, studying her as the flickering candle cast a pool of light where she stood. He told himself that he was merely curious as to which volume she would select, but it was watching Elizabeth herself that mesmerized him. She was unaware, he knew, that her appearance had become slightly disheveled, most likely when she had taken a few naps in the course of the day; and now, loose strands of escaped curls surrounded her face. These created a halo-like effect as they reflected the candlelight, giving her a cherubic appearance that he found enchanting. She moved about with a natural grace, and she seemed almost reverent toward the books, caressing the bindings with her fingertips as if she could discern what was within them by a mere touch—a curious act which Darcy found great pleasure in observing.

A door in another part of the house slammed, and Elizabeth glanced toward the library entrance. Darcy drew further into the shadows, somewhat ashamed of himself for lingering so long and indulging in thoughts and feelings that could never be acted upon, never even be spoken. He determined in that moment, however, that there was no harm in pursuing a platonic friendship with Miss Bennet, so long as he concealed any tendency toward sentimentality toward her. He just wanted to know her better. That was all. He looked up and watched as she read a few passages of the book in her hand, closed it carefully and decisively tucked it under her arm, turning toward the door as she did so.

A few steps more and she would undoubtedly detect his presence. He looked for a way to disappear and was just about to do so when Bingley appeared at the end of the hall. "Darcy!" He called. "There you are! We are waiting for you in the drawing room. Caroline will not begin our card game without you. She was quite insistent that I come to find you."

Elizabeth was now at the door, a look on her face that Darcy found himself unable to interpret. "I am coming." Darcy replied, walking quickly toward Bingley.

"Oh," said Bingley with a grin when he spotted Elizabeth. "I thought you were alone."

"No." Darcy replied, not breaking stride. "I showed Miss Bennet the way to the library to choose a book from your collection. We are finished." He breezed past Bingley, who, with one more glance down the hall at Elizabeth, turned to catch up with Darcy.

Elizabeth, having closed the library door, stood alone in the hallway, watching the two men of Netherfield retreat, her own mind in some confusion as to why Mr. Darcy had remained in the hall.

Chapter Ten

AN ACCOMPLISHED WOMAN

The next morning, with a fresh ice pack newly placed and a dose of pain tonic causing Jane to sleep, Elizabeth once again went to her assigned guest room to change. She drew back the curtains, weary of the gloomy darkness of Jane's room, and turned her face to the morning sun that was just rising above the distant hills. Knowing that Jane would not awaken for some time, Elizabeth determined that a morning walk was all she desired. Additional clothing had come from Longbourn, and Elizabeth chose the warmest of the dresses, a muslin frock that was courser in texture than the others and slightly heavier. With pantaloons and a petticoat, plus her favorite pelisse and hat, she would be warm enough. Holding a pair of gloves in her hand, she returned to Jane's room, where the maid had just delivered breakfast and was stoking the fire.

"Good morning, Susan." Elizabeth greeted her cheerfully. "I am going on a walk in a few minutes. Would you be so kind as to check in on Jane while I am out? I am sure she will sleep, but it would be a comfort to know she will be watched over. I will not be long."

"Yes, Miss Bennet." The maid curtsied and then looked at the sleeping Jane. "I will take care of her as if she were my own sister."

"You are very good." Elizabeth smiled as she hastily ate a piece of toast. "Some fresh air will do much to renew my spirits."

Elizabeth left the house virtually undetected by the other occupants, or so she thought. The morning was bright, with no clouds to obscure the sun, but it was also cold and damp, having rained during the night. A gauzy mist still hung among the autumnal trees, and the grass glistened with water droplets—remnants of the storm. Elizabeth lifted her dress up as she walked, but the day was too beautiful to fuss too much, and as soon as she was clear of the house, she broke into a run, the rush of cool air in her lungs invigorating her. She ran until her heart pounded and she was panting for breath. When the last vestiges of her indoor lethargy had been wiped away, she slowed back to a walk, smiling breathlessly at the rejuvenation she felt, although not yet ready to return to the house.

She continued to walk, feeding off the sunlight and the fresh smell of the rain. She stopped when a large hunting dog suddenly appeared, blocking the path. She looked around for his master, and seeing no one, whistled softly. The dog bounded towards her and she picked up a stick, holding it high above her head to get his attention before she threw it. They played several rounds of fetch, with each return of the stick handsomely rewarded with kisses on the dog's nose and generous petting of his ears. Elizabeth was thus engaged in bestowing her affections on the animal when a sound behind her caused the beast to whine softly and sit at attention. Elizabeth turned with a start, to see none other than Mr. Darcy, astride an enormous black stallion.

"Have you lost your way, Miss Bennet?" He said it perfectly seriously, and yet Elizabeth detected, in the strange tilt of his head, a manner slightly teasing.

"I have not lost my way, thank you." Elizabeth said with a coy grin, "Although, perhaps you have lost your dog, Mr. Darcy? As you see, I have found a handsome one who has become separated from his master." She patted the dog's head and was rewarded as his muzzle sought her hand for more.

"I thought I recognized him. I shall thank you to return him before he transfers his allegiance to you and is completely spoiled for hunting." Darcy's tone was, as before, humorless, yet the glint in his eye hinted to Elizabeth that it was an ill attempt at banter, so she did him a favor and responded lightheartedly.

"You need not fear so," Elizabeth replied. "A dog's heart is as constant as the sun. Once he has given it, it will not be moved, though heaven and earth fall away, he is true. He does not care for your wealth or your position. Your connections mean nothing to him. Were you in rags and ruin, it would not matter, for he loves *you*, not your trappings. You see, you are safe from me; I cannot steal your dog away."

Darcy stared at her for a moment and then, he tipped his hat. "Good day, Miss Bennet," he said, as he turned the horse around and rode away, his dog trailing happily behind him.

Had she overheard the breakfast conversation he wondered? Talk of wealth and position and connections as they related to the Bennet family had perhaps been in poor taste with the two daughters of that very family under the roof. He felt particular shame at his own comments about their marriage prospects, for although they were true, they had also been harsh and unfeeling. She could not have heard them, he realized with relief, for it was during that very conversation he had moved to the window and spotted Elizabeth running into the glade of trees beyond the house. He had feared that she was in some distress and set out to find her, only to find her joyfully playing with his dog, her cheeks rosy, her eyes sparkling and her impertinence intact.

Elizabeth spent the better part of the day reading in quarters with Jane, whose condition at the end of the day was much as it had been in the morning. At half-past six, Elizabeth was summoned to dinner, and the maid came once more to sit with Jane.

The polite inquiries regarding Jane's health from Caroline and Louisa struck Elizabeth as insincere, for they were delivered with such an air of superiority and condescension that it was a great struggle for Elizabeth to remain composed. She did so, however, and upon hearing that Jane was not much improved, Mr. Bingley's sisters spared but a few words of shock and grief over Jane's accident before they moved on to happier subjects. Mr. Bingley was another matter. He bombarded Elizabeth with a myriad of questions about Jane's health until he was satisfied that her recovery was simply a matter of good care and time.

When dinner was over, Elizabeth returned to Jane with no intention of going back downstairs, but having been called upon to return to the group, and with Jane once again fast asleep, she acknowledged that the right thing to do was to join her hosts, although it brought her no pleasure.

She picked up the book she had been reading, and brought it with her, for with no needlework or stationery to occupy her hands, the book secured her faith that the evening would not be wasted.

Upon entering the drawing room, Elizabeth saw that the entire party was playing cards. Caroline invited her to join them, but suspecting that the stakes were higher than she could afford even if she wished to play, she lifted up the book she had brought. "Thank you, but I would rather read; I expect to return to Jane shortly and do not wish to disrupt your game."

"You are very singular for one so young." Mr. Hurst grumbled.

"Do you not care for our society?" Caroline badgered. "Or is the truth more dull?" She turned back to speak to those seated at the table. "Miss Eliza Bennet is a great reader and takes no pleasure in anything else." She tittered slightly as she spoke.

"I deserve neither such praise nor such censure," Elizabeth said, "I am *not* a great reader, and I have pleasure in many things."

"Yes," Caroline said in sugared tones. "I have heard that talk of the militia is of great pleasure to the Bennet household."

"True," Elizabeth acknowledged. "Some of my sisters are indeed pleased at the addition of officers to Meryton society as a result of their being quartered here for the winter, but I do not share their rapture. It is other, more vigorous pursuits that give me pleasure."

"Such as *walking* I suppose," Caroline said haughtily. "I saw you return from your walk this morning. How unfortunate for you that it rained last night; for you can take no pleasure in being found six inches deep in mud."

"If Cleopatra enjoyed a mud bath, why should I not take pleasure in it?"

"Have you no other pleasures to speak of, Miss Bennet? Surely you play the pianoforte."

"Aye, and sing too, but for my own pleasure only. My pleasure does not extend to entertaining, for I play ill indeed."

"Do you hear that brother?" Caroline exclaimed, although looking directly at Darcy. "Miss Eliza plays and sings. I had no idea we were in company with such an accomplished woman."

Bingley laughed heartily and encouraged Elizabeth to play and sing for them.

"I beg you, no," Elizabeth said. "I must return to Jane."

"Nonsense," said Louisa, catching Caroline's drift, "now you must play for us. It would be so disappointing if you decline."

Elizabeth looked at her hosts with some dismay. Mr. Bingley was most eager to hear her play, but Caroline and Louisa's taunts did not make her feel cooperative. Mr. Hurst was grumbling about the card game and their lack of attention to it, but it was Mr. Darcy's face that changed her resolve, for written on it was the firm belief that she would not do it. As soon as she saw this, Elizabeth became determined to contradict his belief.

"If my vanity had taken a musical turn, you would all be in for a grand experience I assure you. I know that you must all be in the habit of hearing the very best performers, but owing to your perseverance, Miss Bingley, I will teach you a lesson, which is to believe me when I say that I play badly." Elizabeth gravely glanced at Mr. Darcy, "And you, sir, I entreat you to keep your breath to cool your porridge, and I shall keep mine to swell my song."

Her performance was pleasing; although by no means perfect, it was far more so than Caroline expected, and after two songs, Caroline thanked Elizabeth for her *display*, and asked her what book she was reading.

"It is a book from your own library," Elizabeth replied, without directly answering her question. "I had read my father's copy some years ago, but I find that I am getting more out of it now, for the questions it poses require some reflection to discern my own opinion on the matter."

Darcy, who had moved to the writing table when Elizabeth was singing, stopped writing, although he did not look up or otherwise acknowledge the conversation.

"And what are these serious questions, might I ask?" Caroline rolled her eyes.

"They tend to the behavior of men, or mankind. Why do men behave in a just manner, or why do they not? Do the stronger elements of society scare the weak into submission, or do men behave justly because it is right for them to do so? Moreover, what of justice alone? Is it a means to an end, or can justice stand alone as a worthwhile aim?" Elizabeth hesitated, seeing that Caroline was not really listening.

"The question that remains to be examined is whether you have, upon reflection, formed an opinion in these matters." Darcy asked, turning in his seat to look at Elizabeth.

"I have, although I expect that my opinion may be altered in the course of my reading," Elizabeth answered. "It is a most enlightening book."

"Miss Bennet, do you paint or draw?" Caroline interrupted.

"Not yet," Elizabeth replied.

"And what foreign languages do you speak? Are you well versed in French, or Italian?"

"No indeed," Elizabeth laughed, "I have had far better uses for my time. If I ever occasion to travel, I will learn enough to get by."

"I believe I must take back what I said earlier, Miss Bennet, about your being an accomplished woman. I have come to believe that you do not deserve the word, for you have paid little attention to those talents and social graces that must accompany a woman of accomplishment." Caroline said rudely.

"Miss Bingley, are you then, an accomplished woman?" Elizabeth inquired sweetly. "For now that I am beginning to understand the gravity of being so accomplished, I should like to know whose example I am to take in the matter."

"If I must name an example," Caroline paused, glancing toward Mr. Darcy, "I give you Miss Georgiana Darcy. She is very accomplished indeed."

"Indeed?" Elizabeth repeated, also looking at Mr. Darcy.

"Yes, my sister is indeed accomplished for her age. The only failing she has at present is the improvement of her mind, through reading." Darcy said firmly. "I may recommend, when she is a bit older and able to get more out of it, that she too explore the pages of The Republic."

Elizabeth felt herself color at the realization that Mr. Darcy had identified the book, and observing that she felt fatigued, she hastily made her excuses and returned to Jane.

Chapter Eleven

A ROOM WITH A VIEW

Elizabeth had not quit the drawing room for twelve seconds before Caroline Bingley declared. "What a tedious chore it is to spend an evening in company with Eliza Bennet. Her country manners, which you call 'charming,' my dear brother, are indeed atrocious. Her refusal to join us at the card table was an affront to civility—if my opinion is of any import."

"I thought the evening went very well," Bingley said cheerfully. "She was as delightful as ever."

"Perhaps to you, she seemed so, but I found her to be insolent in every way. I pray that Jane recovers quickly, for it would be unendurable to continue for many nights in this way. Would you not agree, Mr. Darcy?"

"No," Darcy replied. "I could endure it well, for Miss Bennet was most agreeable company. Any lack of comportment you may have perceived on her part can easily be attributed to her concern for her sister's condition."

"But," Caroline pursued the matter, "that concern is no excuse for her flippant manner of address. She is too mischievous. There is nothing about her to recommend."

"I did not consider her manners untoward. No, indeed, Miss Bingley, her conversation showed a liveliness of spirit that was refreshing, and any mischief she showed *you* was well deserved."

"You say that only because you were not really paying attention, Mr. Darcy. Indeed, you were very reserved tonight, but that is not surprising in light of the society. I am certain I know what you were thinking."

"I imagine not."

"Admit it, Mr. Darcy. You were thinking that it would be insupportable to spend another evening in such a way, in such company as that of Miss Eliza Bennet." Caroline snickered.

"My mind was, I assure you, more agreeably engaged." Darcy said curtly.

"Well?" Caroline prompted after a lengthy pause.

"I was meditating on the very great pleasure which a pair of fine eyes in the face of a pretty woman can bestow."

Caroline blushed slightly. She had received this compliment before, that her eyes were lovely, yet she was gratified that such a statement would come from Mr. Darcy. She fluttered her eyelashes as prettily as she could and pressed him. "If I may be so bold as to ask, whose eyes have inspired these reflections?"

Mr. Bingley looked sharply at his sister, but she did not see it, her attention was so fixed upon Mr. Darcy.

Darcy hesitated, taking stock of Miss Bingley before he casually replied, "Miss Elizabeth Bennet."

"Miss Elizabeth Bennet!'" repeated Miss Bingley. "I am all astonishment. How long has she been such a favorite? Pray when am I to wish you joy?"

"That is exactly the question which I expected you to ask." Darcy replied wryly, "A lady's imagination is very rapid; it jumps from admiration to love and from love to matrimony, in a moment. I knew you would be wishing me joy, for it seems that all it takes to make this leap is the merest hint of admiration." He turned to his friend and speaking softly so that only Charles could hear, he added, "Or a blow to the head."

Charles snorted and flushed, drawing Caroline's attention away from Darcy.

"And you, dear brother, should not encourage Miss Eliza in her *exhibitions*. It does neither of you credit."

༄

The next morning, Elizabeth was concerned to find that Jane still could not sit upright or stand for more than a few moments before she was overcome with dizziness and had to lie down, and that her headache was still severe. Elizabeth related this information to Mr.

Bingley at breakfast, and he immediately sent for Mr. Jones to return to Netherfield to consult on the situation.

In the meantime, Mrs. Bennet had become increasingly distraught that there had been no news from Netherfield regarding Jane's condition. She set out to learn for herself how Jane was doing, in spite of a weak protestation from Mr. Bennet that "No news is good news." Mrs. Bennet flitted about, urging Mary, Kitty and Lydia to hurry, for they were coming too. As much as she wanted to see Jane, she had grown accustomed to the escort of her daughters wherever she went. They served as a balm to her poor nerves; it would not do to make the visit alone.

Elizabeth was in Jane's room when their mother swept in, her younger sisters in tow. They stood around patiently as Mrs. Bennet fussed and stewed over Jane, plucking at her bedcovers as she repeatedly crooned, "My poor Jane. What is to become of you?" Elizabeth's attempts to console her mother were met with stinging remarks about ineptitude in caring for Jane and how wrong it was that Elizabeth had been selected in place of her own mother.

Jane assured their mother that Elizabeth's ministrations had been nothing short of perfect and that she felt significant improvement was nearly upon her, which eventually satisfied Mrs. Bennet. It was at this point that Mr. Jones arrived and after examining Jane, declared that she must remain in bed for at least three more days. He produced an elixir designed to relieve Jane's dizziness to some degree and left it, along with additional instructions for Jane's care.

Afterwards, Mrs. Bennet, with a train of daughters dutifully following behind her, called upon Mr. Bingley and his sisters in the drawing room. She enthusiastically complimented his living arrangements, and asserted, with the confidence bestowed by Mr. Jones' recommendation, that they must trespass on Mr. Bingley's hospitality for *at least* three more days.

Mr. Bingley heartily agreed to continue as host, for he was most happy to oblige and very pleased that he could be of assistance and offer Jane the comforts of his home during her convalescence. Miss Bingley half-heartedly assured Mrs. Bennet that Jane would receive the best of care while Mrs. Hurst nodded and Mr. Hurst snored.

Mr. Darcy had turned to the window nearly as soon as they had entered the room. He gazed silently at the glass during the entire conversation, turning his attentions back to the room only in time to bid farewell to Mrs. Bennet and her three youngest daughters.

Elizabeth had noted his seeming affection for the glazing on several previous occasions with increasing curiosity. She wondered if it was the prospect beyond the glass he enjoyed, or if the view served as some form of escape. Nearly as soon as her family had left, Mr. Darcy had excused himself and quit the room; so Elizabeth, curious as to what had held his attention for so long, took the opportunity to peer outside from the same vantage point that Mr. Darcy had occupied.

The view, she was surprised to find, was not in any way spectacular; in fact, owing to a cover of clouds, it looked rather gray and gloomy. Just as she was mentally convicting Mr. Darcy of using the outdoors as a poor excuse to be unsociable, the sun passed behind a thick cluster of clouds, maximizing the window's reflective properties, which she had not until that moment noticed. She saw, most clearly detailed in the window, the reflection of the chair that she herself had been sitting on. She gasped audibly at her discovery, wondering what it could mean.

"It is a beautiful view, is it not?" Mr. Darcy had re-entered the room and now stood behind her at a barely proper distance. Elizabeth nodded, looking at his face looming over hers in the glass.

"Indeed, although I am certain it is more so when the weather is less foreboding." Elizabeth could feel the heat of his body behind her, in stark contrast to the chill emanating from the windows. She felt a strangeness come over her as she contemplated whether to step to her right or her left, for she could certainly not turn around or step backward due to Mr. Darcy's proximity.

"Does this mean that you will dispense with your walk today?"

"No," Elizabeth replied, "but I shall confine my exercise to the garden paths, for as much as I enjoy a walk, I am not as fond of being rained on."

"Are your walks always solitary?" Mr. Darcy inquired.

Elizabeth blinked, looking downward as she considered her reply in a degree of confusion. Was he asking to join her, or was this just polite conversation? Looking up, with a slight shake of her head, she gave her answer to the glass. "No sir, they are never solitary, for one is never truly alone in nature. There are the birds, and creatures of the wood and glen to console me. Indeed, at times I find myself in the company of a stray hound, or even perhaps, the occasional horseman wandering the countryside."

She only saw it in the rippled glass, and indeed, it was so fleeting that she was not certain she saw it at all. There appeared, for the briefest moment, an enormous smile that crossed his face.

"Touché, Miss Bennet. Would you allow me to show you the garden today?"

"I will if you bring your handsome dog along." Elizabeth said with a slight chuckle.

"And give you yet another chance to steal his affections?" Darcy's tone was droll.

"I could do not do so, sir, even if I tried." Elizabeth smiled before adding, "Although ... it might be amusing to attempt it. He did seem to like it a great deal when I threw a stick for him to chase, and he did receive my attentions most enthusiastically...."

"You must pardon my poor hound's eagerness, Miss Bennet, but you were, after all, kissing him quite profusely." Darcy stepped backward a few steps, opening the way for Elizabeth to remove herself from the window, his face lit, not with a smile, but with a spark of humor in his eyes.

Elizabeth had turned to face him, and that look on his face gave her leave to tease him back. "Then you *must* bring him, Mr. Darcy. It is imperative that I make amends at once, for I do not even know the beast's name, and it will not do to have his reputation tarnished in such a way."

"Apollo. His name is Apollo." Darcy bowed slightly, as if making an introduction. "And I will by all means bring him if it would give you pleasure to see him again and allow you to make amends."

Elizabeth laughed. "Apollo? Upon my word, he is aptly named!"

"How so?"

"Did I not declare him to be as constant as the sun? His very name verifies it. You can have no fear that he and I will ever be anything but friends." Elizabeth laughed again and quit the room.

Bingley, having been the only person who had remained in the room, had observed the scene between them in its entirety and could not withhold comment. "You told me when we first met her that Miss Elizabeth Bennet was not handsome enough to tempt you, yet from where I sat, you were looking very tempted indeed, Darcy."

Darcy looked sharply at his friend. "My sensibilities are intact Charles. Miss Elizabeth Bennet is indeed a charming lady; but I am in no danger of being tempted by her, I assure you. She is ... intriguing, that is all. You need not fear that I have any designs upon her. Your guest is safe."

༄

Elizabeth returned to Jane's room, where she found that Miss Bingley and Mrs. Hurst had joined her sister. Although they appeared to be most companionable toward Jane, Elizabeth suspected that their motive in coming was to access Jane's condition for themselves, for they had looked quite put out that Jane's recovery had not yet progressed sufficiently for transport back to Longbourn. It pleased Jane, however, to have visitors, so Elizabeth excused herself with, "I see that the sun has come out. I believe I shall go for a walk in the garden."

She put on her bonnet and a donned an embroidered wool shawl, hurrying down the stairs with a parasol in hand, hoping that the warming rays of the sun would remain for the duration of her trek through the Netherfield gardens. She came upon the housekeeper, who showed her the way to the best door to access the path into the garden, and soon, Elizabeth was free of the confines of the house.

Two large hedges marked the entryway to the gardens; she was just passing through them, when she heard her name called.

"Miss Bennet!"

She turned around and found that Mr. Darcy was striding in her direction at great speed, with Apollo traipsing along beside him.

"You did not wait for me, Miss Bennet."

"I had thought you were in jest," Elizabeth replied.

"One thing you must know about me, Miss Bennet, is that I never jest," Darcy replied solemnly.

"That is too bad, for I dearly love to laugh." Elizabeth replied, picking up a stick from the ground and tossing it for Apollo to chase. As the dog sprung after it, Elizabeth punctuated her declaration by laughing in delight and ran a few steps to meet the hound on his return.

Mr. Darcy did not attempt to keep up with Elizabeth but trailed behind, noting her vivacity and her natural grace, among other things. He did not attempt to analyze the joyful feelings she inspired in him or how the sound of her laughter made his insides quiver. He was a man of discipline, after all, and in full control of his faculties. He reluctantly acknowledged to himself that he was powerfully drawn to her, but this she could never know! Despite the regard he was developing for her, he could not set aside the expectations of a worthy match imposed on him all his life.

He thought of the stream of women who had unsuccessfully pursued him over the years, yet he could find none to compare with Elizabeth Bennet. How strange it was that she was unimpressed by his fortune and position. She even told him as much, albeit indirectly, in her little speech about his dog. She could not know how those words had stung him, stripped him bare of his own importance, and in the same breath, declared him loveable, if only to his dog. She had declared him safe from her, that she could not steal his dog away, but,

Darcy complained to himself, she had made no such promise about his own heart.

Elizabeth, he noted, hardly knew he was there, although she was clearly enamored with Apollo. He watched, much as he had the previous morning, as she kissed the top of his dog's snout and scratched his ears. He thought of his own mother and how affectionate and warm she had been and considered the great happiness that trait had brought to his father. If nothing else, Elizabeth Bennet could serve as an excellent standard by which to compare legitimate prospects for marriage, for if he could find one such as her who had the requisite fortune and connections, he would count himself a lucky man indeed.

He quickened his pace and caught up with Elizabeth, engaging her in conversation, which seemed to flow effortlessly for her, yet was as witty and fascinating as the lady herself.

Chapter Twelve

THE STUFF OF DREAMS

When Elizabeth returned to Jane's room after her walk, she found her sister fast asleep. She was pleased to see the familiar healthy blush of color had returned to Jane's cheeks. In addition, Jane was sleeping soundly rather than fitfully, as was her previous state.

Retrieving the book from the dresser, she continued her study, for study it was, as she pondered on the application of the book's themes. Justice, she considered to herself, was an elusive object, one she had spent little time considering in her short life. The only serious question of justice to consider at the moment was many miles distant. It would be a happy day indeed when Napoleon was brought to justice; but even then, could justice in his case ever truly be served, considering the evils he had wrought?

Elizabeth sighed. Lack of experience in life may make it difficult to own an opinion on justice, she reflected, for she had never even known a true criminal, or even a scoundrel. No, Meryton had its share in quarrels and strife, and petty crimes did occur from time to time, but overall, her world did not much depend on the scales of justice balancing. *If I met a scoundrel, would I know him as such?* She answered her own question almost immediately, for Elizabeth prided herself on an ability to take the measure of a person in her first impression of them. *Of course I would know him, for evil would be in his countenance and I would discern it in a glance.*

She read for a while, but as soon as Jane stirred, she set the book aside and went to sit on the bed next to Jane.

"Awakening without a kiss, Jane?" Elizabeth teased her sister, "Horrid behavior for a princess!"

"Lizzy, I am no fairy-tale princess as you well know" Jane murmured with a smile. "Although if my dreams were true, I would feel as though I were."

"Dreams, Jane? Of what have you been dreaming?" Elizabeth wiped a loose strand of hair from Jane's brow.

"To be true, I know not how much is dream, and how much is real. It seemed real, although I know it cannot be." A tear escaped the corner of Jane's eye and trickled down her cheek.

"What cannot be, Jane?" Elizabeth tenderly wiped the tear away.

"Mr. Bingley." Jane nearly choked on his name. "In my dream...," Jane stopped and looked forlornly at her sister. "Mr. Bingley...."

"Hush, Jane." Elizabeth soothed, "You must not be melancholy! Mr. Bingley is well and inquires after you whenever I see him, which is often. You may be sequestered in this room, but you are not forgotten."

"Oh, Lizzy, how I long to see him again ... he came to me in my dream and was ever so gentle and kind...."

"Then you must hurry and get well, dearest Jane, for if I am not wrong—and I am never wrong—he longs to see you again as well." Elizabeth patted her sister's hand. "But I must prepare for dinner now. Although I would rather stay here with you, I am to dine downstairs tonight, with the rest of the residents of Netherfield. Mr. Bingley is a joy to know, so cheerful and amiable! It is no wonder he suits you so well. Oh, but his sisters—Jane, I do not understand how you can tolerate them; they are so imperious and superior—I cannot predict how many more days of their airs I can endure."

"Lizzy, they are not as bad as you say." Jane chided. "They are from town and are not accustomed to our ways here in Hertfordshire. We must make them feel welcome."

"As for Mr. Darcy...," Elizabeth continued, "I suspect that there is no one who really knows that man, for he is ... he is ... he is ... I suppose I do not know *what* he is. He is proud, that is certain, but other than that, his character is enigmatic. There is nothing of warmth or generosity in his manners to make him compare with Mr. Bingley. I believe that is it, Jane. He is a cold, passionless man in company, who is so closed off that he has rendered himself unknowable. He does seem to have a tender regard for his sister though, which could mean, but it is by no means certain, that underneath that icy expression and fancy waistcoat he wears, there may actually beat a heart after all."

ঌ

After dinner, Elizabeth again retreated to Jane's room, hoping to spend the evening in quiet conversation with her sister. She picked up the needlework that Mary had thoughtfully brought to her that morning and, aided by the meager light of a candle, set to work, cheerfully sharing selected events from the past few days with Jane.

It was not to last, for barely an hour had passed before Elizabeth was summoned to join those who had assembled for the evening in the drawing room.

"I wish you could come too, Jane, for they like you better than me, and if you were there to delight them, I could sit quietly in the corner and say nothing."

"I should so like to come! My headache has gone, but I am still lightheaded, Lizzy, and it would not do to faint. I would not wish to gain a reputation for swooning, after all, not in front of Mr. Bingley." Jane sighed and then giggled, "Although he might be forced to catch me, and that would be *very* exciting."

"Jane, I do believe you have been too much influenced by the scheming of my mother!" Elizabeth laughed uncontrollably, causing Jane to join her in a fit of giggles.

ঌ

The laughter had raised Elizabeth's spirits, and she entered the drawing room with a light heart, determined not to let her evening be spoiled by anyone.

She need not have feared, for Miss Bingley had noted Mr. Darcy's lack of interest in cards, and so the card table was nowhere to be seen. Mr. Hurst, disgruntled at this affront to his favorite pastime, was already stretched out on a sofa, sleeping. The others were engaged in their own pursuits. Mr. Darcy was sitting at a desk, writing a letter; Mrs. Hurst appeared to be daydreaming as she fiddled with her bracelets and rings. Mr. Bingley was working on the fire. Caroline Bingley was pacing back and forth, stretching her neck to try to see what Mr. Darcy was writing. Elizabeth, who had brought the needlework with her, sat down in the corner, where a candle gave her ample light, and resumed her stitching.

Several minutes passed before Miss Bingley commented to Mr. Darcy on what fine penmanship he had. Elizabeth could not hear his response, but she grinned to herself when she noted that he adjusted his position in order to block Caroline's view of the paper.

"To whom do you write, sir?" Caroline was undaunted. "Your letter appears to be very long."

"To my sister," Darcy replied, not looking up.

At this, Elizabeth found herself drawn into listening more carefully, for she was very curious about Mr. Darcy's sister.

"Oh! Dear Georgiana! How I do miss her. I simply yearn to see her! Please extend my fondest greetings and regards to her. Tell her I hope to see her when we next go to town and that...."

"Perhaps a letter written in your own hand is in order." Darcy interrupted. "There is not room left for me to do your raptures justice."

"Oh, Mr. Darcy," Caroline swept past him, her hand trailing across the desk. "I will just have to save my 'raptures,' as you like to call them, for when I see her next, for I hope it will be very soon—just as soon as I can convince Charles that there is nothing to keep him here, I am sure we will be off to London. I think if we stay, I shall go mad."

Elizabeth smiled to herself again. Was Caroline Bingley so dense that she did not perceive the set down from Mr. Darcy, or was she so desperate for him to notice her that she did not care?

"Why do you smile, Miss Eliza?" Caroline's voice dripped with venom, "Pray, is there something droll upon your mind to entertain us all?"

Elizabeth looked up from her work as she pulled the thread through to finish the stitch. "There is indeed something droll on my mind, but I fear it is for my entertainment alone, Miss Bingley."

Bingley laughed. "Miss Bennet, do tell us what is on your mind, for if you do not, we will all be bored, and find ourselves much as Mr. Hurst is." He laughed again as he turned to poke the log in the fire.

Mr. Darcy set down his pen and turned in his chair to look at her, as if he too wished for insight into what amused her.

"I hate to disappoint, but my thoughts are, after all, my own, and if I keep them, then they cannot betray me, nor can they offend any of you." Elizabeth demurred.

"Offend us?" Caroline was sneering. "Now I must insist on knowing, else I shall be offended indeed."

"Would you be offended then, when offense was not my intent?" Elizabeth replied. "Such a position does you no credit, for it is foolish indeed to perceive a slight where none exists. It is only you who suffers for it, for the one giving offense has no knowledge of it, and hence, no pain from it. What is the point in that?"

"In refusing to answer, you have declared your intent, and so the slight indeed exists, *Miss Eliza*." Caroline retorted.

Elizabeth set her handiwork down and looked directly at Caroline. "Miss Bingley, would you grant me such power over you that I may offend with a word unspoken? That is folly indeed."

Caroline stared at Elizabeth, her jaw slack as she found no ready response. "I am bored with this." She finally sputtered. "Keep your secrets if you have them." Caroline picked up a book from the table, found a seat near Mr. Darcy, and began reading.

Darcy, who had sealed his letter, also picked up a book and began to read. Elizabeth once again occupied her hands with stitching, glancing up periodically at the other occupants of the room. She noted that Mr. Darcy kept looking up from his book at her, forcing her to return her focus to her work. She also found that Caroline Bingley was barely reading at all, for she kept looking at Mr. Darcy and frowning whenever Mr. Darcy looked at Elizabeth. It also did not escape her notice that the book Caroline was holding was from the same series as that of Mr. Darcy's, but this time she suppressed any outward expression of her amusement, lest the previous scene be repeated.

In a short while, Caroline laid the book aside, and invited Mrs. Hurst to join her at the pianoforte so that her sister could play while she sang. They started their performance, which it truly was, for Mrs. Hurst's skill on the keys was impressive, and Miss Bingley put the same airs into her singing as she did into everything else. Elizabeth tried hard to ignore them. Miss Bingley started with some arias, in Italian, but Elizabeth knew that the lyrics were somewhat risqué and found herself somewhat embarrassed on behalf of Miss Bingley, for she was certain that Mr. Darcy well knew the translation. They switched, eventually, to some Scottish airs, which Elizabeth found much pleasanter, although she did not realize that she had begun lightly tapping her toe to the rhythm of the music.

She also did not realize, until he was standing beside her, that Mr. Darcy had vacated his seat and had moved to a position next to her chair, looking down upon her.

"Have you come to inspect my needlework, Mr. Darcy?"

"No." He replied, "I was wondering if you were, perhaps, feeling an inclination to dance a reel?"

Elizabeth smiled up at him, blinked a few times, almost imperceptibly shook her head, and returned to her stitching.

Darcy fidgeted briefly and repeated the question.

"Oh, I heard you the first time, Mr. Darcy." Elizabeth replied, although her eyes remained upon her embroidery. "I just was not certain how to respond, for as much as *I* love to dance, I know that *you* do not enjoy it. It was gallant indeed for you to offer, sir, but it would seem a waste of your sacrifice to spend it upon me tonight." She looked up at him, one eyebrow cocked, with a half-smile on her face, "Therefore, I must decline your offer. Perhaps the next time there is a ball in Meryton, if I am not already engaged to dance, you would oblige me then."

Mr. Darcy nodded his assent, bowed slightly and returned to his chair and to his book, which he did not even pretend to read, for although Elizabeth had refused him, her manner of doing so had been both sweet and arch—such a bewitching combination that he was more tantalized by her than ever. Were it not for the inferiority of her connections, he told himself, he would definitely be in some danger.

"I declare, why should we wait for there to be a ball in Meryton?" Bingley suddenly cried out, clapping his hands as he jumped up from his seat. "Netherfield is perfect for a ball! The drawing room here will make a very fine ballroom, and I am sure that my sisters would be the most gracious hostesses in welcoming all the neighborhood. We must have a ball!"

"Charles, there is hardly enough society in the whole of Hertfordshire to have a really poor ball, let alone an excellent one." Caroline whined. "There are balls enough in London. Let us go to town and enjoy the balls and quality society there."

"I am fixed upon the idea." Charles grinned. "Miss Elizabeth, as you are not already engaged, perhaps you would agree to dance a set the night of the ball—with Mr. Darcy here, as you promised just a moment ago."

Elizabeth, who had certainly not expected such a turn of events, could only imagine how delighted Jane would be at the news and informed Mr. Bingley that should he host a ball, it would undoubtedly be the social event of the year, and that all of the neighborhood would adore him for it. She did not, Mr. Darcy noted with some disappointment, directly consent to the promised dance at his hand.

Charles, having seized upon the idea, quickly became obsessed with it. The remainder of the evening was spent discussing the menu, the musicians, the décor, and, of course, who should be invited. For the first topics, Caroline, Louisa, and even Mr. Darcy obliged him with their opinions. For the guest list, however, Bingley depended on Elizabeth, a task to which she gracefully complied with her knowledge of the neighborhood.

Mr. Darcy was reduced to simply listening, which he did not resent, for he found her descriptions of the various families most diverting and gracious. He had seen the society of Meryton, and knew exactly how it was, yet through Elizabeth's eyes, they all sounded charming, and he found that in spite of his reservations, he began to think of the ball with some degree of anticipation.

Mr. Darcy remained in the drawing room long after Elizabeth had excused herself to return to Jane, yet he appeared to the others to have allowed his mood to turn, and they did not dare disturb him. It was right that they should leave him to his thoughts, for a conflict was raging in his mind.

Never before had he met a woman who was impervious to him. Indeed, women of all types had been paraded before him for many years now, the daughters of the wealthy and the noble elite. He had taught himself to discern the eligible matches from those who were not, yet none who remained had tempted him. They had preened before him, flirted with him, and flattered him, but he was irritated by their manners and suspicious of their motives. He had been as invulnerable to them as Elizabeth Bennet now seemed to be to him.

She could not *truly* be as indifferent as she seemed, Darcy thought, consoling himself. She was willing enough to converse with him, although apparently not eager for it. She did smile at him from time to time, but they were not the type of seductive smiles that women like Caroline Bingley bestowed on him. It was a warm smile—a playful smile that tingled on his skin as surely as her touch did.

It was while he was thus embroiled in thought that the realization came to him that he had deceived himself. He *could not* pursue a platonic friendship with Elizabeth Bennet. It was impossible. He was, in fact, very much in danger of falling in love with her, for even the simple thought of her was eroding his commitment to all that he knew of his place in the world. He was Fitzwilliam Darcy, master of Pemberley, and he could have the hand of any eligible maiden in the kingdom should he desire it—any maiden except for Elizabeth Bennet. He frowned. The only answer was to separate himself from her, for his resolve against her weakened with every moment. Every glance, every laugh, every witty phrase dug him deeper into this pit—a pit that could only lead to acute misery and destruction.

He knew as he took the stairs up to his room that night, it would be hours before sleep would come to him, and when it did, that his dreams would be haunted by the same face that had appeared in them every night of late. They were dreams that he dreaded waking from, dreams of the lovely Elizabeth Bennet.

Chapter Thirteen

THE PERSONIFICATION OF PERFECTION

Perhaps it was Jane's tale of Mr. Bingley's appearing in her dreams that caused it, Elizabeth thought upon awakening the next morning; but it really was terribly rude of Mr. Darcy to impose himself into her own. Then she laughed at herself, for it was ridiculous indeed to suppose that Mr. Darcy's abilities extended to purposeful influence of her dream state, irksome as it was.

She quickly addressed her own toilette, then attended to Jane. She was pleased to see that the brilliance of the bruise on Jane's head was beginning to shift from a dusky purple to bluish green, with a fringe of yellow forming around the edges—further evidence that Jane was healing. Elizabeth was thrilled to find that Mr. Jones had been perhaps too pessimistic about Jane's recovery, for Jane seemed almost herself today, with just a slight light-headedness upon removing herself from the bed, aided by her sister.

"Oh Lizzy, it feels so good to have my feet on solid ground that does not sway beneath me!" Jane exclaimed. "I can truly appreciate your penchant for walking—especially since I owe my current state to relying on a horse for transport."

"Do you remember it now, Jane? What happened?" Elizabeth encouraged her sister to speak as she set Jane down in a chair and began brushing her hair.

"I do remember it, and I will tell you because I know that I must, but you must not laugh at me, Lizzy," Jane replied, watching Elizabeth in the looking glass that hung above the dressing table.

"How could I laugh, knowing what it did to you?" Elizabeth reassured her as she gently detangled Jane's locks.

"I was riding toward Netherfield, but I had let my thoughts run away with me and had completely given Nellie her head when a loud noise startled her. She ran away with me as well, and I lost my seat." Jane sighed, the sort of deep sigh that precedes confession. "Lizzy, my thoughts were run away with Mr. Bingley. I do not know what came over me then, but I know what has come over me now."

"Jane, of what are you speaking?" Elizabeth stopped brushing. "What has come over you?"

"Lizzy...," Jane looked at her sister helplessly as she whispered, "I have given my heart to Mr. Bingley, although I have no true assurance that his regard for me tends in the same direction. If it does not, I do not know what I shall do."

Elizabeth looked at her sister with some shock. To make such a declaration before she was absolutely certain of his feelings was not in keeping with her sister's character. "Jane, how can you say this? Have you come to an understanding with Mr. Bingley?"

"No, Lizzy." Jane smiled serenely. "That is my difficulty. You know that I do not reveal my emotions easily, but my fear is that I will not be able to contain them." Jane paused for a long moment. "When I fell, Mr. Bingley came to my rescue. My mind remains a bit of a fog in the particulars of the event, but what I do remember was that Mr. Bingley held my hand and that he whispered to me—he whispered sentiments that were most tender...." She trailed off, looking at herself in the mirror as she reached up to examine the bruise on her head.

"Jane," Elizabeth cautioned, "foggy memories are no foundation for a declaration of love such as you have made."

"I am aware that I stand upon a thin sheet of ice in so saying, but the memories *have* become clearer. Lizzy, he called me his *beloved,* then he called me his *dearest angel,* and he begged me not to die, for he said that it would *rip his soul out* if I departed from this world. There were other things said too, but I know not how much was dream and what was real. In all of this I find that I now harbor no doubts that Mr. Bingley does have *some* feelings for me. I just have no idea how deeply they flow or if he intends to act on them."

Elizabeth's thoughts were taken back to the scene a few days previous when Jane, delirious from her injury, had summoned 'Charles' to her bedchamber, and he had willingly come, in violation of all the rules of propriety. She thought of Jane's delusions of marriage and children fathered by Mr. Bingley and began to formulate a theory as to the seed of that fantasy. She thought, with new revelation, of the anguish Mr. Bingley had displayed in the hallway. She had seen his attachment to her sister then but had not supposed the depth of it until this moment. She knew that she could not reveal any of this to Jane, but she thought with a degree of relief, Mr. Bingley did not seem the sort of man to dabble with a woman's heart.

Elizabeth's last day at Netherfield was uneventful. Mr. Bingley and Mr. Darcy had left early in the morning to tend to some matters of the estate. Elizabeth had enjoyed an early breakfast and a long solitary walk of the grounds, followed by more time with Jane, during which time she did not even encounter Miss Bingley or Mrs. Hurst.

Late in the morning both she and Jane agreed that Jane was well enough to join the party in the drawing room after dinner. A discussion arose on whether Jane should join them for dinner as well, but Elizabeth was concerned that too much exertion would tire Jane, and being anxious to return to Longbourn, she was not willing to risk a setback.

So it was that Elizabeth announced to the dinner party that Jane would be soon joining them for the evening, but for how long she could not say. As soon as dinner was complete, she returned to Jane's room, where Jane had not only eaten the dinner that had been served but had also refreshed her toilette and arranged her hair so as to cover most of the bruise.

Elizabeth helped Jane down the stairs and found the other ladies, who greeted Jane warmly and, to Elizabeth's surprise, were as kind and sociable to Jane as any she had ever seen. It was a bit of a revelation to realize the degree that she herself must be disliked by Miss Bingley, for if Miss Bingley had treated her with such generosity, she would in all likelihood consider Caroline Bingley to be a fast friend, and she finally understood to some extent why Jane liked her.

A half hour passed in company with the ladies, a sociable, pleasant time where they doted on Jane, told her amusing stories and entertained in a manner most pleasing. By the time the men joined them, Elizabeth had quite forgiven Caroline Bingley for the barbed comments of the past several evenings.

When the gentlemen joined them, Mr. Darcy, upon entrance, greeted the eldest Miss Bennet, congratulating her on her recovery and wishing her well. Mr. Hurst grumbled something unintelligible, but which Elizabeth assumed was a similar sentiment. Mr. Bingley's address to Jane was markedly different from the others. So warm and profuse was he in his well wishes that none could mistake the attention for anything other than devoted ardor for Jane. He insisted that Jane come and sit by the fireplace and built the fire up so that Jane did not add a chill to her other discomforts before he sat next to her, quite as closely as he could, and engaged her in quiet conversation. From her seat in the corner, Elizabeth could only look on with the greatest happiness for her sister.

Miss Bingley attempted once again to engage Mr. Darcy in conversation. Although he was civil, his answers to her many questions did not elicit sufficient response to further the dialogue. Instead, he attended to some sort of business at the desk. Caroline was not easily discouraged, and within moments of the conversation fading would try anew. At length, she turned her attention to her brother, having overheard him mention to Jane the topic of the ball to be held at Netherfield.

"Oh, Charles, I insist you give up on this idea of a ball. You have not sufficiently sought the opinion of the rest of our party, and there are those of us for whom such an engagement would be a punishment." She looked pointedly at Mr. Darcy, aware of his distaste for such assemblies.

Mr. Bingley looked up from his hushed conversation with Jane Bennet, annoyed at the interruption.

"If you mean Darcy," he replied, "he may go to bed, if he chooses, before it begins—but as for the ball, it is quite a settled thing. As soon as Mrs. Nicholls has made white soup enough, I shall send the invitations." He patted Jane's hand to reassure her that nothing could dissuade him from holding the ball.

Mr. Darcy looked up at the mention of his name. "Indeed, I will not go to bed before the ball begins, else I will not be at hand to claim my dance with Miss Bennet."

At this, Caroline glared at Elizabeth, who had glanced at Mr. Darcy with a slim smile. "And what of the other dances, Mr. Darcy? Have you engaged any other pretty partners in advance?"

"No, I have not." Darcy replied politely. "The ball was only decided upon last night."

"I believe in the past that you have stood up only with partners with whom you are particularly acquainted," Caroline prompted, "such as Mrs. Hurst and me."

"Yes," Darcy replied. "But then I discovered that in so doing, I had deprived myself of a very agreeable partner." He looked directly at Elizabeth. "I am reconsidering the wisdom of my previous rule." He then looked at Jane and invited, "Miss Bennet, I should very much enjoy a set with you as well, if you are willing." He smiled warmly at Jane, who nodded graciously.

Miss Bingley's face darkened, but she recovered. Striking as elegant a pose as possible, she began to pace before the desk where Mr. Darcy sat. Noting his lack of interest, she looked around the room and approached Elizabeth.

"Miss Eliza Bennet, let me persuade you to follow my example and take a turn about the room. I assure you it is very refreshing after sitting so long in one attitude."

Elizabeth was surprised, having never before received such a solicitation from Miss Bingley, but the opportunity to stretch her legs was welcome, and so she agreed to it immediately. Miss Bingley's triumph was complete, for she succeeded in accomplishing the true object of her invitation—Mr. Darcy looked up.

He was as aware of the novelty of such a request as Elizabeth herself was. Intrigued by what was to come, he unconsciously set down his pen. Miss Bingley sought to increase her share in his attention by immediately inviting him to join them. Darcy chuckled to himself at Caroline's transparent attempt in attracting his interest.

"I can imagine but two motives for you to parade around the room in this fashion, and were I to join you, I would spoil your plan. No, I shall remain where I am." Darcy smiled.

"Motives?" Miss Bingley pretended shock at such an accusation. "Of what does he speak, Miss Bennet? Do you understand his meaning?"

Elizabeth had looked at Mr. Darcy during Caroline's display and found him looking directly back at her, a smile playing on his lips such as she had never seen. She could not help but smile back at him, feeling deeply that she did indeed understand his meaning.

"No," she finally replied. "I cannot make out his meaning, but you can depend upon this—he will be severe upon us if we press him, but it will disappoint him if we do not."

"Disappoint Mr. Darcy?" Caroline flirted, "Indeed, I would not *dare* to disappoint him. I must have your meaning, sir."

"I am nothing if not obliging," Darcy replied seriously, which evoked a slight giggle from Elizabeth. He continued, attempting to ignore Elizabeth's mirth without success. "I have not the smallest objection to exposing your motives."

"Mr. Darcy, I must have it!" Caroline cajoled.

"You either choose this method of passing the evening because you are in each other's confidence and have secret affairs to discuss or because you are conscious that your figures appear to the greatest advantage in walking. If the first, I should be completely in your way, and if the second, I can admire you much better from where I sit." With a self-satisfied grin, Mr. Darcy sat back in his chair and openly stared at Elizabeth.

Caroline was both thrilled and dismayed at Darcy's reaction, for this was the first time that her provocations had evoked a response from him, but she could not help but realize that it was Elizabeth's presence that made the difference. She grabbed Elizabeth's arm and turned her, so that their backs were to Mr. Darcy. "You were right Miss Eliza; we should not have pressed him, for that was an abominable speech! How shall we punish him for it?" She glanced seductively over her shoulder at Mr. Darcy.

Elizabeth laughed at the thought of anyone punishing Mr. Darcy. "I would not know how to attempt it, Miss Bingley. You have known him far longer than I have. You must know of some weakness in his disposition that we can tease him about. Perhaps his wild imagining about our motives would do."

"No, no!" Caroline declared. "There is indeed no weakness in Mr. Darcy, and he is most certainly not to be teased or laughed at."

"No weakness at all?" Elizabeth teased, "Is your claim truly this, that Mr. Darcy is, in fact, the personification of perfection? Now I am the one disappointed, for I had hoped to find some amusement in his character, some folly to enjoy—I dearly love to laugh, you know. I hope to meet no o others like him, for if all my friends achieve such a state, at what will I laugh?"

Mr. Darcy, the smile on his face waning, replied, "Miss Bingley has given me credit for more than can be. The wisest and the best of men, nay, the wisest and best of their actions may be rendered ridiculous by a person whose first object in life is a joke."

"Indeed, Mr. Darcy, actions of the wise and good variety are not the sort at which I laugh. No, I am not so foolish. The ridiculous diverts me. Follies and foibles are a great source of entertainment, to be sure. Silly whims and inconsistencies amuse me, but these things are what Miss Bingley claims you are without."

"Miss Bingley exaggerates. What she claims is not possible for anyone, but I hope that there is but little of the ridiculous in me. It has been the study of my life to avoid foolishness, and, likewise, I do not suffer fools easily." There was a pained look on his face, as if in so saying he was exposing a weakness himself.

"Of that I am sure." Elizabeth said sweetly, sensing that he was no longer enjoying their repartee. "I cannot imagine that you *could* be made to suffer for a fool's sake, and my teasing you is, after all, not entirely sensible in light of this study you have undertaken. I should not give *the fool* a second thought if I were you." She bobbed a somewhat defiant curtsy in his direction and returned to her seat and her needlework.

She discovered quickly that her task was rendered difficult by the trembling of her hands, a problem she could not account for. Caroline almost immediately distracted the room with her demand for music at Mrs. Hurst's hand. This allowed Elizabeth to recover, to ponder on why she felt so unnerved by the conversation, and to consider why she had suddenly backed down.

She had been poised to strike, to point out his two most obvious faults, to charge him with vanity and pride, and yet, when the moment came to hurl the words at him, she could not do it. In her attempt to explain this to herself, she realized that she instinctively knew that the words would somehow injure him. The guilty, she told herself, take the truth to be hard, for it cuts as deeply as a knife, and although she found his prideful demeanor objectionable, it would not do to make it a point of contention in such a way. A direct assault on his pride, she reasoned, would only harden the man against improvement should he ever realize the fault in himself. In any case, she would not give him the satisfaction of returning his stare tonight, for that would only serve to feed his pride and vanity. Elizabeth kept her eyes cast downward, determined to keep her own counsel and not give Mr. Darcy a second thought.

Mr. Darcy was taken aback by the abrupt end to the conversation just as it was reaching what was, for him, an emotional fever pitch. He had seen in her dark eyes that she had not spoken all. They had danced with the spark of something he could not name, yet it was every bit as tangible as the words she had spoken. She had turned his words back on him, exactly as he had heard her do to others, although he was left unsatisfied by the exchange. She said not to give her a second thought, he mused. That was wise counsel indeed, for any thought of her at all was leading him to dangerous ground, and yet he could not take his eyes off her as she demurely stitched on her embroidery, completely oblivious to the flame she had ignited in Mr. Darcy.

Chapter Fourteen

FAREWELL TO NETHERFIELD

Elizabeth slept with peace that night, content in the knowledge that Jane was recovering well, that Bingley clearly loved her sister, and that the return to Longbourn was upon them. She awoke with felicity equal to that with which she slept and dressed and packed her own things quickly. Consciousness did not come so swiftly to Jane, however, and Elizabeth found herself ready to depart all alone.

It was no matter, Elizabeth sighed, for Jane needed the rest, and they could not go until the carriage arrived anyway. Elizabeth penned the dispatch to Longbourn, requesting it be sent around as quickly as possible. She gave the note to Mrs. Nicholls, who saw to its delivery.

Elizabeth, relishing the opportunity for one last solitary walk around Netherfield Park before breakfast, was soon upon a pathway leading away from the house. The trail, she quickly discovered, put her on a meandering route toward the stables. From a distance, Elizabeth could see the grooms already at their work, although the sun had just come up. The orchards beyond the stables were nearly bare of foliage but looked interesting, and Elizabeth pushed forward with the intention of exploring. Just beyond the stables, as she passed dog kennels, her footsteps triggered the baying of the hunting dogs, and her thoughts turned to her canine friend, Apollo. A detour through the kennels to bid farewell to the hound seemed like a fine idea, for she had developed a fondness for the beautiful animal.

Picking up her dress and petticoat, she navigated a muddy patch between her and the outbuilding. As soon as she passed through the gate, she found herself before five handsome dogs sharing the same enclosure. They were jumping, baying, and raising a ruckus that was certain to catch attention from the stables if it continued, so she hushed them, surprised to find that they settled quickly on her command. When she called to Apollo, he approached her with the same friendliness that he had shown before, and she crouched to pet him as he squirmed with delight at her attention.

"Good morning, my sweet Apollo!" Elizabeth crooned in his ear. "You are looking as fine today as ever." She kissed his nose again, several times, petting him vigorously. "My, but you possess such a handsome coat!" She stroked his back, static electricity from the crisp morning sparking as her fingers passed along his silky fur. "I envy it most wretchedly, but as Mary would remind me, we are not to covet, and here I find myself, jealous of a dog." She laughed, her hands cradling the dog's ears as she rocked his head playfully, and then scratched his neck affectionately, seeking to find the spots that most pleased him.

"Apollo appears to inspire envy all around today, Miss Bennet." The low voice of Mr. Darcy behind her caused Elizabeth to jump and turn with a start, her hands releasing Apollo as she did so. "You promised me most faithfully that you would not steal his affections, and now I find the two of you in a secret liaison behind the stables." He was leaning casually against the kennel doorframe as he spoke. Elizabeth had never seen him in such an attitude, but nearly as soon as she turned to face him, he drew himself erect and was formal once again.

Elizabeth stiffly stood up from her crouched position, her face shifting from the shadows into the sunlight that poured through the cutout windows. She could not tell from his demeanor if he was teasing her or if he was angry. "Mr. Darcy." She curtsied, determined to be composed. "My rendezvous with your hound was no secret; I daresay every groomsman in the stable was on alert. As for your other charge, can a lady not bid farewell to a friend without raising speculation?"

"Farewell, Miss Bennet?" Darcy looked at her, searching her eyes, a strange expression lighting his.

"Yes, Mr. Darcy. I fear we have imposed on Mr. Bingley's hospitality long enough. Jane has recovered sufficiently to travel the distance to Longbourn, and we must return today. I have already sent for the carriage."

Mr. Darcy's face clouded. "Have you informed Mr. Bingley of these arrangements?"

"Yesterday I told him that it was very likely that we would return to our home," Elizabeth confirmed, "as soon as Jane was well enough."

"And knowing that you would leave today, you came to the kennels—to say goodbye to my dog?" Darcy shook his head slightly as if to challenge her account.

Elizabeth raised her chin. "Your eyes, I believe, gave you proof, sir."

"But my ears," Darcy replied, "did not hear the sentiments of a fond farewell expressed. No, I would remember it if they had."

"I was not finished." Elizabeth countered with a raised brow. "Had you not interrupted me, you would have proof enough. Excuse me, sir, I must finish my walk now."

Elizabeth stooped to pat Apollo one last time, making a point to say "good-bye" to the beast before she brushed past Mr. Darcy, coming closer than she would have liked, since he did not step aside to let her pass easily.

§

Elizabeth started her walk on the amber carpet found in the orchards, but she eventually wandered down a lane that rolled with the landscape, taking her past fields populated with lazily grazing sheep. She turned and circled back toward Netherfield, traipsing through a wooded area as she enjoyed the balmy, sunny morning. Returning to the house refreshed and cheerful, she found the rest of the household assembled in the dining room for breakfast.

She greeted them all warmly, and confirmed the news that she and Jane were to away that very morning, which they had all heard from Mr. Darcy. Miss Bingley was suddenly generous in her manners again, no doubt, Elizabeth thought to herself, *because* they were leaving.

Jane went upstairs to pack, and Elizabeth was about to assist her when the footman returned from Longbourn. The reply, written in her mother's hand, refused Elizabeth's request for the carriage. Mrs. Bennet insisted that they must trespass on Mr. Bingley's kindness for at least two more days, for the carriage could not be sent until then, and besides, Jane was not nearly well enough yet.

Elizabeth fumed at her mother's manipulation. The dispatch she had sent to Longbourn had been clear that Jane was well enough to travel. Elizabeth vowed not to submit to her mother's ill-conceived tactics to keep Jane at Netherfield under pretense.

She found Jane in her bedchamber, packing slowly and sadly. "What is wrong, Jane?" Elizabeth could not bear to see her gentle sister's countenance so stricken.

"Oh, Lizzy, surely you must know." Jane sighed, refusing to look at her sister.

"No, Jane, you must tell me."

""I am grieved to be leaving Mr. Bingley, Lizzy. You were in company with him these past five days, and I have had but one evening to enjoy his attentions."

"But, Jane," Elizabeth teased, "his manner with you last night was indeed attentive-his regard for you was spoken in each hushed word that he whispered in your pretty ears. Surely you would rather have him court you at Longbourn than here at Netherfield, with Caroline Bingley hovering about."

"Caroline has only been kind to me, Lizzy. What do you suppose has provoked her against *you*?" Jane asked quietly.

"She vexes me, Jane, she baits me, and although I daily vow not to, I fear that I rise to it—I cannot contain myself." Elizabeth colored in shame. "My opinions offend her, I know this to be so, but there is something more. I believe I have come to an understanding of her cause against me."

"What can she hold against you, Lizzy? I am perplexed." Jane's brow furrowed.

"Miss Bingley," Elizabeth proclaimed, "is in love with Mr. Darcy."

"I believe so too, but what can that have to do with you, Lizzy?" Jane asked, confused.

"Mr. Darcy has been kind to me, Jane. He was the one who counseled me to apply ice to your head when I was distraught, and he had the chaise sent to your room so that I could rest. He escorted me to the library to select the book I was reading, and Miss Bingley knew of it. I have come to believe that her feelings for Mr. Darcy consume her, and she is jealous when he speaks a word to me or even glances in my direction. When he asked me to dance, her color went so crimson that I thought she would have a fit and fall onto the pianoforte in a stupor. She could not detect, as I did, that he was merely mocking me."

"But, Lizzy," Jane frowned slightly, "why would Mr. Darcy mock you? That is absurd."

"Mr. Bingley likes our country manners, as you well know, but Mr. Darcy is accustomed to the sophisticated manners of the ladies of the *ton*. We are a curiosity to him, Jane, nothing more—so he mocks us, just as we made sport of his prideful behavior at the assembly." Elizabeth smiled cheerfully. "Enough talk of Miss Bingley and Mr. Darcy. These matters will be sorted out when we are gone. Our problems loom much larger than petty discords such as these, for Mama has refused to send the carriage."

"Really, Lizzy?" Jane lit up. "Must we stay then?"

"No, Jane. You must apply to Mr. Bingley to borrow his carriage to take us back to Longbourn."

"You are right, of course," Jane said with a pout. "Although I do wish we could stay."

"We have imposed on Mr. Bingley long enough. Besides, how is he to call on you at Longbourn if you are not at home?"

"I will ask him directly, then, to borrow his carriage, for I must be there when he calls!" Jane giggled and looked around the room. "I have finished packing now, and this is as good a reason as any other to seek him out!"

"By all means, go and find him!" Elizabeth laughed, picking up the book she had borrowed. "I must return this to the library."

Mr. Darcy, who had planned to ride that morning, did not do so. He returned to the house to find Charles and report to his friend that the Bennet sisters were to depart that very day. Bingley had taken the news badly and had even tried to plot to delay their departure, but ultimately Darcy helped him see that it was for the best that they go as planned. There was much to do to prepare for the ball, and it would not do to have the distraction of the two sisters in the house. Bingley finally agreed that, for the sake of the ball, he would not oppose their departure.

Mr. Darcy had retired to his bedchamber after speaking with Bingley, for his own feelings on the matter were not so easily resolved. To be sure, he was relieved that Elizabeth Bennet would be removed from the household—his resistance to her grew weaker daily. She could not know what she did to him, he was certain of that. Hers was not the air of a woman bent on tormenting him, yet the effect was the same—perhaps worse. Her playful manner was as natural to her as the breeze that teased her hair, and that lack of artifice in her was as potent as any liquor when it went to his head.

Yet, the thought of her leaving Netherfield depressed him. He conjured up the image of her in the kennel that morning. He had thought, until the very moment when she stood up, that although they sparkled with intelligence and good humor, her eyes were an ordinary shade of brown. Then the sun had struck them, and he witnessed an incredible transformation. Her pupils had shrunk in the sunlight, and the iris of her eye, lit as it was by the morning rays, revealed flecks of green and amber, copper and violet woven in with the brown—strands of color so extraordinary that he literally forgot to breathe for how long he knew not. This was his ongoing experience with Elizabeth Bennet. Nothing was as it seemed in a casual glance; there was always more, and more after that. The depths he dared not fathom.

He opened the parcel that lay on the table in his room. He had made the purchase several days earlier but had not yet sent the gift to Georgiana, for it was all wrong. He extracted the shawl from the package and gazed down at the beautiful garment. For Georgiana, he should have selected one of the lovely pastel shawls, but something had come over him, and he had walked away with this one instead.

The shawl he held in his hands was unsuited for his sister in every way. The silk was a deep red color, like burgundy wine, with wispy gold threads woven into the fabric that shimmered in any light. Petite pink ribbon rosettes bordered the edges, with fine silk embroidery forming a rich ivy-like pattern in satiny shades of green that linked the rosettes in a wild tangle of leaves and vines. The exquisite shawl was dearer by half again the cost of any others the widow had for sale, and yet he had purchased it. He acknowledged to himself that it was as if it were made for *her*, indeed, that the only woman of his acquaintance who could ever do it justice was Elizabeth Bennet. He could not bestow such a gift on an unrelated woman, even if the universe itself declared that Elizabeth only could don it. He would buy another for Georgiana and save this one for he knew not what—he only knew that he did not want to part with it.

Mr. Bingley, although not the cleverest of men, was no fool either. He was sorely tempted to answer Jane that his carriage was not available either, but he could not lie to her in such a way. Instead, he contrived a *minor* falsehood, declaring that of course they could use his carriage but not until nearly evening, for it was undergoing maintenance in the morning. He then sent a footman to the carriage house, ordering some minor service to rectify his deceit by making it a truth instead.

Jane was more than pleased to stay for tea in the company of Mr. Bingley and his sisters. Elizabeth, however, was not. When she learned of the hour that the carriage was to be ready, she declared to Jane that she could not wait. She graciously thanked Mr. Bingley for his hospitality, hugged her sister, and set off in the direction of Longbourn. Mr. Darcy was not seen when she departed, and she did not regret that, for her encounter with him that morning had increased her feelings of unease about the man.

If Elizabeth had known what she was to encounter when she reached her home, she may have reconsidered her decision to walk, or at least taken a more scenic route to forestall her arrival at the gate, for nothing at Netherfield could compare to the horror that sat within the parlor at Longbourn.

Chapter Fifteen

THE ROAD TO LONGBOURN

Fortunately for Elizabeth, providence smiled on her and slowed her step to delay that fateful homecoming, for the road to Longbourn was an ample source of diversion and delight. Her desire to be separated from the increasing vexations at Netherfield had driven her from that house; however, no great urgency to enter the doors of her own compelled her—her normally brisk pace was reduced to what would generously be called a stroll.

The midday sun had warmed the air from cold to simply crisp, and she relished its soothing rays as she meandered along, a chorus of wintering songbirds providing a melody to accompany the rhythm of her footsteps while she imagined herself dancing with a man as suited to herself as Mr. Bingley was to Jane. In her mind he was handsome, although he remained faceless, but he was amiable too, and passionate, although in a gentlemanly way. In her mind's eye, he was tall, although she admitted to herself that this point was negotiable should a shorter man with the right blend of character and intelligence turn up. Did such a man exist? She fervently hoped so and believed that she would recognize such a man upon first introduction or soon thereafter, for he would charm and delight her—of course, he would!

She eventually found herself approaching Meryton, and as she passed the households of friends and acquaintances on the outskirts, she stopped briefly to converse, to wish them good day and to catch up on the tidbits of gossip that the townsfolk were anxious to share. With a smile, she bid goodbye to sweet little Hannah Kettle, the milliner's daughter, and had returned to the road when a harbinger of sorts caused her to stop short. Tied inside the gate of the widow Parks' cottage was a familiar black blood horse. Standing just outside the same was her canine friend, Apollo.

He barked once, as if to greet her, his tail wagging furiously, although he did not move from his place. Understanding dawned on Elizabeth immediately, for she had personally informed Mr. Darcy of the widow's industry. She glanced quickly toward the cottage door, and seeing no one, stepped swiftly to pet Apollo's head a few times and move past the house undetected, for the thought of an encounter strangely unsettled her, and she did not desire it.

"Miss Bennet!" His voice struck her from behind as she passed the neighbor's gate, and Elizabeth stopped and reluctantly turned to acknowledge his salutation with a curtsy.

"Mr. Darcy." Elizabeth tried to moderate her tone in such a way as to acknowledge his greeting without inviting conversation. She found, when she turned, that he was already seated on his mount. He brought the animal forward slowly until he loomed over Elizabeth, and she had to tip her head upwards to see his face, which was in shadow under the rim of his hat.

"Miss Bennet, where is your carriage?" He looked mildly confused.

"The carriage could not be spared from Longbourn." Elizabeth admitted, fearing that he would somehow detect her mother's scheming. "Mr. Bingley's carriage will convey Jane this evening, as soon as it is available."

"Why did you not wait to return with your sister?" Mr. Darcy inquired, as though he were due an explanation.

Elizabeth squirmed slightly, for she could not be entirely truthful without also being impolite. "It is a fine day for a walk, Mr. Darcy." She raised her hand, to illustrate by gesture the fineness of the day.

Mr. Darcy looked around, as though the nature of his surroundings had until that moment eluded him. "Indeed, it is, Miss Bennet." He looked to Elizabeth as if he had something more to say, and so she stood patiently, waiting for him to say it. At length he added, "I rode into Meryton." At this, Elizabeth nodded her head, not entirely astounded at the revelation. Her silent acknowledgement was encouragement enough, however, for Mr. Darcy to dismount and ask, "May I show you the shawl I have just purchased for my sister?"

"But, of course, I would like very much to see it." Elizabeth relaxed and smiled with some surprise at his request. "Mrs. Parks' shawls are so lovely. I confess that I am always taken aback by their beauty."

Mr. Darcy produced a parcel and opened it, revealing a fine woolen fabric the color of crème, with sky-blue threads embroidered into an intricate lacy pattern, embellished with tiny seed pearls throughout. Elizabeth gasped and smiled as she removed her gloves, reaching out to finger the cloth. "Oh, Mr. Darcy!" She exclaimed in a tone more whisper than voice, "It is so very soft! Your sister will be happy indeed to receive such a gift!" She glanced up at him, her eyes shining with sincere admiration at his generosity towards Georgiana. "What a kind brother you are to do such a thing!"

Mr. Darcy, who just that morning had sworn to himself that he would avoid any further contact with Elizabeth Bennet, excepting the promised dance at the Netherfield ball, now found himself gripped by her glance. He knew he must not give in to it, this insane desire to hear her compliments, to hear her whisper his name again. He steeled himself against it, determined not to give himself away and, in so doing, cruelly raise her hopes for something that could never be. He looked down the road into Meryton, realizing he must also be careful not to raise speculation among her neighbors.

Elizabeth saw his eyes stray to the road, and she pulled on her gloves. "I have wondered since we spoke of it if you had come here. It was good fortune for me to encounter you today, for I find myself quite gratified that I could play even a token part in your sister's happiness."

"How clever, Miss Bennet, for you to discover your credit in the matter. I will be certain that my sister knows to whom she is indebted." Darcy was sorry the moment he said it.

"I did not mean...," Elizabeth stammered.

"She will be most thankful to you, I am sure." Darcy muttered, adrift in his disastrous faux pas.

"Good day, Mr. Darcy." Elizabeth curtsied and spun on her heel launching into a brisk walk toward Meryton.

Moments later, she heard the clopping of horse's hooves behind her, and she stole a look across her shoulder to find Mr. Darcy, his horse and his dog all following a few paces behind her. She stopped and turned to face him. "Are you lost, Mr. Darcy? Netherfield is that way." She pointed back to where she had come from and then resumed her walk toward Longbourn.

"It is a fine day for a walk, Miss Bennet." His address sounded oddly apologetic.

"Aye," she replied turning her head to the side, "that it is." She answered cheerfully but did not break stride.

"Miss Bennet!" He called out from where he stood—his voice strangely urgent.

"What is it?" She turned, flustered by his persistence in delaying her.

"It appears that my dog would like to escort you home."

Elizabeth looked downward to see Apollo at her heel. She stopped again and stooped to pet him. "What of your horse? Does he also wish to attend me?"

"Yes." Darcy replied soberly. "Romeo goes where Apollo goes."

"Your horse and dog do not compromise my delicacy, sir," Elizabeth said civilly. "But as you well know, their master must be left behind or *he* will ruin my reputation." She looked at him with exasperation. "Did you not once tell me, Mr. Darcy, that you never jest?"

"I find myself reformed, Miss Bennet." He bowed to her, tipped his hat, mounted his horse and turned it toward Netherfield at a leisurely pace as he called Apollo with a soft, haunting whistle.

❧

Mr. Darcy kept his horse reined to a walk until he cleared the turn in the road that put him out of sight of the town, and then he urged his mount into a cantor, Apollo racing ahead of them. He did not wish to think about this surprise encounter with the second eldest Bennet sister, but his usually disciplined mind had been increasingly uncooperative. Unfortunately, he found that the more he applied his energies to excising the thoughts, the more they persisted.

His behavior was inexplicable. He had left Netherfield that morning specifically to avoid additional contact with Elizabeth before she returned to Longbourn. He merely needed time to regain his composure, he had thought, for the very natural attraction he felt for her would pass once they were separated. It had seemed in the morning to be the rational course—a cathartic ride through the countryside and then an errand to the cottage of the widow, to purchase another shawl for Georgiana. That should be sufficient to keep him away from the house until after the sisters had departed.

He had foiled his own plan, so he could blame no one else for it. When he looked through the window and saw Elizabeth pass by as he completed the transaction, he could have waited a moment to school his feelings, perused the wares or conversed with the lady and her daughter before leaving, but instead he had bolted from the cottage like a schoolboy. Even then, his opportunity to escape was laid before him, for after greeting Apollo, Elizabeth had proceeded toward Meryton with not even a backward glance. That was the reason, he decided angrily to himself, that he called her name. It was the lack of a backward glance.

His own pride had sabotaged him! He had spent so much energy rejecting *her* that it did not seem right that she so easily dismissed *him*. It was not that he actually wanted her to pursue him, but he did want her to notice him, nonetheless, to acknowledge what he dared not acknowledge. Did she not feel the electricity in the air that raised the hair on his neck and threatened to strike him dead when they spoke? Was she impervious to the rush of excitement he felt when she was near, to the connection that stirred his blood when their eyes met? Was it so very wrong to expect that it affected her as well, even though he would not, could not act on it?

It was his vanity that had called her name, that could not let her pass unchallenged, and his stupidity that had insulted her moments later by speaking before he thought. The brief interlude in between his two blunders, however, held a moment he would secretly cherish!

His notion to follow her in an attempt to amend his error was the moment that would truly remain with him, however. He laughed aloud at the thought of it. With Darcy's first step toward Elizabeth, his dog had leapt to catch up with her, setting him on a course that would publicly violate the unbendable rules of propriety. Elizabeth, he realized with appreciation, had gracefully extracted them both from the trap and generously offered him a convenient excuse for his unseemly behavior—that he was in jest. The irony was not lost on Darcy, for he had been, most foolishly, in earnest.

Romeo. Elizabeth was amused as she walked away from Meryton, for the incredibly reserved Mr. Darcy had named his horse for a star-crossed lover. What delicious incongruity, she thought, for Romeo was an impulsive, passionate sort of man, who felt so deeply that he could not live without his beloved. *I have caught you at last, Mr. Darcy. I have discovered something ridiculous in you to laugh at.* She would never say it to him, of course; no, this was a private pleasure—although she might have to tell Jane!

He had behaved oddly, she mused as she closed the distance to her home, much as her father did when he had a great joke he was concealing to spring on them after dinner. Elizabeth conceded that it had been uncharacteristically thoughtful of Mr. Darcy to show her the shawl he had bought for Georgiana—there was nothing to laugh about there, although she felt a slight twinge of envy that the Bennets did not have such a brother to bestow lovely keepsakes upon his sisters. *If Jane marries Mr. Bingley, then I will have a brother!* The thought warmed her heart, for she could not imagine a better brother than Charles Bingley.

She looked up, saw the smoke rising from the chimneys of Longbourn in the distance, and quickened her pace, eager to see if, in her absence, her father had come across some great joke to tell.

Chapter Sixteen

BEHIND THE PARLOR DOOR

Elizabeth peered through the window of her father's study, as was her routine upon approaching the house. She could discern merely from the look on his face the state of the household. If Mary had been sermonizing, he bore a certain weariness. If her mother's nerves were disturbed, he would be so buried in his book that he would not even notice his daughter at the window. If Lydia were making a fuss about a bonnet or gown, his visage was one of amusement, and if some burden were pressing on him, he wore that as well. Today, he was not in his study at all.

Elizabeth entered the house and shed her pelisse, bonnet and gloves into the waiting hands of Mrs. Hill. It was Hill's face that stopped Elizabeth short, for the women looked terrified. She waited while Hill tended to her things, for there was obviously something amiss, and Elizabeth's concern mounted as she noted the trembling of Hill's hands and her general state of agitation.

"What is it, Hill? What is wrong? Is someone ill?" Elizabeth asked quietly.

Hill shook her head, looking in the general direction of the parlor, her mouth open as if she wished to speak, but no words would come.

"Is someone here, Hill? Do we have visitors?" Elizabeth guessed.

Hill nodded and whispered, "Yes, Miss Elizabeth, visitors."

"Who is it?" Elizabeth prompted.

"It is your father's cousin, Mr. Collins, and ... and ... and ....," Hill stammered helplessly.

"My father's cousin, Mr. Collins, and someone else?" Elizabeth confirmed.

"There are four." Hill added.

"Four cousins?" Elizabeth blinked in confusion.

Hill took a deep breath. "No, Miss. Four *visitors*—Mr. Collins and three ladies."

"Do these ladies have names?" Elizabeth began to feel a bit impatient, for it was unlike Hill to be so unnerved and uncommunicative.

Hill drew Elizabeth into the corner and in a low voice, solemnly told her, "They are Lady Catherine de Bourgh, her daughter, Anne, and Anne's companion, Mrs. Jenkinson."

"I have never heard of any of them. Why are they here?"

Hill finally found her voice. "Mr. Collins is to stay at Longbourn for two weeks. The others are travelling on to London tonight. Their carriage needed a repair and is at this very moment being tended to. Lady Catherine is in an ill humor—she is most unhappy about the delay. I served them tea, but there is nothing more that I can do. Your mama is doing what she can, but nothing seems to appease the woman."

"Were they expected?"

"Mr. Collins had written your father of his coming, and Mrs. Bennet had informed me that he would be here for dinner tonight, but they arrived early, and we did not know about the ladies."

"Are the ladies to stay for dinner?"

Hill shrugged helplessly, and Elizabeth realized that she would get no more information from the distraught housekeeper. She encouraged Hill to return to her duties before approaching the parlor door.

"Out?" a shrill voice assaulted her ears through the door. "All of your daughters are out? The youngest before the eldest are married?"

"Yes. My youngest, Lydia, is a great favorite among the gentlemen, and...."

"If your youngest is turning the heads of the men of your acquaintance, your eldest will never marry, of that you may be certain. Had I had another daughter, I would never have allowed such foolishness in my house. It is unheard of."

"Your ladyship, my eldest is very soon to be engaged," Mrs. Bennet said apologetically.

"You are very fortunate, Mrs. Bennet, that Mr. Collins has come. When he informed me of the entailment of this estate, I assured him that it was his obligation to secure his wife from among your daughters. His duty to his family is second only to the responsibilities of his ministry. In marrying a genteel woman, he will set the example for all in his parish. In marrying one of your daughters, Mr. Collins may serve both interests with equal diligence. Such expedient solutions are rare in this world, Mrs. Bennet, and I prize them highly. Where are your other daughters?"

"They are at the neighboring estate, Netherfield Park. My daughter Jane suffered an accident on the grounds there and could not be moved," Mrs. Bennet answered with a quiver in her voice. "My daughter Elizabeth is...."

Elizabeth opened the parlor door and stepped inside, fearing that her mother's nerves would be her undoing.

Mrs. Bennet looked up in surprise at her daughter. "My daughter Elizabeth," she repeated, "is just arrived home from…" she glanced in embarrassment at the Elizabeth's dusty shoes and hem. "Is just arrived home."

Elizabeth scanned the occupants of the room. In the center of their finest settee sat a woman, about the same age as her mother or a little older, dressed in finery fit for court, and she reeked with heavy perfume that nearly caused Elizabeth to choke. The two other ladies were not dressed as finely although their gowns were far more expensive than anything Elizabeth owned. She immediately pitied the youngest, for she looked unhappy and fragile, as though a puff of wind could blow her down. She smiled encouragingly at the poor creature when their eyes met.

The man who sat in an armchair next to the fireplace did not look even remotely related to her father. Mr. Bennet was a distinguished, handsome man, but this man, allegedly a cousin, was difficult to look at. She could not tell his age due to an unfortunate degree of scarring on his round face, undoubtedly from significant boils and other blemishes that he must have suffered in his youth. The effect was blotchy and red, reminiscent of the skin of a toad. His hairline was already receded, and he had combed long strands of thin, stringy hair across his head in an attempt to conceal the exposed scalp. His eyes could barely be seen due to their squint, although he was looking directly at her, smiling with a seamy grin that caused her stomach to turn slightly.

"Are you going to introduce us?" Lady Catherine prompted Mrs. Bennet after a moment of silence.

"Oh, yes." Mrs. Bennet was flustered, and looked like she was about to faint. "Lady Catherine, this is my second eldest, Miss Elizabeth Bennet."

Lady Catherine nodded at Elizabeth, who curtsied and nodded back pleasantly.

"Elizabeth, this is Lady Catherine de Bourgh, Anne de Bourgh, Mrs. Jenkinson and Mr. Collins."

Elizabeth politely acknowledged each of them, trying hard not to laugh at Mr. Collins as he belatedly rose for the introduction. She could hear Lydia and Kitty giggling from their seats in the corner, and she saw Mary smoothing her hair next to them.

"Did you walk home, child?" Lady Catherine scrutinized Elizabeth.

"Yes, I did. It is a fine day for a walk, Lady Catherine." Elizabeth said cheerfully, for she recalled the last time the phrase had been uttered—by Mr. Darcy, and she found herself mysteriously amused by her ability to reference the interlude with no one but herself knowing it.

"Take note, Mr. Collins," Lady Catherine turned to the strange little man. "A sturdy constitution and a resourceful, cheerful disposition are most desirable characteristics for a parson's wife."

"Yes, your ladyship." Mr. Collins simpered.

"It would be well," Lady Catherine continued, "to find a lady who does not always feel entitled to the luxury of a carriage to transport her, one who is not above walking, as befits her station."

Horrified at the implication, Elizabeth said, "I did send for the carriage." She looked meaningfully at her mother, "But it could not be spared."

Lady Catherine looked at Elizabeth suspiciously. "Where is your sister?"

"I have four sisters, Lady Catherine. Three of them sit over there." Elizabeth indicated where they sat, and Lydia paid her for it with a frown. "My other sister, I expect, will be delivered by the carriage from Netherfield Park in time for dinner."

"This is most irregular," Lady Catherine muttered to herself and turning to Mrs. Bennet, said, "I had hoped to meet all of your daughters today, Mrs. Bennet, for Mr. Collins relies upon my guidance in all of his most important decisions."

Mr. Collins nodded in agreement. "Her ladyship is most...."

"We shall not stay for dinner." Lady Catherine announced abruptly, declining an invitation that had not been extended. "I cannot be detained any longer than is necessary." If she sensed the general sigh of relief in the room, she did not reveal it. "My business in London is of utmost urgency. It is a family matter that requires my immediate attention. I believe that my nephew is in grave peril, and his situation requires my intervention as a priority."

"If that is the case," Mr. Bennet said, standing up, "I will go and ascertain the state of your carriage. *Your nephew needs you.*" His manner being most gracious, only Elizabeth detected the note of facetiousness in his address before he quit the room.

Elizabeth tried to imagine what the nephew of such a woman could possibly be like. Was he like his cousin Anne, pallid and sickly? She looked at Anne again, who was clearly exhausted from travelling. It seemed that mention of the nephew had caused her eyes to moisten and her lip to tremble. She looked miserable. Compassion filled Elizabeth's heart for this girl, and for the first time in a long time, Elizabeth was grateful for the nature of her own mother, for one such as Lady Catherine would be much worse.

"Excuse me." Elizabeth curtsied again, "I fear I am covered in dust from my walk and have a need to freshen my appearance." She was out the door in a second, as she had not come very far into the room.

"That one," she heard Lady Catherine say as she left, "holds promise."

With a shudder, Elizabeth fled to the kitchen, where she persuaded the cook to prepare a small knapsack of foodstuffs that could be eaten in the carriage, for her concern for Anne was real, and Elizabeth was a person of action when she saw a need.

She went to her room and hurriedly changed, washed her face and tidied her hair. She raced back down the stairs to the kitchen and helped the cook finish with her gift for Miss de Bourgh, packing it all as neatly as she could. Just as they finished, the de Bourgh carriage passed by the kitchen window on the way to the front of the house. Elizabeth hurried through the entryway to be outside the door when the ladies departed.

Elizabeth intercepted Anne as she came out of the house, calling softly, "Miss de Bourgh." When she turned to face her, Elizabeth stepped forward, and grasped Anne's hand, causing her eyes to widen in surprise.

"Miss de Bourgh, your journey has been long, and it is another twenty miles to London. Please take this with you. I find that when traveling has made me weary, eating even a morsel makes me feel better." She pressed the sack into Anne's hand.

Anne looked at Elizabeth in wonder and replied quietly, so her mother, who was making a production of getting into the carriage, could not hear her. "How very kind you are, Miss Bennet, but my mother does not allow me to eat in the carriage." She looked down longingly at the package in her hand.

"Put it in your pocket," Elizabeth said in a merry but hushed tone, "and eat it when your mother falls asleep. She will never know!"

Anne de Bourgh, who never smiled, smiled. "She will never know!" Anne whispered back at Elizabeth with a grin as she slipped the food into her pocket and turned to climb into the carriage. She settled in and waved goodbye to Elizabeth, thinking to herself that she hoped that Mr. Collins would chose this daughter for his wife, for then she would be a neighbor, and they could possibly even be friends.

Not long after the de Bourgh party left, Jane arrived at Longbourn in Mr. Bingley's carriage, just as the sun was going down. She was escorted by Mr. Bingley, Mr. Darcy and a maid, for Mr. Bingley did not want to risk any discomfort to Jane should any complications arise during the ride. He had persuaded Mr. Darcy to accompany them and brought the maid for the sake of propriety.

Mr. Collins had been shown to the room he would be staying in, to relieve the household of his effusions regarding his patroness, and was not to descend to the lower floor until dinner. When the gentlemen arrived at Longbourn with Jane, they were shown into the parlor for a brief visit. Mrs. Bennet was in the process of supervising the dinner they were laying out for their guest, and Mr. Bennet was in his study, so Elizabeth joined Jane, Mr. Bingley and Mr. Darcy in the parlor.

After they had settled that the roads had been fine, and that Jane had fared well, Mr. Bingley and Jane once again had no eyes or ears for any other. They began quietly whispering to one another as they had at Netherfield, Jane with her sweet, gentle smile adorning each word and Mr. Bingley so enamored with her that he hung on every one of them.

Elizabeth picked up some needlework that her sister had set down and turned slightly to give Jane and Mr. Bingley some privacy. Mr. Darcy walked to the window and stared out at a scene lit only by fading twilight. Elizabeth smiled to herself, for she had caught him in the very act. She looked up at the window, meeting his gaze boldly, for she wanted him to know that his game was discovered and that he could not spy on the room this way anymore—at least not undetected.

Mr. Darcy pressed his lips together, suppressing the laugh that threatened to escape at the challenge in her eyes. He had not desired to come with Bingley tonight—seeing Elizabeth in Meryton had shaken him to the core, and he did not know how much more he could take. Even looking at a warped reflection of her in the ever-darkening glass, her lips puckered in disapproval, her eyes throwing sparks at him wore at his defenses. She intoxicated him when she was near. She was speaking to Jane and Bingley now, her lilting voice chased by an unguarded laugh.

He breathed in deeply, irrationally hoping to inhale a trace of her scent, even though she was across the room, and he did smell something—something familiar—and disturbing. What was it? He looked away from the glass, concentrating on the odor that now permeated his nostrils and made him feel queasy. It took several minutes to place it, for the context was all wrong. Aunt Catherine! It could not be.

He turned abruptly from the window and approached Elizabeth. "Has Longbourn seen any other guests today?" He asked the question casually, with an air of nonchalance that one usually reserved for conversations about the weather.

"Why, yes," Elizabeth responded, somewhat surprised by the odd question. "Our cousin, Mr. Collins, has come for a short stay. He arrived earlier today."

"Mr. Collins?" Darcy looked baffled.

"That is his name. He is the parson," Elizabeth offered, "at a rectory in Kent."

"He came alone?" Darcy inquired, casually again.

"No. His patroness was traveling to London and brought him here," Elizabeth answered.

"How odd—London lies between." Darcy puzzled.

"I thought so myself. I suspect the lady wished to oversee the particulars of Mr. Collins' affairs," Elizabeth replied. Darcy looked at her expectantly, so Elizabeth continued, "She was, to put it delicately, somewhat imperious in demeanor."

"I am familiar with Kent, as I have relations there. Do you know where the rectory is located?"

"No." Elizabeth shook her head with a slight grimace, mentally re-living the quarter hour spent in the parlor with Mr. Collins after the ladies had left. "I know only that it abuts a great estate with grand chimneys and expensive glazing. Rose... something I believe."

"Hmmm." Darcy pretended to ponder on it, slightly ashamed at what was rapidly becoming a deception. "That could be the Rosings Park estate near Hunsford."

"That may be it." Elizabeth nodded.

"Do you remember the lady's name?" Darcy asked.

"I shall never forget it." Elizabeth smiled warmly followed by a tinkling laugh. "Lady Catherine de Bourgh." She said it the way Collins said it, as though it should impress merely by hearing the name.

"Oh yes." Darcy nodded knowingly. "Lady Catherine de Bourgh. Was her daughter, Anne, with her?"

"Yes, yes, she was poor creature." Elizabeth sighed.

"She was not well?" Darcy probed.

"Not at all." Elizabeth shook her head slowly as she pictured the girl in her mind. "Perhaps she was just tired from the journey, but I sensed that she is not happy. She is, I think, proof that great estates with grand chimneys and the finest windows in the kingdom are nothing without loving hearts to fill them." Elizabeth looked up to see Mr. Darcy, looking at her with fierce intensity, and she realized that she might have inadvertently offended him, for she knew him to be the owner of such an estate himself. "Oh, I am sorry, Mr. Darcy. My mouth has run away with me."

Mr. Darcy held up his hand to signal that no apology was necessary. "Was there any talk of why it was necessary to travel to London while Miss de Bourgh was in ill health?"

"Yes." Elizabeth replied with a nod, thinking it appropriate to share what she knew since he seemed to be acquainted with the family. "It had something to do with intervening on behalf of her nephew, who was in some trouble, I think. She did not speak of the particulars."

An uncomfortable look crossed Darcy's handsome face before it turned to the stony mask that she had seen him wear at the Assembly Ball the night they had first met. He chatted with Elizabeth for a few more minutes about the weather, the roads and the upcoming Netherfield Ball, and then the gentlemen departed, not saying exactly when or if they would return.

Chapter Seventeen

UNRAVELED

On the carriage ride back to Netherfield, Mr. Bingley and Mr. Darcy were in entirely different moods, although neither man paid heed to the state of the other. They were each looking out a window into the night, deep in the world of their own thoughts.

The only way Mr. Bingley's day could have gone any better would have been if the Miss Bennets had not returned to Longbourn at all. The loss of the sisters from Netherfield did not truly distress Charles Bingley, for he had joyfully observed that something about Jane's demeanor had materially changed for the better upon her recovery from the fall. The biggest difference he noted was that she no longer bashfully glanced away when he searched her face, but instead, those cornflower blue eyes locked onto his and held them as if she could communicate her feelings directly to his mind. Her serenity was disturbed to be certain, and once, in their hushed conversations, she had addressed him very tenderly as "Charles." She had not even seemed to realize that she had crossed into familiarity, but for Charles Bingley, the sound could not have been more beautiful if a chorus of songbirds had sung his name. In his heart and mind, he allowed himself to be in love with his angel, Miss Jane Bennet, and he knew in the depths of his being that she felt much the same as he.

Mr. Darcy's day had been a disordered mess from start to finish, mostly because, unlike his friend, his heart and mind were in violent conflict with each other. His heart had succumbed days ago to Elizabeth Bennet as the most bewitching creature he had ever encountered, but his mind simply would not allow it to reach beyond that boundary. That word which had never even encroached on his thoughts before was popping into his head with increasing—and alarming—frequency. He vigorously attempted to repress this word with substitutions—*like, admire, respect, regard, esteem* and so on until he was weary of the exercise. Only when he had exhausted himself with the struggle did the word *love* settle itself and find its place among the rest. There was a certain peace in that, but he still could not reconcile his love for her with even a remote possibility of a life with her, and he despaired over the injustice of his dilemma.

Darcy forced his mind to turn to other thoughts. His Aunt Catherine had travelled from Kent to deliver her parson to Longbourn—an obscure country estate in a county she did not like. That was strange enough, but the worst part was that she had now gone to London to meddle with his affairs—again. He was not her only nephew, but he was the only one she ever interfered with. A dark cloud of familiar remorse settled over Darcy, regretting once again that he had gone along with her scheme a decade ago. It had seemed harmless at the time, almost a lark, but his willingness to protect his cousin from a scoundrel in pursuit of a rich heiress had led to the fateful rumors aggressively circulated by his aunt of an *impending engagement* between himself and Anne, rumors that had never ceased even to this day.

His aunt had twisted the fabrication into an expectation and then an obligation that Darcy had spent years and countless hours attempting to amend. He had learned a bitter lesson and sworn from that time forward that the absolute truth would be his standard. His aunt, however, was relentless in her pursuit of the outcome to which she now felt entitled and had gone so far in the past as to confront and intimidate women if she perceived any attachment on his part.

Darcy, who had always prized his privacy, had been forced by his aunt's dogged pursuit of the match to extreme caution as he moved within the society of the *ton*. The added counsel from his father to carefully guard himself from the predatory females within those circles had also proven itself countless times, and Darcy, although he liked the company of women well enough, had developed a barrier of aloofness that effectively insulated him from the feminine wiles and charms that were intended to entrap him.

Aunt Catherine had proven difficult to elude, for although she was rarely seen in London, she exhibited an uncanny ability to detect his movements. That she had left Longbourn a scant half-hour before he arrived was good fortune, indeed, for she could not know of his presence in Hertfordshire, or she would not have quit the county so easily. No doubt, her journey to London was intended to discover his whereabouts, although she could only have one reason to do so.

He was forced to consider what had triggered his aunt's latest round of interference. The only circumstance he could imagine that would impel his aunt to London for the winter was a report of his own serious attentions toward a marriageable woman. Whom, he wondered, only half amused, was the lucky lady? He smiled grimly to himself as he speculated that the object of the gossip was likely Caroline Bingley. The thought of his aunt confronting Bingley's haughty sister was both mortifying and diverting. Lady Catherine de Bourgh had so intimidated and traumatized her other targets that they had literally collapsed into near hysterics at her accusations, insults and threats.

Who was his aunt's informer? Darcy thought it must be someone in his sister's close circle, for she was the only person in recent weeks he had corresponded with on personal matters, and with Georgiana, he was entirely open. He smirked inwardly at the realization that due to Caroline's own insistent prodding, he had repeatedly mentioned Miss Bingley in his letters. That he was staying in her brother's household and had attended balls and assemblies with the same woman must have been sufficient cause to suspect his attachment. His aunt was slipping, he thought, if her paranoia had come to such a conclusion with so little credible information.

Darcy then recalled his last letter to his sister and was stricken with an epiphany. Although he had not specifically named her, he had written in glowing terms of Elizabeth Bennet to his sister, describing a vivacious and beautiful lady in the neighborhood—a young woman of charm and grace, with an intelligence and wit that he had found most refreshing and unusual for a country maiden. Could that reference have been enough to alarm his aunt? A surge of protectiveness for Elizabeth raced through his veins at the thought that he may have inadvertently called his aunt's wrath down upon the woman he loved. He mentally repeated the phrase, silently indulging in that feeling he had never before known—*the woman he loved.*

His heart pounded, his blood boiled, and a painful flood of realizations rained mercilessly on him. Another man would claim Elizabeth Bennet as his wife. Someone else would hold her in his arms, kiss her, take her into his bed and wake to see the sun on her sleep-drenched face. Another man would father her children, make a life with her, daily gaze into the eternal depths of her exquisite eyes. His previous despair was replaced with crushing desperation at his plight. He considered leaping from the carriage and returning to her, declaring himself to her, but he knew that such fantasy could not be.

He looked up at Bingley, who was sheepishly grinning as he dreamily looked out upon a passing landscape he did not really see. He finally understood what his friend must have been feeling as he sat next to Jane Bennet, soaking in her glances, her whispers and her smiles. Darcy grimaced at the realization that he envied Charles Bingley.

Forcing a change in his thoughts again, he turned to memories of his sweet cousin, Anne. He recalled the bright and delightful girl she was as a child. Almost like a faery she had been, her tinkling laughter at his teasing still rang in his ears. It took so little effort to please her then, for she delighted in everything, and although she had always seemed a bit fragile, she had also been lively and energetic, and he had entertained her with stories as they had walked the grounds of Pemberley and Rosings together. As she matured, she had attracted many suitors, and the year Anne came out in society had been particularly trying for him as he considered himself as an elder brother to her. His agreement to the grand deception had stemmed from that protectiveness. He had expected, of course, that a worthy match would be found for his darling cousin in a short time.

What none of them had expected was that she would be stricken with a fever a fortnight later, a fever that nearly killed her. Although her life was spared, the illness had drained all of her liveliness away, and she had remained weak and sickly, rarely going into society again. Darcy gritted his teeth. How cruel of his aunt to subject her to such a journey!

At this moment, some paranoia took root. Perhaps Aunt Catherine did know where he was after all. Had she delivered her parson to Hertfordshire to spy on him? Had she come to the Bennet household by design? It was no matter, he knew what he must do, and he would do it tonight.

Chapter Eighteen

MEETING MR. WICKHAM

Elizabeth discerned that Jane acutely felt the loss of Mr. Bingley nearly as soon as the carriage pulled away from Longbourn. She trailed Jane to her room, pressing the door shut behind them to assure their privacy, and simply asked, "Well?"

Jane blushed and smiled weakly at her sister, unable to conceal the depth of her feelings for Mr. Bingley. "Well. what, Lizzy?"

"You may pretend with everyone else, Jane, but with me, you must disclose all! How went your day after I quit Netherfield Park? I know that you were not subjected to Mr. Darcy's rattling about the house, for, in truth, I encountered him myself on the road to Meryton. Jane, my imagination has run absolutely wild for you and Mr. Bingley all day, and seeing his manner with you upon your return has done nothing but feed my speculation! I am about to go mad for it!"

"Lizzy!" Jane laughed at her sister's dramatics. "It was indeed a very pleasant day, but nothing wild, I assure you."

"He is besotted, Jane." Elizabeth teased. "Admit it—he loves you. A blind man would see it."

"You must promise not to say anything, Lizzy." Jane dropped her voice and paused until Elizabeth reluctantly nodded. "He does wish to court me—as the carriage was being brought around the house, Mr. Bingley very suddenly took my hand in his own. It was very warm, and he was very gentle. He kissed the back of hand in a gentlemanlike way and asked if I would allow him permission ... to speak to my father ... about courting me."

Elizabeth's eyes sparkled with delight. "Jane, that is wonderful! When is he to do it?"

"I daresay he would have done so today, but for our guest. He did not want to seem impolite with a newly arrived guest in the house. I believe he may come back tomorrow. He seemed most anxious to do it." Jane sighed. "He is indeed all that a young man should be, and to be able to receive him at Longbourn as a suitor is like a dream."

"Except that it is real—or soon will be!" Elizabeth exclaimed happily.

"So tell me—who is this Mr. Collins who has come? All I know is his name and that he is to stay here for a visit. What is he like?" Jane asked curiously.

"Well, Jane, he is the sort of man who rather defies description." Elizabeth hedged. "But he is, as I understand, my father's cousin, and the heir of Longbourn when Father dies."

Jane gasped and then suppressed a giggle. "How is it that my mother is not running about calling him names and shrieking of being forced to live in the hedgerows? Does she not despair?"

"Well," Elizabeth paused for effect, "he intends to make one of my father's daughters his wife, as a matter of duty. Mother's opinion of him was vastly improved upon hearing it."

Jane's eyes grew large in shock. "What? I suppose it must be to his credit...."

"Oh, Jane, do not extend him credit until you have at least been introduced! You are altogether too generous with your opinion sometimes." Elizabeth chided. "You are sure to meet him now, for the dinner hour is upon us. Fortunately for you, Mama has eliminated you from the competition for his attentions. Owing to her hopes in Mr. Bingley, you at least, are safe from Mr. Collins. If only I had a Mr. Bingley to offer me such an easy salvation!"

"He cannot be that bad, Lizzy." Jane frowned.

"Let us go down to dinner, and you will see!" Elizabeth laughed. "You know how father and I delight in the ridiculous and absurd. Tonight, our dinner company will offer an abundance of both, you may count upon it, although I will take no enjoyment in it, with his expectations of matrimony hanging over us all like a great dark cloud!"

ᘐ

Seeing Mr. Collins enter the dining room, Elizabeth was struck with the realization that it was only his face that reminded her of a toad. His movement she thought was incredibly similar to that of a duck. This comparison was in large part due to an outward rotation of his legs that caused him to waddle slightly. She censured herself silently for being so critical of characteristics that Mr. Collins could not help. However, it was not long before his manners exposed sufficient oddity in his conduct that his appearance was rendered largely irrelevant.

Mr. Collins was, above all, a flatterer of self. If something deserved praise, he praised it relentlessly, embellishing on its virtues until he had exhausted the topic with a seemingly unending stream of declarations that he managed to turn, before he was finished, to allow him to bask in the glow of how well it all reflected on himself, a humble parson.

His speech initially focused on the charms of the Bennets and the fineness of their house, but he drifted quickly to better, familiar topics, which were obviously well rehearsed. His grand and beneficent patroness, the Right Honorable Lady Catherine de Bourgh, was clearly his favorite topic, for speaking of her granted him the opportunity to inject his own importance into the conversation, along with frequent mention of his large, comfortable rectory, garden and valuable living.

Mr. Bennet was pleased with his guest, for he had supposed, based on Mr. Collins' letters, that he would be a nonsensical man and Mr. Bennet relished the occasions where he was correct. He made the most of the entertainment through facial expressions and gestures aimed at Elizabeth throughout the dinner service. Elizabeth was grateful for her father's merriment, for it eased her discomfort in Mr. Collins' marked and awkward attentions to herself.

Mrs. Bennet was also pleased with him, for he was to marry one of her daughters. This meant that she was not to be thrown out of Longbourn upon Mr. Bennet's demise after all. Her memory conveniently erased her previous distain for the man, and she was, instead, enthralled with his generosity. His stated desire to atone for the sin of inheriting Longbourn through a marital alliance seemed to Mrs. Bennet the perfect, most gentlemanly solution to all of their problems.

After dinner, they took tea in the drawing room, and Mr. Collins pressed "Cousin Elizabeth" into a game of backgammon, which she consented to and soundly defeated her opponent. She then excused herself and retired to her bedchamber early rather than spend further time in company with Mr. Collins.

ஓ

The next morning after breakfast, Mr. Collins requested that Elizabeth accompany him on a walk into Meryton. His purpose was two-fold, to engage her in conversation to further impress upon her his desirability and to establish that like herself, he was of a healthy constitution. His expectation was to remove themselves from the household so he could accomplish these ends in private. He rationalized to himself that there was no want of propriety in so doing, since he was both a relation and a parson and was, therefore. above reproach.

Elizabeth, after establishing that there was no hope of rain, politely agreed to the walk but swiftly enlisted all of her sisters to accompany them. Upon learning that they were not to be alone, Mr. Collins was mildly displeased but willing to make the most of the situation.

Lydia and Kitty raced ahead of them on the road, full of hope that they would encounter officers in town. Elizabeth used her sister's speed as an excuse to pace the walk briskly. She claimed a desire to catch up with her sisters, but she was equally motivated by it being a civil escape from Mr. Collins' pompous prattling. And so it was that they arrived on the outskirts of Meryton with Mr. Collins wheezing and panting for want of breath, thus foiling part of Mr. Collins' plan. This result suited Elizabeth very well, for he could not bore her in such a state.

Mr. Collins expressed a desire to enter the bookstore, for he felt there was a lack of serious reading material in the Bennet household and would not deign to select from among the works in Mr. Bennet's library. Mary concurred that the bookstore would be most pleasant, but Lydia spied Mr. Denny across the street and noted that there was a stranger with him. She demanded that the party go to make his acquaintance, since from a distance, the man appeared to be a gentlemanly, handsome figure—although the two younger Bennets gaily agreed he would be more so if he wore regimentals.

The party followed Lydia, for none of the ladies objected in the slightest to making the acquaintance of a handsome gentleman, although Elizabeth was ashamed of her sister's brazen approach. Mr. Collins expressed a desire to oblige the wishes of his dear cousins and make himself pleasant to them, so they all crossed the street to greet the Captain and his friend.

"Allow me to introduce my good friend, Mr. Wickham." Mr. Denny addressed the group, as soon as they had reached him. "He has come back with me from London, and I am pleased to tell you that he has accepted a commission in the corps."

Mr. Wickham smiled heartily at the sisters and greeted them warmly. His manner was so easy, so unassuming, that although he declared himself delighted and enchanted at the acquaintance, the feelings were even more so on the side of the ladies.

Elizabeth had never met a man so perfect in his address as Mr. Wickham. His countenance, too, was fine to look upon, his eyes merry, his bearing gentlemanly. His conversation was unspoiled by affectation, and he was, indeed, so charming that Elizabeth found herself entranced by the dashing officer. She felt the color rise to her cheeks when he spoke directly to her and was pleased when he shifted his position in the group to be nearer to her.

The sound of horses' hooves caught her attention, and she looked down the road to see Mr. Bingley and Mr. Darcy approaching on horseback.

Mr. Darcy had seen and recognized the Bennet sisters before Mr. Bingley had. Mr. Bingley had spurred his horse to hasten the meeting, and as soon as he was near enough, he called a greeting.

"Miss Bennet! We were just on our way to Longbourn. How delightful to see you here instead! You are well?" Bingley began before Mr. Darcy was even near, for he had slowed his mount considerably.

Jane nodded and replied. "I am well. We have walked into Meryton today to visit our Aunt Phillips."

A round of greetings and introductions ensued, whereby Mr. Collins was introduced as their cousin from Kent, just as Mr. Darcy reached the group. He bowed politely from his seat, and patiently waited as the introductions and civilities continued. He was not actually listening, for he saw no need to further the acquaintance with any of the party before him.

Mr. Darcy had but two objectives. The first was to not even look at Elizabeth. In light of his self-revelations of the night before, he was determined that he would not lose his composure and thereby give himself away. The second task was easier, for it was simply to take the measure of Mr. Collins, his Aunt Catherine's new parson.

Elizabeth, however, held no compunction to looking directly at Mr. Darcy, thinking his manners ill indeed, for his greeting was barely civil while Mr. Bingley was all warmth and affability. It was while she was looking thus at him that Mr. Darcy noticed the man standing next to Elizabeth Bennet.

What she witnessed next was a scene so astonishing that she could not interpret it, for when the two men's eyes met, Mr. Wickham's face turned an ashen white, and Mr. Darcy's, a brilliant shade of red. Mr. Wickham managed to tip his hat and nod his head to Mr. Darcy, but Mr. Darcy was as a statue, not moving or, it seemed, even breathing. He sat upon his horse staring at Mr. Wickham for a long, suspended moment that only the three of them seemed aware of. Mr. Wickham returned the stare, with a smirk on his face as he fidgeted uncomfortably. Finally, Mr. Darcy spoke.

"Mr. Wickham." Darcy's voice was even. "It has been several months now since I last saw you—at Ramsgate."

"Indeed it has," agreed Wickham, relaxing a little.

"And now you have joined yourself with the Hertfordshire militia." Mr. Darcy observed coldly. "I wonder that you did not enlist in the Regular Army to avail yourself of the chance to rout that invading rascal Napoleon."

"That would indeed have been the superior course, but alas, I could not afford the commission. I must of necessity earn my commission in the Regulars first, but then I shall personally chase him down." Wickham replied.

"And what is to be done with him when you have him cornered? Tell me, how does one deal with a blackguard and scoundrel?" Mr. Darcy's eyes narrowed and his voice deepened as he spoke. "Will his evils be published that all may know them? Should he then be executed? Exiled? Consigned to hard labor? What is a sufficient punishment for such a man?"

The tense exchange between Mr. Wickham and Mr. Darcy had silenced the rest of the party, and all eyes were now upon Mr. Wickham, who appeared stricken and unable to speak.

Mr. Darcy continued pleasantly, "My counsel to you, Wickham, would be not to neglect your swordsmanship. You never know when you shall be called out."

At this, Mr. Darcy looked directly at Elizabeth, and his features contorted with a pained expression before he turned his horse and galloped away.

Mr. Bingley excused himself and followed Mr. Darcy.

"Well, now, that was a delightful interlude." Mr. Wickham laughed as soon as they were gone. "If Mr. Darcy is so set against Napoleon, perhaps he should enter the corps himself."

"That was very strange indeed!" Lydia giggled. "If anyone is going to rout Napoleon, it is going to be Denny!"

The gentlemen, excepting Mr. Collins all laughed, and escorted the ladies to Aunt Phillips house, where Mr. Denny and Mr. Wickham begged to leave the party, for they had pressing business to attend.

Mr. Collins found an eager ear with Mrs. Phillips, for she was honored that the parson of such a great lady had come to her home, and took great delight in Mr. Collins' compliments. She discovered that he was a skilled apologizer as well after he spent a quarter of an hour groveling for forgiveness after an inadvertently thoughtless comment was taken as a slight.

ళ

"Darcy, what were you going on about?" Mr. Bingley challenged his friend once they were back in the drawing room at Netherfield. "Who was that fellow?"

Mr. Darcy poured himself a glass of port and drained it. "No one worth knowing."

"But he seemed to me to be a fine chap. If he is a friend of the Miss Bennets, he cannot be as bad as you say." Bingley reassured himself.

"The Miss Bennets," Darcy suddenly looked fierce, "cannot know what he is about, or they would not associate with him. He will ruin their reputations and possibly worse."

"You're serious." Mr. Bingley said in amazement. "What can we do?"

"Nothing," Mr. Darcy replied, "except to warn them somehow. I cannot lay before you all the particulars, but if damnation has its claim on any man, it does upon Wickham. He is a liar, a debtor, a gambler and a seducer. He is guilty of debaucheries of the worst kind against innocents. The Bennets cannot remain untouched by the association if it is allowed to continue."

"If all this is true, you were too easy on him!" Mr. Bingley declared angrily.

"I have good reason not to expose him, Bingley. You must never ask me any more about it, but I do believe that we must take steps to protect Eliz ... the Miss Bennets from that rogue." Darcy went to the desk and took out his writing implements. "I have letters to write for now, Bingley. We can return to Longbourn later, after I am done, for this cannot wait."

Chapter Nineteen

DECLARATIONS OF LOVE

Mr. Darcy watched the express rider racing down the road away from Netherfield until the rider could no longer be seen. He turned from the window and sighed. "Are you quite certain you want to go ahead with this, Bingley?"

"No." Bingley declared somewhat defensively. "I would not speak to Mr. Bennet about courting Miss Bennet—I would far rather speak to the man about marrying his daughter, but I will keep your counsel in the matter and court her first."

"If you must pursue it, which I still have some doubts about, I maintain that courtship is the more prudent course. Time will vet her and prove that the regard you saw displayed after her injury was not merely a delusion born of her fall. If it is truly love that you both feel, the wait will improve it." Mr. Darcy hesitated, and then cautioned. "You are aware, are you not, that it is all the same to her mother. She will undoubtedly have Miss Bennet's wedding clothes purchased before Christmas, even though you are not engaged."

"Yes." Bingley frowned through his amusement. "Mrs. Bennet would steal my thunder and propose to her daughter in my stead, if she could. But it is of no consequence to me what the mother does, for in truth, she does it all for love of her daughter." Mr. Bingley's face cheered again.

"That woman would love her most beautiful daughter to the throne of England," Darcy muttered.

"Then it is my good fortune indeed that the Prince is married and beyond her reach!" Bingley laughed and then became serious. "I have learned something troubling of the Miss Bennets. It explains to a certain extent, their mother—although it cannot excuse her."

"And what would that be? Has their mother escaped from the asylum?" Darcy fixed upon his friend with an insistent eye. "Come, I must have your insight!"

"Then you shall have it." Mr. Bingley agreed and proceeded soberly. "Their father's estate is entailed away from the female line. When he is dead, the six women of that household will be without the comfort of a home, and their income will be just two-hundred per annum. You see, Mrs. Bennet is not so much a fortune hunter for her daughters as we thought. She is only desperate."

"There are few in this world so terrifying as a desperate mother, my friend. I am frightened for you," Darcy said dryly and then added thoughtfully, "The entailment is indeed a shocking revelation. Mr. Bennet should have made provision for them."

"Can you not see, Darcy? When Mrs. Bennet is no longer *so very* desperate, she is sure to be more agreeable." Bingley grinned wildly, as though he had solved the riddle of the sphinx.

"Oh, she will still vex you. If you do marry Jane Bennet, her mother will undoubtedly be desperate for grandchildren." Darcy cautioned.

"On that score," Bingley beamed, "I will be most happy to oblige her."

"Of course, you would. When Mrs. Bennet is caterwauling about your house, I shall hold no sympathy for you, Bingley, nor will I visit. A man would have to truly love a woman beyond any hope of retrieval to humor such a mother-in-law." Mr. Darcy grimaced. "I know I would not."

"When Jane Bennet is my wife, I will not need sympathy from you, or anything akin to it. She is an angel, and I shall awaken every morning to gaze upon heaven itself. The virtues of her own sweet temper will indeed soften any faults that I must endure from her family. Besides, her mother will not be living with us, so the 'caterwauling' as you call it, will *usually* be under another roof, and with five daughters to fret over, once the others marry, she will divide her visits among them."

"It would seem that you have worked it all out." Mr. Darcy remarked.

"Her sister, Miss Elizabeth," Bingley winked at Mr. Darcy, "she is a very pleasant person and much beloved by my Jane. She will undoubtedly visit a great deal. It will be...,"

"... very interesting to see how your sister Caroline copes with the idea of Miss Elizabeth as your sister." Darcy finished Bingley's sentence and then laughed aloud at the thought. "Have you told your sisters of your intentions regarding Miss Bennet?"

Mr. Bingley's face, which had been cheerful, transformed. "I did—just an hour ago, while you were writing your letter."

"How was the news received?" Mr. Darcy asked expectantly.

Mr. Bingley fixed his eye on Mr. Darcy in chagrin. "You should know better than to make me speak of it. Let us instead away to Longbourn where the news will be glad tidings rather than a declaration of war."

"Retreat?" Darcy mocked with a chuckle.

"Fall back and re-assemble," Bingley declared, "in the company of the lovely ladies of Longbourn."

ꟹ

Having returned from visiting Aunt Phillips in Meryton, Elizabeth went to her room to freshen herself. She could not say at what point she became aware of the sound, for when she actually started listening to it, she had the sensation that it had been there for some time, but the sound, soft and muffled though it was, was undeniably that of someone crying.

She stood and tried to get a fix on it, and silently followed it down the hall. A floorboard creaked beneath her, and the sound was suddenly stifled, but too late, for Elizabeth was at the door. She pressed her ear to the door and knocked gently as she uttered the soft query, "Mary?"

There was no answering response, but Elizabeth turned the knob anyway, and entered to see her sister upon the window seat, legs drawn to her chest like a small child. She was cocooned in a large but plain shawl, the fringes dangling beneath her as if extensions of her tears. When Elizabeth entered, quietly closing the door behind her, Mary turned her face toward the window and laid her head on her knees, saying nothing.

"Mary, are you ill?" Elizabeth rushed to her sister. "Tell me, what is wrong?"

Mary did not reply, nor did she raise her head, but was instead overcome by an attempt to suppress her weeping to such a degree that her whole body shook with the effort.

Elizabeth and Mary were not particularly close—not in the way that Elizabeth and Jane were. Although Elizabeth was filled with a compassionate concern for her sister, she knew not how to comfort her. It was as rare to see Mary cry as it was to see her laugh. Elizabeth sat down on the other side of the bench and took the ends of Mary's fingers into her hand, caressing them tenderly as she spoke quietly. "Mary, Mary, it will be all right. You must tell me what is wrong dear sister ... let me help you."

Mary finally lifted her head and looked at Elizabeth, her face red and swollen. She tried to say something, but was unable to utter anything coherent, so she eventually just shook her head, blinking away the tears.

Elizabeth's mind rehearsed the events of the day. Mary had seemed so very Mary-like on the walk into Meryton, meeting the officers, socializing at Aunt Phillips' house and even on their return, although perhaps quieter than usual on the walk back. Had Mary spoken? Quieter than quiet was a difficult distinction, and Elizabeth simply could not recall.

"Mary, did something happen today?" Elizabeth prompted. Mary sniffed loudly and shook her head as a long, broken, "Noo-ooo-ooo-ooo" erupted from her lips.

Elizabeth put her arms around her emotional sister and pulled her close. Mary resisted for a bare fraction of a second before she laid her head on Elizabeth's shoulder and resumed her weeping, while Elizabeth smoothed her hair, and hushed and soothed her as she would a crying baby. Eventually, Mary's tears were spent, and she pulled away, embarrassed at having lost her composure. She wiped at her face with the shawl, removing all traces of her tears.

"Mary, listen to me." Elizabeth held her sister's face in her hands, steadying it so she could look directly into Mary's eyes. "You *must* tell me what is wrong."

Mary swallowed hard and whispered, "Mr. Collins."

"Mr. Collins." Elizabeth repeated. "Has Mr. Collins done something?"

"No." Mary shook her head, and looked down, unable to meet Elizabeth's penetrating gaze.

"Lizzy," Mary suddenly blurted out, "before you arrived home yesterday ... Lady Catherine ... she ... she ... she, well, she liked me best." Mary's chin trembled and came up ever so slightly.

"Oh!" Elizabeth's eyes rounded in surprise. "Mary, are you saying that you actually *like* Mr. Collins?"

Mary nodded and looked out the window again. Elizabeth was rendered speechless, and eventually, Mary began speaking in a hoarse whisper. "I have always thought that if I ever were to marry, it would be to a man of the church. The moment I saw him, I knew that he was a pious man, but I had never dreamed that he would be so noble in his moral character, so confident in his address, so blessed and humbled by the patronage of a great lady. I am smitten, but I am beneath his notice. You are the only one he sees, Lizzy, and you do not even like him. You laughed at him all through dinner last night, and he was our *guest,* Lizzy, our *guest*. How could you dishonor this good man who has come here to amend a wrong not of his making? You do not deserve him, that is the truth, but he will choose you, I know he will." Mary took a deep breath and looked directly at her sister. "We have only just met him, and he is already so very dear to me. How am I to live a lifetime watching you as his wife? I want him to choose *me*."

Elizabeth sat quietly for several minutes, trying to process the feelings that her sister had spoken aloud, trying to fathom the depth with which Mary must feel it to be overcome. Finally, she looked at Mary and spoke. "I am sorry that this has hurt you, Mary. I did not realize, or even imagine, that you liked Mr. Collins. You know that to me he is ridiculous."

"I know." Mary replied softly.

Elizabeth got up and poured some water into the basin on Mary's dressing table. She saturated a cloth, loosely wrung it out and handed to her sister, indicating that she must cool her face and eyes with it. "First, we must have Mr. Collins look at you, Mary. We must give him something to notice. You are actually very pretty, but your hair is always arranged so plainly that it does not flatter you. A softer style, with some curls would look very well on you."

Elizabeth held Mary by the shoulders and directed her to the seat in front of the dressing table. She pulled the pins out of Mary's hair and began brushing it, twirling the locks into different shapes, testing them in the mirror, and then finally, arranging Mary's hair into a loose bun, with thin braids intertwined throughout. She moistened the wispy edges, and turned them on her finger, teasing them into small ringlets that framed Mary's face. Looking in Mary's closet, she was somewhat daunted by the sea of drab colors, but finally, in the back she found a soft pink dress that had previously been Jane's.

"Stay where you are, Mary. I shall return in a moment." Elizabeth said, and hurried to her room where she retrieved a thin gold chain that she then strung around her sister's throat.

"There." Elizabeth said as she turned Mary's face to the mirror. "You are only missing one thing to make yourself truly beautiful."

Mary, who was stunned at what a difference these minor alterations had already made in her overall appearance, shook her head, not understanding.

"Smile." Elizabeth prompted. "Even if it is just a very little smile. There is nothing as enticing on a woman's face as a cheerful countenance. Practice in the mirror for a minute. There is one more thing I wish to get."

She returned a moment later with Jane and in delicate terms explained Mary's dilemma to their eldest sister. Jane was initially surprised at the revelation, but she quickly concurred with Elizabeth that if it would make Mary happy, they should do all within their power to redirect Mr. Collins' attention to the third eldest Miss Bennet.

Chapter Twenty

HIDDEN AGENDAS

Elizabeth, sitting before her dressing table, admired her transformed appearance in the mirror. *I would need far more time to make myself plainer*, she thought with satisfaction. Her hair was arranged in a tightly formed severe bun. She had tamed as many of the tendrils that usually hung about her face as would cooperate, forcing them backwards to combine with the rest of her hair. She wore an outdated dress that she generally only wore to garden in the spring and summer. It was worn and faded and stained—not fit even to turn. She put it on with a smile, and then practiced her frown, for she wished to seem as disagreeable and unsightly as possible to Mr. Collins.

As Elizabeth was admiring her handiwork, the call for all to "make haste" was heard from below. Elizabeth braced herself for what was certain to be a critical diatribe on her appearance as soon as she was seen by her mother. Upon landing at the bottom of the stairs, Hill gave her a strange look but directed her into the sitting room, where Jane, Lydia and Kitty were all peering through the window to witness the approach of Mr. Bingley and Mr. Darcy. Elizabeth joined them at the window, trying not to laugh at Jane's face when her sister noticed the change in Elizabeth.

Mr. Collins cleared his throat as he entered the room, as if to announce himself. The sound startled the sisters and they scattered to their usual seats, except for Kitty, whose seat was now occupied by Mr. Collins.

Mary entered next, self-consciously looking at the floor as she shuffled to her seat, looking up only to gain reassurance from her two elder sisters. There was a pretty blush to her cheeks born of embarrassment, which nicely matched the pink gown she wore and enhanced the effect of Elizabeth's efforts.

Mrs. Bennet came fluttering into the room, her lace mobcap slightly askew. She stopped short when she saw Mr. Collins in Kitty's seat, and then addressed her only standing daughter. "Kitty, you sit there, by the window." She did not of course, wish to risk the possibility that Kitty would take the seat next to Jane. She then cast a cursory eye about the room, and finding it in an acceptable state to receive guests, she moved quickly to her own chair just in time.

Footsteps outside the door gave them warning, and almost in unison, they stood as Hill announced Mr. Bingley and Mr. Darcy to the room.

The air nearly crackled with the tension of the occupants' expectations, for nearly each person present had some agenda or another to pursue. All were keenly felt to be of import by their holder, although several were unaware of the similar or conflicting ideas on the part of any other.

Mr. Bingley was his usual cheerful self, if slightly more agitated than usual. He engaged easily with Mrs. Bennet, who invited the gentlemen into the room. Her welcome of Mr. Bingley was noticeably warmer than that directed toward Mr. Darcy, although her manner toward the latter fell short of being uncivil.

After a cursory pass at the initial pleasantries, Mr. Darcy moved to the window, as was his habit. Normally, Elizabeth would have taken note of this had she not been so very distracted by silently signaling Mary to smile and to correct her posture.

Mr. Darcy stood transfixed, watching Elizabeth in the glass. His recently established rule against looking at her, he rationalized, was really only applied to looking *directly* at her—he allowed himself the exception of the glass.

She had changed, he noted with increasing interest. He could not determine at first exactly what was different, but the effect reminded him of a governess or lady's companion, somewhat austere and spinsterish. What surprised him more than the change itself was his reaction to it. Rather than putting him off as he would have expected, it excited him. What costume was this? What role was she playing with her little grimacing smiles at her sister Mary? With her hair swept completely back from her face, the exquisite lines of Elizabeth's cheekbones were emphasized. The sweep of her jaw gained definition and the curve of her neck was tantalizingly exposed. He realized to his surprise, that the only thing in her face that was actually not perfectly symmetrical was the line of her brows, for one arched somewhat wickedly higher than the other. The feathery edges of her hairline drew a frame around her open face that he wanted to reach out and trace with his finger on the glass. His hands, however, remained firmly disciplined behind his back.

The door of the sitting room opened, and Hill spoke. "Mr. Bennet will see you now, Mr. Bingley."

Mr. Darcy turned and gave Mr. Bingley an encouraging look. He had seen his friend fall for women before, but Bingley's heart had always failed him when it came to facing the young lady's father. This was as far as he had ever gotten before and spoke volumes about the depth of Charles' feelings for Jane Bennet.

Nearly as soon as Mr. Bingley had quit the room, Mrs. Bennet had leapt from her own seat and moved to sit next to Jane. "Jane, Jane, what is he about Jane?" Mrs. Bennet fussed, patting Jane's hand in agitated crooning. Jane tried to quietly calm her mother, hoping that she was giving nothing away in her reassurances that Mr. Bingley had just wished to extend his greetings to her father, but she was sure he would return shortly.

This distraction was the perfect opportunity for Mr. Collins, and he moved as discretely as he knew how, from the seat he had first chosen, to a position on the same settee as Elizabeth, leaving but a small space between them.

"Cousin Elizabeth," he began, "have you never had occasion to travel into Kent?"

"No, sir, I have never done so, although I hear it is lovely." Elizabeth answered, but she was looking fiercely at Mary, urging her with the motions of her eyes to come and take the seat between herself and Mr. Collins. She had a disturbing image of herself mirroring her mother's gestures, but it did not matter. She had promised Mary, and she could only hope that their contrivance would somehow work.

"It is indeed lovely," Mr. Collins effused, "particularly that sweet corner of the county where my own humble parsonage resides." He tipped his head, trying to gain eye contact with Elizabeth. "The most magnificent estate in the whole of Kent of course, is Rosings Park, where my esteemed patroness, Lady Catherine de Bourgh...."

A shadow suddenly loomed over Mr. Collins, and he trailed off as he looked into the visage of Mr. Darcy, who had approached and now stood directly in front of Mr. Collins.

"Mr. Collins? We were introduced, I believe, earlier today in Meryton." Mr. Darcy bowed slightly and was obliged to take a step backward as Mr. Collins attempted to rise.

"Mr. Darcy? Yes, we were indeed, although we did not have the pleasure of conversing at any length, for being in the company of my fair cousins, it was incumbent upon me to attend most diligently to their needs." Mr. Collins voice did not conceal his pleasure that Mr. Darcy had acknowledged the acquaintance nor his desire to impress the great man.

Mr. Darcy looked expectantly at Mr. Collins and finally added, "May I join you?" He stepped forward, indicating that he would take the seat between Mr. Collins and Elizabeth on the settee.

Elizabeth, frowned apologetically at Mary, for there was simply not room on the little bench for four. Mr. Darcy had expressly stated that he was joining Mr. Collins, so Elizabeth returned to her needlework, turning her back to the men as much as she could in the cramped arrangement.

Mr. Collins, who had taken his seat expressly to be near Elizabeth, considered moving to the middle spot himself, but he deferred to the commanding presence of Mr. Darcy, who had already turned to sit and would have landed in Mr. Collins' lap had the parson acted on his impulse.

"Mr. Collins, did I hear you correctly? Is Lady Catherine de Bourgh of Rosings Park your patroness?" Mr. Darcy knew very well that this was the case and had no need of confirmation, but this was the opening he had hoped for. The opportunity was upon him to weigh the purpose of Mr. Collins' visit to Longbourn through casual inquiry, and he was pleased to take it. He felt Elizabeth shift behind him, and he wished her miles away. He could not afford distraction.

"Oh yes!" Mr. Collins' face turned slightly redder than usual. "I am aware, of course, of your connection to her, for she has often spoken of you and her great affection for all of her nephews, but especially that nephew who is the master of Pemberley. She is such a generous and condescending patroness; I count myself truly blessed that the living in Hunsford was granted to a humble man such as I. Why just yesterday, she went miles out of her way to deliver me to this very doorstep, to travel in the comfort of her own carriage, which generosity was, I assure you, beyond my comprehension. I am pleased to advise you that your aunt was in the best of health."

Mr. Darcy blinked, not so much at the behavior of the strange little man, but at the realization that his task was too easy. The man would undoubtedly not just tell him what he wanted to know, but elaborate on it endlessly.

"I am glad to hear it. It is indeed a long journey, and as you said, miles out of her way. May I inquire as to what brings you to Hertfordshire?"

Mr. Darcy felt Elizabeth stiffen behind him. He liked the thought that she was eavesdropping on his conversation as he had done to so many of hers, although he knew it was more a matter of overhearing due to the fact that a person would be hard pressed to fit so much as a potato between them, they were so close.

"I am honored indeed by your interest, Mr. Darcy." Had Mr. Collins been speaking to a lady, he would surely have been thought to be flirting, so sweet was his countenance. "As you must already know, I am related to the Bennet household through my father, who is now deceased." Collins took a deep drink of air and continued. "I am the nearest male relative to my good cousin, Mr. Bennet, who, in having five daughters and not even one son, failed in his responsibility to his family to produce an heir."

"Failed, Mr. Collins?" Darcy repeated.

"Yes, I am afraid he has failed most tragically, for there is an entailment upon this estate, away from the female line, which, it pains me to say, must afflict my fair cousins with more than grief when Mr. Bennet meets his demise." Mr. Collins paused for effect. "I am come to offer them salvation."

"Salvation? I do not understand." Mr. Darcy shook his head.

"When I accepted the living in Hunsford, your aunt, the great Lady Catherine de Bourgh, determined, and rightly so, that I must marry. 'Mr. Collins', she said, 'It is a truth, universally acknowledged, that a single man in possession of a valuable living must be in want of a wife.' Your aunt's wisdom and benevolence toward my humble situation has brought me to the deepest depths of gratitude. I informed her, of course, of my cousin's plight—that of five unmarried daughters with no fortune to sustain them or their poor mother when they suffer the distinct indignity of being turned out of this very home at the time I inherit it."

"I see," said Mr. Darcy. "Is there no remedy for the terms?"

"That is why I am here, Mr. Darcy. Your aunt saw the solution immediately!" Mr. Collins at this point became extremely animated. "I must select, from among Mr. Bennet's daughters, a bride—the companion of my future life. Not only will it redress the loss of the estate from my cousin's family, but it will also heal the breach that has existed for an entire generation. Your aunt, whose condescension defies all description, delivered me here personally, at great expense, so she could meet my fair cousins and bestow upon me her observations and recommendations on which daughter would be the most suitable wife. She is always most attentive to these sorts of things."

"Yes, I believe she is," Mr. Darcy replied. "May I be so bold as to inquire whether my aunt has provided you with her counsel in this matter, or is her assessment to come at a later time?"

Mr. Collins lowered his voice to nearly a whisper and replied, "It is an honor, indeed, to enter into this confidence with you, Mr. Darcy. The ultimate selection is mine, of course, but Lady Catherine did show great favor to the second eldest, Miss Elizabeth Bennet."

Elizabeth shuddered at what she was overhearing, but it gave her hope too. Mr. Collins could make his own choice. Their plan for Mary stood at least a small chance of success.

"The second eldest?" Mr. Darcy's voice had dropped to match the tone of Mr. Collins, although it had developed a hard edge.

"Mr. Collins." Elizabeth turned and peered around Mr. Darcy, interrupting the gentlemen's conversation. "My sister Mary informs me that she is having difficulty with a passage in Fordyce's sermons. Might you be willing to assist?"

Mr. Collins glanced quickly at Mary, who smiled weakly at him, but he turned again and addressed Elizabeth. "My dearest cousin, if it would please you, I would be delighted to help her make it out. I shall return directly."

Elizabeth shared a triumphant smile with Jane as Mr. Collins made his way to Mary's side, where Mary was prepared with the difficult passage the three sisters had identified earlier as being one of great doctrinal import.

It was then that Elizabeth noted that Mr. Darcy was intent on Mr. Collins and Mary. It would not do to have him discover what the three sisters were about, and so, with a sigh, she determined that she must divert Mr. Darcy's attention by any means possible.

Mr. Darcy, upon hearing Elizabeth's breath exhale, shifted his attitude to better engage in conversation.

"Miss Bennet? That was a very deep sigh ... is there some vexation that troubles you?" Mr. Darcy asked curiously.

Elizabeth was somewhat perplexed that Mr. Darcy would broach a topic of such intimacy as her troubles as though he were a dear friend rather than an indifferent acquaintance. "I believe, Mr. Darcy, that I sigh ... deeply ... rather often. It is a very bad habit, I know. I hope that I did not disturb you."

"Not at all" Mr. Darcy mumbled, disappointed that the conversation had died so quickly. He glanced again at Mr. Collins and Mary.

"Although, perhaps...," Elizabeth waited until Mr. Darcy looked at her again, "perhaps you could elaborate on what you said of Napoleon earlier. It put questions into my mind ... of justice. As you know, that is a topic I have put some thought to of late—one of the dangers of reading Plato, I fear."

"Justice," Mr. Darcy looked strangely at Elizabeth, "is a lofty principle, and I believe in it." He shook his head as he spoke. "Sometimes, however, seeking justice for its own sake serves to further injure those who deserve its protection. Napoleon will be stopped, and in his case, justice meted out, but in the world of common men, justice as a principle is not always so easy to apply."

"Justice should always be tempered with mercy," Elizabeth said thoughtfully, "but to abandon the principle merely to prevent pain dishonors those who have been wronged and fails to protect society from the wrongdoer. On this point, we must disagree, Mr. Darcy. The easiness of application should not be a consideration."

"You are young," Mr. Darcy said, his brows knitted together with tension, "and innocent. You cannot know of what you speak."

Elizabeth's eyebrow shot up. "Are you so very old, Mr. Darcy, that your lofty principles are already tarnished with a cynical bent? I am surprised, for whatever other impressions I have had of you, lack of resolve in the face of injustice was not among them."

"Impressions are brittle grounds by which to sketch a man's character, Miss Bennet. I assure you that my resolve is painfully intact." Mr. Darcy's voice carried an intensity that was slightly unnerving. "And as for the rest of my character, I fear that any attempt to sketch it at present would do neither of us credit."

Elizabeth looked up, caught Mary's eye again, and repeated her reminder signals to her sister.

"You mentioned swordsmanship in your address to Mr. Wickham, Mr. Darcy. That was an interesting turn of conversation." Elizabeth pursed her lips. "Your counsel to Mr. Wickham intrigues me. Was your advice to him general or specific in nature?"

"It is in general good advice." Mr. Darcy said, "And in Mr. Wickham's case, it was faithful counsel."

"How are you acquainted with Mr. Wickham?" Elizabeth asked, curious about the handsome new officer. "We were just making his acquaintance today when you came upon us in Meryton."

"I have known him since we were children. He was the son of my late father's steward." Mr. Darcy replied evenly, concerned at the eagerness he detected in her. "We have gone our separate ways."

"He seemed most amiable." Elizabeth reflected.

Darcy's eyebrows pressed together in evident concern, and he spoke with an intensity that exceeded his expression. "Miss Bennet, *please do not involve yourself with George Wickham.* I can say no more, but I beg you, do not give him any consequence." Darcy abruptly stood and returned to his place at the window.

Elizabeth, astonished by Mr. Darcy's behavior, returned to her needlework, pondering the conversation she had just had with him, including his agitation when the topic had turned to Mr. Wickham.

Several minutes passed, during which time Mary managed to hold Mr. Collins captive to the intricacies of Fordyce's Sermons, Jane to maintain her mother's equilibrium, and Lydia and Kitty to giggle about each officer in the Meryton-based militia three or four times. Mr. Darcy managed to brood and stare at Elizabeth in the window glass, and Elizabeth managed to ignore him perfectly well.

At present, the door opened, and Bingley and Mr. Bennet entered the sitting room together. Bingley's face could not conceal his happiness, so the announcement was made to the inhabitants of the room that Mr. Bingley had entered into a state of courtship with Jane, and in addition, he was prepared to host a ball at Netherfield five days hence.

Jane and Mr. Bingley were ecstatic and warmly received the flow of compliments that were directed at them. Lydia and Kitty began whispering about how much more handsome Mr. Bingley would be if he were an officer in regimentals, but that was no matter as the officers would, of course, be at the ball. Mrs. Bennet followed Mr. Bennet to the study, where she insisted upon knowing why it was merely a courtship Mr. Bingley had initiated rather than an engagement. Mr. Collins was put out, for Mrs. Bennet had informed him that Jane was to be *engaged,* causing him to rule out the eldest too soon, which had spoiled his chances at the most beautiful sister. Mary returned to quiet contemplations, quite satisfied with the time she had spent with Mr. Collins. Elizabeth held her needlework in her lap and simply smiled delightedly at the scene before her. Darcy gave up using the glass to observe her and returned to his previous habit of openly staring at the lovely Elizabeth Bennet.

Chapter Twenty-One

MR. DARCY'S DILEMMA

Five Days! *Can a man go mad in five days?* Darcy had been up long before sunrise, pacing the floor, keeping company with his insomniac, unruly mind. Bingley had set the date for the ball, five days hence, and now that the date was fixed, the torture of its anticipation was acute. Five days was not nearly enough to tend to the urgent business at hand, and yet it seemed an eternity away in light of his proximity to Longbourn and the distraction of its occupants.

When Charles Bingley had requested his counsel on letting the Netherfield Park estate, his friend had promised him a pleasant month or two in Hertfordshire, should the house prove acceptable, where he could forget his troubles for a time. To shed his burdens in an idyllic, obscure country setting had seemed, at the time, an offer of respite he could not refuse. He had been, although he would deny it if pressed, deeply weary and in need of restoration of his spirits.

The location had seemed perfect. He knew no one in Hertfordshire and doubted that any of his acquaintance had ever heard of the village of Meryton. His aunt had no connections in the county, and only a select few of his most trusted servants knew the location of his retreat. He had informed but two relations of his whereabouts, his sister, Georgiana, and his cousin Richard Fitzwilliam, in order to maintain his correspondence with them. Here he could hunt and ride and forget, for a time, the grief and trauma of the past year. In some degree of anonymity, he could evade the soul-crushing social press of London and remove himself from his Aunt Catherine's increasingly annoying interference in his life.

It was a disaster. His aunt, who he was certain had never entered the county in her life, had suddenly appeared at the neighboring estate with her new parson—their cousin, no less! He could not have foreseen that. *At least that idiotic clergyman seems oblivious to my evasion of Aunt Catherine, fool that he is, or he would call my aunt back to Meryton in a trice.*

Meryton, Darcy thought, must be a capital place for evasion. He reflected on the several months he and Richard had unsuccessfully chased George Wickham to seek some private retribution on him. Wickham deserved to pay dearly for his dalliance with Georgiana, but the search had been fruitless. George Wickham had escaped them and disappeared. To find him suddenly in Meryton, speaking to those same neighbors from Longbourn, had been a shock and an unforeseen windfall of opportunity, which he was already pursuing.

Oh, those neighbors from Longbourn! How much better it would have been for him had he remained unaware of that house, and most particularly, of Elizabeth Bennet. She had ruined him. Thoughts of leaving Hertfordshire to avoid her presence depressed him, thoughts of staying to be near her tortured him equally. She haunted his dreams by night; she ignited his passions by day. Never before had he allowed himself to indulge in unattainable fantasies, and yet of late, he found himself drifting into that realm, a place where Elizabeth Bennet was graced with better, nobler relations and a fortune of her own. In that place, he could seek her hand without censure, and his duties and obligations to his family were not offended, for her place in society was no longer so decidedly below his own.

Duty to family—what an insidious concept inhabited that phrase! The darkness that had gripped him the evening before returned and filled him with nausea at the knowledge that Mr. Collins would most certainly make an offer of marriage to Elizabeth. He knew her duty to her family would only be served with acceptance. There was no way out for her, yet the thought of Mr. Collins bedding Elizabeth as his wife could not be borne. It was unthinkable. Mr. Darcy was filled with an inexplicable rage toward Mr. Collins. Salvation indeed! What was salvation if it took its recipient to misery? There was only one answer—*Elizabeth must refuse him! Defy her family and act in her own best interests!*

He knew he could not dare to hope that she would refuse. Just last night, he had seen with his own eyes that Elizabeth had changed her appearance to better appeal to Mr. Collins' sensibilities of propriety. Her dress had been modest and humble, her hairstyle plain. What could explain it if not her desire to prove herself an acceptable parson's wife? Jealousy ripped through Darcy like a blade, to know that she had never done the same for him—taken extra care in her appearance to please him—but had done so for the sanctimonious, odious Mr. Collins. Worse, it was humiliating to know that she never would, for she could never know of his growing love for her. He must bear that burden alone.

Mr. Darcy looked through the window toward the rosy lavender light of the breaking dawn. Although Longbourn was three miles away, he imagined he could see the smoke rising from the chimneys there. What was Elizabeth doing? Was she still abed, her hair tousled, her exquisite eyes still touched by sleep? Was she seeing to her toilette, washing herself in the floral waters that made her smell like spring? Perhaps she was dressing, slipping into a frock that would tantalize him with the way it clung to her pleasing figure.

Yes. He answered his earlier question. A man could easily go mad in five days with such thoughts as these.

He turned his thoughts to Pemberley, that grand haven of hearth and home. As much as he loved it, the great house felt so empty with his father gone and Georgiana at school. The solitude at Pemberley had driven him back to London, with its myriad attractions and diversions. Charles was there, and it had for a time driven away that deep loneliness that relentlessly dogged him to introduce Charles and his sisters into the circles of society that his own position afforded. Charles' gentlemanly behavior and cordial manner, combined with the fortune he had inherited from his father had allowed the Bingleys to gain some footing in town. Their superior manners gave them an air of respectability, and their fashionability distracted from their roots in commerce. Eventually, after calling in favors and gentle, persistent persuasion directed at those in power to decide, he had obtained the coveted vouchers to Almack's on their behalf.

Caroline Bingley had, Darcy realized in hindsight, allowed this social triumph to alter her—Louisa, somewhat less so. As the daughters of a successful tradesman who could afford to do so, they had been sent to fine schools and dressed in fine clothes. According to what Charles had told him, his sisters had been subjected to much disdain and snobbery due to their lower station in society, in spite of their family fortune. Upon finding a degree of acceptance in London, they now demonstrated the very attitudes of superiority that had so cruelly mortified them and genuinely appeared to have forgotten that the Bingley fortune was acquired through trade.

Mr. Darcy recalled with a shiver that he had initially been impressed with Caroline's beauty, grace and comportment in society—else he would not have assisted the Bingleys in gaining access to the *ton*, for his own reputation was tied to that act. It was not until they had come to Hertfordshire that their vicious natures were fully exposed, although their oft-times callous treatment of Charles had led him to suspect that there was a certain meanness about Caroline in particular. Noblesse oblige was bred into you, and Caroline was proof of it.

Caroline. Darcy sighed. She was naively convinced that she would someday be the mistress of Pemberley. That had become evident these past weeks as she spoke with increasing possessiveness of his estate, pretended a greater intimacy with his sister than she had, and had flirted outrageously with him. Her behavior toward Elizabeth Bennet was unpardonable, but through it, Caroline had revealed her perception of Elizabeth as a rival. This was amusing in a way, for as the daughter of a tradesman, Caroline was below even Elizabeth Bennet in station. Her fortune could not purchase a revision of heritage and history, however much she might wish it—just as all of his wishing could not change the situation of Elizabeth Bennet.

With her family estate entailed away from her line, one uncle an attorney, and the other in trade, her connections, although respectable, were not sufficiently elevated to recommend her as an eligible marriage prospect for a man in his position. It was perverse! The magnificent and spirited woman of his every desire was torn away from him merely by her situation in life!

His every desire. The phrase repeated itself mercilessly in his head, along with the dream-born images of those desires. He saw it all, clearly, indelibly written in that part of his mind that remained open to possibilities. It is there that his lovely bride, Elizabeth, graciously receives their guests as mistress of Pemberley. In that private world, they confide in one another, tease one another, growing ever dearer to one another as the years pass. She would kiss their children the way she kissed his dog, with affection and abandon and tenderness ... and he would watch her and marvel that this wonderful woman was his own. He dared not think, not consciously anyway, of the intimacies that they would share as man and wife. It was too much loss to bear.

It came to this. He, Fitzwilliam Darcy wants Elizabeth Bennet as his wife more than he has wanted anything in his life, yet cannot harbor the slightest hope of having her. He is powerless to change her situation.

Mr. Collins, who is perhaps the most ridiculous person he has ever met, also desires to marry Elizabeth Bennet. Through a cruel twist of ill-fated luck, in all probability he will be successful in that quest. Knowing that the union would resolve much of her family's burden, it would seem best for all were he to step back and allow another to claim what he cannot, yet the thought of it was abhorrent to his every sensibility. He knew that he had no right to interfere, and yet, as the sun cleared the last dusky colors from the sky, that is exactly what Mr. Darcy determined he must do, although the means whereby he was to accomplish it was yet to be discovered.

Chapter Twenty-Two

RIBBONS, LACE AND NOTIONS

"Five days, girls!" Mrs. Bennet exclaimed happily at breakfast. "The ball is in five days, and we have a great deal to do! Lydia, we must make over your blue gown with new ribbons and lace! You shall look so well in it then!"

"Five days!" Lydia groaned. "I must wait *five whole days* to dance with the officers? It will seem like a year, I am certain!"

"You can still *speak* with them, Lydia." Kitty reassured her. "One but has to walk into Meryton to speak with the officers."

Mr. Bennet looked over his glasses at Kitty. "I am certain that the officers are about more important errands than to speak with silly girls in the street, my dear."

"Mr. Bennet, we must make the best of the militia's being quartered so close while they are here." Mrs. Bennet admonished him. "Besides, the girls must go to Meryton for the ribbons and lace for the ball. If the officers are standing about in the street, it would not do to snub them. It would not be civil."

"Let them go then," Mr. Bennet sighed, "but I beg you—spare me further talk of ribbons and lace, madam; spare me the lace. I would rather talk of your nerves than to speak of lace."

"Mary." Mrs. Bennet turned to her third eldest daughter curiously and sniffed. "You look very well today."

Mary, who was unaccustomed to compliments about her appearance, colored and replied with a degree of discomfiture, "I have recently read a passage in Fordyce's Sermons, Mama, about the divine nature of our personages as temples. Care in our appearance, so long as it is modest and not excessive, cannot be censured, for indeed, the natural beauty of God's own creatures should not be inordinately suppressed."

"Yes, yes, that is all very interesting, Mary." Mrs. Bennet looked around the table at her other daughters. "Jane! What a glow there is upon your cheeks! I daresay Mr. Bingley can have no doubts that you are the most beautiful girl in the entire world! But, of course, he already knows this full well, for why else would he single you out for courtship if you were not so beautiful?"

Jane, although very accustomed to compliments about her appearance, also blushed. "Thank you, Mama."

"Miss Lizzy." Mrs. Bennet frowned at her second eldest. "Where *did* you find that dress? It does not look well on you at all. You look quite ill-favored and unfashionable today. You must change, if not for your own sake, you must consider the reputation of your sisters. And your hair, Lizzy! What have you done with your hair? That will not do at all!"

"My dress, Mama," Elizabeth replied with a smile, "is most serviceable and will do very well about the house. My hair likewise will do fine. I have promised Mary that I will help her with her dancing this morning, and this arrangement is more fixed than my usual, so I may better apply myself to Mary's lesson."

"What a fine idea!" Mrs. Bennet exclaimed excitedly with a clap of her hands. "You must *all* practice your dancing, for my girls must be the most elegant at the ball! You must all be admired for the fineness of your dancing, or I shall be greatly disappointed."

Mr. Collins entered the dining room as this exchange was occurring and looking around the table, bowed slightly. "Am I to understand that the morning's activities at Longbourn are to include a dance rehearsal? If I may be of service to my fair cousins in practicing the steps, I am at your disposal, for I believe, and I know that Lady Catherine would support me in this, that an understanding of all of those social graces we are called upon to demonstrate in society are our duty to perform. My participation in your preparations for the ball would be an honor, indeed, for I am certain that it cannot fail to improve your performance as well as mine."

"We cannot practice *too* long, Lizzy," Lydia pouted. "We must have time to look at the shops; and do not forget that we are to go to Aunt Phillips' again today. She has invited the officers, and they have accepted. I would far rather play cards with them today than to dance with my sisters."

"That is an evening engagement, Lydia." Elizabeth reminded her sister. "There will be time enough for cards *and* dancing." She then turned to their cousin and answered his offer. "Thank you, Mr. Collins. You are welcome to join us in our practice."

After breakfast, the sisters, tailed by Mr. Collins, repaired to the sitting room, where they rearranged the furniture to make room to conduct their rehearsal. Lydia and Kitty were paired, and Elizabeth declared that she would play the music so that Mary could practice, with Jane as the instructor. Mr. Collins, after an ingratiating bow to Elizabeth at the piano, was paired with Mary, and they spent the next hour marking the steps and figures of the dance.

At the hour mark, they stopped for some refreshment, and both Jane and Elizabeth seized upon the opportunity to compliment Mr. Collins and Mary on what a fine couple they made in the dance and how well suited they were as partners. It was not, in fact, insincere, for while Mr. Collins was clumsy and forgetful of the steps, Mary was patient and forgiving of his errors. Their strides being rather well matched, the effect was not altogether dreadful, particularly after they had practiced the most difficult portions a few times.

The encouragement was well placed in Mr. Collins, for having a high opinion of himself, he took any compliment aimed at him as absolute. "I hope," he cried enthusiastically, "that I may expect to dance with all of my fair cousins at the ball!"

Lydia, who was behind him, rolled her eyes in annoyance, but the only one of the Bennet sisters who replied to Mr. Collins was Mary. Mary only spoke after Elizabeth poked her side, but upon this prompt, she said, "Mr. Collins, it would be an honor to dance a set with you." Then, as he was opening his mouth to respond with another stream of platitudes, Mary smiled at Mr. Collins. It was not a vague smile nor an insipid one. It was a smile filled with warmth and admiration and perhaps even a little bit of silliness. Such a smile had never been bestowed on the Reverend William Collins in the whole of his life. Had Mary spoken to him in Latin, he could have interpreted it, but her countenance in that moment was beyond comprehension to him. It struck him, though, and sufficiently so that he was momentarily discomposed and rendered into the unlikely state of speechlessness.

The group returned to their practice, and both Elizabeth and Jane, reflecting on the activity later, observed that Mr. Collins had settled in the second hour, into seeming quite content to practice with Mary, and somewhat improved in his general manner, having ceased for that period with the banal commentary to which they had become accustomed.

ஒ

The daytime trip to Meryton was a fruitful one. The walk into town was much as it had been on the previous day, with the exception that Elizabeth and Jane were determined to keep Mary walking next to Mr. Collins while keeping themselves as distant as possible.

What ensued would have appeared to a casual onlooker to be as orchestrated as any dance, for there was a distinct rhythm to the changes in position, falling behind, moving forward and constant switching of places as they strolled into town. If Mr. Collins was frustrated by the chase, he did not reveal it, causing Elizabeth to muse on whether he was accustomed to walking partners who avoided him. The sisters were not required to offer much in conversation, but Elizabeth and Jane, when there was a break in Mr. Collins' speech, would interject and ask Mary's opinion on a matter related to the parson's rambling, and she proved herself in this most admirably.

In town, all five sisters successfully acquired ribbons, lace and other notions to embellish their gowns and hair for the Netherfield Ball. Mr. Collins elected to visit the bookstore during the lady's foray into the various shops, which, although of great interest to the feminine gender, were not particularly appealing to the parson.

The walk back to Longbourn posed additional opportunity for discourse between Mary and Mr. Collins, and Elizabeth was pleased with the small progress they were making. She was certain that Mr. Collins had warmed in his attitude toward the one Bennet sister who wished for his attentions.

At length, when the conversation waned, Elizabeth broached a topic that had been on her mind since the previous evening.

"Mr. Collins," Elizabeth opened, "am I correct in recalling that your patroness, the Lady Catherine de Bourgh, was on an errand of great import? She was serving the needs of a relation who was in some peril was she not?"

"My dear Cousin Elizabeth! Your compassion in recalling the tender mercies that great lady has bestowed upon her nephew does you credit! Indeed, you are correct, for nearly the moment she learned of the dire circumstances her nephew has found himself in, she was most determined to come to his aid and intervene with all the power of her position and status in society to bring an end to the hazard he was in, with all haste."

"This nephew—is he in mortal danger?" Elizabeth inquired with concern.

"I cannot say, dear cousin, for I do not know the particulars. Her Ladyship is, among her many other estimable qualities, the very soul of discretion," Mr. Collins answered. "Indeed, my understanding of the situation is perhaps less extensive than I had believed, for it was my impression that the nephew she was to rescue was the very master of Pemberley, the illustrious Mr. Darcy. Since the man is at present in residence in this neighborhood, and as I have seen with my own eyes that no distress imperils him, I must conclude that the nephew of her benevolent errand must be one of the sons of her brother, the esteemed Earl of Matlock."

"Her Ladyship is Mr. Darcy's aunt?" Elizabeth confirmed the detail she had overheard the previous evening.

"Oh yes, indeed, and soon to be his own mother, for her daughter, Miss Anne de Bourgh, the heiress of Rosings, is affianced to Mr. Darcy, and although the date of their nuptials is not at the present time set, it cannot fail to be soon." Mr. Collins beamed.

"Mr. Darcy is engaged ... to Miss de Bourgh?" Elizabeth breathed out in astonishment. "Upon my word, I had never imagined such a thing!"

"Indeed, when that day comes that they are joined in the bonds of holy matrimony, the great estates of Pemberley and Rosings shall be joined with them." Mr. Collins exclaimed enthusiastically. "The annals of history will most certainly extol the marriage as one of the spectacular matches of our age!"

"I am sure that they shall, Mr. Collins." Elizabeth said softly, with a weak smile. "I am sure that they shall."

൞

The promise of the militia at Aunt Phillips' house assured the punctuality of the Bennet family, and the five sisters and their cousin were transported by carriage at the appropriate hour to the Phillips' home. There they found, to the delight of some, that a number of the officers were already assembled.

Mr. Collins resumed his praise of Mrs. Phillips' house and the society therein as soon as they arrived. Four of his cousins, who had tired of hearing him, quickly left him conversing with Mary and Mrs. Phillips, who was enamored with hearing her house compared favorably with the great estate of Rosings, once she understood the grandeur of it.

Elizabeth, upon seeing Mr. Wickham in the midst of the gentlemen, had much the same reaction as she had the first time they had met, on the street in Meryton. She was struck with the handsomeness of his face and figure and had to secretly agree with Lydia that the red coat improved him beyond measure. His smile, which preceded him in his approach, was all that was charming, and his address to her so genuinely easy that she fell quickly into conversation with him as though they had long been friends. She was very inclined to find him amiable and had very nearly forgotten Mr. Darcy's caution about Mr. Wickham altogether.

Elizabeth, in comparing Mr. Wickham to the other gentlemen in the room, found that he exceeded the best of the others put together in conversation, in humor, in countenance and even in the air with which he carried himself. He was, although a lowly officer in the militia, the very personification of a gentlemanly person and superior to the others, she was sure. She was also sure that every female eye in the room was upon him, and she was exceedingly pleased when, after he had attended to the obligatory social greetings owed to the room, he declined to play cards and seated himself next to her away from the tables.

Elizabeth, being of a curious nature, had given much thought to the scene that had unfolded on the street between Mr. Wickham and Mr. Darcy and wanted nothing more than to understand it. She did not dare broach the topic directly, however, but determined that she would attempt to get to know Mr. Wickham better and see if she might find an opening.

"Mr. Wickham," she said, after the initial pleasantries had passed, "I understand from Mr. Darcy that you are of long acquaintance, having grown up together."

"That is very true." Wickham replied genially. "My father was the steward of the Darcy estate when I was young."

"Oh yes." Elizabeth paused. "You father is no longer in service there?"

"He died when I was still a lad," Mr. Wickham said with a warm smile. "It was old Mr. Darcy who saved me then. He did not turn me out of the house, instead treating me as though I were his own son. I had a wonderful youth and love Pemberley as my own home."

"Pemberley—is it a large estate?" Elizabeth inquired.

"It is a fair prospect, indeed, Miss Bennet. It is stately and grand and is accompanied by the most beautiful grounds and property I have ever seen." Mr. Wickham had a faraway look, and Elizabeth waited a moment before she spoke.

"You said that old Mr. Darcy treated you as a son...?"

"Ah," Mr. Wickham said with a laugh, "you are recalling, no doubt, that my greeting from Mr. Darcy yesterday was not so very fraternal." Mr. Wickham sighed. "We were indeed like brothers once, Miss Bennet, but that has come to an end. Tell me—how long have you been acquainted with Mr. Darcy?"

"About a month. He is here with his friend, Mr. Bingley." Elizabeth replied.

"And how do you like him?" Mr. Wickham probed. "What are your impressions of the man?"

"It is certain that he is very proud...," Elizabeth started, "... and vain to be sure. But such an attitude is the purview of the rich, I suppose." She paused thoughtfully. "He has, in truth, been very kind to me, in spite of his haughty demeanor. If I had known him longer, I may even be inclined to call him a friend. I spent above four days in company with him at Netherfield, and he was very gentlemanly, even though my presence was an imposition to the household."

"Indeed?" Mr. Wickham weighed her words. "And how do the people of Meryton like him?"

Elizabeth laughed. "He is a proud, disagreeable man, as you well know. That is plain to be seen by anyone. He has generously patronized several of the local businesses, however, and that may have improved opinions generally. Now that you have broached the subject, I suppose I should ask—how do *you* like him, Mr. Wickham?"

"It would not truly be fair for me to give my opinion of him. Mr. Wickham said. "I have known him too long and too much has passed between us—I cannot be impartial. I loved his father though, as the very best of men, and his passing was a tremendous loss for me in countless ways. Do you know how long Mr. Darcy is to remain in Hertfordshire?"

"His friend Mr. Bingley has declared himself in courtship with? my sister Jane, and we expect that *he* will remain for some duration. Mr. Darcy's plans I do not know, but I have not heard of any intention to quit the county soon," Elizabeth said.

"Oh." Mr. Wickham had a look of consternation. "Mr. Darcy and I are not on the best of terms. It shall not be pleasant to have him in residence while I am quartered here, but if he is distressed by it, he must go, not I."

"I did observe the manner of your greeting one another yesterday. What could he have meant by what he said to you?" Elizabeth flushed slightly at her boldness in asking.

"I am sure I do not know," Mr. Wickham said. "His address astonished me greatly. I did perceive some great resentment in what he spoke, the cause of which I am at a loss to identify. If anyone has a cause for hostility, it is I, not he. Mr. Darcy has greatly wronged me."

Elizabeth's curiosity was piqued, and yet she knew that pressing the matter was an affront to delicacy. Mr. Darcy's cautionary words of the evening before now returned in her mind to disquiet her, and she mentally rehearsed his plea that she not involve herself with the man or give him consequence. It was not just this that worried her, for she then recalled his caution against sketching a man's character on impressions. It had been of himself he spoke at the time. However, upon consideration, it seemed applicable in the case before her as well. She certainly had good impressions of George Wickham, despite having known him for only a very short time. She was unsettled and unsure now. Mr. Darcy had obviously been communicating a specific message to Mr. Wickham in Meryton, and while his words had not been specific, he had clearly sent a potent message of distrust to Mr. Wickham. She looked nervously at the charming officer by her side and found herself set upon a most unlikely course.

"Mr. Wickham, I am sorry for you if you are at odds with Mr. Darcy, but I am certain that he is a good and fair man. I know not what wrong you claim against him, but if there was some illegality, you should seek redress in the law. If it is something else, amends may always be made. Please do not burden me with your argument tonight, or put me in a position between you, for I am disposed to like you both."

Mr. Wickham's cheerful façade failed him, but he rallied quickly. "Miss Bennet, I am sorry. I should not have darkened this lovely evening with my woes. You are perfectly right in what you say. I shall consider your counsel, and perhaps in due course, amends shall be made."

Their conversation continued for but a few more minutes before Mr. Wickham excused himself to play at cards with the company.

Chapter Twenty-Three

AN INADVERTENT DESIGN

Elizabeth lay silent and warm in her bed. The soft patter of a gentle rain striking the glass of her window was the only sound to hear in the darkness. The house was still: it was too early to rise. The fragments of her dream floated elusively in her misty consciousness, beyond recall, but near enough that the essence remained, taunting her to make meaning of it.

Mr. Wickham had been in the dream, like the sun, sparkling, cheery and warm. He beckoned, and she had felt herself drawn to him She remembered that much. There had been another presence though—darker, brooding and powerful enough to pull her, as if with some invisible force, into his orbit. She closed her eyes again, wishing the act could return her to the place where it had seemed real. It had not been a nightmare, or even an unpleasant dream. It *had* been confusing, but it had also been thrilling, like standing on the edge of a precipice in the wind.

She felt her heartbeat quicken and her breathing become shallow as a pair of eyes came into focus in her mind. The eyes she knew well, for they had stalked her relentlessly whenever Mr. Darcy had been in company with her. In her dream, she remembered with a degree of clarity, his eyes had mesmerized her, locked onto her and whispered to her. It was so strange. His lips moved not, his stance remained proud and haughty, but his eyes *did speak* to her. They had glistened with meaning; they had called her name. Elizabeth.

She tried to rouse herself, to break free of the half-dream she had fallen back into, but although her mind was seemingly alert, her body was unresponsive to any attempt at movement. Mr. Darcy's eyes drew closer. Elizabeth had no recourse as his relentless gaze bore into her. She could do nothing but match the intensity of his stare. There was nothing else to look at, nothing else to do. His eyes were then seemingly joined by the rest of the handsome face, so close she could feel his breath play in her hair like a breeze. His countenance had transformed from the familiar aloof mask into a visage filled with tenderness and longing. She felt her own expression change to mirror his as her resistance to the image in her mind melted away. She could feel his strength, and his passion too, for it burned in his eyes like a flame. How long they looked at each other this way, she could not tell—time in a dream is fluid—it had seemed an eternity.

Waking again as the room filled with morning light, Elizabeth could not recall how the dream had ended, but this time the pieces did not shatter with wakefulness. They lingered instead, in her memory, to ponder and reflect on through the day.

❧

Elizabeth was the last to enter the dining room for breakfast. Her father had already eaten and left, but the rest were discussing the events of the previous evening with great animation. Elizabeth took a seat as far from Mr. Collins as possible. She lazily spread some jam on her toast, nearly oblivious to the noise her sisters were making, her mind pleasantly engaged in puzzling over her dream.

"Lizzy!" Lydia broke into her reverie. "Lizzy, what did you say to poor Wickham last night? It took us nearly half an hour to get him to laugh again after *you* ruined his spirits."

"We spoke at some length of his childhood. Perhaps he was feeling nostalgic," Elizabeth replied.

"That's right!" Lydia exclaimed. "He told me too—all about how Mr. Darcy used him very ill. That is not nostalgia, Lizzy. That is his poor heart being broken."

Elizabeth looked impatiently at her sister. "We have known Mr. Wickham but two days, and even I can see that he does not bear the countenance of a heartbroken man, Lydia."

"He told me you would not hear him." Lydia countered. "You did not want to hear the truth about Mr. Darcy and his cruelty toward Mr. Wickham—though I cannot imagine why." Lydia stood as she pounded her hand on the table. "Mr. Darcy was jealous of Wickham, and then he cheated him! Poor Mr. Wickham was denied his rightful inheritance and income because Mr. Darcy was mean and vindictive! Wickham was *forced* to join the militia!"

Elizabeth pressed her lips together disapprovingly. "Lydia, lower your voice." She glanced up at Mr. Collins, who was paying close attention to the conversation. "Lydia, if there is a dispute between Mr. Darcy and Mr. Wickham, they must be the ones to settle it." Elizabeth could see Mr. Collins nodding his head in agreement, as he chewed a mouthful of food. That could not stand. "Besides," she added lightly, "you said you loved the sight of Mr. Wickham in his regimentals. You must be sure to thank Mr. Darcy for forcing Wickham to enlist."

"Humph." Lydia puffed her cheeks as she plopped back into her chair. "I will thank Mr. Darcy to take his leave."

Elizabeth looked sharply at her youngest sister, willing her to stop speaking.

"What? I am only saying what we are all thinking—even you, Lizzy, if you would admit it." Lydia defended. "Mr. Darcy adds nothing at all when in company. He may be very rich, but he is dreary and too stuffy. The officers are much more pleasant."

"Lydia, dear," Mrs. Bennet interrupted, "I have been thinking. You have made a number of acquaintances among the officers of the regiment, but they have not yet come to call at Longbourn." Mrs. Bennet paused, waiting for her words to have their desired impact. "You must invite them to tea."

"Oooohhhh yes!" Lydia squealed and Kitty giggled. "Mr. Denny and Mr. Wickham, and, of course, Captain Carter! We must serve cake, Mama! Nothing but cake will do, you know."

"You shall have your cake, Lydia, if you invite them for tomorrow." Mrs. Bennet nodded approvingly. "Jane, why did Mr. Bingley not call yesterday? The very day after your father consents to his courtship, he fails to call. It is a disappointing beginning."

"Mama," Jane said sweetly, "Mr. Bingley had some urgent business in London which he had planned to attend to after the ball. When I informed him that we were to go to Aunt Phillips' home last night, since he had not been invited, he took the opportunity to see to his affairs in town early so that he would not be obliged to leave Hertfordshire for several weeks. I am certain he will call today."

"I suppose that is all right." Mrs. Bennet sniffed.

"Mr. Collins." Mary's voice was just above a whisper, and her face flushed slightly when everyone at the table turned to look at her. "Mr. Collins," Mary spoke more loudly and with a most unusual shade of determination in her tone. When the object of her address finally responded by looking at her, she continued. "Mr. Collins, it has occurred to me that we have been remiss. We have not considered that as a clergyman, you will be expected to call upon our own parson, Mr. Timmons, during the course of your stay at Longbourn. I thought, perhaps, you might fulfill this obligation today, when the road is drier."

Mr. Collins colored slightly and answered with his usual verbosity that Mary was correct and that such a call would certainly be the appropriate thing to do. Mary then advised Mr. Collins with a boldness that astonished her mother and sisters that she would happily oblige him with her company on his walk to the rectory in order to provide detail on Mr. Timmons' recent sermons. This, she assured him enthusiastically, would provide a common ground for their discourse and serve to make him at ease in the visit. Although Mr. Collins seemed surprised and slightly reluctant, with much encouragement from Mary, seconded by Jane and Elizabeth, he did at length agree to the outing.

Within the space of two hours, Lydia and Kitty had gone to Meryton to make the invitation to tea, and Mary and Mr. Collins had walked out with them, to go together as far as the rectory. Mrs. Bennet had gone to the kitchen to discuss the evening meal and the requirement of cake for tomorrow's tea.

Jane sat by the window watching for Mr. Bingley with one eye as she stitched on a sampler with the other. Elizabeth sat near her, the light from the window illuminating the delicate pattern of her embroidery as she placed the tiny stitches in a new handkerchief.

"What is that pattern, Lizzy?" Jane asked, glancing at Elizabeth's handiwork. "I do not recognize it."

"The whitework pattern is my own design Jane. I am hoping to finish it in time for the ball at Netherfield. As soon as I have done the stitching, I will trim it with lace to match my gown." Elizabeth smiled at her sister. "I am wearing the gold-threaded muslin our Aunt Gardiner gave me last year. I have not had a chance to wear it since she took us to that ball in London last spring. What will you wear Jane?"

"My white silk. I am re-trimming it with new ribbon, and I think it will turn out well." Jane turned to look out the window, and the movement she detected was what she had hoped. "He is come!" Jane's face blossomed with her smile as she turned to watch the approach. "He is not alone, Lizzy."

Elizabeth stood and looked out the window, tipping her head to the side slightly as she softly uttered, "Romeo."

"What did you say?" Jane peered at her in confusion.

"The horse, Jane. Romeo is Mr. Darcy's horse." Elizabeth smiled to herself as she muttered her reply.

Jane glanced out the window at the approaching riders. "Mr. Darcy does not seem like a romantic." Jane observed. "He must be a complex man."

"I think you may be right, Jane." Elizabeth drew closer to the window until she stood so close that her breath condensed on the pane as she spoke, her eyes fixed on the black horse and rider. "He is a complicated man, to be sure." The sight of the two horsemen transfixed her, Mr. Bingley posting to his horse's trot, while Mr. Darcy was regal and erect in his seat as his horse moved in a smooth, ambling gait.

"Come, Lizzy, we must move away from the window—they will see us! We must not stare!" Jane urged as the men drew nearer.

"I believe Mr. Bingley already knows you like him, Jane. There is no need to hide it. It may even please him to know you are eager for his company." Elizabeth tipped her head toward her sister as she spoke but kept her eyes trained on their gentlemen callers as amusement crossed her face. "And as for Mr. Darcy, he will not notice us—he comes for Bingley's sake. I am sure his mind is engaged in loftier pursuits than spotting the spies in the window."

In this assessment, Elizabeth erred, for at that moment, the gentlemen were in fact highly aware of the two eldest Bennet sisters tracking their approach. In the case of Mr. Bingley, it was exactly as she supposed, but if she could have perceived the bent of Mr. Darcy's thoughts, she would have been greatly astonished.

To *him*, she was as a specter in the glass, a vision of a warm and welcoming heart standing watch in the windows of Pemberley, waiting for his return home. It was not a great leap to contemplate the loving embrace that would greet him inside the door nor the sweet fragrance that would fog his mind as he held her close and cherished the comfort of her arms as they wrapped around him. Salutations would be spoken only after his lips had been satisfied upon hers and even then uttered between his address of kisses on the lovely face of his precious wife.

The shock of the word penetrated and jolted him from the reverie as surely as if he had fallen into a lake of ice. Elizabeth Bennet could never be his wife. Of all the bitter truths he had ever known, this one cut the deepest and caused the sharpest pain. What had begun as admiration and evolved into love had crossed into an agony more acute with every encounter. If seeing her thus in the window could plunge him to despair, how could he bear to speak to her? How could he bear not to?

This was the state of Mr. Darcy's mind as he dismounted and with Mr. Bingley approached the entrance to Longbourn as he braced himself against his traitorous emotions.

Jane and Elizabeth were seated, innocently looking as though they had been industriously stitching for hours, when Mr. Bingley and Mr. Darcy were announced and shown into the room. The ladies stood, setting down their handiwork, and curtsied, welcoming the men formally and graciously, but as soon as Hill had closed the door, Mr. Bingley closed the distance between himself and Jane in great strides.

"Miss Bennet." Mr. Bingley took up Jane's hands in his as he looked ever so happily into her eyes. "I have counted the hours since we were last together, and they have been far too many!"

Pink crept into Jane's cheeks as she fought to maintain her composure. "For me as well, Mr. Bingley."

At this, Elizabeth turned away, seeking to give her sister and Mr. Bingley at least a semblance of privacy, and discovered that Mr. Darcy had picked up the hoop of her embroidery and was studying it with apparent curiosity.

"Are you generally so fascinated with needlework, Mr. Darcy?" Elizabeth's eyes sparkled with merriment as she held out her hand to receive the article.

"No," he replied as he returned it to Elizabeth. "It is the pattern that caught my eye. It is unusual."

Elizabeth looked down at the pattern of loops and swirls she had designed. "Is it? It is not so very unusual, I daresay, but perhaps not common either, for I composed the lines myself." She proceeded to sit, taking up the hoop and needle, to resume her stitching.

It was then that she saw them—the elements in the pattern that were as inadvertent as they were prominent. This was undoubtedly the source of Mr. Darcy's interest in the pattern. Embedded quite unmistakably in the design of pulled eyelets and tucked ridges were the letters "E" and "D," interlaced and connected in the appearance of bold initials.

She continued stitching as she felt the color creep into her cheeks. It was not mortification that tinged her face with a rosy hue, but the laughter that she was attempting to suppress.

"Miss Elizabeth?" Mr. Darcy had seated himself near her own chair and looking at her with alarm. "Are you quite alright?"

She looked up at him, her eyes almost wet with tears of hilarity. They sparkled dangerously as she nodded, grasping inwardly to retrieve the breath that eluded her without revealing her laughter to Mr. Darcy. She did not want him to suppose that she was laughing at him when her own blunder had caused it.

"Excuse me." Elizabeth dropped the hoop beside her as she stood and removed herself from the room before she lost all control. A step into the outside air gave her release, and she gulped the air in with great rushing breaths as her laughter escaped her, rippling waves of mirth that subsided gradually as she leaned against a tree and composed herself.

After several minutes, she straightened herself to return to the house, only to discover that Mr. Darcy had followed her outside and had, it seemed, witnessed her loss of control, the offending embroidery hoop once again in his hand.

"Miss Bennet," he said softly as she moved to pass him on her way back to the house. "I did not intend to be discourteous a moment ago. The design is quite enchanting." He handed the hoop back to her awkwardly. "Please forgive me if I offended you."

"I could hardly refuse forgiveness when you beg it with such politeness," Elizabeth said with a raised brow as she received the article yet again, "but I assure you, an apology is quite unnecessary. There is nothing to forgive."

"If I did not upset you, may I inquire as to what was the cause of your ... distress?" Mr. Darcy asked in confusion.

"That was not distress, sir." Elizabeth said as she continued walking toward the house. She waited for him to come alongside her before she added, "I am certain it cannot surprise you, for I told you myself that I dearly love to laugh, even if the object of the joke is myself."

"Why did you leave the room?" Mr. Darcy asked. "Surely you could have laughed among friends."

"Mr. Darcy, we are both aware that proper comportment does not allow for an attack of gaiety such as I have suffered to be exhibited in company. I required a moment of privacy." Elizabeth replied.

"What was the source of this ... attack of gaiety as you call it?" One corner of Mr. Darcy's mouth turned up as he asked the question.

"There it is." Elizabeth chuckled. "I knew you could not restrain yourself from asking! If you know the answer—as well you may—it is most ungentlemanly of you to ask me to own it."

"Let us assume I do not know the answer." Mr. Darcy pressed, his hint of a smile widening slightly.

"If that is the case, I believe the proper course of action would be to allow a lady to keep her secret," Elizabeth retorted triumphantly, "and never to broach the topic again."

"Then I shall not force you to own it, Miss Bennet. I would not wish to be accused of ungentlemanly behavior. The lady's secret is safe." At this, he genuinely laughed and escorted her back indoors to the sitting room, an uncharacteristic grin plastered on his face.

The next half an hour was spent in relaxed conversation. Jane and Mr. Bingley continued contentedly talking quietly between themselves, but Elizabeth found that the strange tension between herself and Mr. Darcy was somehow gone.

Elizabeth boldly continued stitching on her handkerchief, although holding it at an angle that obscured Mr. Darcy's view of it. They discussed several books they had both read, and Mr. Darcy told Elizabeth a little about his sister, Georgiana, whom he had seen briefly the day before when he was in London.

"Did you also see your aunt in London, Mr. Darcy?" Elizabeth enjoyed asking the question, for the last time they had spoken of Lady Catherine he had not disclosed the relationship.

"Yes, as a matter of fact I did," he responded with a nod and a shrug, "and my cousin Anne as well. She sends her regards to you and your family."

"It must have been a great joy to see her." Elizabeth replied, allowing a slight air of smugness to creep into her tone as she kept her eyes focused on her needle. "I understand that you are engaged to Miss de Bourgh."

At this, Mr. Darcy looked intently at Elizabeth. It took a moment of silence, but eventually she looked up, blinking at the flutter of déjà vu that stirred in her stomach as their eyes met. "It is a lie." Darcy's voice was guttural as he locked his eyes onto hers. "I am not engaged to Anne."

"Oh." Elizabeth said softly as she broke the gaze and dropped her eyes in confusion. "I must have been misinformed."

"Anne told me you were kind to her." His voice had lost its edge. "She was exceedingly grateful."

Elizabeth shifted uncomfortably. "I was glad to be of some assistance. She did not look well."

"She also told me some incredibly diverting stories about your cousin, Mr. Collins." Mr. Darcy chuckled, trying to return to the ease of their previous conversation. "I would be willing to share them with you someday when you are in need of a laugh, but you must promise not to run away if the laughter overcomes you."

"It is not fair to exploit Mr. Collins in such a way—it is too easy." Elizabeth said, with an arch in her brow and her tone. "If you must make me laugh, let it be at you alone. I do not believe you can do it, but if you do, I promise to stay and laugh. I am obliged to warn you, though, that Miss Bingley will not approve."

Mr. Darcy's brow furrowed for a moment, and he answered seriously. "You have raised the stakes to a point of pain, Miss Bennet. Remind me to never play against you at cards."

"Mr. Darcy, at cards you would have the advantage." Elizabeth laughed at him. "I bet in jokes and giggles, which cost me nothing. At cards, where money is required, your threshold is unlikely to be exceeded. As you well know, I have no money to squander at the tables."

"I did not mean to...," Mr. Darcy stammered.

"Do not distress yourself so, Mr. Darcy." Elizabeth continued to laugh, "I am not seeking your sympathy. I much prefer my currency, for when you lose, your money is gone, but I may retain my good spirits and humor, even when it is spent."

"True," Mr. Darcy said, "but laughter cannot secure your future."

"That is where Mr. Collins comes into the equation." Elizabeth said sweetly. "He is the heir of Longbourn, and in his marrying one of its daughters, the future is secured for all. You need not concern yourself with the matter."

"Has he made an offer?" Mr. Darcy's face returned to the mask Elizabeth hated.

"He has only just arrived, Mr. Darcy. It would hardly be proper for him to offer in so short a time." Elizabeth stood as she spoke, agitated by the turn in the conversation. "I must excuse myself now. I have enjoyed our conversation today very much. I sincerely hope the pleasure will be repeated again in the future." She curtsied and went to her room upstairs, taking her embroidery with her.

Chapter Twenty-Four

STARS & CONSTELLATIONS

Elizabeth's bedtime routine of brushing and braiding her hair was barely complete when Jane knocked quietly and joined her in her bedchamber, as happened most evenings, if Elizabeth had not already gone to Jane's room first.

"Oh, Lizzy!" Jane cried out softly as she closed the door behind her, "What a day we have had at Longbourn!"

"Never has there been a day such as this one." Elizabeth laughed as she shook her head in agreement. "Having a suitor is very agreeable, I daresay, if his name is Mr. Bingley."

"Oh, Lizzy, Mr. Bingley is everything wonderful!" Jane sighed happily, "But I fear that I behaved very selfishly today. When we are together, I forget myself. Was Mr. Darcy difficult to entertain? It appeared that he distressed you...."

"Jane, you must not fret!" Elizabeth giggled, "I was discomposed, to be sure, but it was no fault of Mr. Darcy's, unless one can assign blame for an observant eye."

"Observant eye? What did he see, Lizzy?" Jane was clearly puzzled. "Was I not in the room as well? Am I so blind?"

Elizabeth retrieved her embroidery hoop and handed it to her sister. "It was the handkerchief. My design intrigued him. If you study it, you will see what I myself missed when I drew the pattern, and even as I stitched on it did not realize was there. Mr. Darcy noticed it with but a glance."

Jane took the article and moved closer to the candle to examine it. Suddenly, her eyes rounded and she gasped. "But it is so plain! What did he say?"

"He said nothing, except that he found the design unusual." Elizabeth started to laugh again. "Imagine my horror, dear sister, when I discovered these initials, stitched by my own hand, and exposed by Mr. Darcy! I cannot imagine what thoughts he entertained, but I do wish I could have been looking at his face, for I am certain it was a sight! I was so consumed by the absurdity of what had happened that I was forced to quit the room or else fall upon the floor for lack of breath!"

"That was when you left? We all thought you had been upset, although we had no idea what could have made you so." Jane suddenly paled. "Mr. Darcy followed you! I should have gone after you myself, but Mr. Darcy said ... he said...," Jane put her hand over her mouth. "He picked up your embroidery, said something nonsensical about constellations and stars and said most emphatically that he would speak to you and put your mind at ease. When you returned, it seemed to be so, and I did not give it another thought."

"That is because your thoughts were all wrapped up in Mr. Bingley!" Elizabeth teased and, after a moment's pause, added, "Jane, now you have made me wonder, for Mr. Darcy said nothing to me of stars. Can you not remember what he said?"

"Goodness, I was not paying him much heed." Jane blushed. "Let me think." She sat quietly, and after a moment of contemplation said, "I think it was something like 'Men look at stars and see constellations to order the sky. I have foolishly seen heaven in a handkerchief.'" Jane pondered for a moment and shook her head. "What do you suppose he could have meant by it?"

Elizabeth took the hoop from Jane and fingered the pattern, tracing the letters that had been a moment ago the cause of great levity. "I suppose he must have thought that he imagined the letters in the design the same way men see constellations in the sky, by connecting random points. That is a great relief to me, for I would not want him to think me presumptuous."

"You have never cared what Mr. Darcy thought before, Lizzy. Has something changed?" Jane challenged her.

"Do not be ridiculous, Jane. I cannot have him think so—he is already far too conceited. It would be a great disservice to the man to add to his vanity when it is already as bloated as it is." Elizabeth retorted. "If only there were a remedy for a pride such as his, I would serve that to him in an instant!"

"As you did to poor Mr. Collins at dinner?" Jane laughed at her sister. "After all our work to get him to notice Mary, he could not be pried from your side tonight. You were very nearly rude to him, and he was too obtuse to notice."

"*Poor Mr. Collins?*" Elizabeth complained. "I say poor *Mary* for liking such a man. The tragic thing is that he improves when in Mary's company. I cannot say how she does it, but it is uncanny. He is undoubtedly the stupidest man in all England, and yet Mary has managed to elicit some almost intelligent discourse from our cousin."

"You must allow for the difference in Mary's temper." Jane counseled. "Mary must see good in him, or she would not desire his attentions. I have never seen her so intent on achieving a specific end as she is now. We must continue to help her. Consider, this—if she can improve him in one conversation, imagine how enriched he would be with a daily dose of Mary."

"But Jane, it is our unhappy lot to be burdened with such an odious cousin. Think on this—could we bear to call him brother? I am very uncomfortable to think that I have thrown Mary into his path as a means to save myself." Elizabeth frowned. "Yet she really does seem to like him. I cannot understand my own sister."

"You have told me many times, Lizzy, that only the deepest, most profound love would induce you into matrimony. If Mary finds herself bound to Mr. Collins by these same feelings, you cannot fault her for the same standard to which you hold yourself." Jane persuaded.

"You are right, Jane." Elizabeth conceded. "I am delighted that you also seem to have had the good fortune to find yourself profoundly in love. You are in love, are you not?"

Jane blushed and looked away from her sister. "I believe I am. If love is marked by tender feelings of admiration and regard, as well as a stirring of passions that I did not know were within me, then I confess; I am most happily in love. You must promise, Lizzy, not to repeat it to anyone, not until we are engaged."

"I promise." Elizabeth laughed. "Although it is written on both of your faces, etched so deeply in every glance, that your secret, though safe with me, is not really safe at all."

&

Mr. Darcy, upon his return to Netherfield, was relieved to find that responses to three of his express letters had been delivered in the course of the day. These, combined with the two he had retrieved from his London house gave him much cause for reflection.

From his cousin Richard came the reply that he would come to Meryton as soon as his leave was approved. When he arrived, they could together determine the best course of action for the "Wickham problem."

From his steward at Pemberley came the assurance that although Lady Catherine de Bourgh had attempted to learn of Mr. Darcy's whereabouts through them, including threats and intimidation, the information had been faithfully withheld, and he could be certain that she would not receive intelligence through his estate in Derbyshire.

From his solicitor in London, he received confirmation that the land agent responsible for letting the Netherfield property to Mr. Bingley had been cooperative in making a guarantee that the transaction would be held in strictest confidence, and that they could not be traced to Hertfordshire by inquiries made by outside parties.

From his cousin Lady Sefton, he was given the most helpful information, for as one of the great patronesses of Almack's, she was privy to the rumors and gossip of the *ton*, even though the London season was past. Some had linked his name, as he had suspected, to that of Caroline Bingley, although Lady Sefton stated that she did not believe the rumors to be legitimate. She informed him also that his aunt, Lady Catherine de Bourgh, had been in attendance at several functions in recent weeks, making similar inquiries about Miss Bingley and had made frequent references to her own daughter as her nephew's intended.

Last came the reply he had from Mrs. Annesley, Georgiana's companion. He had spoken to her personally when in London, for fear that someone in close proximity to his sister had gained access to her correspondence. From Mrs. Annesley, he learned that the lady's maid serving Georgiana was discovered to be related to an upper housemaid at Rosings and had, when questioned, confessed to sending her cousin letters containing confidences shared with her by young Miss Darcy. The maid, Mrs. Annesley informed him, had been discharged and replaced upon the discovery, much to Georgiana's dismay.

No one in any of the letters had ever heard of Mr. Collins, although Richard had generously offered to interrogate him once they had finished their business with Wickham. Darcy smiled to himself at the mental image, which rapidly evolved to a slightly more sinister thought. *I will interrogate Collins myself. He will feel as though he has been through the Inquisition before I am done, and then I shall let Richard have a go. That should chase that disturbing little man off for good.*

The letters left him agitated. Georgiana would feel betrayed, a painful setback for his dear sister. If Wickham were not so close, and if Caroline Bingley had not become so aggressive in her pursuit of him, he would be tempted to bring his sister to Netherfield, but with the situation as it was, this course could not be considered.

At least there was the consolation that George Wickham was trapped. The cost of resigning his commission was too high, and it was not likely he would make such a personal sacrifice—so Darcy could patiently wait for Richard to come before he made any move there.

His aunt, he felt certain, would have difficulty tracing him, since it appeared that his measures to block her had thus far proved successful. She would be furious but no more so than he was for her ongoing insistence on advancing the lie that he was to marry Anne.

Darcy stopped to consider why he had felt compelled to refute the engagement rumor to Elizabeth Bennet. It would have served him much better to let it stand, for if she had noticed his struggles—and he was certain she could not have failed to—she would have an easy explanation as to why he had not made any move for her in spite of his obvious regard for her. It was a perfect foil to his potent emotions, which threatened to betray him at any moment. Why had he not simply allowed her to believe it?

This question he did not wish to face, for it did not reflect well upon his own character. He could assuage his guilt by claiming it was the lie he objected to, but he had let others believe it in the past when it had served to do so. No, the truth was more insidious. He wanted Elizabeth Bennet to see him as free of entanglements, as master of his own destiny. Why it mattered he did not examine more closely, for it became painful to acknowledge that what he wanted Elizabeth to believe of him was the lie, for free he was not, and his destiny was bound up in obligations and expectations enough to sink a ship.

As was hers. The more he thought of the entailment on Longbourn, the angrier he became at the trap that made Mr. Collins an eligible suitor for a woman such as Elizabeth. More tragic still was that she seemingly had no alternative.

Clarity struck Mr. Darcy, as it had done with increasing frequency of late. His aunt was stopped for the time being, Wickham would wait until Richard arrived. Georgiana was safe. When analyzing the troubles that preyed upon his mind, one alone was fixed as the urgent, immediate priority. Very soon, Elizabeth Bennet would be lost forever to Mr. Collins unless something was done to prevent it. This probability, he admitted to himself, threatened his own happiness severely, for it seemed as a deep abyss for the woman he secretly loved to fall so low and be doomed to a life of misery by circumstance. He could be satisfied, he told himself, if she were to marry a man who was worthy of her, but not Mr. Collins. He did not deserve her.

His plan to deal with Mr. Collins, which had been formulating in his mind from the moment he had become aware of Collins' intentions toward Elizabeth, must be put into play tomorrow!

Chapter Twenty-Five

OF WOODLAND SPRITES & MERMAIDS

For the second night in a row, Elizabeth awoke from a dream in the pre-dawn hours. She lay still, as if her quietude would prevent the hazy remnants from departing. Most of the images escaped, released by her increasing consciousness, but the sweetness of the dream stayed with her. The impressions from the first part of the dream were gone, although there were vague memories of trees and a river and a fish, but in the end part, she could clearly remember an embrace, her head pressed against the broad expanse of a masculine chest, strong arms wrapped around her, a refuge of safety and security. She had heard his beating heart against her cheek, but upon awakening; she recognized it as the wild pounding of her own. In her dream, a gentle hand had lifted her face upward and familiar eyes had gazed into hers as a single finger traced her lips. He had descended slowly, his eyes never breaking away until his lips pressed against hers.

Elizabeth Bennet had never before been kissed by a man—not even in her dreams, and the shock woke her. Her lips still tingled from the kiss that had not happened, and she blushed in the darkness at the pleasure it wrought. She pressed her fingertips against her mouth as if to cool the heat that lingered.

Sleep would not return, and her mind would not remove itself from the man who had sheltered her in his arms and flaunted propriety when she could least resist him. He had taken liberties and compromised her, and to her chagrin, she had enjoyed it. She could not hold Mr. Darcy accountable for things he had not actually done, but neither could she easily forgive him for making her feel so weak and vulnerable in that very hour.

Her insomniac mind became as a carriage with runaway horses, barreling through every moment spent in company with him, every word and every glance. He was always haughty—except when he was not. He was always disagreeable, although with time he was becoming less so. He frowned too much, but she had also seen him smile—a great improvement to his dour expression. He was too intense, too brooding for comfort, and yet she found her spirits oddly fed by his intensity, her curiosity piqued by his brooding. He was an interesting case for observation, she decided uneasily.

She thought upon the scene that had unfolded around her embroidery. Had Mr. Darcy somehow influenced her pattern for the handkerchief? She did not think so—it was an accident, a coincidence, for she had begun it nearly a month earlier when she had barely known him. Either way, he had not seemed upset by it, and she knew he had noticed it even though he did not openly concede it. Upon reflection, it almost seemed to please him. That was very strange—nothing pleased Mr. Darcy.

She had briefly considered altering the design, but she worried that she would ruin it in so doing, so she had, instead, worked by the light of her bedroom window that day to finish the stitching. Today she would sew on the trim, a piece of lace given to her by her Aunt Gardiner a few years previous. It had started as trim on a gown, but when Elizabeth's frame had become more womanly; the gown was passed to Mary, although not before Elizabeth had reclaimed the lace. It had been made, her aunt told her, in the village of Lambton in Derbyshire, where she had grown up, and because the lace was dear to her aunt, it was dear to Elizabeth.

Eventually, Elizabeth acknowledged to herself that she was fully awake, and although the hour was early, she rose and dressed, determined to clear her mind with a brisk walk in the mists of the early morn. She did not bother to dress her hair but left it in the thick plait she slept in. She would return and style it before the household was even awake.

༄

Mr. Darcy was also awake, although no pleasant dream had beckoned him from slumber. His mind was a frenzy of thought as he paced the floor, churning through George Wickham, Mr. Collins,

Caroline Bingley, Bingley and Jane Bennet, Miss Elizabeth Bennet and her handkerchief—and her eyes—and her laughter—and her ... mother. He thought of his aunt, Lady Catherine, and his cousin, Anne. He wondered when his other cousin, Colonel Richard Fitzwilliam, would arrive.

He thought of Georgiana, and her pleasure at receiving his gift of the shawl, and he thought of the other shawl he had purchased, and wondered if its intended recipient would ever even see it. He stewed over what Wickham had done to Georgiana, then he thought of Miss Elizabeth again, of the way she raised her eyebrow at him, the way she pursed her lips when something displeased her and how he wanted to crush her mouth with his own when she did so.

He thought of Pemberley, of how empty it had felt when he was last there, and of how long it had been since the great estate had been graced with a mistress. He thought of Elizabeth, of her wit, her grace and composure, and the way that she had won his dog's heart with her wild kisses and petting and fetching games. Apollo whined and thumped his tail at mere mention of her name now. The dog's allegiance was not so constant as Elizabeth had promised it would be.

Eventually, Darcy acknowledged to himself that he would go mad before his five-day limit if he allowed himself to continue, so although the hour was early, he dressed, determined to clear his mind with an early morning ride through the rolling lands of Hertfordshire.

❧

Elizabeth crept into the kitchen and took a crust of bread, wrapping it in a cloth before she pocketed it, along with an apple. She donned her least fashionable, but warmest, outer attire. Made of tightly woven wool, the hooded scarlet cloak would protect her from the damp air well. She pulled the hood over her head and quit the house noiselessly.

The sun was not yet up, but the faint traces of dawn were sufficient to light the path, and she ran toward Oakham Mount with the sureness of one who had taken the route many times. Alone, she could release her energies with a sweet freedom she did not know when scrutiny was upon her. She ran, and skipped, and hopped onto rocks, leaping from them as though, for an instant, she could fly, as her cloak billowed around her on the descent. The further she went, the better she felt. Her worries seemed smaller, the outlook, brighter and the day, more promising with every step.

When she arrived at the base of the mount where rising ground loomed ahead of her, she slowed her pace in order to make the climb without becoming winded. The sky along the horizon was now tinged with a rosy hue, an augur of the coming daybreak. Elizabeth rested for a moment on a boulder, preparing to begin the uphill climb and anticipating the beautiful view she knew awaited her. She felt steady now; her exercise had vanquished the tensions that had driven her from the house. It had also warmed her, and she pulled the hood off her head. The cool air felt good in her hair, which was now clinging to her neck, due to the dampness that collected as she ran. She pulled her braid out of the cloak and freed the strands, running her fingers through them to allow the light breeze to cool her further.

It was as she sat upon the rock, releasing her tresses from bondage, that Apollo came, bounding up to her excitedly. He barked once and turned in a happy circle, his tail wagging and his canine mouth turned up to resemble a smile.

Elizabeth knew now, as she had not in her first meeting with the hound, that his master would be near, and she felt a strange flutter in her stomach as she looked for him down the path. She could detect no sign of Mr. Darcy, so, after quickly re-braiding her hair, she turned her attentions to his dog, renewing their acquaintance in much the same manner as she had made it.

She did not know that Mr. Darcy had been following her red-cloaked figure at a distance for some time, intrigued with the abandon with which she traveled. He committed to memory her flying leaps, the little twirl she made in the path, and the joyous appearance of her taking a loping run down a descending slope with her hands in the air and her head thrown back in sheer delight.

When his path had merged with where she walked, there was no restraining his dog once he caught her scent, and Darcy sought cover in a copse of trees, reticent to be discovered. He had watched her, fascinated, as the lengths of her dark hair spilled across her shoulders. He had held his breath when she had searched for him, wondering if it was disappointment he witnessed before she welcomed his dog with all the enthusiasm he expected.

Mr. Darcy knew he could not remain hidden for long, so after a few indulgent moments, he urged his horse back to the path, and approached the scene casually, as though it were the most natural thing in the world to encounter an acquaintance by accident at the base of the mountain before sunrise.

"Miss Bennet." He nodded from atop his mount, unable to contain his smile at the sight before him.

"Mr. Darcy." She acknowledged him somewhat reluctantly as she hugged his dog. "Have you lost your way yet again?"

"Perhaps." He said with a smirk. "Although I believe it is just my dog I have lost."

"You seem in good spirits today." Elizabeth observed.

"I am," he replied with an uncharacteristic grin, "in excellent spirits. I took a ride in the woods and find myself come across a woodland creature I cannot identify. If I were by the sea, I would say it was a mermaid, come out of the water and combing her hair upon the rocks. As there is no water, I am left to wonder if you are a sprite… or a nymph."

Elizabeth laughed. "I am no sprite, Mr. Darcy. If I were, I would have disappeared before you came upon me. I had not anticipated that the wandering threesome would wander *this way* so early. You have caught me unawares."

"Pleasantly so," Darcy said, relaxing in his saddle. After a brief pause, he asked, "Threesome?"

Elizabeth laughed again. "How else am I to think of you, sir? There is my canine sweetheart, Apollo, come to raise the sun in the sky, and the equine lover, Romeo, who has followed me once before, and there is you. That is three."

"A sweetheart, a lover, and me." Darcy raised his eyebrows in amusement. "You did not characterize me as you did the others."

"How would you have me do so?" Elizabeth wondered, tipping her head, squinting her eyes, and pursing her lips together. "Their taciturn master?"

Darcy frowned. "No." He dismounted and approached Elizabeth. "I would far rather be something else. Would you be so kind as to try again?"

"Oh dear." Elizabeth sighed, strangely affected by his approach, and unsettled too, at the realization that she wanted to say something that pleased him. She tapped her cheek as though deep in thought, while Mr. Darcy stood before her, holding the reins. "I suppose I will grant that some would find you handsome. You will have to settle for 'their handsome master,' or take 'taciturn' back as implicit."

Darcy shook his head in mock amazement. "Did you just call me handsome, Miss Bennet?"

"Do not make me repeat it, or I will deny ever saying so." Elizabeth retorted. "I was under some duress at the time." She jumped up from the rock. "I am going to finish my walk to the top of Oakham Mount now. I would not miss the sunrise, Mr. Darcy."

"You have not missed it." Darcy tipped his head to the east, as the golden rays of the morning sun crested on the horizon. "You can see it where you stand. It is beautiful, is it not?"

Elizabeth looked, and seeing that he was right, shrugged her shoulders. "I am going all the same. Good day, Mr. Darcy." She patted Apollo's head and started away.

"Miss Bennet!" Mr. Darcy called after her. She turned around and looked expectantly at him. "Miss Bennet, may I accompany you? I have long desired to see the view from the top of this mount. It would be a pleasure to do so in your company."

Elizabeth nodded her agreement, but said, "You do realize that our doing so alone is not proper ... yes, I suppose you do. I will allow it, but must beg you to speak of this to no one. I have a reputation to consider."

"How could you think I would speak of it to anyone, when I am so very taciturn?" Darcy said with a sly grin. "Your characterization of me is your guarantee."

"Ah, but I have revised it at *your* insistence." Elizabeth replied. "Handsome men are known to be very bold in bragging of their conquests. I require your word of honor as a gentleman that you will be silent about this."

"I am not a braggart, and you are not a conquest, Miss Bennet." Darcy was in earnest. "I have no desire to defeat you. You have my word that I will keep *this* secret as well as I have *your previous one*, and that I would do nothing to harm your reputation."

Elizabeth nodded her acceptance of his reply and then walked briskly, too much so for conversation, as Mr. Darcy followed with Romeo behind him and Apollo running circles around them all. The walk was companionable, with the light of day ever brighter as they climbed.

As she walked, Elizabeth was reflecting on how surprised she was that she did not resent the intrusion on her solitude. She was also amazed that although just a few hours had passed since she had dreamed of being kissed by Mr. Darcy, she was not uncomfortable in his presence. After all, he did not realize that he had kissed her. That was one secret he would *never* know.

Darcy's thoughts were on a parallel to those of his companion. He thought of how he had ridden out in the morning to escape his thoughts, especially thoughts of Elizabeth Bennet, and how when he had spotted her red cloak, he had had no alternative but to pursue her. He had no regrets that he had done so. Being near her was a guilty pleasure, one that he embraced in the moments when he could and only fought when they were apart.

It was as he was thus musing that Fitzwilliam Darcy was forcefully struck with an epiphany. *I cannot live without Elizabeth Bennet.*

It was at this very moment that they reached the summit, and Elizabeth said softly, "Look, Mr. Darcy. Is the sight before you not a fair prospect? I do not know how to bear it sometimes, to gaze upon such beauty and not be able to ever hold it, to be limited to just looking. It seems a hardship."

"Yes," Mr. Darcy said, looking at Elizabeth, the sunlight glinting off her hair, and her face flushed from exertion. "I believe I understand how you feel."

Suddenly, Romeo stepped between them and nuzzled his head against Elizabeth's side with a soft whickering sound.

Elizabeth laughed and mumbled something about him being a lover. Reaching inside her cloak, she produced the apple she had brought for her breakfast.

"Your horse, Mr. Darcy," she giggled sweetly, "while it would appear he seeks my affections, he is in fact, bent on stealing my apple." She held the fruit out in her palm for the animal to take.

"He is a stupid horse," Darcy replied. "He has taken the lesser prize."

"I think not, for all I have left is a crust of bread. I would gladly share it with you if you are hungry." Elizabeth dug into her pocket and produced the little bundle, unwrapped the bread and broke it in two. She offered a piece to Mr. Darcy.

He looked at the crust thoughtfully before accepting it and ate it in silence, surreptitiously watching Elizabeth eat hers.

Elizabeth did not miss his furtive peeks at her, for she was engaged in the same pastime of watching him. He seemed so unassuming and at ease, he hardly seemed to be the same man whom she had contemplated upon awakening. When they had both finished, Elizabeth joked, "Had I anticipated a picnic, I would have stolen the cake Mama had Cook make for tea."

Darcy shook his head. "The bread was perfect, Miss Bennet. Sometimes, when a man is hungry, a piece of bread is all it takes to tide him over. I find myself very satisfied."

"I am glad." Elizabeth responded sincerely. "And now I fear I must return to Longbourn, before I am missed."

"I will walk you home," Darcy replied, "although I will stop out of sight of the house ... for the sake of your reputation."

"That is not necessary, Mr. Darcy. It is too far out of your way—I would not have you trouble yourself on my account." Elizabeth turned to begin the descent.

"Miss Bennet, I am not accustomed to being refused." He stopped speaking when she glared at him over her shoulder. "Miss Bennet," he tried again, "it would please me if you would allow me to escort you home."

"That is a little better, Mr. Darcy, but there is a problem. You are too slow!" With a laugh, Elizabeth raced down the trail. Apollo kept pace with her, but Darcy, leading his horse, dared not go so quickly and had to content himself with a silent prayer that she would not break her neck.

At the rock where he had first come across Elizabeth, he mounted and spurred the steed, catching up with Elizabeth before she had made much distance.

She laughed when he reined in his horse in front of her, blocking her path. Elizabeth stopped and bent over to catch her breath, panting from running as fast as she could. When she had breath to speak, she looked up at the man who sat stern-faced in the saddle and smiled charmingly. "You have won, Mr. Darcy. I am defeated. You may escort me home, although you may not brag about your victory."

Darcy was on the ground as soon as Elizabeth spoke. "You are mistaken, Miss Bennet. If anyone has been defeated today, it is I. I have waged a fierce battle and have lost, although I am not sorry for it."

Elizabeth walked around Darcy and his horse, shaking her head in confusion. "Walk me home or not, it is your choice."

Mr. Darcy walked alongside Elizabeth until they were just out of sight of the house, neither of them making conversation. He bid her goodbye, and mounting the horse once again, he sped back to Netherfield, his mind and heart full of Elizabeth Bennet.

Chapter Twenty-Six

WAITING FOR TEA TIME

"Good morning, Mr. Darcy!" Caroline exclaimed as he joined his breakfasting friends, "We had quite despaired of seeing you at all this morning. It is so unlike you to remain abed so late. Are you unwell?"

"No," he replied cheerfully, "I am exceptionally well. I went for an early ride to exercise my horse and dog and am quite refreshed."

"You must be famished." Caroline said, "May I indulge you with a pastry this morning?"

"No, thank you, just some tea." Darcy shook his head with a faint smile. When Caroline appeared ready to object, he added. "I ate some bread earlier and have no appetite for pastries."

"Some toast then?" Caroline offered.

"As I said," Darcy scowled slightly at Caroline, "just the tea."

"Speaking of tea," Bingley interrupted, "I am to call at Longbourn later this morning for tea. Would you join me, Darcy? I believe there is company enough to occupy you, although perhaps not so high as you like."

"I cannot imagine intentionally spending more than five minutes in company with the Bennets." Caroline sniffed. "Mrs. Bennet is without exception the most alarming example of ill-bred manners I have ever encountered. Do not count on me to accompany you, Charles. I will entertain Jane Bennet here anytime you like. I do not understand your wishing to go to that house, although I believe Mr. Darcy appreciates the 'fine eyes' to be had there."

"One goes where one is happy, Caroline." Charles grinned. "I am as happy when at Longbourn as anywhere in the world."

"I am not happy hearing you even speak of Longbourn, Charles." Caroline abruptly stood up. "I will find another room where the conversation does not turn on such an insufferable topic as this. I do hope you get past this infatuation with Jane Bennet quickly. She is a nice enough girl, but she is not for you. You will see soon enough, and your ridiculous infatuation with her pretty face will fade, as it always has before. Come, Louisa."

Louisa obediently followed her sister out of the room, looking apologetically at Charles as she went. Mr. Hurst wordlessly dropped his serviette on the table and left a moment later.

"If I had known that happiness would clear a room, I would have tried it myself years ago," Darcy said dryly after they had gone.

"It did seem remarkably effective." Charles laughed. "Caroline apparently does not wish to visit the Bennets, and she would certainly prefer you stay at Netherfield instead of accompanying me to Longbourn."

"Then I must accompany you or resort to hiding from your sister in the library. She does nothing but tease me, and I do not like it." Darcy said. "I would as soon *see* the fine eyes as hear endlessly about them."

"Miss Elizabeth?" Charles chuckled. "She is a lively girl, and I like her very much. Miss Bennet tells me that her sister is too spirited and headstrong for their mother but that her father adores her as his favorite daughter."

"Their father seems gentlemanly enough." Darcy reflected. "I wonder that the estate is not more profitable. The property is sufficient, I believe, to have done much better."

"I have thought the same." Bingley acknowledged. "He does not appear to be much engaged in improvements."

"Perhaps he is not motivated to undertake improvements. It would take but a year to see an increase in income if it were done right." Darcy looked out the window toward Longbourn. "Then the dowries of his five daughters would not be so meager."

Bingley laughed. "I care not a whit about Miss Bennet's dowry, Darcy! I have money enough for us both! Why deny myself the greater treasure of felicity in marriage simply because she cannot add to my fortune? I assure you that when I am holding her in my arms, I will *not* be thinking of money."

Darcy's expression clouded. "How can you know that she is not a fortune hunter—that when you are holding her in your arms, that *she* will not be thinking of money?"

"If money makes her happy," Bingley shrugged, "then I shall be its willing bearer. However, I do not believe she is like that."

"You could do better." Darcy informed him. "She has no connections."

"Neither did I, until you became my friend. If she will have me, let my connections increase hers, then no one can ever say that she has none, for the name of 'Darcy' is sufficient connection for anyone." Bingley grinned, as though the answer were so easy that a simpleton could have seen it. "I hate to ride upon your coattails, my friend. I hope you do not begrudge it."

"You are as a brother to me," Darcy replied soberly and shook his head. "I do not begrudge it."

"Are these your only objections to my lady?" Bingley clapped Darcy on his shoulder. "You cannot doubt her affection for me. I should make her an offer!"

"No, I do not doubt." Darcy said, "I have seen her attachment to you. These were my main concerns, but as your friend, I caution you not to act rashly. A proposal of marriage is serious business, and cannot be honorably retracted once made. Let it be courtship for a time. No harm may come from waiting."

"No harm, perhaps, except that my heart may burst!" Bingley declared.

"That would surely make a mess." Darcy laughed. "Wait, but do not wait so long that you die first."

"You must know that time will only deepen my devotion to her, and abject desire will prevent postponement sufficient to bring death." Bingley said with a smile. "You *are* coming with me today, are you not?"

"I believe I shall." Darcy replied with a nod and a smile. "I have a favor to ask of you now, and I hope you will oblige."

"You have indulged me most graciously today," Bingley said cheerily. "I cannot imagine that I could refuse you anything."

"My cousin, Colonel Fitzwilliam, has agreed to come to Hertfordshire to assist me in some personal business. He expects to stay at the Inn in Meryton, but I would ask if he might instead make use of a room here at Netherfield. He is a pleasant fellow, perhaps even more jovial than you are. You are certain to enjoy his company immensely."

"But this is splendid!" Bingley cried. "Of course, I will oblige! I will tell the housekeeper to prepare a room. When is he to arrive?"

"I do not know exactly. It could be soon." Darcy replied.

"This cousin, I believe, is the son of an earl is he not?" Bingley said with his eyebrows raised.

"Yes," Darcy replied, "the second son of the Earl of Matlock."

"Oh ho! Caroline will be most impressed!" Bingley said, beaming. "She cannot fault me for a lack of decent company with such a man as this under our roof! She may even be distracted from her grand attentions to you, Darcy. I hope you do not mind."

"Thank you, Bingley." Darcy said thoughtfully. "You well know that I would not mind such a diversion at all, although I cannot predict how Richard will feel about it."

"Look here, Darcy!" Bingley pointed out the window. "A carriage approaches."

Darcy recognized the carriage in a glance. "Richard has always had impeccable timing." He muttered with a shake of his head. "I have never figured out how he does it. Come and meet my cousin Bingley—today is proving to be an interesting day indeed."

Elizabeth heard her mother calling for her as she approached the house. Her walk, having taken longer than usual, brought her home just as her family was gathering for breakfast, and she hastened her steps.

"Lizzy! Where is that child?" Mrs. Bennet's voice carried down the hall as Elizabeth removed her cloak.

"I am here, Mama." Elizabeth peeked into the dining room. Her family and Mr. Collins were all seated and already eating. Mr. Collins looked up at the sound of her voice, and his eyes widened when he saw Elizabeth, her cheeks pink from the cold and her dark hair hanging in a loose rope.

"Lizzy, you cannot come to breakfast in such a state!" Mrs. Bennet scolded. "Do your hair, girl! You are too wild today!"

"Yes, Mama." Elizabeth bobbed a curtsy at her mother and withdrew.

"I am so sorry, Mr. Collins." Mrs. Bennet apologized. "Lizzy knows better—I think she must have gone for a walk and forgotten herself."

"Your daughter, Mrs. Bennet," Collins said graciously with a slow, sideways nod of the head, "is uniformly charming. I take no offense, for walking is beneficial exercise, and she is to be commended for making it the first business of the day. While the rest of the household was still asleep, Cousin Elizabeth had already risen."

Mary looked across the table at Mr. Collins, her eyes slightly narrowed, her expression thoughtful. "Mr. Collins, I believe you are correct."

Mr. Collins, hearing his name, turned to listen, and shook his head, uncomprehending.

"A walk, Mr. Collins." Mary smiled in sweet agreement with her cousin. "My sister has exercised while we breakfasted, and you have most convincingly persuaded me that if we do likewise and exercise during *her* repast, our day will have begun nearly as productively as hers. We may still reclaim the morning. You are so astute to have thought of it!"

Mr. Collins blinked twice and then nodded graciously to Mary. "Cousin Mary, your swiftness in discerning my meaning does you credit. Indeed, a walk after a meal aids digestion and returns the mind to a state of alertness by increasing one's circulation."

"I am most indebted to you, Mr. Collins." Mary said, dabbing the corners of her mouth with a napkin. "I will be ready to go in five minutes." She rose from the table and quit the room, Mr. Collins speechlessly watching her departure.

Mrs. Bennet watched her daughter go as well, a quizzical look on her face, as Lydia and Kitty whispered and giggled of the coming teatime with the officers and Jane and Mr. Bennet continued their breakfast, lost in their own thoughts.

❧

Colonel Richard Fitzwilliam accepted the invitation from Bingley to stay at Netherfield, sent his carriage back to the inn in Meryton for his trunks and was now settling into his room.

Darcy knocked on the door to Richard's temporary quarters, nearly bursting with the need to counsel privately with his cousin.

"Come!" Richard called out, and when Darcy stepped through the doorway, Richard frowned at him. "Oh, it is just you, Darcy. I thought perhaps that the fetching Caroline Bingley had come to compromise me." Richard laughed, "Egad, that woman knows how to assess a man in an instant. I have been weighed and measured, although she was in such haste she quite forgot to look at my teeth."

Darcy shut the door before he laughed. "How I have missed you, Richard!" He slapped his cousin on the back. "You had better lock your door tonight, or Miss Bingley might put such a plan into play—or determine to finish her inspection and come to check your teeth!"

"So, have you saved a piece of Wickham, or have I come too late?" Richard asked with a gleam in his eye. "If you have moved without me, I may just have to trounce you in his stead."

"Wickham is intact—for the time being." Darcy replied. "As a gentleman, I could not call out the son of a servant. Denied a duel, I did not have the heart to cheat you of your share of his hide."

"So what is the plan, or were you waiting for me to come up with the ideas?" Richard asked.

"I am always open to your ideas, Fitz. Many of my best memories are the product of them." Darcy grinned. "But today, we will just toy with Wickham. His anticipation of our second act will be acute before we are done."

"Zounds, I like the sound of this!" Richard grinned broadly. "What do you propose?"

"I have it on the best authority that George Wickham will be taking tea today, at a local household." Darcy started.

"So it is to be a tea party, eh?" Richard raised an eyebrow.

"As I was saying, he has been invited by some neighbors, a household comprising five rather lovely, unmarried daughters." Darcy continued.

"A tea party in paradise? I should have come sooner!" Richard exclaimed. "What are we waiting for?"

"Tea time, Richard." Darcy smiled indulgently. "There is more to tell, if you will quit interrupting me."

"Do tell." Richard sat down and leaned back. "I shall not interrupt again."

"As I said, there are five daughters in the Bennet family." Darcy paused, and Richard pressed his lips together to prove his promise. "The eldest, Miss Jane Bennet, is considered the greatest beauty in the county, and Bingley is courting her."

"We have an in!" Richard exclaimed, slapping the table.

Darcy shot a dark look at his cousin. "Oh! Sorry," Richard said, "please continue."

"The youngest, Miss Lydia Bennet, is not yet sixteen." Darcy nodded at Richard meaningfully. "The Bennet family estate is entailed away from the female line, with no male son to inherit. The heir to Longbourn is none other than our aunt's parson, Mr. William Collins."

"Now there's a coincidence for you," Richard mumbled.

"Mr. Collins is presently a guest at Longbourn, delivered to their door by Aunt Catherine herself."

Richard's eyes widened, but he did not speak.

"Mr. Collins, it seems, has been advised by our aunt that he must marry one of the Bennet girls to satisfy the entailment while keeping the estate in the Bennet family," Darcy said.

"A reasonable solution—for once our aunt has made some sense." Richard smiled at the thought. "I am astonished—I did not think it possible."

"Mr. Collins is, and I say this with all due respect owed to his station as a clergyman, the most absurd man I have ever encountered," Darcy replied.

"Ah." Richard laughed. "I should have known Aunt Catherine was incapable of sense. How silly of me."

"Mr. Collins has, I believe, focused his attentions on the second eldest Miss Bennet. Miss Elizabeth Bennet. And she appears to be receptive to him."

"The number of ladies in the house dwindles too quickly. From five, we are down to three—two if Wickham takes one. We had better go now, before they are all gone!" Richard laughed.

His laugh was met with a fierce glower from Darcy.

"What is it, man?" Richard asked uneasily. "Have I said something wrong again? Has Wickham already taken one? I shall string him up the nearest tree if he has!"

"No." Darcy swung a second chair to face Richard and sat down in it. "No, I do not believe Wickham has compromised any of them yet. They have no fortune to tempt him, but they do possess a myriad of other charms which he would have no hesitation to abuse. Wickham may still be a danger to them and most certainly to the daughters of the village merchants."

Richard folded his arms and narrowed his eyes, waiting for Darcy to continue.

"Let me tell you a little more of the Bennets." Darcy resumed. "The second eldest…"

"Elizabeth." Richard confirmed.

Darcy nodded. "Miss Elizabeth Bennet." Darcy swallowed and tugged at his cravat. "The second eldest, Miss Elizabeth Bennet...."

"I believe you have established her name and position," Richard said smugly, "and that Mr. Collins has singled her out."

Darcy turned red. Richard grinned and added, "And that she has a myriad of charms to recommend her. And that she is lovely."

Darcy looked at his cousin helplessly and spoke so softly as to barely be heard, marking his statement with a nearly imperceptible shake of the head. "I do not know what to do, Richard. She has bewitched me."

At this, Richard's jaw fell open, a gaping hole from which no words or laughter could escape. Finally, Richard composed himself, closed his mouth, crossed his leg and waited for Darcy to continue.

"She is unlike any woman I have ever met." Darcy finally said.

"I would expect no less," Richard replied, "of a woman capable of bewitching the impenetrable heart of Fitzwilliam Darcy."

"I am not made of stone, Richard." Darcy replied.

"I will be sure to put an end to those rumors at my earliest convenience." Richard said. "But you have told me nothing of her. If I am to meet her, I think you must prepare me, lest I too am smitten by her charms. You may be able to fend this Collins fellow off, but I could give you a challenge if you do not persuade me against it."

Darcy smiled. "I thought her rather ordinary when I first met her. I cannot recall why."

Richard nodded his head encouragingly.

"She is artless, yet so witty and intelligent that I was soon captivated by whatever she said."

"A good beginning, to be sure." Richard nodded. "Is she an accomplished woman?"

"She plays the pianoforte some, and when she sings, her air is unaffected and natural—her voice is angelic. It pierces me to the soul."

"Pierces you?" Richard seemed impressed. "And what of her manners?"

Darcy smiled. "In company, she has a way of putting others at ease—including me."

"This is interesting." Richard laughed. "I wonder how she managed it."

Darcy shook his head, with no answer to the question. "She is not afraid of me. She has laughed at me even, and she actually refused let me walk her home. Twice. She declined to dance with me as well."

"I like this girl!" Richard exclaimed. "She is not daunted by your imperious manner? Do you think we could perhaps recruit her to join the King's Army? If her heart does not fail her with you, she is braver than half the men in my regiment!"

Darcy rolled his eyes impatiently. "Richard, I am warning you."

Richard put his hands up in surrender. "She is braver than I as well!"

Darcy laughed. "I think she *is* brave. And she is kind—to her sisters, and upon observation, to everyone she knows."

"Has she been kind to you, Cousin?" Richard's eyebrows emphasized his query.

"If torture can be considered kindness, she has been exceedingly so." Darcy half laughed, half grumbled.

"What means of torture has she employed?" Richard looked as though he enjoyed the question too much.

"She has made me love her, Richard. I am undone." Darcy looked miserable.

"That is wonderful!" Richard exclaimed. "What have you done with Collins?"

"I have not acted on my attachment to Miss Bennet. There were complicating factors." Darcy shrugged. "She does not know of my affections."

"So you are made of stone after all," Richard said softly.

"She has no fortune, Richard. She has no connections. Her family ... well, to put it in the mildest terms, country manners can be rather ... irregular by the standards of polite society." Darcy frowned.

"Shocking." Richard mocked him.

"Stop that." Darcy put his head in his hands, his elbows rested on his thighs. "I have struggled as you can never know to repress my feelings for Miss Bennet. It will not do. It has all been in vain."

"Why in heavens name would you do that?" Richard asked sincerely. "Do you need more money?"

Darcy, head still in his hands, shook it. "No."

"Are your connections lacking? Is being my cousin not enough for you?" Richard asked.

Darcy raised his head up and glared at Richard.

"Some would say that country manners are charming." Richard grinned.

"Aunt Catherine would not say so." Darcy countered.

"Oh!" Richard cried, "I have been so captivated by the tale of Miss Bennet that I nearly forgot to tell you. I saw Aunt Catherine in London yesterday." Richard looked as if he would burst. "I have never seen her so...," he stopped speaking, puckered his faced and looked at the ceiling mid-sentence.

"So ... what?" Darcy finally asked impatiently.

Richard shrugged. "... enraged. She has been blocked at every turn. She personally went to the Bow Street Police Office and demanded that they find you and deliver you to her."

"What?" Darcy shouted abruptly.

"They ejected her from the Police Office. She was *most seriously displeased*. I do not envy you when she finally catches up with you. She also seems to have some sort of quarrel with Miss Bingley." Richard enjoyed delivering the news immensely. "I do not believe she has any idea of Miss Bennet."

"Au contraire." Darcy said. "Aunt Catherine is the one who told Mr. Collins that Elizabeth Bennet would make him a fine wife."

"This just gets better and better." Richard clapped his hands. "Can we go to tea now?"

Darcy looked skeptically at his cousin. "You had better behave yourself, Fitz!"

"I know you're really serious when you call me that." Richard laughed. "So let's see, at tea today, there will be, five Bennet sisters and I assume their mother. Then we have Wickham, Collins, Bingley, you, and me?"

"Possibly Mr. Bennet and two other officers from the militia I believe." Darcy nodded. "You outrank them of course."

"That's how I like it." Richard laughed heartily rubbing his hands together gleefully. "Never underestimate the power of rank, cousin. You may have a massive fortune, but I believe I outrank even you!"

"And you never allow me to forget it." Darcy laughed. "It is truly a wonder they let you command. Do they realize how very juvenile you are?"

"Of course not, Darcy." Richard shook his head. "Does Miss Bennet realize you are not an arrogant brute?"

"Miss Bennet is very bright, and she does not suffer from a lack of understanding." Darcy paused, his eyebrows furrowed in frustration. "Except when it comes to me. I have hinted broadly more than once that I admire her, yet I have failed to impress—which is, I admit, for the best."

"Do you believe she holds any particular regard for Mr. Collins? Perhaps she does not understand because her heart is not free to do so." Richard speculated.

"No." Darcy replied. "She holds no attachment for him, but may feel an obligation to her family due to the entailment. When you meet them, I am certain you will agree on this count."

"Do you have any idea of her liking you?" Richard asked.

"It is difficult to discern. In some ways, I wonder if I am as blind to her feelings as she is to mine. I see clues that she may like me, yet they are confusing at best. I saw her this morning, walking. We conversed briefly, and I thought it was going well. Then she did the most astonishing thing. She ran away from me."

"What did you do?" Richard asked, amused once again.

"I had no alternative but to chase her." Darcy replied.

"No alternative?" Richard raised an eyebrow. "You were *forced* to chase a lady?"

"She had my dog." Darcy glared at his cousin. "That is to say, the dog ran off with her."

"I must say that your approach to wooing is unique." Richard chuckled. "I am most eager to meet the lady who has inspired my cousin to take chase. Can we go now? I find myself very, very thirsty."

"I will get you some water," Darcy replied, "or some wine."

"Only tea will do, Cousin." Richard laughed. "Only tea will do!"

Chapter Twenty-Seven

YOU, ME AND A CUP OF TEA

"Make haste! Make haste!" The Bennet household had echoed with the phrase all morning. Mrs. Bennet, who Elizabeth was certain would be hoarse before teatime arrived, was in her element. Three officers of the militia had accepted Lydia's invitation to tea, and the prospect of gentlemen callers, most particularly dashing red-coated officers, set the heart of the mother of five unmarried daughters aflutter. When she added their eligible houseguest, Mr. Collins, and the most excellent Mr. Bingley to the guest list, their gentlemen callers were equal in number to her daughters. Mrs. Bennet was certain their prospects would be raised from the single occasion alone.

She considered the possibility that Mr. Bingley would bring his friend, Mr. Darcy, with him, and hoping that her husband would elect to join their party for tea, she made certain to provide ample seating in the sitting room, where they would entertain. This had caused some degree of last-minute furniture rearranging in order to provide multiple intimate conversation areas, in which the men might become better acquainted with her daughters. She was quite satisfied with the result.

With the house at the ready and preparations for the refreshments complete, Mrs. Bennet turned her attentions to her daughters. She summoned them all individually for private inspection, giving each her approval or directions for making themselves more suitably outfitted for the occasion. Only Lizzy gave her any trouble, and she sent her second eldest back to her room with the maid to redo her toilette in a more feminine, alluring way, over Elizabeth's objections that mid-day tea did not require primping equal to a ball.

Mary, her mother was surprised to note, had blossomed considerably in recent days, having simultaneously discovered curls, lace and smiling, evincing a subtle yet distinct softening of her formerly staid appearance and demeanor. Mrs. Bennet congratulated herself on persevering with the daughter who had seemed a lost cause and thought that she would do well to marry an officer.

Mr. Collins had made himself scarce during the commotion, preferring the solitude of his guest quarters to the uproar of a household of incomprehensible females.

Fifteen minutes before the appointed hour, Lydia and Kitty could be found pacing and giggling in front of the second-floor window at the front of the house. The youthful residents knew this spot as 'the crow's nest', a name Elizabeth had bestowed at the age of twelve, during a period of fascination with pirates. The window, which afforded the best view of the road from Meryton, was wide enough for all five sisters to peer out together if two sat on the sill.

The cry soon went up from Lydia that the officers were not far off, creating a flurry of activity. Doors were slammed, stairs were rapidly traversed, pictures that were not crooked were straightened, and all members of the household, including Mr. Bennet, were convened in the sitting room forthwith.

Mr. Collins' entry into the sitting room had been unusually vigorous. Coming through the threshold, he launched himself with the clear intent to acquire the seat next to Elizabeth, with the surety of a bolt flung from a bow. He was intercepted by another female cousin, Mary Bennet, who, upon the man's catapult toward her sister, leapt from her seat with earnest intent to redirect his trajectory. This she accomplished by exclaiming his name with great force, causing him to draw up with a degree of shock. Having thus engaged his attention, she sweetly, yet with a hint of sternness, informed him that she gravely needed to obtain his counsel on a personal dilemma and required his attendance to that end.

Mary's invitation, unanticipated as it was, left Mr. Collins with a dilemma of his own. He could preserve his reputation of impeccable manners, or he could rudely decline Mary and proceed to claim a seat next to the woman he hoped to make his wife. Ultimately, although openly dismayed and slightly agitated, and with a longing glance over his shoulder at Elizabeth, Mr. Collins meekly accompanied Mary to a seat by the table, where her small arsenal of books was stacked in anticipation of a lengthy conversation.

Shortly thereafter, Mr. Wickham, Mr. Denny and Captain Carter were announced to the room by Hill. The officers were greeted effusively by Mrs. Bennet. Captain Carter and Mr. Denny remained politely attentive to her pleasantries, but Mr. Wickham scanned the room of Bennets distractedly, until his eyes fell upon Elizabeth Bennet, who stood by a small table near a window, her person lit by the sunlight streaming through the glass, her face friendly and open. She held in her hand a small white cloth, the project she was working on trimming with lace as they kept company.

His desire to be seated near her was accomplished as soon as it was civil to break free of the welcome, and George Wickham joined Elizabeth with the swaggering confidence of a man well accustomed to admiration from the ladies. He had reflected much on the end of their previous conversation and was determined to use this opportunity to overcome it to full advantage, for it was a blow to his pride that her admiration was not fully given. He employed an excessive degree of charm, greeting her with a kiss on the back of her hand, locking eyes with her as he did so—a maneuver he had perfected by practicing it on the hands and hearts of many a maiden.

"Miss Elizabeth, your loveliness today takes my breath away. You are all that is good and beautiful in the world. Were I to be stricken at this moment, I would die a happy man." He whispered the compliment hoarsely, a heated expression burning in his pale gray eyes.

Elizabeth withdrew her hand nervously and, returning to her own chair, invited him to be seated as she occupied her hands with a return to the trim on her handkerchief.

He seated himself without even looking away from her face. He took in the tinge of pink his greeting had evoked and pressed for more intimacy by moving his chair slightly closer to hers, talking all the while of how greatly he had anticipated coming to Longbourn after Lydia had issued the invitation, his voice hushed, although infused with an air of urgency.

"I feel that we have much to say to each other, Miss Elizabeth, for I wish to discover all that there is to know of you. I feel so at ease with you. I pray that I am not being too forward, for I would not wish to offend your delicacy, but a soldier's life is not all heroics, you know. We must face the possibility that each day will be our last."

Elizabeth looked at him curiously. His discourse was far more dramatic than their last encounter, and she wondered what had inspired the change. Her eyes fell to her needle as she placed another stitch. He took her silence as encouragement.

"The peril of my situation gives me courage, Madam, to speak what is in my heart. Our acquaintance has been but of short duration, I well know, but surely you must feel it as well." He paused to swallow and took a deep breath. "I have seen it in your eyes; I know what I have seen." He nodded, as if to assure them both. "I dare hope that you find me in some way agreeable." He stopped, waiting for her to acknowledge it.

"Is it the unrest of the local population that has inspired your fear, or are you to subdue the French today, Mr. Wickham?" Elizabeth asked mildly as she pulled the thread in her lace taut. "I had been under the impression that the militia was quartered here to train and renew their strength. I wonder at this peril you speak of."

Wickham's eyebrows shot upward at the challenge. "Does not my devotion to King and country serve as sufficient endorsement of my sincerity?"

"Would you have me believe that to merely don a red coat infuses a man with sincerity?" Elizabeth replied. "I would sooner believe that donning the attire of a clergyman bestows wisdom and humility." She glanced over at Mr. Collins as she said it.

"My red coat, Miss Elizabeth, is indeed a poor second to the attire of a clergyman. That was my fondest wish, you know, to take a living in the church." Wickham shook his head sadly.

"Truthfully?" Elizabeth's eyes widened as she looked up briefly from her sewing.

"In truth, the desire was instilled in me by my godfather, old Mr. Darcy" Wickham said. "He intended me for the church, and I was set upon the idea from a young age." He looked out the window with some melancholy, as though he could see the lost dreams of his youth through the panes.

"How came you to be a soldier instead? The path seems far afield from that of a churchman." Elizabeth puzzled, briefly distracted from the task in her hand.

"Ah." Mr. Wickham said lightly. "I fear you have discovered the source of my quarrel with young Mr. Darcy."

At this moment, the door opened and Hill announced the arrival of Mr. Bingley, Mr. Darcy, and Colonel Fitzwilliam to the occupants of the room.

Jane sighed happily and beamed at Mr. Bingley, her eyes inviting him to the seat she had carefully guarded next to her. Elizabeth squirmed in her seat, vaguely uncomfortable at the thought that Mr.

Darcy would see her sitting with Mr. Wickham. Lydia, Kitty, Mr. Denny and Captain Carter turned all together at the mention of a colonel in their midst. Mr. Collins and Mary were so deeply engaged in some sort of debate that they barely glanced up at the arrivals. Mrs. Bennet greeted Mr. Bingley warmly, politely acknowledged Mr. Darcy, and pursued the introductions of Colonel Fitzwilliam, who was dressed in his regimentals and lent the uniform much distinction. Mr. Wickham blanched and sat very still.

Mr. Bennet immediately noticed the change in the dynamic of the room and closed his book in order to observe. Mrs. Bennet, oblivious to any tension, introduced Colonel Fitzwilliam to the room, rapidly firing off the names of those who were present, leaving the colonel grateful that all he needed was to locate one person.

As soon as the newcomers had dispensed with their obligatory greetings, Mr. Bingley took the seat next to Jane. Colonel Fitzwilliam took a direct course towards Elizabeth and Wickham. The only unoccupied seat remaining was next to Mary and Collins, but Mr. Darcy did not take it. He moved instead to the window next to the one where Wickham and Elizabeth were sitting and gazed out of it, as he was often wont to do.

Colonel Fitzwilliam, with barely a glance at his cousin and not even acknowledging Wickham, effortlessly moved an empty chair from the position next to Wickham to the other side of Elizabeth. It was done so quickly that she had barely blinked before he was seated beside her.

"So you are the famous Miss Bennet." Colonel Fitzwilliam opened with such gentlemanly ease that there was no awkwardness to his approach. "I have heard so much of you that I find myself captivated before you have even spoken. I pray that you speak to me now, to justify my belief in your myriad charms."

Elizabeth could not help but laugh. "Colonel Fitzwilliam, is this some military strategy you employ? I am disarmed, sir, but have no inclination to summon any of my 'myriad charms' by way of your command." She resumed her attentions to the handkerchief in her hand; the lace trim was now very nearly affixed.

Colonel Fitzwilliam chuckled, nodding his head approvingly. "Well played, Miss Bennet. I shall discover your charms by other means." He slapped Wickham on the knee. Both Elizabeth and Wickham jumped. "What do you say, George? Have you any advice for me on how best to discover this fair lady's charms?"

Elizabeth had not realized that the two men were acquainted, but she now noticed how distinctly uncomfortable Mr. Wickham appeared to be as he soundlessly shook his head. She detected, as well, a slight trembling of his person, which seemed to imply that he was afraid.

"You are fortunate that he has declined, Miss Elizabeth." Colonel Fitzwilliam leaned toward her as if confiding a secret. "Mr. Wickham here has a great understanding of the means whereby a young lady's charms may be discovered."

Fitzwilliam now turned his attention directly to Wickham, and Elizabeth watched in amazement as the colonel's air of geniality and warmth vanished into what she could only assume was that of a practiced commander. It was also the first moment when she saw any similarity in the demeanor of the two cousins. "Who is your colonel, and how long have you been in his regiment?"

"Colonel Forster." Wickham's composure had dissipated. Great beads of sweat rolled off his face. He swallowed a great gulp of air, causing Elizabeth to wince at the sound. "I ... I ... I ... took my ... my ... c ... c ... commission about a ... a ... a ... week, a week ago." He was visibly shaking. Elizabeth wondered why he was so afraid of Colonel Fitzwilliam.

"Colonel John Forster?" Fitzwilliam pressed, and was rewarded with a weak nod. "Good man. I am acquainted with him. Please be so kind as to tell him that I shall call upon him tomorrow." Wickham forlornly nodded again.

The colonel then returned to face Elizabeth, all traces of his formal bearing gone, and he casually engaged her once again in pleasant conversation, during which time he surprised her with his knowledge of many personal details. They spoke for about ten minutes, after which time tea was served.

Elizabeth had finished applying the lace to her handkerchief and set the completed project on the table next to her in order to drink her tea. Wickham made his escape to join Lydia, Kitty and the other officers. His exit from the group served to vacate a chair next to Elizabeth, which Darcy looked at but did not take. He did turn to face the room as he stood with his tea and cake, which Elizabeth thought was a far more social move than she had expected of him, as he had spoken nothing since his initial entrance into the room.

Elizabeth sipped on her tea and chatted with the colonel, who she suspected had taken a fancy to her, as he continually said things to make her laugh and obviously enjoyed his success. She glanced around the room as much as she politely could, taking in the sight of Bingley and Jane, their heads nearly pressed together as they engaged in a fervent conversation. She observed Lydia and Kitty, laughing and giggling with the officers, although Mr. Wickham had not regained his spirits and barely ventured a smile in the course of the hour.

After Mr. Collins finished his third cup of tea, he moved to the chair that had been vacated by Wickham. Elizabeth noted with amusement that this seemed to perturb Mr. Darcy, who became more rigid, stern, and slightly redder in the face than he had been the moment before Mr. Collins changed his seat.

Why Mr. Darcy would react in such a way to the silly parson Elizabeth could not pretend to understand, but she enjoyed it, somehow, to think that he did. She looked at her father, who winked at her. He too had noted the odd effect, and they enjoyed a private joke together that neither of them understood.

Fitzwilliam was unperturbed by the addition of Mr. Collins to their little group, and after acknowledging that he was indeed a nephew of Lady Catherine de Bourgh and a son of the Earl of Matlock, he resumed his conversation with Elizabeth.

At some length, Mr. Collins inquired after the health of the colonel's brother, the eldest son of the earl. Fitzwilliam replied that his entire family was well. This caused some degree of apparent anxiety on the part of Mr. Collins, who muttered something unintelligible about a letter, and Elizabeth realized with a degree of interest that, in resolving this inquiry, all three nephews of Lady Catherine were accounted for; and none appeared to have recently been in any peril whatsoever.

What it could mean, she did not know, but Mr. Darcy suddenly approached the group and stood looming over them. Mr. Collins looked up at Mr. Darcy, the action emphasized by Collins beginning at Darcy's feet, and continuing until Mr. Collin's head was completely tipped back, his mouth slightly agape.

Colonel Fitzwilliam leaned back in his chair and looked up his cousin with some amusement. Elizabeth wondered what private joke the two men held between them.

"Mr. Collins." Darcy broke his silence. "My cousin, the colonel, had the distinct honor of seeing Lady Catherine just yesterday in London. He tells me she was much engaged in pressing matters related to her family."

Mr. Collins looked at Fitzwilliam, who grinned and nodded his head to confirm it.

Mr. Darcy then spoke with some warmth to the parson, although his authority was as if forged of iron. "I myself was in London but four days ago and also saw my aunt at that time. I understand that when last you saw her, she was much concerned about *me*. Her information was from an idle and false report. There is no need for you to concern yourself further on the matter. It is settled."

Mr. Collins looked nervously between the two gentlemen before launching into speech. "I am much obliged that you have made this known to me, for just today I have dispatched a missive to my esteemed patroness, wherein I made known to her my progress on the errand I am here to perform. I felt it my duty to inform her, Mr. Darcy, that I had encountered you, her nephew, here in Hertfordshire, and assured her that there was no cause for concern, as you were in temporary residence with a very respectable family, that of Mr. Charles Bingley and his sisters." He drew in a lungful of air and continued. "I had not known, of course, that the matter was already resolved, but it puts my mind at ease that she had heard the news so many days ago, as she was most distressed when I saw her last."

Mr. Darcy's eyes hardened and his jaw clenched. "Mr. Collins." Darcy's voice was no longer warm. "Your interference in my personal affairs is insupportable. Regardless of anything she may say to the contrary, my aunt has no claim upon me. Your letter disclosing my whereabouts is a breach of my privacy that I shall not soon forget. You would do well not to cross me again, for next time I may not be so forgiving of your trespass." He bowed stiffly and added, "Excuse me."

Mr. Darcy crossed the room and stood before Mr. Bennet to beg a moment of his time in the study. This was readily agreed to since Mr. Bennet had tired of the company and appreciated the excuse to leave. The two men removed themselves from the sitting room, whereupon the three officers indicated that they must return to their camp straightway. They thanked their hostess for a lovely time and were escorted out the door by Lydia, Kitty and Mrs. Bennet, where they stood together outside, delaying their departure with idle conversation.

Mr. Collins took advantage of the exodus and quit the room as well, saying nothing as he left. Jane and Mr. Bingley remained, still speaking softly between themselves. Mary remained at the table reading a book, and Elizabeth and the colonel resumed their conversation.

"I say, my cousin certainly knows how to inspire a rapid conclusion to an otherwise pleasant tea-time," Colonel Fitzwilliam commented as they watched the door close behind Mr. Collins. "But that is all right with me. I like it better this way."

"How so?" Elizabeth smiled. "Did you not enjoy yourself?"

"Too much I think." Fitzwilliam replied with a mischievous grin. "How could I not when much of the conversation featured you and me and a cup of tea? It was a great pleasure, to be sure, and I daresay that I enjoyed it far more than Darcy did. I have never seen him so unsociable as he was today."

"Really?" Elizabeth was surprised. "Mr. Darcy's manner seemed to me as it has ever been in company."

"If that is true," Fitzwilliam reflected, "there must be something very different in the company in Hertfordshire. He seemed most peculiar to me."

"I suppose it is our 'country manners' that offend him," Elizabeth said with a shrug, "Mr. Bingley has told Jane that Mr. Darcy does not like the society in the country, and I believe he spends far too much time comparing."

"By what calculation do you arrive at this conclusion, Miss Bennet?" Fitzwilliam seemed intrigued.

"It is no calculation." Elizabeth laughed. "Rather than make conversation, Mr. Darcy would far rather lord over any assembly and glare at anyone whose behavior displeases him. I know this because he glares at me a great deal when in company."

"I had thought you were friends," Fitzwilliam replied. "I believe you mistake my cousin."

"That may be true. I confess that he puzzles me exceedingly." Elizabeth confided. "He is an enigmatic man, Colonel. Tell me, as one who knows him well, why did he stand about for the entire visit and say nothing except to insult Mr. Collins?"

"I cannot answer that," Fitzwilliam smiled, "without revealing a confidence."

At that moment, Mr. Darcy re-entered the room but only to summon the colonel and Mr. Bingley to take their leave and return to Netherfield.

After their guests had all left, Elizabeth returned to the sitting room to set it to rights. She moved the furnishings back to their regular places and tidied up the various artifacts in the room. She was nearly finished when she thought to retrieve her completed handkerchief and discovered, in horror, that her beautiful whitework treasure with the Lambton lace trim had vanished from the table.

She searched on the floor and in other places around the room, but the little kerchief she had made for the Netherfield ball was gone.

Chapter Twenty-Eight

WHERE REPUTATIONS COLLIDE

The call to the evening meal at Longbourn came in the same way and at the same time as it ever did. The food was much the same as always, and the seating arrangements were regular, yet it would long be remembered as the most unusual dinner conversation ever held in that house. Mr. Bennet, whose presence at the table was typically one of good cheer, was sullen and brooding in his demeanor.

Mrs. Bennet opened the dinner conversation in her usual way, having not yet noticed the change in her husband's manner. She effused liberally on the great delights of having had the officers for tea and repeatedly declared how well her daughters had looked and how much admired the girls were by the officers. Mr. Bennet frowned at his wife with such a look of disapprobation that when she finally looked at him, her voice faded away before she finished her sentence, and she nervously returned to her bowl of soup, suddenly out of tongue.

Lydia quickly took up the raptures her mother had relinquished, and for a full minute all that was to be heard around the table was a rapid babbling of the officers names and repetition of the fine compliments they had paid to her. Mr. Bennet cleared his throat, and seeing a heretofore unknown fury in his gaze, Lydia was struck with silence as well, although she was not beyond pouting over it.

Elizabeth looked with curiosity and concern at her father, for she had never seen him like this before in all her life. Her father had remained in his study after his meeting with Mr. Darcy, and Elizabeth suspected that her father's foul temper was attributable to the same. She tried to catch her father's eye, convinced that he would direct some signal of reassurance her way, but when she did meet his eye, the same glower that had silenced her mother and sister was bestowed upon her, and she looked away, disquieted by the knowledge that her father was certainly unhappy.

Mary, who up to that point had seemed quite intent on her meal, abruptly spoke to Mr. Collins across the table. "How pleased you must be, Mr. Collins, at the great favor Mr. Darcy showed you this day at tea."

Mr. Collins, whose expression reflected pleasure in the beginning of her phrase, fell markedly in the end of it. He frowned and blinked, unprepared to respond. "Cousin Mary," he began, "I have not the slightest idea of the favor of which you speak, for, indeed, Mr. Darcy showed me none."

Mr. Bennet raised his eyebrows, his furrowed look tempered by his expectations of Mary's producing a response. He had to wait for it, however, due to Elizabeth's interjection into the conversation.

"Upon my word, Mary, how could you speak so? Mr. Darcy's manner toward Mr. Collins was cold and unfeeling!" Elizabeth cried, "All who heard it felt the judgment in his words."

Mr. Collins turned to look at Elizabeth, his face filled with gratitude at her defense of him. "Thank you, Cousin Elizabeth." He wagged his head as he spoke, in a strange bobbing motion that was intended to convey appreciation but emphasized his ridiculousness instead. Seeing this, Elizabeth fell silent.

"Mr. Collins." Mary waited to continue until he reluctantly turned back to her. Then she smiled graciously at him, evoking a small smile in return. "Mr. Collins, you are an astute man, and I am certain that upon reflection, you will come to see what transpired in a more prudential light."

Mary had now gained Mr. Collins' rapt attention, his curiosity over some alternative meaning momentarily overcoming him. His attention was not isolated, for her sisters and parents were riveted as well, waiting skeptically to see if Mary could magically turn insults into compliments.

"One has first to acknowledge that Mr. Darcy is entitled to an expectation of privacy, which you must agree we would all desire for ourselves." Mary began, with silent nods around the table acknowledging that this was a fair wish. "His unease at discovering that his privacy had been compromised, however unwittingly, is some excuse for his being uncivil. Are we all not prone to a moment of temper when unhappy news is relayed to us?"

Mr. Collins frowned at the implication that he had done wrong, but he was uncharacteristically silent, allowing Mary to continue. "Had this same event occurred with a less even-tempered man than Mr. Darcy, you may have been subjected to far harsher treatment, but Mr. Darcy was indeed gracious, for once he had expressed his displeasure at your indiscretion, he rightly put you on your guard against a repeat offense, and said that he forgave you. This he did despite your lack of apparent remorse or apology." Mary smiled with understanding and compassion at Mr. Collins. "You have received, at the hand of one of the most illustrious men in the land, a kind and valuable lesson, Mr. Collins, one that will serve you well in your ministerial capacity and was delivered with very little pain to you under the circumstances. Do you not call that favor?"

Mr. Collins reddened slightly and then smiled weakly. "Indeed, Cousin Mary, I believe you are correct; he has shown me favor indeed. I confess, dear cousin, that I had not considered his words in this way, but you have helped me to see that the occurrence may prove beneficial and instructive if I take it as such. Nay, it cannot fail to be so upon introspection and reflection. I shall call it favor, indeed! Yes, Mr. Darcy's generosity, although not equal to that of his aunt, is nonetheless not to be dismissed as less than a grand gesture, the magnitude of which I am only now beginning to appreciate more fully."

"You are a godly man, Mr. Collins." Mary smiled once more at him. "Perhaps you have unquestioningly given too much weight to the words of your noble patroness. There was a hint in Mr. Darcy's address that perhaps there is more than one view that can be taken of his affairs with his aunt. This is often the case in family matters, I believe, which may prove to be complex. Wisdom dictates that future dealings involving Mr. Darcy will not assume full comprehension of his situation. I have great faith in you, good sir. I am most certain that as you are a cautious and prudent man, further reproach from him will not be necessary."

"Mary, of what do you speak?" Mrs. Bennet asked curiously.

"Mama," Mary replied solemnly, "we have just spoken of Mr. Darcy's insistence on discretion in his private affairs. It would be insupportable to discuss them further."

Mrs. Bennet looked at Mr. Bennet, who nodded his head in agreement with his daughter. "Mary, you may just demonstrate some sense yet. I will be glad for it, as I have something to relate to all of my daughters which will require a great deal *more* sense than has been shown of late."

"What is it, Papa?" Elizabeth asked with some relief, for the suspense of not knowing the cause of his attitude had been difficult to bear.

"They are not glad tidings, of that you may be sure. It is a matter of some delicacy, and I would normally approach it only within the bounds of immediate family. However, it is rather urgent, and so, I will speak frankly and rely on Mr. Collins' discretion." Mr. Bennet looked meaningfully at Mr. Collins.

Mr. Collins nodded his assent and eagerly tuned his ears to hear what delicate and urgent matter Mr. Bennet was about to relate.

Mr. Bennet looked with great seriousness at his five daughters sitting around the table. His eyes lingered on Elizabeth and again on Lydia before he spoke. "I had, until today, thought that an officer in the service of king and country could be esteemed to be of highest moral character. Indeed, the general expectation is that regardless of whether they are of noble or gentle birth or arrived at their rank by exception, as officers, they behave as gentlemen. I have sadly learned that this is not always the case. There are some in the ranks who are debtors and gamblers, and worse yet, there are seducers to be found among them as well."

Mrs. Bennet gasped at the last word. Elizabeth, Jane and Mary all looked to their father with alarm. Kitty looked nervously at Lydia, and Lydia looked bored. Mr. Collins dropped his spoon into his soup, which made a loud clattering sound and flung droplets of the liquid on his person. He immediately attempted, in a somewhat comical fashion, to remove them with his napkin, which activity to some extent, although not entirely, mitigated the tension that had been wrought by Mr. Bennet's declaration.

Mr. Bennet continued. "It has been brought to my attention that one such man has been in our very midst today." He paused for effect. "This will not do. From this day forward, none of my daughters will speak to, keep company with, or in any other way associate with Mr. Wickham."

Silence reigned at the Bennet table for a full minute, if not two. Mrs. Bennet's eyes looked as if they were to vacate their sockets so far did they bulge outward, and Jane looked worriedly at Elizabeth. Elizabeth was suddenly attentive to eating her soup, to hide her shock at what her father had said. Mr. Wickham a seducer? The sweet and charming things Mr. Wickham had said to her that very day were ringing in her ears and tormenting her with the thought that perhaps she had been the target of his next seduction. While she did not believe he would have been successful, she had to admit to herself that his manners were most engaging, and had he persisted, she may have naively been tempted to succumb. She was grateful that she would never know.

Mr. Bennet chased away the long silence with an additional speech. "This information, from a trustworthy and reliable source, is not to be doubted, nor will I entertain any questions about it. In exchange for the warning on behalf of my daughters, I am sworn to secrecy on the particulars that have convinced me of the veracity of the report. I will not be gainsaid in this declaration, and, indeed, any defiance will result in confinement to the house until such time as the militia has left Meryton. This means, of course, that should you encounter officers, whether it is on the road, in a house or at a dance, if they are in company with Mr. Wickham, you are not to engage in any social intercourse whatsoever."

Lydia whined loudly at this but was silenced once more by her father's impatient glare in her direction.

"Lizzy, am I understood?" Mr. Bennet asked pointedly.

"Yes, Papa." Elizabeth muttered self-consciously, wondering at her father's behavior. She had never seen him so stern, and she speculated that Mr. Darcy's business with him earlier in the day had been the impetus of this bad humor. There was too much evidence to doubt it.

"You are wrong, Papa!" Lydia pouted. "It is not fair! Mr. Wickham is a perfect gentleman and very amiable. Mr. Darcy has treated Mr. Wickham infamously, and I know that he has now slandered him as well, for we all saw you go together with him into your study! Would you honestly believe such a disagreeable man as Mr. Darcy over Mr. Wickham?"

"Silence!" Mr. Bennet stood up from the table, his napkin cast down as he rose. "Lydia, you were warned, and now you shall feel it. You are confined to the house until such time as the militia has departed."

"But the ball!" Mrs. Bennet and Lydia spoke in unison.

"What of the ball? You shall not go to the ball but shall remain at home with Hill." Mr. Bennet grumbled at Lydia. "I will not be moved, and I am in no mood to be contradicted." He looked around the table. "Does anyone else wish to defend Wickham? I am certain your sister would appreciate the company during the ball. Kitty? Have you nothing to say?"

"No, Papa." Kitty shook her head.

"Mrs. Bennet?" Mr. Bennet challenged his wife.

Mrs. Bennet looked thoughtful and sweetened her expression as much as she could. "Surely there is no reason to deny Lydia attendance to the ball, Mr. Bennet. We have re-trimmed a gown for the occasion, and all the officers are set upon dancing with her. They will expect to see her there. How are we to explain it?"

"The officers will find some way to resolve their disappointment with some other young lady at the ball. I will not be prevailed upon, Mrs. Bennet. Do not attempt to persuade me, or Jane may well be the only Bennet allowed to go." Mr. Bennet excused himself and quit the room.

The rest of the household did not recover their spirits during the meal, and the rest of the dinner was eaten in an awkward, uncomfortable silence.

"Oh, Jane, that was the most unbearable meal of my life!" Elizabeth declared to her sister in Jane's bedchamber that night. "I was already distressed, and seeing Papa so out of sorts has only made it worse. Today has been a dreadful day, indeed."

"Certainly not the whole day, Lizzy." Jane smiled. "Tea-time was pleasant enough."

"You are, as always, correct Jane; although in retrospect, viewed with my father's revelations of Mr. Wickham, it casts an entirely different light upon the tea as well." Elizabeth sighed. "I did have a lovely walk this morning though. I climbed to the top of Oakham Mount and there saw the sunrise. The colors in the sky were splendid, with golden rays and streaks of rose and saffron. The day began with great promise."

"It does sound lovely, Lizzy. Nevertheless, the tea must have held some other pleasure—I saw that Colonel Fitzwilliam was very attentive to you." Jane said encouragingly.

"I am astonished, Jane, that you were even aware of his presence. I thought you only had eyes for Mr. Bingley." Elizabeth laughed. "I did not expect you to notice!"

"I heard you laughing and looked up. There you were, seated by the colonel, his eyes fixed upon your face as though you were a masterpiece of a great artist. Mr. Collins sat near and appeared for all the world as though he would speak to you but could not find his voice. Mr. Darcy was standing by the window listening and watching most intently, seemingly content to observe. You certainly held their attention, which did *not* please my mother. I believe she wished for the colonel to join with Lydia and the officers in their conversation."

"I did enjoy meeting the colonel, Jane. He is a man of good breeding and taste and as gentlemanlike a person as I could ever expect to meet—except when he was teasing Mr. Wickham. There was something odd in their conversation, which I had assumed to be merely playfulness between old friends, but my father's disclosure about Mr. Wickham leads me to believe that there was something more."

Elizabeth looked at her sister, who seemed unable to fathom what 'something more' could mean.

"Jane, there is something else that troubles me." Elizabeth began. "My handkerchief, the one I was to take to the ball—it has disappeared."

"You must have misplaced it, Lizzy. I will help you look tomorrow." Jane reassured her sister. "Needlework does not grow legs, but you do tend to be careless and absently leave things about."

"No, Jane. I took it to tea to trim it with the Lampton lace from Aunt Gardiner. When it was completed, I set it on the table. After everyone had departed, I discovered that it was missing." Elizabeth's sadness was apparent. "I fear it is gone."

"Could there have been some accident? Perhaps it was pocketed by someone who mistook it as his own." Jane suggested.

"Men's handkerchiefs are not commonly trimmed with lace in such a way as a lady's kerchief is. The only persons who were near me were Mr. Wickham, Mr. Collins, Mr. Darcy and Colonel Fitzwilliam. None of these could have mistaken it as his own."

"But why, Lizzy? Why would anyone wish to take it?" Jane puzzled. "I do not understand."

"I have spent the evening pondering this same question, Jane, and either one of the men is simply a thief, or there is some other motive at work. Mr. Wickham was beginning to show me his attentions, and we know that Mr. Collins has singled me out, even though Mary is trying very hard to gain his favor. The colonel seemed to fancy me, or rather I fancied him and hope that he fancied me. I think that it is possible that one of them considered it as a prize—a token." Elizabeth frowned. "I think I should dislike a man very much who would steal from me as an expression of regard. I have heard of it being done, but I do not like it."

"You must admit it is romantic." Jane smiled.

"I shall admit no such thing! I want it back—that is all. How am I to determine who has taken it?" Elizabeth frowned. "Perhaps I must confront them all. Will they admit it if a challenge is issued?"

"Lizzy, it should not be attempted! If they have not taken it, you will offend, and if one of them has, he will be forced to add a lie to the sin of stealing." Jane admonished. "No, you must let it be known that you desire it back, and he will certainly return it to you."

"If it is returned of his own free will, I will forgive, but if it is not, and I discover who has taken it, he will certainly learn that Elizabeth Bennet is no easy target for a petty thief!" Elizabeth declared with great determination and fervor. "He will learn that heaven is not the only destination to be had in a handkerchief!"

"Lizzy!" Jane cried. "You must not speak so!"

"I speak truth, Jane." Elizabeth fumed. "I *will* have it back!"

The evening at Netherfield was very different from that of Longbourn. Miss Bingley had come upon a new strategy in her pursuit of attention from Mr. Darcy. She was clearly determined to stir him to some great jealousy by means of flirting outrageously with his cousin.

Colonel Fitzwilliam was a willing accomplice in her charade and made great sport of returning her banter in kind. He was not serious, of course, but the resulting repartee was dazzling, and it moved the others of the household in various ways.

Mr. Bingley was desperately unhappy with his sister for her overtly coy behavior and not pleased at all with the colonel for encouraging her in it. Bingley's mild attempts to disrupt their game had little effect except, perhaps, to spur his sister on.

Mr. and Mrs. Hurst spoke barely at all, and Mr. Darcy, other than finding occasional amusement in the antics of his cousin, was largely unmoved by any of it and retired early for the night.

Since obtaining a reaction from Mr. Darcy was the point of Miss Bingley's behavior, the entire company followed suit soon after and retired as well.

Not long after Mr. Darcy had arrived at his chambers, a knock sounded, and he found his cousin at the door. Entrance was granted, and Colonel Fitzwilliam entered the room, his countenance lit with merriment. He threw himself into a chair, his sprawling figure a distinct contrast to the reserved upright one of his cousin. "Had I known the delights I would find in Hertfordshire Darcy, I would have joined you weeks ago!"

"Delights?" Darcy frowned. "Of what do you speak?"

"Oh come now, you know of what I speak. Caroline Bingley for one has been a great source of amusement. She *likes* you, Darcy!" Richard teased.

"True, but hardly delightful, Fitzwilliam." Darcy shook his head.

"Then there was Wickham. I would just as soon have started with a sound thrashing, but I must say that your idea to merely toy with him first gave me great satisfaction. To see the rascal lose his composure as he did was worth postponing his appointment with my fist." Fitzwilliam balled his left hand and tapped it into the palm of his right with a grin.

"He has feared you since we were lads. I was not surprised that his reaction to you today was potent." Darcy mused.

"I do not recall why...," Fitzwilliam wondered aloud.

"You had caught a fish that was unusually large, and Wickham threw it back into the river. You did not take this action well." Darcy replied. "I believe it was above three weeks before his bruises from the trouncing you gave him that day had abated. He has lived in mortal fear of you ever since. Surely you knew that."

"I had forgotten." Fitzwilliam roared with laughter. "We were but children!"

"Has he ever crossed you since that day?" Darcy asked pointedly. "I daresay he has not."

"And now I have thrown his own pretty little fish back into the stream. I do not expect he will find Elizabeth Bennet on his hook now." Fitzwilliam laughed softly.

"I trust that Wickham's 'hook' will find not one of the Bennet sisters," Darcy replied soberly. "I have spoken with Mr. Bennet, and upon securing his assurance of secrecy, I warned him against Mr. Wickham, giving him enough of the particulars that he could be in no doubt of the danger. He was most violently distressed. I anticipate he will forbid his daughters to grant any audience to George Wickham in the future."

"There are many fish in the sea, cousin. You have saved but five." The colonel frowned. "We cannot easily expose him without great harm coming to Georgiana, but I believe we must do what we can. I will begin tomorrow by revealing what we know of his character to his colonel. Perhaps military discipline will reform him—after I have soundly beaten him for what he did to my cousin, that is."

"I have not the taste for vengeance that you have." Darcy replied. "It cannot undo the heartbreak of my sister, nor can it restore her confidence to what it was."

"If you were to marry, Georgiana would have the gentle influence of a sister to help her overcome it." Fitzwilliam said meaningfully. "Perhaps someone witty and lively would do."

Darcy began to pace. "I see what you're about, Fitz. You will have me regret my confession to you before long."

"I cannot restrain myself, Darcy. To see you standing apart from Miss Bennet today, mooning over her from the window while three other men held her attention was pathetic." Fitzwilliam hesitated before continuing. "If you have a design on her, you must at least make it known. She thinks you hold her in contempt. However did you manage that?"

"Contempt?" Darcy was astonished. "How came you to this understanding?"

"Merely by conversing with her. You should attempt the same sometime, Darcy—she is a most pleasant conversationalist. She said that you glare at those who displease you, and that you glare at her a great deal. Is that not contempt?"

"We have spoken," Darcy said defensively. "I am full aware of her charms in conversation." He spun on his heel to pace the other direction. "I do not *glare* at her!"

"You glared at her today." Fitzwilliam countered.

"That is your fault, Fitzwilliam. How could I not be unhappy when you were at her side, enjoying her smiles and laughter? I was glaring at you!" Darcy retorted in frustration.

"My cousin is jealous!" Fitzwilliam roared with laughter. "Perhaps you will not be so when you learn what I have done for you."

"What have you done?" Darcy stopped pacing. "I do not like the tenor of your voice, Fitzwilliam. What mischief have you been up to?"

"I have collected a token for you, something to give you courage, to inspire you to do better, for at present, I fear she will not have you, should you make an offer." Fitzwilliam reached into his pocket and paused, raising his eyes to his cousin to be certain of the attention his gesture deserved.

"Fitzwilliam...," Darcy growled impatiently.

With a flourish, Colonel Fitzwilliam extracted a lady's handkerchief from his pocket, a dainty, lacy one, pristine and white. He held it to his nose and sniffed. "It smells like her. Lavender and roses and a bit of something else, I think."

"Give me that!" Darcy cried, as he forcefully took it from his cousin. He laid the cloth open in his hand, the fine lace edges dangling off the sides of his palm and fingers as he looked upon it in awe.

"What devilish impulse caused you to take this?" He whispered in anger and gratitude.

"As much as you watched me speaking to your beloved, your eyes strayed to the kerchief even more. I thought you wanted it." Fitzwilliam shrugged.

Darcy held it to his face and inhaled deeply. "It is true what you said. This cloth holds her fragrance. I could easily become intoxicated by it." He spread it out on the table. "Look at it, Fitz. What do you see?"

Without leaving his chair, Colonel Fitzwilliam stretched his neck to study the cloth. "The lace looks familiar."

"Does it?" Darcy looked again. "So it does, although I do not know why. Look at the pattern in the cloth, man."

"It is simple, yet elegant. It shows a refined degree of taste." Fitzwilliam commented.

"Why did you choose this moment to be both blind and obtuse? Darcy grumbled at him. Fitzwilliam looked again, closer.

"But ... that looks like...," Fitzwilliam's eyes rounded in surprise, and he looked up at his cousin with a grin. "*She likes you*!"

"I cannot keep this." Darcy sat wearily in an armchair. "She has certainly already noticed it is taken. What must she think?"

"She did not see me take it. She will hardly know what to think." Fitzwilliam shrugged. "Any lady who has had an admirer has suffered the loss of some small article or another. I have a whole drawer full of gloves and handkerchiefs and fancy hairpins I have pilfered from ladies I was keen on."

"I am sure they would have given them to you had you asked, and you would not have had to resort to petty thievery." Darcy shot his cousin a dark look. "I am sure you meant well, but I would not wish Miss Bennet to think of me so. We must devise a way to return it."

"Another great adventure at Longbourn!" Fitzwilliam smiled apologetically at his cousin. "We shall return it tomorrow, and your reputation shall be restored ... somehow."

Chapter Twenty-Nine

THE HOSTAGE HANDKERCHIEF

After Richard quit the room, Darcy readied himself for bed but found himself not in the least fatigued. He stoked the fire and paced the floor, his mind agitated and troubled, yet not settled on any particular source of trouble; there was so much to dwell on.

Having been accustomed to maintaining strict regulation of all of his affairs, it was disturbing to have multiple aspects of his life so irretrievably beyond his firm control. He attempted to order his thoughts, but tonight they were stubborn, flighty thoughts, and did not yield to the mental discipline to which they were usually subject.

Eventually, he retrieved a paper and a quill and committed his list of troubles to written form, solidifying the concerns that had eluded his conscious mind. This exercise, in one regard, returned a sense of power. He could name them, write them, and solve them, as he had always done. On the other hand, the answers he sought were not readily apparent. The complex tapestry of his situation seemed ever more so with each addition to the list, where his adversities overlapped and interwove with his hopes and wishes in a frustrating interplay of circumstance.

It was ironic, Darcy thought, shaking his head with a wry grimace, that his aunt would likely come to Hertfordshire to confront Caroline Bingley rather than Elizabeth Bennet. He had a moment of self-reproach for this, but only a moment. Caroline Bingley clearly considered herself deserving of social interactions with not only the gentry but with the aristocracy as well. It would be a lesson she brought upon herself, to be brought low by his aunt, and he was loath to deny her the experience, painful though it might be. The thought of a similar confrontation between his aunt and Elizabeth Bennet filled him with abhorrence, but, fortunately, his aunt had no cause to suspect his attachment to Miss Bennet.

The mere thought of Elizabeth's name plunged Darcy into a tumult of raw emotion. Since he confided his attachment to Elizabeth to Richard, the concerns that had previously plagued him, those of family duty, position and status—all the worries that had prevented him from acting previously—seemed nothing at all.

Had these obstacles been removed even one day earlier, Darcy thought with bitter relief, he would be preparing to speak to her father, to declare to Elizabeth all that was in his heart, and to make an offer of marriage immediately. The possibility that she might refuse him had been so far from his mind that when Richard had told him of Elizabeth's belief in his contempt, he had been shocked and grieved at the knowledge. The tender feelings he had nurtured for her and the depth of his regard had belied any possibility that she did not requite his love or even recognize his admiration for her.

Fury raged at the understanding that he had wrestled so deeply with nearly uncontrollable passions over this woman and she was, the whole time he had suffered in violent torment over her, utterly indifferent to him.

His anger was quickly followed by disbelief. Women of the first circles, women of noble lineage—those who were infinitely more eligible than Elizabeth Bennet, had pursued him, to no avail. How was it that the only woman he had ever met who had ignited such a flame in his heart and mind did not see his worth? He knew that there was no defect in matters of status, connections and fortune, so what did he lack? His character was widely known to be above reproach; it was unthinkable that there could be any question of integrity. His mind went back to the morning at Netherfield when he had caught her admiring his figure. He was certain there was no lack of attraction to his appearance on her part and no lack of open admiration on his either. Had she really believed his silent gaze of admiration was one of contempt?

He pondered how, in the early conversations he had enjoyed with Miss Bennet, he had labored to hide any symptoms of obvious sentimentality despite the potent, passionate feelings she stirred in him. He replayed in his mind not only those moments of success in this control but also numerous interludes when his determination to conceal his affections had failed and he had been more open. *Had she noticed nothing?*

His self-evaluation had been in vain. Upon reflection, there was only one logical conclusion. His manners, he knew were prone to be detached and aloof; his demeanor, at times, arrogant. His air must have reflected the assurance of his own superiority, for in all the ways he had ever believed mattered, he was, in point of fact, a superior man. It was only now, considering that his conduct was the source from which of her opinion of him had flowed, that he recognized any folly in behaving in a manner that was consistent with the actual order of the world. It was his own pride and conceit that had sabotaged him, had set Elizabeth's mind against him, and although he did not know how to begin to repair the damage wrought by his behavior, he convinced himself that it was possible. To think otherwise was not a consideration he would entertain.

Darcy wiped the ink from his hands, and after staring at it for several minutes, reverently picked up the handkerchief that lay spread on the table. The cloth told him that she had felt *something*. Stitched in her own hand was a tangible, prophetic symbol of her destiny joined with his. He held the cloth against his cheek, closing his eyes as he indulged in the feelings that swept over him in so doing. He shifted his hand, bringing the crumpled cloth to the center of his face. The motion was slow and deliberate, although his hand trembled with the rush of raw emotion engendered by the act. In one sense, the sweet token of the woman he adored calmed him, although his heart raced at the faint scent of her that lingered in it. He hardly realized that he had pressed his lips against it, his gentle kiss upon the cloth so unconsciously made that it was only as he released it that the thought occurred to him. Once returned to Elizabeth, the cloth that he had privately worshiped would be held against her face, and she would unwittingly receive the kiss he had secretly bestowed in the folds of white embroidery and lace.

The thought pleased him so well that a second and third kiss were impulsively added before he returned it to the table. He spread it out once more to see the pattern and reassure himself yet again that he had not imagined it. There was a part of him that did want to keep it, but he then looked back at the list he had penned and realized that nothing on the list was more urgent than restoring the handkerchief to Elizabeth and changing her opinion of him.

Elizabeth had been awake a good portion of the night, for although she lay still in the dark, thoughts of Mr. Darcy galloped wildly in her mind through the hours, in alarming bursts that alternated between clarity and confusion. The cascade had been triggered by Jane's suggestion that the theft of her handkerchief had been some sort of romantic gesture. Jane had not mentioned Mr. Darcy's name—that had been Elizabeth's conclusion alone, but, now, the weight of the idea pressed on her like a great stone.

Men like Mr. Darcy are not romantic about poor country maidens! Elizabeth chastised herself for entertaining the thought at all, yet as soon as she denied it, she recalled that Mr. Darcy had looked at the folded handkerchief on the table frequently during the tea. His declaration to Jane and Bingley that he had seen heaven in the little cloth made him a suspect—except that she could recall no point in time when he was close enough to it to have picked it up. *There. It could not have been Mr. Darcy.* Elizabeth reassured herself, the thought somehow comforting. *If not Darcy, who?* This echoing question was not explored, for even in her rebuttal of the theory, she harbored no doubt that Mr. Darcy was somehow responsible. *Perhaps he had an accomplice. Colonel Fitzwilliam?*

'*I thought you were friends.*' Colonel Fitzwilliam's bold response to her assertion that Mr. Darcy did not like her crowded its way into her head. '*I believe you mistake my cousin."* What could the colonel have meant by saying this if not to disclose that she suffered from a want of understanding of Mr. Darcy's opinion of her? He could not tell her more, he had said, without revealing a confidence. Had Mr. Darcy been the source of the confidence?

Recollections came to her mind of their encounter that morning. Mr. Darcy had teasingly accused her of being a "sprite." Was there some romance in such a claim, she wondered. He had said it while looming above her on his great stallion, and it had not felt romantic at the time, but then she had called his dog her sweetheart. She blushed in the dark at how he may have taken it, when followed by her reference to his horse as a lover. This was followed by what seemed now in the darkness to be more than it had that morning. *He asked me to characterize him!* The conversation, in the hazy light of approaching dawn, had seemed a whimsical moment. *I said he was handsome.* Elizabeth, recalling how she had threatened to withdraw the compliment, felt one small chuckle bubble out of her throat in light of her own cheeky impertinence with the man.

The rest of the morning rushed upon her, and suddenly, it seemed that he had openly declared *something,* although it was impossible to say exactly what. Elizabeth realized that as they had basked together in the morning light her heart had been touched—a little, although in the moment she had denied the feelings that had threatened her equilibrium. It was for the best, she knew, for Mr. Darcy was too much of a gentleman to encourage her to hope for romance when such a match held no advantage for him. The colonel's claim of his belief in her friendship with Mr. Darcy suddenly made perfect sense!

Mr. Darcy, she concluded, did enjoy her companionship, although he did not fully reveal it in company. His pleasure in their conversations was evident, and his intentions were clear that he wished to pursue a platonic cordiality. Such a relationship must be beneficial to them both if Jane and Mr. Bingley continued to progress toward marriage, for as Jane's closest sister and Mr. Bingley's dearest friend it would not do for them to be unpleasant in their relations.

There, in the still of the night, in the confines of her own heart, she felt a small pang of disappointment that it could never be more, for somewhere in her muddle of thoughts, she came to the realization that she was rather fond of Mr. Darcy. His kindness, the gentle way he spoke to her, the dignity with which he carried himself, these things were slowly crowding out her initial impressions of pride and arrogance--not entirely, but enough for her to acknowledge, if only to herself, that knowledge of his good opinion of her was sweet. She had not sought his good opinion; in fact, on several occasions her actions should have driven away any hope of it. However, with some little evidence that she had nevertheless attained it, she was more inclined to be benevolent in her opinion of him as well.

As for the handkerchief, she was back to where she had started. She had no proof that it was Mr. Darcy, and his character was so inherently honest that it was simply not consistent with his nature to steal or to engage an accomplice in theft. She did not believe Mr. Collins was clever enough, which left the colonel and Mr. Wickham as the only remaining suspects.

The change in Mr. Wickham's behavior toward her had been suddenly so forward that she wondered at it. Her father's revelation at dinner that Mr. Wickham had engaged in past seductions was some explanation but not a satisfactory one. As bold as they had been, his declarations had also been flattering, and she could see in looking back on them, Mr. Wickham had been attempting to lead her directly back to an attempt to relate his history with Mr. Darcy. This, she speculated, may have been his motivation, to win her loyalty in taking sides against Mr. Darcy.

Mr. Wickham, who had been only mildly disconcerted by the presence of Mr. Darcy, certainly had been discomposed by Colonel Fitzwilliam. There was truly a history of some kind there, and the undercurrent of hostility was great. *Did Mr. Wickham take the handkerchief in retaliation for my unwillingness to hear him?* It was a possibility. She realized with chagrin that she did not know his character well enough to rule him out as the thief.

Colonel Fitzwilliam had charmed Elizabeth from the moment she met him. She reflected on the way his eyes had twinkled with a good-natured mischief and how he had put her immediately at ease. She hardly knew him, yet she already trusted him. A thought occurred to her that she had been inclined to trust Mr. Wickham implicitly as well, until Mr. Darcy had warned her against him. Now, by virtue of his association with Mr. Darcy, she felt no compunction in granting Colonel Fitzwilliam her trust and good opinion with less than a day of acquaintance, in spite of his mischievous countenance. Yet Elizabeth could not rule him out as one who would steal a handkerchief. She did not think he would do it with any malicious or even romantic intent, but would he do it as a lark? She could believe it very well indeed. Of course, she told herself, once he knew how she treasured the lace on it, if he had taken it, he would not hesitate to return it.

After many hours of wakefulness, her mind awhirl with thoughts that would not be set aside, Elizabeth finally dozed and eventually slept in the hours just before dawn. It soon became a heavy, dreamless sleep that would hold her exhausted body captive to the bed late into the next morning.

ঌ

Darcy awoke before dawn again, filled with desire to see Elizabeth. He dressed and rode out to the base of Oakham Mount, initially hopeful for a repeat of the previous morning's good fortune. He knew before he arrived that she would not be there, for he did not see her figure upon the path, but he remained out, riding in the vicinity until the sun was well up, and the foggy mist that had veiled the path had burned off. He had brought Apollo, considering him an ambassador of goodwill with Elizabeth, and it seemed to Darcy that he was not the only one disappointed at the lack of sprites in the Hertfordshire countryside that morning.

Chapter Thirty

THE WINDS BEGIN TO BLOW

Elizabeth woke with a start, the sound of raised voices and a slamming door jarring her from a deep slumber that could have easily held her for another hour. She tried to make sense of it from beneath the warm comfort of her feather quilt, but as the fog of sleep lifted, so too did her ambivalence to the sounds emanating from below stairs. As soon as she raised herself up to sit on the edge of the bed, the frigid air in her chambers was incentive to rapidly dress for the day, see to her toilette, and join her family for breakfast.

"Lizzy, are you unwell?" Jane said with concern as soon as she entered the dining room.

"I am well," Elizabeth replied with a slight shake of her head. "I had some trouble sleeping, that is all."

"Humph." The sound came from within Mrs. Bennet's chest, expressing disapproval. "You will not secure any dance partners if you cannot be bothered to sleep well, Lizzy. Beauty requires adequate rest, and you should take care to sleep tonight, or you will not be fit to be seen at the ball!"

"Yes, Mama." Elizabeth smiled sweetly at her mother as she prepared herself a piece of toast. "I shall not rest until I rest." She looked around the table. "Where is Papa?"

"He went to his study." Lydia giggled, "After his concession."

Elizabeth arched a dubious eyebrow at her sister. "Concession? What concession?"

"Just that I may go to the ball after all." Lydia burst out with a great smile. "Mama worked on him, of course, but she was not successful at all." Lydia frowned. "He was completely unmoved when I entreated him." She pointed at Jane. "But then Jane said that it would make her unhappy if I could not be there, and Kitty said the same. Then Mama said she too, and he allowed that I could go."

"Did he say why he relented?" Elizabeth asked.

"Well, he frowned a great deal at me throughout, and said I was silly at least five times." Lydia pouted slightly. "But he seemed to think it was unfair to Hill more than it was unfair to me, which was ungenerous of him, I think. The very moment he conceded, he left the table straightway in a foul temper. I think I shall avoid his study this morning lest he change his mind again, but he will be over it soon enough—certainly before the ball."

Elizabeth looked with consternation at Jane who nodded her head acknowledging it and offered an explanation. "Lydia was desperate to go to the ball."

"Do not look so put out, Lizzy." Lydia teased. "There will be enough dances with Mr. Wickham for both of us I daresay."

"I was not thinking of Mr. Wickham, and you must not either. Do not forget that Papa has forbidden us to even speak to him." Elizabeth glanced at Mr. Collins, mortified at the conversation that was taking place before their relation. "I was recalling how badly you conducted yourself at the Assembly Ball. Netherfield is very elegant. I hope that you will behave yourself in a more ladylike fashion tomorrow night than you did then."

"You are not my mother, Lizzy! I shall be as merry as I please, and you can say nothing about it!" Lydia retorted. "So ha-ha-ha, when I am dancing with the officers, you...," Lydia looked wickedly at her sister, and then at their guest, "may dance with Mr. Collins! He is not so jolly as the officers, but he has practiced all the steps now, and will make a fine partner for *you,* I am sure."

Mr. Collins colored and looked as though he would reply, if not for the mouthful of food interfering with his speech. He satisfied himself with a simpering grunt, a slight nod, and a wan smile sandwiched between his puffy, stuffed cheeks.

Mary intervened. "I believe Mr. Collins said that he will dance with all of his cousins, did you not, Mr. Collins?"

Collins, still chewing, could only add another grunt and nod to reply in the affirmative.

"I am very much looking forward to our dance, Mr. Collins. You do make an excellent partner." Mary fluttered her eyelashes as she smiled at Mr. Collins. It was not an intentionally flirtatious flutter, but rather a slightly nervous batting. Combined with a mild flushing of her face and her voice trailing to a whisper by the time she said 'partner', her delivery of the bold pronouncement was so demure and sweet that it seemed almost coquettish in its appeal. Mr. Collins stopped chewing and swallowed the contents of his mouth in one great lump.

Mrs. Bennet interjected, "Why yes, Mr. Collins! I am sure all the girls will be vastly happy to oblige you with a dance! Have you a mind as to which of the girls you would dance with first?"

Mr. Collins, whose expression revealed a degree of residual discomfort in speaking, replied. "Cousin Elizabeth, I believe should have the honor. Cousin Jane will, of course, be engaged for the first with Mr. Bingley, so as the next in seniority to Jane, you must be my first choice." He looked at Elizabeth and smiled triumphantly.

"I am sorry, Mr. Collins." Elizabeth replied quickly. "I have already promised the first set to Mr. Darcy, when I attended Jane at Netherfield." She blushed a little knowing that although Mr. Darcy had claimed a dance, he had said nothing about it being the first. "Perhaps, you will dance with Mary first, as she is next in seniority to me."

"I am greatly disappointed to hear this." Mr. Collins frowned slightly at Elizabeth before turning his attention to Mary. "Cousin Mary, would you do me the honor of reserving the first dance for me tomorrow?"

Mary was pleased and showed it, expressing great pleasure with her acceptance of the invitation. Mrs. Bennet narrowed her eyes slightly at Elizabeth. "So you're to dance with Mr. Darcy? Now there is a turnabout! I must say that I should like to see that arrogant man take the floor with one of my daughters, for he refused to stand up with any of them at the Assembly Ball, and it is very nearly an admission of how wrong he was."

"Mama, you mistake him. Mr. Darcy knew no-one but his own party at the Assembly," Elizabeth defended, "his offense was not intentional."

Kitty suddenly stiffened and sat up straight in her chair. "Mama, do you hear that? There is a carriage in the lane!" She jumped up impulsively and ran to the window, peering out in an attempt to discern the visitor. "It is that lady! The one who brought Mr. Collins!"

Colonel Fitzwilliam and Mr. Darcy rode to Meryton shortly after breakfast. Having dined with the officers on a previous occasion, Darcy knew where the commanding officer was quartered, and they called upon the man at precisely twelve o'clock.

Their visit was short—but twenty minutes in duration. Colonel Forster, who recalled his previous acquaintance with Colonel Fitzwilliam, was pleased to renew the friendship. It did not take long for the callers to turn the conversation to the business that had inspired their visit, and with uncommon gravity, they related what they knew of Mr. Wickham's character and history of scandals in the various areas in which he had resided. No specific mention was made of Mr. Darcy's connection to Wickham, other than they were from the same neighborhood in Derbyshire, and that one young lady injured by Mr. Wickham was also from the area.

In the several months that the cousins had spent tracking Wickham from Ramsgate, although they had not located the man himself, they had collected a litany of evidence against him. Upon disclosing what they knew, Colonel Forster was solemn. He was highly aware that the situation was political, for he was responsible to maintain adequate ranks in the militia, but the goodwill of the merchants and people of Meryton was critical for the duration of the time they were to be quartered in the village. To knowingly harbor an officer who would endanger the reputation of the entire militia and harden the general opinion against them was serious business.

Colonel Forster thanked them for bringing the charges against Mr. Wickham to his attention and assured them that he would pursue some action to prevent Meryton or its residents from falling prey to any mischief from his officer. His first act, he declared, would be to assign Mr. Wickham to some duty the next evening, effectively preventing him from attending the ball that the officers had all been invited to at Netherfield.

The two gentlemen left the colonel's quarters reassured that Mr. Wickham's activities would be curtailed to some extent; however, they were not assured that the colonel took the matter as seriously as they would have liked. It took only a few inquiries to determine which inn Wickham was housed in, and the men paid their second call of the morning shortly after the first.

Mr. Wickham would most certainly have declined to see them had he been in his room. However, he was standing by the road with several other officers when Colonel Fitzwilliam and Mr. Darcy approached the inn. Wickham greeted the men civilly, and they did likewise, although those present would later say that they had felt a distinct enmity in their address from the start. They would also say that following a brief private audience with his callers, George Wickham was a changed man. The charm and amiability he was well known for was strained, and his address became more frequently sullen and morose instead. This transformation resulted in much speculation by those who knew him in the militia and by others in Meryton as to what had transpired between the men, but it would be some time before the truth of the matter would be known to anyone except the three men from Derbyshire.

Mr. Bingley became increasingly impatient for the return of Fitzwilliam and Darcy to Netherfield. The preparations for the ball the next evening had engaged the full attention of his sisters and the staff, and he could discover no corner of the house where he did not find himself in the way, with the exception of his own quarters, to which he had confined himself since breakfast.

His thoughts were not on the ball, however. They were on his lovely Miss Bennet, and although he was more at ease when making calls accompanied by a companion, he eventually decided not to wait for his friends to return but to set out for Longbourn alone.

It was as he was approaching Meryton that he observed a grand carriage. Drawn by four handsome bays and attended by smartly dressed footmen, he saw it leaving the little village going the opposite direction as he. The conveyance was out of place in the countryside, but his mind was so directed on calling on the Bennets that he scarce looked twice as he passed it.

After Lady Catherine left Longbourn, the household was in an uproar. Mr. Collins had expected that she was there to insist on his decision regarding a wife, but she had not even mentioned it. She had instead, swept into the house, discomposed the entire family and all the servants with her sudden arrival, dispensed with the pleasantries and demanded to know in which house in the neighborhood her nephew could be found.

Mr. Collins, ever anxious to please, had offered that not one, but two of her esteemed nephews—Mr. Darcy and Colonel Fitzwilliam—could be found as houseguests at Netherfield Park. Upon gaining the directions to that estate, she took her leave of the Bennet house with no further ado, departing in the same abrupt and imposing manner in which she had arrived.

Mrs. Bennet was both delighted that such an important person had called at Longbourn a second time and unhappy that the visit had been unsatisfactory. It could hardly be classified as a social call, yet Mrs. Bennet actively sought to identify any elements that could be used to turn it into a triumph to be shared with Lady Lucas and Mrs. Phillips.

Mr. Collins seemed quite beside himself with anxiety and relief upon the departure of his patroness, and seemed suddenly determined to accelerate his success in winning Elizabeth's favor. It did not take long for Elizabeth to tire of his attentions, and she retired to her bedchamber, where she knew that Mr. Collins could not follow. Jane, however, did follow, and the two sisters marveled together over what had transpired in the course of the morning.

"What could it mean, Lady Catherine coming here?" Jane wondered. "She seemed so determined."

"I do not know for certain." Elizabeth mused. "But it may have something to do with her daughter, Miss de Bourgh. Mr. Collins told me that Mr. Darcy is engaged to his cousin, but he told me that he is not. I suspect that her mother is of the opinion that he is. I confess to wondering how Miss de Bourgh looks upon the matter. It seems a hopelessly convoluted mess."

"Lizzy, how grateful I am to hold no doubt of Mr. Bingley's affections. He is such a steady young man." Jane smiled blissfully. "I am grateful too that he does not have a terrifying aunt chasing him about the countryside. That would be dreadful!"

"One cannot help but feel some compassion for Mr. Darcy, I suppose." Elizabeth ventured. "His aunt is rather imposing after all. I am certainly glad she is no relation of mine."

"Has your heart softened toward Mr. Darcy?" Jane's eyes widened hopefully.

Elizabeth laughed at her sister. "Jane, you know what I think of him, but I am now determined to allow myself to like him, at least a little. He is, after all, Mr. Bingley's friend, and we are bound to see him if you are being courted by Mr. Bingley. There is nothing so annoying as constantly being civil to a person one dislikes, so I am of a mind to like him just well enough to be a friend, and I believe that will suit him also, for he has been somewhat more amiable of late."

"That will please Char ... Mr. Bingley." Jane smiled contentedly.

"You must not tell Mr. Bingley anything about it." Elizabeth warned. "I do not wish to give the wrong impression."

"What, that you're entirely reasonable and not nearly as stubborn as you seem?" Jane teased. "No, we must not spread that about the county!"

A few minutes later, the call came from below that Mr. Bingley was approaching the house. Jane stood to go, but Elizabeth was suddenly reluctant. "I am in no temper to keep company with Mr. Collins. Would it trouble you if I did not join you today?"

"No, it would not trouble me, but I cannot speak for my mother. If you are not to come to the sitting room, you had best quit the house altogether, or Mama will make you come." Jane replied.

"I do believe that I am a bad influence on you, Jane!" Elizabeth laughed. "You go down to Mr. Bingley, I will go for a walk, and perhaps Mr. Collins will oblige us all and spend some time with Mary."

Jane nodded happily and left the room, while Elizabeth prepared herself to go out. She tiptoed down the stairs and after retrieving her pelisse and gloves, went to the kitchen, where she filled a basket with provisions from the larder. Her mother, as mistress of Longbourn, had a duty to see to the well-being of their tenants, but it was an obligation she frequently neglected. In recent years, Elizabeth and Jane had often performed the visits in her stead. Elizabeth knew that if her mother were upset about her abandoning the callers at Longbourn, she would also be appeased when she learned that Elizabeth had done so while fulfilling the duty to visit their tenants. Leaving through the back door, Elizabeth could not be seen from the sitting room and was soon well out of sight of the house.

❧

Leaving Meryton after seeing Mr. Wickham, Colonel Fitzwilliam and Mr. Darcy concluded that Mr. Bingley would have most likely become impatient and gone to visit Longbourn without waiting upon their return, so they likewise set out for Longbourn.

Carefully folded and tucked into the pocket nearest his heart, Darcy carried Elizabeth's handkerchief. He had not told Fitzwilliam of his plans to return it, nor had he set his mind to the way he was to accomplish it, only that it must be done. His mind wandered to it constantly as they rode. He composed in his mind little speeches to say as he returned it, but none of the approaches gratified him, for he could envision Miss Bennet challenging whatever he said. He did not wish to inflame her anger against him but rather to please her. Eventually, Colonel Fitzwilliam could bear the silence no longer.

"One would think you were on your way to the gallows, Darcy. I know that you do not enjoy Mrs. Bennet's company, but surely your anticipation of seeing Miss Elizabeth is a happy affair."

"It would be, I grant you." Darcy said, "If I were not faced with the prospect of returning the wretched handkerchief that you stole."

"So you're to return it? Will you tell her how you came by it?" Fitzwilliam asked casually.

"I do not know." Darcy scowled. "I would not wish her to think I took it."

"Blast it man, why ever not? She thinks you hold her in contempt. If you prove yourself to be just a bit of a scoundrel, it will make you even, and you can start anew." Colonel Fitzwilliam laughed.

"But I am not a scoundrel." Darcy grimaced. "Nor am I likely to be convincing as a pretender. I cannot deceive."

"Then you had best tell her the truth." Fitzwilliam grinned. "I *am* just a bit of a scoundrel, and I am sure she will believe it of me. Would you like me to return it to her? I will gladly tell her why I took it...."

"No!" Darcy nearly bellowed. "You have done enough damage!"

The colonel struck his balled fist long ways against his heart. "I am hit!" He cried dramatically, "You have pierced me!"

"This is not a time for hilarity, Fitz. Your antics make me weary today." Darcy shook his head.

"The first thing you must know about women, Darcy, is that they like men who are in a good humor. You must shed that serious attitude and discover the delights of pleasing a lady with your attentions." Fitzwilliam nudged his horse to go faster. "I will be glad to show you how it is done!"

Darcy, alarmed at the implications of Fitzwilliam's offer, spurred his horse as well, and the two cousins raced the last half mile to Longbourn.

Chapter Thirty-One

I HAVE FOUND YOU AT LAST

Although Colonel Fitzwilliam had the advantage of an early lead, Darcy's magnificent steed possessed superior speed and stamina, and so it was Darcy who arrived first at the gates of Longbourn. The race had invigorated him, and he vaulted from the saddle with energy and an excitement born both of the exercise and his deep desire to see Elizabeth. When his feet acquired the ground, it occurred to him that the ride may have disheveled his appearance, and he spent a moment brushing off the dust and straightening his attire. He reached for his handkerchief to wipe the sweat from his brow, and in his haste, very nearly mopped his face with the stolen, lacy one in his pocket, but he caught himself in time.

He had just finished the task of making himself presentable again when Colonel Fitzwilliam came walking his horse down the lane. He was in a state of complete relaxation, leaning back in his saddle and loudly singing "The British Grenadiers." He stopped his horse as he approached Darcy. Peering down at his cousin, he laughed, "Darcy, you will not be making a favorable impression on the ladies of the house by arriving to call in such a state. Whatever were you thinking?"

At this, Darcy rolled his eyes and shook his head, for he knew that Fitzwilliam had been hard upon his heels. The colonel must have reined in prior to their final approach in order to put on this show of nonchalance. "Fitz, you are a chucklehead!"

Fitzwilliam gracefully dismounted. "If you wish to war with slanderous insults, you should surrender now. You know I am better at it than you, you old nincompoop."

"Nothing as easy as surrender now that *you have* begun it! I will defer the war until later, you bacon-brained fatwit. For now, exchanging insults with you holds far less appeal than what waits beyond that door." Darcy nodded with a grin at the entry to Longbourn. It had been many years since he and his cousin had played at this game, but when they were young men, Fitzwilliam, several years his senior, had used it to provoke him, and they eventually had made great sport of it.

Fitzwilliam agreed to the temporary truce, and clapped his cousin playfully on his back as they walked to the house. "I am heartened that you took my advice about being in good humor, Darcy. Your manners improve considerably under my tutelage!"

Darcy ignored his cousin.

Their horses were entrusted to the groom from the stable that approached to take them, and soon Darcy and Fitzwilliam were announced to the Longbourn household.

"Mr. Darcy! Colonel Fitzwilliam!" Mrs. Bennet seemed surprised by their arrival. "You are very welcome." She bobbed a curtsy and sounded as though they were less welcome than "very." The two men bowed in answer to her tepid greeting. She then added tentatively, "We had thought that you would be occupied with your own callers at Netherfield."

At this, Mr. Bingley left Jane's side and crossed the room. "It is your aunt, Darcy. Miss Bennet has informed me that she was here in search of you. She has gone to Netherfield to find you."

"That is unfortunate for her, for it is plain to be seen that I am not presently to be found at Netherfield," Mr. Darcy replied. "With no prior introduction to your sisters, she will be forced to leave her card and depart. Such a circumstance will displease her to no end!"

"What do you suppose her business in Hertfordshire is?" Bingley wondered aloud. "Could not most dealings be transacted via post? This is too far from London for a mere social call."

Darcy and Fitzwilliam looked at each other meaningfully. "I will see to my aunt. She is undoubtedly here on some family business, which she deemed urgent enough to require her personal attention." Darcy replied to Bingley, who nodded his acceptance of Darcy's reply. Darcy then returned his attention to the group assembled in the sitting room. His eyes swept across their faces expectantly, but he hid his disappointment that Miss Elizabeth was absent from the party.

Bingley did not miss the expectant look on his friend's face, however, and leaned toward Darcy so that he would not be overheard. "Perhaps now would be a good time to address that business with your aunt. Miss Elizabeth has gone for a walk." Darcy nodded, and turned to Mrs. Bennet as Bingley returned to sit by Jane.

Darcy spoke warmly to his hostess, saying, "Mrs. Bennet, I pray you will forgive me for not staying. If it would be acceptable to you, I will call again at a later hour, once I have attended to some personal affairs." He bowed slightly as he said it.

Mrs. Bennet eyed him suspiciously; however, it was evident that the colonel was not planning to leave, and this arrangement suited Mrs. Bennet quite well, so she graciously accepted Darcy's apology, and turned to engage Colonel Fitzwilliam in conversation.

As soon as he was clear of the house, Darcy turned his horse and doubled back toward the lands to the rear of Longbourn. His general sense from their conversations was that most of Elizabeth's walks began either toward Meryton, or into the fields, hills and woods in the other direction. Since he had not passed her on the road coming from Meryton, he guessed that she had gone the other way.

He rode aimlessly, scanning the property around him for some time. Being late November, the fields had long since been harvested and would lie fallow until spring. The wooded bands that separated the fields were all completely barren of foliage, and the golden-red carpet of leaves beneath them was now faded, their colors muted echoes of what they had been just a month before. Although it was mid-day, he saw no movement other than some sheep in the distance. As he searched, what had begun as a certainty that he would find her soon became desolation at the possibility that he would not.

He stopped his horse and together, man and beast stood still, he scanning the vast countryside as his horse patiently waited. Finally, he saw some movement along one of the paths. The curve of the land obscured his view, but he could make out a figure sufficiently well that he pressed his leg into Romeo's side, and together they took off toward the person moving along the path, Darcy's heart hopeful that it was Elizabeth Bennet. It was not.

Instead, he found a young lad gathering kindling. When he was close enough to be heard, he called out to the boy. "You, there!"

The boy stopped, wide-eyed and looked up at Mr. Darcy, his mouth agape.

"Do not be alarmed, my boy." Darcy said as he came to a stop. "Have you been long in the woods today?"

The boy closed his mouth and nodded, his eyes still saucers.

"Tell me, please, have you seen Miss Bennet along this path?" Darcy asked, softening his voice.

"Yes, sir, she was here, sir, not an hour ago." The boy looked hopeful.

Darcy retrieved a few coins and asked, "Where did she go?"

The boy pointed down the path. "The cottages," he said. "She will be ta the end of the row by now."

Darcy leaned down in his saddle and dropped the coins into the boy's upraised hand. "I am much obliged!" He made a soft clucking sound, and he was soon cantering toward the cluster of small homes he could now make out in the distance. He slowed his pace to a walk as he approached the buildings. A stray chicken squawked loudly as it flapped its wings and moved out of the road. A small brown dog barked from behind a scraggly hedge, and the curtains fluttered behind the panes as a hand parted them slightly.

A moment later, a man came toward him from the second cottage. He stopped in the middle of the road in front of Mr. Darcy, no welcome on his face, his hands on his hips.

"I am in search of Miss Bennet." Darcy said after a moment of silence. "Pray, have you seen her?"

The man's demeanor changed instantly, and still saying nothing, he led Darcy to the gate of a cottage. Nodding his head sideways to indicate that she was inside, he turned and walked back down the road. Darcy tied his horse to the branch of a tree and approached the cottage door. It swung open before he could knock.

A young woman stood before him. "Who are you?" she asked curiously.

"I am looking for Miss Bennet. Is she perchance inside?" Darcy tried to look over her shoulder to see into the dark interior.

The girl nodded once and replied, "Yes."

"May I come in?" Darcy asked in such a way that he could not be denied. The girl simply stepped aside and admitted him to the small home. He could hear Elizabeth's lilting voice, around the corner from the door, and the sound itself put a hint of a smile on his face. He removed his hat and stepped further inside, peering into the small kitchen where the family was assembled.

Elizabeth's back was to him, and Darcy surmised that she was holding an infant, for she was rocking and bouncing slightly as she spoke to the woman seated by her at the table. Two small children milled about the table, and one sat underneath it.

"A weak infusion of tea, made from the herbs I have brought you, should take care of the colic. It is what my Aunt Gardiner has used with her children, and it never fails." Elizabeth lowered her head to croon at the baby. "What a sweet little one! Such a precious one you are, Hannah! Oh look, she is smiling at me." Elizabeth reluctantly stood and gently returned the baby in her mother's arms. "I must be going, but I have enjoyed our visit today, Mrs. Miller. I dearly love children, and yours are all a true delight. Please, let us know if there is anything else you stand in need of. Good day." Elizabeth picked up her now-empty basket from the table and rose.

"Miss Lizzy." One of the children tugged at her dress.

Elizabeth looked down at the little girl, who shyly held up a perfect pheasant tail-feather to her. "It is beautiful, Lottie. Thank you." She smiled encouragingly at the girl and curtseyed to her as she placed the feather in her basket. The little one returned the gesture, and Elizabeth turned to leave with a whimsical look on her face. She stopped short at the sight of Mr. Darcy by the door.

"Miss Bennet." Darcy bowed. "I have found you at last."

Elizabeth looked shrewdly at Mr. Darcy, highly aware of the presence of curious onlookers from the Miller family. She did not wish to inflame any gossip among her father's tenants, for it would not take long to spread to Meryton from there. "How kind of you to find me, Mr. Darcy." She quickly led him from the house, and when she reached the tree where his horse was tied, she finished the thought, "I was unaware that I was lost. I pray you, enlighten me on why you are here."

Darcy looked at the woman who stood before him quizzically. Her eyes were twinkling dangerously, but her eyebrow arched in challenge, and her tone hinted at displeasure. How was he to interpret her? "Miss Bennet, I did not mean to imply that you had lost your way, but rather that I have been most anxious to speak with you." He held his breath, hoping that she would respond favorably.

"I see." Elizabeth stroked the side of Romeo's neck and patted it. "We should not talk here." She started to walk briskly past the row of cottages. Darcy quickly untied the horse and caught up with her when she was nearly clear of the buildings, walking at her side as he led Romeo.

"Mr. Darcy, you are fully aware, I am certain, that you and I walking alone together risks both of our reputations. Tongues will wag." She turned to face him. "You should at least get on your horse."

He frowned. This was not how he had envisioned the conversation. "Miss Bennet, I will get on my horse, but only because you wish it. Tongues will wag regardless." He mounted and nudged Romeo's head ahead of Elizabeth, so that Darcy was still side by side with her.

"You said you were anxious to speak to me, Mr. Darcy. I will hear you now." Elizabeth said with an upward glance.

"I am indeed anxious to speak with you." Darcy began, "However, I find myself at a disadvantage."

"I think that riding up there in all your state gives you a distinct advantage." Elizabeth replied. "You should speak now while you have it."

"Miss Bennet, I will wait to speak until I can see your face. I cannot speak to your bonnet."

Elizabeth turned her face to look up at him. "Mr. Darcy, be warned. If I walk this way, I am bound to stumble. You said you must see my face, and you have it now. Does this please you?"

"I would not have you stumble, Miss Bennet." Darcy replied. Elizabeth turned her head back to facing forward. Darcy rode alongside her in silence, analyzing. Even this conversation, incomprehensible as it was, delighted him as much as it vexed him. At length, he stopped and dismounted again. Elizabeth also stopped and looked at him expectantly. He was surprised to see a smile on her lips and an amused look on her face.

"Miss Bennet, I was serious when I said that I needed to speak with you." Darcy planted himself in front of her and stood his ground in the path.

Elizabeth's eyes shifted nervously, but she raised her chin and said archly, "Do you mean to frighten me with your satirical eye, Mr. Darcy? I must warn you that my courage always rises with every attempt to intimidate me."

"I am not afraid of you," Darcy said, a trace of humor crossing his features. "Will you hear me now?"

Elizabeth nodded and clasped her hands in front of her, around the handle of the basket. "I will."

"I must insist that you allow me to speak my peace before you reply."

Elizabeth pursed her lips and said nothing.

Darcy took a deep breath. "Miss Bennet, a few days ago, I followed you from your house, afraid that you were in distress, but found you overcome instead by laughter. You claimed that the reason for your amusement was a secret, and although I had a theory, it seemed indelicate at the time to press the matter. Do you recall this?"

Elizabeth grudgingly nodded, her lips still pursed.

"My theory related to the embroidery work you had in a tambour frame. I had commented on its unusual design, which I fear was the source of your laughter. I know not whether the pattern was intentional or not, but I did see that the initials E and D were a prominent element. I confess Miss Elizabeth, that I was astonished to see it. Is your middle name Deborah?"

Elizabeth, blushing now, shook her head.

"Diana?" Darcy guessed.

Another shake, her lips pursed so tightly that she looked almost comically puckered for a kiss.

"Does your middle name even start with a 'D'?"

"No." Elizabeth glared at him. "If you want me to be silent, you must stop asking me questions!"

"Of course." Darcy nodded, tipping his head to the side with a boyish charm. "I will press you no more on the secret I allowed you, but am bound to reveal my own secret, in light of a certain event. In telling you, I acknowledge that I may open myself to ridicule, but that cannot be helped. I must confess to you now, Miss Bennet, that I was fascinated, or rather, *intrigued* by the mystery of what the 'D' might mean."

Elizabeth's eyes narrowed ever so slightly, and she folded her arms across her chest, the basket now nestled in the crook of her elbow. In her eyes, however, Darcy saw not surprise at his revelation, but a spark of bewildered comprehension, so he continued.

"When I was at Longbourn yesterday, it appeared as though you were adding lace trim to the very same handkerchief, although I could not be certain. When you set it down on the table, I had hoped to discern it but could not make out the pattern from my vantage point, although I studied it several times in an attempt to detect whether it was the same cloth." Darcy paused, knowing that she was now expecting him to confess that he took it, and he secretly relished knowing that he had not. "My cousin, Colonel Fitzwilliam, noticed my interest in the article, and in what can only be characterized as a sorely misguided act, he picked it up when your attention was diverted. He gave it to me when we returned to Netherfield." Darcy reached into his pocket and handed Elizabeth the handkerchief without ceremony.

Elizabeth gasped, her eyes widened in astonishment. "Colonel Fitzwilliam took it? Oh, Mr. Darcy! You cannot know how I grieved at its loss." She reached for the handkerchief that was extended to her. Her head was bowed, so that Mr. Darcy could not perceive her expression, but she reverently opened it and refolded it, running her gloved fingertips across it contemplatively. With both hands she pressed it against her chest and raised her head, her eyes were closed, but when she opened them, they sparkled with unshed tears and her chin trembled with emotion. "I was not certain I would ever have it back." Elizabeth whispered her fear. "The lace was a gift to me from my aunt when she married my uncle. It is a very fine piece of lace." She held the cloth out for Darcy to see it. "It comes from the village of Lambton, where my aunt lived."

"Lambton, in Derbyshire?" Darcy asked.

Elizabeth nodded. "Mr. Darcy, you must allow me to thank you for restoring the kerchief to me." She held it against herself again, emphasizing how she cherished it. "When I discovered it was gone, I was greatly distressed, but now all I can feel is relief and gratitude." She raised her eyes to meet his, merely to emphasize the statement. She had no way of knowing that the ribbons of color in her irises were magnified by the moisture that clung to her lashes, although she was highly aware that her emotion caused her lower lip to tremble dangerously, which she attempted to suppress by pressing her lips together.

In Darcy's face, Elizabeth had expected to see the glimmer of friendship that Colonel Fitzwilliam had assured her was there. Instead, she discovered eyes that searched hers with an unexpected warmth and intensity. For several suspended seconds, she was drawn into them, her mind numb to all else. A sudden strangeness in her stomach caused her to inhale sharply, and look away with an involuntary shiver. She shifted uncomfortably as she found herself without words and unwilling to return his gaze.

"Are you cold?" His low voice assaulted her ears with a gentleness and a nearness that caused her insides to quiver in a way she had never experienced before. She shook her head as she unconsciously bit her lip and dared a glance upward again. His eyes had remained fixed resolutely on her face, and this time, she took her courage not from intimidation, but from the softness in his expression.

"I am not cold, Mr. Darcy," a demure smile played on her lips, and she set the handkerchief into her basket. "However, I would be warmer if I were permitted to continue walking."

Darcy stepped aside and waved his hand in a gesture for her to continue. "By all means." He fell into step beside her. After a few minutes of walking in silence, he spoke. "Miss Bennet, are you aware that I am from Derbyshire?"

Elizabeth suppressed a laugh. "Yes, Mr. Darcy, I believe that *everyone* is aware of this."

"Are you at all familiar with Derbyshire?" Darcy inquired.

"Not at all," Elizabeth replied. "My aunt speaks of it, but I have no personal knowledge. I understand there is a wild beauty that is quite different from what is seen in Hertfordshire."

"That is mostly true, although Hertfordshire is not without its share of wild beauty." Darcy said, "I find that I often prefer wild beauty to that which is tame." He glanced at Elizabeth and continued speaking. "The grounds of my home in Derbyshire, for example. Much of the landscape is exactly as nature intended, with little interference."

Elizabeth smiled sideways at him. "Do you spend much of your time there?"

"Not in recent months." Darcy replied. "Pemberley...," he trailed off, not wishing to speak of his loneliness there or divulge his dream to banish the solitude by bringing Elizabeth home as the mistress. "Pemberley is but five miles from Lambton."

Elizabeth stopped and looked at Darcy with some astonishment. "Only five miles?" She retrieved the handkerchief from the basket. "Have you seen lace such as this before?"

Darcy nodded. "Many pieces of lace exactly like it may be found within the walls of Pemberley ... my mother's touch."

"Oh." Elizabeth worried that she had crossed into too personal a topic and fell into silence as she resumed walking. It was not until Darcy spoke again that she noticed the faraway look on his face.

"My mother was the very soul of Pemberley. When she died, darkness fell. My father was inconsolable, and my sister was raised by nannies. I was sent away to school, and the joys of coming home could not compare to what had gone before. Do not mistake me, my father was the best of men, but his heart was broken when my mother died, as was mine."

"I did not intend to invade your privacy," Elizabeth said somewhat nervously. "It saddens me that you lost your mother at so young an age."

"I would not have you be sad for my sake." Darcy replied. "I much prefer your laughter to your tears."

"If that is so, then say something ridiculous, and I will oblige you." Elizabeth said, relieved at the opportunity to lighten the mood through teasing.

Darcy looked at her in consternation. "Nothing ridiculous comes to my mind."

"Speak to me of follies and foibles then." Elizabeth grinned.

Darcy shook his head. "I know some pretty sonnets to recite if that would amuse you."

"That will not do, Mr. Darcy. Sonnets are dreary, mournful things—lamenting, yearning, striving but never striking a chord of humor, and rarely even of love as I perceive it. They would certainly fail to make me laugh." Elizabeth laughed. "You may have to resort to this." She reached into her basket and extracted the feather, holding it out toward Mr. Darcy.

She did not expect him to accept it—the offer was purely in jest, however he plucked it from her hand and deftly slid it into a pocket in his coat. "Thank you, Miss Bennet." Darcy said, slightly smug. "I had not expected you to be so very helpful."

"I am not ticklish." Elizabeth said. "Perhaps you intend to fill it with ink and write sonnets with it, to prove me wrong."

"No." Darcy shook his head. "I would prove you right with some dreary, mournful verse, and I cannot do that. However, I will make you laugh with it. Perhaps I will add it to one of Miss Bingley's hats, or even one of my own. You will have to wait and see."

At this, Elizabeth did laugh, for the thought, she told him, was indeed ridiculous. They fell into easy conversation and covered the distance quite companionably. They came near Longbourn, and Darcy belatedly told Elizabeth he had matters to attend to, asking if she would permit him could call on her later at Longbourn. Elizabeth, in some bewilderment, agreed, and he mounted his horse and sped away toward Meryton.

Chapter Thirty-Two

THE DAY THE BLUE VASE BROKE

Elizabeth had but a short walk to Longbourn once she had parted ways with Mr. Darcy. Watching him ride away left her with a strange sensation, similar to stepping away from the comfort of a warm fireplace into the frosty air of a winter night. She hastened her steps, noting from the length of her shadow that it was later than she had realized.

Once indoors and free of her bonnet and pelisse, Elizabeth stopped by her father's study to report on what she had learned of the tenants, for there was some illness in several of the homes she had visited.

Afterward, she listened carefully from the study door to discern the location of Mr. Collins. He was speaking loudly with Mary, which provided Elizabeth the chance to seek an alternate direction whereby she could avoid encountering him.

It was not that she wished to slight him; however, his attentions had become increasingly marked. She remained civil to him, but never more than that. In spite of this, his behavior seemed guided only by his expectation of being well received, rather than any evidence of it.

She returned the basket to the kitchen after retrieving her handkerchief from it. As she was hanging the basket, Mrs. Hill entered.

"Beggin' your pardon, Miss Elizabeth, but have you seen Miss Jane? She was searchin' for you a moment ago, and we thought you had not yet returned." Hill looked slightly agitated.

"No, I have not seen her, Hill. Can you tell me where she is?"

"She is in the dining room, Miss." Hill nodded toward the door.

Elizabeth thanked the housekeeper and made her way to the dining room, careful not to make any noise that might alert Mr. Collins to her whereabouts. She peeked through the door and found Jane alone, her face reflecting a degree of anxiety uncommon for her sister.

"Jane?" Elizabeth said softly as she entered the room. "Is something amiss?"

"Oh Lizzy!" Jane's relief at her sister's arrival was evident. "I hardly know! What a to-do there has been here today."

"What has happened?" Elizabeth asked, suppressing her alarm.

"It all began with Lady Catherine. We had thought that Mr. Darcy had gone in search of her, but shortly after he left, she returned to Longbourn. She was in high dudgeon, for she had expected to find Mr. Darcy at Netherfield."

"He was not there." Elizabeth stated, for she knew he had been with her.

"No." Jane responded. "Which circumstance displeased her most seriously. She could not press for admittance to a house where she knew no one, so she returned to Longbourn to retrieve a means to an introduction. She was most determined to be accommodated."

"Who did she take?"

Jane sighed. "She seemed to have Mr. Collins in mind when she arrived, but upon finding Colonel Fitzwilliam and Mr. Bingley here, she would only speak to the colonel, until he introduced Mr. Bingley, and then she insisted that they both return to Netherfield with her at once." Jane pressed her hands to her cheeks as if to cool them. "She was most urgently in search of Mr. Darcy! She continually inquired as to his whereabouts. When they could not answer to her satisfaction, her displeasure grew. Poor Mama, the whole conversation was a hardship on her nerves, and she took to her room nearly as soon as they departed."

"And you, Jane. What worries you?" Elizabeth asked with concern.

"It is true; I *am* worried—about Mr. Bingley. He seemed most discomfited by the manner in which she spoke to him; he was not himself at all. When he attempted to be amiable and gracious with the lady, she said he was insolent and should show more deference to one such as she, who is his superior in every way. Poor Mr. Bingley." Jane's shoulders sagged. "I would not have him appear so disheartened as he did in that moment."

"And what of the colonel?" Elizabeth wondered, "Did she speak in the same manner with him?"

"She was quite put out with him over something, although I do not know what. She glared at him, looking fierce and frowning." Jane shook her head for lack of understanding. "We do not know the colonel well, but he grew in my esteem today, for he was kind where she was harsh and he was amiable when she was disagreeable. He spoke gently to her and tried to sooth her. She would have none of it, of course, but Colonel Fitzwilliam treated her almost as he would a mother. It was most endearing."

Elizabeth smiled at Jane's description. She would allow Jane her good opinion of the colonel and never tell her that he was the one who had stolen her handkerchief. She did hold the handkerchief out for Jane to see, however. "Jane," she said, "I have been spared any further distress over my missing kerchief. As you see, it has been found, and all my fretting over its disappearance was for naught. I am so very pleased to have it back, especially the lace, which is now dearer to me even than before."

"Lizzy, I am glad! Now you shall have your handkerchief for tomorrow night's ball after all! You must be very pleased." Jane beamed. "How was it restored to you?"

"The mode is of little importance." Elizabeth brushed the question aside. "I am curious about one thing though. Did Lady Catherine have anything to say to Mr. Collins?"

"Yes," Jane nodded, "although we do not know what was said. When her carriage arrived, Mr. Collins did not wait for her to be announced to the household. He made haste outdoors to greet her nearly as soon as the carriage door opened. You cannot doubt the attitude of his welcome, for it was all deference to his esteemed patroness, yet we could see from the window that she was in a temper. What she spoke must have been dreadful, for Mr. Collins was crestfallen and dejected upon hearing her and has been out of spirits from that moment."

"Poor Mr. Collins." Elizabeth said.

"Poor Mr. Collins indeed!" Jane cried. "After Lady Catherine's departure from the sitting room, he made haste to quit the room himself, and broke Mama's blue porcelain vase when he ran into the table!"

"The blue vase? Oh, Jane!" Elizabeth sat down shaking her head. "No wonder Mama took to her room!"

"There is more." Jane said. "Mr. Collins attempted to pick up the pieces of the vase, but he was shaking and trembling most fiercely, and a particular shard had an edge like a blade. His hand was cut deeply, and his bleeding was profuse. *That* is when Mama took to her room!"

"What then?" Elizabeth asked with mounting distress.

"I assisted Mama to her room, for we thought that she would swoon! Hill, I think, took up the pieces of broken vase and cleaned the blood from the floor. Mary stayed with Mr. Collins to bind his wound." Jane replied. "I do not know what has become of Kitty and Lydia; they have made themselves scarce since Lady Catherine took Mr. Bingley and the colonel away."

"What you have endured Jane!" Elizabeth comforted her sister. "I am sorry I was not here to help you bear it."

"I shall bear it well, Lizzy, for Mr. Bingley has promised that he will return today." Jane blushed. "I find I can bear almost anything with such a prospect before me."

༄

Mr. Darcy entered Netherfield through the smaller entryway nearest the stables. It was in the stables that he learned that Mr. Bingley, his cousin, and Lady Catherine were all assembled in the house. He did not doubt that they were waiting upon him, and he felt the weight of it.

He took the rear stairway two steps at a time to the upper floors, where he went directly to his bedchamber. It was not that he wished to avoid the encounter so much as to postpone it by a few moments. His pleasant conversation with Elizabeth still stirred in his heart, and he laid the feather he had plucked from her hand on the dressing table, fingering it slightly with a smile as he replayed the scene in his mind.

"Speak to me of follies and foibles," she had said to him, and his only thought was that she, Elizabeth Bennet was his greatest weakness, and he was too deeply in love with her to think himself ridiculous for it. Then he laughed aloud from sheer joy, for although she had rebuked him for a breach in propriety in seeking her out alone, she had not run away from him this time, and to his great relief, she had accepted the handkerchief without reproach. Her gentle teasing had delighted him, and the feather was a trophy he would not part from easily. It represented so much to him, for it would remind him of the babe in

her arms and the other sweet child who had offered it as a gift for her kindness. To witness Elizabeth tending to the needs her father's tenants put him in mind of his own tenants, who had not been blessed at the hand of a gentle mistress since his mother's passing.

He picked up the feather again, and twirled it between his fingers, his thoughts turning to the promised dance he would claim with her one night hence. When he had originally extracted the promise of a dance from her, he had considered it a victory in their verbal duel. When he had reminded her of it the next day, he had thought it the only pleasure he would take in Charles' ball at Netherfield. Now, he was nearly giddy with anticipation of taking her to the floor. He envisioned her as his graceful partner, their eyes upon each other as their movements matched in time and step with the music. Their hands, he knew, would clasp and release throughout the intricate series, and she would be close enough that her intoxicating fragrance would swirl delicately in the air around him. Darcy's heart beat a little faster; his breath came a little heavier merely imagining the thrill it would be.

He dallied with the thought of daring a second set. He did not care who noticed that he singled her out, for in truth; she was to him, the only woman of any interest who would be in attendance, and when they were not dancing, he hoped to follow Bingley's example and spend as much time as possible in conversation with the woman he hoped to win.

A knock at the door interrupted his reverie, and his valet advised him that his presence was awaited in the drawing room. He allowed the valet to retie his cravat, and went down to join the party assembled in the drawing room.

Upon entrance into that room, he took in the scene before him, assessing the situation with his usual care. His aunt, although a guest, seemed in command of the whole room. She was seated in an armchair, sitting stiffly upright, with Anne and Mrs. Jenkinson seated on a settee beside her. Miss Bingley and Mrs. Hurst were seated together on a sofa, and Charles was seated alone on another. Colonel Fitzwilliam was standing by the fireplace, one leg crossing the other as he casually leaned against the mantle, holding a drink in his free hand. Mr. Hurst was inebriated and sitting at a table, nursing his cup.

Darcy greeted the party with politeness and seated himself next to Bingley.

"Nephew," Lady Catherine intoned, "it is a great relief to have finally found you. Much has happened since you left me in London this week past."

Darcy looked at her placidly. "All is well?"

"Not as well as should be." Lady Catherine replied coldly. "As you will recall, I had expected to formally announce your engagement to Anne while we were in town."

"I recall that you had expressed the wish, Aunt." Darcy answered, "But it is a wish that neither Anne nor I share. I told you this when I last saw you." Glancing around the room, it was evident that the only person enjoying the conversation was Colonel Fitzwilliam, who raised his glass in a silent toast, although Miss Bingley was excessively attentive. "This matter can be of no concern to others." Darcy said abruptly, "For what purpose are you in Hertfordshire, Aunt Catherine?"

"What cold greeting is this?" Lady Catherine appeared affronted. "I am here on an urgent matter related to your interests. You are in dire need of counsel, and I, as almost your nearest relation, I am here to provide it."

"Counsel?" Darcy's face was as stone.

"Why yes. Did Richard not tell you? I spoke with him in London but a few days ago." She glared at Colonel Fitzwilliam across the room and addressed him briefly. "What game are you playing at? I will not be treated in this manner!"

"Of course, Richard told me he saw you." Darcy replied. "But why have you come *here*? I am in need of no counsel I assure you. You must have been misinformed."

"Are you not contemplating engagement to another?" Lady Catherine raised an eyebrow threateningly. "I had heard reports in London that you are often seen in company with that lady there." She nodded toward Caroline Bingley.

Darcy stood and approached his aunt. "This is the urgent counsel? To press me on the nature of my acquaintance with Miss Bingley? Aunt Catherine, you have gone to great trouble for nothing."

Lady Catherine looked at Caroline, whose cheeks had turned bright red. "She does not think it is nothing."

"You have my assurance that your concerns regarding Miss Bingley are unfounded. Is there something else I may assist you with? What do you require?" Darcy asked with a hint of impatience, for he was ready to dispatch his aunt's party back to London.

"It is unfortunate that you were not so cooperative when last I saw you, but I am known throughout Kent for making the most of an unfortunate situation. One must do so to be content. It would pay you to heed my advice in this." Lady Catherine blinked her eyes several times, and continued in an imperious tone. "I am fatigued. Please show me to my bedchamber now if you please, to rest before dinner. Anne will do the same."

"What?" asked Mr. Darcy incredulously.

Lady Catherine haughtily replied. "Do not be daft nephew. Your host, Mr. Bingley, has graciously extended an invitation to remain at Netherfield, both as recuperation from our journey, and to enjoy the music and society of the ball to be held on the morrow. You shall dance the first with Anne, of course, before she has tired."

"It is true. They are to stay." Caroline nodded to Darcy as she dispatched a footman to summon the housekeeper, and then addressed the three ladies from Kent. "Your trunks have been delivered to your rooms, Lady Catherine. Mrs. Nicholls will escort you. We dine at six."

"Very fashionable," Lady Catherine muttered as she rose to follow the housekeeper.

Little was said until the newly arrived guests had left the room. Once their footsteps had faded in the distance, a commotion ensued.

"How did this happen?" Darcy turned to Bingley. "This should not be!"

"I do not recall." Bingley replied apologetically. "It all happened so fast. One moment we were making introductions and the very next, she was invited to stay for the ball."

"How did she know there was to be a ball?" Darcy's usual success at suppressing his emotions was in peril.

"The ball is not a secret, Mr. Darcy." Caroline admonished. "Our preparations are too obvious to be mistaken. Having ladies of such distinction at the ball will lend an air of elegance, especially alongside Colonel Fitzwilliam and you, Mr. Darcy. Do you not think so, Louisa?"

"Why yes, although it cannot be compared to an affair in London." Louisa smiled in agreement, and her husband roused for a moment, raised his glass and muttered "elegance" before he laid his head back on the table.

Darcy looked at Caroline as though she had gone mad. "Do you know what you have done?"

"Of course I do, Mr. Darcy. I have made your relations welcome in this house. Would you have it otherwise?" Caroline challenged.

"Of course not." Darcy replied with a frown that implied he would.

"Your aunt arrived with her mind set against me, Mr. Darcy." Caroline continued, "I will do all within my power to change her opinion, and make myself acceptable to her."

Darcy moved to the window, staring out of it, unspeaking for a long time. The others talked among themselves, but eventually, Darcy felt the presence of his cousin at his side.

"We had promised to return to Longbourn this evening, for tea after dinner." Colonel Fitzwilliam opened the conversation, his voice too low to be overheard. "I fear that our plans for tonight have been foiled. Lady Catherine will expect us to remain and entertain her."

Darcy nodded. "You do realize that Miss Bingley knew what she was about, I am sure. She is not oblivious to my interest in Elizabeth Bennet, and she will find a way to turn our aunt's suspicions away from herself and toward Miss Bennet. It was observable in her countenance."

"Caroline Bingley could be a good sort of woman, if someone would but tame her." Fitzwilliam chuckled. "If her fortune were fifty thousand instead of twenty, I would call myself Petruchio and tame her myself. It would be amusing to try, although there is something off about her that makes me think such an attempt would not be without its peril."

Darcy laughed softly. "One day, Fitz, you will strike an idea that has merit. Apparently, today is not that day."

"How is this for an idea? I will ride to Longbourn to personally express our regrets, and be back in time for dinner." Fitzwilliam suggested.

"Good idea, wrong rider!" Darcy replied somewhat forlornly. "We must send Bingley. Mrs. Bennet will forgive him, and the explanation coming from him will be more acceptable since he is formally courting Miss Bennet."

The colonel nodded and within minutes, Mr. Bingley was on his way to Longbourn. It was with a longing, heavy heart that Darcy watched him go.

His only consolation was that tomorrow was the ball. Darcy determined to take his aunt's advice. It was an unfortunate situation that his aunt was to be at the ball, but he would find a way to make the most of it.

Chapter Thirty-Three

THE NETHERFIELD BALL PART ONE

Dawn was a gray, dismal affair the morning of the ball. Dark clouds hung low, obscuring the sun, and the air was heavy, despite occasional gusts of wind that signaled the approach of a storm. Elizabeth rose with the faded light, despite her promise to rest. A distant thunderclap had delivered her from slumber, the sound calling to her as if by name. The panes of her windows rattled against the wind, and she wrapped a blanket tightly around her shoulders when she stood to look out upon the bleak beginning of the day.

'What a contradiction this grim sky is,' she thought, *'to how I feel!'* Exultant anticipation radiated throughout her being at the very thought of the impending ball. Her belief in her own indifference to Mr. Darcy had shattered the previous evening when Mr. Bingley had arrived to express regrets that the Netherfield party would not call at Longbourn that evening after all. Disappointment at the loss of Mr. Darcy's company had burned in her chest so fiercely that it had consumed her mind the whole of the evening. In those hours, the cast of their recent conversations transformed, and she marveled that she had known herself so poorly. She wondered too, if her perceptions of the man she now yearned to see were also skewed.

A faint sound, carried on the wind, broke into her thoughts, and she strained to hear it. It came again, haunting and mysterious. Elizabeth searched the gray world outside her window for some clue to the source. A dark movement in the distance drew her attention as she heard the sound again—the bay of a hound—at the same moment as she saw a lone rider astride a black stallion approaching Longbourn. His pace was unhurried. His seat on the horse was upright and dignified despite the blasts of wind that raged around him. Elizabeth's mind told her it was an illusion, that the intensity of her thoughts had conjured an apparition of Mr. Darcy's appearance in the faint light. She moved closer to the window, her breath frosting the pane as her forehead pressed against the cold glass, peering wistfully at the figure she half expected to vanish at any second.

He did not disappear. He stopped some distance away, his horse prancing lightly in place while Mr. Darcy seemed simply to stare at the house. It was far too early for a social call, but Elizabeth instinctively knew that he was there for her. She hesitated for one suspended second, as her guarded, proper self, warred with the girl who simply wanted to go to him.

Elizabeth dressed swiftly, fearful that he would be gone before she could reach him. She left her hair in its tousled side-plait, and flung on the same hooded cloak as she had worn a few mornings earlier as she raced down the stairs. Soon, she was at the road, although the hedgerows made her blind to the spot where she had seen Mr. Darcy. She ran, holding her hood with one hand, until coming around a bend, she saw him, still soberly looking at Longbourn. She halted abruptly, her eagerness dampened by the look of shock on his face when he saw her.

"Miss Bennet!" He exclaimed. His surprise at her sudden appearance was evident. "This is no sort of day for an early morning walk!"

Elizabeth curtseyed slightly in an attempt to compose herself before she responded. "Nor is it a good sort of morning for a ride, Mr. Darcy, yet here you are."

"Yes." Darcy nodded as he knit his eyebrows in consternation. "Here I am."

"I observed your approach from my window." Elizabeth smiled warmly. "I hope you bear no ill tidings."

"Oh." Darcy shook his head slightly. "No. No ill tidings."

"May I inquire as to why you *are* here, Mr. Darcy?" Elizabeth asked curiously.

"I could not sleep." He shrugged and looked at her with that same intensity as he had on the path from the cottages the day before.

"I am pleased that you are here." Elizabeth said, with a step forward. "I had hoped to speak with you before the ball." He nodded at her, so she continued. "It is about my cousin, Mr. Collins."

"Mr. Collins?" Darcy frowned.

"Yes." Elizabeth said, although a gust of wind carried the word away as her scarlet cloak billowed around her. She quickly pushed it down with both hands as another puff filled the hood with air and swept it off her head.

Darcy's dismount from the saddle was so immediate that he was standing in front of Elizabeth before she had finished wrestling her hood back on, and suddenly, his hands were gently tugging at the sides of the woolen covering, assisting her in the task. Elizabeth colored and muttered, "Thank you." She reached up with one hand to hold the hood in place as Darcy reluctantly released it.

"We must first get you out of the wind." Darcy said, with a nod of his head toward Longbourn. "Then we will speak."

Elizabeth turned and began to walk, her face still warm. Mr. Darcy positioned himself to her side, protecting Elizabeth from the full force of the wind. She felt something touch her hand, and looked down to find Apollo walking at her other side. She extended her fingers to stroke the top of his head and thought to herself with some amusement that she must look a fright, but Mr. Darcy had not seemed to notice it.

Approaching the house, they came alongside the garden wall, where the air was calm. Mr. Darcy stopped walking and turned to look at the windswept beauty before him. "I believe you had something you wished to say, Miss Bennet."

"Oh yes." Elizabeth found herself unable to look directly at him, her earlier boldness now standing on quivering legs. "I wished to speak with you about the ball."

Darcy nodded. "I have been looking forward to our dance with great anticipation."

Elizabeth breathed a sigh of relief that Darcy had broached the topic first. "It is our dance that I must speak of."

Darcy held his breath, fearful that she would decline the promised dance after all.

"I do not wish to be too forward, Mr. Darcy," Elizabeth began, "but I find myself in a difficult situation. My cousin, Mr. Collins, expressed a desire to dance the first set with me." Elizabeth looked to his face at this moment and caught a distinct hardening of his jaw, but she had begun, and was determined to finish. "Although you had not specified the dance, I felt, that having promised myself to you, I could not commit to Mr. Collins."

Darcy could not suppress his delight, and the corners of his mouth turned up ever so slightly. "Where is your difficulty, Miss Bennet?"

"I am afraid that I told Mr. Collins I was to dance the first set with you. I know that this was presumptuous of me, and I am mortified that I must confess this to you, but...," Elizabeth stopped speaking when she felt Mr. Darcy's hand grasp hers and hold it in his own. Her bare fingers curled slightly around his gloved ones in reflex as his thumb firmly folded over her delicate grip on him. Somewhat discomposed, she stared down at where they were joined as a stain of deepest rose crept back to her cheeks.

"It shall be in the first dance, then, that your promise will be fulfilled." His voice was reassuring, and he placed his other hand over the top of hers, so that both of his hands now enclosed it. "Would it be too much to ask," he hesitated and tightened his hold on her. "Miss Bennet, would you do me the honor of dancing the supper set with me tonight as well?"

Elizabeth was astonished and drawing her hand out of his clasp, she looked him directly in the eye and gasped, "Mr. Darcy, you must realize how that would be taken!"

"I do." He replied gravely, although a hint of mischief tugged at one corner of his mouth. "I am most pleased to dance the first with you; however, it leaves me void of anticipation for the remainder of the evening. I will have several other partners between the first dances and the supper set, as will you. It is perfectly proper."

"It is perfect fodder for idle gossip, Mr. Darcy. Speculation and rumor will unavoidably tie our names together, proper or not, should we dance a second set." Elizabeth frowned and shook her head.

"This offends you?" Darcy questioned her with a slightly squinted eye.

"Not at all, but I had thought it would offend you!" Elizabeth raised her chin defensively, even as her thoughts ran wild with his meaning.

"You have my assurance that it does not." Darcy corrected and then pressed her with a charming degree of uncertainty. "What is your answer?"

Elizabeth nodded almost imperceptibly, her eyes locked onto his, searching for understanding as he reached up to position her hood again. "Good." He said softly, his gloved fingertips brushing against her cheek as his hand withdrew.

"I must return to the house." Elizabeth said as she stooped abruptly to pet Apollo, who was sitting at her feet. She wrapped her arms around the animal's neck and murmured, "Goodbye, my dear, sweet Apollo." She stood and found Mr. Darcy's eyes still intently upon her.

"Until tonight, Miss Bennet." Darcy bowed in a formal, gentlemanly gesture of farewell.

"Until tonight, Mr. Darcy." Elizabeth curtseyed and stepped back out to the road, sparing one look over her shoulder before she lowered her head against the wind and hastened back to Longbourn.

The household at Longbourn was much consumed for the better part of the day with their preparations for the festivities of the evening, and Elizabeth found ample time to dress with great care. Her hair, which she generally maintained with simple styles, was formed into a particularly elegant arrangement and adorned with dainty jeweled hair ornaments.

Elizabeth found herself immensely grateful to her aunt Gardiner. The small collection of lovely accessories she owned were mostly gifts from her fashionable aunt. A pair of pearl teardrop earrings and a matching strand of pearls were among the treasures bestowed by her relations when Elizabeth had last visited them in London. They were selected specifically to complement the gold-threaded Indian muslin gown acquired for a dress ball she had attended, together with the fine white kid gloves.

Upon her arrival at Netherfield, Elizabeth spoke briefly to Caroline and Louisa, who were both alarmingly gracious as they welcomed the guests. Mr. Bingley had been standing next to his sisters greeting their guests, but he abandoned the reception line in favor of escorting Jane into the drawing room. He offered his other arm to Elizabeth, and together they went through the doors, where the room had been prepared in stunning splendor for the ball.

Elizabeth began covertly searching for Mr. Darcy. She maintained her movement through the crowded room and had just found her friend Charlotte Lucas when she heard the sound of Mr. Collins' voice calling to her.

"Cousin Elizabeth!"

Elizabeth made a point of introducing Miss Lucas to Mr. Collins, and as soon as they were engaged in a civil dialogue, she excused herself, in fear that Mr. Collins would engage her for a dance, knowing that she could not politely refuse. She approached the end of the room and found Lady Catherine de Bourgh seated regally in a large armchair as if she were holding court. Elizabeth approached her, and with a deep curtsy, expressed her delight that Lady Catherine was in attendance at the ball. This pleased Lady Catherine, who had expected far more attention and deference than she had thus far received. Elizabeth inquired after Miss de Bourgh and, upon learning that Anne was in attendance, excused herself to go in search of her.

Her search for Anne was interrupted by a masculine voice, spoken in her ear from behind.

"Miss Bennet, you look positively ravishing this evening!"

A smile swept pleasantly across Elizabeth's face as she turned to face the owner of the voice. "Colonel Fitzwilliam!"

The colonel took her gloved hand and kissed the back of it in a practiced movement. "Miss Bennet, I ask you, how is a man to remain composed with such a greeting?"

Elizabeth smiled. "You must find a way, Colonel, for the room is full of officers tonight, and you must not be outdone."

"Ah, but I am already outdone. My cousin informed me that he has engaged you for the first set, and I am too late to ask for your hand as the ball is opened. I am a persistent fellow, however, and pray that you will reserve the second set for me." Although he spoke of disappointment, Colonel Fitzwilliam grinned at Elizabeth as if the second set were a grand prize.

"I would be delighted." Elizabeth smiled with pleasure at him before glancing around the room again. "Have you any idea where I may find Miss de Bourgh?"

Colonel Fitzwilliam's brows shot up in surprise at her question. "You have met my cousin?"

"Yes" Elizabeth replied, "but once. I should like very much to renew our acquaintance, however, and was in search of her when you found me."

"Come with me." Richard beckoned her to follow, and they wound their way through the assembling crowd to where Anne was resting on a chair in a quiet corner. Mrs. Jenkinson was seated nearby. He positioned himself somewhat protectively to the side of his cousin upon reaching her. "Anne," he said quietly, "I believe you have already been introduced to Miss Elizabeth Bennet."

To an onlooker, the greeting between the two females would have seemed that of old friends. So great was the delight of Miss de Bourgh at the sight of Elizabeth that her attitude was excited, her greeting, so animated that one could forget for a moment the fragility of her health due to the flush of color in her cheeks and the sparkle in her eyes.

Colonel Fitzwilliam stood by them, his admiration for Elizabeth growing with each moment as she drew shy Anne de Bourgh into easy conversation. Not since her illness had he seen such a thing happen, and he stood in open awe at the scene before him. Several minutes passed thus, and he minded not at all his lack of share in the conversation, so great was his enjoyment of his cousin's pleasure in it.

They would have continued for some time were it not for the cues that the first dance was imminent. "Anne," Richard interrupted, "you have promised the first dance to me, and I believe we must take our places." Anne and Elizabeth looked up to see that Mr. Darcy now stood next to the colonel, having apparently been there, unnoticed, for several minutes.

Darcy held his hand out to Elizabeth. "The hour is at hand, Miss Bennet," he said with a bow. "I have come to claim you."

Elizabeth placed her hand into his to be led to the floor, slightly perturbed at the possessiveness of his declaration. She was, however, secretly pleased at the surprised looks of others in the room to see that she was the chosen partner of the distinguished Mr. Darcy for the opening dance.

She honored him with a curtsey and a smile to begin, and although he only reciprocated with the requisite bow, she was beginning to understand the nuances of his expressions well enough to know he was gratified by her smile. She knew also that the care she had taken in her appearance was not wasted on Mr. Darcy, for there was a look in his eyes that threatened her knees with weakness and her lungs with a forgetting of their function.

She rallied, as the familiar motion of the steps and strains of the music restored her calm, and she relinquished any nervous tendency and instead determined to enjoy the dance. She glanced around her and saw Jane dancing with Bingley, her eyes alight with contentment and happiness. Mary, she noted, was partnered with Mr. Collins, who was bumbling the steps already. Colonel Fitzwilliam was with Anne, who was surprisingly graceful and competent on the floor. Caroline Bingley was standing up with one of the officers, as was Lydia, although Lydia seemed blissful while Caroline seemed resentful in their respective countenances.

Turning her attention back to Mr. Darcy, she found that his eyes had not left her while hers had strayed.

"Mr. Darcy," she said lightly as they passed, "if you are as hungry as you appear to be, there are refreshments to appease you."

"I am not hungry." He denied with a shake of his head, as he gracefully turned and looked quizzically at Elizabeth.

"In that case," she said, as their hands joined briefly, "I beg you not to look as though you would consume me."

Now separated, Darcy could only look at Elizabeth as he contemplated his answer.

When they drew near again, he replied in a whisper barely audible above the music. "Trust your eyes, Miss Bennet."

At this unexpected response, Elizabeth chuckled. "Perhaps we should speak of the dance instead—of the number of couples or how pleasant private balls are compared to public ones."

"Private balls are far more pleasant, it is true, especially when one is particularly acquainted with one's partner." Darcy smiled pleasantly.

"You are very agreeable tonight." Elizabeth commented. "Do you enjoy dancing after all, Mr. Darcy?"

"Not as a rule" he answered as their hands clasped yet again, and this time, he held it longer than the dance called for, requiring Elizabeth to gently tug to break free and get out of step.

"Is your enjoyment gained then, in tormenting me?" she asked when she had caught up with the dance.

"If I torment, it is not to abuse my partner, but rather because I am distracted by her." Darcy replied.

"So I am to blame? That is ungenerous! Will you step on my toes next?" Elizabeth challenged him with a tinkling laugh. "The courtesy of a warning would be best."

"I think," said Darcy with thinly veiled mirth, "that I would prefer to take you by surprise."

The dance separated them once more, and this time it was Elizabeth whose mind raced, searching for a fitting reply. When they drew together once more, their arms crossed and both hands connected as they circled each other in time with the music. Elizabeth waited until they had gone around before she said, as they broke free, "I do not like surprises, Mr. Darcy."

"You will like mine," he replied confidently as they took their place in line.

Elizabeth glanced over at him with some degree of alarm, fearing a reappearance of the conceited man she had first encountered in Hertfordshire several weeks prior. "You are very bold tonight, Mr. Darcy. What assurance do you have that I would welcome surprises from you?"

Darcy made no answer and seemed discomfited by the turn of the conversation.

At that moment, Sir William Lucas came by them, and on seeing Mr. Darcy, he stopped to compliment the couple on their dancing. "This is capital indeed! Such superior dancing is not often seen in the country. It is evident that you belong to the first circles, Sir! Allow me to say, however, that your fair partner does not disgrace you! I must hope to have this pleasure repeated often and soon, perhaps when a certain desirable event shall take place!" Sir William glanced from Elizabeth to Jane and Bingley meaningfully. "What congratulations will then flow in! But you must return to the dance now, Mr. Darcy! You will not thank me for detaining you from the bewitching conversation of Miss Elizabeth for long. Carry on! Carry on!"

Darcy acknowledged the man with a slight bow. "Thank you, Sir William. I do have great hopes of dancing again with Miss Bennet very soon." He glanced up at Jane and Mr. Bingley and his expression softened. "Including, as you say, at a certain desirable event, should it take place."

Sir William crossed the floor, dodging those still engaged in the set, as Elizabeth and Mr. Darcy joined back in the dance.

"I was wrong, Mr. Darcy." Elizabeth said sweetly across her shoulder as they passed, and when he returned, he approached with a skeptical expression, as though he did not believe he had heard it. Elizabeth continued. "Your response to Sir William just now was a great surprise, and you were perfectly right. I did like it ... very much indeed. I find myself in some anticipation of the next surprise, if another is yet in store."

She said this as the first dance of the set concluded, and following some applause for the musicians, the couples lined up for the second.

When Elizabeth looked back up at Mr. Darcy, she found a transformed man, for he was beaming at her unabashedly. She looked first to the right and then to the left to see if there were something in the room that had caused his transformation. Just as the dance began, she realized with sudden clarity that it was her expression of approval that had done it.

This was a revelation of no mean proportion to Elizabeth, for she had not thought that a man of Mr. Darcy's status and position would care for her approval, and she determined to test her discovery forthwith.

"Mr. Darcy, I hope you do not think me bold in saying that Sir William was correct. Your dancing is indeed very fine." Elizabeth commented as they entered the first formation.

Darcy looked oddly at her. "Thank you," he replied, "as is yours."

Elizabeth, her eyes dancing impishly added, "I particularly admire the arrangement of your cravat tonight. It looks very well on you."

Darcy's eyes widened slightly, adding emphasis to the smile already on his face. "I am glad you approve, Miss Bennet."

They passed the next several minutes simply dancing, Elizabeth smiling and lively, and Mr. Darcy unable to remove his eyes from her. Eventually, during a lull in their progression in the set, Elizabeth ventured again.

"Mr. Darcy, may I express to you how fond I am of your dog Apollo? He is truly a delight." Elizabeth's sincerity could not be doubted.

"Apollo is equally fond of you, Miss Bennet." Darcy's eyes registered that he had caught onto her game.

"And Romeo! Such a handsome mount I am sure I had never seen!" Elizabeth added enthusiastically.

"He is a pleasure to ride." Darcy smiled indulgently, waiting for her next statement.

"You have a fine seat on him, Mr. Darcy. His rider is well-matched." Elizabeth was grateful that the dance turned her back to him at that moment, for she felt her face turn warm at her forwardness, and her several steps alone in the progression of the dance allowed her to breathe deeply and reconsider her course. She ceased with her compliments and continued to dance, each step made in perfect grace, each pass by Mr. Darcy marked by a glance upward to his handsome face.

"You do not ride, Miss Bennet?" Darcy asked after several more minutes had passed with only the music to accompany the perfectly synchronized harmony of their motion.

"No, I do not." Elizabeth replied with no apology.

"May I inquire as to why not?" Darcy asked patiently as he rose up on his toes and turned into the next sequence of steps.

"I prefer to walk," Elizabeth said, looking askance as her part in the dance took her near to Mr. Darcy.

"Would you like to learn to ride?" Darcy tipped his head to see her face.

"I have never desired it." Elizabeth turned her head to the side, unwilling to look at him and relieved that the dance moved them apart at that moment.

"Would you allow me to teach you?" Darcy offered.

"I have no suitable mount, Mr. Darcy." Elizabeth replied, "And I hardly think that a man such as you would understand the horror of riding side-saddle."

"I taught Georgiana." Darcy replied.

Elizabeth shook her head. "I do not feel safe on a horse."

"You will be safe with me," Darcy said.

"How many ways must I refuse before you relent?" Elizabeth laughed.

"How many times must I offer before you accept?" Darcy countered with a smile. "It is not in me to back down, Miss Bennet. Once I have set my course, I persist."

"Mr. Darcy, it is my course you are setting, not your own." Elizabeth replied. "It can mean nothing to you if I choose not to ride. Why *do* you persist, sir?"

Her question marked the end of the second dance of the set, and Darcy left it unanswered. He took Elizabeth by the hand and led her from the floor; his reluctance to separate from her was palpable.

"Miss Bennet, I look forward to the supper dance. Please enjoy your evening until then." He bowed, and walked away.

The next set with Colonel Fitzwilliam passed quickly, for he was entertaining and lighthearted, elevating Elizabeth's spirits with each passing moment. The last few minutes of their dance, however, came to an abrupt end, despite the continuation of the music.

"Miss Elizabeth," Colonel Fitzwilliam said, as they skipped with another couple in a circle, "may I ask what it was that rendered Darcy so serious toward the end of your dance with him?"

"He made me an offer I was not prepared to receive, Colonel." Elizabeth answered with a dismissive laugh.

Fitzwilliam's eyes popped with astonishment. "He made you an offer in the middle of a dance? How peculiar! If I may be so bold, what was your reply, Miss Bennet?"

"I refused him, of course. I know my own mind," Elizabeth replied, "although he was most persistent. I believe I would be refusing him still if the dance had not ended."

"I must ask you, Miss Bennet, if there is any hope of persuading you otherwise?" Fitzwilliam's face had drained of all color. "I know my cousin is not always well spoken, but I cannot believe he has no hope of success."

"Do not be alarmed, Colonel. I explained to Mr. Darcy that I never desired it, and although he seemed disappointed, he took it well enough." Elizabeth smiled encouragingly. "Besides, he has asked me to stand up with him for the supper dance, and I suspect that he will press me on the matter again at that time."

"You do not know my cousin, Miss Bennet. Once refused, he will not raise the question again." Colonel Fitzwilliam shook his head sadly.

"That is not what he said to me." Elizabeth replied, shaking her head. "He insisted that he would not back down, but that he would persist in his offer until I accepted."

"He did?" Fitzwilliam shook his head in disbelief. "I know my cousin well, and I assure you that should he once make addresses to a lady, his pride would prevent a second offer if the first was refused."

Elizabeth suddenly stopped dancing and stared, open-mouthed, at the colonel as the color first drained from her cheeks and then was restored to a brilliant hue when the stain of mortification cast a blush upon them.

"Are you unwell?" asked Fitzwilliam, alarmed at the sudden change in his partner. He removed her from the floor, finding a chair upon which he made her sit and drew another chair close for himself. After some several minutes of attention, he found her color turning to normal.

Elizabeth looked around the room to assure herself that no one would overhear their conversation before she began. "Colonel Fitzwilliam, there has been a dreadful misunderstanding."

"I should say so!" Fitzwilliam appeared slightly relieved.

"I must tell you that the offer made tonight by Mr. Darcy was not, as you mistakenly appear to believe, a proposal of marriage." Elizabeth rushed to say it. "He offered to teach me to ride a horse, which offer I did not accept. That is all."

Fitzwilliam closed his eyes, as though in so doing his *faux pas* would vanish. When he opened them, all signs of levity were gone. "Miss Elizabeth, I fear I have done great harm tonight, for I *did* mistake your meaning and, in so doing, have given away that which was not mine to give. I know not how to repair what I have done." His head drooped sadly, and he shook it in disbelief.

He looked across the room to where Darcy was dancing with Caroline Bingley and then back to Elizabeth. "Miss Bennet, my cousin is an exceptional man—the best of men. There is not time to elaborate on this point but only to assure you that it is so. I mistook your meaning because I know that Darcy has come to regard you in a way that transcends casual acquaintance."

"What are you saying?" Elizabeth shook her head, for although she understood the words, she did not comprehend what she was hearing.

"He is never going to forgive me for this." Richard muttered under his breath, "He may never speak to me again." A deep sigh escaped his lips, and he said, "My cousin is in love with you, Miss Elizabeth, deeply, passionately, ardently in love."

Chapter Thirty-Four

THE NETHERFIELD BALL PART TWO

Fitzwilliam Darcy met the final strains of music with relief. It had been a punishment to stand up with Caroline Bingley—a dismal half-hour of marking time to music, made worse by the tantalizing presence of Elizabeth Bennet, her vivacious smiles and witty conversation bestowed on her partner, Colonel Fitzwilliam, in the second set of the evening.

Envy, where he was not the object of it, was a new experience for Mr. Darcy. His only relief from the dull ache it burdened him with had been the two brief interludes in the dance when he and Caroline had been part of a triple that included Elizabeth and Richard. The fleeting series of steps before the progression moved on had been a torment, for too soon Elizabeth had drifted away again to the next triple.

Darcy witnessed the moment when Elizabeth had faltered in the dance from across the room. He had tracked her through the weaving dancers as Richard walked her off the floor and seated himself familiarly next to her. Darcy's feet and arms had continued going through the motions of the dance with Caroline, yet his eyes strayed continually to where his beloved Elizabeth tipped her head toward Richard in animated conversation. They were clearly in one another's confidence, and as the music faded away, both Elizabeth and Richard turned and looked at him.

Richard's face, which Darcy noted for but an instant, was apologetic, but Elizabeth's expression he could not readily understand, although he perceived a profound shift in her countenance. The demure tilt of her head, the shine in her eyes, the almost-smile that played on her slightly parted lips combined with a lingering gaze that nearly brought him to his knees.

"Mr. Darcy." Caroline's voice purred in his ear and brought him out of his reverie. "I believe the dance has come to an end." She snapped open the fan that dangled from her wrist and fluttered it rapidly, just beneath her eyes. With some impatience, Darcy realized that in an uncharacteristic show of bad manners, he had neglected to escort his partner from the floor.

"So it has." He nodded, reluctantly breaking his eyes from the vision that had mesmerized him, and offered Caroline his arm. He delivered her to the table where the refreshments were available between dances as rapidly as he was able.

"Did you hear Mrs. Bennet during our dance, Mr. Darcy? It was shocking!" Caroline sniggered, "But of course you heard her—that voice could shatter glass. Those Bennets are positively medieval!" Caroline said as she raised a cup to her lips. When no reply was forthcoming, Caroline turned to discover Lady Lucas standing where Mr. Darcy had been, eyebrows raised in a manner that left no doubt as to whether she had been overheard.

When Mr. Darcy took Caroline Bingley on his arm after the dance had concluded, Elizabeth Bennet fled. She had whispered a soft "Please, Colonel, I beg you, excuse me," to a distraught Colonel Fitzwilliam. She stood and shrugged with a shake of her head in answer to Jane's quizzical look across the room. Her short residence at Netherfield when Jane had been injured worked to Elizabeth's advantage in navigating the house as she left the noisy, well-lit rooms and sought a place of solitude in the darkened corridor that led to the library.

The library itself was not her destination, but rather a nook by a window near it. A cushioned bench had been fitted to the recess in the wall, and although Elizabeth had not availed herself of the spot previously, she had noted it and instinctively sought it now.

The cool air in the passageway brought sweet relief to Elizabeth's cheeks as she tucked her body into the quiet alcove and stilled herself. The faint strains of the music in the distance added to the serenity of the otherwise quiet corner.

So much had changed, so quickly. She needed to contemplate the meaning of it all and sort, yet again, her feelings. In light of what Colonel Fitzwilliam had said, and she had no reason to doubt his word, her mind was free to allow thoughts she could never before have fully entertained.

The thought of joining with Mr. Darcy in dance had filled her with joyful anticipation only that morning, and knowing that he too was eager for it had increased her expectations of a pleasurable evening. Such a leap as this, though, she had never pondered. She had realized, of course, that he found her interesting and, eventually, that he liked her. She even allowed that he was partial to her, but *love*? Not just a vague inclination, or even a fine, stout love, but a *deep, passionate, ardent love!*

Her heart pounded with the realization that Mr. Darcy had, in fact, attempted to communicate the depth of his regard directly for some days now. Tender moments in his company, conversations that hinted at his admiration, smoldering expressions that caused her stomach to flutter, and all the kindness conveyed in his actions toward her collided in her mind to deliver her to the inevitable conclusion that it must be true. Mr. Darcy loved her.

Do I love him in return? She pressed her fingers against her temples as if the pressure would clear her thoughts and reveal the answer. She felt some urgency to discover it, for when she had looked to the dance floor after Colonel Fitzwilliam's disclosure, her eyes had met those of Mr. Darcy. She had seen in that moment not arrogance or pride but an anguish and vulnerability in his eyes that she never would have supposed was there.

The sound of approaching footsteps prompted Elizabeth to quiet her breathing. She could see a dim pool of light getting nearer and could soon make out a single candle lighting the path of its bearer. She saw the flame rise higher, and a soft voice called out, "Miss Elizabeth?"

Upon hearing her name specifically called, Elizabeth felt obligated to reply. "I am here." A hastening of steps soon brought Anne de Bourgh to stand awkwardly before Elizabeth.

"Miss Eliza, what are you doing here?" Anne asked, "Are you unwell?"

"Oh no," Elizabeth replied, "I am well, or I think that I am. The drawing room was peculiarly warm, so I came here to cool myself—that is all. What brings you to this hallway, Miss de Bourgh?"

"I came in search of you." Anne said, "My cousins were distressed when you disappeared."

"Your cousins?" Elizabeth echoed.

"Yes, my cousins. The tall, handsome men you have been dancing with this evening." Anne laughed quietly.

"Why should my leaving cause distress? I have already danced with both ... I do not understand." Elizabeth shook her head.

Anne set the candle down and sat next to Elizabeth on the bench. "I will tell you if you will return to the ball with me."

"I only stepped away for a few minutes" Elizabeth replied, "I had not quit the ball entirely."

"Indeed, I can see that, but you have foiled their plan nonetheless." Anne smiled.

"Plan?" Elizabeth frowned slightly.

"It would not have been necessary if it were not for my mother." Anne began, "She became insistent about certain expectations for tonight, and my cousins were not pleased nor were they inclined to comply with her demands. For that matter, nor was I." Anne drew in a deep breath. "I believe you are aware that my mother intends that Darcy and I marry."

"I had heard it." Elizabeth acknowledged.

"This idea has poisoned her mind of late. She has become obsessed with it, even though no offer has ever been made, nor is it likely to be. She has forgotten reality and speaks of little else, at least to me. She is determined to see the two estates joined together."

"What is your position?" Elizabeth asked gently.

"I am sick of hearing of it. Darcy is as a brother to me, and the idea of marriage to him feels very wrong. We would both be miserable in such an arrangement, and even if we could get past our unhappiness, I could never provide an heir. Five physicians, three of whom my mother took me to see in London these past weeks, have informed us that my constitution is too weak to carry a child. To attempt it would mean certain death for me."

"Oh no!" Elizabeth cried out, "This is terrible! I am so very sorry to hear this!"

"Do not be sorry for me. I am reconciled to it even if my mother is not." Anne sighed. "She wishes to announce an engagement between myself and Mr. Darcy this very night. Hence, the plan."

"Oh yes, the plan." Elizabeth nodded.

"The plan must necessarily include you, Miss Elizabeth, for in addition to my engagement, my mother has made it clear to Mr. Collins that he is to secure the promise of your hand without any further delay."

"She has?" Elizabeth shook her head. "I cannot understand why Lady Catherine would invest herself in whom I marry, but in this, she must accept disappointment. I am not inclined to receive addresses of that nature from Mr. Collins, should he attempt them."

Anne laughed merrily. "My cousins are unwilling to subject you to the prospect of even one dance with Mr. Collins! As part of the plan, they had recruited Mr. Bingley to dance the third set with you—before you disappeared."

"I never had any idea of slighting Mr. Bingley." Elizabeth sighed with a frown. "That was rather high-handed of your cousins to interfere with my dance partners in such a way. I am perfectly capable of handling even such a partner as Mr. Collins."

"You must not be upset, Miss Elizabeth! Their interference was well meant." Anne cried out in some dismay.

"So this plan—was it merely to prevent Mr. Collins from dancing with me?" Elizabeth inquired curiously.

"Oh no." Anne smiled. "They are also determined to prevent my mother from engaging you in conversation past your initial greeting. Mother already traumatized poor Miss Bingley earlier today. I was not there when mother spoke with her, but Miss Bingley was distraught for several hours afterward. She retired to her quarters, but her unhappy rantings could be heard in the hall for quite some time. My cousins suspect that Miss Bingley may have directed mother's attention toward *you*, Miss Elizabeth."

"I do not understand." Elizabeth shook her head in confusion.

"They believe that Miss Bingley hinted to my mother that Darcy favors you with particular regard. Mother suspected, of course, that Miss Bingley was merely attempting to divert her attention, but after the first set, when she observed you and my cousin on the floor, she must have been convinced. When Colonel Fitzwilliam escorted me to my mother's side, we were both subjected to a vile discourse on your use of 'arts and allurements' to ensnare Darcy's affections during the dance."

"Upon my word!" Elizabeth stood and faced Anne in frustration. "How is it that so many persons openly declare this affection when I hardly know of it myself?"

"I may be speaking out of turn, but, Miss Elizabeth, it is written on your faces." Anne said hesitantly with a sweet reassuring smile. "I have never seen my cousin in such a state as he is in tonight. He has borne a heavy burden for many years and became serious and too sober under its weight. Tonight his countenance is lit, and his eyes are for you alone. Anne searched Elizabeth's face in the dim light. "I do not pretend to know you equally well, but it did appear that you met his attentions with pleasure...."

Elizabeth felt heat rise in her cheeks, and she looked down the hallway toward where the sounds of the ball emanated. "Miss de Bourgh...."

"I am sorry." Anne interrupted, flustered. "I have said too much. You must understand that his happiness is of utmost import to me...."

"I understand" Elizabeth replied sincerely. "I believe it is time we set these things aside and return to the ball. It would not do to distress your cousins further." Elizabeth picked up the candle and offered her arm to Anne. "I would be honored if you would call me 'Elizabeth.' You have most certainly acted as a friend to me tonight."

"And you must call me 'Anne.'" She linked her arm through Elizabeth's elbow. "I have few friends, Elizabeth. I am most gratified to count you among them."

When Darcy saw Elizabeth return to the drawing room, arm-in-arm with Anne de Bourgh, he was filled with relief. The sight of the two women, talking and laughing, seemingly oblivious to all others, seemed nearly a miracle. When Anne had insisted that she should be the one to search for Elizabeth, Darcy only agreed on the grounds of propriety. His doubts had been profound, and he had spent the better part of twenty minutes ruing the decision, wishing he had gone to find her himself. Now, seeing how easy Anne was with Elizabeth, his thoughts naturally turned to his sister. He was certain that if Elizabeth had so easily drawn out Anne, she would do the same with Georgiana. An overwhelming contentment came over him, as it seemed that his decision in favor of Elizabeth Bennet was reaffirmed at every turn.

The fourth set of the evening found Mr. Darcy paired with Jane Bennet, as he had engaged her for a dance on the same night as he had extracted the promise from Elizabeth. Mr. Bingley, a most amiable partner, took Elizabeth to the floor for the set, and Colonel Fitzwilliam found a willing partner in Miss Catherine Bennet. Mr. Collins, having failed to reach Elizabeth in time to procure her hand for the dance, approached Charlotte Lucas instead and was rewarded with a pleasant partner as well.

The spectators were no less occupied. Lady Catherine, in particular, watched both Mr. Darcy and Elizabeth Bennet with rabid interest. Although they were not paired for the dance, their glances strayed often toward each other—often enough to displease his aunt immensely. Anne de Bourgh also observed the dancers from a seat near her mother, smiling blissfully each time her mother frowned. In spite of this, the dance was otherwise uneventful, and the half-hour of the set passed quickly.

It was not quickly enough for Mr. Darcy, however. The supper dances were to follow, and he longed to stand up with Elizabeth once more. That she would be seated next to him for supper following the set was almost more anticipation than he could bear. His pulse raced every time she drew near, and each look they shared bestowed his imagination with fresh fuel.

At the conclusion of the set, Darcy and Bingley, anxious to restore themselves to the partners of their preference, chose a course that intersected with the other on the floor, affecting an early exchange in their companion. This act thwarted Mr. Collins' intention to approach Elizabeth in another attempt to gain her hand for a dance. Having now danced with his cousins Mary, Lydia and Kitty as well as with Charlotte Lucas, he was faced with the dilemma of either standing down for the set or selecting from among his previous partners. Since he had no introduction to any other young ladies in the room except Anne de Bourgh, he was limited in his choices. He did not dare risk Lady Catherine's wrath by asking Anne to dance and could not dance with Charlotte again so soon, so he (hoping to impress Elizabeth with his stamina) opted to engage Mary again, for the supper set.

After a brief rest period, where light refreshment was imbibed and light conversation enjoyed as well, the dancers returned to the floor.

Mr. Darcy, standing across from Elizabeth as the couples lined up, was aquiver with an expectation of an encounter at least as agreeable as the previous dance, and he hoped even more so. She was a vision of ethereal beauty. The golden threads woven into her gown shimmered in the flickering candlelight as the gauzy frock floated around her shapely, slender form. The jewels in her hair also caught the light, in vivid contrast to the deep brown locks that held them, and the delicate pearls that encircled her neck perfectly framed the tantalizing hollow at the base of it. Darcy imagined that he could detect her quickened pulse in that notch, and his fingers tingled with the temptation to reach out and touch the velvety spot animated by Elizabeth's beating heart.

Elizabeth regarded her partner amid conflicting emotions. The knowledge that she had gained, that Mr. Darcy loved her, affected her deeply, and although she had enjoyed conversing with Anne, it had come at the expense of her opportunity for quiet introspection. Now, standing before him, Elizabeth was highly aware that beneath the composed exterior of Mr. Darcy's face, there raged a passion for her that she had neither considered nor understood. The thought of it was daunting, and yet she felt her courage rise within her—she was equal to it, she knew, and Darcy's declaration, *You will be safe with me.* repeated in her mind as an assurance that indeed, regardless of the depth of his emotions, she had nothing to fear in his company.

The music began, and from the moment of her profound curtsey, Elizabeth danced *for* Mr. Darcy. Not with the air of submission or seduction, but rather, she carried herself as one who felt cherished and desired to nurture and explore the feelings it inspired in her.

Several minutes passed with no spoken word passing between them, and yet, there seemed to each as though an unseen cord connected them, a tether that grew painful and taut when the dance drew them apart, and which softened and became less insistent when proximity slackened its grip. The intensity of this eventually became too much for Elizabeth, and she broke the silence by commenting on the general splendor that the Bingleys had effected on Netherfield for the ball.

Darcy, unwilling to release what was for him akin to an enchanted moment, replied with his agreement of her observation and fell silent.

A minute later, Elizabeth resumed the conversation with serenity. "It is *your* turn to say something now, Mr. Darcy. I commented on the beauty that surrounds us, now you might say something of...."

"The beauty that is before me?" Darcy interrupted, his expression neutral.

Elizabeth offered him a faint smile for the compliment. "That is not what I meant at all, Mr. Darcy. I would thank you not to tease me, or I might miss the steps of the dance and embarrass my partner."

"That would be impossible," Darcy replied, repaying her smile with one to match it.

"Oh, I assure you that I could very well confuse the dance should I become distracted," Elizabeth replied, her eyes twinkling as she turned away from Darcy in the dance.

"But you would not embarrass me in so doing—that is the material point." Darcy countered when she returned.

"Perhaps, in this I should test you," Elizabeth said archly as the steps brought her near to him.

"I would not perjure myself, but a test from you would not be unwelcome, should you desire it," Darcy said evenly as their distance grew again.

Elizabeth laughed at him across the floor. "Mr. Darcy, I could scarcely arrive at a challenge equal to your abilities. Besides, I still await the fulfillment of a certain promise you made but yesterday. We can count that as a test if you like. If you manage that one, I will devise some amusing quest for you to try your hand at next."

The dancers formed into a row, and Elizabeth and Darcy walked side by side, their hands joined at their sides. "I have already fulfilled it, and merely await your discovery of my efforts to learn if it will suffice." Darcy said with a grin, unseen by Elizabeth. "What quest would you devise, I wonder?"

"Not so fast, sir!" Elizabeth said as they turned to face each other, "If you have already done it, how am I to discover it?"

"I believe the usual mode would be with your eyes." Darcy said indulgently.

Elizabeth immediately looked at Caroline Bingley, whose turban was adorned with a fluffy, white ostrich feather. She peered at Louisa next, who wore no feathers at all. She scanned the room and could not detect it. "Am I to understand that the feather is in this room?" Elizabeth clarified.

"No." Darcy replied. "The feather you gave me is out of sight. However, a number of identical plumes are indeed in this very room, placed by my hand."

"And they will make me laugh?" Elizabeth beamed, delighted at the thought.

"That is my hope, Miss Bennet, since you love to laugh so dearly." Mr. Darcy smiled warmly. "I have grown fond of hearing you laugh, so we both shall be rewarded when you detect it."

The color rose in her cheeks at this, for it occurred to her how very much it pleased her that proud Mr. Darcy had gone to the trouble of concocting something ridiculous, simply to hear her laugh at it. She directed her attention, aside from keeping time with the dance, to searching out the room for the feathers. She would not beg him for a hint, although she was sorely tempted to.

She first checked the heads, jackets and gowns of all she could see and then examined the floral pieces for any sign of pheasant tail-feathers in the arrangement. Her eyes tracked along the moldings and scanned the hanging portraits and their frames. No sign of the token appeared to her eye. The longer she looked, the more it seemed to please Darcy. Then she saw Colonel Fitzwilliam watching her and knew in an instant that he understood exactly what she was seeking.

In the brief interval between the first and second dances of the set, she approached the colonel and suggested that he ought to offer her a clue, since he was obviously an accomplice. He glanced over Elizabeth's shoulder where Darcy stood a short distance away, watching them converse.

"My cousin would very likely object, Miss Elizabeth, to my giving it away." The colonel informed her but added with a smirk, "Which is why I believe I shall. I have already divulged one of his secrets tonight; I might as well sink the ship entirely."

"Remind me never to trust you with any of my secrets, Colonel. You are far and away too free with them." Elizabeth teased.

"You may be right, Miss Elizabeth. I am told—mostly by Darcy—that my discretion is wanting, but in this, I can see no harm. I will only plant the idea, and you must puzzle it out. That is fair, and then Darcy cannot accuse me of giving it away." The colonel lowered his voice to a conspiratorial whisper. "The answer is 'man'. Recall the riddle and the location of the treasure you seek will reveal itself."

"I should never have accused you of being too free with secrets, Colonel! That does not help me at all." Elizabeth pouted prettily. "Can you not give me a better hint than that?"

"Enough, Richard." Darcy spoke from behind Elizabeth. "The dance resumes in a moment, and I require Miss Bennet's hand for it. We must return to the floor." He gently took Elizabeth's hand and led to where the couples were lining up for the second dance.

"How long were you standing behind me, Mr. Darcy?" Elizabeth asked as they took their places.

"Long enough to know what you were about, Miss Bennet." Darcy chuckled. "Have you any idea of the clue Richard gave you?"

"It seems familiar somehow, but I have not yet sorted it out. Pray, would you care to enlighten me?" Elizabeth bestowed her most charming smile on Mr. Darcy.

"I would by no means suspend any pleasure of yours," Darcy said kindly as he bowed for the beginning of the dance.

"You must suppose that I take pleasure in solving mysteries," Elizabeth replied in consternation. "In this case, I do not have enough information to arrive at the answer."

"But you do," Darcy said confidently.

Elizabeth pursed her lips at this reply, and they fell into silence yet again. The particular dance in which they were engaged was complex, and she was content with no conversation, since this enabled her to resume the examination of her feelings. The more she thought on them, the more she found herself shedding her first impressions of the man in favor of the man she knew from their more recent encounters. While the first was proud and arrogant, too elegant and too critical for her liking, she now knew him to be a man of great reserve and dignity. He was intelligent and thoughtful, and although she had not expected it, there was even some humor in him that she had missed at first. His manners had changed very little, and, yet, in knowing Mr. Darcy better, her opinion of him was improving. Although she could not yet concede that she loved him, it was clear to Elizabeth that she had grown to like him very much. She wondered how she would know, should it ever happen, if her feelings crossed into love.

"I have it!" she suddenly cried out as the elusive answer suddenly appeared in her mind, startling Mr. Darcy and several of the couples around them.

"Do you?" Darcy seemed pleased.

Elizabeth craned her neck toward the entryway to the drawing room, but too many stood in the way, and she could not see the object she sought. "I do, I am certain of it," Elizabeth replied. "I find that my studies of the Greek tragedies were not for naught. 'Man' is the answer to the famous *riddle of the Sphinx*!"

"So it is." Darcy smiled again.

"Mr. Bingley has a bronze statue of the Sphinx at the threshold of this very room!" Elizabeth declared triumphantly, attempting to spot it yet again while still maintaining her part in the dance.

"Yes, Miss Bennet, he does." Darcy said blandly. "Would it please you to examine it?"

"Very much." Elizabeth nodded, and when the strains of the dance wound to a close, Darcy and Elizabeth went together to the entryway, where Elizabeth found, to her great amusement, that the figure of the Sphinx was adorned with a freshly made pheasant tail-feather headdress. Her dainty laughter rang out on that end of the hall, attracting the eye of all within hearing distance.

Mr. Darcy offered her his arm with gentlemanly charm, and Elizabeth took it gracefully as Darcy explained, "Now that you have had your laugh, Miss Bennet, it is time for supper."

The young couple walked amiably together to the dining room as many eyes followed their progress. The intimacy of their attitude could not be mistaken—all who were present saw the same, and while there were some who were pleased and happy for the young couple, there were others who set it in their minds at that moment that they must be separated as quickly as possible.

Chapter Thirty-Five

THE NETHERFIELD BALL PART THREE

Walking to the supper room on Mr. Darcy's arm, Elizabeth found herself suddenly aware of the great immensity of the man and of the physical power exuded by his person. She felt a passing moment of lightheadedness, and her grip tightened in an effort to steady herself. This was answered by a slight flexing on his part, which response was unseen, of course, to others, but which served to reinforce Elizabeth's own notice of the potent effect the contact had on her.

Elizabeth was soon seated with Mr. Darcy on her right and Colonel Fitzwilliam on her left. Jane and Mr. Bingley were across the table from Elizabeth, and so evident were Mr. Bingley's besotted attentions to Jane that Elizabeth was quickly under the conviction that an engagement was imminent. Mrs. Bennet, who had concluded the same, was freely declaring her great anticipation of the nuptials to Lady Lucas.

Lady Catherine, who was seated with Anne not far from Mrs. Bennet, was openly shocked at the mercenary tendencies shown by Mrs. Bennet, who enthusiastically spouted self-gratulatory effusions of the inevitable matches of Lydia and Kitty and perhaps even Mary to other rich men they would meet through the connection of the wealthy Mr. Bingley. Elizabeth, she loudly explained, was soon to be engaged to Mr. Collins, which match was the best *that* daughter could hope for, and certainly good enough for her—she was unlikely to recommend herself to one like Mr. Bingley as Jane had.

As her mother's conversation became louder, Elizabeth's mortification grew, for it was clear that all within earshot of Mrs. Bennet, including Mr. Darcy and the colonel, were riveted by every word. Elizabeth detected with dismay an increasing gravity on the part of both gentlemen as they listened to her mother. With her hands under the table, she nervously unbuttoned the opening on her mousquetaire-style gloves and tucked the finger portions in, so that she would not soil them when she ate. She fixed her eyes on her white soup and gave great attention to it, grateful that at least Mr. Bingley and Jane were oblivious to all that went on around them and therefore spared the vexation that was attached to overhearing such a speech.

The room, she noted, was a trifle warm, and consumption of the soup increased this sensation to a degree that Elizabeth soon felt a dampness on her neck. She longed to return to the cool corridor by the library. She set down her spoon and determined to wait for the soup to cool before she returned to it. With no soup to hold her attention, and unable to bear the embarrassment any longer, she engaged the colonel in conversation.

"Colonel," said she, "I have been wondering what part you played in that great joke with the feathers, since you knew enough to point me to it."

"Miss Elizabeth, I have spent my cousin's patience for speaking out of turn today, so you must direct your inquiry to him, lest it come to blows." Richard chuckled. "Although I do confess to being more skilled with glue than he, in the execution of his scheme."

"Perhaps," Elizabeth smiled teasingly, "if you tire of a military career, you should consider millinery, or haberdashery, where your talents with the placement of feathers would do you credit."

At this, the colonel laughed loudly, drawing the attention of Mr. Darcy to their conversation. The three conversed quietly with each other, and Elizabeth was soon enamored with the ease with which Colonel Fitzwilliam extracted amiable and pleasing dialogue from Mr. Darcy. She found herself charmed first on the right hand, and then on the left, as the two men vied for the honor of her soft laughter and witty conversation.

Lady Catherine, seated at sufficient distance that she could not overhear what they were saying, was perfectly able to observe the nature of their interaction and made no attempt to suppress her displeasure at the slight to Anne, who had not even been taken to the floor by Mr. Darcy in the course of the evening. Anne, however, was perfectly pleased to watch the pleasant discourse between her cousins and Elizabeth Bennet from her place at the table.

Lady Catherine soon found an ally in that same woman she had upbraided so thoroughly earlier in the day. Having now witnessed several instances of the favor Miss Bennet was shown by Mr. Darcy, Lady Catherine determined to engage Caroline Bingley in her task of diverting Mr. Darcy's attentions away from his charming companion.

Caroline had to but whisper in Charles' ear to encourage her brother to open the night's entertainments, for many a young lady had come prepared to exhibit their talents on the pianoforte should the opportunity arise. The first to rise to the occasion was Mary Bennet, who, having brought several pieces of music, which she conveniently had with her at dinner, leapt to her feet and hastened to the instrument as soon as Mr. Bingley made the invitation.

Elizabeth braced herself for the worst. Mary, whose skill on the pianoforte was admirable, was not blessed with an equal gift for song. The air she chose to perform was, however, remarkably suited to her voice, and when she was done, the applause, although not exactly enthusiastic, was sufficient encouragement for Mary to launch into a second number. Elizabeth stiffened and tried to catch her father's eye, hoping for some intervention before Mary exposed herself to ridicule. Her father smiled at her and winked when she saw it, and Elizabeth took her napkin into her lap and wrung it desperately, to relieve her anxiety over Mary's display. Suddenly, she felt a warm hand lightly touch her fingers, and she immediately knew it to be Mr. Darcy who had reached out to still her—under the table and unseen by anyone. She glanced up at him, and he pressed his lips together in such a way as to resemble a smile without actually being one. It was, however, the unwavering warmth in his eyes that reassured her, and she was able to endure the remaining part of the number quite well. When Mary was finished, the hand withdrew, the moment passed, and Elizabeth, who had been astonished at the boldness of the gesture at first, keenly felt the loss of his comforting touch when it was gone.

Mr. Bingley promptly suggested that Mrs. Hurst play while Miss Bingley sang. Their performance was so superior to the one that had preceded it that the discrepancy could not be missed by anyone. Elizabeth could not help but notice that the operatic song Caroline sang with great affectation was also bold and flirtatious. Miss Bingley unabashedly looked at Mr. Darcy with great intent as she sang, and Elizabeth was forced to turn away in vicarious mortification at the spectacle.

She once again noted the warmth of the room, and felt a trickle of dampness form on her brow. She drew out her handkerchief and discretely swabbed the droplet away. Mr. Darcy smiled at the appearance of the lace-trimmed cloth, but the smile soon faded as he realized that in the hour they had been seated, the color in Elizabeth's cheeks had deepened while the rest of her complexion seemed to have paled. Several of the wispy curls that had escaped from her hairstyle were clinging to her glistening forehead, held there by a thin, dewy film of moisture.

As Caroline finished, Charles turned to Elizabeth and invited her to perform next. Although Elizabeth had not prepared for such an opportunity, she felt bound to repair the damage done to the Bennet name by Mary. As there were several of her favorite numbers which she had committed to memory, she nodded and rose from her seat.

As she stood, she wondered that she had not noticed the peculiar effect of the lighting in the room before, for there were several peculiar spots that seemed to float in the air—they were dark, almost black. They expanded rapidly in her view and as they did, Elizabeth felt a strange recurrence of the lightheadedness she had encountered when entering the supper room. That same unsteadiness which had afflicted her in that moment caused her to sway as she took her first step from her chair. The blackness came before she knew that her legs had failed her, and she fainted like a rock into the arms of Mr. Darcy.

Chapter Thirty-Six

THE END OF THE BALL

Mr. Darcy relived the moment a thousand times in the hours that followed, when Elizabeth had swayed and then dropped, nearly to the floor. It was instinct that he had reached for her, and in the fleeting moment that her fallen form had lain, limp and lifeless in his arms, he knew a moment of desperation that penetrated him to the core. Time had seemed suspended as an unnatural silence enveloped the room. Those who were near to them gathered around, looming over them in a tight circle. Chaos then ensued in a cacophony of voices that surrounded them on every side.

Mrs. Bennet wailed—her unrestrained declarations of Elizabeth's imminent demise were the first sound to be heard in what rapidly became a chorus of conflicting reactions. Mr. Bennet was clamoring to make his way around the table, calling loudly to Mr. Darcy to unhand his daughter as he pushed past people and tripped on chairs. Mr. Collins began a stern diatribe on the evils of overindulgence in wine by the gentle-born young lady in social settings such as a ball. Lady Catherine's strident voice could be heard above the din, accusing Elizabeth of shamelessly swooning as a willful bid for Darcy's attention. Jane stood, looking over the table at her sister as she cried out helplessly, "Lizzy! Lizzy!" Mr. Bingley was instructing the footmen to bring a chaise to the adjoining salon, while Miss Bingley and Mrs. Hurst were indiscreetly proclaiming their shock at

Elizabeth's wanton display. Mr. Hurst complained loudly about the disruption to his dinner, and Anne de Bourgh began softly crying. Mary quietly asked whether it was advisable that she should perform again, since Lizzy was not able to do it.

It was at this moment that a slightly drunken Lydia skipped into the room, holding some indiscernible item aloft. She was trailed by Kitty. Three officers pursued them, including Mr. Denny, who was calling out in a temper, "Give that back!" Lydia stopped suddenly, having nearly tripped over her fallen sister. "Whatever is Lizzy doing on the floor?" she asked incredulously, as the parties behind her collided into her back, nearly knocking her down on top of Elizabeth. When no one answered her directly, she said, "La! What a joke! I wonder that I did not think of it first. I imagine I would have a dozen officers coming to my aid should I have swooned!" She giggled, and turned around to run the way she had come, crashing into the others briefly before she twirled and danced out of the room, calling "If you want it back, Denny, you must catch me first!"

To all of this commotion, Darcy was nearly oblivious as he clung to Elizabeth. His lips were nearly in her hair as he attempted to shift her weight so he could raise her from the near-prone position with no harm to her, and no one but the unconscious maiden in his arms was near enough to hear the whispered endearments he used as he called her to awaken. At what seemed to him an interminable length of time, (but was in fact no more than a moment) Elizabeth's lashes fluttered, and he felt her stiffen as consciousness returned. She drew in a deep breath, nearly gasping for air to fill her lungs.

Colonel Fitzwilliam bent and began to lift Elizabeth from the other side, as Mr. Bennet arrived at the spot and aided in raising her from behind. As soon as she was upright, the men released her, and Darcy was obliged to steady and support her once again as she wobbled on legs suddenly weak.

Mr. Bennet, on seeing this, stepped forward and removed his daughter from the gentleman's grasp, whereupon he assisted Elizabeth alone into the next room, jealously guarding her against additional aid from either Mr. Darcy or Colonel Fitzwilliam. The footmen had arrived with the chaise and placed it at Bingley's direction near the fireplace. Elizabeth was set down upon it, despite her feeble protests that she was well. She was not well, however, and after her attempt to rise up resulted in another near collapse, she agreed, at her father's insistence, to recline on the lounge.

Mr. Bennet closed the doors to the salon and conferred with Bingley and Darcy on what must be done. Bingley's distress was severe as he bemoaned that the only bedchamber not currently in use by residents or guests of Netherfield was the nursery, and it was filled with unused furnishings at present and not nearly ready for use as a sick room.

Loud evidence of Mrs. Bennet's nervous condition suddenly filled the room as Jane entered with a glass of negus and a napkin. Thankfully, the sound faded again when the door closed behind her. She moistened the cloth and pressed the cool compress gently against Elizabeth's forehead and cheeks as she soothed her sister, and encouraged her to sip from the cup.

For her part, Elizabeth's fevered mind was beginning to comprehend what had occurred, and her mortification at the knowledge was acute. Coupled with the debilitating nature of the symptoms that had overtaken her, she keenly felt her inability to demonstrate her fitness, or even to object to decisions being made for her without so much as offering a choice or asking her approval.

Had she been in a state to do so, she would have insisted on being heard, but it was difficult to keep her eyes open or to speak, and soon she involuntarily dozed under Jane's ministrations.

At length, a knock on the door was followed by the entrance of Colonel Fitzwilliam, who had come to inquire after Elizabeth on behalf of her mother. It was now evident that Elizabeth was gravely ill with a fever. The colonel felt for her pulse and declaring it to be dangerously low and rapid, insisted that they send for the apothecary as a matter of urgency. When Mr. Bingley explained the dilemma of the lack of a bedchamber for Elizabeth, Colonel Fitzwilliam immediately volunteered to vacate the room he was lodged in to accommodate her.

Mr. Darcy began to challenge him for the honor, but a glance at Mr. Bennet silenced him, for there was a ferocious look in his eye that brooked no argument—his favorite daughter would *not* be nursed at Netherfield.

The colonel excused himself to return to Mrs. Bennet, and as he opened the door, Mr. Collins stood in his way, with an evident expectation of gaining entrance to the salon.

"Excuse me," said the parson with a sanctimonious tone, "I have come to ascertain the condition of my cousin's daughter and to console with her in her hour of need, for indeed, a swoon is a most distressing event, and I am certain that my presence would offer her welcome comfort and serenity of mind." He tried to step past Colonel Fitzwilliam, but the colonel did not allow him passage.

"She is unwell," Colonel Fitzwilliam said. "It would be best for her to rest. Her sister is caring for her at present, and she is well attended."

"You do not understand," Mr. Collins countered, his face reddening at the rebuff. "On the morrow, I intend to offer for her hand and in this have been encouraged by her most excellent mother and my noble patroness, your very own aunt, Lady Catherine de Bourgh. Under this certainty of intention, it is imperative that I am at the side of the companion of my future life in such an hour as this. It is my right and my obligation."

"Mr. Collins," the colonel replied patiently, "I mean no disrespect, but you are not betrothed to Miss Elizabeth at this hour, and therefore not entitled to the access you seek. She is not to be disturbed."

"Fitzwilliam!" Lady Catherine appeared suddenly behind Collins and pushed her way past the parson without ceremony. "What is this? What goes on in this room, Nephew? Am I to understand that the young lady has taken ill?"

"You are correct, Aunt. She is indeed ill." Fitzwilliam nodded, as he continued protectively blocking entrance to the salon.

"This is highly irregular!" Lady Catherine's temper began to rise. "How dare she risk Anne's health in such a thoughtless and callous manner? This is not to be borne! She must be removed from this house at once! What is being done? Has her carriage been called for?" She fired the questions off without waiting for any response. "You must remain as far away from her as possible. I know of these things! Where is Darcy?" She tried to peer past the colonel into the room. "That young lady must be dispatched this very hour!"

The colonel stepped forward, forcing his aunt to take a step back, allowing him to close the door firmly behind himself. "Arrangements are being made, Aunt. We must not interfere."

Lady Catherine sniffed. "Anne and I shall not stay at the ball! Advise Mr. Bingley that we have gone to our rooms and shall most certainly not return to the lower floors of this house until tomorrow noon, providing that Miss Bennet is no longer on the premises. I will not risk Anne!" She turned on her heel, and beckoning to a reluctant but obedient Anne, they quit the ball.

࿐

With Elizabeth removed to the salon, the ball proceeded for most of the guests. For those who had not seen it, it seemed as if nothing had happened at all, although the amiable and solicitous host was notably absent from the festivities, along with Mr. Bennet, Jane, Darcy and Colonel Fitzwilliam.

Mr. Bingley strove mightily and unsuccessfully to convince Mr. Bennet to allow Elizabeth to stay at Netherfield, as her condition was deteriorating rapidly. The apothecary, Mr. Jones, eventually arrived and settled the argument, for he declared that she was not fit to be moved farther than to a bed in the same house. He declared her to be in great danger from a putrid infection that would be made worse by the cold air that would certainly be encountered should they attempt to transport her on a winter night. Jones consoled them with assurances that her youth and strength of constitution would work in her favor; with proper care, she would likely recover completely.

In hushed tones so as not to disturb her, the two cousins resumed the debate over which would sacrifice their apartment to make room for Elizabeth. Although Colonel Fitzwilliam was formidable on the battlefield, his tenacity was no match for the determination of Mr. Darcy, and the housekeeper was ordered to ready Mr. Darcy's suite for its new occupant with all haste. This exercise was watched with a degree of severity by Mr. Bennet, for whether he perceived it or imagined it, he nonetheless observed a significant attachment to his daughter in the chivalry of the men and had the fleeting thought that he would be wise to guard the door of her room. It was only fleeting, however, for he rapidly concluded that it would be too much trouble to execute such a precaution. Moreover, as these were respectable gentlemen, surely it was unnecessary.

Elizabeth, in the meantime, fell into a fitful, nearly delirious slumber. As her angelic sister Jane did her best to make her comfortable. Jane gently removed her necklace and earrings, then took the pins and ornaments from her hair, combed the locks with her fingers and twisted them into a loose braid.

When the housekeeping staff announced that the room had been made ready, the cousins once again were at odds. Neither Mr. Bingley nor Mr. Bennet possessed sufficient strength to carry an adult lady up the stairs, and none were inclined to entrust the task to the footmen. The remaining candidates for the transport were therefore Mr. Darcy and Colonel Fitzwilliam. After some quiet, yet animated, discussion between the two in the corner, Darcy approached Mr. Bennet and offered to carry Elizabeth upstairs under close observation by her father, lest any question of impropriety be raised. Mr. Bennet reluctantly conceded, his concern for Elizabeth overruling any concern about appearances.

Darcy slipped his arms beneath Elizabeth and lifted, cradling her against his chest, as Bingley opened a side-door that led to the stairway. Mr. Bennet followed immediately behind. Jane too followed, for she was to stay and offer the same service to Elizabeth that her sister had performed for her one month earlier in the same household.

Darcy was outwardly calm, his face inscrutable as he rapidly made his way down the hall and up the stairs, trailed by her worried father and sister, but what thoughts were racing through his mind! The heat of her fever could be felt through all their layers of clothing, particularly where her head pressed against him. He looked downward and saw rivulets of perspiration trailing slowly down her forehead, and he knew that her danger from the fever was significant. He could feel, too, her heartbeat, fluttering and racing as though paced by a hummingbird's wings. He remembered the same from when Anne had contracted the fever that had stolen her health. A grim, dark spirit of fear nearly overtook him, but he rallied. *Elizabeth is strong,* he told himself. *She will not be weakened as Anne was.*

When Darcy placed her on the bed, the faded impressions of a hundred forgotten dreams pressed hard upon him. This was not the vibrant Elizabeth of those dreams, and yet carrying her in his arms up the stairs, her breath warming his breast, her body nestled against his stirred a visceral response. The very act of lowering her into his bed excited strange feelings of tenderness, protectiveness and longing that he knew must not be revealed to anyone, lest by his thoughts alone she would somehow be compromised.

He stood and excused himself from the room with the civility of a stranger, leaving her to the care of her father, sister and the apothecary. In his heart and mind was a vow that never again would he be obliged to leave her side at such a time; although he was not at liberty to declare it, he knew, truly knew, that *she needed him.*

The remaining hours of darkness had been an ordeal for Jane. After the men had quit the room, Jane removed Elizabeth's gown, gloves and slippers and worked relentlessly to cool the fever that raged in her sister.

Elizabeth moaned, muttered and mumbled as she tossed weakly in the bed throughout the night. Jane could not distinguish most of what her sister said, but one truth was evident. Descended into the confused dream-state of delirium, Elizabeth was obsessed with Mr. Darcy. She spoke unintelligible words meant for him, she grumbled about him, and, most confusing to Jane, she called out for him with alarming frequency.

Had they been at Longbourn, Jane fretted, this would be easily concealed. At Netherfield, however, discretion with such a secret would be impossible to ensure, for as soon as a servant or visitor observed her and heard her speak, it could not be kept from anyone. Although it was a simple matter to excuse the words as coming from a fevered mind, it was also evident to Jane that the foundation of these ramblings was, in fact, solidly laid.

Jane locked the bedroom door, lest anyone enter and unwittingly find Elizabeth undressed or, even worse, discover her secret, for as Jane thought upon the constitution of the household at present, there was but one she felt she could trust with it. She hoped that Mr. Bingley would come to speak with her soon, for she was certain that he would know what to do. He would know how to protect Elizabeth from his sisters and from Lady Catherine and her daughter. Jane hardly believed them capable of malice, but she knew that Elizabeth would object if they were aware of what she indelicately uttered in an unguarded state.

If Elizabeth would not wish those ladies to know of it, how much less would she wish for Mr. Darcy and Colonel Fitzwilliam to hear of it? How was she to safeguard her sister's dignity alone? Bingley would be discrete, she thought, and she needed an ally in the house. She would seek his counsel at first light.

Mr. Darcy had returned to the ball. The only persons remaining were in the card room, constituting mostly officers from the militia, and a few local families, including the Bennets. Mrs. Bennet was excessively displeased that Jane had not been able to dance again with Bingley and that Elizabeth was to stay at Netherfield. She had no comprehension of the severity of her daughter's condition, and seemed to think it nothing at all that Elizabeth would have a 'little fever.'

The person most distressed at Elizabeth's unscheduled removal from Longbourn, however, was Mr. Collins, who, having given up at playing cards, sat forlornly in the drawing room with Mary, who was doing her best to cheer him with assurances that this adversity would strengthen them and that the lesson to guard one's health must be learned by all. Faith, she told him, must be the order of the day.

Darcy wandered back to the dinner room, which had been cleaned and restored to its normal order. He then returned to the adjoining salon, which had not been disturbed since he had taken Elizabeth upstairs. Closing the door behind him, he went in and sat upon the chaise where she had rested, placing his head in his hands in a tormented moment of despair. It was then, with his head hanging low, that he saw it on the floor. That little white cloth he had last seen clasped in her hand before she had fainted had been lost by its owner and delivered yet again to his hand. He unfolded the crumpled handkerchief and spread it out on his leg.

The last time he had spoken to Elizabeth of it, he had hoped for her to tell him that the design had been purposeful, that she had sewn the initials E.D. intentionally, but tonight, looking at it with an honest eye, he knew that she had not. No, Elizabeth had not consciously crafted it as a fond hope sent into the ether. Instead, he now knew that if the constellation in the handkerchief were to mark a particular destiny, he must imbue it with that meaning himself by doing all in his power to fulfill it. As soon as she was well enough to see him, he would propose to Elizabeth Bennet, beg her to relieve his torment and consent to be his wife.

Chapter Thirty-Seven

THE EFFECTS OF INTERFERENCE

Jane dozed, slumping in exhaustion against the side of the bed next to where Elizabeth lay. The night had passed, and the soft light of morning gradually lit the room as the last candle on the bedside table sputtered with its final flicker of flame. Elizabeth moaned and shifted, awakening Jane enough for her to hear the soft clicking of the doorknob as someone tried it from outside.

Jane was instantly alert and hurried to the door, hoping that it was Mr. Bingley on the outer side. The knob rattled again, and she undid the lock and opened the door a crack, to peer into the dim corridor. She saw not Charles Bingley but, instead, Anne de Bourgh, wide-eyed and anxious, peered in at Jane, then cast her eyes over her shoulder, as though fearful of being seen. Having apparently satisfied herself against that worry, she pushed urgently against the door, and Jane stepped back instinctively, reluctantly allowing her entrance. Anne turned and locked the door behind herself before speaking to Jane.

"Miss Bennet, how is Elizabeth? I could not sleep for worry! I begged the housekeeper for information when I awoke, and she informed me that Elizabeth had taken ill and was not to be moved, that indeed, you were both still at Netherfield, and that Mr. Darcy had sacrificed his room for her comfort." Anne spoke rapidly, in hushed tones. "Pray, tell me, and do so quickly else I too may faint from fear for her! What is her condition? The last I saw of her in the dinner room, she looked very ill indeed."

Jane looked soberly at Anne. Her naturally trusting nature wanted nothing more than to believe that Anne's concern was genuine. "She is not well at all, Miss de Bourgh. A fever holds her in its grip and has done so all this night long."

"Oh!" Anne cried with distress. "I suffered from such a fever once and recall the fearful pains and terrible dreams it brought. This is most unhappy news indeed. She must be made well!"

"Mr. Jones gave us every reason for hope when he saw her. My sister is strong, and she is not prone to illness." Jane smiled courageously. "She shall be well; I believe she shall with all my heart."

"Miss Bennet, you look dreadfully tired." Anne took Jane's hand. "Have you been up all night with her? Someone must relieve you. Shall I call for a maid?"

Jane shook her head vehemently. "That will not do at all. I must keep vigil with my sister until the crisis is past, for I cannot trust it to anyone."

Elizabeth began to murmur and shift in the bed, prompting Jane to return to the bedside. Jane raised her up gently as she pressed a glass to Elizabeth's lips, urging her to take a few sips of broth. She freshened the cloth that had fallen from her sister's forehead and dabbed it against her cheeks first, then placed the cool compress again across her brow.

Anne watched from where she stood by the door. Her hand covered her mouth as if to suppress all the horror she felt, as Jane tenderly nursed her sister. Suddenly, Elizabeth began to thrash about, her mumbling more pronounced. Jane hushed her, but it was to no avail, for Elizabeth did the thing that Jane most feared. She called, clearly and plaintively for Mr. Darcy. Not just once, but three times she cried out before she began to sob, and her words became unintelligible once more.

Jane looked at Anne with trepidation.

"I can plainly see," said Anne calmly, "why a maid will not do to sit with her. Your sister would not wish the household to hear of this."

"No." Jane shook her head gravely. She walked across the room and took Anne by the arm, whereupon she walked her to the furthest corner of the room, and with their backs turned to Elizabeth, Jane made her case. "The fever has stirred such talk in my sister as she would never utter if she had her senses about her. She knows much more of the world than I ever thought, Miss de Bourgh. She has broadened her mind with extensive reading and is, no doubt, the wiser for it; some of the things she has spoken this night would be certain to shock her relations! To this, I must add the fear, which you have just heard for yourself, that in the hidden world of her heart, she holds certain feelings for your cousin, Mr. Darcy. I have heard of your engagement to him and am sensible of the distress this may cause in such a case as yours. I must beg you to preserve my sister's reputation and speak of this to no one."

"First," said Anne prudently, "we may better take this conversation to the private sitting room that adjoins the bedchamber." She opened a door that Jane had assumed led to a closet, which revealed not only a very comfortable room but also a table that already had a breakfast for Jane on it. The two women stepped into the room, and with a look back through the crack to make certain Elizabeth was all right, Jane closed the door most of the way, barely leaving it ajar. "Second," Anne continued, "it must be established that I am not engaged to Mr. Darcy. Third, my greatest hope at this moment is that your sister will be well again. She must abandon this notion that she must suppress her feelings for my cousin."

"Miss de Bourgh, you cannot be serious." Jane gaped at her. "My sister maintains propriety in all that she does and guards her deepest feelings with care, as any proper young lady does."

"My cousin also guards his feelings well—too well sometimes," Anne said. "It is an admirable quality, of course, that his emotions are under good regulation, but in this case, it is simply not to be borne, not when he has such a hope of happiness."

Jane frowned. "It is a hard thing to love someone, I suppose, when one wonders if the sentiments are requited."

Anne smiled pensively. "I loved a man once, nearly ten years past. I was persuaded by my mother to pretend that I did not, for she maintained that he was only interested in my fortune." Anne sighed. "It broke my heart when Mr. Fellows went away. He was convinced by a lie that I did not love him and that I was soon to marry Mr. Darcy instead. I fell ill not long after he left, and *I wished that I would die* to end the suffering of my broken heart. I had not the will to rally my spirits against that dreadful fever."

"Oh, I am so very sorry." Jane clasped her arm in sympathy. "Did you ever hear from him again?"

"Yes, I did." Anne replied quietly. "He lives but eight miles from Rosings on an estate that is about the same size as your family estate of Longbourn. He married a woman of small fortune, and she bore him three beautiful children. She died in childbirth giving him a son some three years ago. Several months ago, he called on me, I believe with the thought of renewing his addresses. My mother was furious that he had the presumption to raise his eyes to me yet again, and she drove him away."

"He came back, all those years later? How remarkable!" Jane sighed. "Do you still love him?"

Anne shrugged. "I hardly know—it has been so long now. I confess that when I saw him at Rosings, standing up to my mother, that moment of hope was the greatest happiness I have known in many years. So you see, you must allow me to help you care for Elizabeth, to restore her to health, for as long as we remain at Netherfield. I do it to spare others the sorrow that befell me."

"I did not expect this of you, Miss de Bourgh. I am at a loss for words." Jane replied. "But you have already done me a kindness by showing this sitting room to me, for I can feel at far greater ease admitting persons to this room while maintaining my sister's privacy in the other. If I may, I would prevail on you to find Mr. Bingley and send him to this room."

"I will do whatever will be of help." Anne curtseyed to Jane. "I will summon Mr. Bingley now and return shortly to sit with Elizabeth so that you may rest. You many depend on my silence as to anything I hear in this chamber.—I am ever so grateful that I may be of some small service to my friend Elizabeth."

~

Morning dawned too early for the remaining females at Longbourn the day after the ball. The rooster crowed, but they did not stir. The morning sun, low as it was in the sky, had chased the shadows away, but drawn curtains were sufficient remedy for that inconvenience. Breakfast was cold on the sideboard before the bedraggled Bennet sisters and their mother faced the day.

Mr. Collins and Mr. Bennet had long since broken their fast and made some good use of the morning hours, although they too were moving slower than the usual pace.

"What word from Netherfield, Mama?" Kitty asked quietly. "Will Lizzy and Jane come home today?"

"Hill just handed me the letter, for heaven's sake! Kitty, give me a moment before you begin your pestering!" Mrs. Bennet broke the seal and read parts aloud as she skimmed through it. "Elizabeth is too ill to be moved ... Mr. Jones la, de, da ... send clothing for Jane...." She looked up from the letter—"Well, that at least is good news. Perhaps with Jane at Netherfield, Mr. Bingley will get on with the business of proposing to her as he ought to have days ago!" She returned to the letter. "Clothing for Elizabeth ... la, de, da ... they do not know how long it will be ... the footman will wait la, de, da." She folded the letter and laid it on the table. "It is very clever of Lizzy to become ill while at Netherfield, for her sister's sake. Of course, it is just a trifling little fever and she will be well soon enough, but we must make the most of it while we can. Hill!"

While the requested articles were being gathered and packed by the maid, a sharp knock was heard at the main door of Longbourn. Mrs. Bennet was surprised to hear it, for who would call the morning after a ball? She nonetheless left the dining room and instructed Hill to deliver the visitor to the drawing room. Upon entering the drawing room, she found that Mr. Collins already occupied the room, quietly reading. She greeted him and then turned to discover who was at the door.

"Mr. Jones, the apothecary," Hill announced solemnly, "has come to call on Mr. Bennet."

"Oh." Mrs. Bennet said impatiently, "Mr. Bennet is in the study. Take him there."

Mrs. Bennet returned to the dining room and listened with eager joy as Lydia and Kitty regaled her with the pleasures of the ball. Suddenly, Mr. Bennet stood in the door, a deep frown etched on his face.

"What is the matter, Mr. Bennet?" Mrs. Bennet cried out with alarm. "Do not vex me with such a look, my poor nerves cannot take it!"

"I bear no good tidings today, Mrs. Bennet, but news of a serious nature. Mr. Jones has just informed me that our tenants, the Millers, also suffer from this fever, and that their baby, little Hannah was the first to be taken ill with it. She passed from this world during the night." Mr. Bennet paused to determine his wife's understanding.

"Oh, the dear sweet child. She was such a favorite with the girls!" Mrs. Bennet said with detached sadness. "I will have Hill send them a pie, to console them for their loss."

"Mrs. Bennet." Mr. Bennet interrupted. "I must tell you that Lizzy was at the Miller cottage a few days ago and held the babe in her arms but a few hours before the fever struck the child."

"Oh, my poor Lizzy!" Mrs. Bennet cried, gripped suddenly with an awareness of his full meaning. "Is she also to die? Are we *all* to die of a fever in our beds? What are we to do, Mr. Bennet? What are we to do?"

Mr. Bennet appraised his wife for a full minute before he spoke. "Mr. Jones instructed me to ensure that we all drink a glass of elderberry wine before bed every night for a week and drink a cup of strong lemon balm tea as a tonic three times a day for the same. I have instructed Hill to send some in right away. I advise you to drink it." Mr. Bennet looked over his glasses at his wife. "He also said to have cook use extra onions and garlic in our soup for several days at least. I know you despise them, but he assures me that this measure will help prevent the spread of the fever to this household. Mr. Jones returns now to Netherfield, where they will be informed of this development as well. The poor man has been up all night, I fear." Mr. Bennet turned and went back to his study, leaving his youngest daughters to calm Mrs. Bennet's nerves.

Lady Catherine did not remain upstairs as she had promised just hours before, but instead, appeared in the dining room at Netherfield as soon as the servants opened the doors. It was not her appetite she sought to gratify—she was in high dudgeon over the deviation of affairs in the household from her explicit instructions.

Caroline Bingley was the first unfortunate resident to enter the room following its occupation by Lady Catherine.

"Miss Bingley!" The older woman said sternly. "The servants have informed me of most alarming news! Am I to understand that Miss Elizabeth Bennet remains under this roof?"

"I am sorry to distress you, madam, but so she does." Caroline replied civilly.

"This is not to be borne!" Lady Catherine scowled and glared at her. "Who dared to disobey? I made it very clear that the Bennet girl must be removed!"

"The apothecary declared it unsafe to move her." Caroline replied. "It does seem rather extreme to keep her here, with her own house but three miles away, but my brother would not risk it."

"Unsafe?" Lady Catherine's eyes narrowed. "If she is in such poor condition, then it is most certainly unwise for us to remain in the house. I shall depart within the hour with Anne and my nephews. It is insufferable to be dangerously exposed in such a way and as guests in the house no less! I am not used to such treatment as this! I must find my daughter immediately. Have you seen Anne? She was not in her room when I awoke."

"No, Lady Catherine. You are the only person aside from the servants I have seen this morning." Caroline raised a cup of tea to her lips. "Shall I send a footman to search for her?"

Lady Catherine paused. "And what of my nephew, Mr. Darcy? Where is he?"

"He could be in nearly any room in the house except for his own chamber. When the requirement for a bed for Miss Elizabeth became apparent, there was not one available. Mr. Darcy surrendered his. I know not where he slept last night." Caroline smiled to herself, fully aware of the impact of her words.

Lady Catherine's eyes bulged in fury. "My nephew was deprived of his bed? Do you know who he is? He is the master of Pemberley! His lineage was seeded with nobility! How dare that country upstart take the bed of one such as he! She could have slept in the servant's quarters! Thoughtless, pretentious girl! She is a disgrace!"

"Aunt Catherine." Darcy stood in the doorway. "Have you something to say to me?"

"My nephew!" Lady Catherine calmed slightly. "What disappointment you must feel at the unfortunate turn of events last night. It cannot be helped, but no matter, a country ball is not ideal to announce an engagement in any case. We must make plans, dear boy, for I grow impatient. We must begin the wedding arrangements at once."

"I will not marry Anne," Darcy said firmly. "This pretense must cease, Aunt Catherine."

"But your mother! She desired it!" Lady Catherine insisted.

Darcy replied with directness. "My mother never spoke any such thing to me. She loved Anne dearly while she lived; indeed, she treasured that niece who was her namesake, but never once did she say she desired an alliance of our houses. The engagement you are so fixed on has never been anything but a lie. It does not exist, and it does none of us credit to give further voice to it."

"This is because of that Bennet girl!" Lady Catherine growled. "I saw the way she behaved with you! She may be practiced in the arts and allurements of the coquettish female, but I trusted you to be above such trickery. She has drawn you in! Can you not see that she is beneath you? She is as far beneath you as this daughter of a tradesman is!" Lady Catherine pointed at Miss Bingley with disdain.

"We are not discussing Miss Bennet or Miss Bingley." Darcy replied with cold civility. "We are discussing your daughter, Anne. I have been patient with you, Aunt. For ten years you have pressed the matter, in spite of my denials and protests against any understanding. There is no engagement between Anne and myself nor will there ever be. I do care for her, as though she was my own sister, but that is all. If you do not cease with your interference in my life, I will be forced to take actions which may be unpleasant to us all."

"Do not change the subject, Fitzwilliam Darcy. We *are* discussing Miss Bennet." Lady Catherine huffed. "In spite of my best efforts at encouragement and persuasion, for ten years you have delayed your marriage to Anne. It has not escaped my notice that it is only since the wiles of Miss Bennet have turned your head that your denials and protests against the marriage became convincing to any degree. Will you turn your back now on what you owe to your family? Your obligations and duties are clear, and a marriage to one such as this penniless country maid would bring shame to us all!"

"Is it your assertion, Aunt, that I must seek your approval before I make an offer of marriage to anyone?" Darcy drew himself to his full height.

"As almost your nearest relation, it is only right that I know the intimate details of your affair, and guide you in any actions which have an effect on our family name and reputation!"

Darcy's jaw was rigid as he spoke formally and coldly to his aunt. "I owe you no such deference. Do not believe that my allegiance to you shall overcome my devotion to the lady I choose as my bride. Make no mistake, the choice is mine, and mine alone to make. You will honor she who bears my name and my children when the time comes that I take a wife, or you will not be welcome at Pemberley."

"Shall you elevate Miss Bennet to be mistress of Pemberley? Are you engaged to her?" Lady Catherine pressed angrily.

"I am not engaged to anyone at present." Darcy frowned at his aunt. "And I am not likely to disclose to you any design to become so prior to the event. Do not think that I am unaware of the unpardonable abuse you have imposed on any lady you suspected of finding my favor. Even Miss Bingley, who is the sister of my dearest friend and your hostess in this house, was subjected to it, undeservedly so."

"Do not be so ungrateful, nephew! Someone must keep their head. Men are never disposed to discover the truth once they believe themselves in love. I have done it in your service." Catherine arched her brow haughtily at Mr. Darcy.

"Aunt Catherine, I believe that you expressed a desire to depart Netherfield. In this, I bow to your greater wisdom. I shall, of course, remain here, as shall Colonel Fitzwilliam. I will see to it that your carriage is made ready immediately. I believe you said you would go within the hour. Shall you require assistance in packing your belongings?"

"I have changed my mind." Lady Catherine glared at Darcy. "I am not going anywhere!"

Darcy had found that the library at Netherfield was a place he could retire for solitude, and it is there he went to cool his temper after his conversation with his aunt.

Shortly after he went to that room, Mr. Jones arrived at Netherfield, and was shown to where Jane, Mr. Bingley and Anne de Bourgh were convened in the sitting room of Mr. Darcy's suite. Mr. Jones shared his distressing news, gave Mr. Bingley the same advice as he had given Mr. Bennet, and after examining her, dispensed some additional medicines for Elizabeth's care to Jane, cautioning her that Elizabeth's condition may worsen before it improves. Mr. Jones did not linger and, so, left before Mr. Darcy was even aware of his arrival.

It was in the library that the housekeeper found Mr. Darcy when the letter arrived for him from Meryton. The letter bore a seal with a distinctive "W" design and was addressed to Mr. Darcy in the familiar, extravagant hand of George Wickham.

Chapter Thirty-Eight

MR. WICKHAM'S REVENGE

The household at Longbourn was unusually quiet. Mrs. Bennet had retired to her room complaining of her nerves, attended by Mrs. Hill. Mr. Bennet was firmly ensconced in his study, the door closed, which was a certain sign he did not wish to be disturbed. With Jane and Elizabeth at Netherfield, only Lydia, Kitty, Mary and Mr. Collins remained downstairs. The three sisters soon went to the drawing room, with Lydia in great hopes that it would not be long before the Lucases called at Longbourn to take some tea and discuss the ball. She speculated that there was a good chance that some of the officers they had danced with would not be able to stay away and would call as well. Mr. Denny, in particular, she happily claimed, was half in love with her already and would surely call today.

Mr. Collins looked up from his book when they entered, his features contorted into what a generous person might call concern as he stood to acknowledge the entrance of his youthful cousins.

"Good morning." He spoke formally with a sideways nod of his large head. "I understand that your esteemed apothecary, Mr. Jones, called upon Mr. Bennet not half an hour ago, followed by sounds of the apparent distress of your mother shortly afterward. While I am never prone to pry into the private affairs of anyone, I must humbly say that, in this case, I feel that it is right to make an exception. With my position and standing in the community as a clergyman, I feel uniquely qualified to bless my fair cousins with my insight and understanding. Pray tell me, did Mr. Jones bear news of Miss Elizabeth? Is she to return to Longbourn today? I must speak to her without delay on a matter of great import."

Lydia turned her back to Mr. Collins, rolled her eyes at Kitty and quietly snorted before whispering. "How droll our cousin is! He is so serious—do you suppose he is to make Lizzy an offer? La! Would not that be a fine joke?"

Kitty's eyes widened at the thought and Mary, who had heard Lydia, smiled with deliberate sweetness at Mr. Collins, walking over to where he stood. She nodded at him before she seated herself determinedly in the chair next to where he had been sitting and opened a volume of the New Testament, which she had brought with her. Seeming not to know what else to do, Mr. Collins returned to his chair and his book.

Mary read quietly for several minutes, and then, not looking up from her book, she spoke. "Mr. Collins, Mr. Jones did indeed bear news today, sad news of a tenant in one of the cottages."

Mr. Collins swallowed audibly, a pained expression on his face. "Tenant?"

"Yes," Mary replied. "Elizabeth had visited the cottage a few days ago. Their baby died in the night of a fever."

"What was Cousin Elizabeth doing at the cottage?" Mr. Collins seemed perplexed.

"Mr. Collins, as the future master of Longbourn, you cannot be ignorant of the duties this will demand of you and your wife. Your tenants are what make the estate profitable. It is through their toil that food is on the table and clothes are on our backs. Elizabeth was attending to their needs, fulfilling my mother's duties in her stead, as she has often done. The tenants are very fond of our Lizzy."

"Much as a parson's wife visits the parishioners, I imagine." Mr. Collins nodded knowingly. "Her compassion does her credit."

Mary shook her head and returned to reading the Bible. Mr. Collins returned to his reading as well, although the escalating sounds of Lydia and Kitty's conversation on the other side of the room prevented him from paying heed to the book.

"I do not!" Lydia was arguing. "You're just saying that because I danced more than you at the ball."

Kitty pulled a face. "You do so! That button is almost as big as your nose."

"I would have seen it in the mirror when I dressed." Lydia said triumphantly. "You are a liar. Liar, liar, liar!"

"Go look in the mirror now if you do not believe me." Kitty pouted. "There is a grog blossom, sure enough! I believe it is growing larger every minute."

"Mind your tongue Kitty—I will do just that!" Lydia stormed out of the room, Kitty watching her anxiously. A moment later, a loud shriek was heard, and Lydia came running back into the drawing room.

"What am I to do, Kitty, oh what am I to do? The officers will come, and I cannot let them see me with this hideous pimple on my nose! It is a monstrosity! What am I to do?" Lydia turned, suddenly remembering that Mr. Collins was in the room. She started to giggle, and taking Kitty's hand, she pulled her sister out of the room; this was followed soon after by the sound of feet on the stairs.

Mary smiled serenely after her sisters left the room, although Mr. Collins was discomfited by the scene he had just witnessed. At length, Mary spoke.

"Mr. Collins," she said as she pressed the volume of scripture open in her lap, "are you well versed in the Epistles of Paul to the Corinthians?"

"I have studied all of God's word, Cousin Mary," Mr. Collins replied.

"There is a passage in Chapter 6 of Second Corinthians. It warns against being unequally yoked. Could you explain what it means to me?" Mary handed him the open book, pointing to the referenced passage.

Beads of perspiration formed on his head, and he pulled out his handkerchief, and mopped his damp forehead before he spoke. "Yes, well, as you said, it is a warning. It tells us that the believers should not marry those who are unbelievers."

Mary nodded patiently. "That makes perfect sense. What of the next part?"

Mr. Collins peered at the book before him. "It is but more of the same, my dear cousin. Do not fret yourself about this passage. I am certain that these warnings are such that *you* heed them by intuition and have no need to be commanded in them."

Mary blinked slightly and turned to look at him curiously. Never before had she heard Mr. Collins express a thought that had not dripped with excessive verbiage. "I have been pondering on the principle itself, Mr. Collins. My thoughts have traveled to the metaphor, to that of the yoking of persons whose situation and character are unsuited. It behooves us all, I believe, to seek a companion with which we would be *equally yoked*. Do you agree?"

"Tis a fool who would do otherwise." Collins nodded, the spark of a future sermon forming in his mind. "It is a solid principle upon which to judge, that is certain. It would serve to guide many who may otherwise raise their hopes to the wrong person."

"Ah, but we are all fools in matters of love, Mr. Collins. It is too often seen that an unsuitable match is discovered too late, after the nuptial vows have been spoken, and the blush of infatuation has faded. The scales fall from the eyes then, and they see the poor nature of the match too late." Mary hesitated, collecting her thoughts before continuing. "If the solid strength of a plow horse is harnessed with the lively spirit of a thoroughbred, the fields will never be plowed, nor the race won. Both beasts are good in their respective sphere, but in temperament and purpose they are unequally yoked if put together."

Collins looked at Mary, his eyes narrowed. "I see what you are saying, Cousin Mary, although it is difficult to discern your intent. Do you seek my counsel on a particular case, or are we speaking in general terms?"

Mary looked away again, her gaze focused through the window at some distant point. "It is indeed a particular case. There is one in my circle who pursues a most imprudent match. In circumstance and station, a marriage would appear equitable to both parties, but I know that it would not be so—their dispositions are not at all alike. They could never be happy together, but I cannot interfere." She sighed and shook her head sadly.

"Your generosity of spirit does you credit, cousin." Collins declared. "If you believe I may be of service, I am willing to offer my assistance. You may well know, my station in life as a clergyman grants me the opportunity to guide such persons that I may encounter away from troubled waters such as these. If you would introduce me to the gentleman in this instance, I will counsel with him, and perhaps help him to come to an understanding—to see the foolishness of the match."

"I would that you could do so, sir, but I am not at liberty to disclose the identities of the persons of which I speak, for they are in our midst and would certainly detect my interference. Perhaps, now that you are aware of it, you will perceive it through observation and reflection and may act accordingly of your own volition." Mary looked into his eyes and smiled. "I believe it is in you to work this out. I shall speak no more of it."

Mary retrieved the Bible and set it on a table, laid open to the passage they had discussed. "I must go and see to my mother. Thank you for your company, Mr. Collins. I do feel better for having spoken with you about the matter." She curtseyed and quit the room hastily, lest the shaking of her limbs give away the emotions she felt at her own boldness in speaking so with Mr. Collins.

Mr. Collins turned to examine the biblical passage again. The challenge set before him by his cousin was a welcome diversion from the book he was reading. He flattered himself with the thought that she had recognized his superior abilities as a clergyman and turned his mind to the task set before him by Mary Bennet.

❧

Charles Bingley, Anne de Bourgh and Colonel Fitzwilliam sat together in Darcy's private sitting room, each sipping on a cup of lemon balm tea. In the adjacent bedchamber, Elizabeth Bennet rambled incoherently through her fever, with her sister diligently attending to her needs. The walls and door muffled the moans and mutterings that she was making, but it was too late to keep what she said a secret—Anne had heard them for herself, Jane had confided them in Mr. Bingley, and the colonel had diligently wormed the truth out of them.

"Anne," Colonel Fitzwilliam ventured, "why do you suppose your mother has not tracked you here yet? I expected her to drag you away some hours ago."

Anne nodded and a mischievous look crossed her features. "I shall tell you why. She believes I am asleep in my room, exhausted by the ball. She has taken to her room as well. She said something about not letting anyone pack her belongings or send her back to Kent. It was a most peculiar conversation. She was seriously displeased about something. I confess that I did not press her."

"She had a quarrel with Darcy—that is what she was displeased with." Bingley said with a frown. "Speaking of the man, where is he? It is not his nature to stay away. What do you suppose keeps him?"

"I was wondering this as well." Colonel Fitzwilliam stood and immediately strode toward the door. "I will locate him. He can never manage to hide from me for long."

❧

Colonel Fitzwilliam's hunt for Darcy was brief. He encountered the housekeeper at the bottom of the stairs, and upon enquiring after Mr. Darcy's whereabouts, the colonel was escorted by her to the library door.

Colonel Fitzwilliam swung the library door open quietly with a gentle knock on the panel as he did so. It was doubtful that Darcy would be asleep in the day, but knowing that Darcy had been deprived of a bed overnight, he could not be certain. One glance at the long sofa testified to its vacancy, and Richard scanned the room to determine his cousin's location. He spied a lone black boot protruding from a wingback chair. With the chair being faced away from the door, all of Darcy but the telltale boot was effectively obscured.

"Darcy?" Colonel Fitzwilliam entered the room and approached his cousin tentatively. There was something odd in the angle of the boot that testified to a different posture in the chair than was customary for his always-proper cousin. The colonel came around the chair to find Darcy leaning back, nearly slumped in the chair. His coat, waistcoat and cravat had all been flung over the back of another chair, and Darcy's appearance was disheveled and despondent. He looked up at Richard and frowned.

"You look awful!" Richard informed his cousin and, trying to raise Darcy's spirits, added, "Please tell me *you are* not going to faint, because I am not certain I can catch you."

Darcy rewarded him with a faint smile. "I am not ill, Richard."

"What is it, man?" Richard insisted. "Tell me at once what has brought you so low! Has something happened?"

"I have received a most disturbing letter and am in desperate need of your counsel." Darcy handed the letter to the colonel; the paper was damp and wrinkled from being clutched in Darcy's hand. "It is from Wickham. You might want to sit down before you read it."

Colonel Fitzwilliam, letter in hand, moved to the window where the light was better and sat. He smoothed the paper out on his thigh before he began to silently read.

Master Fitzwilliam Darcy,

You may well be surprised that I would approach you with correspondence so soon after your assault on my person in Meryton. Did you perchance believe that threats would cause me to withdraw from society as a convenience to you? I must inform you that our confrontation has had the opposite effect. Your challenge has strengthened my resolve for justice in the matters that lie between us.

It was only my love and admiration for your father, who indeed treated me as his own son, which kept me from seeking that justice until now. I confess that I had harbored a hope that the brotherhood we had shared in our youth would be restored in time. I foolishly believed that when your sister accepted my marriage proposal some months past, a beginning had been made to this end. How joyful I was at the prospect of lawfully securing my place in that family which I already considered my own. Your denouncement of our betrothal was a cruel blow, not just to your sister's tender heart, but to my own happiness as well.

After some months of desolation over my lost love, I resolved to begin anew and was joined with the Hertfordshire militia at the urging of a friend. I was, at that time, assured of the pleasant companionship of my fellow officers and the hospitality of the good people of Meryton. I made significant investment in the purchase of my regimental uniform, with full intent of remaining honorably with the regiment for some duration.

Had I known of your residence in the vicinity, it is probable that I would have declined the commission, knowing, as I do, of the implacable resentment you bear toward me. It is not in my nature to anticipate any evil disposition in you – at least not sufficient to compel you to poison my superior officers against me. Yet I have discovered that such has been done, with malicious disregard for my reputation in the community in which I was to reside for the winter. In spite of our past history, I had not thought you as low as this. The defamation of my character at your hand has forced me to resign my commission and quit the county. This is due in no small way to the refusal of even the innkeeper to extend the credit that is afforded every other officer in the regiment. I am informed that the denials are entirely founded in your slanders against my name, which my Colonel was compelled to disclose to the town in order to protect the general standing of the militia. I do not fault him in this – you are to blame.

As I was preparing for my departure, under the dark cloud of your obstruction, the officers billeted in the same inn as I returned from the private ball held last evening at Netherfield Park. My ears were filled with their tales of the ladies, the dancing, the food and the wine. You may imagine my interest when they informed me of the peculiar degree of attention you paid to Miss Elizabeth Bennet. It was the opinion of several who were in attendance that you fancied yourself violently in love with Miss Elizabeth, and that she appeared to their eyes to return your regard. Am I to wish you joy? I assure you that I am not so generous of spirit upon consideration of the great harm you have inflicted on me.

You first deprived me of my own chance at felicity in love and have twice removed the means whereby I am able to support myself in even the meanest of circumstances. I find myself inclined to repay you for your officious interference in kind, and have now arrived at the point of this letter.

During the time that I was at Ramsgate with Georgiana, I found her to be eager for my attentions. She, being somewhat reserved in nature, was deeply moved by my declarations of love but unable to reciprocate them audibly whilst she preserved her natural delicacy. Desiring to know of her true feelings, I urged her to express them, so she penned a letter, declaring not only her devotion and love but communicating in most animated language the depth of her passion and desire to elope and be wed to me. She mentions in the letter certain improprieties that took place between us, which you may interpret as compromising in nature. I assure you that at the time they occurred, these liberties were taken with full expectation that we would be married ere long, but since that event did not take place as planned, the exposure of the letter would be highly damaging to what is generally known of your sister's character. My character, having been thoroughly disparaged by you already, can suffer no additional harm from such revelations.

You are probably thinking that I am now to ask for monetary rewards for my silence regarding the truth of what occurred at Ramsgate. You are correct in this thought, although it is primarily for my own comfort, and not as a punishment to you. In truth, the loss of money would be insufficient pain to one who has so much of it, so the details of these transactions are not to be included in this letter. They will be provided to you at such time as I have secured an untraceable means for the transactions to take place. Today, I will instead tell you the true cost of my silence.

The letter and the truth contained therein about your sister shall remain secret so long as you remain wholly unconnected to any woman, most particularly the delightful Miss Elizabeth Bennet. Should you court, become engaged or marry, you will regret it as soon as it is known, for I will expose Georgiana's folly to the world, using the letter written in her own hand as evidence of it. I have many friends in Derbyshire, Hertfordshire and London, and you may be certain that I will hear of any attentions that single out any lady of your acquaintance. You deprived me of the woman I loved, and I will exact my revenge in its full measure and deprive you of the same.

I warn you against any attempt to detect my location or involve legal authorities in the matter. These actions will invoke my wrath and I can promise that you will regret your actions should they occur. You will hear from me again soon regarding the financial arrangements previously mentioned.

Sincerely yours,

George Wickham

"I will kill him!" Colonel Fitzwilliam cried as he finished the letter. "I will track him down like an animal; then I shall run him through with a blade before I put a bullet through his black heart!"

"You will not kill him, Richard. If you did so, you would have blood on your hands." Darcy said firmly. "We must find a way to separate him from the letter and destroy it. In the meantime, we must not provoke him further."

"I will strangle him—a bloodless death will leave no trace on my hands!" Richard growled.

"I cannot allow you to murder him by any means, Fitz. Think how the scandal would affect poor Georgiana." Darcy reasoned. "We will first verify that such a letter does exist. We must not forget that among his other charming qualities, Wickham is a liar, and this may be a ruse. I must speak to Georgiana privately."

"That is all very rational, Darcy." Richard paced. "Have you no occupation in all this that befits a soldier? I need to *do* something!"

"You shall." Darcy said ominously. "While I am in town speaking to Georgiana, you must work with Bingley to evict Aunt Catherine from Netherfield. Jane needs a bedchamber, as do I. Lady Catherine and Anne must depart immediately. That is your task."

"Thunder and turf, Darcy, you are cruel! You leave me to wrest with that bitter old woman while you go to London?" Richard grumbled. "Next time we play, I am the general and you are the foot-soldier!"

"How is Elizabeth?" Darcy changed the subject as he began replacing his discarded garments in preparation for an immediate return to town.

"So it is 'Elizabeth' now is it?" His cousin teased, "When did she cease to be 'Miss Elizabeth', hmmm?"

Darcy rolled his eyes and said with some impatience as he buttoned his waistcoat, "Not now, Richard!"

"Very well. Darcy, I will tell you what you ask. Miss Elizabeth is much as she was when you last saw her. Her sister is caring for her, but the fever has not yet broken, and she remains in a delirium." Colonel Fitzwilliam then related all that Mr. Jones had said about her care and told him of the tenant's child who had died, which had an immediate impact on Mr. Darcy's demeanor. He stopped tying his cravat and looked at the colonel in shock.

"The baby—it died?"

The colonel nodded and then paused, weighing his next words carefully. After this brief hesitation, he divulged to his cousin that which he knew Jane did not even want Darcy to know. "She is calling for you, Darcy. I do not know what you have done to warrant it, but somehow you are on her mind. Go to London, as you said, but first, go to Miss Elizabeth. Do not let her call go unanswered."

With a nod to his cousin, Darcy raced from the room without another word, his cravat in dreadful disarray.

Chapter Thirty-Nine

YOU SAID YOU LOVE ME

Fitzwilliam Darcy was not the sort of man who ran indoors. He made no exception today, although his stride was longer and his pace brisker than usual as he closed the distance from the Netherfield library to the stairway leading to the upper floors. His attention was trained on an unsuccessful attempt to tug his cravat into a semblance of order as he hurried through the hallway, and he did not even notice the echo of his footsteps on the floor. Caroline Bingley, however, did.

"Mr. Darcy." She met him at the bottom of the stairs. "I had nearly despaired of seeing you again today. After that frightful scene with Lady Catherine, a lesser man would have gone into hiding."

"Miss Bingley." Darcy drew up short and stiffly bowed in a formal greeting, glancing up the stairs as he did so.

"The housekeeper tells me that they moved your trunks to Colonel Fitzwilliam's room. Did you find a bed in which to sleep, or were you forced to roam the halls all night?" Caroline teased.

"I thank you for your concern, Miss Bingley. I am sufficiently rested." Darcy said brusquely. "Please excuse me." He stepped sideways, toward the staircase.

"Mr. Darcy," Caroline snickered, calling him back. "I was extremely amused to discover the wig of feathers on my brother's prize statue. Whatever possessed you to do it?"

"Do not be fooled, Miss Bingley." Colonel Fitzwilliam's approach had been silent and startled Caroline. "You may be very surprised to learn this, but my cousin is not as bold as I. He would not have dared such a venture alone." He nodded at Darcy, who took his signal and, without another word, went up the stairs.

Caroline watched Darcy's retreating figure, her brows knit in consternation. "Mr. Darcy seems out of sorts today. It is insufferable that a man of his station should be deprived of his accommodations. I cannot understand why the Bennets did not take Miss Elizabeth home with them to Longbourn. They are such a tiresome family, do you not agree, Colonel?"

Colonel Fitzwilliam turned thoughtfully. "Tiresome?" He shook his head decidedly. "I do not think they are tiresome."

"Oh?" Caroline smirked. "And how would you describe our country neighbors, if not tiresome? Surely you are accustomed to finer company than the Bennets."

"Your country neighbors have a certain liveliness rarely found in the first circles." Colonel Fitzwilliam smiled warmly. "Finer company may be fine indeed, but the society here in Hertfordshire most definitely has its charms."

"Their manners are boorish, and there is no evidence of breeding among them at all." Caroline tsked.

"But surely ... Miss Bingley, what are you saying? Could it be that you do not approve of Charles courting Miss Bennet?" Colonel Fitzwilliam asked cautiously.

"Not at all!" Caroline rolled her eyes in disgust. "Jane Bennet is, I grant you, a sweet girl, but her family is beyond the pale! I had hoped to persuade my brother to return to town immediately after the ball. I suppose now, with Miss Elizabeth ill under our roof, we cannot close the house for the winter yet. How I *long* to leave this place and return to the society of town!"

"Must you stay? Why not just leave?" The colonel asked, genuinely curious.

"My brother needs me to run his household." Caroline replied haughtily, "But that is not why I remain. To be frank with you, Colonel, if I leave, Charles is likely to make an offer to Miss Bennet, and I cannot allow such a thing to happen. It is only through my diligent persuasions that he has not done so already."

"You object to her so strongly?" Richard squinted slightly.

"My brother's fortune qualifies him for a far better match than the likes of Jane Bennet." Caroline sniffed. "There were some among the *ton* who were quite interested in him last season. I daresay it will raise all of our fortunes considerably when he marries a lady with superior connections and an ample dowry."

"Your brother's fortune also allows him a degree of freedom in his choice of a bride." Colonel Fitzwilliam smiled. "If I were in his place and could afford to disregard the size of a lady's dowry, a match to one of the lovely daughters of Longbourn would be a most agreeable prospect indeed."

ও

Darcy's long legs advanced up the stairs two at a time, as soon as he was no longer in view of Caroline and the colonel. His only thought was of reaching Elizabeth. He had spent the night pacing the floor of the library, torturing himself with worry, wondering if he had somehow missed some sign that Elizabeth was ill earlier in the evening. His greatest desire was to be of some use to her now, but he felt strangely unable to act.

When his cousin had informed him that Elizabeth was calling for him, he felt as a man shaken from a stupor. The knowledge served as a call to action, and he did as his protective instincts dictated—he raced to her side with no apparent thought of appearances or propriety.

Arriving outside the suite, he found that both the bedchamber and the adjacent sitting room doors were closed. He tried the knob directly into his former bedchamber. Finding it locked, he moved to the other door and impatiently threw the door open, bursting in on Jane and Mr. Bingley, who sat together on a small sofa.

Bingley's arm was tenderly encircled around Jane's shoulders, and Jane's head was leaned against his chest in an exhausted state of slumber. Bingley grinned sheepishly at Darcy and signaled him to be quiet, lest Jane awaken. Darcy nodded his understanding and closed the door softly behind himself.

The door to the bedchamber was open, and the minor disturbance of Darcy entering the sitting room brought Anne from Elizabeth's bedside to discern the source. She saw her cousin with a degree of both relief and concern. Glancing over her shoulder at Elizabeth, she stepped into the sitting room and shut the door.

"You should not be here," Anne said quietly before admitting, "but I am glad you have come."

"Why should I not be here?" Darcy replied gruffly.

Anne gestured graciously for him to sit. He instead took a step toward the bedroom door.

With a sigh, Anne replied, "The fever has loosed her tongue, and her sister," Anne nodded toward the sleeping Jane, "diligently protects against the repercussions of her unguarded state. If Miss Jane Bennet were awake, you know full well that she would refuse you—she would deny you entrance."

"Miss Bennet is *not* awake, however, so her refusal is not forthcoming." Darcy pointed out with another step.

"It is not proper." Anne replied, shaking her head as she leaned against the door protectively. "She is not fit to be seen." Darcy closed the distance between them, his cousin the only obstacle to entrance. Anne raised her chin, defying him. "Elizabeth would not wish it—for you to see her like this. No woman would."

"Stand aside, Anne." Darcy said, his voice quiet but stern. "I know that she has asked for me, and I *will* see her."

Anne glared at him stubbornly, their eyes locked. "It is too soon!" She insisted, "She asked for you in delirium cousin. You must wait until the fever has broken, when she has her wits about her."

Any person inclined to doubt that the two descended from the same bloodlines before would see it clearly now, in their bearing and the unwavering look in their eyes. Both were determined in their course—she in defending the doorway, while he was resolved to gain passage. Several minutes passed in this posture of silent challenge. Anne's fists clenched until her knuckles ached while Darcy's jaw became ever more set in response to her defiance.

Suddenly, Elizabeth's voice was heard from within the bedchamber, and both Anne and Darcy turned at the sound. Anne, eyebrows raised for emphasis, shook her head in warning at her cousin as she opened the door to return to Elizabeth. Mr. Darcy disregarded her warning and followed her into the darkened room unbidden.

Anne moved directly to Elizabeth's bedside, replacing the cool, damp cloth laid across her forehead with a fresh one. "Hush, Elizabeth, I am here." Anne soothed, wrapping her arm underneath Elizabeth's back to raise her up slightly. "You must drink this." She raised a glass from the bedside table to Elizabeth's lips and tipped it, making certain several sips were taken before she returned Elizabeth to the pillow.

Darcy watched in silence from the foot of the bed, his face an emotionless mask.

"You should leave." Anne said to him as she wrung out another cloth and pressed it against Elizabeth's neck and face. "For the sake of propriety if nothing else, you must go, Fitzwilliam."

At the sound of his Christian name, Elizabeth repeated it in a barely audible murmur. "Fitzwilliam."

His eyes, now fully adjusted to the dark, met with Anne's. "I will not leave until I have spoken to her." Darcy replied. "You know me too well to doubt my resolve, Anne. No-one outside our circle will ever know—you may be assured of my secrecy."

At the sound of his voice, Elizabeth's eyelashes fluttered, and she moaned, turning her head to the side.

Anne hesitated for a moment, clearly weighing the wisdom of what he asked. "You know that I would trust you with my life, Fitzwilliam, and in this dark hour, I will now trust you with hers. I pray that I am not mistaken in doing so." With another glance at Elizabeth, she nodded, affirming her decision as she rose up out of the bedside chair. She patted Elizabeth's hand softly before she quit the room, leaving the door ajar.

Darcy walked slowly from the foot of the bed to the side of it, his eyes never leaving her face. He took in the sight of her, so small and pale except for her cheeks, which were unnaturally red from the fever. Her lips were cracked and peeling. Her eyes seemed sunken in her face, framed by dark circles of gray skin. Her hair was still twisted into a loose braid, but many strands had worked their way free. Some were strewn across her pillow, but others clung to her skin—dark tendrils pasted to her fevered brow with sweat.

"Oh, my Elizabeth!" He cried softly as he sank into the chair beside her and took her hand in his. With his other hand, he felt her face, flinching at the heat emanating from it. He turned the cloth that Anne had placed there and gently stroked the hairs away from her forehead.

Her eyes opened just a sliver. "Mr. Darcy." Her parched lips barely moved as she said his name.

He tightened his grip on her hand. "It is I."

She stared at him through unbelieving eyes for a long moment. "Are you an angel?" Elizabeth whispered in confusion as her dull eyes opened a little wider. Her gaze drifted to the wall beside her as she struggled in vain to comprehend. "You must be an angel ... I saw you die." A tear trickled from the corner of her eye.

Understanding of her belief came to him, and he shook his head in denial. "No dearest Elizabeth. I am no angel." Darcy spoke as he would to a child. "I live—feel my hand in yours! Look into my eyes. You have had a terrible dream—that is all. I live!"

Her eyes turned again to him, and for a moment, Darcy thought that he had overcome her belief in his death. His heart sank when she spoke with sadness. "The battle was fierce," Elizabeth mumbled as she closed her eyes again and turned her head away, releasing another tear as she softly wailed. "You fell, and all is lost."

Darcy spoke again, louder and deeper. "I am here, Elizabeth." He wrapped his other hand around their clasp, and gently tightened his grip. "Hear my voice. I live, and so do you. I did not fall, I did not die." He gave her hand a gentle shake. "Do you hear me?"

Her eyes remained closed, but her brows knit together. "I thirst." The words came under her breath, distant and disconnected from their conversation.

Darcy repeated what he had seen Anne do, putting his arm beneath her, raising her up and placing the glass to her lips. "Drink, my love." He held her close as he coaxed the liquid down her throat, murmuring encouraging words with each successful swallow. She relaxed after the first few sips, and responded obediently to his command for her to continue until the glass was empty. When the task was done, and he started to lower her to the pillow, she turned her head against him and inhaled deeply.

"Oh, my dear Mr. Darcy," she began to sob in her delirium. Darcy hesitated, thinking that she was perhaps, finally speaking to him. Her next words struck him with force, for they made it clear that she still thought him dead. "I shall never see him again." A fresh round of tears broke through as her one free hand grasped at him and found the dangling end of his cravat, which she pulled and held to her bosom, as though it comforted her. "Why?" She gasped the question and opened her eyes again. They were trained on Darcy's face but seemed unable to truly focus, and then she spoke, looking at Darcy, but obviously seeing something else. "Why him, dear Lord? I loved him, and now he is dead, and he will never know." Her eyes filled with tears again, and her body was wracked with sobs that testified to the depth of what she was feeling, even though it had no foundation in reality.

"This will not do!" Darcy whispered to Elizabeth. "Forgive me for the liberties I am about to take my darling!" He pulled back the counterpane, slid his other arm beneath her knees and stood with the softly weeping Elizabeth in his arms. He carried her to the doorway leading to the sitting room.

"Bingley, stop sitting around—make yourself useful man! Miss Elizabeth's fever is severe. Have your people fill the tub with cool water right away. There is not a moment to lose!"

Mr. Bingley jumped up with a start, waking Jane. "Cool water?" He questioned. "Whatever for?"

"Just do it," Darcy barked. "Quickly!"

He turned to his cousin. "Anne, lay out a fresh night dress for Miss Elizabeth. This one," he said, "will soon be wet, and she will require another."

"Miss Bennet, may I counsel with you regarding your sister?" He beckoned to Jane who hastened to join him as he returned to the bedchamber. He sat in a large upholstered chair in the corner, still holding Elizabeth in his arms. Elizabeth had stopped crying and was dozing against his chest. Jane entered, some trepidation in her expression as she regarded the man cradling her sister.

"Mr. Darcy...," Jane began, "I cannot allow...."

Darcy shook his head to interrupt her. "Miss Bennet, I know this all seems very untoward; however, I beg you to hear me out."

Jane nodded hesitantly. "I will hear you. I pray that your explanation is persuasive indeed. I do not wish to have to take this to my father." She looked with some horror at the intimate way her sister lay in Mr. Darcy's arms. "If she were not so very ill, I would consider her compromised by you already, Mr. Darcy. I suppose that some allowance must be made for circumstance."

Darcy nodded his understanding and continued. "I would tell you of the housekeeper at my estate in Derbyshire, Mrs. Reynolds. She came to Pemberley when I was a small child, and I can tell you that she is very good and wise. She always keeps an herb garden, and we rarely required the services of the apothecary or physician because Mrs. Reynolds always had a remedy." He shifted Elizabeth's weight slightly and continued.

"There was one winter that a fever swept through the village of Lambton, sickening many of its people. Our servants, having done business in the village, contracted the fever, and it was not long before many in our household were violently sick. Unfortunately, the apothecary was also ill, and so was unable to dispense anything to relieve the suffering, even to Pemberley. The fever took the lives of many elderly persons in the village and a few babies and children. The fear of death was upon us all."

He looked carefully at Jane to determine if she was following him before continuing. "I contracted the fever and was soon in a similar state to how your sister is today. I also was delirious and suffered hallucinations. A fever that produces such waking dreams is very dangerous—as you well know."

Elizabeth moaned, and Darcy stopped speaking to Jane as he comforted Elizabeth, while Jane looked on in astonishment. When Elizabeth had calmed, he continued. "Mrs. Reynolds, against the advice of all, insisted that I be placed in a tub full of cool water as a means to reduce the fever. She was warned by many that this treatment would turn the fever to pneumonia and possibly kill me, but she stood fast, and the fever abated as a result. This was of necessity repeated several times over the course of my illness, but each time, it cooled the fever and delivered me from delirium. This is what I wish to do for Miss Elizabeth—that which was done for me. I know it seems an unusual course to take, but I ask you to trust me in this. Do I have your blessing to proceed?"

Jane nodded. "Your judgment is sound, Mr. Darcy. If you believe it will help my sister, I will agree."

"Good." Darcy said. "I will lower her into the tub, but you and Anne must tend to her from there. When the fever is sufficiently reduced, she will regain her senses, but she will still be very weak and require assistance in changing to dry bed-clothes and returning to the bed."

Jane nodded. "I understand." She eyed Mr. Darcy and Elizabeth warily again but returned to the sitting room once more, making certain the door was wide-open, and she had a seat with a direct view.

❧

Darcy, Bingley and the colonel paced in the hallway the entire time Jane and Anne were assisting Elizabeth, which exceeded an hour by nearly half again. Very little was spoken among them, as the outcome of the cooling bath was foremost on their minds. When Jane finally opened the door to call them back to the sitting room, their relief was obvious, for the look on her face told all.

"Come in!" Jane beckoned them urgently. "It has worked! It is almost a miracle! Lizzy's mind is no longer in a muddle, although she is definitely still quite unwell."

The three men filed into the room, and as soon as he was in the room, Jane grasped Mr. Bingley by both of his hands. Her joy in the moment was evident as she declared, "Oh Mr. Bingley, I am so very, very happy. Lizzy will be well! I must thank you for all the good care my sister is receiving here in your house." She smiled up into his face, her affection for her sister feeding her affection for Mr. Bingley. "You are so very kind; I do not know how to thank you well enough!" She sighed and looked shyly down at the floor.

Mr. Bingley, a boyish grin on his face, assured her that she was very welcome and that it was his pleasure. The two were once again lost to the presence of anyone else in the room as Jane spoke quietly to Mr. Bingley of what happened during the time they were separated.

Anne emerged from the bedchamber and quietly said to Darcy, "Cousin, Miss Elizabeth has requested an audience with you. Are you able to accommodate her request?" This was said with a hint of mischief, for she knew all too well what his response would be.

Darcy, with a grateful nod, brushed past her without answering. He pulled the door closed behind him.

Elizabeth was sitting up in the bed, her eyes shining in the dim candlelight, as Darcy returned to the bedside chair. He took her hand again and gazed silently into her eyes. At length, he offered to get her a drink, which she gratefully accepted, and after slowly drinking two full glasses, she laid back against the pillows.

"Mr. Darcy," Elizabeth finally spoke with a weak smile. "I think we must have some conversation, but I am very tired and cannot think of anything to say. Perhaps you could begin this time."

He looked at her blankly. It seemed that he also could think of nothing to say, for he opened his mouth as if to speak, but then closed it again, his lips pressing together in frustration. He stood and paced across the room, turning to see that Elizabeth had followed his trek with her eyes, waiting patiently for him to speak. He crossed to the window and moved the curtain aside, as if he expected to see something of interest on the grounds. When he dropped the curtain, he turned again and returned to the chair, although he stood behind it as he looked again at Elizabeth, words eluding him as he battled with the wave of emotions he was feeling. Finally he spoke. "I must inform you, for the record, that I am not dead."

"Oh." Elizabeth's lips made the same shape as the sound. "I am glad for that." Her eyes averted, and she absently picked at the fabric of the counterpane. Darcy returned and sat in the chair next to her, pulling it forward so he was as close as possible.

"You seemed to think that I was dead." He said, looking at her expectantly.

"I suppose I did." Elizabeth replied, not meeting his gaze. Eventually she glanced up at him. "That you are here, declaring yourself as among the living tells me that what I saw must have been a dream, but Mr. Darcy, it seemed so very real. It was a great battle on a vast and bloodied battlefield. You were astride Romeo and together you defeated many enemies." She lay back against her pillow, and closing her eyes, continued to speak. "But then there was a man dressed all in black who came onto the field. He was in the shadows—I could not see his face, but you seemed to know him. He raised a pistol and shot ... oh, it does not matter." She opened her eyes and looked at him again. "It was not real."

"Is this when I fell?" Darcy asked gently.

Elizabeth nodded, tears forming in her eyes. "Shot through the heart."

Darcy reached out and took her hand. "There is but one thing that has penetrated my heart, Miss Bennet, and it is not a bullet."

Elizabeth wiped her tears away, her eyes wide as she took his meaning.

"Do you remember anything else of these dreams?" Darcy asked.

Elizabeth nodded, and trying to compose herself, sweetly teased, "I thought you were an angel."

"I am no angel." Darcy frowned. "If I were, we would not be alone in a bedchamber."

"Mr. Darcy, I assure you, if I were to make an indelicate sound, we would not be alone for long." Elizabeth replied quietly. "The door may be closed, but you may be assured that my sister is on the other side of it."

The sides of Darcy's mouth twitched as though a smile were attempting to appear. "Then let us make only delicate sounds, Miss Bennet."

Elizabeth laughed softly. "Only delicate sounds then, Mr. Darcy. We are agreed."

"What else do you remember?" Darcy asked. "I daresay that is a safe topic."

"Perhaps." Elizabeth replied, "I do remember it, although it is unclear, as if I am seeing it all through a thick fog."

"But you *do* remember." Darcy pressed. "Do you recall what you said when you thought you would never see me again?"

"Well... yes, I think so." Elizabeth stammered slightly. "The words are hazy."

"I beg you not to trifle with me through talk of hazy words." Darcy replied, his voice thick with emotion. "I know you were delirious when you spoke, but then you said that you love me. You are not delirious now, and I must ask you—can it be true?"

"Oh." Elizabeth looked at the wall, color flooding her cheeks. "How am I to answer such a question?" She returned to her occupation of tugging at imaginary threads on the counterpane.

"Much depends, Miss Bennet," Darcy said quietly, "on your answering it honestly."

Elizabeth closed her eyes once more. "I was utterly convinced that you were dead, Mr. Darcy. I cannot convey to you the depth of my despair."

"Did you mean what you said?" Darcy whispered urgently.

Elizabeth sighed deeply as she resigned herself to full disclosure. "Yes." It was barely audible. "Yes. I meant it."

Darcy reached and took her hand from atop the counterpane, and raising it to his lips; he kissed her fingers, curled around his own, and then he kissed the back her hand. He then turned it over, and with his fingertip, he lightly drew the image of a flower in her palm, and gently kissed the center. "Miss Bennet, I am not at liberty to openly declare an attachment today, but you must know that my attentions toward you are not capricious. Certain obstacles must be dealt with before I can make my love for you known to the world, but I must tell you here and now, with God as our witness, that I do love you as well, most ardently."

Elizabeth withdrew her hand. "The obstacles you speak of, will you not tell me what they are?"

Darcy retrieved her hand again. "I do not wish to burden you, but I will tell you that it has to do with my sister. I would very much like you to meet her."

Elizabeth smiled. "I would like that as well. Perhaps after Christmas."

"I was thinking of later this week." Darcy replied. "I will go to London and return to Netherfield with her in a few days."

"You are to leave?" Elizabeth asked forlornly.

Darcy froze at the sound of her plaintive question. He mentally rehearsed his options before he replied, "Dearest, I must. I wish that it were not so, but perhaps it is for the best." Darcy said, "You must rest, and if I stay here, it would be a torment to us both. I cannot continue to come to your bedchamber—the servants will talk even if our friends do not. It truly is best that I go...."

"Mr. Darcy, it is not fair." Elizabeth replied.

"Not fair?"

"It is not fair that you extracted a confession of a most intimate and personal nature from me, and now you leave before I can do the same." Elizabeth arched an eyebrow.

"Oh. By all means, I am at your disposal. What am I to confess?" Darcy asked with surprise.

"There is one other thing I remember." Elizabeth's color deepened. "When you spoke to me, and thought I did not hear, your form of address was familiar. Did you not call me 'Elizabeth'?"

"I confess that I did." Darcy nodded.

"May I ask why?" Elizabeth puzzled.

"How can you not know why?" Darcy pulled his head back, feigning astonishment. "I have thought of you as 'Elizabeth' for some time now."

"You have?" Elizabeth's astonishment was not feigned. "But surely we are not so well acquainted as to justify the use of Christian names."

"Miss Bennet, rules of propriety may dictate that which I speak aloud, but in the purview of my thoughts, I am sovereign."

"I cannot pretend that this does not surprise me, Mr. Darcy—I am astonished, and yet, I have a favor to ask, and I hope you do not think me too bold in asking. Will you say it aloud for me to hear now, while my mind is clear?"

Darcy looked into Elizabeth's eyes. "In private, perhaps, when it is just you and me, I will say it whenever it pleases you, my dearest, loveliest, Elizabeth." Darcy raised his hand to her face and held her cheek in his palm. "What will you call *me* when we are alone?"

"That is simple." Elizabeth smiled as she unconsciously leaned her head into his hand. "We should not be alone at all, but should the occasion arise, I am prepared for it. Your name is Fitzwilliam, and that is who you now are to me, and who you ever shall be." She raised a finger to her lips in thought. "You added a few sweet adjectives to my name, the least I can do is the same for you." She tipped her head to the side, and said, "You are my kindest, noblest Fitzwilliam." She nodded happily. "Yes, that will do for now, but I may change my mind in the future. This was very short notice."

Darcy stood and kissed her gently on the forehead. "I will hurry back to you from town, I promise."

"And I shall try to be well when you return, Fitzwilliam." Elizabeth smiled lovingly at him as she spoke his name. "It would not do for me to be ill when I meet your sister!"

"There are a great many other reasons you need to be well, Elizabeth." Darcy said softly. "We have much to say to each other when you are well."

Darcy backed silently to the door where he would leave, his eyes never leaving the woman he hoped to make his wife. Upon reaching the door, he opened it, only to find that Jane, Bingley, Anne and the colonel were all pressed up against it. Only the colonel actually fell.

Chapter Forty

AWAY TO LONDON

Darcy looked down at his cousin on the floor and dryly said, "I have not known you to be a praying man before this. Miss Elizabeth's fever may have done some good, if it has driven *you* to your knees! I must implore you to say your amens, however, and rise. There is much we need to speak of."

"Amen." Richard said emphatically, with a nod, and rapidly found his feet. "I will meet you in my chambers, Darcy. We will be undisturbed there." He hastily beat a retreat from the room.

Jane, Bingley and Anne had all stepped back, leaving a clear path for Darcy to pass into the sitting room. He bid them all to sit and then he secured the door to the hallway before he spoke.

"Anne," he said gravely, "Miss Elizabeth did not actually request to see me, did she?"

Jane and Mr. Bingley looked at Anne together with astonishment, while Anne looked guiltily down at her hands, which lay folded neatly in her lap. "Not exactly," she finally admitted, "but I thought it would be good for her spirits."

"You may have been right in your belief, but the means was very wrong." Darcy frowned. "She was not prepared for it."

"She did ask if you were still near, cousin, and was most assuredly comforted in my answer that you were. With her fever gone and Mr. Jones' draught in her, she was surely sufficiently lucid to speak with you. We—none of us—ever imagined that you would close the door." Anne looked at him defiantly. "I made certain that she wore a dressing gown over her nightdress. She was not inappropriately attired."

"I am not angry, Anne. I suspect however, that Mr. Jones' draught contains ingredients that weakened Miss Elizabeth's natural reserve." Darcy raised his eyebrows. "Although she seemed perfectly rational, her speech was slower—her words slightly slurred. When she awakens, she may very well be distraught to recall what she has revealed."

Jane gasped. "Mr. Darcy, if what you say is true, she will be mortified!"

"She well may be, Miss Bennet; however, what she has said changes nothing of my regard for your sister." Darcy replied. "She said nothing indelicate or untoward. She was perfectly ladylike."

"I should go to her." Jane said, moving toward the bedchamber. "I thank you for your assistance today, Mr. Darcy, but I think it may be best if you leave now."

Darcy nodded, watching Jane as she quit the room. He then turned back to Anne. "It is already past tea-time. Your mother will discover that you are not in your room as she has believed, and her wrath will shake the rafters of Netherfield if she finds you in a sick room. I think you too must go."

Anne nodded. "You are correct, cousin. I will go and will pretend to have been sleeping late for my mother's sake. Heaven only knows how many times I have done so before! I can only hope that my assistance today has been of some service to Miss Elizabeth."

She looked strangely at her cousin—a searching look, a hopeful look, and then she continued, awkwardly, to share the thoughts that had been on her mind in the course of the day. "There is something so very singular about Elizabeth Bennet—she is quite extraordinary. I know that this is not lost on you, cousin, for I can see in every look that you love her, and I believe that her feelings are the same." Anne shifted uncomfortably and crossed her arms over her chest before she continued. "You may be one of the most eligible marriage prospects in all of England, but even I can see that you are barely worthy of her. I love you as if you were my own brother, but I see your faults as any sister would. They are nothing to me, of course. I admire you all the same, yet I will lay them before you—because I know that no one else will!" Anne stood and began to pace. "You are too proud. I have lived all of my days in a household of pride, and the pain it has caused could fill volumes." She gave him a foreboding look before she continued. "Too often, your arrogance turns to a selfish disdain for the feelings of others. Elizabeth is a compassionate and caring woman—she will *not* be able to respect you if she discovers this trait." She had looked at the door as she spoke and lowered her voice, as though Elizabeth might overhear her and discover it from this very conversation. "As for your high station—look to my mother and you will see the toxic effects of the preservation of rank. She may remain high and mighty, but her throne of nobility is a cold and lonely place." Anne shuddered, and Darcy realized the depth of loneliness this must have brought to Anne as well. "I have seen you reject the daughters of dukes and earls without ceremony, cousin, and I am certain you feel Miss Elizabeth is beneath you. For once, listen to your heart instead of that conceited head of yours, William. Elizabeth Bennet is not merely your equal, she is your superior in many ways, and a love match with her would secure you a lifetime of happiness. There. I have said my peace and will say no more."

Darcy, who had listened patiently, replied, "Anne, I have never heard such a speech from you in all our days! I am certain it took a great deal of courage for you to do it." He looked at her intently. "You are perfectly right in everything you have said, and I can only reply that I value your counsel, my dear cousin, and will take your words to heart."

Anne had anticipated many possible responses from her austere cousin. This was not one of them. She ran to him and gave him a quick hug as she whispered, "Thank you!" She immediately turned to the door and with a backward glance informed him, "I will go find mother now."

This left Mr. Bingley and Mr. Darcy alone in the room. They regarded one another for a full half a minute before Bingley spoke.

"The key, I suppose, to understanding the heart of a Bennet appears to be that one must catch them when they are out of their wits." Bingley said with a laugh.

"Perhaps you can laugh now, but it was not so very long ago when you were quite beside yourself about Miss Bennet's injuries." Darcy frowned. "Miss Elizabeth is not yet out of danger, Charles. I beg you to be serious."

"Not out of danger? Has her fever not yet broken?" Bingley's eyes were wide with astonishment.

"Not naturally broken Bingley. The fever will undoubtedly return. If she keeps her wits, the medicine from Mr. Jones will suffice, but if she loses touch again, the bath must be repeated as soon as possible. You should assign a dependable maid to assist Miss Bennet in the task."

"Of course, Darcy." Bingley nodded in agreement. "Sarah will do very well."

"As pleasant as it may be to have Miss Bennet sleep on your shoulder, you know full well that this will not provide adequate rest. While her sister is still in any danger, you should have a chaise and some bedding brought to these rooms. We did the same for Miss Elizabeth when Miss Bennet was recovering, do you not recall?" Darcy chastised. "It will not do for both of them to be sick."

Bingley nodded. "I should have thought of that. I will see to it at once."

"I must go to London on urgent business, Bingley, and will be absent for several days. I have charged the colonel to see that Lady Catherine and her daughter are removed from Netherfield in my absence. This will free their rooms for both Miss Bennet and me."

"Excellent! That is a capital plan!" Bingley clapped his hands. "With all due respect, your aunt does not make a pleasant houseguest. She has the servants in an uproar."

"I have another favor to ask of you." Darcy looked at his friend apprehensively. "I have reason to believe that it is unwise to leave my sister in London at this time. She is presently ensconced in my residence in town with her companion, but there is some unpleasant business afoot, which would harm her greatly. I would like to bring her to Netherfield with me when I return."

"But, of course!" Bingley smiled happily. "We should be such a merry party with your sister among us!"

"This returns us to the matter of accommodations. I may yet require assistance from the colonel, so I do not wish to send him away prematurely, but my sister will require a room."

"Oh yes. I never thought that eight rooms would be insufficient when I leased this estate. It seemed more than adequate at the time." Charles eyebrows knitted in frustration.

"I have a suggestion, but your sister may not like it." Darcy replied.

"My sister?" Bingley's eyebrows shot up in wonderment. "Of what do you speak?"

"Mr. and Mrs. Hurst are each in use of a bedchamber. If they would be willing to share, this would free a room for Georgiana." Darcy said. "I fear your sister may resent the loss of her privacy."

"It is a perfect solution, Darcy. My sisters are far too coddled. Such economies will do Louisa good. I will see that it is carried out before you return." Bingley nodded.

Darcy grasped his friend by the shoulders, shaking him slightly. "Thank you, Bingley! I will return your hospitality come summer! You must visit Pemberley."

Bingley nodded, a plan forming. "If I may extend that invitation to my sister Louisa in exchange for her cooperation, I believe she will endure Mr. Hurst's snoring as long as need be!"

Darcy smiled. "By all means. Invite both of your sisters if that is what it takes to secure the comfort of my sister. Whatever it takes Bingley!"

Darcy strode to the door. "I must leave immediately to make it to London tonight. I will see you in a few days."

Jane had found Elizabeth sleeping—a surprise, considering that Mr. Darcy had just left her bedside moments before. She was disappointed in this, for she longed to speak to her sister. She contented herself, instead, with tending to Elizabeth's comfort. When she had done all she knew to do, she noted that Elizabeth kept to one side of the bed, so Jane laid herself down on the other and quickly fell asleep.

Darcy went directly to Colonel Fitzwilliam's chambers, entering without knocking. Richard sat in a chair reading a book, one leg crossed on the other, nearly making a table for the book.

"Ah, Darcy." Colonel Fitzwilliam looked up and smiled. "You neglected to call for your carriage. I took care of that for you. It should be at the door very soon."

"Thank you." Darcy nodded.

"Assuming that you will be at your London residence, it hardly seemed necessary to pack a wardrobe for you, but I had your valet put together a few of your personal effects in that bag." He nodded toward a black valise on the table. "I can think of nothing else you need."

"I thank you once again." Darcy bowed slightly. "Have you any further thoughts on Wickham?"

"Aye." Colonel Fitzwilliam scowled. "I have thought of no less than six bloodless ways to hasten his voyage to hell."

"That is a last resort, Fitz. You are too eager to see the man die." Darcy replied. "There must be another way."

"Another way?" Fitzwilliam gripped his stubble-covered chin thoughtfully. "I am certain there is another way. Give me but a moment, and I will think of a seventh." He counted off on his fingers as he spoke. "So far I have strangulation, poison, suffocation, a lightning strike, drowning and starvation." He looked up at Darcy, squinting. "Here it comes—another stroke of genius is upon me ... I have it! Wickham will freeze to death! I will remove his coat and tie him up—leave him in a barn ... walk away. I would not even be near when he finally succumbs to the cold."

"Richard, you cannot possibly entertain such a thought." Darcy rolled his eyes. "We are gentlemen, you and I. We cannot lower ourselves so."

"Have you a better idea?"

"I will speak with him first. I am hoping he will come to his senses, although I harbor no illusions about his character. He has turned out very bad!" Darcy shook his head. "I cannot imagine when his heart turned, but he has crossed all boundaries now. One thing is certain—he will receive no more money from me, as a matter of principle. Nor will he succeed in barring me from Miss Bennet. He has no right to interfere in our lives in such a way. As soon as I discover more about the letter, I will know what must be done. I must, in all of this, protect my sister from him!"

"Georgiana will not be safe from him until he is dead. Now if you would just let me...," Fitzwilliam began.

"No!" Darcy stopped him. "Can you not see that intentional injury to Wickham is an affront to my father's memory? I may despise the man, but my father loved him. I will find a peaceful solution. I must!"

"If you change your mind cousin, you know I am happy to personally install him in Beelzebub's regiment. His uniform will even be free!" Fitzwilliam slapped his knee. "That is better than he deserves, you know."

"If I change my mind, you will be the first to hear of it." Darcy bowed, picked up the valise and as he went through the door, he turned. "In the meantime, you may focus your scheming on dealing with Aunt Catherine!"

"Is that it? Am I dismissed so easily?" The colonel smirked.

"No. There is one more thing. Keep that abominable Mr. Collins away from Elizabeth Bennet!" Darcy growled as he pulled the door closed behind him.

Lady Catherine was, at that very moment, in a rage. Darcy could hear her loudly railing about Anne's exposure to the fever as he slipped past the bedchambers occupied by his aunt and cousin. He felt a bit guilty about leaving them to Colonel Fitzwilliam, but he knew the colonel was competent and would manage his aunt far better than he himself could.

Fortunately for him, the carriage pulled up to the door at the very moment he descended the stairs. He boarded it and was away before even Caroline Bingley realized he was leaving.

Darcy's thoughts were on fire with all that pressed upon him. He wearied his mind with his concern for Georgiana, his rekindled hatred of Wickham, frustration that his aunt had imposed herself at Netherfield and the idea that Mr. Collins was still expecting to marry Elizabeth. He worried himself that Jane was left with only Charles Bingley to stand between Caroline and whatever mean agenda was on her mind. He pondered on how best to approach Mr. Wickham and wondered anew whether there was actually such a letter as Wickham had described. Part of him disbelieved that his sister was capable of all that Wickham claimed, but the other part knew how easily she was led. He felt a wave of nausea surge, just considering the possibilities he could encounter.

When he had exhausted all other avenues of thought, he permitted his mind to stray to Elizabeth. It was a strange realization that he had now seen this women at her very worst and that even in that moment, he found her beautiful beyond description. How very different that was from the first time he had seen her and had found her wanting. "*Unfathomable,*" he whispered to himself.

It was different too from their later encounters when he thought that he loved her. Now he realized he had he had only just truly crossed into that realm, where nothing else mattered but her comfort, her well-being—her happiness. He desperately wished that he could turn the carriage and return to her side, but he knew that he must forge ahead and deal with Wickham.

He hoped that she understood his intentions—that he had made himself sufficiently clear. He could not afford to propose to her formally until Wickham was no longer a threat, for she would be obligated to share such tidings with her family, and news of an engagement would most certainly reach Wickham.

He allowed himself to dwell on their final conversation. He had realized that she was drugged immediately, when he saw the dilation of her eyes as they shone in the candlelight. He felt some abhorrence that he had taken advantage of the situation, of not leaving when he knew that she might be too forthcoming. He had stayed, however, and learned what he needed to know. He set aside most of the shame he felt, for had he not spoken of what was in his heart to her as well?

Darcy turned his mind to the future. Elizabeth loved him—surely, she would accept his offer and they would marry as soon as it could be arranged. Would they spend Christmas together as master and mistress of Pemberley? Would Georgiana love Elizabeth as her new sister? Would Elizabeth come to love Pemberley as he did? Would she be happy so far away from her family? He knew the answers to his thoughts were all yes, and his mind soon drifted to more indecorous thoughts.

He pondered on their happy engagement and planned the times and places where he could steal a kiss or two before the wedding night—when he would finally take her to his bed and make her his wife. He thought tenderly and passionately about that night, when all that was forbidden to them now would be sanctioned by the church and in the eyes of God. He understood, perhaps for the first time in his life, why the marriage bed was a sacred place. In spite of his lusty thoughts—and he did suffer from those—he pondered on the great gift it was for this woman to entrust every part of herself to his care, and he vowed never to betray that trust.

Long gone were any thoughts of her lack of fortune, low connections, disapproval from his family and the improper behavior of hers. All he could think of now was the joy of sharing his own good fortune with his lovely Elizabeth, of taking her proudly on his arm and introducing his bride to all he knew and of filling the halls of Pemberley with children that bore a resemblance to them both.

Eventually, he dozed in the carriage, but the dreams that followed as he rocked and swayed on the finely appointed seat were but an extension of the happy thoughts he nurtured in his heart.

Chapter Forty - One

INTRIGUES, LIES & DECEPTIONS

It had been many years since Anne de Bourgh had dared to defy her mother. Defiance, as defined by Lady Catherine de Bourgh, constituted any contradiction, any act causing her displeasure, and any behavior deemed rebellious or against the expectations of the great lady. Having chosen her path in defying her mother that morning, Anne felt a turn inside herself, a metamorphosis in her mind that both terrified her and freed her.

She had hoped to avoid any unpleasantness by returning to her room unnoticed, but her mother had been waiting in her chamber when she slipped into the room, and a great quarrel had occurred. Lady Catherine, astonished by her daughter's defiance, expressed her displeasure at Anne's treacherous betrayal, her disregard for her own health and her pathetic friendship with "that Bennet girl." She then railed against the idea that Anne would play nursemaid to a person who was hardly worth her notice.

Lady Catherine had expected Anne to react with her familiar submission. She was sorely disappointed in the outcome. Not only did Anne retain her composure, she insisted that her friendship with Elizabeth Bennet would not be so easily dismissed, that she admired her new friend greatly, and that assisting in her care had been a privilege, and not a hardship at all.

Lady Catherine forbade Anne from returning to Elizabeth's room on grounds of Anne's own health and attempted to extract her promise of obedience. Anne, who had never challenged her mother on any point since the age of two, stood her ground now. She would not make the promise. Lady Catherine attributed Anne's obstinacy to the influence of Miss Bennet.

Lady Catherine, now in high dudgeon, confined Anne to her room and stated that she knew exactly what to do. Anne shuddered at the threatening tone in her mother's declaration and almost gave into the demand, but ultimately, she held fast. It was not until Lady Catherine stormed out of the room, slamming the door behind her, that Anne collapsed on the bed, weeping and distraught over the confrontation with her mother.

Caroline and Louisa were alone, enjoying a satisfying exchange of criticism and gossip in the drawing room when a footman announced the arrival of Mrs. Bennet, Miss Mary Bennet, Miss Catherine Bennet, Miss Lydia Bennet, and Mr. William Collins. Caroline agreed to see them and then grimaced at her sister as soon as the footman's back was turned. "How I suffer here in Hertfordshire, sister," she groaned. "I hope Charles sets his sights on London soon. I cannot endure another moment with the Bennets." Louisa nodded sympathetically.

Upon entrance into the room, Mrs. Bennet took charge of the conversation.

"My goodness!" She declared, "We did not expect to find such a small party assembled here, with a house as full as Netherfield Park has been in many a year. You do both appear completely recovered from the ball. Such stamina is a blessing, I assure you. I have been exhausted all day from it. I found a need, however, to venture out, so that I may bring some additional clothing for Jane and Elizabeth. It is so very *gracious* of you, Miss Bingley, to provide care for my Elizabeth after her fainting spell last night. Pray, how fares she today?"

To this question, Caroline did not know the answer, so she simply replied, "Mrs. Bennet, you have come all this way; perhaps you would like to visit her and satisfy yourself as to her condition."

She gestured for the footman to show the way, and following a series of curtsies, the entire company from Longbourn filed out of the room behind him. They said not a word among them as they were led up the stairs. The footman knocked on the door to the sitting room and after a pause with no answer, entered the room, which was empty. The footman knocked on the closed door to the bedchamber, which was opened just a crack by the maid, Sarah. She slipped through the door, pulling it closed behind her.

She spotted the group assembled and curtseyed before she spoke. "The Miss Bennets are sleeping now and are not to be disturbed, by order of Mr. Bingley."

"Not to be disturbed?" Mrs. Bennet squawked. "I am their mother and will see them if I please. Not to be disturbed, indeed! It is the middle of the day, after all. Inform Miss Bennet that I have come this moment, and do not give me any more impertinent answers, or Mr. Bingley will hear of it!"

Sarah colored, curtseyed and retreated into the bedchamber. Mary, Kitty and Lydia removed themselves to the available seats, but Mrs. Bennet stood impatiently at the door, while Mr. Collins stood beside her, flushed with anticipation.

A few minutes passed before a sleepy Jane opened the door and stepped into the sitting room.

"Mama, what are you doing here?" She rubbed her eyes and waggled her head attempting to shake the grogginess away as she asked the question.

"Why, I have come to see how *Miss Lizzy* is doing." Mrs. Bennet retorted. "May I not call upon my very own daughter?"

"Mama, Mr. Jones was here but half an hour ago and gave Lizzy another dose of his draught, which makes her very sleepy. He said that to recover, it is best that Lizzy rest as much as possible. Her fever is not so high as it was, but she is still very ill. I beg you not to insist on seeing her today. Tomorrow would be better." Jane replied.

"She is well enough to see her mother." Mrs. Bennet insisted. "I will see her now. You may wait with your sisters." She pushed Jane aside, stepped into the room, and with a gesture for Jane to clear the entryway, pulled the door closed behind her.

Jane went and sat on the settee, alarmed by her inability to dissuade her mother from the unwise course of waking Elizabeth. Kitty, seeing her distress, moved to sit by Jane and gave her a gentle hug of reassurance. Lydia sat on the sofa, holding her hand in a strange position in front of her face, while Mary, also upon the couch, watched with a serious expression as Mr. Collins remained expectantly by the door to the bedchamber.

Several minutes passed, during which time the muffled sounds of Mrs. Bennet waking Elizabeth up could be heard through the door, distressing Jane further. At length, her heavy footsteps could be heard, and the door opened.

"Elizabeth will see you now, Mr. Collins." Mrs. Bennet said somewhat smugly. She opened the door to admit him and then pulled it closed behind her as she joined her daughters in the sitting room.

&

Anne de Bourgh was determined to show her mother that she could not be ordered about as if she were still a child. She left her room as soon as she had composed herself and went downstairs to the drawing room where she found Miss Bingley and Mrs. Hurst quietly conversing.

"Oh Anne, do come in!" Caroline smiled with an insincere graciousness. "We were just speaking of you."

As Anne entered the room, Mr. Bingley arrived behind her.

"Louisa," he said, "I must speak to you and your husband as a matter of urgency. Would you be so kind as to locate him and join me in the study?" His sister nodded and stood, quitting the room behind her brother, leaving Anne and Caroline alone in the drawing room.

"So," Caroline began in sugared tones, "your mother tells me that you are engaged to your cousin, Mr. Darcy."

"She tells everyone that." Anne replied. "It gives her much pleasure to do so."

"Have you an engagement ring? I would dearly love to see the sort of ring that Mr. Darcy presents to his intended bride. It must be very beautiful." Caroline said.

"I have no ring." Anne stated serenely.

"Oh? That must be very *disappointing*. It is the latest fashion, after all, for a man to present his intended with a ring." Caroline probed, "Pray, when are the nuptials to take place?"

"No date for our marriage has been set." Anne said with a smile.

"No date?" Caroline echoed.

"As you are so curious about it, I will tell you that I believe Mr. Darcy will announce a wedding date very soon."

"You poor dear." Caroline cooed. "No ring and no date. You must be beside yourself."

"Not at all." Anne blinked innocently.

"When did he propose?" Caroline asked, her eyes squinting slightly.

"Did my mother not tell you? She usually tells people that part as well." Anne said with a laugh.

"No." Caroline frowned. "Perhaps you would tell me."

"Well, my mother would tell you that the engagement is of a *peculiar kind,* that our union was *planned from the cradle*." Anne replied, as if she were confiding a great secret. "The idea is to unite the de Bourgh and Darcy legacies into a grand and powerful estate that will signify nearly the largest in all of England."

"So it is a marriage of convenience?" Caroline smiled in spite of herself.

"Some would say it is." Anne confirmed, "But not I. My cousin would never marry for convenience alone. He hides it well, but I assure you, he is a passionate man."

Caroline's eyes widened, and she sought Anne's confidence. "Do you *love* him?"

"I have known him all my life, Miss Bingley. What is there not to love?" Anne replied with a composed smile.

"Does he love you as well?" Caroline's composure was now somewhat threatened.

"He loves me as much and in the same way as I love him Miss Bingley. You must not worry about that. He will not be in a loveless marriage if I have anything to say about it." Anne reached out and patted Caroline's hand.

"I do hate to change the subject, but I faithfully promised my dear cousin that I would continue with the lemon balm tea." Anne said. "He does not wish to see me fall ill as Miss Elizabeth did."

"Of course." Caroline smiled. "I will order some for myself as well.

ஓ

Colonel Fitzwilliam had remained in his quarters after Darcy left. He had two purposes in doing so. The first was to drink a glass of Port wine to relax himself and the second was to determine what his strategy would be. A good military man never begins a campaign without a strategy, preferably a good one. He paced and pondered for an hour before a smile lit his face and he thumped his fist on his table with excitement.

"How did I not think of this before?" He cried aloud. "It is too easy!"

He set out at once to find his aunt. He started his search in the drawing room, where he found Caroline and Anne quietly sipping tea.

"Cousin Anne, do you know where I may find your mother?" Colonel Fitzwilliam said with a bow.

"No, I am sorry I do not." Anne shook her head.

"I believe she had planned to stay near her chambers today." Caroline grinned. "This morning, Mr. Darcy threatened to have the servants pack her belongings, and she seemed quite determined that it would not happen."

"Thank you." He bowed again and quit the room, bound for the stairs. In the hallway, however, he heard raised voices echoing from the direction of the study, and fearing that his aunt was causing trouble, he quickly arrived at the study door. He heard the usually quiet Mrs. Hurst, nearly in hysterics, as she insisted that she could not, under any circumstances share a room with her husband.

Convinced that his aunt was not a party in that conversation, he returned to the stairs and soon found himself outside his aunt's chambers. He closed his eyes and knocked loudly at the door.

"Who dares disturb me?" Lady Catherine said loudly. "Go away."

"It is I, your nephew, Richard." He injected urgency into his voice, knowing that this would pique his aunt's curiosity.

"Come." She answered irritably.

With a deep breath, the colonel turned the knob and entered the small sitting room, where his aunt stood in the center.

"Aunt Catherine, I have not seen you all day. Are you well?"

"No." She said sternly. "I am not well at all. It has been a most distressing day." She imperiously set herself in the middle of a long settee by the fireplace and repeated, "A most distressing day!"

"Oh." Richard said, and seated himself in an attitude of sympathy near to her. "Is there anything I can do to ease your distress? Would you like me to order some tea or a glass of wine?"

"Wine at this hour? That would not do!"

"Some tea then? We have been drinking lemon balm on the advice of the apothecary." Richard offered.

"Lemon balm?" Lady Catherine's eyebrows rose as though the suggestion were scandalous. "These apothecaries are not to be trusted. Lemon balm is too mild. One must drink hyssop tea to prevent infection! Someone should have asked me. Why was I not consulted?"

"I will call for some hyssop tea for you." Richard replied. "And advise the household of your recommendation."

He left the room for a few minutes and returned. "It should be here shortly. Now, tell me what vexes you Aunt Catherine, and I will do what I can to help."

"Oh nephew, your attachment to me is such a comfort. I am distressed by so many things. My nephew Mr. Darcy has not yet announced his engagement to Anne, and due to this dreadful business with that Bennet girl's sick room, I am undone. It is not to be borne, and yet Anne has defied me and exposed herself to the illness in nursing her. If Anne sickens and dies from another fever, what will I do? She is all I have in this world, except, of course, Rosings and my dear nephews."

"These are heavy burdens indeed, Aunt." Richard soothed her. "How may I be of assistance?"

"You must convince Fitzwilliam to marry Anne." Lady Catherine declared. "And it must be done immediately."

"I cannot." Richard shook his head.

"Why ever not?" Lady Catherine sat up in an even more stiff posture than she had been and glared at him. "He may listen to you, although he does not listen to me."

"Did you not know? Darcy has gone to London." The colonel patted his aunt's hand. "I do not know when he is to return."

"London?" Lady Catherine gritted her teeth as she spoke. "He leaves Anne and me here in this house of disease while he goes to London? This is not to be borne! He said nothing of London this morning. Order my carriage, nephew, and call for the servants to come pack our things. Anne and I will return to London as soon as all is ready."

"As you wish, Aunt Catherine. I am happy to assist in any way that I can." Richard stood. "I will send Anne to speak with you. I am certain you wish to advise her of the change in plans."

"Yes." Lady Catherine sniffed. "And I shall make her drink some hyssop tea as well. The lemon balm will do nothing!"

Richard smiled indulgently at his Aunt and quit the room. "Too easy." He muttered under his breath as he walked away.

He had not taken three steps before Sarah, the maid who had been helping with Elizabeth, breathlessly stopped him in the hallway. She made a hurried curtsey and delivered her message. "Colonel Fitzwilliam, begging your pardon, sir, but Miss Bennet asks that you come to Miss Elizabeth's room—as a matter of urgency."

"What is it? Has she taken another turn?" He asked, alarmed.

"No sir. Miss Bennet said to tell you that her cousin, Mr. Collins, is in Miss Elizabeth's room at this very moment. Mrs. Bennet brought him to see her, and it could not be helped."

Colonel Fitzwilliam turned and ran toward Elizabeth's room without another word, the young maid but a few steps behind him.

Darcy awoke as his carriage reached the outskirts of London, when the familiar sounds and smells of the city stirred him. It was already dark, a light drizzle of rain was turning to mist in the streets, and the first traces of fog hung in wispy trails along the walkways. He was filled with foreboding as he looked to the dark alleyways leading to the labyrinth that was the underbelly of London. Wickham, he assumed, was hidden somewhere in the seamy parts of the city, and a bitter tang entered Darcy's throat as he thought about the man who had once been his friend.

By the time the carriage swept down the crescent row where Darcy House dominated the terraces, his anticipation of seeing Georgiana had overcome any trepidation he felt regarding the conversation they must have. He eagerly descended from the carriage and entered his house straightway.

The dining room immediately off the entryway was lit, and inquiring after his sister as he shed his coat and hat, he learned that Georgiana and Mrs. Annesley had only just begun their supper. He instructed his housekeeper that he would join them, which sent the servants scurrying to accommodate the directive immediately.

Georgiana had stopped eating to listen when the front door had been opened. When Darcy entered the dining room, she leapt from her seat at the table with a soft squeal and welcomed her brother with an enthusiastic hug. Although she was a young woman now, the mode of their greeting had changed little in the past decade. He fondly wrapped his arms around her and kissed the top of her head, after which he gripped her face in his hands and looked into her eyes with all of his brotherly affection. "Are you well?" he asked gently.

"Oh yes, I am better every day." Georgiana replied with a shy smile. "Mrs. Annesley is very kind, and I am learning a splendid new concerto on the pianoforte. We did not know you were coming—this is a great surprise, dearest brother, to find you here with us in London." She hugged him again.

"I did not know I was to come either, until this morning." Darcy replied. "There is much we need to speak of. Let us eat, and afterward, I would speak with you privately."

Georgiana looked at him curiously and nodded. "But, of course."

The meal passed pleasantly, with Georgiana quietly answering her brother's questions about how she passed her days, how she was doing in her studies, and who had come to call. After the meal, rather than separate for any length of time, he invited her directly to join him in the library, which also served as his study when he was in town.

She followed him meekly, with the demeanor of a child who knew she was in trouble, but uncertain as to why. By the time he closed the door behind her, she was trembling. Darcy wrapped his arms around her again and comforted her. "Do not fear, little one." He soothed. "You must know that I love you." She nodded, and they sat next to each other on a settee.

Darcy extracted a handkerchief from his inside pocket; he held it out for his sister to see.

She took it, curiously, spreading it open in her palm to study the whitework embroidery. "Oh brother, this is so beautiful! Have you brought me another gift from Hertfordshire?"

"No, sister, I am not giving this to you, but I wish to tell you something about it. It belongs to a lady in Hertfordshire named Miss Elizabeth Bennet." Darcy explained.

"You have written of her! She is the one with four sisters, is she not?"

"The very one." Darcy nodded indulgently. "And she embroidered this handkerchief these past weeks. She finished it but a few days ago."

"Why do you have it? A lady would not give up a treasure such as this ... oh! Did she give it to you as a token? Do you carry it for love?" Georgiana smiled up at her brother with a knowing smile.

"Do not let your imagination run away with you, Georgiana. She dropped it, and I retrieved it. I will be returning it soon."

"Oh." She looked back and studied the handkerchief. "Did you not say that her name was Bennet? Why is there not a "B" in the pattern here? What does the "D" represent?"

"I do not know." Darcy admitted. "Miss Bennet is somewhat mysterious at times. This is one of those mysteries." He smiled indulgently at his sister. "I was wondering if you would like to help me return it."

"How could I do that? Is she now in London?"

"No, dearest. I thought that perhaps you would like to visit Hertfordshire and stay for a few weeks at Netherfield Park. My friend, Mr. Bingley, was most pleased at the idea of your visit, and I think you would enjoy it there."

"And I shall meet the mysterious Miss Elizabeth, shall I not?" Georgiana smiled happily at her brother.

"She would very much like to make your acquaintance." Darcy nodded. "I think you shall like her."

"When do we leave? I must begin to plan!" She cried happily.

"In a few days, I hope." Darcy replied with a soft smile. "But first, we must speak of something less pleasant, which is of a serious and urgent nature."

"What is it? I see this distresses you! What do you speak of?" Georgiana's countenance shifted to concern.

"I wish I did not have to ask this question of you, but I must." Darcy shook his head. "Please know that I am not angry with you, but I must insist that you speak truthfully. I did not press you on these things those months ago, but I must do so now."

Georgiana nodded silently, her eyes wide with uncertainty.

"Last summer—when you were at Ramsgate with Mr. Wickham—did you ... that is ... what did you ... I mean to say ... did he commit anything improper on your person?"

"Oh." Georgiana blushed. "Not terribly so, dear brother. He did kiss me once—when I agreed to marry him, but it was very fast. I told him that I wished to wait until after our vows for anything more, and he went no further. Is that what you needed to know?"

"You are a good girl, my dear." Darcy smiled at her. "Did you, during this time, write any notes or letters to Mr. Wickham?"

"Not exactly." Georgiana replied. "But I did once write a letter *for* him."

"What does that mean?" Darcy asked abruptly. "There is a letter?"

"Well, yes." Georgiana nodded with some fear. "George—I mean Mr. Wickham, told me it was necessary for us to travel to Scotland—in case someone stopped and questioned us. He told me everything that I was to write, and then he was to carry it with him in case it was needed."

"What did it say?"

"I hardly remember." Georgiana frowned. "I suppose it said that I loved him and wanted to marry him. There was something about our elopement being of my own free will. He had me write that my parents were dead and that my governess and companion, Mrs. Younge, was aware of all the particulars."

"Was there anything more?" Darcy pressed her. "Think carefully."

"I do not believe so." Georgiana shook her head. "He did ask me to put in a part about being compromised, to prove that the elopement was necessary, but I told him that was silly. One did not have to be compromised to go to Gretna Greene, and since I was of the minimum age, I felt that adding a lie to an otherwise truthful document would be a mistake."

"What happened to the letter?"

"Mr. Wickham took it. I imagine it is gone now. We did not marry, after all." Georgiana shrugged her shoulders. "There is nothing to be done with such a letter now."

"Have you seen or heard from Mr. Wickham since Ramsgate?"

"Well, yes. It was only today, but earlier, of course. Mrs. Annesley and I saw him in the park. He was wearing a red coat and looking very fine. He came to speak with us and said he was on leave from the militia. He asked me many questions about you and was ever so friendly. I do not believe he is angry that we did not marry at all, which was a great relief for me."

"That will be all for now, Georgiana. You may plan to leave for Netherfield in a few days. I will let you know when I have concluded my business." He turned to the pile of correspondence that sat on the desk.

"Fitzwilliam?" Her soft voice interrupted.

Darcy looked up. "Yes?"

"Thank you for the blue shawl you sent me." She said with a shy smile. "I love it and think of you whenever I wear it."

Darcy came around the desk and hugged his sister once again. "That shawl is very special to me as well. I believe we will both be happy when you are using it. Very happy indeed."

Chapter Forty-Two

THE PROPOSAL OF MR. COLLINS

My mother has lost her mind. Elizabeth sat, propped up in the bed, her mouth agape as Mrs. Bennet fluffed the pillows behind her, raising her daughter to a near sitting position. Mrs. Bennet then smoothed out Elizabeth's hair with a quick finger-comb and tied the top of her dressing gown closed.

"Mama, stop this." Elizabeth protested. "I am very tired."

"No," Mrs. Bennet muttered under her breath, and then tugged on the end of the ribbon. "We had best leave him with a little view. Nothing shocking." She spread the top of the dressing gown wider, exposing Elizabeth's neck. "Oh, that's better."

"Mama, what are you doing? Elizabeth re-tied the ribbon as best she could with fumbling fingers. "I do not want to see *anyone* right now."

"Miss Lizzy, you must listen to your mother, and do as I say." Mrs. Bennet puckered her lips and nodded firmly at her daughter. "I know what I am doing, and you must trust me. For once in your life, set aside your foolish notions and do the right thing for your family." Her face softened and she sat down next to Elizabeth on the bed. "You would not want your poor mother to starve in the hedgerows now, would you? I realize it is not the best time for it, but Mr. Collins will be returning to Kent soon, and we must make the best of things while he is here."

"Mama, let Jane come to me. I need Jane." Elizabeth pleaded, closing her eyes. "Send Mr. Collins away. I will not see him."

"I will do no such thing, Miss Lizzy!" Mrs. Bennet exclaimed in a whisper. "You will see him! He has come all this way, eager to speak with you! Deny him an audience, indeed. Are you determined to put me into an early grave? My nerves cannot take much more of your obstinate ways. You are too willful—too headstrong! The world does not change for one such as you; you must change for it, and you will start today."

"No, Mama, I beg you." Elizabeth's eyes locked desperately with her mother's. "He could have nothing to say to me that I want to hear."

Mrs. Bennet glared angrily at Elizabeth. "It wounds me deeply that of all my girls, it is you who will be the mistress of Longbourn someday. Your ingratitude is shameful—do you hear me? You must embrace your good fortune with a thankful heart. I *insist* you grant him an audience as he has requested." She marched determinedly to the door to the sitting room and swung it open. "Elizabeth will see you now, Mr. Collins."

Elizabeth watched helplessly from the bed as her mother departed. From the dim light of the darkened bedchamber, the silhouette of her mother passed through the doorway into the adjacent sitting room, crossing paths with Mr. Collins as his shadowy form stepped through the threshold.

Although her mind was affected by the sedating drugs administered by Mr. Jones, Elizabeth found herself with full clarity regarding one truth. Mr. Collins was here to propose to her. She felt a peculiar detachment from the impending proposition, and calmness settled upon her as she resolved to simply get the business over with as quickly as possible.

He approached her bedside. "My fair cousin, Elizabeth," he began, his hands wringing together slightly, "I have come to you now in what is otherwise a time of distress to bring to you such happy tidings that I am sure they will improve your spirits and your health ere long."

"Please sit, Mr. Collins. I cannot see your face." Elizabeth replied, her eyes squinting.

"Oh, yes, of course." The chair that was next to the bedside was a woman's chair, and Mr. Collins looked upon it with some disdain before he set himself down on it. "As I had begun to say, I have looked upon this moment with the greatest anticipation. I am certain that you know of the reason I traveled from Kent to visit my cousins at Longbourn, for it has not been a secret by any means, but I feel it my duty to explain, leaving no misunderstanding between us, the reason I am here before you today.

You may well be aware that it is less than a year since I was granted the living at Hunsford. Divine providence itself has blessed me not only with a valuable living but with a most generous patroness, as well, who has condescended most graciously to lend her considerable wisdom in advising me on the matter of matrimony. On the point that I must marry immediately, she has been most insistent, and upon learning of my inevitable inheritance of this estate when your father is no longer earthbound, she persuaded me that the only honorable course was to marry one of his daughters in order to spare you all from the fate that our ancestors did not. But this you must already know." Mr. Collins reached out to take one of Elizabeth's hands, which were folded together on the bedclothes.

"I must beg you not to be so familiar, Mr. Collins." Elizabeth said as she pulled her hand away.

"You will not consider my touch too familiar when we are married, Miss Elizabeth. Do you not recall, on the day we first met, how taken Lady Catherine de Bourgh was with you? She favored you above your sisters, recommending you from the very beginning as the ideal partner of my future life. You must see what an honor this is to have been noticed by such an esteemed lady as she. Therefore, I have singled you out in my attentions and intentions, for I am as faithful a man as there ever was, and once my course is set, I am true to it. Knowing that Lady Catherine approved of you, I have observed that in company, your behavior is above reproach. You are intelligent and energetic, and your concern for those within your sphere—all of these commendable qualities highly recommend you as the ideal parson's wife. Why, the courage it took for you to hold a dying baby in your arms and comfort her family in the hours before her death—this spirit of generosity and compassion is an example of the goodness of your nature, although in future, I hope that you will exercise more caution. It will not do for you to become ill again."

"Dying baby?" Elizabeth shook her head, her features contorted. "Who? Of what do you speak?" She began to tremble. "Not, not, not ... oh, no!" She began to cry, her hands covering her face. "No, no, no, oh, little Hannah, no!"

"Do not be distraught cousin. The babe is with our Lord now. There is nothing to mourn." Mr. Collins said with a shake of his head. Elizabeth made no reply but continued to weep.

"As I was saying, you possess all of the traits I desire in a wife, and I am convinced that marriage to one such as you will increase my own happiness tenfold. My contentment in the marital state cannot fail to benefit my efforts as a clergyman and shepherd to my fold. It is good fortune, indeed, to have discovered one so well suited to my desires in the very household of my inheritance. There are many lovely and amiable young ladies in the neighborhood of Hunsford from whom I could select, but knowing that my good fortune upon your father's demise could bring ruination to so many who do not deserve it, I consider that an alliance between us provides a most fortuitous solution to the whole business. Due to matters of distance, and of commitments to my parish, I believe a short engagement is preferable."

Elizabeth removed her hands from her face and looked with astonishment at Mr. Collins, tears cutting trails down her cheeks.

"Mr. Collins, you assume too much. You have made no proposal." Due to her crying, Elizabeth's breath was coming in spasms as she spoke.

"Oh yes, of course. This is an honor that every young lady dreams of, no doubt, and I would not do you the discourtesy of denying you your tender moment. It is uniformly charming that you should ask for it! I first must assure you of the violence of my affections. I am sensible of your situation in life, and in consideration of the fact that nearly every worldly good within the walls of Longbourn will become mine upon inheritance, it would be unseemly for me to make any demands upon your family by way of a dowry, however much society may expect it. You shall never hear me complain of this when we are married. Miss Elizabeth Bennet, I pray that you will do me the honor of accepting my application for your hand in marriage and consent to be my wife."

Elizabeth suppressed her anger at his audacity. "I see in all that you have said that you approach me with good intent and, therefore, have discharged any duty you may have felt toward our family due to the entailment. I thank you for your consideration of our welfare, truly, I do, but although it may pain you to hear it, I must decline your offer, Mr. Collins. In light of my own feelings in the matter, I cannot do otherwise. I must beg you now to leave and never say a word more of this to me." Elizabeth looked at him wearily.

The beaming visage of Mr. Collins was rapidly transformed to one of disbelief. "Miss Bennet, think of what you are doing!" Mr. Collins said angrily. "I realize that it is common for fashionable females to make a display of their elegance by refusing a proposal the first time it is made, but for one in your situation, this is a dangerous game—you are in no position to refuse. You must know that mine may be the only such offer you shall ever receive, and in refusing me, you condemn your mother and sisters to poverty of the severest kind. Your father's health may be excellent today, but we live in an uncertain world, and I shall perhaps not feel so charitable toward my cousins when he dies if I have been spurned by his daughter. I now make my offer a second time, but this shall be my last."

"I play no game, I assure you. Indeed, as a rational creature, I abhor the very idea of tormenting a decent man merely to gratify my own vanity. I am not that sort of woman. My answer to your offer is once again, *and will always be,* no." Elizabeth closed her eyes. "Please go, Mr. Collins. It was ill-advised for you to visit me today."

"You are not well." Mr. Collins stood up decidedly. "It is clear to me that this fever has addled your mind, which has impaired your ability to answer truly, for I *am* an eligible match in every respect. No, you cannot be serious in a refusal! There is too much at stake. When you have recovered, I will approach you again and expect at that time that you will have regained your senses. I am persuaded that you will then accept my offer, and I will lead you to the altar with all due haste, for it is not a wise thing for a man to live alone. I am truly lonely, dear cousin, and I am determined that you shall be my solace and my comfort. I pray you do not think me indelicate when I tell you that, from the moment we first met, thoughts of our marriage have brought me great hope in the brightness of the future." He leaned across the bed toward her.

Elizabeth's eyes snapped open, lit with indignation. "Mr. Collins, what you speak of will *never* be. Step back this instant or I shall scream."

Mr. Collins' face contorted as if he were in pain. "You are the chosen companion of my future life cousin, Elizabeth. We have not yet taken our vows, but I am deeply attached to you already—you will most assuredly be my wife. Lady Catherine approves of you, and your mother has encouraged the match."

His expression clouded as he began to realize that his designs were to be circumvented. He was overcome with desperation. Confusion at Elizabeth's refusal, fear of Lady Catherine's reaction to his failed mission, and pent-up desires stirred by his imaginings of married life drove Mr. Collins in that moment to a most uncharacteristic course. "You have lit the fire of passion in my heart cousin, and even Adam partook of the forbidden fruit when tempted by a woman. If I compromise you now, nothing could prevent me from claiming that which is rightfully mine. I will not need your acceptance—your wise and excellent parents will insist on the marriage." He sat down on the edge of the bed. "It is not my preference, of course, but if there is no other way...."

"Mr. Collins!" Elizabeth exclaimed, "You are a respectable man! You must desist before your actions are irrevocable!" She opened her mouth to scream, but his hand clamped across her mouth, muffling the sound that would call for help. She widened her eyes at him, hoping to call him back to reason as the look on his face twisted into a leer. She was too weak from her sickness and the drugs to fight him effectively, and she was nauseous with fear and uncertainty at what might happen next. She struggled under the bedclothes to free herself, but this only excited his determination.

"Unhand her this instant!" Colonel Fitzwilliam roared from the doorway. It was but a fraction of a second before he was upon Mr. Collins. He wrapped his arms around Collins' chest and pulled him backward, away from Elizabeth. Collins' legs kicked wildly in the air as the colonel turned and thrust the parson into the sitting room, where Mrs. Bennet hovered near the doorway, a hopeful look on her face. Her other daughters too were there, astonishment and mortification written on their faces.

"Miss Bennet," the colonel commanded Jane, "attend to your sister. I shall deal with Mr. Collins." He held Mr. Collins by the arm and led him roughly out of the room.

They ran into Mr. Bingley in the hallway, and after one look at the two men's faces, Bingley's color deepened, and he bade the colonel follow him.

Mr. Collins was almost submissive as he was escorted to Mr. Bingley's study by the two gentlemen, although he spoke without pausing, barely taking so much as a breath.

"Take care, take care, my dear Colonel, I beg you!" Mr. Collins attempted to break free of the ironclad grip that held his arm. "You know full well that Miss Elizabeth is my intended bride! I informed you of that myself—last night at the ball. Had you listened to me then, this scene would likely have been unnecessary. It is of no matter, however; I am fully of a disposition to forgive your interference. I am certain the nephew of my esteemed patroness would have nothing but the best of intentions, so in the spirit of generosity that your aunt has so frequently bestowed upon me, I am prepared to let bygones be bygones. You see before you the happiest of men, for I have proposed to my fair cousin, and she was in raptures at my offer, raptures! She was on the very verge of accepting me when you burst into the room and removed me from her side. I cannot imagine what came over you in that moment, for I was myself in great anticipation. My expectations of hearing her utter the words I have long waited to hear were dashed in that moment when you tore me away from her. I demand that you return me, so that I may have her answer!"

"She could not have been about to accept you, Mr. Collins, with your hand covering her mouth." Colonel Fitzwilliam spoke barely above a whisper in Mr. Collins ear. He released Collins and pushed him into a chair in Bingley's study. "If she were in such raptures over the offer, pray tell us why you were about to force yourself on her?"

Bingley, who had been listening intently to this point, blanched and turned to Mr. Collins. "Is this true, sir?"

Collins frowned at Colonel Fitzwilliam. "He is painting a black picture, indeed, Mr. Bingley, but it was not as he makes it seem. When a couple becomes engaged, surely there is no evil to be had in a chaste kiss if their tender feelings deem it appropriate in the moment."

The colonel's eyebrows raised in disgust. "There was nothing chaste in what you were about."

Mr. Collins licked his lips nervously and blinked rapidly, his eyes darting about the room, looking everywhere except directly at the colonel. "You misunderstand. My feelings for my fair cousin are natural and just. When we are married, all this will be forgotten."

"*What* will be forgotten?" The colonel leaned forward and placed his hands on the armrests of the chair where Mr. Collins sat. Mr. Bingley stood behind the colonel, looking over Colonel Fitzwilliam's shoulder at the now-quivering parson. "Have you, a man of the cloth, a man who has taken orders in the Church of England, a man who represents our Lord and Master in the ministry—have you compromised Miss Elizabeth Bennet today?

"N-n-n-n-n-no," Collins stammered.

"Did she accept your proposal of marriage?" the colonel pressed.

"I-I-I t-t-told you before, you interrupted us before she c-c-could do so." Mr. Collins replied belligerently.

"Did she, in point of fact, refuse your offer, Mr. Collins?" The colonel's face was mere inches from Collins.

At this question, the simpering parson sat bolt upright. He squared his shoulders and looked directly into the face of his challenger. "I do not owe you answers, Colonel. You are not her family, although I am. You have no connection whatsoever to this woman, while I am presently residing in her family home at the invitation of her excellent parents."

"Shall we summon my *aunt,* Mr. Collins? Perhaps you would like to explain the events of your failed proposal to *her*."

"That will not be necessary." Mr. Bingley spoke. "You may not owe explanations or answers to the colonel, but you do owe them to me. This is my house, Mr. Collins, and you have intruded upon it, in the guise of family, and attempted to compromise a young woman who is currently defenseless and under *my* protection."

The colonel was astonished at the transformation in Mr. Bingley. He was most certainly angry, and it was evident that this was not an emotion frequently entertained by his amiable host. Bingley began to pace as he spoke, as though a great force had built up within him.

"Did she refuse you?" Bingley stopped pacing and stared directly into Collins' face, his tone making clear that he would not tolerate an evasive answer.

"Why, yes, in the beginning." Collins replied nervously. "But females are notoriously fickle. I am certain that she was soon to decide in my favor."

"On what grounds do you base this conclusion?" Bingley asked through gritted teeth.

To this question, Mr. Collins made no reply but sat despondently upon the chair, uncharacteristically silent. At length, Mr. Bingley resumed speaking.

"Mr. Collins, I never expected to be placed in this position, but you leave me no choice. You will return to your carriage and await the rest of your party from without the house. You shall never be granted entrance into my home again." A frowning Mr. Bingley then summoned two footmen to escort Mr. Collins out of Netherfield House.

When he was gone, Mr. Bingley turned to the colonel and said with a sigh, "I wish I could do the same to my sister."

The colonel laughed. "Let us forget Mr. Collins *and* your sister for the moment. I believe we need to notify your other guests that their companion awaits them in the carriage."

"Yes." Bingley smiled. "I must give Mr. Collins some credit however. He most determinedly attempted that which I have not found the courage to do. I am not to be outdone by a man such as he. Today will be a good day after all."

Chapter Forty-Three

WHAT COMES WITH THE TIDE

Mr. Bingley had thrown back another glass of port to improve his resolve on several fronts and to calm the unusual racing of his heart and strange quivering of his limbs. These symptoms combined with a curious agitation that left him with the unusual desire to strike something.

He returned to the sitting room, eager to dispatch Mrs. Bennet and the three younger Miss Bennets back to Longbourn with their reprobate cousin. He did not, however, expect to find Caroline and Lady Catherine together with the Bennets in the sitting room. Jane, he rightly assumed, was in the bedchamber with Elizabeth.

"Mrs. Bennet," Lady Catherine was saying coldly, "In good faith I encouraged Mr. Collins to marry one of your daughters and even came to Hertfordshire myself to visit with them, for a woman is able to discern more of another woman in a day than a man can perceive in a month. For this trouble, I have been heartily disappointed in his prospects of choosing a wife from your progeny. Your eldest daughter smiles too much but speaks too little. Anyone can see that she is beautiful, but nothing else of her stands out at all. As for your second eldest, Miss Elizabeth, her opinions are altogether too strong for one so young. This does not recommend her as a suitable wife for anyone at all. You must rein her in, or she will most certainly end a spinster. Your third," Lady Catherine nodded toward Mary across the room, "well, I cannot remember her name—but she is a plain, insipid child of no accomplishment whatsoever. She will take care of you when you are old; that is the best you can hope for with that one. Your two youngest are perhaps the worst of your ridiculous offspring. They are silly and unrefined—wholly unsuitable for the dignified attitude the wife of Mr. Collins must own, although they might entrap one of those local officers with their flirtatious manners. I am ashamed of you, madam, for having raised five such daughters. You should have taken better care of their education. I cannot, in good conscience, approve Mr. Collins' offering for any of them. I fear that our trip to Hertfordshire has been in vain."

Caroline stood behind Lady Catherine, her posture unconsciously mimicking the aristocrat. Her lips were pressed together, and she nodded her head in agreement with every utterance.

Mrs. Bennet's eyes were wide with astonishment at being spoken to in such a manner. She made a deep courtesy and attempted a rebuttal. "Your Ladyship...."

Lady Catherine's hand flipped into the air to cut her off. "Mrs. Bennet, do not add excuses to your shame. Your daughters are now all but grown. They are past the age where you may reclaim them. Now, I must speak to your daughter Elizabeth before I quit the county. Please take me to her, for I must have an audience with her this moment. I insist."

Mr. Bingley's symptoms flared once more, for having heard Lady Catherine's speech toward Jane's mother, and knowing what she had previously said to Caroline, he was certain that Darcy's aunt was intent on verbally abusing the fevered sister of his beloved Jane, and very possibly Jane herself.

"Lady Catherine," Bingley stepped into the room and spoke with an amiability he did not feel. "I understand from Colonel Fitzwilliam that you will be departing Netherfield to return to London within a few hours. May I say what a great honor it has been to have entertained you as our guest? We are most obliged to have enjoyed your distinguished presence among us, most particularly at the ball. You and your lovely daughter were a most welcome addition to the festivities." He smiled at her charmingly. "I am informed, Lady Catherine, that you might be willing to make some recommendations on additions to my library, which I am most anxious to improve."

Caroline, who had entertained visions of Lady Catherine dressing Elizabeth Bennet down, stamped her foot slightly as she said, "Charles, Lady Catherine has requested an audience with Miss Eliza. Perhaps she could lend you her literary advice afterwards."

Bingley, whose temper was back to an even keel, was determined not to allow it. "Oh yes." He smiled graciously at Lady Catherine. "Unfortunately, Mr. Jones administered a sedative to Miss Elizabeth barely an hour ago. I fear that she is not awake to receive visitors at present and will not rouse for several hours. I am certain she will be most pleased when I relate your desire to see her, no doubt to wish her well." He bowed to Lady Catherine and swept his hand toward the door. "If you will follow me, I am most eager that you take the opportunity to inspect the library now."

Lady Catherine narrowed her eyes and frowned. She looked at the closed door of the bedchamber, clearly displeased. "Your apothecary is mistaken in his approach. Sedation is an unwise course for one who is ill. It is far better to allow a natural state of rest in these cases. You will tell him this when he returns, of course."

"But, of course." Bingley repeated with a nod and a smile.

Her frown deepened, and she turned back to face Mrs. Bennet. "You would do well to teach your daughters not to aspire to a marriage beyond the sphere they were born to. I believe that you, Mrs. Bennet, are ample proof of this principle should they require an illustration of the foolishness of such a course. It is a pity their mother was not gentle-born. They might have turned out better."

"Lady Catherine." Bingley stood holding the door open for her, and with a sniff, she raised her chin up and swept out of the room. Bingley turned to Mrs. Bennet and quietly said, "Please accept my humble apologies, madam." He nodded to her kindly. "I have anticipated that Miss Elizabeth would be indisposed to visitors, and have sent Mr. Collins to await you in the carriage. I hope to call at Longbourn myself in but a few hours to speak to Mr. Bennet on a matter of some delicacy. I depend on your graciousness to advise him to expect me."

"Oh, yes, Mr. Bingley, I am sure he will be happy to oblige you," Mrs. Bennet said delightedly. "Come along, girls." She signaled to her daughters. "We will see ourselves out."

Darcy prowled like a panther in his study at Darcy House, restless and brooding. *Something is wrong.* Like a thunderstorm, the premonition swept over him relentlessly, yet there were so many troubles he was attending to that he could not with any degree of certainty identify the source of his disturbed feelings. At least he knew that Georgiana was well and happily anticipating her escape to the country with her brother. It was a relief to know this much, at least.

Of Wickham, he had received no news yet, but a dozen hired men were scattered through the city looking for information or for sign of him. Georgiana's encounter with him in the park revealed that he was lurking and unquestionably aware of Darcy's presence in town. If he did not locate Wickham, he had no doubt that Wickham would eventually be overwhelmed by his own avarice and contact him directly. Darcy had no patience to wait for it, however.

He had entrusted his cousin and friend to see to the well-being of Elizabeth and was satisfied they would protect her well, but he had left her before she had recovered, and fevers, he well knew, could be unpredictable. "No," Darcy said under his breath as he shook his head for emphasis, "Elizabeth is strong. It is not Elizabeth." Yet the recollection of her falling in a dead faint into his arms, of her delirium from the fever, and her uncontrollable shivering when he had lowered her into the water belied his confidence in her strength, and his heart was gripped with worry that he had left her too soon.

Lady Catherine, he hoped, had already quit Netherfield. He wondered for a fleeting moment of humor what scheme Richard had cooked up to dislodge their aunt from Bingley's house, but this delivered him to yet another possibility. Was Anne well? Knowing her constitution, he recognized that nursing Elizabeth had been a serious risk—was his gentle cousin taken ill with the fever? Was this the source of the dark cloud that pressed upon him? Could Anne survive such an illness? Darcy shuddered at the implications and pushed the thought away.

Could something be amiss at Pemberley? He could not shake the oppressive feelings, and he once again rehearsed in his mind every possibility, every situation he was engaged in, every person he loved. When the burden became more than he could endure, for the first time in many years, he prayed. It was while he was on his knees, pleading with his maker for guidance and strength that he heard loud voices. He leapt to his feet as the sound of a fist pounding on the front door further interrupted his solitude. He cracked the door of his study and listened as the butler and footmen questioned whether to disturb Mr. Darcy. He moved to the foyer to investigate, and upon his inquiry, the men stepped aside, revealing the body of a man, in torn, blood-soaked clothing, lying in an oddly twisted heap on the doorstep.

He heard one of the younger footmen wonder, in a dread-filled whisper, who the man was and whether he was dead. As if in response, a moan emanated from the injured man, proving, at least, that he was not dead. The sound triggered a visceral response in

Darcy, as he answered the other half of the man's query. "It is Wickham. Bring him in at once. Put him on the dining room table." He pointed at the young footman. "Fetch Dr. Fogg immediately." The men carried Wickham in as instructed and dispersed, no doubt to clean the blood from their uniforms before it stained them. This left Darcy and the butler alone with Wickham.

"Shall I have a room made up for him?" The butler asked quietly.

"No. He cannot stay here." Darcy answered quietly. "Have one of the older maids come and clean him up a bit, however." Wickham's face was bloodied and swollen beyond recognition. There was no question, due to its position, that his right leg was broken. Darcy stared at the man who had once been as a brother to him, and although he expected to taste the bile of hatred in his throat, he was instead filled with profound sorrow. "George," he whispered and shook his head sadly, "what have you done?"

Alone in the room with Wickham, Darcy went through his pockets and found little—certainly no money, some evidence of debts incurred, but nothing useful in discerning what had happened. As Darcy was searching, Wickham's eyes opened slightly, and the hatred that Darcy could not summon contorted Wickham's face. "This is your fault," Wickham whispered through his pain.

"Where is the letter, George?" Darcy demanded with urgency.

Wickham made a weak sneer on his bruised and bloodied face. "It will cost you." His lips barely moved.

"Who did this to you?" Darcy asked soberly.

"You did," Wickham replied, closing his eyes with a grimace.

The maid entered with a basin of water and a bundle of clean rags. She gingerly began wiping blood and debris away from his face with a dampened cloth. Darcy watched in silence.

When Dr. Fogg arrived, Darcy related what little he knew and quit the room early in the examination. At length, the butler brought the physician to Darcy, who had retired to the study to work on correspondence.

"Well?" Darcy stood as he spoke, emotionless.

Dr. Fogg was grave. "You were correct that the beating was severe, Mr. Darcy. I have administered the strongest drug I have for pain. It is unlikely that your friend will survive the night."

This, Darcy did not expect, and his astonishment at the news was apparent. "Can nothing be done?"

"For his external injuries, certainly, and we could set his leg with reasonable success, but there are signs that he has sustained injuries internally. I have seen symptoms such as these before, Mr. Darcy, and survival is nearly impossible. Whoever did this to him wished him to suffer an agonizing death." Dr. Fogg frowned. "You must notify his family at once if they are to say goodbye to him."

"He has no family." Darcy replied quietly. "There is no-one to come for him, and I cannot allow him to remain in my house."

Dr. Fogg nodded his understanding. "He will not feel much pain if you move him soon. The public hospital will take him if he has nowhere else to go."

"I do not know where he is living, sir, or who would take him in to die." Darcy glanced toward the dining room door. "I need your assurance that he will suffer as little as possible, sir." Darcy replied. "I will pay for the medicines to achieve it."

They heard a sound in the dining room, and the two men, realizing that Wickham was in that room alone, entered with haste, only to discover that George Wickham had not even lasted the hour, and now lay dead upon the table. Darcy's feeling of foreboding was not resolved in this, but remained more potent than before.

When the Bennets and their guest arrived at Longbourn, they did not keep company with one another. Mrs. Bennet eagerly sought Mr. Bennet to advise him of Bingley's expected visit and to share news of Elizabeth's condition, although she was strangely silent on the matter of her conversation with Lady Catherine. Kitty went to her chambers to nurse her headache. Lydia, assuming that some officers must have been smitten with her at the ball, also returned to her chambers to refresh her toilette to look her finest when the officers came.

Mary sat at the pianoforte and began to play. The tune was a melancholy one, which Jane and Elizabeth would have noticed had they been there, but there was no one in the house to recognize Mary's sadness. She had played but a quarter of an hour when tears began to form, and she quickly wiped her eyes and left the instrument, going instead to the sitting room where she resumed reading the second volume of Fordyce's Sermons.

A few minutes later, she heard the door creak open and looked up to discover Mr. Collins had entered the room. She returned to reading her book and did not look up again until she realized that Mr. Collins was now standing directly in front of her, with a marked intention to speak. She set the book down and looked at him expectantly.

"May I be of some assistance, Mr. Collins?" Mary asked quietly.

"Cousin Mary," Mr. Collins launched into his speech. "I come to you now, greatly relieved, for I have a matter of great importance to discuss with you, which I was unable to speak of earlier due to considerations of seniority within your family."

"Of great importance, you say?" Mary replied, with a slow blink. "Pray continue, sir."

"As I had begun to say, I have looked upon this moment with the greatest anticipation. I am certain that you know the reason I traveled to visit my cousins at Longbourn, for it has not been a secret, by any means. I feel it my duty to explain, leaving no misunderstanding between us, the reason I am here to speak with you today."

Mary nodded. "I would not wish there to be any misunderstandings either, Mr. Collins."

"You may well be aware that last Easter I was ordained and am now settled at Hunsford. Divine providence itself has blessed me with not only a valuable living, but also with a most generous patroness, who has, in gracious benevolence, lent her wisdom in advising me and rendered her assistance in the matter of selecting a wife. On the point that I must marry, she has insisted, and upon learning of my inevitable inheritance of this estate, she persuaded me that the only honorable course was to marry one of my cousin's daughters in order to spare you all from the fate of being without a home. Of course, these things are of no surprise." Mr. Collins shifted his weight nervously.

"The final choice is mine, and after having weighed the matter, and given great thought to the various virtues to be had among you and your amiable sisters, I find, my dear cousin, that you, of all your sisters, are the most suited to become the companion of my future life. You are in possession of a pleasant, steady character and have evidenced great discipline in your reading and educational pursuits. Your modesty is, of course, a highly valued attribute, and your interest in the doctrines and great sermons do you credit."

"What are you saying, Mr. Collins?"

"I am saying that you possess all of the traits I desire in a wife, and I am convinced that marriage to one such as you will increase my own happiness tenfold. My contentment in the marital state cannot fail to benefit my efforts as a clergyman and shepherd to my fold. It is good fortune, indeed, to have discovered one so well suited to my desires in the very household of my inheritance. Cousin Mary, I am offering for your hand and humbly request that you consent to be my wife. Due to matters of distance, and of commitments to my parish, I believe a short engagement is preferable."

Mary smiled. "Mr. Collins, my life has been one of great uncertainty, for I have had little hope of meeting a man who would be a suitable match for me. Since you first arrived at Longbourn, it has been my fondest wish that you would offer for me, and I have thought of little else, for I too perceived that you and I would be well matched. It is a double sorrow for me that I must decline your proposal."

"Decline?" Mr. Collins was stunned. "You are not serious!"

"I am completely serious. I know not what happened this morning between you and Elizabeth, but I am not so dull that I cannot hazard a guess. I am persuaded that your manners were not above reproach, which a parson should always be. Nevertheless, I believe we could have resolved this question among ourselves. However, the second point, of which you are presently unaware, creates an insurmountable barrier." Mary's composure was perfectly contained.

"Of course, it can be resolved. The events of this morning are nothing more than a common misunderstanding. It could have been made by anyone. What is the barrier of which you speak?" Mr. Collins appeared convinced that no other barrier could possibly exist.

"Lady Catherine is that barrier," Mary replied. "Your patroness declared this very morning that not one of us was an eligible match for you. I know that you esteem her too highly to contradict her direction in the matter and that had you known of this, you would not have spoken to me of marriage. As for myself, although I could tolerate it for a short duration, the daily disapproval of Lady Catherine would be more than I could bear, even if you were able to overcome her declaration."

"Oh." Mr. Collin's presence shriveled in the face of this information. "I thank you for your honesty, Cousin. I must reflect on what you have told me, for as you said, I did not know." He abruptly quit the room.

❧

Mr. Bingley watched with relief as Lady Catherine's carriage pulled away from Netherfield. He was filled with an unfamiliar sense of pride at having successfully manipulated her to leave Elizabeth's sickroom and in having spoken so forcefully to Mr. Collins. He felt powerful and strong—he was eager to talk to Jane now, before these newfound feelings faded. He fairly ran up the stairs to find her, a grin plastered on his face that grew with each passing moment. Today would be the day he became the happiest of men. Today would be the day he offered for Jane Bennet's hand in marriage.

Chapter Forty-Four

A BEGINNING, A MIDDLE AND AN END

The police arrived while Dr. Fogg was still writing down the details of Wickham's death. The man himself was not yet cold on the table when the officer arrived, having been summoned by several passersby who had first attempted to pursue the rough-looking men who had dumped what had appeared to be a dead body at the door of Darcy House.

The general noise and commotion drew Georgiana down the stairs from her chambers where she had been packing. Darcy noticed her as she descended, and he broke away from the others, calling for his housekeeper to take her back upstairs and stay with her until he could come. Unfortunately, the officer was not a sensible man, and, having no concern for the delicacy of the young lady's feelings, insisted that she remain for questioning.

Darcy managed to conceal the sight of George Wickham laid out on the table by directing Georgiana to his study, guiding her gently away from the doors to the dining room. It was his intention to privately disclose George's identity to his sister there. However, the officer's boisterous interrogation of the butler was underway near the front doors, and Georgiana learned of the reason for the disturbance of the household by overhearing him loudly repeat, "... so Wickham was bloodied but still alive when you found him."

Georgiana stumbled, but Darcy quickly steadied her and conducted his sister to the study where he saw her to a chair, talking softly, hoping to comfort. He poured her a small glass of wine to calm her nerves and reached to retrieve a cloth from his pocket for her tears, as his sister was now silently weeping. He first produced Elizabeth's handkerchief, but he quickly found his own for his sister's use.

Holding the lace-trimmed article in his hand stirred a profound reaction in Darcy, and from it, he drew strength and courage to face the ordeal that lay ahead. It was not that he feared himself incapable of doing it on his own—far from it, but in that moment, he discovered the sweet joy of knowing he was not truly alone, that although Elizabeth was not physically near to him, she was still somehow there in his heart and mind, giving him purpose. He tucked the handkerchief back into the pocket nearest to his heart.

He reached out and embraced his sister. "You must listen carefully, Georgiana, and be strong."

Georgiana looked at him, through wide, red-rimmed eyes and nodded her head.

"I would protect you from this pain if I could, but a man's life was forfeit, and the police will insist on knowing the reasons. I fear that the secrecy with which we have guarded your dealings with Mr. Wickham will soon come to an end. I hope to persuade the authorities toward discretion, but you must do as I say."

Fresh tears welled up in her eyes, and he took her hands in his as she hung her head in shame and fear. "Do not fear, Sister. You have had no part in his death." He took her chin in the crook between his thumb and finger, raising her face to look at his. "I know that speaking with these men at all will be difficult for you, but remember that you are a Darcy, and you will find the courage. You must answer truthfully any question you are asked, but do not offer more. I will be close by at all times."

"I cannot do it, Brother. Can you not make them go away?" Georgiana's lip trembled.

"It would not be wise to do so. Disguise of every sort is my abhorrence, and in this case, it would imply our guilt where there is none. It will not do to raise their suspicions, dear one. We must face their questions and trust in the truth."

The officer knocked at the door and opened it immediately. "I will see the young lady now."

Darcy stood and strode across the room, closing the door behind the officer. "You will interview my sister here in the study, sir." Darcy spoke respectfully, but was firm. "I am her guardian; I insist that it be so, and in my presence."

"Very well, so long as you do not interfere, you may remain."

Georgiana was pale, and her whole body shook with terror. The officer looked at her with some chagrin that he was obliged to speak to her at all.

The officer took the seat vacated by Darcy, and Darcy took a position by the wall where he could observe and see both parties clearly. His face was stern as he stood as a sentinel for his sister.

"What is your name?" The officer began with the easy questions first. His surprise was evident when she responded with difficulty.

"I am...," Georgiana swallowed and began again. "My ... my ... my ... n-n-n-name is Miss G-G-Georg-Georg-Georgiana D-D-D-Darcy."

The officer glanced over at Mr. Darcy, who nodded his confirmation as he stood in an intimidating stance, his feet apart, hands locked together behind his back.

This, the officer quickly realized, could take much longer than he had planned. He changed tactics by question number two. "The man who died here tonight—Mr. Wickham—did you know him?"

Georgiana looked at her brother for assurance, her eyes blinking uncontrollably before she answered. "Y-y-yes." She pressed her lips together and looked to her lap.

"How long have you known him?"

"F-f-forever," Georgiana gasped.

"If I may, sir," Darcy interrupted, "Mr. Wickham was the son of my late father's steward. My sister has known him since infancy, as one of the household."

"I see. Thank you." The officer turned back to Georgiana. "Did you like Mr. Wickham?"

Georgiana once again looked at her brother, this time with some alarm, but again, he nodded for her to answer. "Y-y-yes sir, I ... I ... I ... did."

"Do you know anyone who wished him dead?" The officer wanted to be at an end of the interview, his impatience at Georgiana's stammering clearly evidenced in his tone.

"I ... I ... I ..." Georgiana paused, "I d-d-d-do not th-th-think so."

"Sir," Darcy broke in again. "My sister has received quite a shock this evening. She is but sixteen years old and knows none of the particulars, as she was upstairs through the whole of it. I beg you to excuse her—I can tell you far more than she."

This was all the persuasion the officer needed to terminate his inquiry. Of the innocence of the maiden he was certain, and the promise of Darcy's cooperation was sufficient incentive to grant Georgiana's release.

Mrs. Annesley waited for Georgiana outside the study and took her upstairs as soon as the door opened. Darcy watched with concern from the doorway as his sister was escorted away. Georgiana's stammer had not been so pronounced since the period right after Ramsgate, and he feared that the death of Wickham in such a manner would set his sister's recovery back dramatically. This concern he could not dwell on now, however, for the officer awaited him.

The officer annoyed him, and Darcy knew full well that he would be within his rights to eject the policeman and demand a Bow Street investigator immediately. His conversation with his cousin Anne preyed on his mind, however, and he determined to practice better manners by humoring the officer—at least for tonight.

Returning to the study, Darcy offered the officer a glass of port, which was accepted. Darcy moved to the window, looking out upon the small garden area in the rear of the townhouse as if he could see it in the darkness that had already fallen. He waited for the other man to speak.

"Mr. Darcy, you said that you could tell me of Wickham. The time has come for you to reveal what you know."

"Tell me what you wish to hear, sir, and I will tell it." Darcy replied, turning to face him.

The officer frowned. "Begin with your connection to Wickham."

"As I said, he is the son of my late father's steward. We grew up together," Darcy replied. "After we attended Cambridge, our lives took different paths, and these past several years I have avoided contact with him."

"The son of a steward received a gentleman's education? Your father must have paid a generous wage." The officer remarked.

Darcy looked at him blandly. "Yes, sir, he did."

"I take it from what you say that you have not seen Wickham in recent years. How long has it been?"

"I said that I avoid contact. It does not follow that I have not seen him." Darcy replied. "In point of fact, I saw him just a few days ago."

"You did?" The officer became more alert. "Where did this meeting occur?"

"In Hertfordshire," Darcy answered.

"That is far from Derbyshire, is it not? What were you doing in Hertfordshire?"

"I was a guest in the home of a friend. I was unaware that Wickham had joined himself with the Hertfordshire militia until I encountered him in the village of Meryton, where the militia is quartered for the winter." No emotion passed across Darcy's face as he spoke.

"I see." The officer jotted a few notes. "Was your meeting cordial?"

Darcy shifted his weight, "Reasonably so."

"That is not exactly a yes, Mr. Darcy. I must ask you to elaborate."

"We were not friendly. I was not pleased to discover him making the acquaintance of a family of young gentlewomen, and I issued a mild warning not to meddle with them."

"Meddle?" The officer's brow shot up.

"Mr. Wickham has earned a reputation, to put it frankly, as a seducer nearly everywhere he goes. Being new to Meryton, the town did not yet know what he was."

"Was this warning privately made, or public?" The officer squinted at Darcy, observing him closely.

"Public, although I was not explicit. I later visited him privately to assure that he took my meaning."

"And did he—take your meaning?"

"He did. He resigned his commission and returned to London shortly thereafter," Darcy replied, turning again to the darkened glass.

"And you followed him here?" The officer speculated.

"Yes, I did." Darcy said.

"For what purpose?"

"To speak with him. Nothing more." Darcy answered firmly.

"That is a long journey for a conversation." The officer observed. "Of what did you wish to speak?"

"A private matter." Darcy replied.

"Mr. Darcy, a man has died. I cannot let your answer stand. You must answer the question."

"It is a family matter, sir, and can have nothing to do with these proceedings." Darcy shook his head.

"Answer or I shall be forced to arrest you on suspicion of murder."

Darcy rolled his eyes in irritation and considered again the possibility of ejecting the insufferable officer. "Mr. Wickham claimed to be in possession of a letter. I merely wished to ascertain the contents of the letter."

"And once you retrieved the letter, you had him killed?"

"I did not kill Mr. Wickham, nor was I party to his death." Darcy was emphatic.

"Your maid said that he accused you of the deed before he died." The officer countered.

"He did, sir. In his dying words, he was true to his nature, and maliciously lied." Darcy nodded, turning his head to look over his shoulder at the officer.

"Are you now in possession of the letter?" The officer clearly expected that he was.

"No. The conversation I had come for did not occur before Wickham's demise. I remain in the dark about the letter."

"What do you know of it?"

"Wickham claimed it was damaging to my family." Darcy said in clipped tones.

"Extortion?" The officer probed.

"Yes."

"Do you have any proof of his planning to blackmail you?" The officer pressed.

"Yes."

"What proof have you?"

Darcy looked at the man resignedly. "I have a letter from him, detailing his case. I came to London to discern the truth before I determined a course of action. I have already discovered his letter to contain lies."

"Where is this letter?"

"It is in my possession."

"You must produce it, as evidence." The officer said seriously.

"Evidence that Wickham was a scoundrel? I can produce a hundred witnesses who would swear it." Darcy replied.

"Evidence that you have a motive, sir, to see him dead." The officer answered coldly.

"It was not I!" Darcy thundered and followed more calmly, "Wickham was a man of excessively happy manners, which enabled him to acquire friends quickly, but his vices—gambling, debt-leaving, fortune hunting and debaucheries—insured that he made many enemies as well. I am not your man."

"But he did die under your roof." The officer said pointedly.

"He was brought here injured. I tried to help him, but it was too late." Darcy replied.

"Why was he brought here?" The officer accused. "That he was delivered to your very doorstep in such condition implies your involvement. It is manslaughter, at least, if not outright murder."

"I only just arrived in London last night. I sent men into the city today in search of him. They were instructed to discover him, but not approach. They will confirm those directions to the last man." Darcy defended himself. "I gave no order to harm him. I do not know why he was brought to my house."

"Do you know anyone who wanted him dead?"

Darcy did not immediately reply.

"Have you heard anyone voice a threat on his life?" The officer sensed that Darcy was holding back. He sat down, leaned back and crossed his leg, as though he would wait patiently for the answer. "I had a cat once, who was a great mouser. She would catch the mice, kill them, and drop their carcasses at my door—as a sort of gift, I think. Did someone leave a gift on your doorstep, Mr. Darcy?"

"I think not." Darcy shook his head. "The only person I ever heard speak of killing Wickham knew that I did not want it, and he stayed his hand."

"Who was this person?"

"He could not have done it. He is not in London." Darcy replied.

"He has a name, I presume." The officer would not relent. "You must give it to me."

"Colonel Richard Fitzwilliam." Darcy answered after a moment's pause. "He is my cousin and the second son of the Earl of Matlock. He did not do it. He is a good man, a noble servant of king and country."

"What was the good colonel's interest in seeing Wickham dead?"

"He saw the letter I received from Wickham." Darcy replied.

"Ah yes. The letter from Wickham. I must have it."

"I told you, it has nothing to do with this investigation. I beg you to allow me privacy in this matter, sir." Darcy's tone belied any idea of begging.

"Produce the letter or surrender yourself to arrest. Those are your options." The officer gritted his teeth.

Darcy hesitated, his temper rising at the attitude of the man. He could, with very little trouble, ruin the officer's career over this behavior. He struggled mightily for restraint against that course before he finally took a deep breath, heaved a frustrated sigh, and went to his desk where he unlocked a small drawer and retrieved Wickham's letter. "I must insist upon your discretion in the matters related in this letter, sir. You will understand in a moment."

The officer stood to read the letter, which he read through not once, but three times. When he had finished with it, he folded it and put it in his pocket. "So Wickham compromised your sister. I assume she is the girl who went upstairs a moment ago?"

Darcy nodded. "Although the letter implies that he compromised her, on her word, a chaste kiss was all that ever passed between them.

Nevertheless, he imposed on a shy, reserved young lady who trusted him as a friend. He persuaded her that he loved her when it was her inheritance of thirty-thousand pounds that he desired. You can well imagine how she came to believe herself in love with him—he has a smooth tongue and has practiced this deception on others before her. With no experience in such matters to guide her, and a paid companion who failed to protect her, they very nearly eloped last summer. It was only through the grace of a well-timed visit that the plot was discovered before they went to Scotland." Although Darcy recited the facts with little emotion in his demeanor, the officer detected pain and sorrow in the man's eyes.

"Now I understand why you were not immediately forthcoming with Wickham's letter, Mr. Darcy. His death resolves a number of problems that afflict you, is this not true?"

"Not at all, I assure you. It increases my problems by half again at least." Darcy replied.

"By what calculation do you say this, Mr. Darcy?"

"Previously, my only concern was to contain the damage from the letter and prevent Wickham from ruining my sister's reputation. They say that every man has a price, sir, and of Wickham, no statement was ever truer. I would have secured his cooperation with only the pain of drafting a note to satisfy his greed. Now, with his death, my entire family will undoubtedly suffer from scandal. Particularly, sir, until I clear myself of the charges you have laid at my door. Your suspicions are understandable considering that Wickham was determined to undermine my happiness." Darcy began to pace in the short space in front of the window.

"My sister has already suffered deeply from the events I related to you. I fear that if you chose a course other than discretion, she will be exposed to all of society, partaking in ruin and disgrace of the acutest kind. My own intentions of betrothal must of necessity be postponed until these matters are resolved, for I cannot subject my intended or her family to the scrutiny and gossip that will naturally follow such a death in my own household."

"Your intended is this Elizabeth Bennet he speaks of? Was she acquainted with Mr. Wickham?"

"To some extent. It was she and her sisters I spoke of making his acquaintance on the road in Meryton the day that I warned him."

"Is she aware of Wickham's latest interference?" The officer's eyebrows rose, marking the question with the possibility of Elizabeth as a suspect.

"She most certainly is not, nor is her family. Only Colonel Fitzwilliam and I know of it."

"Then I must speak with the colonel. Where may I find him?"

"I sent an express requesting my cousin's immediate presence in London just moments before you arrived, while the doctor was making a more thorough examination of his body. Knowing the colonel as I do, I predict that he will not wait for morning to come but will arrive on horseback sometime during the night. I daresay that he is the sort of man that the highwaymen do not trouble."

"I shall return, then, in the morning." The officer made another note. "I respectfully advise you not to leave the city until such time as the question of who killed Mr. Wickham has been fully investigated."

"Of course." Darcy agreed with a frown.

"Now, I must determine what to do with the man's body. The doctor informed me that he has no family to claim it."

"If I may be so bold, sir, I am as close to family as Wickham had on the earth, unless you count the numerous bastards that he sired, and they can do nothing for him now. I should like to do this one last service, on behalf of my father, who was much attached to Wickham. I will pay to transport his remains to Derbyshire and arrange for burial in the churchyard near his own parents. The death will be recorded in the parish register at Kympton."

The officer looked curiously at Darcy. "Very well, sir. I will allow it."

After Mr. Collins had spoken with Mary, it was not long before his absence from the household was noted by Mrs. Bennet. She questioned Lydia and Kitty, and Mr. Bennet as to whether they knew of his whereabouts, for she wished to speak with him about Lady Catherine. He was not to be found, and Mrs. Bennet's distress over his disappearance echoed through the hallways, driving Mr. Bennet to his study and Lydia and Kitty outdoors. The servants too found occupation in distant corners of the house.

It was but two hours later when a note came from Lucas Lodge requesting that his belongings be sent to him there, for he would no longer reside at Longbourn. The man from Lucas Lodge had brought a cart, with instructions to wait for the trunk. Mrs. Hill found that his trunk was already packed, and so it was that without so much as a farewell, Mr. Collins quit Longbourn.

As the Lucas's cart was being loaded with Mr. Collins' trunk, a visitor arrived. His visit was unexpected, although not unwelcome.

His arrival did much to calm Mrs. Bennet's nerves, and Mr. Timmons, the local parson was invited to join the family in the sitting room.

A visit from the parson was not unprecedented; however, it had been some time since he had come to attend the Bennets at Longbourn. Mrs. Timmons had died giving birth to their first child two years previous, and he had faithfully observed a period of mourning for the first year. His emergence from that period was not so obvious as it would be for most, since he always wore black regardless, but he was, in fact, missing the benefits of companionship and domestic bliss that marriage had previously afforded him.

When Mary Bennet had brought Mr. Collins to visit him, he was surprised to discover the young lady well versed in scripture and doctrine. Her quiet demeanor had caught his attention, and her obvious desire to live by the word had touched him. He had never truly noticed her before, for she was nearly invisible to him as the plainest in the family of five sisters, but on the day she came with Mr. Collins, she seemed prettier than he recalled.

From the moment that visit had begun, he had quietly observed her and found her to be exactly the sort of woman he knew he could be happy with, although he thought, perhaps, Mr. Collins had perceived her value and developed an interest in her. It had been his good fortune today to see Mr. Collins on the road, walking toward Meryton. He had engaged the parson from Kent in a friendly conversation, and upon learning that Mr. Collins' visit at Longbourn was over, Mr. Timmons had set out shortly afterward to initiate his suit in hopes of finding favor in the eyes of one Miss Mary Bennet.

Bingley stood at the threshold. In reality, it was at the threshold of the sitting room to Darcy's old quarters, but today, he felt it to be the threshold of his entire life. He knocked at the door, paused a moment, and admitted himself to the room. Jane sat in a chair near the fire. It was evident that she had dozed there, for she jumped with a start when the door opened.

Bingley closed the door behind him. "How is Miss Elizabeth?" he asked quietly.

"She is sleeping, Mr. Bingley. She is still quite unwell—the fever is back." Jane worried. "Sarah is with her now, keeping her as cool as she can."

"I will have another bath prepared shortly. That seemed to provide a more lasting effect, did it not?" Bingley offered.

Jane looked shyly away. "Thank you, sir, it did."

"Miss Bennet." Bingley crossed the room to where she sat and extended his hand to assist her to a standing position. When she stood before him, he raised her hand to his lips and lightly kissed her knuckles before he released her. "Do you know why I am here, Miss Bennet?"

Jane blinked innocently. "To inquire after my sister, I think."

At this response, Bingley unsuccessfully fought back a smile. "No." He shook his head with mock seriousness. "I am come to inquire after you. How are *you* today, Miss Bennet?" He looked directly into her eyes.

"I am well." Jane blushed and broke the gaze.

"You look well." Bingley replied. "You look very well indeed." A cheerful grin began to spread across his face in spite of his attempt to be solemn.

"Thank you." Jane fidgeted slightly. "Has Lady Catherine gone?"

"Miss Bennet, I do not wish to speak of her. I wish to speak only of you." Bingley lowered his voice. "When we first met at the Assembly Ball, I knew that I had met an earthbound angel. You are all that is lovely and gentle and kind, Miss Bennet, and as I have come to know you further, I have been witness to your affectionate nature and determination to see all that is good in the world."

Jane looked up at Mr. Bingley, her eyes shining with the realization of what was happening.

"I am blessed, Miss Bennet, with sufficient means to provide for you, and establish a home wherever you wish to settle. I promise to care for you and love you to my dying day if you will accept my hand in marriage." The grin had disappeared from Mr. Bingley's face, replaced by an earnest, hopeful expression, as he waited for Jane's reply.

"Did you say you love me?" Jane whispered.

Bingley nodded, "I did."

Tears began to well up in Jane's eyes but did not fall. They instead clung to her pretty lashes and made them sparkle as she nodded her head in return, echoing the movements he had just made. "I accept your proposal, Mr. Bingley. I accept your hand and your heart and—well, all of you!" She giggled daintily and blinked, releasing the tears, which now spilled down her cheeks. "I love you too." She added softly.

"Are you saying yes?" Bingley's grin was back. He took both of her hands in his and just held them as he stared into her face in wide-eyed rapture.

Jane, nodding her acknowledgement to his question, matched his grin with a serene smile. They stood this way, foolishly staring at each other for several minutes. Finally, Jane spoke. "I must go to my mother and tell her."

"Your mother will certainly be happy for our news," Bingley said, "But I must go to your father and obtain his consent. Do you think he will have me as a son-in-law?"

Jane smiled at the ridiculousness of the question. "Oh, he will have you if my mother will." Then they laughed together. Jane became serious afterward and said, "If we can see to Elizabeth's fever before we go to Longbourn, it will ease my mind. It will be all right to leave her with Sarah for a few hours."

Bingley agreed and ordered the bath, leaving Jane to attend to Elizabeth while he went downstairs to order the carriage to take them to Longbourn. He then paced in front of the doorway for five full minutes. Occasionally a little skip worked its way into his stride as the joy of knowing that Miss Bennet had accepted him overflowed to his feet.

Suddenly, he bounded up the stairs, making double time as he took the climb two steps at a time, arriving back at the doorway to the sitting room. The servants were still bringing water for the bath, so after a moment's hesitation, he opened the door.

"Jane!" he called excitedly, and she came out from Elizabeth's chambers.

"Mr. Bingley? Is something wrong?" she asked with alarm.

As if in response to that question, Charles Bingley took Jane's face in his hands and pressed his lips against hers in a swift, gentle kiss. He released her and grinned at her astonished expression. "Nothing is wrong—not at all! You have made me the happiest man who ever lived, and I wish you to be as happy as I. I pray that you will forgive me for taking such a liberty, but in the absence of an engagement gift, it did seem the ideal way to accomplish it." He grinned again at her, clearly pleased with himself.

Jane smiled shyly at him. "Mr. Bingley, I am very happy, but you must refrain from kissing me until we are wed. When we talk to my father, let us seek a short engagement, so that you may resume your liberty taking at the earliest possible moment. I am all aflutter."

Mr. Bingley readily agreed.

Chapter Forty-Five

REAL OR IMAGINED DREAMS

Jane helped Elizabeth back into the freshly made bed, smiling contentedly to see how much her sister was improved from the bath, which had once again cooled the fever. Elizabeth lay back against the cool pillows with a small sigh.

"Jane, do you suppose Mr. Jones will approve my return to Longbourn soon? I do so miss having the rest of my family near—the comfort of your presence is all that keeps me easy here, Jane—I can plainly see that I have put someone out of their bedchamber."

Jane did not reply, although she looked troubled as Elizabeth spoke.

"There remain a number of personal articles about the room," Elizabeth waved her hand toward a shelf that contained several articles. "Although I have slept most of the time I have been here, I am certainly not blind when I *am* awake, although the room is dark enough to make me feel as though I am. I am truly mortified to think of it. The sooner I go, the sooner the room may be restored to its occupant."

"Hush, Lizzy. Mr. Darcy was most willing to give his room up for you." Jane chided her sister gently. "You must not be ungrateful, after what has been done for you here. You are *not* yet well enough to go, not while the fever persists. You must rest and get well."

"This is Mr. Darcy's bedchamber?" Elizabeth gasped. "I cannot stay here!"

"You cannot do otherwise." Jane replied and began to prepare another draught for her sister, which Elizabeth noticed and immediately protested.

"Jane, please, I do not wish another dose! The draughts fog my mind, truly, and give me such dreams as you would not wish to hear. Besides, I have already slept far too much. Please just sit and talk with me."

Jane stopped with her preparations and, instead, sat in the chair at Elizabeth's bedside, taking up her hand. "Lizzy, I have been so worried for you, and Mr. Jones said that sleep would help you recover. If you will take the medicine for the fever and the sleeping draught together, I will tell you something that will most assuredly bring you great happiness, as it has already done for me."

"Tell me first, Jane, so that my mind is perfectly clear when you tell me, for happy news will do me far better than rest."

Jane moved to the edge of the bed and took both of Elizabeth's hands in her own. "Mr. Bingley...," Jane started.

"He has made you an offer!" Elizabeth cried out, and Jane responded with enthusiastic nods of her smiling face as little squeaking giggles burst from her lips. "I knew that he loved you!" Elizabeth exulted. "When did this happen? What did Papa say? And Mama? She must have hardly known what to say—for now her dream has come true, and I will not have to worry of what she will say when I refuse Mr. Collins."

Jane looked quizzically at Elizabeth. "Mr. Bingley proposed just a few minutes ago. We are preparing to return to Longbourn as soon as you are settled, so that Mr. Bingley may gain Papa's consent, and I may share the news with Mama. I could not bear to miss seeing her face when she learns of it. I am so very, very happy, Lizzy—it is nearly too much joy to bear, too much good fortune to be true!"

Elizabeth reached her arms out, and the two shared a sisterly embrace before Jane pulled back and set her hands on Elizabeth's shoulders.

"Lizzy, I am very glad be the means by which such peace and security may be brought to our family, and we shall speak of that more in a moment, but something you said just now has confused me. Did not Mr. Collins already make you an offer?"

"When would he have had an opportunity to do so, Jane? I have been here with you since the ball." Elizabeth replied.

"Then what did he say to you? Mama said he was to propose...," Jane shook her head in bewilderment.

"You are confused, Jane. I did not dance so much as one step with Mr. Collins, which is a great relief, and thankfully, I have not seen him since the ball, for he is at Longbourn, and I am here," Elizabeth said.

"But, Elizabeth," Jane wrung her hands as she spoke. "Mr. Collins came here with Mama this morning and had an audience with you—alone. Mama insisted that it was quite within the bounds of propriety, since he was a kinsman and a clergyman. She told us as we waited outside the door that it was his plan to propose to you. Do you not recall what he said?"

"Mama was here?" Elizabeth's eyes widened.

"Lizzy, she was here this morning and spoke with you before Mr. Collins did" Jane said quietly. "Try to remember."

Elizabeth sat, her eyebrows knit together in frustration as she tried to recall the event, but at length she let out an exasperated noise. "I dreamt of Mama coming to tend to my fever, but that is all. What did she say?"

"I do not know," Jane said. "She was alone with you, as was Mr. Collins."

"I was alone with Mr. Collins? I do not like the sound of that, Jane, not at all! I cannot recollect *seeing* him, let alone *speaking* with him. I most certainly hope that I did not accept his proposal! Pray, at what hour did they come?"

Jane thought for a moment. "I daresay it was but a few minutes after I had given you a sleeping draught when Mr. Collins, Mama, Mary, Kitty and Lydia all arrived. You had not yet gone to sleep, and I was certain you would be happy to see Mama. I did not know she was to send Mr. Collins in to speak with you until it was too late.

A soft knock at the doorframe caused Elizabeth to look up, her face beaming with unmistakable joy, as for a short moment, the silhouette and stature of the man, caused her to believe the visitor was Mr. Darcy. Jane did not see her sister's expression, having turned around to face the door.

"Colonel Fitzwilliam," Jane greeted him graciously. "How fare you this day?"

Standing in the doorway, Colonel Fitzwilliam did not fail to see Elizabeth's countenance fall when she realized she had mistaken his identity. "Ah, Miss Elizabeth, I am glad to see that you are awake." He said, with a gentlemanly bow that reminded Elizabeth once more of his cousin. "I apologize for having overheard a part of your conversation just now. It was unintentional, but perhaps fortuitous. Am I to understand that you do not recall your conversation with Mr. Collins this morning?"

Elizabeth nodded with a disturbed frown. "I do not remember seeing him at all."

"That must seem very strange, but I assure you that you are not going mad. I have seen this same phenomenon in soldiers who have been administered opiates, which no doubt your sleeping draughts contain," the colonel replied thoughtfully. "I may yet be of some service to you, Miss Elizabeth. Mr. Collins himself told me that he had indeed made an offer of marriage to you and that you refused him. Mr. Bingley was also present when he spoke of your refusal and can verify what I say. I tell you this with some trepidation and a warning that I believe he intends to renew his addresses at his earliest opportunity."

"Upon my word," said Elizabeth with an anxious laugh, "it is a fine state of affairs to discover that I have refused a proposal that I cannot even remember receiving. I suppose that so long as he did not compromise me, my refusal by your word shall stand for now."

Colonel Fitzwilliam looked cautiously at Jane before he spoke again. "Mr. Collins is by no means to be trusted, Miss Elizabeth. You must not allow yourself to be alone with him, or you may find your fears realized."

"Oh, no!" Jane cried, "You are wrong! Mr. Collins is a very good man and would never compromise anyone, although his manners *are* rather peculiar. He is certainly not a good match for Lizzy, but we were hoping to turn his attention to Mary, who likes him very much."

"I am not wrong," Colonel Fitzwilliam said seriously to Jane before he turned to face the bed once more. "Miss Elizabeth, I suppose we must now ascertain whether your memory is intact for other conversations that occurred in this state as well."

"I fear I do not remember much that has transpired since the ball." Elizabeth looked sad. "I know that I have suffered some very strange delusions from the fever and now am left to wonder if any of my memories are genuine, or if they are *all* imagined."

Colonel Fitzwilliam looked at Elizabeth, a warm smile on his face. "My cousin Darcy visited you. Do you recall a conversation with him?"

Elizabeth blushed. "I do."

"That was real," Colonel Fitzwilliam said with a laugh. "You may trust your memory on that count, at least."

"Oh," Elizabeth said with a secretive smile. "It is a happy thought, indeed, to discover that I did not imagine it."

"Do not concern yourself with occupying these quarters, Miss Elizabeth," the colonel reassured her. "Darcy has gone to London to take care of some business matters and collect his sister, Miss Darcy. He should return in a few days' time."

"Oh, yes." Elizabeth beamed. "He did inform me that he is to bring his sister. Please tell me what she is like."

"She has grown to be much like her brother in many respects," Colonel Fitzwilliam began. "Like him, she is tall, with a reserved nature. She adores children, and...."

"Does Mr. Darcy adore children?" Elizabeth interrupted.

"Well, yes, Miss Elizabeth, as a matter of fact, he does, provided that they are not *too* naughty." The colonel's eyebrows rose knowingly. "I suspect that you were something of a mischief maker when you were young, were you not?"

Elizabeth laughed gaily. "I shall not answer you, sir! If I deny it, you will not believe me, and if I confess it, you will press for details. No, please continue telling me of Miss Darcy."

The colonel chuckled at Elizabeth's reply and continued, "She is a lovely young lady and very accomplished on the pianoforte, although she does not like to perform for others very much. She sings quite well for one so young. Sometimes her brother even joins her for a duet."

"Mr. Darcy sings?" Elizabeth was incredulous.

"Oh, yes, and quite well too, although never when in company. One must creep up quietly to hear him sing." The colonel laughed. "He is a man of many talents, but he has a nice bushel under which he conceals all but the very dull talents."

"You have heard him sing?" Elizabeth was skeptical.

"Many times—but only because I am an excellent sneak."

"Do you also sing?" Elizabeth teased.

"I do, but only in company with the hounds—they are the only ones who will sing with me.

"Colonel, we must *force* him to sing a duet with his sister!" Elizabeth declared. "I must hear it for myself!"

"It is far likelier, madam, that you could coax him to sing a duet with *you*."

"Excuse me, Colonel." Jane interrupted, "I need to give Elizabeth her medicine now, and she will fall asleep soon after. Thank you for visiting her, but you must go now."

"Very well." The colonel grinned at Elizabeth. "There will be time later for me to divulge more of my cousin's secrets to you, I am sure."

Mr. Bennet was relaxing over a book and a glass of port when a knock came on the study door. "Enter." He called, although he rolled his eyes at the interruption.

"Mr. Bennet," said Mrs. Bennet—more calmly than was her wont, as she smoothed the front of her dress. "I need your advice."

"You seek my advice?" Mr. Bennet put down his book and looked at his wife sternly. "Do not sport with me, Mrs. Bennet."

"Do not be ridiculous, my dear, I would never sport with you, but find myself puzzled over what I must do." She primly sat on a chair near to her husband. "I was very rudely set down today."

"I do not have the pleasure of understanding you. On which circumstance do you seek my counsel, your state of puzzlement or to redress the question of your set down?" Mr. Bennet looked over the top of his reading glasses at his wife. "I have never known you to be missish about such things."

"Oh, Mr. Bennet, do not tease me today. I am quite beside myself already, and you do not know—you cannot understand how I suffer. You cannot help but know that they are two sides of the same coin!" Mrs. Bennet plucked nervously at her sleeves and straightened her mobcap as her carefully collected composure began to collapse. "When we were at Netherfield today, Mr. Collins was to propose to Lizzy, but Colonel Fitzwilliam came and took him away, in a most high-handed manner. Then, what do you suppose, but that Lady Catherine came to the chambers to call on Elizabeth while we were still there. At first, I thought she paid our Lizzy a compliment, her being a great lady as she is, but very soon, I realized that she was in high dudgeon, although for what reason I cannot say. I do not think the woman is quite well in the head!"

"Many people are not, my dear Mrs. Bennet; there is nothing you can do about that," Mr. Bennet remarked dryly. "Pray continue."

"Well, when she learned that Elizabeth was indisposed and could not see her, Lady Catherine was incensed and turned her anger on the rest of our daughters, insulting each one in turn, declaring them unsuitable for consideration by Mr. Collins—even your precious Lizzy was not spared."

"She insulted our daughters, did she?" Mr. Bennet took a sip of his port. "Well, I am not happy to hear of her disapproval, but it is over and done now, and since she has done us a great favor, I am disposed to think kindly of her."

"Favor?" Mrs. Bennet cried out indignantly. "How can you say such a thing?"

"Now that Lady Catherine de Bourgh has rejected our daughters, not one of them must face the prospect of marriage to my ridiculous cousin. It is hard enough to call Mr. Collins a kinsman, but, after all, one's relations are wholly a matter of chance. One's spouse is another matter entirely, and I believe I could not endure calling Mr. Collins my son by choice."

"You will not think so kindly of her when I tell you this—Lady Catherine was very rude to me." Mrs. Bennet sniffed. "She is an abominable woman! It is no wonder Mr. Darcy is so very high and mighty coming from a family such as that. No doubt, they think they are better than we are—even that colonel fellow—he was horribly officious with Mr. Collins. Such ungentlemanly behavior I have never seen!"

"Then we have escaped a dreadful fate, Mrs. Bennet, for the future Mrs. Collins, whoever she may be, will most certainly enjoy the close supervision and patronage of Lady Catherine. Let it be someone else's daughter." Mr. Bennet chuckled.

"And someone else's daughter will be the mistress of Longbourn while we starve in the hedgerows!" Mrs. Bennet wailed.

A knock at the door interrupted the conversation, and upon an invitation to enter, Hill opened the door and announced, "Mr. Bingley to see you, Mr. Bennet."

ꟹ

Colonel Fitzwilliam received the express from Darcy house a mere quarter of an hour after Bingley and Jane had boarded the carriage to Longbourn. He ordered that a horse be readied immediately and went to his room to pack a few belongings. Darcy's message was short and cryptic, leaving his cousin impatient to depart for London. He re-read the letter.

Richard,

Wickham is dead. There will be uproar, and I require your assistance. Please return to London with all haste.

Fitzwilliam Darcy

The colonel wrote a slightly longer note to Bingley informing him that urgent business had called him away, but that he hoped to return in a few days. He addressed several other items of business, particularly as it related to the watch-care of Elizabeth, and left the note on Bingley's desk in the study. He then went to the drawing room, where Caroline and the Hursts were much occupied with being idle.

"Ah, Colonel!" Caroline called out to him as soon as he entered. "Please do come join us, for we need a fourth, and you will do nicely."

"Miss Bingley," he replied. "It is my rule never to play cards in company. I always win, and someone invariably accuses me of cheating, when in fact, my military training for strategy is where the credit must go. In either case, you would find yourself poorer if I play."

He then informed the party that he did not have time to do their game justice anyway, for he was to leave Netherfield and return to London immediately. There was a general air of disappointment among them, for the levity that he had brought to the household had been a welcome change from the boring conversations they had fallen into of late.

It took him another quarter of an hour to extract himself, for nearly as soon as he said he must go, Miss Bingley would attempt to prevent it. *She would make an excellent spy* he thought, his mind turning over recent observations and conversations with Miss Bingley that weighed heavily—there was something unsettling about the woman, but try as he might, he could not identify with precision the source of his unease.

When he was finally able to quit the drawing room, he went upstairs to where Sarah was watching over Elizabeth, who was once again fast asleep.

"Sarah," he instructed, "you are to allow no-one admittance until Miss Elizabeth's sister has returned to nurse her. Lock the door behind me, and do not open it for anyone but her sister or Mr. Bingley. I have retrieved the spare door-key from Mr. Bingley's study." He held up the key to show her and set it on the table. "No one in the household will be able to gain entry unless you grant it."

Sarah's eyes were wide as she listened to his instructions. "Yes, sir." She replied to the colonel, whose orders left no question of disobedience. "Begging your pardon, but what if it is Miss Bingley at the door? She is acting as mistress for her brother, and if I refuse her...."

"You must *not* open the door for Miss Bingley." The colonel repeated his directive in full again and added, "You may inform her of my instructions and appeal to her brother if she threatens you in any way." Colonel Fitzwilliam smiled at the young maid. "It is just a precaution. If you follow my instructions, all will be well."

Caroline Bingley watched from the window as Colonel Fitzwilliam rode into the winter twilight. She reviewed the locations of each person in the household. Darcy was gone away, and now the colonel had, as well. Lady Catherine and Anne had also departed, and her brother and Miss Bennet would likely be gone for at least another hour, as he had taken her to Longbourn to see her family, although it was now too late for visitors to call at Netherfield. She turned and saw Mr. Hurst dozing on the sofa, and her sister, Louisa, was practicing a new piece of music on the pianoforte. Dinner would not be for another hour.

"The time has come." Caroline muttered to herself with a self-satisfied smile. "I am to be the mistress of Pemberley someday and cannot leave matters to chance."

She returned to her chamber with purpose, pleased with her own foresight to prepare for just such an opportunity as that which now presented itself.

Chapter Forty-Six

SCHEMES PUT INTO PLAY

Caroline was astonished to find the door to Darcy's former quarters locked. Rapping on the door impatiently, she demanded entrance. Putting her ear to the door, she could hear movement behind it, but no voice acknowledged her presence.

"Sarah! I know you are in there with Miss Elizabeth. Open this door at once." Caroline's annoyance was evident as she rattled the doorknob to emphasize her displeasure.

"I cannot," the timid reply came from behind the door.

"Has the door malfunctioned?" Caroline challenged her.

"No, ma'am," Sarah replied quietly.

"Then why can you not open it?"

"Colonel Fitzwilliam ordered me not to, and I dare not disobey." Sarah's voice quivered as she replied.

"Colonel Fitzwilliam has no authority in this household, Sarah. I am the mistress here. You will obey *me, and only me,* do you hear? I *insist* that you open this door!" Caroline screamed as she kicked the door angrily.

"I cannot," Sarah replied again.

"This is insupportable! You are dismissed from this moment, you ungrateful, insolent little wretch! You are no longer a servant in this household, and you will receive no recommendation for your service here. Depart at once and never return," Caroline declared loudly.

No response came from inside the chamber.

"Sarah!" Caroline screamed. She slapped at the door and rattled the handle again, and then stopped suddenly, changing to low, threatening tones. "I know where to find a key to this room, Sarah. You shall surely regret your defiance when you hear this. You have already ruined your own employment; if this door is not unlocked, with you nowhere to be seen, when I return, your mother and brother shall also be dispatched—as a result of *your* insolence!"

Sarah stood behind the door, her hand resting upon the doorknob. She was trembling—the implications of Caroline's threats filled her with dread, and after she heard Caroline storm away, she gripped the handle tighter, prepared to flee when she felt a hand on her shoulder. She turned to find Elizabeth behind her.

"You are very courageous, Sarah, but I cannot allow you to lose your position for my sake. You must do as she says—Miss Bingley is your mistress."

Sarah looked at Elizabeth wide-eyed. "Miss Elizabeth, Colonel Fitzwilliam instructed me to open the door only for your sister or Master Bingley. He made me promise!"

"I cannot imagine why," Elizabeth replied. "I am certain he just meant me to rest, and he would not wish you to be dismissed. He understands as well as anyone that you must have something to live on."

Sarah frowned and shook her head. "He brought the spare key here, to keep her from opening the door." She pointed to the key that lay on the table. "I am forbidden to admit her, Miss Elizabeth, even if the mistress threatens. I will not go back on my word."

"How very curious! The colonel would not so instruct you without cause." Elizabeth wobbled slightly where she stood. "I fear that I must sit down—my strength is by no means what I wish it." As Sarah was assisting Elizabeth, the sound of footsteps outside the door heralded Caroline's return.

Muffled voices alerted them that Caroline was not alone, and then the jangle of keys and the rattle of the lock informed them that their security had been breached an instant before the door swung open to a triumphant Caroline, who swept into the room, quite astonished to see Elizabeth sitting in the outer room.

The housekeeper stood behind her with a ring of keys. She was glaring at Sarah, displeased that a member of the household staff had defied the mistress on her watch. She signaled with her head that Sarah should leave, but when Sarah attempted to do so, Caroline caught her by the arm, yanking her around to face her directly.

"What was this about?" Caroline demanded. "What mischief are you up to, and where is the stolen key? What other items have you stolen from this household, you ungrateful little thief? Go with Mrs. Norris now, but you are not to leave until there has been a full accounting of your misdeeds." Caroline roughly cast her toward the housekeeper, who ushered her from the room.

Caroline turned to face Elizabeth. "My dear Eliza, it appears that you are recovered."

"I am a little better, thank you." Elizabeth replied politely. "I am obliged to inform you, Miss Bingley—the key you accused Sarah of stealing is there, on the table. I understand that it was Colonel Fitzwilliam who put it there, not the maid."

Caroline walked to the table and picked up the key, twirling it in her fingers. "It is of no importance, I assure you. I cannot have a servant disobey me or there would be open revolt. Such disgraceful behavior will not be tolerated in *my* household."

"I see." Elizabeth muttered. "You would prefer that she break a promise to another to accommodate your orders."

"Yes, I would. If you had ever run a household yourself, you would perfectly understand, but as you have not, you must trust me in this. Colonel Fitzwilliam is a guest and has no right to elicit such oaths from the staff in *my* employ. He seeks to undermine me and was mistaken in so doing. He has cost that maid her living."

"Have you no compassion for the girl?" Elizabeth inquired, "She was in an impossible situation."

"Perhaps, but it is of no concern to *me*. It is done now. She would have been discharged anyway, for we are soon to return to London for the winter." Caroline waved her hand dismissively. "I cannot tolerate another day in the country! There are too many prying eyes and wagging tongues in this county by far."

"What was your urgent business in my quarters, Miss Bingley? It must have been a matter of great import for you to make such a case of gaining immediate admittance." Elizabeth asked with a weary sigh. "I had been asleep before your knocking at the outer door woke me."

"I came out of *concern,* dear Eliza. With my brother and your sister gone to Longbourn, I feel it was my Christian duty to ascertain your condition. After all, if you need to see Mr. Jones again, the hour to summon him is nearly upon us."

"Thank you, but I do not require Mr. Jones." Elizabeth replied with an attempt at civility she did not feel, "Is there any other matter that brought you here? I should return to the bedchamber if we are finished, Miss Bingley."

"I wish to visit you." Caroline said, coldly. "You have been a guest in this house, of which I am presently acting mistress for two days now and have been well attended to be sure, but now you are alone."

"You are most observant. I am indeed alone." Elizabeth nodded, thinking, *I am alone because you sent Sarah away.* "I thank you for your consideration, Miss Bingley. It was most kind, but I daresay Jane shall return soon. I do not require your attendance."

"There is another reason for my visit, Miss Eliza. I am perfectly aware of how many persons were in this room yesterday, and considering the number, I discerned that the decanter of elderberry wine we provided according to Mr. Jones' directions was certain to be low." Caroline pointed to a tray on the table with the nearly empty vessel. "I see that my anticipation was indeed correct. I have brought more. The new bottle is in the hall; I shall go get it now." Caroline smiled with forced sweetness as she turned to retrieve it.

"That is very thoughtful, Miss Bingley, but you have underestimated the efficiency of your staff. A footman delivered a new bottle on the instruction of your butler this morning, and Jane is to refill the decanter on her return. There shall be adequate time for it to settle before we drink our evening cup." Elizabeth said.

"Nonsense," said Caroline, "we were forced to buy the wine in Meryton since we had not anything so crude as elderberry in the wine cellar here at Netherfield. It is of an inferior quality and the amount of sediment in these bottles is shocking. We must pour it now and give it more time."

"By all means," said Elizabeth sweetly as she gestured toward the table. "The bottle is just to the left of the decanter there. There is no need to go for another."

Caroline frowned but transferred the liquid from the bottle and replaced the stopper, her back turned to Elizabeth as she worked. When she had finished, she posed the question, "How do you like the room, Miss Eliza?"

"I beg your pardon?"

"The room." Caroline turned with a slight smirk. "These *are* Darcy's chambers, you know." She inhaled deeply. "The room still bears his distinct aroma. You are surrounded by it. Does that not please you?"

"I had not noticed." Elizabeth shook her head. "I have been too ill to take particular note of the smell. It could have been a fish market, and I would have slept through it."

"Come now, we are both women," Caroline said with a smirk. She tipped her head as if to enter into a confidence with Elizabeth. "Do you not take pleasure in lying in Darcy's bed? Is there not some delightful essence of the man that lingers on the pillows?"

"Miss Bingley, I beg you to forgive me for not answering such an indelicate question. In return for the favor, I shall forgive you for asking it," Elizabeth replied evenly.

"I *knew* it." Caroline shrugged. "I *knew* that you were violently in love with him. Oh, you poor, pitiful creature—Darcy would never ... oh, but you thought he would, did you not?" Caroline laughed feebly. "Louisa said that you would believe he could love you, but I gave you more credit."

"Upon my word, I know *not* of what you speak," Elizabeth replied as she turned toward the bedchamber door.

"Do you not?" Caroline teased. "If that were so, you would not withdraw so easily—you would desire an explanation. No, I see well enough that you believe he cares for you, although he does not regard you well enough to declare it openly." She drummed her fingers on the table as she added, "I wonder why he would wish to appear indifferent, if he is not. What do you suppose he means by keeping it secret?"

"If he were to harbor such a secret, what will you accomplish in exposing it?" Elizabeth shrugged and replied archly. "What do you propose I do if it is true? What if it is false? What then? Pray tell me how I should act in regards to a secret so well kept that you must speculate it into existence."

"I daresay that you *think* you know how to act," Caroline sneered. "This is why men should not marry below their station—you simply do not understand the ways of men of society—that is dismally evident. There are the ladies whom they marry, and there are the others whom they use for their pleasure and cast aside when they lose interest." Caroline gasped as though sudden realization was upon her. "Miss Eliza, you poor thing—have you already given yourself to him? I suspected that this is not the first time you have been in his bed, Why else would he trouble with you as long as he has? You sad, naïve country maid—*if you are still a maid*, you may rest assured that when it comes to marriage, his head will rule. He will select a woman of breeding, of accomplishment, of fortune...."

"You mean that he will choose you," Elizabeth replied calmly. "If that happens, I shall wish you joy."

"I *shall* be mistress of Pemberley." Caroline smiled victoriously as she held out her hand and inspected her fingertips. "And you—you shall be derided and pitied, your reputation tarnished with whispers of impropriety and disappointed hopes."

"You, the mistress of Pemberley? I think not Miss Bingley, for yours are not the words of a gentle born lady. Whomever he marries, Mr. Darcy's 'head' is certain to require that she is at least that—fortune and connections aside, you cannot sustain your pretense to be a gentlewoman unless you first acquire some manners." Elizabeth curtseyed and retired to the bedchamber, closing the door behind her.

As soon as Elizabeth was out of sight, Caroline reached into the slight cleft between her bosoms and withdrew a small key. She promptly went to the small writing desk in the corner and used the key to open the bank of drawers it held. She rifled through the top drawer, extracting a journal and a stack of papers, which she promptly sat at the desk to read.

The journal had occupied her attention for a quarter of an hour when she turned a page and found two folded papers tucked between the leaves. The first she unfolded and discovered what appeared to be a charcoal rubbing of some sort of embroidered design, which she did not examine closely—she assumed it to be some trivial enclosure sent in a letter from Darcy's sister, but the second paper, it constituted a list written in Darcy's elegant hand. She studied the contents of the list carefully.

Wickham—in Hertfordshire
Aunt C.—leak / hunting / will find
Anne—confirm status
Collins—proposal
C. Bingley—trouble / reproach
E.D. handkerchief—<u>must</u> return
E.B.—opinion / walking / dance
Georgiana—write letter/ visit
Fitz—assist with W
Col. F.—visit

The list puzzled her as much as it intrigued her. Some names where obvious, others more cryptic. Was "C. Bingley" a reference to her or to Charles? E.B. was obvious, but who was E.D.? What status was he to confirm with Anne? What did it all mean?

She heard the distant sound of her brother and Jane entering the doors of Netherfield, his merry voice ringing loudly in the entryway. She hastily returned the journal and papers to the drawer, which she locked. The exception was the list, which she folded into a smaller size and tucked into her dress along with the two keys. She was careful to avoid detection as she left the room and picked up the rejected bottle of elderberry wine as she passed the table in the hall. Returning to her own chambers at the end of the corridor, Caroline was both disappointed and pleased with the outcome of her call on Elizabeth, but far more distracted by the meaning of the entries in the list she had acquired, so she retired to her chambers to study it further.

"Charles, I must go to Elizabeth." Jane giggled slightly as she pulled herself from his embrace.

"You are an angel of mercy to your sister," Bingley replied with a cheerful smile as he released her, "and an instrument of torment to *me* now that we are engaged."

"Do not say it! Can I cause you to be in torment when I am so very happy?" Jane sighed. "I am glad Papa agreed to a short engagement, although Mama was certainly wishing for more time to prepare. In all honesty, dearest, she began planning our wedding the day you obtained Papa's consent to court me, although I told her it was too soon." Jane let out an involuntary squeal. "Oh, Charles! I shall be Mrs. Bingley for Christmas!"

"Yes, you shall." Bingley raised her hand to his lips and kissed her knuckles. "Never have I seen you so joyous, Jane! We are fortunate, indeed, for a Christmas engagement brings great opportunities, my angel. I shall trim the halls of Netherfield with mistletoe in every doorway!" Charles declared.

"You shall not need it," Jane blushed, "when we are wed."

"I will not wait for Christmas Eve, Jane. We deck the halls tomorrow!" Bingley declared, his eyes dancing at the genius of his idea.

"That is too soon." Jane laughed merrily, even as she attempted to scold him.

"Negotiations are in order, I suppose. I will settle for one early sprig of mistletoe, strategically placed." Bingley smiled mischievously.

"I will not be here at Netherfield for you to use it! Have you forgotten? I return to Longbourn as soon as Elizabeth is well enough to go," Jane reminded him.

"Then I shall place it at Longbourn," Bingley whispered the sly threat victoriously.

"Oh dear!" Jane cried, "You must not tease Mama so! If she were to see us kissing beneath the mistletoe, she will expect that you want to ... um, hmmm, she will expect that you intend to marry me." Jane trailed off with a delighted giggle. "You are determined?" Jane bestowed a shy smile on him, and he was undone.

"Very," Bingley said with a cheeky grin as he stole another kiss from sweet Jane, whose reluctance decreased ever so slightly with each romantic encounter with the amorous Mr. Bingley.

The hour was late when Colonel Fitzwilliam arrived at the outskirts of London, later still when he reached Darcy House—yet upon his approach, the glow of candlelight in the front window bid him welcome. He had not yet alighted from his steed when a stable-hand appeared to see to the animal, and the butler opened the doors, greeting him as politely as if he were arriving for high tea.

He declined the offer to refresh himself and went directly to Darcy's study, where his cousin had patiently awaited his arrival. The door was ajar, and Fitzwilliam could see Darcy bent over the desk, writing. At the sound of footsteps, Darcy looked up from his work, set the pen down and leaned back in the chair.

"How is Miss Bennet?" Darcy asked solemnly.

"She is very well. By now I believe her engagement to Bingley is official," the colonel said, fingering some books on a shelf. He turned, and seeing Darcy scowling, added, "Perhaps you meant the *other* Miss Bennet? She was sleeping under the care of the maid when I left. I believe she was a little better."

"Aunt Catherine?"

"She returned to London as soon as her prey left the field." Fitzwilliam picked up a book and thumbed through it. "She was really quite *put out* with your sudden departure."

"That is excellent—I am glad she came away. What news of ... Collins?" Darcy asked, almost as an afterthought.

"Well, now, there *is* a bit of news, to be sure." Fitzwilliam stepped to the far side of the room, away from Darcy. "Mr. Collins came to the house with the Bennets while I was speaking with Aunt Catherine. I did not know he was in the house."

"What does that mean; you '*did not know*?'" Darcy stood, his eyes riveted on his cousin.

"In some respects, I cannot tell you exactly what it means—I do not know all the particulars...."

"Particulars? What particulars?" Darcy's face reddened. "You were supposed to protect her from him!"

"I will tell you what I know if you will just calm yourself." Fitzwilliam sat down, maintaining an erect posture. "Are you quite certain you wish to hear it? You will not like it."

"Cease with this prevaricating, Fitzwilliam, and get on with it."

"Very well. When I came across Collins, he was in the bedchamber alone with Miss Elizabeth, who was reclining in the bed, fully covered by the bedclothes. He was leaning across her, as though he had been sitting just a moment before, although one of his hands covered her mouth and the other pinned her down as she struggled against him."

Darcy fell backward into his chair and covered his face with his hands, exhaling loudly. "Was she...?"

"Compromised?" Fitzwilliam suggested and shrugged his shoulders. "The harpies of the *ton* would say yes, but for practical purposes, no, it did not go that far. I interrogated Collins thoroughly, and I am satisfied that we got to the essence of the matter. The incident began when he proposed to her, and when she refused him, he would not believe she was sincere. He was pressing her for a different answer when I arrived—I believe in the aroused state he was in, he well may have compromised her—had I not intervened."

Darcy raked his hands through his hair. "The man must be publicly disgraced, exposed and removed from his position. It cannot stand!"

"Would you expose Miss Bennet as well?" Fitzwilliam asked gravely. "Aunt Catherine would most certainly use such knowledge against her."

Darcy looked pained. "Did he harm her?"

"I do not believe so." Fitzwilliam crossed his leg, relaxing slightly.

"I could kill him." Darcy said softly, through gritted teeth. "So help me, if he so much as bruised her, it may take your entire regiment to stop me from vengeance."

"I am the fierce one who threatens death to scoundrels, Darcy." Fitzwilliam scolded. "You are the one who keeps a cool head and prevents it. That is the order of things."

"You need not remind me of it." Darcy replied grimly. "Your threats against Wickham were of great interest to at least one officer of the law."

"Turned me in, eh?" Fitzwilliam chuckled. "First I was cheated of the opportunity to dispatch Wickham, and now I am betrayed by my favorite relation. This is not a good day! It should be simple enough to sort out, however. There is nothing there to hold their interest. By what means was he killed?"

"His assassins were not so imaginative in their means as you would have been." Darcy replied. "I believe he was bludgeoned to death."

"How came you to hear of it?"

"He was left, nearly dead, upon the doorstep of this house. He died within moments, but not before he named me as his killer in front of a witness." Darcy frowned. "That was a lie, but I know not who it was that did it."

"Whoever did it knew enough of your object to bring Wickham here." Fitzwilliam stood and began to pace. "An accomplice, perhaps?"

"I openly sent men into the streets in search of Wickham. Half of all London knew of my desire to locate him," Darcy railed against himself.

"Then half of all London is suspect, I imagine," Fitzwilliam replied cheerily. "That narrows the field considerably—only half the city."

"I was the prime suspect for a short time." Darcy frowned and then added with a slight smile, "Now it is you."

"You, a suspect for murder? Preposterous! Which runner had the audacity to level such an accusation?" Fitzwilliam finally appeared bothered by what Darcy was saying.

"It was not a runner, Fitzwilliam, but the first policeman on the scene—an officer of no true consequence. I sent a dispatch to Sir Vincent Parker at Bow Street once the officer quit the house. Justice will prevail, and I suspect we may never see that particular officer again."

"Why did you not eject the man from the house? He had no right!" Fitzwilliam was indignant.

"Cooperation, cousin, establishes that I have nothing to hide. I have already disclosed any incriminating facts they may stumble upon in an investigation, which he is certain to relate to his superiors. In particular, it is possible that Bow Street will discover the letter Georgiana wrote to Wickham, so I told them of it myself first."

"So there is a letter." Fitzwilliam sighed and shook his head. "We must find it before anyone else does."

"Agreed," Darcy replied with a firm nod, looking meaningfully at his cousin. "It has been over seven years since we engaged in such a venture—I never expected to do so again. Our costumes from before are woefully unsuitable."

"If that is code for 'they do not fit anymore,' never fear. I will acquire new ones in the morning." Fitzwilliam suppressed a laugh. "You are no longer the slight youth you once were."

"You speak as though *you* are." Darcy half-smiled. "I am more concerned about putting on vulgar manners than I am in finding coarse attire. We are no longer practiced, and have never done it for serious reasons, but for sport only, and even then only in our youth."

"It is like riding a horse, Darcy. Once you learn to do it, you never really forget, and our former adventures will serve in good stead for the matter at hand." Fitzwilliam laughed. "What shall we call ourselves?"

"Fools?" Darcy suggested.

"When it is over, we may have the luxury of saying so, but for now, I shall be Smythe, and you shall be Hedgecock." Fitzwilliam said with a grin. "We are both George, to remind us why we are doing it."

Darcy snorted. "Hedgecock, I know full well, means 'son of Richard'—your ruse to make me your subordinate has failed. I will choose my own name—I will be Pratt." Darcy replied. "We must wait until after Sir Vincent has gone to don our disguises, and then we may be about our business. Although I abhor the very thought of this masquerade, I have given the matter much thought, and it is for the best. It will be a relief when we have brought Wickham's machinations to an end."

"Aye," said Richard sympathetically, "and a relief to return to Hertfordshire. It must be hard to be away from her at such a time."

"It is," Darcy replied as his thoughts turned back to Elizabeth. "Richard, I am unsettled and restless, as though there is something I have missed—some hidden danger lurking to injure me or those I care for."

"I have felt the same." Fitzwilliam replied. "I sense that something is amiss at Netherfield. How well do you know Bingley's sisters?"

"Very well, I think," Darcy replied, knitting his brow at the question. "What do you imply?"

"There is a look about Miss Bingley that I do not trust. She looks upon you with a mercenary eye, and at Miss Elizabeth with malevolence when she believes no one observes her."

"It is true that she has spoken ill of Miss Elizabeth, seeking my agreement; indeed, she has so spoken of the entire Bennet family." Darcy reflected. "I suspect, although I have no evidence to support it, that she harbors a hope that I may offer for her hand."

"In truth, she is envious of your attentions toward Miss Bennet. You are not so naïve as to believe that a woman of her temperament will calmly stand aside, are you?" Fitzwilliam prodded. "She will act."

"This is impossible, Richard!" Darcy began to pace. "I cannot possibly be in two places at once. I must tend to matters here before I can return to Hertfordshire, but now you tell me that she may be in some danger from Caroline Bingley? What am I to do?"

"I left a note for Bingley," Fitzwilliam said. "I could not specifically accuse his own sister without cause, but I did warn him that only the maid or Miss Bennet should be left alone with Miss Elizabeth. I can only hope that he takes my meaning."

"She cannot remain at Netherfield under these circumstances." Darcy declared firmly. "I will send my best carriage tomorrow, first to Mr. Jones to arrange it, and then to convey Miss Elizabeth and her sister back to Longbourn. She will at least be safe at home."

"There is only one problem with that plan." Fitzwilliam replied.

"What?" asked Darcy impatiently.

Fitzwilliam laughed. "Bingley may never forgive you."

Chapter Forty-Seven

IS THIS NOT LOVE?

Jane arrived at the bedchamber where her sister slept, happier than she could ever recall being. So anxious was she to tell Elizabeth of their mother's delight at the news of the betrothal that when Elizabeth did not rouse upon the opening of the door, Jane crept over to the bed to discern if her sister might be sufficiently awake to give excuse to disturb her. She discovered her sister sleeping soundlessly. Indeed, Elizabeth lay so still and quiet in the bed that Jane was immediately alarmed, and she reached out to discover whether breath was still upon her sister's lips. She discerned that it seemed shallow and she laid her hand on Elizabeth's neck, relieved to find the pulsing of her heart to be steady and strong.

At Jane's touch, Elizabeth's eyes reluctantly opened and she granted her sister a sleepy smile.

"Well? Did my father manage to frighten Mr. Bingley away, or did he grant consent? I hope it is the latter, for I have become quite enamored of the idea of his being my brother." Elizabeth sat up with a delighted smile.

"He consented most heartily, Lizzy, and Mama—she would have died and gone to heaven she was so carried away with the thought of Mr. Bingley as my husband. She was somewhat preoccupied with pin money and carriages to be sure, but Charles did not even mind. In fact he, quite agreed with everything Mama said. It was so amusing, dear Lizzy. I am sorry that you could not be there!" Jane sat dreamily on the side of the bed. "Mama failed to mention fine clothes and jewels, and Mr. Bingley, he took Mama by the hand and said, 'Do not forget that I shall dress your daughter in silks, madam, and adorn her lovely neck with pearls and sapphires. She shall have the very best of everything!' Mama was very nearly overcome! I wonder what is the opposite of nerves. Whatever it is, Mama had a very bad case of it!"

Elizabeth's contentment at Jane's good fortune was evident as she sat smiling in the bed. "I know that you are not thinking about such material concerns as Mama—what are your thoughts on the matter?"

"I scarcely know what I feel, Lizzy. I know that Mr. Bingley is the kindest and most amiable of men, and I do hold to the deepest belief that we will be very happy together. I shall devote all of my attentions to making him content in his situation," Jane sighed. "He has sworn to do the same, so we shall go about our days seeing to one another's comfort. Is this not love?"

"It well may be, Jane, but if it is not, it is a worthy second to it. Such unselfish devotion cannot help but thrive in your hearts and become love, if it is not there already." Elizabeth put her hand over Jane's. "Did they agree to the short engagement as you had hoped?"

Jane nodded. "Oh yes, just long enough to publish and read the banns, and the wedding shall be upon us. Our wedding is but three weeks and two days away, provided the church is available."

"So soon?" Elizabeth's eyes widened in astonishment. "There is much to be done!"

"For my part, it can wait until you are well." Jane replied. "Mama has already begun planning, and you may be assured that all her practice with entertainments will culminate on the day of my wedding, whether or not I am in the thick of it."

"Mama does take delight in entertaining—that is undoubtedly true." Elizabeth withdrew for a moment into her thoughts. "Jane, I am loath to turn to more solemn things, but something occurred here in your absence that must be rectified at once."

"What is it, Lizzy?" Jane's countenance fell. "What has happened?"

"I wonder—Is Miss Bingley aware of the betrothal?" Elizabeth pondered.

"Why, yes, Charles told her and Mrs. Hurst of our engagement just a moment ago." Jane looked curiously at her sister. "She was less delighted than my mother, but that could be said of anyone."

"It was so strange, and I am at a loss to provide an explanation for what transpired. Miss Bingley came to visit me in this room while you were away at Longbourn. I had been asleep, but she would not be turned away, although Colonel Fitzwilliam had instructed Sarah not to open the door to anyone but you. Caroline was incensed at the insubordination of her servant and has discharged Sarah from service for it." Elizabeth shook her head sadly. "I cannot fault Sarah for what occurred. She should not have lost her employment for my sake. Can nothing be done?"

"I shall explain what happened to Charles—he will know what to do. Do not fret, Lizzy, for at the very least, I am soon to be mistress of this house and can undo what was done myself." Jane patted Elizabeth's hand. "All shall be well. What else did Miss Bingley have to say?"

"Very little." Elizabeth shook her head. "Her visit here was very odd. She seemed most intent on making certain we had sufficient elderberry wine, which she insisted on pouring into the decanter herself, although she did not even inquire as to whether we required more lemon balm, which was consumed at a pace far exceeding the wine. She even brought a bottle of the wine with her and seemed rather distraught that there was a new bottle already in the room. It seemed so very out of her character to be attentive to such a thing that I cannot help but say that it raised my suspicions immediately."

"Perhaps she is feeling remiss as your hostess and wished to make amends," Jane said thoughtfully.

"I do not believe it, Jane. She said vile things to me that I will not give further voice to through repetition. I have always felt her to be unpleasant. I now believe her beyond mere rudeness. She is possessed of a truly vicious character," Elizabeth said vehemently.

"She is to be my sister!" Jane cried out, aghast at what Elizabeth was saying. "You are being unkind!"

"I may be unfeeling in so saying, but she will not spare you her wrath when she unleashes it." Elizabeth frowned. "In fact, I would not put it past her to have meddled with the wine. She stood in the way, Jane, so I could not see her pour it, and she was indeed behaving most surreptitiously when she did it."

"You mistake her, Lizzy. I shall prove it to you." Jane removed the stopper from the decanter and poured a cup of the sparkling red liquid into a glass, swirling it slightly as she breathed in the aroma. She shook her head slightly with some surprise and sniffed it again before she dipped her finger into it and touched her tongue to the droplet on her fingertip, skewing her face at the unpleasant taste. "It is laced with laudanum. I thought I could smell it, but the bitterness is undeniable." Jane set down the glass, blanching with shock. She picked up the phial that Mr. Jones had dispensed the tincture of opium in and discovered it to be empty. She turned, holding the small, flat vessel up for Elizabeth to see. "She has added all that remained in the phial to the wine! It was not even a quarter gone!"

"I did not consider her to be as bad as this!" Elizabeth's astonishment was evident, as she returned to the bed, pale and trembling. "If two drops makes me sleep for hours, what would a larger dose do? Oh Jane, do not leave me tonight. Spend the night here in the room with me. Together we shall be safe."

"This is serious indeed, Lizzy. I must go and tell Charles about Sarah and about the wine. Such treachery cannot be borne. Indeed, I know that he will not allow such behavior, from his very own sister and in his house—of that I am certain! I shall return Lizzy, after I have related these doings to my intended."

Picking up the decanter of elderberry wine as she departed, Jane quit the room and went in search of Mr. Bingley.

Elizabeth found herself in such a state of agitation over their discovery that she knew she would be unable to rest until the matter had been resolved, and she set about tidying up the sitting room. She lit a few candles, as the daylight was rapidly fading, and set the room to order quickly. She noticed, as she came around to the small writing desk in the corner, that there was a folded paper, which had fallen onto the floor beneath it. Picking it up, she discerned from the outside that it was not written upon, but bore instead some sort of design or pattern. She unfolded the paper and discovered a delicate charcoal rubbing in the pattern of her handkerchief, slightly smudged but nonetheless recognizable. This, she realized, must have been taken before Darcy had returned the cloth to her. She could only assume that he had made it as a keepsake.

She left the paper on the table and turned to the bedchamber, doing the same service there that she had performed in the sitting room. With the room lit by candlelight, it was brighter than it had been even during the daytime, with the shades and curtains drawn, and as she looked about the room, she realized that more than a few articles remained from Mr. Darcy's residence in the room. She began to wander, idly picking up any item that appeared to belong to *him,* as if some connection to him might be formed merely by holding his belongings. Eventually, she peeked into a drawer and found, to her delight, a perfect pheasant tail-feather within. She replaced it pulled open the drawer beneath it, and found therein, pushed back into the farthest corner, a parcel loosely wrapped in brown paper. She could see well enough that it contained a fine fabric, and as she raised the candle to get a better look, the material shimmered in the flickering glow.

"What is this?" Elizabeth cried softly, as she impulsively pulled the fabric from its wrapper. She held in her hands, the softest cloth she had ever felt. The beautiful, deep wine color was offset, she could see, by threads of gold in the weave. She opened it up and discovered an embroidered shawl of such exquisite workmanship and softness that she could not help but wrap herself in it, just for a moment. Was it another gift for his sister, or some elegant lady of the *ton,* perhaps? The last thought sobered her, and she carefully folded it and returned it to the wrapper, sorrowing that she had ever seen it.

She pondered on the disparity of the three articles she had discovered in Mr. Darcy's room. The rubbing represented her handkerchief, which, although of high sentimental value to her and, apparently to Mr. Darcy as well, was of no true monetary value. The feather, too, was a common thing—a single fallen plume from a wild bird, easily replaced a thousand times over. The shawl, on the other hand, must have cost Mr. Darcy very dearly and was the sort of item she never had any expectation of possessing. Her two meager contributions to his collection were nothing to what he could acquire in an instant with little thought of the expense.

Never had Elizabeth Bennet felt so poor as she did in that hour. To this feeling, she added the knowledge of the sudden, inexplicable departure of Mr. Darcy and the harsh, cutting words of Miss Bingley, until her mind knew not what to think. Was her reputation already tainted—did others think that she was compromised? She had heard sordid tales of innocent women who had fallen prey to pretty words and romantic gestures, only to be cast aside when they had foolishly surrendered their virtue. Was Mr. Darcy playing a cruel game with her? Indeed, Mr. Darcy had *not* proposed marriage but had left her nearly as soon as she had acknowledged her feelings for him, and with no witness, no one to vouch for what was spoken between them.

The more she thought upon it, the more firmly she believed that the tender regard she had held for Mr. Darcy was evidence of her own gullibility. This quickly restored her original belief that a man of his station would never lower himself to accept a woman of her societal sphere as a viable prospect for a wife and that she had been skillfully duped by a man well versed in the ways of the world. Then her reason sallied forth. *No! This is too ungenerous!* Her heart rebelled against her mind in attributing such duplicity to the man. To this was added another thought—that even if his declaration of love was sincere, he must by now regret having uttered it, knowing the degradation it would be to his family if he were to make an alliance with one who brought nothing to the union but her charms and whose own relations were so decidedly below his own.

In these thoughts, Elizabeth was truly grieved, for she doubted not her own conviction of whether she loved Mr. Darcy. She did—utterly and completely. She had succumbed to his kind heart, his unequalled intelligence, his informed mind, his confidence and the passion she sensed simmering beneath the surface of his composed demeanor. What had once seemed arrogance, she now perceived as reserve; what had put her off as pride she had come to appreciate as an inborn, stately dignity. His earnest, steadfast gaze felt as a flame on her flesh, and she had discovered the heady torment of desire blossom within her—along with the realization that she was never as purely happy as she was when in company with Mr. Darcy.

She could not bear the devastating truth in what Caroline Bingley had spoken, but there it was—articulated by a heartless shrew who did not deserve the honor of being correct. But when it came to marriage, Elizabeth well knew that Darcy's head would indeed overrule his heart. He could have anyone he chose, and he would choose well—it was his nature to do so. The woman who took her place at his side would undoubtedly bring a fortune and connections as assets to the match and possess an advanced education and a pedigree of noble birth to parallel Mr. Darcy's. She would certainly be beautiful, but added to these attributes, Elizabeth wished for him a gentle soul—one who would care for him in the same manner as he cared for those he loved. She hoped the future Mrs. Darcy would be a woman of good humor, who would see through his moods and delight him when the weight of his position pressed upon him. She now realized, upon deepest reflection, that it could not be her, regardless of how much she desired it for herself.

What if Mr. Darcy allowed his heart to rule instead? The thought flickered in Elizabeth's mind like the dappling of sunlight through the trees on a breezy day. *What if he does propose to me after all?* She could not bask in the thought for long, for nearly as soon as she thought it, she was assaulted by the knowledge that such a match would bring him scorn and derision among his equals in society, and she could not allow herself to be the means to so harm him. If he were to ignore all of this and marry her in spite of expectations imposed by his birthright, would even five years pass before he came to resent her? Could she live happily knowing that she had been the means of bringing him so low? Elizabeth, weary in body and disconsolate in mind, lay down on the bed and surrendered herself to slumber in order to escape the sorrow of the reality she had only just come to realize.

୬

Sir Vincent Parker appeared at the doors of Darcy House promptly at seven in the morning, and he was ushered straightway to the study, where Darcy and Colonel Fitzwilliam awaited his arrival.

The Bow Street officer did not waste any time with small talk. After a cordial greeting to Mr. Darcy, whom he already knew, and an introduction to Colonel Fitzwilliam whom he knew only by reputation, he bowed respectfully to both men, and made a short apology for the events of the previous evening. He assured them that the officious policeman who had attended the scene had been thoroughly reprimanded for overstepping his bounds and would not be further involved in the investigation.

To this, Darcy generously replied that although the officer had spoken with more authority than he had right to, he had observed a keen mind for investigation in the man, and that he hoped the misstep would not cost the man future opportunity in his career. This statement was unexpected by both the Bow Street man and the colonel, but the point was duly noted by the officer while his cousin merely registered astonishment.

Sir Vincent was a dapper and surprisingly jovial man, who, upon Darcy's methodical recitation of the previous evening's events, informed him that he had never heard a second telling that so accurately matched the first, which he had previously read in the officer's report. That being out of the way, he proceeded to ask for information on various aspects of Wickham's past. It was immediately apparent to both Darcy and Fitzwilliam that George Wickham was not unknown at Bow Street.

After the briefest possible explanation of what had transpired between Wickham and Georgiana from Darcy, Sir Vincent divulged that Wickham had been occupied in a number of fraudulent schemes, not the least of which involved eloping with young heiresses to gain access to their fortunes. In this, he was aided by a woman of questionable character—a woman who presented herself in society as a widow. Although the woman went by several names—Mrs. White, Mrs. Smith and Mrs. Younge—that they knew of, they were by no means certain of her actual identity or her current whereabouts. She was known to carry on her person immaculate but forged letters of recommendation, used to engage herself as a governess and companion—the means by which she imposed herself on families in need of such service.

It was believed by Bow Street that in Mr. Wickham's short period of studying the law, he made connections with men who are now working attorneys. Their theory was that this was the means whereby Wickham discovered young ladies of recent inheritance.

When Sir Vincent mentioned Mrs. Younge carrying on her person letters of recommendation, Darcy was convinced of the idea that Mrs. Younge was the holder of Georgiana's letter and that she was the key to resolving the matter. This thought he did not mention to the officer, however, but a glance at Fitzwilliam convinced him that his cousin had the same thought as he.

The interview with the Bow Street officer concluded when Darcy called for the butler, instructing him to facilitate the cooperation of any in the household whose testimony was of interest in the investigation. Sir Vincent, a man of impeccable timing as well as impeccable dress, departed the house just as breakfast was placed upon the sideboard in the dining room. The two men ate hurriedly, but the colonel—long used to rushed meals with his soldiers, was done and gone to obtain costumes for their adventure before Darcy's toast had even turned cold on his plate.

It was eleven o'clock in the morning when the two men began dressing in their disguises. They changed upstairs in the nursery room of the house, for the staff rarely went into that room.

When they first donned the clothing of common men, they had still not appeared common at all, despite fabrics that chafed and ill-fitting cuts of the cloth. Once they had rubbed some soot on the collars and cuffs and roughed up the elbows and knees with glass-paper, the clothing took on a more worn appearance and was marginally more convincing. They gave the same treatment to some hats and shoes that were several years out of fashion and added a thin layer of grime to their faces as well. The transformation was now complete, and they both declared that they would not recognize one another at first glance. Darcy worried that they had overdone it, but the colonel felt that they had achieved the perfect look—beneath the notice of the higher classes, but well within the spectrum one commonly saw on the streets of London.

It took a bit of practice to modify their posture adequately, and then they turned to work on their speech. Colonel Fitzwilliam was very good at it, having spent more time among those of lower ranks, but Darcy simply could not adapt well enough to convince, and Fitzwilliam finally told Darcy in exasperation to pretend that he was mute, for he would surely give them away at the first word.

They left the house through the servant's area, where delivery persons came and went during the day as a matter of course. Colonel Fitzwilliam had obtained some sacks of vegetables along with the clothes, and the two men shouldered them in a way that combined with their hats, hid their faces, and they marched directly into the basement of Darcy House from the back stairway and "delivered" the produce as they passed through to exit. They blended well enough with the bustling hive of activity that no one appeared to take notice of them, and soon they were outdoors, at the base of the stairs that led to the street.

From their vantage point below, they could see that a carriage had arrived in front of the house, and they cautiously peered up through the wrought-iron fence that enclosed the area to discover, to their chagrin, that the carriage bore the crest of the house of de Bourgh. They could see the footman at the door, announcing Lady Catherine's visit, and they could also see, in shadowy profile, the great lady herself watching the door through the carriage window.

Fitzwilliam whispered to Darcy that this would be a grand test of their disguises, and with no hesitation, he bolted up the stairs, with Darcy trudging in mock weariness behind him. "Pratt, old man, do hurry up, we do not have all day!" Fitzwilliam turned so that his back was to the carriage as he berated the man behind him.

"Bah!" Darcy waved his hand dismissively, and he hunched down a bit to let the rim of his hat mask his face. "Smythe, you goat, I will come as it pleases my feet to do so and no faster!"

In this manner of mild harassment, the cousins walked undetected, right past the carriage of their aunt, who was disappointed to learn that she had missed catching her nephew at home. As instructed, the butler reported to the footman that the Darcy carriage had departed early that morning, and he could not say when it was to return. The news was received by Lady Catherine loudly enough that Darcy could hear her put voice to her displeasure as he made his way away from her. He was thankful to note that it did not occur to her to visit Georgiana alone, and within minutes, the de Bourgh carriage rolled right past the two men, Smythe and Pratt, as they made their way to where Fitzwilliam had a hired carriage waiting.

Chapter Forty-Eight

PRATT & SMYTHE IN LONDON

When Elizabeth awoke the next morning, although her eyes were closed, she had the distinct impression of a person hovering over her. She lay still at first, slightly panicked as she listened to the breathing, but she finally peeked through barely open lashes to discover Jane smiling above her.

"Lizzy! You are awake!" Jane sat on the bed next to her sister. "You slept so soundly last night that I was very nearly worried that something more than the wine was amiss! You made not a sound, nor did you move about in the bed as you have the past few nights." She placed her hand against Elizabeth's forehead, "It is as I had hoped—you do not have the fever this morning. I think you may soon be well!"

Elizabeth sat up. "I do feel better Jane—not quite myself, but ever so much better than I have these past few days. Tell me—did you speak with Mr. Bingley about Caroline?"

Jane turned somber as she nodded to affirm it. After a full minute passed in silence, Elizabeth prompted Jane. "Well?"

Jane shook her head woefully. "Oh Lizzy, I was so worried about what to say to him. I went downstairs to the drawing room, and Mr. and Mrs. Hurst were there, but my dear Mr. Bingley was not there with them, so I asked Mrs. Nicholls if she knew where he had gone, and she said I might find him in his study. When I came upon him, he was—well, he was so pale Lizzy; I knew not what to think!"

"Oh no!" Elizabeth cried. "What was wrong Jane? Was he ill?" Her countenance reflected her worst fear—that she would transmit her fever to those who had cared for her.

"No, no, he is well." Jane reassured her. "He had just come across a letter left for him by Colonel Fitzwilliam." Jane sighed deeply. "The colonel had expressed—most apologetically—a worry that Caroline may wish to harm you. I shall not go into the particulars of what he said, but when I showed the decanter to Charles and told him what had passed between you and Caroline, as well as of our discovery, he was terribly shocked."

"What did he do?" Elizabeth asked quietly.

"Well, at first, he was so astonished by it all that he did hardly anything. His color changed though, from very pale, to a most worrisome shade of red. I could tell that he was in every way attempting to school his feelings, but I worried that he would go into some sort of fit if he did not calm himself." Jane blushed. "So I determined that, as his future wife, it might be acceptable, nay, advisable for me to ease his distress."

Elizabeth giggled at that. "Jane, what did you do?"

Jane sat down in the chair at Elizabeth's bedside. "Not very much. I just reached out to him and took his hand into mine and told him that you were well, which was the most important thing, but that he must go to speak with his sister, for such behavior cannot be tolerated." Jane looked down at her lap, as a smile erupted on her face. "Lizzy, if you could have heard what he said to me then, you would have no doubt that we will be as happy together as two people can be."

Elizabeth shook her head, as she encouraged Jane to continue. "What did he say?"

"He said that I gave him courage, that for many years Caroline had done as she pleased—insulted him, defied him, cut his friends and spent his money, but that he had been afraid of her all his life. He said that, with me by his side, she would no longer have such power over him, and that this act against you, Lizzy, was beyond the pale. And then what do you think, but he came around the desk—very abruptly, I must say—and kissed me!"

"Oh!" Elizabeth cried, "he did not!"

"Well, yes," Jane smiled dreamily at her sister, "he kissed me most passionately, like a soldier going to battle might kiss his beloved under the fear that he may not live to kiss her again."

"Mr. Bingley? We are still talking about your charming and unassuming Mr. Bingley, are we not?" Elizabeth shook her head.

"And then," Jane's eyes shone, "He marched out of the room and went straight upstairs to Miss Bingley's chamber door."

Elizabeth listened, wide-eyed. "I do not believe it!"

Jane nodded "I followed right behind him—he was in such a state that I was afraid he might do something foolish! He pounded loudly on the door with his fist and demanded that she open it, so that he might speak with her."

"Did she?" Elizabeth almost whispered.

"She would not open it. She told her brother to go away and come back when he was not drunk, which he was not, but judging by the sound of her voice, she most definitely was."

"What did Mr. Bingley do then?"

"Why, he accused her of poisoning your wine and trying to kill you." Jane replied. "He told her that he was ashamed of her and that she would answer for it sooner or later, so she might as well open the door."

"Did she?"

"No. Charles soon discovered that she had taken every key to her room in the household, so no one can open the door. She is still shut inside, for Charles posted footmen in the hallway to alert him the moment she came out. She started to open the door but once. When she saw the footmen, she locked it again," Jane replied. "You were very safe last night. Not only did I come and sleep in this room with you, but Charles posted footmen at your door as well. He is very angry at his sister."

"I cannot imagine Mr. Bingley angry, Jane," Elizabeth said with a shake of her head. "He is too amiable."

"I expect that you cannot imagine him passionate either," Jane smiled sweetly. "Charles loves his sister, Lizzy, but he loves me too, and he knows that when we marry, he shall have four new sisters to look out for. He already cares for you dearly and will not allow Caroline to harm you. I am certain of this."

By two o'clock, Darcy and the colonel had made their way through over a dozen pubs and taverns with no success in finding any information on Wickham or Mrs. Younge. They were careful only to sip at their drinks in order to prevent inebriation from sabotaging their goal, although they were not entirely unaffected—the sheer number of sips amounted to a less than fully sober state—which merely added to the authenticity of their costume.

Neither man had allowed this lack of early success to discourage him, and it soon paid off—they struck a chord of resonance in Covent Garden, when the mention of the name George Wickham triggered a marked change in demeanor of some people with whom they spoke. The cousins were immediately regarded with suspicion and distrust as soon as the name was spoken.

The reactions were visceral and generally resulted in aborted conversations marked by a string of vulgar epithets, threats and gestures aimed at the intruders—Mr. Pratt and Mr. Smythe. They moved on when this happened, but it was soon evident that word of their presence in the neighborhood preceded their movements. They became increasingly aware of the unfriendly stares of the inhabitants of the street. What they could not yet discern was whether the reactions were due to a generally held animosity toward Wickham or they stemmed from a misguided instinct of his friends to protect him.

As the behavior of those they encountered changed, so did the manner of the two gentlemen. Mr. Smythe took his swagger and his voice to new heights, while Mr. Pratt became more silent and stiff as they ventured into what was becoming an increasingly hostile situation. He took to grumbling his objections at Smythe, his face dark with frustration.

They had just made a hasty departure from a pub on Drury Lane, when the colonel whispered to Darcy. "Do not look backwards, Pratt; I believe we are being followed."

"Of course, we are," Darcy muttered. "Some ruffians, no doubt, bent on beating us senseless for sport."

"You are too cynical, Pratt. He is just a boy and an urchin, at that." Richard laughed at his cousin.

Despite the colonel's warning not to, Darcy turned and looked behind them. Twenty feet back, there stood a youth, perhaps twelve years old. His clothing was dirty and ragged and far too thin for winter. Underneath a slightly askew cap were two alarmed eyes of the palest blue. The boy had stopped walking the moment Darcy turned, and he stood ready to flee. They stared at each other, boy and man, each believing that the other may hold a key to what they searched for, and each rooted temporarily in his place by fear. The boy's fear seemed primarily that of pursuit, but Darcy's fear was that they would frighten the boy away and be unable to find him again, a thought shared by Richard—who stood motionless behind Darcy. The colonel watched in astonishment as his tall, austere cousin gradually lowered himself, one knee on the ground before he tipped his head, beckoning the boy to approach.

From his position behind Darcy, Richard could not see the transformation of Darcy's expression, but he did see as Darcy reached into his pocket and produced a coin, which he held up—an act that was tracked by the sober blue eyes of the lad. His expression was that of one who contemplated what appeared to be a worthy offer. After a brief hesitation, the lure of the coin won over his caution, and he boldly closed the distance and reached for the shilling, which Darcy pulled back as he did so, denying the boy his prize.

"You want this coin, boy?" Darcy asked quietly. The child nodded, even as he danced lightly on his toes, ready to run.

"I will give it to you, after you have answered a few questions. Do we have an understanding?"

"Yes, sir." The boy said quietly, looking around to see who else might be on the street to see him talking with the stranger.

Darcy, seeing the boy's discomfort, replied, "Let us step aside to a quieter place. Do you know somewhere we could talk?"

The boy nodded, and with a look over his shoulder to see if they followed, he led the two men to a storefront half a block away, where faux marble columns provided a semblance of privacy.

"I see that you are clever." Darcy half-smiled as he once again lowered himself to the same height as the boy. "This spot is perfect. What is your name?"

"Davey."

"Davey is what you are called then ... is your Christian name David?" Darcy asked kindly.

"Aye." The boy nodded.

"Very good. You are named for the courageous boy who killed a giant with a stone between the eyes. You have no stones with you today, I hope." Darcy chuckled softly.

"No, sir," the boy replied seriously.

"My head and I are very glad to hear it. My friend is Mr. Smythe," Darcy pointed to the colonel, "and I am Mr. Pratt. We came here in search of another man, Mr. Wickham. Have you heard of him?"

"Aye," the boy said nervously. Darcy noticed that for all his bravado, he was quivering.

"Do not fear, Davey; we will not harm you." Darcy tried to be reassuring. "Did you see Mr. Wickham, yesterday perhaps?"

The child nodded, almost imperceptibly. "Me mum sent me ta find 'im."

"Your mum? What does she want with Mr. Wickham?"

"My sister, sir, 'as sprained 'er ankle." The boy blushed.

"Was Mr. Wickham the one who did it?"

"'Aye, 'e tol' 'er they'd be yoked afore she showed." Davey whispered seriously.

"So your mum wants to find Mr. Wickham so he will marry your sister?" Darcy asked kindly.

"Aye." The boy said fervently.

"When did you last see him?"

"T'was yesterday, same time as now."

"Do you recall where it was that you saw him?"

"Aye, 'e was gowin inta the Bucket o' Blood."

"The Cooper's Arms*, on Rose Street? You are certain?" Darcy smiled victoriously.

"Aye, 'e went in, but I dinay see 'im come out."

"Thank you, Davey, you have done well." Darcy went back into his pocket. "Here is your shilling as promised. As for finding Mr. Wickham, tell your mum that Mr. Pratt said to go see the housekeeper at Darcy House. Here is the address." He placed a small card into the boy's hand with the coins.

Davey nodded his understanding, pocketed the shilling and card, thanked Mr. Pratt profusely, and disappeared into the throng of people.

"Mr. Pratt, you are suddenly good with children?" Richard teased as soon as the boy was gone. "I wonder what other hidden talents my cousin will discover in his pursuit of domestic bliss, eh?"

Darcy stood up and turned to the colonel. "I advise you to focus, Mr. Smythe, on the task at hand. You are too easily distracted. That *was* a stroke of good luck that you spotted the boy! Now we know Wickham was at The Cooper's Arms. Do you believe he was fighting, or gambling?"

"Drinking," replied the colonel, "and it was not luck, but my keen abilities of observation that spied the child. You owe your *luck* to my military training, Pratt."

"I shall send a letter of thanks to Prinny." Darcy said dryly as he began walking west. "I am certain he would love to know that his officer's training was put to such good use in detecting a lad with no training whatsoever."

"That is where you are wrong, Pratt. Living on these streets, that boy has been in training since he was born." Richard lengthened his stride and pushed ahead of Darcy. "You would be wise to learn a lesson or two from that child—when we get to The Cooper's Arms, we should not openly declare our purpose."

"All that military training has left you sadly devoid of tact, Smythe—do they not teach you diplomacy? I am not accustomed to being shut down so, but it is of no matter, as I agree that discretion is the order of the day." Darcy nodded. "*You* should likewise mind your tongue. We will discover more listening."

"Did your men make it to Rose Street in their inquiries yesterday?" Richard inquired.

"No, although they covered several parts of Covent Garden, they thought it did not seem promising. Sanders and Stewart mentioned inquiring at the brothels on Hart Street for him but did not speak of Rose Street. They were so close—perhaps he was warned." Darcy frowned.

"If so, it could not have been much of a warning—it did not spare him." Richard sighed. "I do not think he was warned—ambushed perhaps."

"That is one possibility," Darcy replied thoughtfully. "From the time that boy saw him enter the tavern to the time he was left for dead upon the doorstep at Darcy house, it could not have been more than five hours. Smythe, I fear that discovering what befell Wickham in his last hours may not in fact lead us to Mrs. Younge. How we are to discover *her* is constantly on my mind."

"We are following a trail, Pratt. Be satisfied to go where it leads." Richard counseled.

Quiet fury surged in Darcy's eye. "Satisfaction will come only when I have put that blasted letter to the flames and set the deeds of Wickham behind me forever. He perpetrated much evil in his short life—I refuse to accept his torment from the grave!"

"To grant him such power would be insupportable, indeed." Richard replied calmly. "We will bury his deeds with him, and Georgiana will be safe from his treachery.

"All of England is safe from his treachery now, although I must wonder how many foolish women he used ill and abandoned." Richard shook his head.

"I do not wish to contemplate it, Smythe," Darcy replied. "The heartache he has wrought just to the house of Darcy is sufficient for my lifetime."

"There is the turn off to Rose Street ahead," Richard said. "It is time to enter the lion's den."

Rose Street barely qualified as a street—it was, in fact, a dim, narrow alley, littered with the dregs of humanity. The cobblestones in front of the Cooper's Arms pub were darkened with dried blood for at least thirty feet from the threshold, and the stink of rotting garbage, stale urine and unwashed men combined to generate a distinctly unpleasant stench. Pratt and Smythe approached the doors, passing clusters of filthy, drunken men staggering to and from the place, stepping over one who had fallen from overconsumption. They closed the distance in silence, each mentally and physically preparing for what lay ahead.

The view through the dirty glass panes revealed that the place teemed with rowdy men, and despite the cold weather, many stood outside to consume their pint. Pratt pushed the doors open and stopped in the threshold as he was assaulted with smoke, billowing so thick that faces beyond a few feet away were obscured in the swirling haze.

"Go." Smythe hissed and gave Pratt a helpful shove from behind to propel him past the doors and into the room.

They worked their way through the crowd, careful not to incite anyone's ire as they moved toward the narrow bar, where the bawdy and bold jostled and jockeyed for position. Pratt and Smythe, after assertive, slightly impatient maneuverings, eventually arrived at their destination. Their size, soberness and comparatively imposing presence attracted the barkeep's attention, and he waited relatively quickly and with no mean degree of curiosity on the two strangers.

Smythe ordered a pint of strong beer for each and signaled to Pratt that they should move away from the counter. They soon stood away from the bar in a recessed nook, which insulated them slightly from the din. Smythe gleefully mirrored the ill-mannered actions of the carousers around them, while Pratt stared morosely into the depths of the liquid in his cup, appearing to be lost in thought—although he was instead tuning his hearing to the drunken conversations taking place around them.

He learned that they had just missed a particularly brutal fight in the back room, but that another was to take place shortly. Smythe was easily persuaded to change their location to the back room, and they—along with at least half of the noisy crowd—migrated to the cave-like venue where the fight would soon begin.

The tenor of this group was different. Fully inebriated, they were possessed of a shared lust for the violence that was soon to unfold, and when it did, they erupted as though this were the Roman Amphitheater and the sparring men gladiators of old. For Smythe, the mood stirred his warrior self, the manly revelries calling to his baser instincts. It was with great fortitude that he resisted giving into it altogether. Pratt, however, was disgusted by what he saw. A swarm of men whose greatest aspiration was their next pint of beer or gin garnished with the spattering of blood from some poor fool's broken nose or worse. Pratt drew himself to the back wall, where he forced himself to watch the fisticuff fight, half-heartedly raising his glass of beer to the cheers that erupted each time a bare-knuckled blow landed well from either party.

His attention was soon diverted, however, to the hollered discourse between the two old codgers in front of him, who freely complained that this fight was nowhere near as exciting as yesterday's unscheduled fight between 'that swell Wickham' and a man they called 'the Frenchie." The fight, Pratt learned, had been over gambling debts owed by Wickham, who at first had tried to get out of it. Wickham, they reminisced, had fought like a madman, all the while screaming that he would be able to settle within a week—that his ship had come in. The two men cackled like old women over that, speculating with lewd suggestions about the name of the ship, where it had docked, and in which seas it had sailed.

He was frustrated for some time that the men were so well entertained by their own vulgar humor that they disseminated no new information about Wickham. Then, as if these very thoughts had reached out and extracted the desired information, they spoke of four hoodlums who had saved Wickham from the Frenchman and carried him away through the alley that ran next to the pub. Their next turn of phrase caused Pratt's blood to chill in his veins, as the men speculated as to whether the four had actually collected the handsome reward they expected from Fitzwilliam Darcy.

Pratt rather abruptly drank the rest of his beer, and when he lowered the glass from his lips, he discovered that their musings had invited others nearby to join in their discussion about what Wickham might have done to capture the particular attention of one of the richest men in England.

Their prattle ran the gamut—from the uncomfortably close guess that Wickham had probably meddled with Darcy's sister to the repetition of the stories Wickham had spread in other places about Darcy's being jealous of him. There was even an absurd rumor that Wickham and Darcy were partners in crime and that Wickham had crossed him. Pratt was relieved to discover that nothing they said was rooted in any fact at all. It was strange to discover the eager interest with which perfect strangers discussed his business as though he were something to them.

The fight had ended, and the poor sod who had lost was being dragged away by two men, one arm draped around either of the other men's shoulders. The room began to drain of its bawdy humanity, whose empty cups begged for refilling, but the men he was overhearing stayed, their thirst having not yet overcome their interest in the topic at hand.

Smythe joined Pratt and began edging him out of the room, but Pratt shook his head and broke away, returning to where the men still congregated. Pratt soon injected himself in their discourse by introducing himself, while Smythe stood by and marveled at the sight of Darcy casually speaking to anyone without the benefit of a proper introduction. He informed them that he had heard them speaking during the fight and then spoke convincingly to the men of his boyhood friend, George Wickham, and his distress at hearing he had missed encountering Wickham there by just a day. He dispatched Smythe to acquire additional drink for his new "friends" as he pressed the men for whatever they could remember.

The men knew nothing more, but others in their midst stepped forward, greedily spilling what they knew in return for drink. By the time Pratt and Smythe quit the pub, they knew exactly where to find Mrs. Younge and had obtained the names of the men who had taken Wickham away.

Elizabeth knew not what to say to her mother, whose distress at finding Jane and Elizabeth suddenly returned to Longbourn had triggered a fresh attack of nerves, and she had shut herself in her room. Elizabeth did not console her mother, for she did not know how to interpret the event herself.

It had been mid-morning, shortly after breakfast, when Mr. Jones had suddenly appeared at Netherfield and, after a cursory examination, declared Elizabeth sufficiently fit to travel to Longbourn. The household staff had, without notice, descended on the room and efficiently packed the Bennet sisters' belongings within moments of the arrival of the apothecary. The sisters were ready to depart in less than half an hour without having even assisted in the preparations.

It was obviously clear to everyone, including Elizabeth, that she had not truly recovered from her fever and that her departure was premature. No one said this aloud, but it was intimated in the actions of the staff, and in the concern expressed by all that Elizabeth not exert herself by packing or become chilled in stepping too far away from the fireplace. This was perhaps the most confusing aspect of their being dispatched to Longbourn—the suddenness.

Mr. Bingley had seemed distraught when advising Jane that they were to leave but had declared it for the best, considering that he must determine how to deal with Miss Bingley in light of recent events. His disappointment at their separation, he assured Jane, would be overcome by his calling upon her faithfully at Longbourn until their wedding

When Jane and Elizabeth stepped out the doors of Netherfield, Elizabeth's astonishment was complete. Mr. Darcy's fine, enclosed carriage stood at the ready to convey the sisters to Longbourn, with several thick, soft blankets to keep them warm as they made the short journey. The footmen stood by to assist the ladies into the carriage, but Mr. Bingley had stepped forward and insisted on giving them the hand-up himself. Ever gracious and charming, his eyes showed the distress he felt at their departure.

Now in her bedroom, Elizabeth saw herself in the mirror for the first time since the night of the ball, and she was momentarily stunned to see how pale and gaunt she looked after just a few days of illness. She looked wearily at her trunk. She knew that she could let their lady's maid put her clothing away, but she sighed with the knowledge that if she wanted it done as she preferred it, she would, of necessity, perform the task herself.

Elizabeth opened the trunk to unpack it, and resting on top was the beautiful gown that she had worn to the ball. She carefully hung it and returned to the trunk, restoring her clothing and accessories to their customary place in her dresser or closet. As she lifted her last nightdress from the trunk, she gasped to discover that the staff at Netherfield had mistakenly packed the shawl she had found in Mr. Darcy's dresser. She stared in disbelief at the exquisite item—even lovelier in the daylight of her room.

Not wanting any of her sisters to see it, Elizabeth hastily closed her bedroom door before she reached into the trunk and, with an attitude close to reverence, lifted it out. She wrapped it around her shoulders and turned to see herself in the looking glass. She was again astounded at the beauty of the garment, which hung in soft, elegant folds from her arms. The color proved to be perfect with her complexion, adding a soft pinkness to her pale skin. She sat down on the bed, the shawl still wrapped around her body, and pondered on the man who had purchased this shawl. She once again wondered whom it was for and considered that she should immediately wrap it up and return it to Mr. Bingley to restore to Mr. Darcy.

"He will not miss it," Elizabeth whispered to herself as she rubbed a corner of the cloth against her cheek. "Not while he is away in London." She tightened the shawl around herself and, closing her eyes, tried to imagine what it would be like to have Mr. Darcy's arms hold her tightly. Then she scolded herself for such thoughts. She quickly removed the shawl and folded it, hanging it up behind her ball gown where it was not likely to be noticed. She turned around to close the empty trunk and noticed a folded paper that had been directly beneath the shawl on the floor of the chest. Turning it over, she saw that it was a letter, sealed with Mr. Darcy's insignia. On the front, her name was written in his elegant hand.

This was an unexpected event indeed. How the letter came to be there, Elizabeth could not imagine, considering the absolute breech of propriety it represented. Her curiosity would not be denied, however, and she broke the seal and unfolded the letter. She did not have time to read so much as the first sentence before Lydia burst into her room, forcing Elizabeth to fold the unread letter and slip it into a drawer.

"Lizzy, Lizzy, you will never guess what has happened!" Lydia was short of breath, as though she had been running for some time.

Elizabeth just shook her head, her eyebrows raised to match the alarm in Lydia's voice. "Lydia, it is true—I will never guess."

"I must tell you then, for more than one thing has happened while you were away!" Lydia giggled nervously and then looked sober. "Well, none of it is good news to be sure. The first thing I must tell you, and you will be very surprised, is that odious Mr. Collins has asked Charlotte Lucas to marry him ... and she has accepted him!"

"Charlotte? Mr. Collins? I do not believe it!" Elizabeth felt queasy. "Surely Charlotte is better and wiser than this!"

"That is not even the most distressing news, Lizzy! Kitty and I were just in Meryton, and we went to speak with Carter and Denny, and the officers are all in an uproar! They are inconsolable, you see, because of what has been done! You will not believe it, for it is shocking—shocking, indeed! I daresay it is the most shocking thing I have ever heard in all my life! Lizzy, I know he was your favorite as much as he was mine—he is the one we were all so much in love with, the one who everyone in Meryton praised to the skies—Mr. Wickham ... he is *dead! Murdered they said!* Colonel Forster received an express from Colonel Fitzwilliam this morning, and it is all very mysterious, and no-one knows who did it...."

"Lydia, you must not joke about such things!" Elizabeth scolded.

"It is not a joke, Lizzy—my heart is broken!" Lydia whined and stamped her foot. "He told me we would elope to Scotland in the spring, and I would be Mrs. Wickham, and that is all ruined now!

"Lydia!" Elizabeth glared at her youngest sister. "Is it true? Is Charlotte to marry Mr. Collins? Is Mr. Wickham is truly murdered? You are not making these things up?"

"Truly!" Lydia replied. "I must go and tell Mama!"

"You must *not* tell Mama—not like this, lest you aggravate her nerves further. Go to Papa and tell him first, and he will decide how to tell Mama. She is already beside herself because Jane has gone from Netherfield. I do not know what such news will do to her."

Lydia frowned. "You are right. Mama wanted *you* to marry Mr. Collins, and she wanted *me* to marry Mr. Wickham—well, she would have wanted it if she had known—and now two of her fondest dreams have been taken from her. I will tell Papa, as you said."

As quickly as Lydia had intruded, she was gone. Elizabeth retrieved the letter Mr. Darcy had written from the drawer and moved to the window seat, where the light was better. She stared at the folded paper in her hands. Mr. Darcy had arranged for her abrupt removal from Netherfield before he had even returned from London. Was this not a clear signal that he had thought better of the feelings he had expressed? What if this letter stated exactly that? Elizabeth had already come to terms with the thought that Mr. Darcy could not act on the sentiments he had previously expressed, and holding the letter in her hand, she suddenly feared that the contents would be tangible proof of what she had realized must be. She found herself unable to face that prospect in her current state, so she determinedly returned the letter to her drawer and, although it was barely noon, lay down on her bed and promptly fell into an exhausted sleep.

*"The Cooper's Arms" was the former name of the current "Lamb & Flag" pub. In the early 19th century, it was informally called "The Bucket of Blood", a reference to the bare-knuckled fisticuff fighting that took place both in a back room, and in the street in front of the establishment.

Chapter Forty-Nine

LETTERS THREE

Mr. Bingley watched, standing forlornly on the Netherfield entrance porch until the carriage taking Jane and Elizabeth Bennet back to Longbourn was long out of sight. When he returned to the interior of the house, he inquired first after his sister and was assured by the butler that Caroline remained sequestered in her bedchamber. Upon hearing this news, he returned to his study, where he retrieved once more the letter he had received from Darcy's coachman that morning. He sat behind the big desk and read it again, slowly. With a heavy heart, he called for a footman to summon Mr. and Mrs. Hurst once again to speak with him in the study.

Upon their arrival there, Louisa, who rarely showed a sign of temper, was prepared to make her case, and launched into her tirade before Charles had a chance to so much as greet his sister.

"Charles, I am fully aware that the Bennet sisters have now departed, along with Lady Catherine and her strange little daughter Anne. There are now sufficient rooms, I believe, to accommodate all the guests in residence as well as those who are yet to arrive, and I demand that Mr. Hurst and I be restored to our original two rooms immediately. If this is not done, we shall make each other mad before the day is out!" Louisa said with great animation. "Is this not so, Mr. Hurst?"

"Eh?" Mr. Hurst looked at his wife in confusion. "I was rather enjoying it."

Louisa's cheeks tinged with color, and she turned to face her brother again. "Quite mad. I shall be quite mad."

Charles, who had patiently waited for his sister to finish, replied, "I pray that you do not say such things, Louisa. It is not seemly under the circumstances we now find ourselves in."

"Whatever can you mean, Charles? The circumstances we now find ourselves in are that, for the first time since the ball, the household is set to return to normalcy. I am greatly relieved by it, and will be even more so when I have achieved the privacy of my own bedchamber once again."

"Louisa, are you aware that Caroline remains in her chambers and will not come out?" Charles asked quietly.

"But, of course I am." Louisa sniffed. "The entire household is aware, and the way even the servants gossip here in the country, I expect that all of Meryton knows it too."

"There is more to this business than what the gossips may have to say, and it is time that you heard the whole of it, sister. I beg you to sit, for you may require such support before I am finished with what you are about to hear. You must prepare yourself for something very dreadful." Charles looked at his sister meaningfully, and she realized for the first time that his mood had been somber from the moment of their entry. She sat in a chair, and her husband followed suit.

"I wish you to think back to when our eldest sister, Annabelle, was about the same age as Caroline is now." Bingley said.

"Do not speak of her!" Louisa cried. "I cannot bear it!"

"You were very fond of her, I know," Bingley conceded gently, "but if we do not wish the same fate for Caroline, we must open our eyes, Louisa."

"It cannot be—Caroline is not at all like Annabelle!" Louisa began to cry.

"You think she is not, but Annabelle was the light of all of our lives before...," Charles trailed off and looked away from his sister, softly adding, "... before she was not."

Mr. Hurst, who rarely paid any attention to anything, was paying rapt attention to *this* conversation. "Who, pray tell, is Annabelle, and what happened to her?" He finally asked.

"Annabelle is our eldest sister." Louisa muttered through her tears. "She is in Bedlam."

"What?" Mr. Hurst burst out loudly. "And what has Annabelle to do with Caroline?"

"Annabelle was very beautiful, very accomplished." Charles began, "She was all that our parents wanted for us all to be. She did not have a friend such as Mr. Darcy to introduce her into London society as we did, but eventually, she caught the eye of a wealthy, landed gentleman from Shropshire, and they married."

"Why have I never heard of her?" Mr. Hurst huffed. "I have a sister and brother that I have never met?"

Charles nodded the affirmative to Mr. Hurst before he continued. "She greatly desired to be in London for her first season as a married woman, and her new husband obliged her by renting a townhouse in a fashionable neighborhood. At first, all was well." Bingley sat down behind the desk, his posture erect as he continued relating the tale. "Annabelle was well received—not in the first circles, mind you, but in her own level of society, quite well. Unforeseen disaster happened, however, when another man—a powerful duke—met her at a dinner and liked her appearance and manner. Even though she was a married woman, he took her as a lover."

Louisa gasped and buried her face in her hands. "Do not speak of it aloud!"

"Louisa, silence is what started it." Bingley replied to his sister. "Although she was not married to him, she began to fancy herself as the duke's wife. He ensured that Annabelle—and her husband—were invited to the finest parties and balls of the first circles of society. If her husband knew of Annabelle's infidelity, he did not so speak, and this went on for over a year. The doctors said it was the pressure created by this double life that was the beginning."

"The beginning?" Hurst held onto the arms of his chair with white knuckles.

"The beginning of her decline. Annabelle began to suspect that all in the household were spies, sent to watch her by her husband. She also began to claim herself a duchess and insisted upon being addressed as such. She seemed to be of the strong belief that she was surrounded by others who were of the same status, and she regularly conversed with unseen persons, whom she claimed that *she* could see perfectly well. At first, her husband pandered, but one day she tried to kill him with a knife, declaring that her invisible friends had told her that if she did not kill him first, he would undoubtedly kill her. He sent her to Bedlam, and he returned to Shropshire with their baby daughter—not even knowing if he is the child's father or if it was the duke who sired her. We have not seen or heard from him since, but Louisa and I have been to visit Annabelle in the Bethlem Hospital several times. Caroline would never go."

Mr. Hurst sat in shock as his wife quietly wept next to him.

Mr. Bingley picked up the letter from Mr. Darcy and read excerpts of it to his sister and brother-in-law. It detailed observations made by Colonel Fitzwilliam about Caroline's behavior. Darcy expressed his primary motive in writing the letter as a concern for the safety of Jane and Elizabeth Bennet, whom Caroline had made veiled threats against when in company with the colonel. Bingley then spoke to his relations of the decanter of elderberry wine that Caroline had heavily laced with laudanum—sufficient, he had been informed by Mr. Jones that morning, to cause a person to stop breathing with only a few sips of the wine.

"Oh, Charles, you will not make her go to Bedlam!" Louisa cried, "Not Caroline!"

"Of course not, but she cannot stay here with us either. If the pressures of society are what caused Annabelle's mind to descend into chaos, then could it be the same with Caroline? The preparations for the ball, Lady Catherine confronting her most cruelly, my admiration of and offer of marriage to Miss Bennet, Mr. Darcy's admiration of Miss Elizabeth—could these events be the foundation of descent into madness for our sister Caroline?"

"Mr. Darcy admires Eliza Bennet? Are you certain?" Louisa repeated. "Caroline has told me daily that he is to offer for her at any moment! She has her heart set upon being the mistress of Pemberley! She complained about how deluded Anne de Bourgh was in her belief that Darcy would marry her."

"It is Caroline who suffers delusions," Bingley read from the letter in his most Darcy-like tone. "Caroline believes that I am in love with her and have designs to make her my wife, which belief is not grounded in reality."

"I knew it!" Mr. Hurst exclaimed, looking at his wife, "I knew your sister was crazy!"

"Her attachment to Mr. Darcy does not make her mad, Charles." Louisa defended.

"Read the letter, Louisa, and then tell me what you think." Charles handed the letter across the desk to his sister.

After her perusal of the letter, and acknowledging that she recognized much of the behavior described in it, even Louisa was finally convinced that all was not well with Caroline.

Her siblings could not bring themselves to consider Bedlam as an alternative, and so, together, they determined that they must hire a nurse experienced in the care of such persons and send Caroline away to the seaside where she could recuperate, and, hopefully regain her clarity of mind. Recovery, they had been assured by the doctors caring for Annabelle, was possible with time and adequate care. The Isle of Wight in Hampshire was settled on, for both its natural beauty and the requirement of nautical transport to come or go. Caroline would be easier to contain, they reasoned, on an island, and they resolved that once Caroline was settled there, they would remove Annabelle from Bedlam also and send her to join Caroline at the shores of the sea, where hopefully, both would regain their senses in the peace and serenity of nature.

Pratt and Smythe were well pleased with themselves, having attained the information to take them onto the next part of their quest, and they were, perhaps, not paying adequate attention to their surroundings as they made their way down Hart street to return to Drury Lane where Mrs. Younge was reputed to be in residence. This inattention proved to be unfortunate.

"Well, boys, it appears as if you have been out to play," Sir Vincent Parker spoke loudly at them from behind.

The cousins turned to face the Bow Street officer, and Colonel Fitzwilliam extended his hand with a sheepish grin. "Indeed we have, sir, and enjoyed ourselves immensely. I am Mr. Smythe, and my friend here, is Mr. Pratt."

"I am certain you are both aware, *Mr. Smythe,* that it is a crime in London to disguise yourself and impersonate another man." Sir Vincent said with a wry smile as he shook the colonel's extended hand.

"We impersonate no other man, sir—our impersonations are fiction; hence, we are innocent of any crime," the colonel said cheerfully. "Perhaps you should now drag us off to your office at Bow Street, however, so that our innocence may remain a secret."

"I should rather follow you to the home of Mrs. Younge. If what I overheard is to be believed, you are on your way there at this moment." Sir Vincent nodded knowingly at them, his eyebrows raised. "We have been seeking her out for some time now, and if we succeed in apprehending her, I believe we may come to an understanding regarding your innocence of fraud in appearing thus."

"You bargain, sir, as though you presume us guilty." Colonel Fitzwilliam laughed heartily. "You misunderstood our errand, however. We do intend to locate Mrs. Younge at the earliest possible moment, but for now we seek the four scoundrels who were last seen with Wickham—that is what we are about."

Sir Vincent looked at the colonel through narrowed eyes. "I do not believe you, but I will play your game. Of whom do you speak, *Mr. Smythe*?"

The colonel indicated that they should walk, and then he looked around to see if anyone was paying untoward attention to them before he spoke in hushed tones to Sir Vincent. "They are the ones who carried him away after he fought the Frenchmen at The Cooper's Arms. They seemed to expect to collect some reward from Mr. Darcy for delivering Mr. Wickham to him."

"How very opportune that they should profit from the man's misfortune," Sir Vincent replied, "How came they by this expectation?"

"The man's misfortune?" Darcy snorted in disgust. "I daresay Wickham put himself in that circumstance by his own hand. He was challenged over gaming debts, sir, and this was not the first time his creditors have come to claim their pound of flesh when he did not pay."

"As for the reward, *Mr. Pratt*—did Mr. Darcy in fact offer one?" Sir Vincent asked with a frown.

"In fact, he did not." Darcy replied.

"Do you know their names?" The officer inquired.

"We do." Darcy replied. "They are all called Mr. Morris, as they are four brothers—Thomas, Samuel, Jonathan and Edmund."

"Morris, you say? I know these blokes—there are not enough brains between them to produce a single rational thought!" Sir Vincent muttered. "They get themselves into trouble at Bow Street from time to time, but never something so serious as murder...."

"Do you perchance know where they live?" Colonel Fitzwilliam pressed him.

"That I do." Sir Vincent nodded and turning down a side street, began to make his way rapidly. He waved his hand in the air indicating that they should follow; so Darcy and the colonel hurried to catch up with him. They walked together at a brisk pace, in silence, for a quarter of an hour before arriving at the ramshackle residence of the Morris family.

Mrs. Morris, upon seeing the Bow Street officer approaching, had stepped through the doorway, wiping her hands on her apron as she approached the three men. Nearly as soon as he saw her, Sir Vincent called a greeting, and when their paths met, he said, "Mrs. Morris, it is my pleasure to introduce you to Mr. Smythe and Mr. Pratt. They are here as agents of Mr. Darcy, who has discovered that it was your sons who delivered Mr. Wickham to his door last night." He turned to face his companions. "Gentlemen, this is Mrs. Morris."

Mrs. Morris quickly got a gleam in her eye and called over her shoulder to the house for her sons to come out. They were brawny, large men, easily as tall as Darcy and Fitzwilliam, although much dirtier, as though they had not seen a tub since the onset of winter. When her progeny had assembled, their mother turned back to Sir Vincent and requested that he repeat what he had said about the reward.

"I said nothing of a reward, madam." Sir Vincent replied. "I merely said that my companions, Mr. Smythe and Mr. Pratt are here as agents of Mr. Darcy."

There ensued some general grumbling amongst the Morris brothers, about trickery and being cheated, and they postured aggressively, as though they might assault their guests with no provocation beyond the perceived deceit.

"Ah, stow it!" Mrs. Morris finally yelled at her sons, who did. She was now in a temper and, hands on hips, she demanded that Sir Vincent tell them what his business there was, or leave.

"Mrs. Morris, perhaps you did not know. I am sorry to tell you this, but Mr. Wickham expired shortly after your sons abandoned him at the doors of Darcy House." Sir Vincent said smoothly. "We are here to investigate his *murder*."

The general alarm among the Morris brothers was extreme, yet they dared not move from where they stood. They began to argue vehemently amongst themselves about which of them was to blame. After several minutes of their bickering, during which time no enlightenment regarding the actual events came forth, Sir Vincent stepped in to question them.

They freely admitted that they had taken Wickham away from the pub after the fight. Their claimed reason for doing so was that two of them had separately run into men earlier that day who were looking for Wickham. They were instructed that if they came upon any information on his whereabouts, they should go to Darcy House to report it, and they would be handsomely rewarded if the information proved true.

Two of the Morris brothers were acquainted with Wickham, and when they spotted him fighting at the Bucket o' Blood, they reasoned among themselves that if Darcy would pay handsomely for information to find him, how much more generous would that rich gentleman be if they delivered the man himself? This question elicited more accusations of blame amongst the brothers, along with additional pushing and cussing between them as their narrative eroded into language so vulgar that it could not be easily understood by gentlemen unacquainted with such colorful language.

Their mother once again silenced them but changed her tactics by addressing questions now to just one son, Samuel Morris, and from him, the story came forth with clarity. Mr. Wickham had initially expressed his gratitude for their rescue from the fight in the pub, and gladly boarded a hired cab with the four brothers to distance himself from the scene. His face, they said, was much covered in blood and swollen, and he held onto his side, obviously in severe pain. When they had gone some distance, he said they were far enough away, and asked to be let off, but the brothers instead told him where they were taking him. When Wickham heard their destination of Darcy House, he became angry, declaring that they were delivering him into the hands of his sworn enemy. They did not relent, however, and Wickham unexpectedly leapt from the moving carriage.

Jonathon and Thomas had followed him out of the cab, running back to the place where he had jumped. They found Wickham, collapsed and groaning in pain at the side of the road, his leg broken. Despite the broken bone, returning him to the cab required the muscle and fists of all four brothers, as Wickham fought valiantly against them. By the time they arrived at Darcy House, Wickham had not only calmed but was passing in and out of consciousness, and the brothers suspected that their efforts to subdue him had gone too far. In fear, they had discarded him on the doorstep, rapped on the door, and fled, all thoughts of the hoped-for reward fleeing with them.

The discovery of the events of the last hour of Wickham's life had sobered Darcy. He pondered on Wickham's dying answer to his question, "Who did this to you?" Wickham had replied, accusing Darcy, "You did." It was impossible to know if the injury that had killed Wickham had been inflicted by the Frenchman, acquired in the ill-fated leap from the carriage or in the overly harsh blows of his rescuers turned captors, but Darcy felt his own burden of guilt keenly. The idea had seemed so absurd when Wickham had said it, yet now he recognized the possibility, and he was struck with the realization that a man's truth was painted from the perspective where he stood, colored by his bias, the brush-strokes of his character being the source from which the image developed. In that moment, Darcy realized that in his dying breath, Wickham had, in all probability, believed that Darcy truly was to blame.

"What makes you so serious?" Fitzwilliam put one hand on Darcy's shoulder. "Surely you are looking forward to seeing Mrs. Younge again."

Darcy looked up, and realized that they were nearly to her residence. They had made their way back to Drury Lane after bidding farewell to Sir Vincent, who had returned to Bow Street, and they now stood before the large wooden door that marked the threshold of Mrs. Younge's current residence.

The colonel knocked loudly on the door, and it swung open to reveal an elderly woman within. Just behind her was Mrs. Younge, who upon seeing Mr. Darcy, cried out in distress for her to close the door, but Darcy wedged his foot inside the doorframe. With small effort he pushed the door back open, and the cousins found themselves within the entryway of the household, unwelcome though they may be.

It was quickly apparent that Mrs. Younge did not have any understanding as to why the two men were at her door, dressed as they were. It was also evident that she was expecting Mr. Wickham to arrive there at any moment; indeed, she had been under the belief that the knock at the door had been the same.

Upon the revelation of Wickham's fate, Mrs. Younge fell heavily down onto the nearest chair, but this was her only outward expression that anything was amiss. She stared dumbly at the men who had delivered the news—her former employer whom she had deceived, and his cousin. She was surprised to find some degree of compassion in their faces.

It was then that she confided to them that she knew something of Wickham's plan to make them pay for Georgiana's letter, although she could not approve of further harming that poor child. She confessed that like he had so many others, Wickham had deceived her also, with the promise that when they had together amassed sufficient fortune, she was the one with whom he would truly elope. At first, she had believed him sincere, but as she watched him spend or gamble every penny they acquired, she had realized her trust in him was in vain. She was strangely without evidence of feeling as she spoke, and her speech tumbled out as though she had lain awake for many nights rehearsing what she would say should such a moment arise.

At length, she walked to the fireplace, and going to a box on the mantle, she retrieved a paper from it. She handed it to Mr. Darcy without ceremony, but with an apology for her part in the scheme, which was to harbor the letter to prevent Mr. Darcy from discovering it.

He unfolded it, scanned its contents and cast it immediately upon the fire. He leaned heavily upon the mantle and watched it burn until there was no trace left of the offensive document, and then turned with what may have resembled satisfaction and declared that the letter was no more.

He reached into his pocket and retrieved his coin purse, which he set on the table. "Mrs. Younge, I do not expect we shall ever see one another again, but I leave with you this token of gratitude that you have delivered to me, with no expectation of reward, the very item that I was seeking. I hope that you have learned something from this misadventure and will seek an honest living in future. I will leave you now."

With their mission of destroying that letter accomplished, Smythe and Pratt hired a cab and returned to Darcy House.

Elizabeth lolled in the familiar comfort of her own bed, the residual achiness from her recent illness accentuating the feeling of her soft bedding that enveloped her as if in a cloud. She woke gradually, and still sleepy, she wondered at the strangeness of the light in her room. It was somehow wrong—as dim as pre-dawn, yet with a brightness that did not whisper of the coming of a new day. She stretched, resisting the wakefulness that was coming until she realized that she was fully dressed within the folded counterpane. She sat up with a start as the recollections of time and place returned. A dull pain settled in her throat as the turns of her world from the past few days rushed into her mind in an overwhelming cacophony of thought and emotion.

She stood and tidied her bed before moving to the window. A light skiff of snow had fallen, flurries of flakes still swirling past the windowpane. The gnarled gray bones of the tree outside her window shimmered where the light dusting of tiny white crystals were illuminated by the light of late afternoon. It was a peaceful scene, yet it somehow caused Elizabeth to recall the windy morning of the day of the ball when, looking through this same window, she had seen Mr. Darcy on the road. Although she knew it was impossible, her eyes were compelled to seek that place she had seen him. The current emptiness of the road echoed the hollow place that twisted inside her when she thought of him. Looking back out the window, she caught the faintest hint of her own reflection, and recalled, with some melancholy, Mr. Darcy's use of a darkened pane to spy on her. A streak of purple lightening flashed in the sky, striking somewhere on

Mount Oakham. It seemed a mystical reminder of the morning he had come upon her at the base of the mount and they had together shared the glory of the sunrise and a crust of bread.

Then she remembered the letter. Her eyes were drawn to the drawer that held the letter, seemingly by the same pull that had turned them to the road just a moment before. The letter from Mr. Darcy, she realized, intimidated her more than the man himself ever did. "My courage always rises!" Elizabeth whispered aloud, determined not to be daunted by a piece of paper. She retrieved the letter from the drawer and returned to the window seat, where there was still enough light to read.

She had already broken the seal, so with slightly trembling fingers, Elizabeth unfolded the letter and began to read.

My dearest Elizabeth,

I have been gone but two days from Netherfield, and already it seems as though an eternity has passed. I know that some would think it wrong of me to write to you when we are not yet properly engaged, but I felt it necessary, for reasons that will soon become clear.

I pray that you are well and sufficiently recovered for the travel back to your home, which you must know was for your protection. I assume that if this letter has made it into your hands, you will already be at Longbourn, safe in the arms of your family. My cousin, Colonel Fitzwilliam, had observed some strangeness of behavior on the part of Miss Bingley, and it was his expressed opinion that she meant you some harm. With his own return to London, he advised that the wisest course would be to remove you from that location where Miss Bingley might have any power over you, so this morning, I dispatch my carriage along with this letter, entrusted to Mr. Bingley to ensure that you receive it when you are well away from Netherfield.

I hope, upon the return of my carriage to London, that I, along with my sister will soon be bound for Hertfordshire ourselves. It is for this reason that I am compelled to write this letter.

Colonel Fitzwilliam tells me that you do recall some of the conversation that occurred between us before I departed for London. It is with that knowledge that I write this letter in the strictest confidence of your goodness, and faith in your ability to conceal what I must tell you.

You may have heard of it by now, but if you have not, let me be the one to tell you, that Mr. Wickham is now dead – by whose hand I know not. This is for me some great sorrow, due to his connection to our family many years hence, but I confess that I feel also some relief, to know that he will no longer be a danger to young ladies in Meryton or anywhere else in England.

This danger was felt most keenly in my very own household, when last summer, Mr. Wickham, in pursuit of my sister's fortune of thirty-thousand pounds, followed her to Ramsgate and convinced her that they were in love. He ultimately persuaded Georgiana that they must elope to Scotland. Fortunately, by the grace of God, the scheme was discovered before their departure, and Colonel Fitzwilliam and I were able to separate Mr. Wickham from her. As you may well imagine, the shame of her humiliation at his hand was a devastating blow to my sister, who at the time was not yet sixteen.

Georgiana was at home with me when Mr. Wickham was brought to the doorstep of Darcy House with severe injuries to his person. He passed to the next life less than an hour later. She did not see him but is greatly traumatized by the event. My sister is, much like myself, somewhat reserved in company, and these events have preyed greatly upon her. My purpose in bringing her to Hertfordshire is, frankly, so that she may be in company with you, as I feel that your kind and lively nature will do much to improve both her spirits and her confidence, which are at present sadly undermined. It is my hope that the sisterly affection I have observed between you and the eldest Miss Bennet may soon extend in like manner to Georgiana. An acquaintance with the eldest Miss Bennet may similarly benefit my sister, for I have observed her to be gentle and gracious in all circumstances.

Due to this history, it is imperative that no mention is made of Mr. Wickham in Georgiana's presence. How this may be best accomplished, I leave to your judgment, knowing that I may trust you to protect my sister against further heartache and scandal.

When we last spoke, I informed you that I was not at present free to openly declare my attachment to you. Of the obstacles I spoke of then, but one remains, and as I write this, I have great hopes that the resolution for this is at hand. When I return to Longbourn, it is my intention to more fully make known to you the depth of my regard and to discover whether I have found sufficient favor for you to allow me to teach you to ride horseback, which answer I was not able to receive due to your sudden illness at the ball. Your initial refusal has vexed me greatly, and I will employ every means at my disposal to persuade you to say yes. I intend, also, to return to you your lovely handkerchief, which was dropped from your hand sometime during that evening, and which treasure is once again in my possession.

I look forward to seeing you and your father very soon and to introducing you to my sister on that occasion.

Warmest regards,

Fitzwilliam Darcy

When Elizabeth had finished reading the letter, she read it completely through again. Her shock at Mr. Darcy's revelation about his sister was nothing compared to other things that seemed implied in his letter. She returned the letter to the drawer and determined to join her family downstairs before they came up in search of her. They must never know of this letter.

Chapter Fifty

RETURN OF THE DARCYS

Six o'clock found the Bennet family assembled in the dining room for their evening meal, and Mrs. Bennet was in top form from the moment their repast began. Her discourse began with effusions on Jane's upcoming wedding. She rhapsodized on the gowns and the decorations, the luncheon and the guests. *Mama is determined to squeeze six months of talk into three weeks!* Elizabeth mused but remained unnaturally quiet as she attempted to force herself to eat.

Mrs. Bennet eventually mentioned that she had sent an invitation to Mr. Bingley and his sisters to join them at Longbourn for the meal, but that his reply declined her offer, citing urgent family business. She pressed Jane for her intelligence on the matter, but Jane's eyes grew large, as she claimed no knowledge of his personal family affairs. This response was not well received, as Mrs. Bennet insisted that this would not do, and that Jane must begin at once to train Mr. Bingley to counsel with her faithfully in all matters of import. As she said it, Mrs. Bennet directed a meaningful look at her husband, who did not in any way acknowledge the remark—until she had looked away.

Then Mr. Bennet caught Elizabeth's eye and smirked, rolling his eyes at the implication that Mrs. Bennet had somehow achieved this state of confidence from her own husband, in which look Elizabeth found herself discomfited. The realization of her own hopes for a match where open discourse was the rule was the foundation for her unease. The little appetite she had mustered fled, and she resorted to sipping from her cup and stirring her soup in order to appear occupied with the meal.

Fortunately for Jane, Mrs. Bennet's mind had flitted to another topic entirely, settling on Mary. She informed the room of her delight in the discovery that several of their neighbors had noticed that Mr. Timmons had paid some distinct attention to Mary during the service on Sunday, and she had great hopes that this was proof that Mary had caught his eye. This inevitably led to the topic of Mr. Collins.

Mrs. Bennet glared at Elizabeth as she spoke of the great loss it was to their family that Elizabeth had refused Mr. Collins' proposal. When informed that Elizabeth had no recollection of the encounter, Mrs. Bennet was astonished, and wailed about the tragic end to his addresses, no doubt, she complained, at the insistence of Lady Catherine, who had altogether too much influence over the man.

Upon this declaration, Mr. Bennet dabbed at the sides of his mouth with his napkin and inquired after the roast pheasant before adding that he would not have granted consent to Mr. Collins to marry any of his daughters, so it was no great loss that he had desisted in his pursuit.

This fueled Mrs. Bennet into a frenzied tirade. She proclaimed her shock at the discovery of the mercenary nature of Charlotte Lucas, accepting a proposal of marriage from him the very day after he had proposed to her Lizzy. This, she suggested, was due to the example of the same fault in her mother, Lady Lucas, who undoubtedly courted Mr. Collins' favor on Charlotte's behalf the moment Mr. Collins arrived at the doors of Lucas Lodge.

Mr. Bennet frowned at Mrs. Bennet, with one eyebrow raised impatiently at his wife. "Do you begrudge the loss of an ill-suited husband for your second daughter or the loss of Longbourn to someone less deserving?"

"Both!" Mrs. Bennet declared. "And to Charlotte Lucas, of all people. Why she is as plain a girl as was ever born and practically on the shelf! She will do no honor to your ancestral home, Mr. Bennet. Can you imagine what the children of Charlotte Lucas and Mr. Collins will look like? They cannot hope to produce a child half so beautiful as any one of our girls!"

"Mama!" Elizabeth interjected. "I had not desired Mr. Collins' attentions and refused his offer—or so I am told, for I have no recollection of our audience at all. You should not have brought him to Netherfield at all Mama—we are fortunate that I have not suffered the disgrace of being compromised at his hand! I do not know by what means he persuaded Charlotte to accept him, but...."

"Have you not heard?" Lydia, who had been ignoring the conversation, broke free of her daydream and excitedly informed her family, "Mariah Lucas called on us today, this very morning. We had not seen her since yesterday, and I was afraid she should hear the news that some blasted scoundrels had murdered Wickham from someone else before I could tell her!"

"Lydia, watch your tongue!" Elizabeth corrected.

"La! You may watch it as easily as I!" Lydia retorted as she stuck her tongue out at her sister before continuing. "I saw Mariah coming to Longbourn from the window, and Kitty and I met her on the lane—we ran the whole way! There is a fine to do at Lucas Lodge just now—that is what she came to tell us." Lydia paused and took a deep breath. "Just yesterday, Mr. Collins proposed to Charlotte, but that is old news, no; this news is even more shocking than that! Mr. Collins...," Lydia looked around the table until all eyes were fixed on her. "Mr. Collins took to bed just hours ago with a fever. Mr. Jones has examined him and is of the opinion that *he caught the fever from Lizzy*!"

Elizabeth was mortified. "It is not possible!" She protested, shaking her head. "I held that infant for some length of time, and so I can understand how the sickness passed to me, but how could it have passed from me to Mr. Collins? He came into the room, I know, but Colonel Fitzwilliam informed me that I had refused his offer. I do not understand how this could be."

"Well, Lizzy," Lydia assumed an air of superiority born of having information everyone wanted to hear. "Mr. Collins was talking like a drunken man in his delirium, and it led Charlotte to the opinion that something scandalous may have occurred between you and Mr. Collins. He is by no means clear in his meaning, but he kept repeating something about 'My cousin's warm breath upon my hand.' Mariah even heard this for herself! Mr. Jones said that if it is not just the rambling of a fevered mind, but that you did indeed breathe upon his hand, especially if your lips touched it, it could very well be the means whereby Mr. Collins contracted the fever! Was his hand upon your lips, Lizzy?"

"Upon my word! I have no recollection, Lydia—I simply cannot say." Elizabeth sighed and asked with a miserable countenance. "How ill is he?"

"The onset was as sudden with him, apparently, as it was with you!" Kitty broke in. "The things he was saying in delirium were not proper, and they sent Mariah as far from the room as she could go in the house. Charlotte, as his betrothed was determined to nurse him, but Mr. Jones would only let her cool his brow for a short while before even she was sent away. Mr. Jones is to send someone else to nurse him—I do not understand the reason. Mariah said they are all to drink lemon balm tea and drink elderberry wine, just as we have done. She does not like lemon balm, not at all, and is most put out."

"It is so strange, Mama; did Mr. Collins not drink the lemon balm as we all did?" Jane inquired. "I have not felt a moment of illness, and I was with Lizzy much longer than Mr. Collins was."

"No, he did not." Mary said quietly. "Mr. Collins said that Lady Catherine always recommends hyssop tea instead of lemon balm for the prevention of sickness, and so that is all he would drink. He said Mr. Jones knew nothing next to his patroness' vast knowledge of such things."

"Mr. Collins should be well in a few days." Elizabeth said hopefully. "I am not yet fully recovered, but I am much better, and thus far it only took a few days, thanks to Jane's excellent care."

"Mariah said that Mr. Jones declared Mr. Collins even more ill than you were, Lizzy!" Lydia added. "Mariah said that his eyes have rolled back into his head several times, and he has had more than one moment of seizure in which he nearly landed on the floor! Sir William was forced to sit on him to keep him abed! If the fever does not break, he could die!"

"Do not say such things, child!" Mrs. Bennet scolded, and then with full composure turned to her husband. "If Mr. Collins *were* to die, to whom would the entail fall, Mr. Bennet?"

Now both of Mr. Bennet's eyebrows were raised. "I am sure I do not know, madam, but one should not ask such indelicate questions before a man is in the grave."

"Mr. Collins has mentioned your eventual death, husband, on numerous occasions. He has asked about the value of the silver and the paintings, and how many servants we could afford. I fail to see why I cannot contemplate what might happen if the reverse were to happen and *he* was to die! It is of no consequence, however—if you do not know, I will ask my brother, Mr. Phillips." Mrs. Bennet declared. "We must prepare for the possibility of the worst!"

"We should have done that years ago, Mrs. Bennet, by setting aside some money for the future, but instead it has been frittered away on gowns and ribbons and lace and who knows what other silly whims you have had. However, if it will give you peace of mind, I shall make a discrete inquiry with my solicitor in London, for we have never considered such a possibility. This is a vexing question, indeed."

"Lydia," Elizabeth spoke gravely, "have you spoken to Papa about the plans you had made with Mr. Wickham for the spring?"

"Hush, Lizzy, he does not know of them." Lydia whispered back to her sister. "It is of no consequence now."

"What is of no consequence? Of what do you speak?" Mr. Bennet looked with some stern demeanor at his youngest daughter over the top rim of his glasses.

"It is nothing, Papa," Lydia murmured.

"It is *not* 'nothing,' Papa. Lydia, you must tell him." Elizabeth prompted between gritted teeth.

"It was a joke, Lizzy; can you not take a joke?" Lydia demurred.

Every feminine head at the table was now turned to Mr. Bennet. "I am fond of a good joke, Lydia, and I insist upon hearing this one." Mr. Bennet raised his eyebrows impatiently toward his youngest daughter.

"All right, I will tell you!" Lydia spoke resentfully, with an angry look at Elizabeth. "I was full in love with Mr. Wickham, and he with me, and now he is dead. That is all."

"I have sadly neglected your education if you believe this to be a joke, child." Mr. Bennet narrowed his eyes at Lydia. "What, may I ask, is the funny part of it?"

"If you must know, the funny part never can happen now, but I will tell you anyway so you can see it truly would have been a great joke—on all of you! My dear Wickham and I were to elope to Scotland in March! You would not have known where to find us, for we were to leave in the night, and be married before any of you could catch up with us! When you next saw me, I would be Mrs. George Wickham, on the arm of the handsomest officer in the regiment! I laugh now just thinking of it!" Lydia giggled as she resumed eating.

"Lydia," Mr. Bennet said calmly, "At what point *exactly* did you come to this arrangement with Mr. Wickham?"

Lydia, slightly piqued at what she took as a challenge to her story, declared, "It was the day before the ball. He said he was to go to London to buy a pretty ring for me, with the word 'beloved' inscribed in it, and that I was not to lose patience, for he would return in short order. I was to keep it a secret, he said, but I can see no point in keeping the secret of a dead man. I was engaged even before Jane—I was first in that at least!"

"You have no proof of this," Elizabeth murmured with a grimace, "promises such as this, when spoken only in private and not declared openly are not really promises at all."

"Lydia, my dear, do you not recall that I forbade you any contact with that officer?" Mr. Bennet scowled. "And now I discover that immediately after I declared that you not see him at all, you made a secret plan to *elope* with him? How did you manage to convince me to let you even go to the ball? I surely do not remember, but it is of no matter. I have learned my lesson, and you shall feel the pain of it."

"Do not be rash...," Mrs. Bennet broke in timidly.

Mr. Bennet held his hand up at his wife. "Stay your tongue, Mrs. Bennet; I will not be dissuaded this time as I was before the ball. I perceive that my youngest is not merely silly, nor is she simply a determined flirt. She is a disobedient and calculating child. This wild behavior will not be borne for another moment in my household. Lydia, from this day forward, you are no longer 'out' in society, and will not be so until you are seventeen years of age, and then only if I am impressed that you have reformed. You will not be allowed to be in company unless you have been expressly invited. You are not to leave the grounds of Longbourn unless you are accompanied by me, or someone I have approved. Not even your mother may take you from the house without my consent."

"Papa!" Lydia wailed, "It is not fair!"

"And yet," Mr. Bennet set his utensils down firmly with a loud clank, "in spite of your protests, I am unmoved. It is done, and it is done for the best." He wiped his mouth with his napkin and threw it down on the table. "The next outburst from you, Lydia, shall be met with a penalty that will by no means be pleasant."

Lydia, who had stood up in protest, sat heavily in her chair, a pout upon her face and her arms folded in frustration. Mrs. Bennet was aghast, but wary of speaking out against Mr. Bennet when he was in high dudgeon. The first to find her tongue was Elizabeth, who claimed that the meal had fatigued her, and she excused herself, retiring at once for the evening. Only Jane perceived a degree of melancholy in Elizabeth's countenance, but when Jane went to her sister's bedchamber, she found Elizabeth sound asleep.

Mr. Bingley could no longer postpone the inevitable confrontation with his Caroline. He ordered a tray of food to take to her, and soon stood outside the door of her suite. Bingley knew from previous conversations with the footmen guarding her door that she had accepted meals delivered to her antechamber while she was locked in the bedchamber. He knocked at the door to the antechamber and heard the click as the lock was undone. This was followed by the sound of her footfalls as she raced to the bedchamber, the slam of that door, and the rattle of the key in that door as she locked herself in with the bed.

He entered and set the tray on the table, arranging it as he thought the servants would do, and then went loudly to the door, which he opened and noisily closed, although he did not actually quit the room. Instead, he stepped behind a large tapestry that hung on the wall between the two doorways. He quietly sidled along the wall behind the tapestry, intensely focused on not sneezing from the dust that loosened from the cloth, the fine particles swirling into his nostrils as he moved along. In this, he was successful, although he could still feel a sneeze looming. When he reached the edge of the tapestry that hung by the bedchamber door, he waited.

At length, she cautiously unlocked the door to the bedchamber. From his hiding place, Charles could see Caroline as she poked her head through the doorway and searched the room to detect if anyone was there. Apparently satisfied, she finally came out. On tiptoe, she crossed to the unlocked doorway to the hall, and locked it with a key she held in her hand. She then moved to the table and examined the contents of the tray Charles had brought. At length, the sneeze overcame him, and, although she jumped, Caroline acted as though she had not heard it. Charles stepped out and crossed the distance to the table, promptly seating himself casually in the second chair, preparing himself a plate as though it were high tea.

"Are you quite well, Caroline?" Bingley finally ventured.

"I am." Caroline said. "Why do you ask?"

"We both know you have behaved badly, Caroline. I am here to hear your reason, or excuse, or story—whatever you have to offer to explain it," Bingley replied, slightly agitated.

"I have not behaved badly; I cannot imagine what you are referring to. For bad behavior, you should check in on the family of your intended. I believe you will find enough bad behavior to satisfy your need for discovery there."

"Tell me about the wine, Caroline." Charles looked intently at his sister. "You have always been so clever."

"Oh that." Caroline feigned amusement. "I cannot take all the credit, Charles. There we were in the room with Eliza...."

"We?"

"I cannot tell you if you constantly interrupt!" Caroline snapped. "There we were, in the room with Eliza Bennet, our well-laid plan foiled by your butler—inadvertently I believe—because he had sent a fresh bottle to the room already. There she was, the trollop who had clearly aspired to usurp my place with Mr. Darcy, and I could not pour the wine I had earlier prepared with a sleeping draught for her into the decanter. Fortunately, Mr. Jones provided a solution to my dilemma. I substituted some laudanum and added it to the wine sent up by the butler."

"Where is the bottle of wine with the drought?" Charles asked impatiently.

"I drank it." Caroline said apologetically. "I knew you were angry at me, so I locked the room, but I was hungry even after the paltry supper that was sent. I reasoned that I would not feel the hunger if I were asleep, so I drank the bottle of wine and slept quite peacefully."

"You drank the entire bottle?" Charles gasped.

"Yes, of course I did. The elderberry wine is actually quite delicious. I was astonished!"

"Why did you put the draught in the wine bottle, Caroline?" Charles' mind was racing as he attempted to understand what his sister was telling him.

"I obtained the draught from Mr. Jones for my own insomnia, which has plagued me of late. They work very well, particularly if I drink some wine with them. I am out for hours." Caroline replied.

"But you attempted to place the wine in Elizabeth's quarters." Bingley challenged. "She already had both the draughts and laudanum to assist her in sleeping."

"Can you not see, Charles? Adding just a bit to her dose would only make her sleep longer. Mr. Darcy cannot speak to her if she is fast asleep, and poor Jane was looking tired too. The dose would not even be a full one with one glass of wine. You make too much of it."

"Why did you add the laudanum to the decanter?"

"I already told you—since the butler was so efficient, I had to think quickly. I was not the one who thought of it. *He* thought of it."

"He? He who? The butler?" Bingley pressed.

"Not the butler. My friend. I do not recall his *name.* I am not certain that he even has one, but he talks to me. Gives me ideas. Consoles me. Him."

"What did he say?"

"That the laudanum was on the table, and it would do the job just as well." Caroline replied matter-of-factly. "He told me to hide what I was doing from Elizabeth so that she would drink it, and then she would sleep for a very long time."

"The amount you put in that bottle was lethal." Charles replied angrily.

"Oh? Is Eliza dead then? Did Jane drink some as well? I say good riddance, I will tell you now that he said we would never recover from such a match, and that I would never find a suitable husband with such relations as the Bennets. He is right, you know."

"They are not dead Caroline. Jane detected that the wine was tainted and they did not partake of it. They have returned to Longbourn." Charles shuddered at what his sister had said.

"Oh, that is good! Now we can quit this horrid county of Hertfordshire and return to London!" Caroline clapped her hands.

"You will have to go without me." Charles replied. "I must stay for my wedding to Jane Bennet, but after what you have done, it is impossible to allow you attendance to that happy event. Louisa and her husband are to take you into town tomorrow morning. They are planning a delightful trip to the Isle of Wight and will allow you to come with them, since you shall not attend the wedding."

"I want to stay in London," Caroline pouted. "Louisa will listen to me. We can delay the trip until the season is past. Then at least I will be able to see Mr. Darcy and he may resume our courtship at his earliest convenience."

"Mr. Hurst is quite determined to go, and my house in town is to be redecorated to suit my new wife's tastes. It will be quite impossible for you to stay at my London residence for more than a few days." Bingley said firmly. "You will go with Louisa. We have planned a few surprises for you in London. I know how much you like surprises."

"Very well, Charles, I will go and distance myself from those awful Bennets. I wish I could believe you are not serious, but I see that you are perfectly so. He tells me it is too bad they did not drink the wine, but there will be opportunities in the future, I am certain, to amend my failure." Caroline selected a few more items from the tray with a frown. "The staff may pack my belongings after I go to the drawing room."

"I will have the carriage come around at nine," Bingley replied, looking at his sister with sorrow. The conversation had confirmed his fears. In addition to her belief that she would be mistress of Pemberley, Caroline was hearing voices and having trouble sleeping. Caroline's beginning was much the same as Annabelle's had been.

Although they had not departed until daylight was upon them the following morning, Darcy watched Georgiana, who was fast asleep in their carriage, in spite of her insistence that she had slept well the night before. He contemplated on his good fortune. His business in London had ended better than he could have hoped and faster than he could have imagined possible. The Wickham problem would haunt his sister no more, and the path was clear for him to declare himself to Elizabeth and bring his addresses to the culmination of a proposal.

He indulged in thoughts of her, flashes of her face passing before his eyes in a constant stream. Her dancing eyes, her lips pressed together, the arch of her brow, her head tipped ever so slightly to the side—his mind relived their moments together and wove them into a tapestry of future felicity.

The delights of a marriage born of a love match next paraded incessantly in his daydream. Visions of Pemberley interlaced with memories as he pictured Elizabeth walking amid the gardens and pathways of her new home. He thought with contentment of introducing his bride to the Pemberley library, music room, conservatory, and art collection. He imagined her in their dining room as hostess to the company they entertained. He conjured her in a beautiful gown, adorned in the Darcy jewels, atop the stairs. Together, with her on his arm, they would descend to open their home for their first ball.

His mind wandered further to the children they would eventually have. He imagined dark-haired daughters with sparking eyes that could not be denied and fine strong sons who would one day carry on the Darcy legacy. Thoughts of taking his *wife* to their bed and initiating the activities that would produce those children elicited a grin of ecstatic anticipation on his handsome face. He cooled his thoughts and expression by considering all the many topics of conversation they would engage in. Elizabeth seemed very determined to converse, and he had no more objections to the sound of her voice falling on his ears than he would have to her lips pressing against his own.

The rocking of the carriage eventually lulled Darcy into a doze, where the object and scenes of his reverie took seemingly tangible form. He enjoyed very pleasant dreams all the way back to Netherfield. In this state, he did not even see the Bingley carriage when they passed on the road or hear Caroline's cries of "Mr. Darcy!" fading into the distance.

Chapter Fifty-One

FAMILY TIES

Elizabeth excused herself from the company of her family immediately after the evening meal and returned to her bedchamber, burdened by a vague despondency over the seemingly insurmountable obstacles that barred even the faintest hope of that future which would constitute her greatest happiness. The tallow candle sputtered and released a swirl of black smoke as she set the flame on the table next to the nook of the window seat. The yellow light was dim but provided adequate illumination for another reading of her private letter from Mr. Darcy. His correspondence had occupied her mind throughout the past hours since she had first read it.

The small fire from earlier in the day was out, leaving the room cold, for the staff had not yet distributed the embers from the larger fireplaces among the bedchambers. Elizabeth readied herself for bed quickly, and, shivering at the chill in the air, she impulsively reached in her closet to the place she had hidden the wine-colored shawl and withdrew it. She wrapped it almost reverently around her shoulders as she retrieved the letter and sat in the same fashion as she had since childhood, with her legs tucked beneath her on the window seat.

The shawl and the letter came to me together, however accidental that event was she thought, defending her action to herself. *It is only fitting that they remain paired when the letter is examined*. She tugged the shawl resolutely around her shoulders and prepared to read the letter yet again. Her eyes first scanned the page as a whole, noting how very much like the man his hand was. The powerful angle and uniform shape of the letters were striking—the penmanship was as elegant as any calligraphers might be, yet masculine in form, and perfectly legible.

Although she had read the letter twice through before dinner, indeed, certain parts of it were already indelibly fixed in her mind, she felt as she had upon her first reading, somehow worried about what she might find there.

My dearest Elizabeth, So familiar a greeting carried an intimacy that felt to her nearly forbidden, and yet she thrilled at his use of her Christian name while a faint echo played in her mind of similar words spoken at her sickbed.

His next lines confused her, particularly the passage that spoke of their being *not yet engaged*. By this, did he imply that he was in fact to offer for her at some future moment, or did he mean to impress upon her the undecided nature of their acquaintanceship? She recalled the cruel declarations that Caroline Bingley had made to her about Mr. Darcy's ultimate choice in a wife. *Is he putting me on my guard not to assume what is not formally established?*

She read on in the letter, warmed by the confidence he expressed in her character, for it signified some degree of esteem, intimated that he regarded her with sufficient trust to disclose such private matters to her. She was pleased that he wished to introduce his sister to her and flattered, to some degree, at his expressed hopes in their friendship, yet there was something troubling in that request. She could not immediately discern the source of her discomfort on the matter, but it niggled at her nonetheless.

Although Lydia had told her, and she had previously read the letter, she was still shocked nearly to disbelief at the suddenness of Mr. Wickham's demise and the apparent mystery that surrounded his fate. She was rocked to her core, yet again, by the disclosures about the dealings of Mr. Wickham with Miss Darcy. Elizabeth recalled her brief friendship with that amiable and charming man with a fresh perspective, for while Mr. Darcy had personally advised her to give no consequence to Mr. Wickham, she had thought him to be a pleasant and agreeable acquaintance. In retrospect, perhaps he was too smooth in his manners to be trusted.

She chastised herself for having failed to speak privately with each of her sisters and set her mind to do so in the morning, to explain that they must not mention Mr. Wickham in Georgiana Darcy's presence. This she felt could be best accomplished by preying on their sympathies in describing Wickham as having been raised as nearly a brother in the house and assuring her sisters that it would sorely grieve Georgiana should they mention Mr. Wickham or anything related to him. In this sound advice she could speak to her family with no mention of any letter from Mr. Darcy and yet accomplish the task he had entrusted to her.

Her eyes turned back to the letter. The last paragraph was cryptic and was the source of some anxiety to Elizabeth, for she could not make out his meaning. She felt certain that Mr. Darcy was saying something important to her without saying it exactly. *It is peculiar that he should renew his idea, especially as I was so adamant in my refusal! Surely he does not intend to pursue his offer to teach me to ride—that was playful jesting from the dance, a topic that should have been left at the ball.* Perhaps, she reasoned, that this was yet another ploy to express the platonic nature of their relationship. Did he mean to impress upon her his determination to restore the distance dictated by the disparity of their individual stations? As she pondered this question, the answer to her discomfort in the earlier part of the letter came. The purpose of the letter was clear—Mr. Darcy merely wished to enlist her aid in helping his sister overcome the events that he had disclosed in the letter.

She re-read the letter now and saw with clarity all that he was trying to say—to gently advise her that she should not anticipate any further addresses but prepare, instead, to be of service to his sister, who was in need of consolation and a friend. This she would gladly do for him and be honored by the request. Indeed, she knew that she could not refuse him anything. He could not know the heartbreak she harbored—she would not betray her feelings for him again in light of his indifference. Now that she had detected his meaning, she was sure she could be at ease in his presence, for she would know how to act.

She returned the letter to the drawer, snuffed the candle, and slipped beneath the counterpane of the bed, the shawl still wrapped securely around her body. She lay awake, contemplating the possibility that, as early as tomorrow noon, Mr. Darcy and his sister might be returned to Netherfield.

୨

The next morning after breakfast, Elizabeth sought out each sister, and her parents, as well, in turn for a private conversation about their upcoming introductions to Miss Darcy, for she was determined not to fail in this assignment to insulate Miss Darcy from comments that would injure her. She began by sharing what general information she knew of Miss Darcy and cautioned her sisters against overwhelming the shy girl, who was raised with no sisters and only one elder brother. She added, as if it were an afterthought, that Mr. Wickham had been raised in the same household and was as a brother to her when she was young. Upon hearing of Miss Darcy's childhood attachment to Wickham, each of her family solemnly agreed not to mention him, lest they provoke her tender sentiments and bring further trouble to her in so doing.

Lydia, in particular, was anxious not to stir up remembrance of that fellow within the house, for their father, rather than forgetting his promised penalties, was piling them on, sentencing his youngest daughter to many hours of study, of practice, and even to chores in the household. He was in such a foul temper over Lydia's disobedience that even Mrs. Bennet dared not intervene on Lydia's behalf.

Neither had Kitty escaped their father's wrath, for it had become known after Elizabeth had quit the meal that Kitty had been privy to all of Lydia's anticipation of an elopement, and she was included in all of the punishments that Lydia bore, although Kitty accepted it meekly while Lydia chafed against each assignment.

Following the interviews, Elizabeth was disconcerted to realize that, although she had only been about for a few hours, weariness chased her, and she was once again obliged to rest. Mr. Jones had warned her of the possibility of fatigue following her illness and admonished her to heed her tiredness in order to recover fully. She fought valiantly against it, but by late morning, she admitted defeat and so informed Jane before she returned to her bedchamber. She was fast asleep when the party from Netherfield arrived at Longbourn.

Kitty first raised the alarm as the carriage entered the drive, but Mrs. Bennet took up the cry, and all of the occupants of the house, save Elizabeth and her father, rapidly converged and assembled in the sitting room. When Hill announced their guests, five of the Bennets rose calmly from the seats where they had appeared to be thoroughly engaged with tasks of sewing and other needlework.

The family stood nearly in unison as Mrs. Bennet stepped forward to greet them. Miss Darcy was introduced to those Bennets present, as was her companion, Mrs. Annesley. Everyone engaged in those pleasantries attendant to introductions, but when no Elizabeth was named among the daughters, Georgiana looked nervously at her brother.

Mr. Bingley, a great smile on his face stepped up and inquired. “You are all well I hope?”

"Very well." Mrs. Bennet replied graciously. "Except for Lizzy, I should say. She is not herself since the fever."

At this, Mr. Darcy's eyes widened slightly. "Shall I summon a physician from London?"

"You are very kind, Mr. Darcy, but that is not necessary. Mr. Jones has advised that there is a minor outbreak of the fever in the neighborhood, and he has warned us that it will be some few weeks before Lizzy is fully recovered." Mrs. Bennet gestured for her guests to be seated as she reassured them. "It is not an epidemic, mind you. As it turns out, the illness is not passed easily, and those who are preventing it with lemon balm and elderberry appear not affected at all."

"It is excellent that the illness may be prevented," Mr. Bingley declared. "I would hate for such a thing as an epidemic to interfere with the wedding."

"Now that you bring it up," Mrs. Bennet said with delight, "there are orders of business regarding the wedding that cannot be delayed! Come, Jane. Come, Mr. Bingley. We will repair to the parlor so as not to be disturbed in our preparations." She stood and walked to the doorway, beckoning to Jane and Mr. Bingley. Jane blushed with some mortification that her mother had jumped to the object of her preoccupation so immediately, with not even an offer of refreshment, but Mr. Bingley was all smiles as he offered his arm to Jane for the brief walk to the parlor.

"Lead the way, Mrs. Bennet; I am certain we can resolve any matters of nuptial-related urgency in short order and join the company shortly." Mr. Bingley then lowered his voice to a whisper that only Jane could hear. "Perhaps," he said with a boyish grin, "we shall find a suitable location for the mistletoe in the parlor!"

The departure of those three wedding planners left Mr. Darcy in the room with Georgiana, Mary, Kitty and Lydia. He walked to the window, as was his habit, and stood with his back to the ladies, who quickly disregarded his presence. His concern about exposing his sister to the younger Bennet girls was quickly allayed. It was evident by their gentle manners toward his sister that his letter to Elizabeth had born fruit—the girls were all perfectly well behaved, and kind and welcoming too. Mary inquired after her musical studies, and Kitty asked her about town. Lydia admired her frock and inquired after the latest fashions, as it was apparent that Georgiana Darcy was outfitted in apparel more current than what was typically seen in Meryton.

Georgiana blushed and stammered some at first, but she soon was at ease in their company, giggling at Lydia's jokes along with

Kitty. Darcy watched them in the glass, gradually relaxing as he observed his sister respond favorably to the unaffected welcome she received in this household. He quietly moved to a seat by the table and, with some agitation, sat down. He picked up a book that sat on a nearby table and thumbed through it. He set it back down and listened while Lydia told a humorous story about a cat that hid her kittens in the barn. Kitty interjected frequently with details Lydia had left out, and Georgiana was spellbound with the tale.

While the young ladies were thus engaged, the door to the sitting room quietly opened, and Elizabeth entered. Mr. Darcy immediately stood and bowed to her, his eyes seeking hers as he greeted her. "Miss Elizabeth."

She curtseyed in response. "Mr. Darcy."

He crossed the divide rapidly, relieved at her appearance in the room, but on his approach, her eyes turned away from him to Georgiana, and she smiled at the girl with great warmth before she turned her expectant gaze back to Mr. Darcy.

"My sister," Darcy said, wishing not to take his eyes away from Elizabeth.

Elizabeth laughed softly. "I am aware of who the young lady is, Mr. Darcy. I was very much hoping to be favored with an introduction—if it is not too much trouble."

"Oh yes, of course." Darcy blinked himself out of the stupor that threatened him. He made the introductions, and Elizabeth drew Georgiana away from the younger girls. Taking her by the hand, she lead her to the set of chairs that Jane and Mr. Bingley had so often occupied, where they could converse quietly, undisturbed by others in the room.

Elizabeth put the young girl at ease nearly the instant they met, her conversation so generous and her manner so warm that Georgiana's expression was soon more animated than Darcy had seen it at any time since she was a child. Elizabeth's eyes, which he had always found so enchanting and intelligent, twinkled with what seemed to be genuine affection for Georgiana within moments of their first greeting. Darcy marveled at the transformation that Elizabeth had effected on his sibling. Georgiana looked up at him once, as if to reassure her brother of her well-being. Darcy's delight at the outcome of the first meeting of the two women he loved most in the world nearly overcame his reserved demeanor, but he remained composed and rewarded Georgiana's gesture with a faint smile and a nod.

The door to the sitting room opened again, and Mrs. Bennet entered, followed by Mrs. Hill with a tray of refreshments. Mrs.

Bennet fussed and directed the other woman in her preparations, which Darcy observed with some amusement. Several minutes later, Jane and Mr. Bingley also returned to the sitting room. Jane had a strange, rather shocked, expression on her face, which Elizabeth did not notice, due to the depth of her discourse with Miss Darcy.

When the refreshments were ready, Mrs. Bennet proved herself a gracious hostess. This Mr. Darcy noted with some degree of astonishment, for the same woman had certainly served him on previous occasions, yet he had not until today noticed the ease with which she performed her duties. In one unguarded instant, as Mrs. Bennet handed him a cup of tea, Mr. Darcy bestowed on her a smile of approval and appreciation. A gleam appeared in Mrs. Bennet's eye as the gentleman from Derbyshire found favor in it, and she immediately began to consider which of her remaining three daughters would best suit Mr. Darcy as a wife, for she already considered Mary as good as taken by Mr. Timmons.

"Mr. Darcy." Mrs. Bennet began as soon as the refreshments were distributed, "It is very good that you are back from London. Your sister is a lovely girl, and I see that she and my Lizzy are well on their way to becoming fast friends."

"Indeed, madam, so it would seem," Mr. Darcy replied with a glance toward where Elizabeth and Georgiana remained engrossed in conversation. "I believe that my sister has enjoyed meeting all of the Miss Bennets today."

"Of course she has!" Mrs. Bennet exclaimed. "My girls are as good as any you will find anywhere, and better than some others in the neighborhood. That is why I do not care one farthing that Charlotte Lucas is to marry Mr. Collins, for else she would surely have ended an old maid, which I would not wish on anyone."

"Nor would I," Mr. Darcy agreed. His interest was piqued by the news of the betrothal, and he inquired, "I had not heard of Mr. Collins' engagement. Pray, where is your cousin? I should like to wish him joy."

"He is not here, Mr. Darcy," Mrs. Bennet admitted. "He left Longbourn a few days past and is presently a guest at Lucas Lodge." She hesitated for a moment before adding, "But you must not call on him there, for he is at present indisposed."

Darcy grew stern. "If I may presume to ask, what is the cause of his indisposition?"

"Why, Mr. Collins is stricken with the fever." Mrs. Bennet replied. "He is, in fact, gravely ill." She eyed Mr. Darcy nervously.

"I am sorry to hear it." Darcy said politely. He silently reflected on the events Colonel Fitzwilliam had disclosed about his last encounter with Mr. Collins.

Mrs. Bennet, having decided just moments before that Elizabeth was the best candidate for Mr. Darcy, was now struck with a new worry. Rumors that Mr. Collins had compromised Elizabeth were entirely possible due to Mr. Collins' feverish talk, probable, in fact, if one considered Lady Lucas' shocking lack of discretion. She cleared her throat to be certain she retained Mr. Darcy's attention. "Oh!" Mrs. Bennet ventured with a slight laugh, "I hear that the fever has produced wild imaginings in Mr. Collins. He has uttered a good bit of utter nonsense in his delirium. I am certain he will be most diverted when his health is restored."

"Fevers are known to produce such effects." Mr. Darcy acknowledged. "One should not give too much credence to words spoken by one so stricken." Darcy abruptly looked at Elizabeth, his thoughts turning back to the sweet conversation at her bedside before he went to London. He had hung on her words of love the entire time he was away. *Do I give too much credence to what she said in such a state?*

"Exactly so," Mrs. Bennet replied with some relief that she had averted disaster. She turned her attention then to Jane and Mr. Bingley, leaving Darcy to his own thoughts.

∽

When the visitors from Netherfield departed, Jane drew Elizabeth aside. "Oh, Lizzy, much has happened in the past day! My poor Mr. Bingley has put on a brave face, but he is grieved, sister, grieved! He has had to send Caroline away!"

"Away? Before the wedding?" Elizabeth puzzled.

"Oh yes." Jane wrung her hands. "She departed for London this morning with Mr. and Mrs. Hurst, where they are to arrange for a physician to examine her. Lizzy, she is quite mad!"

"Jane, are you certain?"

"After Mama left the parlor, Mr. Bingley asked me to remain for a moment. He was very serious—I have never seen him so upset. He proceeded to tell me that there is another Bingley sister, an older sister named Annabelle."

"Why have they never mentioned her?" Elizabeth wondered aloud.

"It is because ... oh Lizzy, I can hardly bear to say it. Annabelle is in Bedlam." Jane pressed her lips together to prevent herself from weeping.

"Bedlam? Oh no, Jane, but this is terrible!"

"And now Charles fears that the same demons that have taken Annabelle's mind prey on Caroline. A voice told her to put the laudanum in the wine, Lizzy." Jane whispered. "He asked me if I still would have him, with such a family! Oh, my dear, dear Mr. Bingley, he was so worried."

Elizabeth embraced Jane, who accepted the comfort gratefully. "Jane, perhaps it is not wise to marry him. What if these demons were to afflict him as well?"

"Charles will not go mad, Elizabeth. I can assure you of that," Jane said resolutely.

"But how can you be certain? With two sisters...," Elizabeth shook her head, dread in her eyes.

"They are half-sisters, Lizzy." Jane did not pause for questions, but rapidly told the essential elements to her sister. "Their mother had three daughters very young, and then began to act very strangely. Before his father realized she was not right in the head, she took her own life. The girls were all small children and do not truly remember her well. Charles' father married again, and Charles is the product of that union, not the first." Jane parroted back the information that had just been given her. "Old Mr. Bingley wished to elevate his family's station once he had made his fortune, so they did not mention the first Mrs. Bingley to anyone at all due to the shameful mode of her demise. Charles did not even know of this history until after his father's passing, and it was all in a private letter given only to him. His sisters do not even know of it. He showed me the letter, Lizzy. Ever since the eldest was sent to Bedlam, he has lived in fear that this secret would emerge."

"I will not divulge it to anyone," Elizabeth promised. "What is to happen to Caroline?"

"I do not know. She is to be examined in town, and if they can avoid Bedlam, they will do so, but she cannot be allowed near those she might harm. Charles said they might send her to an island, if it can be arranged. We should hear more from the Hursts in a few days." Jane gave her sister a weak smile. "I believe all shall be well, Lizzy. I am only glad that it was discovered before she did any harm to you, or to anyone else."

"Will this not cast a pall over your wedding, Jane? Are you certain you should not postpone it?" Elizabeth prompted. "Perhaps you should wait until this matter is all resolved."

"Nothing shall cast a shadow of any sort over my wedding!" Jane exclaimed. "I am to be Mrs. Bingley, and I am marrying the dearest, most amiable man in all of England. I only wish such happiness for you, my dear sister, for I cannot sleep at night, so great is my anticipation."

"Then I am happy for you," Elizabeth cheered. "What are you to say when people inquire after Caroline?"

"I will not lie, Lizzy. She has gone back to London with the Hursts, and, due to urgent family business, they cannot be present at the wedding." Jane smiled, her serenity restored.

"I cannot say that I will miss their superior ways at the wedding, but my heart does break for Mr. Bingley and for Caroline too. I daresay her life will not be what she hopes for."

"Do not worry about Mr. Bingley." Jane said sweetly. "I daresay that I may find a way to console him when we are married!"

Upon their return to Netherfield, Georgiana repaired to the drawing room, eager to try out the pianoforte, and Bingley went to his study. Darcy, noting that, for a winter day, it was fine out, declared that it had been too long since he had gone for a ride.

He was soon astride his mount Romeo and, together with Apollo, they covered the grounds around Netherfield. Tensions fell away as the exertion worked out the stiffness that had formed over the past few days of less physical pursuits.

Whether it was consciously done or not, he did not know, but Darcy soon realized that he was on the road to Meryton. His destination, he knew, was Longbourn once more, for he had been unsatisfied with the brief interaction he had with Elizabeth, who had spent the duration of their visit at Georgiana's side.

Once he acknowledged to himself where he was going, he urged Romeo back into a canter, and he closed the distance between himself and his beloved with an urgency born of the deepest yearning to see her face, hear her voice and to gaze into her eyes.

Soon the smoking chimneys of Longbourn Manor appeared in the distance, and he slowed to straighten his hat and make certain that all else about his appearance was in order. His heart raced with anticipation. He did not know how he would prevent himself from sweeping Elizabeth into his arms and taking her lips with his. As he was contemplating this act, which seemed increasingly more alluring every minute, her realized that the darkness that had pressed on him in London, that sense that something was wrong, had faded almost to oblivion. All that he could imagine to be wrong had been resolved, and nothing was left but to make Elizabeth an offer and marry her with the same haste that Bingley had set about to claim her sister as a bride.

He was now at the very spot where he had met Elizabeth the morning of the ball. Today there was no wind, but as if on cue, Apollo began to bay. Darcy snapped his whip lightly on Romeo's flank and made the short distance to the entry gate as Apollo bounded after them.

In the house, Kitty heard the sound of the hound and searched the window for a visitor. She loudly reported to the household that Mr. Darcy was back, and that he had come alone.

This was perceived by Mrs. Bennet as a good sign, and she determined to do as well for Elizabeth as she had for Jane. She sent the maid to fetch Elizabeth from her room, for the earlier visit had exhausted her and she had lain down again. She instructed the maid to tidy Elizabeth's hair and make sure that her dress was not wrinkled before she entered the sitting room.

When Hill announced Mr. Darcy, the sitting room contained the same residents as had attended earlier in the day. Mrs. Bennet and four of her daughters were there, missing but Elizabeth. He greeted them all politely, and although it had been just a few hours since he had been there, he inquired after Elizabeth's health.

"Oh, she is on the mend." Mrs. Bennet replied. "She is well enough, that is, although not quite herself...."

"Thank you Mama." Elizabeth said from the doorway, her hair untidy and her dress slightly wrinkled. "Mr. Darcy, you are returned. Have you forgotten something?"

As the eyes of four sisters and a mother turned to await his answer, Mr. Darcy realized his mistake. He had anticipated a more private conversation than this! "Indeed I have Miss Elizabeth, and I have made haste to rectify it."

Elizabeth invited him to sit, in a chair opposite the settee, where she sat—joined by Jane and Kitty. Mrs. Bennet could clearly see that Mr. Darcy wished some privacy, and after making a point of the pleasantries, she excused herself from the room. She thought that, to be less obvious, she might drain the room of its excess occupants one at a time, so every few minutes she sent a blushing Hill into the room to summon a daughter until only Elizabeth and Mr. Darcy remained.

For once, Elizabeth was grateful for her mother's scheming.

"I received your letter, Mr. Darcy." Elizabeth began. "I thought that my sisters did exceedingly well in remaining discrete about Mr. Wickham's death, did you not think so?"

"Yes. They were a delight," Mr. Darcy answered with a smile as his eyes unrelentingly bore into her visage.

"And my first meeting with your sister, I trust, was as much a pleasure for her as it was for me," she added with sincerity. "I did not know exactly what to expect, but I found her all that is wonderful."

"And a third person took pleasure from your meeting," Darcy said softy. "I was tremendously gratified to see the two of you finally meet."

"I am glad you approved," Elizabeth said. She raised her eyes to his but looked away with uncertainty. "There was another item besides the letter that came in the trunk, Mr. Darcy. I believe it was packed by the Netherfield staff in error, and I must restore it to you."

"What was it?"

"It is a shawl. A beautiful shawl."

"The red one?" Darcy smiled.

Elizabeth nodded.

"What makes you think it was an error?"

"It is not mine," Elizabeth replied. "The rest of the articles in the trunk were all mine, and I saw the shawl in a drawer in your room, so I believe the staff mistakenly thought it belonged to me."

"Did you look through my bureau?"

"I did." Elizabeth could not suppress a slight grin.

"The shawl should be yours," Darcy answered. "I would like to see it on you."

"Mr. Darcy!" Elizabeth gasped. "It is too fine! Such a costly gift would be a scandal!"

"Did you try it on?"

Elizabeth colored and looked away.

"I bought it for Georgiana," Darcy said, "but realized that the only woman of my acquaintance who could ever wear it was you. So I returned to the widow and bought the blue one for my sister."

Elizabeth's eyes widened, and her color deepened.

"I could wait no longer for you to have it."

The cruel words of Caroline Bingley, hinting that Elizabeth was wanton, echoed in her mind, and she knew that accepting the shawl would begin the destruction that would ruin her reputation forever. "It is a beautiful garment, Mr. Darcy, but you must realize that it is impossible for me to accept it."

"Impossible?" Darcy shook his head, not comprehending.

"Yes, impossible! Surely you know this! What are you to me? You are the friend of my sister's intended. I cannot accept a gift of such magnitude from a man so wholly unconnected to me. To do so would disgrace us all!" Elizabeth said bitterly. "It is cruel, indeed, to toy with my feelings in such a way."

"Unconnected?" Darcy repeated as he stood. "Elizabeth, I can think of no two people more connected than I desire us to be!"

The poisonous words spoken by Caroline had taken root, and in pain, she flung them at Darcy. "You want me in your bed, sir? Is that what you say?"

"Well ... yes," Darcy replied, confused.

"I will not be a mistress! I will die an old maid before I would do such a thing!" Elizabeth cried and jumped up from the settee, to quit the room before tears fell.

She did not go two steps before she felt a hand around her wrist that stopped her progress.

"Unhand me, sir." She whispered, her eyes closing to release the tears that would no longer be denied.

"I beg you to hear me." Darcy said as he relaxed his grip.

"No. The answer is no." She turned to face him.

"I must beg you to reconsider your answer." Darcy said solemnly. "Perhaps it would serve us both if I were allowed to pose my question before you make such a hasty response."

Elizabeth shifted her eyes in a gesture Darcy recognized as begrudging agreement.

It took him a few moments of changing expressions and attempts at a beginning before he finally spoke. "In vain I have struggled," he began, "but it will not do. My feelings will not be repressed. You must allow me to tell you how ardently I admire and love you."

Elizabeth arched a brow but remained silent.

"I pray that you will forgive me my initial reluctance in pressing my suit with you. There were—obstacles—to my acting on these feelings, obstacles that now I see were no obstacles at all, but foolish prejudices that prevented my making any serious design on you at the start."

"Are you soon to arrive at your question?" Elizabeth asked, slightly annoyed at his beginning. "I cannot answer a question that is not asked."

"Patience." Darcy replied. "I intend to ask this question but once in my lifetime, and I should like to get it right."

Elizabeth's eyelashes fluttered at this response, and she calmly seated herself once more on the settee, although the fluttering of her heart could be detected as a vein on her neck pulsed.

He stared for a long moment at her, thinking through the many things he had rehearsed to say, but instead, he spoke to the primary misunderstanding he knew of. "I would not have you be my mistress, except in the capacity of mistress of Pemberley, which is the natural role for my wife! I love you passionately, my dearest, loveliest Elizabeth, and you may take your time in answering my question, if time is what you need, but you will have your question now." He drew a deep breath and returned to his chair—although he sat forward on the seat as far as he could, nearly closing the gap between them. He took her hand in his, and when she resisted, he raised it to his lips and kissed the back of it before he released it. "Elizabeth, I beg you to relieve my suffering and ease my torment. Please, will you do me the honor of accepting my suit for your hand in marriage?"

Elizabeth stared at him in astonishment, her lips parted as if to speak, but no words escaped them.

"Have you nothing to say?" Mr. Darcy finally broke the silence. "Am I to expect an answer?"

"Mr. Darcy, you cannot be serious!" Elizabeth exclaimed. "I am well aware that your family will have imposed expectations on you to choose your wife and the mother of your heir from among those who are at the very least your equal in society. The daughters of the nobility are at your feet, sir, and my father is but a country squire."

"You are gentle born, are you not?" Darcy inquired with a calmness he did not feel.

"I am." Elizabeth nodded.

"Do you love me?" Darcy pressed his suit.

"That is not fair, Mr. Darcy—you know that I do! I have always desired a marriage for love, but now that I am faced with the possibility, I see that there is more to consider. I would not have you disappointed and injured when your family and all of society turns against you for marrying a country maiden of small fortune and low connections. I could not bear the heartache it would cause you!"

"Did I not tell you that I had obstacles to overcome? These objections are nothing to me, I assure you. I had never thought that a marriage for love would be possible in my case, but I know now that nothing less can be acceptable. When we are married, your fortune and your connections will be unrivaled! The misfortunes you cite may be heavy to some, but, I assure you, my thoughts on future marital felicity with you have vanquished any doubts I may have harbored early in our acquaintance. I am resolved to devote my life to your happiness, even at the peril of my own."

"You are very eloquent, Mr. Darcy, but I believe that I must invoke your offer of time, that I may think more on your offer. I am not prepared to agree to this at present. I am not myself." Elizabeth muttered as the tears returned.

Darcy withdrew Elizabeth's handkerchief from his pocket and pressed it into her palm. "Let your tears stain this, my darling, and I shall pray that someday they shall be tears of joy when we are wed."

To this Elizabeth could not reply. Instead, she took the handkerchief and dabbed at her eyes in a vain attempt to stem the tide of emotion that flooded unbidden through them.

Darcy was anguished that he had been the cause of her tears, and soon expressed the act which he least desired to do. "I fear that my presence is not a comfort to you, Miss Bennet. I will leave you now."

Chapter Fifty-Two

SAY YES

Darcy did not go two steps before he felt a slight pressure on his arm. He stopped, and Elizabeth withdrew her hand. "Please." Elizabeth whispered. "Please do not leave me."

"You wish me to stay?" Darcy turned and their eyes met, his hopeful, hers wide and glistening. She looked down as she granted him a barely perceptible nod. He returned to the chair across from her, relieved by her plea but at a loss for its interpretation.

His return calmed Elizabeth, and a steady composure settled onto her as she dried her eyes. "There, you see, I am well. I do not know what came over me," she assured him with a weak smile, although her skin was pale and her lip presented a tremor that caught Darcy's attention.

"Indeed, you are not well. Is there nothing I may do for your present relief? Some wine perhaps?"

"No, thank you." Elizabeth shook her head. "Spirits will not resolve my dilemma."

"Dilemma?" Darcy asked.

"Your proposal, Mr. Darcy. Surely you are aware of the dilemma it presents," Elizabeth said wearily.

Darcy shook his head and replied frankly, "I presumed that any hindrances to our match were on my side alone. Pray enlighten me as to the source of the perceived conflict on yours."

"You told me once that it had been the study of a lifetime to avoid foolishness, and that you do not suffer fools easily." Elizabeth said, "You will be considered by all of society to be a fool if you take a wife of such low station as I. I cannot allow myself to undermine that which has been the study of a lifetime."

"It is true, until that day, this was my course." Darcy acknowledged. "On that occasion, as I recall, you painted yourself the fool and counseled that I not give you a second thought—which advice I did not take. I believe I have thought of nothing but you from that day forward. My studies of late have indeed broken with patterns established for a lifetime, much to my improvement."

"I would not have you change for my sake, Mr. Darcy." Elizabeth said, blushing.

"Nonetheless, I am an altered man," Darcy replied. "I have changed not for your sake, however, but for my own. How else am I to win your affections than to shed those distressing imperfections in my character?"

Elizabeth, having recollected their conversation at Netherfield, pursed her lips with a degree of amusement and replied, "Mr. Darcy, if you succeed in exalting yourself to perfection, you leave nothing ridiculous for me to laugh at."

"Then tell me what I must do to be acceptable to you," Darcy replied. "I would crawl on the floor and let you scratch my ears if you would bestow an ounce of the same affection on me that you have to my dog."

Elizabeth laughed at the image this painted in her mind, and she replied with some gaiety, "That would be ridiculous, indeed. Would you lick my face as well?"

Her joking inquiry had quite the opposite effect on Mr. Darcy than what she had expected, for his countenance changed suddenly, and he became, to her eye, very serious.

"Elizabeth, you are too generous to trifle with me. If these reservations you harbor cannot be overcome, please tell me at once. One word from you will silence me on the subject forever."

"I beg you to keep your own counsel," Elizabeth said archly. "You admonished me to be patient but a moment ago. Have you forgotten so soon that you promised me time to consider your proposal? It has been less than five minutes, sir."

"I did not expect you to hesitate." Darcy replied honestly, his disappointment that she had, evident in his looks.

"How could I do otherwise?" Elizabeth replied gently. "Our alliance will be seen as an abomination by your family, indeed by anyone who believes in the preservation of rank, Mr. Darcy, and despite my tender feelings for you, I must consider that the duration of our acquaintance has not been long. How am I to truly know your character in so short a time? What do you know of me that assures you of mine?"

"You are no doubt aware of my reserve in company." Darcy said. "I have not the talent to converse easily with strangers. This does, I admit, create a measure of difficulty in the avenues of social intercourse. However it also frees me to observe others most carefully. I formed a high opinion of you very early in our acquaintance. I know all that I need to know—my regard for you is fixed. I will gladly address any doubts you may have of my character if I could but know what they are."

Elizabeth rolled her eyes. "The problem lies not in doubt of your character, but rather that your character seems too good to be true."

"Were you not of the belief that I would have you as a mistress?" Darcy softly questioned. "Is this not evidence of doubt in my noble character?"

Elizabeth colored deeply. "Do not repeat what I said! It is truly evidence of doubt, but not in you—not exactly. Miss Bingley said that...."

"Miss Bingley? Do not give credence to anything that woman may have said!" Darcy said with a wave of his arm. "Her intentions could only have been malicious! Is that what this is about, then? Were it not for Bingley, I would have never met her, and now I wish I never had! The only woman I have ever cared for—will ever care for—is you! What must I do to settle this in your mind, Elizabeth? I adore you! I worship you! All that I have or ever may have is yours. You have reduced me to this; I am but a beggar at your feet. Let the world concern itself with our differences, but we must never speak of them again. We both know that you never threw yourself at me, but the other way around! Show me some mercy, I entreat you, and agree to be my wife!"

Elizabeth looked directly at Mr. Darcy. Her astonishment at the raw emotion of his outcry eliminated any consideration of a response, and she gaped at him, unblinking as his gaze bore through her, insisting on some reply. This moment of mutual staring lasted long, and Darcy, who had always prided himself in being under good regulation, began to realize what he had done. His mind told him that he had gone too far in pressing the matter, but his passionate heart was aflame with the need to have it resolved. H stepped closer to the woman who had captured him. "Please, Elizabeth." He reached out impulsively and touched her soft cheek.

"Fitzwilliam." Elizabeth did not realize she had breathed his name as she searched his eyes; the intensity that burned in them caused her to tremble and she finally looked away. "You wear me down sir. How am I to be sensible in the face of such persuasions? How am I to deny you anything?"

"I would not have you deny me." Darcy's fingers stroked downward lightly until he cupped one side of her face in his hand. She tipped her head slightly into the comforting warmth of his palm as he continued. "But neither do I wish you to bend to my will."

Elizabeth reached up and removed his hand from her cheek, although she did not release it but instead lowered it to where she could take it in both of hers. "That is very good, Mr. Darcy, for I am assured by my mother that I am willful, headstrong and stubborn to a fault. Did I mention obstinate? That too is numbered among my weaknesses. You could not force me."

"Oh, there you are wrong." Darcy said gruffly, drawing closer. "I could very well force you to accept me."

"I should very much like to know how." Elizabeth's full attention was on the masculine hand in her grasp.

"Do you not remember when I came to your bedchamber at Netherfield? We were alone for some time in your room and with you in your nightclothes too, with a closed door between the world and us. I believe I shall have compromised your reputation beyond repair—if word of our scandalous liaison were to get out. One word to your father and our fate would be sealed." This provoked such an expression of alarm in Elizabeth's countenance that he hastily added, "Do not worry—I have no intention of mentioning it, unless...."

"Unless what?" Elizabeth raised a brow.

"Unless Mr. Collins were to make known his own visit to your chambers and claim to have compromised you himself. His threat to do so, although not fulfilled, was made before the colonel could remove him from your chambers." Darcy shrugged. "Should that happen, then I would have to inform Mr. Collins that I compromised you *first*!"

"Oh, dear heavens, that must not happen!" Elizabeth cried with mortification. "I was very nearly unconscious—I had no say in who came into the room!"

"That is not entirely true," Darcy replied. "I came to your bedside because you called for me."

"I do not remember calling for you." Elizabeth retorted. "Much of those first days are not clear."

"I shall enlighten you at once. You called for me, and I came to you. Now you are compromised, and I must marry you immediately." Darcy said drily, although a slight grin tugged at his lips on one side.

Elizabeth perceived that he was teasing her and airily replied in kind, "I liked it far better when you were waiting for my answer!"

"I wait still." Darcy said softly, returning his hand to her face. "In truth, I will wait until you will have me. I am spoilt for anyone but you now, for my own heart, I know, to be as constant as the sun. Once I have given it, it will not be moved. Though heaven and earth fall away, I will be true. I do not care that you have no great fortune or any high connections. I love you and none else. You promised me once that I was safe—that you could not steal away my Apollo, but I was never once safe after I met you, for it is my heart you have stolen. You have bewitched me, Elizabeth, and I am yours forever."

"That is not fair—you have used my words against me!" Elizabeth said half laughing as she boldly looked into his eyes, astonished to find herself unable to look away once they had met.

"And pretty words they are indeed. I well know the effect they had upon me." Darcy replied with a cheeky, dimpled grin. "Will you say yes now? I see the answer in your eyes already, dear one, but I must have it upon your lips to be content."

"Oh." Elizabeth colored. "My lips?"

"You torment me! It is just one word, Elizabeth. I am beginning to wonder at this obstinacy you are accused of. I think it might be epic."

"Oh." Elizabeth murmured defensively. "I am not so *very* obstinate. Willful, perhaps,...."

Darcy could bear it no longer, and he leaned forward and silenced her ramblings by taking her lips with his own, gently and chastely. It was so quick that Elizabeth barely had time to gasp before he broke away. "Yes," he prompted, "the word is yes. I must have it." He leaned in as if to kiss her again.

"Mr. Darcy!" Elizabeth cried softly.

"Fitzwilliam," he corrected her, his lips a whisper away from hers. "Say yes, Elizabeth."

"I cannot think." Elizabeth breathed.

"Do not try." He nuzzled the side of her face. "Say yes."

"I will be compromised. This is not proper." Elizabeth shut her eyes against the sight of him and found herself overwhelmed instead by his scent and his nearness.

"You are already compromised, my dear. This time there is no fever to steal it from your memory. If you love me as you said before, say yes to me now."

"You are incorrigible," Elizabeth accused, weakening.

"I am not, but I could be if you wish it." His lips brushed her cheek. "Say yes."

"Is this how you will win all of our arguments when we are married?" Elizabeth challenged.

"When we are married?" Darcy ceased his administrations and sat back, his eyebrows raised expectantly.

"Yes." Elizabeth replied sweetly and echoed it with another, resounding 'Yes.'

At this moment, Darcy's joy could not be concealed from anyone, and he leapt from his chair, pulling Elizabeth to her feet as well. He placed his hands on her shoulders and slid them down her arms to take her hands up in his. He raised them to his lips and pressed several kisses on the back of them, squeezing them lightly. "Elizabeth, how I have dreamt of this day! I will make you very happy. I vow it to be so, for you have this moment delivered me to the very pinnacle of happiness myself! The sun has come out for me!" He kissed her hands again but then grimaced. "I must speak to your father." He blanched. "What if he denies me consent? In the eyes of Mr. Bennet, am I good enough for you, Elizabeth?"

"I suppose you must find out, Fitzwilliam. He is in his study. Do not concern yourself overmuch; he is not so obstinate as I, but he has been less predictable of late. I think you have some courage and some audacity, which he will enjoy very much—let him see it. If he believes you will entertain him as a son-in-law, you may stand a chance!" Elizabeth smiled in delight at the prospect of Mr. Darcy approaching her father to ask for her hand.

"Fine words of encouragement these are." He feigned a frown but then brightened. "If he will have Bingley as a son, perhaps he is not such a terror as I thought. I will go, my future wife, and face your father. Now that I consider it, persuading you was more difficult than your father ever may be!"

"I recommend that you not attempt to convince him with a kiss as you did with me. He would not like it!" Elizabeth giggled daintily as she opened the door to allow Mr. Darcy passage to the hallway.

Chapter Fifty-Three

TERMS OF ENGAGEMENT

Darcy had not ventured far past Elizabeth before she called him back. She pressed her crumpled, slightly damp handkerchief into his hand. "Mr. Darcy," she said when he raised his eyes questioningly to hers, "please take this with you. It is the work of my own hands, as you know, but I think it will give you courage! When my father scowls at you, or smirks, or however he attempts to disarm you, you may think of it and know that I sent you into the lion's den bearing this token of my ... regard for you."

"Regard?" Darcy repeated as he smoothed the handkerchief out in his hand.

"Yes. It is a token of my ... affection for you." Elizabeth colored at her boldness.

"Affection?" He carefully folded and tucked it in the inside pocket of his waistcoat. He looked at her expectantly. "It is much more than that to me, dearest Elizabeth. It is an emblem of our certain future; I heartily believe it to be so! Can you not see? The design unconsciously wrought by your hand shall be consciously fulfilled by mine. Regard and affection you say on your part, but for mine, it is a token of love and our future felicity in marriage!"

"That was a sweet speech, Mr. Darcy." Elizabeth smiled at him tenderly. "With such sentiments as these on your part, I may never desire the handkerchief returned, but insist that you keep it always as a token of my love, forever tucked away in the pocket nearest your heart."

Darcy laid his hand over his chest where the handkerchief was concealed. He bowed to Elizabeth, a small smile gracing his lips as he turned and walked quickly down the hall to the door of Mr. Bennet's study. His firm knocking on the door echoed slightly, and Elizabeth could hear her father's deep voice as he bid Mr. Darcy enter. From where she stood, she watched as Mr. Darcy gave a little tug at his cravat before he disappeared from her sight.

❧

Mr. Bennet's invitation to Darcy to enter was spoken with civility, although it lacked the usual warmth of the patriarch. This formality did nothing to dissuade Darcy from his errand, and he stood before his intended's father quite unaffected by the tone directed at him.

"I wonder, Mr. Darcy, if your purpose in coming here is to inform me of some other scoundrel from the militia who should be avoided by my daughters as it was the last time. That was good of you to warn me about Wickham, although he very nearly ruined my Lydia anyway! Does Denny or Carter now have some design on one of my daughters, eh?" Mr. Bennet looked over the top of his glasses at Darcy and raised his brows in a silent challenge.

"No, Mr. Bennet, the man with a design on one of your daughters is standing before you." Darcy replied cautiously.

"Oh ho! Mrs. Bennet was right about you! My own dear wife was here in my study but five minutes ago, telling me to prepare for your approach. I will spare you from hearing what she said, but suffice it to say that I shall never hear the end of this, not until I am cold in my grave." Mr. Bennet grumbled slightly. "She will crow about it endlessly and...," he trailed off and sat back in his chair, looking up at the tall, proud Darcy, who stood before him. "Port, Mr. Darcy?"

"None for me, sir, but I would not presume to suspend any pleasure of yours. Please yourself, I pray you."

Mr. Bennet stood and poured himself a glass, pouring one for Darcy too, despite the fact that Darcy had declined. "In case you change your mind," he said as he moved the cup six inches closer to Darcy. "Let us hear about this design of yours."

"Mr. Bennet, I have asked Miss Elizabeth to be my wife, and she has agreed. I am here to obtain your consent to wed your daughter."

"She has no dowry to speak of, Mr. Darcy, nothing to tempt a man such as you." Mr. Bennet said, as though this response dismissed the topic entirely.

"Of this, I have long been aware." Darcy replied, "I assure you that I have sufficient income to support your daughter with ease and will grant her a generous allowance in lieu of the proceeds from a dowry as a term of the marriage settlement. You need not fear for her comfort or protection; I am well able to provide both."

"I do not doubt this." Mr. Bennet nodded, "My greatest concerns are not strictly monetary. Elizabeth is a country maiden. She has spent almost no time in town, has rarely traveled any distance from Hertfordshire, and has been raised in a society that is confined and unvarying. Should she marry you, the expectations of society in the first circles will create some great pressures, I think."

"I am certain she will adapt," Darcy said brusquely. "Miss Elizabeth always behaves impeccably in company. Her comportment will draw no undue attention, I assure you."

"The wife of Mr. Darcy will most certainly draw attention." Mr. Bennet said. "Elizabeth should taste the life she has agreed to before she is committed to it through sacred vows, uttered before both God and man. I would not have her jilt you, but neither would I have her enter into such a married state as you offer blindly, not when the lifelong happiness of a most beloved daughter is at stake."

"What do you propose? How is this understanding to be gained?" Darcy gritted his teeth. "Are you denying your consent?"

"Calm yourself, Mr. Darcy! I grant my consent, of course I do, but I must impose conditions." Mr. Bennet poured himself some more port.

Darcy exhaled loudly and pressed his hand over his heart-pocket before proceeding. "Name your conditions, sir."

Mr. Bennet nodded. "After Jane's wedding, Elizabeth will return with her aunt and uncle to London and spend one season in town. There, she shall attend balls and soirees as arranged by her aunt and uncle. I advise you to arrange for invitations from those of your circle, as well, if you are serious about introducing her to that society. If she still desires to marry you at the end of the season in June, the wedding may proceed with no further impediment."

"Why such a delay?" Darcy demanded. "If it is a merely a London season you wish for her, she may spend the season in far better style as a married woman than as an engaged one. What you ask is unreasonable, sir. An engagement of six weeks would suffice, but six months? This cannot be justified as a rational course, Mr. Bennet. It is unwise."

"You claim your own course is rational, Mr. Darcy, yet you fail to see the folly in it. I could not bear to see Elizabeth caught in a marriage where she was unhappy. Your ability to support her—even, I daresay, provide her with a life far above the one to which she was born is not in question. Her contentment in the world to which she would be relegated, however, is not so certain."

"I will devote myself to her happiness; of this you may be assured." Darcy said stiffly.

"I can well believe it of you, but I must insist. There is one additional aspect of this condition we have not yet discussed, and that is the matter of secrecy."

"Our engagement will be publicly acknowledged, on this point I will not bend."

"We are in agreement on that point, at least. I would not condone a secret engagement. She will be introduced into society as your betrothed—no one in society will know that it is conditional upon her desire following the season ... not even, Elizabeth."

"You would require me to keep the nature of your consent a secret from her? Such a beginning cannot be wise, Mr. Bennet." Darcy objected. "I wish for our marriage to be laid in a foundation of mutual trust. To withhold this information is a betrayal from the very start. Can I not persuade you against the condition? I will agree to withhold the disclosure of this stipulation from the ears of the world, but Elizabeth, at least, should know of it."

"I would not burden her enjoyment of the season with the weight of such a decision. I am resolved that she is not to know and insist on your cooperation in this. In June, I will visit with her, and if she is content to move forward, you may proceed with whatever haste you deem appropriate. If, however, she harbors doubts—as she well may, they must be resolved or my consent shall be withdrawn."

"Mr. Bennet, this is most irregular!" Darcy said with a frown and began pacing the small expanse of floor available. "I mean no disrespect, sir, but I must inquire as to your reasoning. You will allow Bingley to marry Miss Bennet nearly the very moment the reading of the banns is complete, yet you impose this unhappy wait on us? It is unjust, sir, to treat your daughters so differently!"

"The justice of my decision is not open for debate, nor is it subject to negotiation. My mind is made up." Mr. Bennet raised a brow at Mr. Darcy, as if daring him to object further. "Elizabeth shall have a season."

"I might point out, sir, that the primary motive for a young lady to have a season in London is to secure a match from among the eligible bachelors present." Darcy stopped his incessant march to and fro across the study and glared at Mr. Bennet. "This motive can no longer apply to Miss Elizabeth upon her engagement to me!"

Mr. Bennet peered at Darcy over his glasses. "Perhaps not." He removed his glasses and set them on the desk. "Of course, you realize that the season consists of more than this. London is a source of extraordinary diversions. With the theater and opera, in addition to the balls and opportunities to dine, any young person would desire the chance to partake of these delights before they settled into married life, but this is not the reason I insist on this. It is the society that concerns me. Mr. Darcy, I understand that you have personally gained a degree of favor in the *ton*, a position that is highly envied by some whose status is above even your own. The expectations imposed on one who moves in those circles are nearly tyrannical when compared to what Elizabeth has experienced in Hertfordshire. Surely you realize that she will never be accepted of her own accord in that society. Her manners will matter not. With no dowry or so much as one worthy connection to her name, she will be ostracized by those who will see an alliance with you as ascension to a higher sphere than that to which she was born. She must see that sphere for what it is."

Darcy replied softly. "Mr. Bennet, we would spend the majority of the year at Pemberley, not in London. Her association with that society will be insignificant."

"Can you deny that she will encounter scorn among those in your circle? From the mothers who have pined to call you their own son to their daughters who have preened and primped for your benefit? Elizabeth will be the one who dashed their dearest hopes, which will not endear her among them, you may be sure! In the event of a hasty marriage, there will forever be whispers of scandal, rumors that my daughter used her feminine wiles to capture you! No, I could not bear for her name to be so tainted. Although it be false, it will not matter." Mr. Bennet replaced his glasses. "A season will reveal to her the nature of her anticipated associations. She may then make an informed decision."

Darcy sighed, concern creasing his brow. "You do not think she will be happy in such a marriage as I offer?"

"Elizabeth is accustomed to being *liked* Mr. Darcy. Indeed, in Hertfordshire she is admired and respected wherever she goes. While she may display a remarkable resiliency in the face of intimidation, to be slighted is another matter entirely, particularly if the insult is undeserved. It is your good fortune that you never gave her offense—she may have never overcome it."

"Of course she is liked. Who upon knowing her could withhold their good opinion?" Darcy smiled at the thought of his own determination to resist her charms. "She shall be a triumph in London, Mr. Bennet, of that you may be certain." Darcy smiled at the father of his bride-to-be. "It is said that a June wedding is fortuitous, smiled on by the mythical goddess of marriage, Juno. Of course, I am no worshiper of the Roman gods—merely a student of the legends. It is but a small consolation; however, I shall console myself with the idea. We shall marry in June, upon the satisfaction of your condition. I must however, insist on a condition of my own."

"Do you?" Mr. Bennet's brows shot up in surprise. "What would that be?"

"While her wit and vivacity will shine as brilliantly as any among the *ton,* her wardrobe is dreadfully lacking for such a venture as you prescribe. If my intended is to be paraded before *le bon ton,* I insist that she be attired in clothing befitting her station as my betrothed. Consider it as her armor against the arrows of the opposition. I shall provide *you* the funds to do it. In this way, there is no question of the propriety of her outfitting, as it shall be her father who pays for her fashionable purchases in the eyes of the world."

"Mr. Darcy, I ..." Mr. Bennet spluttered.

"I know—she will not like it, particularly as she will believe it is through your sacrifice that she is extravagantly clothed," Darcy acknowledged grimly. "But, it cannot be helped. Her introduction to that society will be measured in large part by first impressions. You, sir, are an observer of persons—surely you cannot doubt the truth in what I say. Miss Elizabeth will find no possibility of acceptance in those elite circles unless she is presented as an equal. By your decree, she is to decide whether she can be happy in those circumstances. Dressed as a country maid, she will certainly be rejected before they can truly know her. Dressed as their equal in wealth and circumstance, her natural graciousness and charm will sweep her into the very bosom of that society without impediment. If she decides against it then, at least I shall have the satisfaction of knowing that it was not simply for want of a suitable frock."

"Mr. Darcy, I have five daughters. I can hardly dress Lizzy as a peacock while the others are as drab as peahens. My wife...."

"I suppose such a disparity would hardly inspire sisterly affection." Darcy pondered. "I shall include sufficient funds that your other daughters and even your wife may find additional fabrics and ribbons and lace at their disposal. This will have to suffice, as any more would raise suspicion as to the source."

"I do not know how you did it," Mr. Bennet muttered, glaring with some resentment at Mr. Darcy. "I had devised a plan that would expose the folly of this match to Lizzy, and now I am astonished, sir, to find that due to your designs on her, I shall be obliged to endure the subject of *lace* in perpetuity instead. This is a cruel blow to my peace of mind, but I suppose I must endure it, as I have no means of escape other than the closed door of this study."

Mr. Darcy extended his hand to Mr. Bennet, who reluctantly grasped it, and they agreed to the terms with a handshake first, but then Mr. Bennet presented Mr. Darcy with the cup of port that had been poured earlier, but which had gone untouched until then. Darcy nodded, and the two men raised their cups and downed the port to seal their contract. Upon the completion of this rite, Mr. Bennet set his cup heavily on the desk and spoke grimly. "On your way out, please send Lizzy in to see me, Mr. Darcy. I wish to speak with my daughter."

❧

Mr. Darcy's exit from the study was an event of which the entire household was aware. Elizabeth stood just outside the door, anxiously waiting Mr. Darcy's return from her father's den. Her mother had joined her in the hallway shortly after Darcy had entered, and within a few short minutes, the assembly included the remainder of her sisters, Mr. and Mrs. Hill, the cook and the lady's maid.

Upon his entrance into the hall, he exclaimed, "I had not expected to run the gauntlet today. Visiting Mr. Bennet was quite enough!" This declaration dispersed the occupants of the crowded hallway, except for Elizabeth and Mrs. Bennet. "Miss Elizabeth, your father has requested your presence in his study." He bowed to her slightly as she searched his face for some indication of his success, but, instead, she encountered a look of firm resolve not to give his emotion away.

Elizabeth's eyes danced at the challenge of discerning. "Mr. Darcy, my father has requested my presence, and I will go to him, but I must know—do I go to him as one engaged, or shall I face him with disappointed hopes?" She tilted her head and arched a brow, her lips pursed in expectation of the answer.

"You are engaged," Darcy nodded, as Mrs. Bennet gave a little shriek and ran into the drawing room.

Elizabeth and Darcy could hear her announcing their news to her sisters, and Elizabeth smiled indulgently down the hallway in the direction of the drawing room before she turned her countenance, her eyes lit with delight, on Mr. Darcy. "That is very good news."

Darcy's expression thawed at the evidence of his beloved's pleasure in her circumstance and a gentle smile crossed his lips. It was with this impression that Elizabeth turned and made her way to her father's study.

৵

Elizabeth had suspected that her father did not look on a match with Mr. Darcy favorably, an attitude that she failed to understand, so the frown that creased his brow when she next encountered him was no source of astonishment. Yet she found herself inexplicably saddened by this proof of his displeasure in her engagement. In the face of the intimidating prospect of the interview with her father, she braced herself and raised her chin in what he would recognize as a distinctly defiant attitude.

"Elizabeth, are you out of your mind to be accepting this man?" Mr. Bennet began. "He is rich, to be sure, and although your mother has most efficiently driven the importance of wealth into all of my daughter's heads, I have always believed you to have more sense than the other four put together. It is too hard, too hard by far, for me to see you, my dearest Lizzy, subjected to a marriage where you cannot be happy. How has this happened? Has he imposed himself on you?"

"Father, you are mistaken. I never thought that Mr. Darcy would consider one such as me for a wife, so I have not been open in the least about my feelings for him, but I am far from indifferent to him. You need not fear that I might be unhappy with him. He is not what I thought him to be in the beginning. I thought him too proud then, but I was wrong. Indeed, he is the best of men, and I anticipate that the sources of joy and consolation I shall find as his wife will bring me happiness of the deepest kind." Elizabeth smiled with sincerity that belied any concern on her part.

"Yes, I can easily believe that you will be a most amiable wife for any man, and I daresay there shall be no reason to repine regarding your marriage itself. It is the society you shall be forced to endure that I fear for you. You know that I do not enjoy going to London, but have you not ever wondered why?" Elizabeth shook her head. "It is because the so-called society in town is populated with the most vicious creatures that England can have ever seen. Men and women alike take great sport in reducing lovely maidens such as yourself to a point so low that many never recover. You witnessed for yourself the poisonous nature of Lady Catherine de Bourgh. Consider this. She has not lived in town for over twenty years. Her talons have not been sharpened and honed as they would have been had she constantly been in such company as you will face. These people will seek to destroy you, my Lizzy. Did you even consider this before you agreed to marry Mr. Darcy?"

"I did not." Elizabeth admitted slowly. "My considerations were centered on the implications for Mr. Darcy among those of his circle. As for my part, the sources of happiness that would stem from taking my place as his wife are considerable. I cannot see how the opinions of those so wholly unconnected to me would make any difference to my answer."

"Oh, you do not, not now, only because you speak of that of which you know nothing. You can have no understanding of the devastation their contempt could inflict on you. For this reason, although I have given my consent to Mr. Darcy, I have done so on the condition that you are to spend the upcoming season in London. It will give you experience, my dear, experience you will sorely need if you are to ascend to the position in society you will occupy as the wife of one who, I admit, is among the most illustrious men in the land. You have not been prepared for such a life. I never considered it possible, which I now realize was due to ignorance on my part." Mr. Bennet looked across the rim of his glasses. "One season cannot change that, but at least you will enter your marriage with a knowledge of what you face. Caroline Bingley's worst is nothing compared to what you will encounter among the *ton*."

"Father, you cannot mean what you say!" Elizabeth cried out defiantly. "I wish to marry Mr. Darcy as soon as it may be arranged. I love him, father; I love him ever so dearly! I have pondered deeply on the implications of our alliance, and it is he who shall make the greater sacrifice. How can we impose such a wait upon him? He will have duties to attend in Derbyshire."

"Lizzy, do not attempt to persuade me otherwise. I have informed Mr. Darcy that you shall spend the season in London, and he has agreed. Then you may marry—in June, if all goes well."

"Oh, Father, how can you vex us so? I am mortified!" Elizabeth covered her face with her hands, to cool her cheeks.

"You will see my dear—this course is for the best. You must trust me." Mr. Bennet walked to his daughter and embraced her. "The time will pass quickly, you may be assured of this. In any case, you may discover that the diversions and entertainments of London are greatly to your liking. Console yourself in this."

"My consolation, Father, is in knowing that at the end of it, I shall marry the best man I have ever known. I shall think of that before every ball, every theater engagement, every time I walk out—it shall be the joy of knowing it brings me a day closer to becoming Mrs. Darcy that will enable me to endure it. To this, I might add that I shall fare well in that society. You shall see. I will be content!"

❧

Upon quitting her father's study, Elizabeth went to the sitting room. Her mother and sisters were all in attendance, and upon her entrance, her siblings cried in unison, "Lizzy!"

Elizabeth felt the press of their presence immediately, as Lydia and Kitty leapt from their seats and ran to her, bouncing with excitement on their toes.

"Lizzy, Lizzy!" Lydia exclaimed with a quick glance over her shoulder at their mother, "I am to be your bridesmaid, am I not?"

"And I!" Kitty echoed.

"And we shall have new gowns—first for Jane's wedding, and then for yours! Oh, how very smart we shall be at all the balls and assemblies!" Lydia gushed.

"And new gloves, too." Kitty added. "And slippers, if Papa will buy them."

Mary stayed in her seat, watching the scene with a demure smile, as did Jane, who beamed at her sister from across the room.

"Of course, he shall buy you new things!" Mrs. Bennet's voice rang out over the hubbub. "What else is a wedding for, if not to be dressed in your finery?"

"A wedding is to enact the state of marriage," Mary intoned soberly. "It is the union of a man and woman in the sight of God, to bring forth children as the fulfillment of the commandment to multiply and replenish the earth. It is to provide companionship for the man and security and a home for the woman."

"That may well be," Lydia said with a giggle, "but there is no commandment that says I may not attend the wedding in a new and fashionable frock!"

Elizabeth glared in frustration at her youngest sister. "Lydia, do not count upon a new dress for my wedding soon, Papa has…"

As she was speaking, the door to the sitting room opened and Hill announced that Mr. Timmons had come to call. The ladies of the household, with knowing glances at Mary, hastily returned to their places upon the entry of Mr. Timmons, except for Elizabeth, who excused herself with some relief and slipped out of the room before Mrs. Bennet had launched into the pleasantries she loved to bestow on any suitor of a daughter.

Elizabeth raced to her bedchamber and retrieved the red shawl. It was far too elegant for everyday, but she swept it around her shoulders and ran in a less than ladylike manner down the stairs and out of the front door, her eyes searching the drive to the house. Seeing no one, she next ran to the gate and peered down the road, hoping to catch a glimpse of Mr. Darcy before he was out of sight.

It had been too long, she realized, as the lonely stretch of road before her bore no traveler, not on horseback or in a carriage. Disappointment overcame her in that moment, and she leaned wearily against the gate, closing her eyes in an attempt to conjure his face in her mind. She realized after a moment that she felt a presence there with her, and she opened her eyes to discover two large brown ones staring unblinking back at her from below. With a slight whine, Apollo thumped his tail on the ground as Elizabeth turned and looked around them before she crouched down and called the beast to her.

"Apollo! How I have missed you!" She crooned in his ear as she scratched the sensitive place beneath it and petted his head and chest. "How is it that you are alone yet again?"

"Stealing my dog's affections again, Elizabeth?" A soft, deep voice spoke from behind her, and she whirled around to find Darcy atop his mount looking down on her.

Elizabeth's eyes danced with delight. "I am trying," she said teasingly. "Without much success, I think, for Apollo is terribly attached to you. I am practicing all the same, however, for did you not beg me to bestow some head pats and ear scratches on *you?* I fear that you will find no satisfaction in my abilities—they were learned upon a dog and must be shamefully displeasing to you."

Darcy laughed heartily and dismounted. "You willfully misunderstand my meaning, but I shall forgive you for such infractions when we are wed," he said, approaching her. His eyes shifted to the cloth that was wrapped around her shoulders. The golden threads woven into the shawl glinted in the fading light, and he reached out, fingering the softness before his hand trailed down her arm. "It looks very fine upon you, as I knew it would."

Elizabeth colored but steadfastly looked into Darcy's face. "I intend to wear it whenever I am inclined to please its giver, which I expect to be often. I shall probably wear it out before six months are up!" Her lip quivered. "Six months! How are we to endure it?"

"Do not be troubled." Darcy's face had clouded with some emotion unfamiliar to Elizabeth. "I daresay that I have not courted you properly anyway, and I intend to do so now. The next six months shall be the sweetest you have ever known, although not better than what is to come after, I assure you. At the end of it, your father will be satisfied and we shall become husband and wife. Six months is nothing, dearest, not when we may anticipate a lifetime."

"Mr. Darcy," Elizabeth began, "I mean ... Fitzwilliam." She fidgeted. "There is so much I do not know about you. I should very much like to...," she looked into his eyes, and finding encouragement there, she continued. "That is, I was hoping ... thinking ... wondering ... well, as much as has been spoken of Pemberley, I have never seen it, and it is, after all, to be my home, and I shall be mistress in that house. I thought perchance that we might..." Darcy's eyebrows rose expectantly, prodding Elizabeth to complete her request. "I was hoping that we might visit Pemberley ... soon."

"Nothing would delight me more." Darcy said, beaming with pleasure. "We must discuss this with your father, for he has declared you must have a full London season. Perhaps at Easter, when springtime has at least touched the grounds, we could venture to visit there. You may have become bored with London by then anyway."

Elizabeth laughed. "I thought you preferred town!"

"I shall prefer wherever you may be found," Darcy said quietly. "I wish never to part from you. If you are in town, I shall seek every opportunity to remain in town. If you are in Hertfordshire, I shall follow you here and quarter with the militia, if need be. When we are married, I think we shall remain at Pemberley for the greater part of the year, if it suits you."

"I believe I would like that, and it will be far more practical than your following me everywhere like a lost puppy." Elizabeth's eyes shone as she tipped her face up to look into Darcy's, but a gust of wintery air caused her to shiver just then; the shawl was decorative and not designed for warmth.

Darcy raised his eyes to examine the deserted road. He gave a little tug on Romeo's reins, and the horse stepped forward, blocking both the wind and the view of the house. "Are you cold?"

Elizabeth nodded. "A little."

He instinctively stepped closer to her, setting his hands protectively on her arms. "You must return to the house, Elizabeth. You are recovering from your illness—a chill may cause a relapse."

One step forward, and Elizabeth had crossed the invisible line of separation dictated by all the conventions of propriety. She pulled the shawl snugly around her shoulders, her arms crossed over her chest in so doing. Darcy's hands naturally slid around to her back as she came into the warmth of his embrace. Both stood motionless, overwhelmed by the proximity to the other, and by reluctance to do or say anything that would break the spell of their nearness. With a sigh, Elizabeth rested her head against Darcy's chest, and his arms tightened around her in response.

"I am not cold now," Elizabeth whispered contentedly into the lapel of his greatcoat.

"No, nor I." Darcy replied with a quiet chuckle. "You astonish me at every turn. We cannot stand here like this forever, although I find myself tempted to attempt it."

"No, I suppose we cannot," Elizabeth said as she nestled her head more firmly against him.

Several minutes passed in silence before Romeo stamped his foot impatiently. Apollo whined, and the couple reluctantly stirred. Darcy relinquished his tight grip upon her and held her loosely instead. Elizabeth turned her face upward, and in an unexpectedly raspy voice uttered, "I shall return to the house now. Good-night, Fitzwilliam." She looked into his eyes and discovered them glittering back at her with such tenderness that she hesitated in breaking away from him but instead stared at the mesmerizing appearance of his face.

It was but an instant later that the tenderness that had illuminated his eyes captured her lips as he lowered his head and pressed his mouth urgently against hers. Elizabeth gasped at the sensations that exploded within her at this contact, and Darcy's arms tightened once more, pulling her into him as his kiss became raw and passionate. It lasted just half a minute, but when he released her, Elizabeth was wide-eyed, with cheeks that rivaled the reddest rose.

"Oh!" she exclaimed breathlessly, gaping at Mr. Darcy with some degree of shock. She shook her head slightly, as one does when waking up from a dream and then an enormous smile overtook her face—she could not have repressed it had she tried. "Oh!" she repeated. "That was ... lovely." She did not mention the warmth that had enveloped her entire being. She looked up at him shyly. "Do you think you could do that again?"

At this, Darcy laughed and complied with her request, this time finding Elizabeth's soft mouth eagerly responding beneath his lips. "I must go now," Darcy said resolutely when he finally broke away. He grasped her bare hand in his gloved one. "I believe you may be right, Elizabeth. Six months will be much to endure."

He mounted in an effortless motion and whistled softly to Apollo as he started off for Netherfield, glancing back to see Elizabeth making her way back to the house before he urged Romeo into a canter.

Chapter Fifty-Four

DREAMS COME TRUE

"Mr. Bennet, a word?" The door to the study squeaked as Mrs. Bennet pushed it open just far enough for her face to peer in at her husband.

A slight frown crossed the weary features of his face. "What now, Mrs. Bennet? Have you not enough lace to trim a wedding hat for the pig?"

Her face brightened. "Stuff and nonsense! Of lace, I believe we have sufficient, but there *is* something that we have need of. Should the wedding fall upon a day that is overcast, we shall need more wax candles. A dreary house on such a day would be insufferable, and tallow will not do! I know that we have exceeded the funds you extended for the wedding, but I assure you this is essential!"

"Another essential expense?" Mr. Bennet sighed. "It would seem that I am doomed to endure frivolity in the budget yet again, but I suppose our guests cannot eat their breakfast in the dark. Now go, before I regain my senses and revoke it all. Shut the door behind you—I am in dreadful need of some peace."

Mrs. Bennet departed with a satisfied air, and Mr. Bennet patted the pocket of his waistcoat, where a key to the lock on the study door provided no small degree of comfort and assurance that should he choose to exercise the option, he could secure a modicum of peace quite readily.

He could, from his reading chair, hear the decidedly boisterous voice of his wife calling out orders to various persons as she raced from one task to the next. Mrs. Bennet was a woman possessed of great energies, which she had faithfully devoted for the past several weeks to acquiring the finest of wedding clothes for Jane. Her attentions were now turned to planning the wedding breakfast and ensuring that Longbourn was in a state of spotless perfection to receive their wedding guests three days hence.

Kitty and Lydia, who had initially been delegated an excessive number of wedding chores by Mrs. Bennet, had appealed to Mr. Bennet for relief, which he had granted in the form of assignments of an academic nature. His two youngest daughters had thereafter devoted themselves with surprising steadiness to their education. Mr. Bennet harbored no delusions that this would continue after the wedding, but he was pleased for the time being at their compliance, particularly that of Lydia, who demonstrated far greater capacity and intellect than he had thought his youngest and silliest daughter capable of.

Mr. Bingley had become a fixture in the Bennet household, his amiable nature and cheerful countenance a dramatic foil to Mr. Bennet's ever more cantankerous demeanor. He was pleased to assist Lydia and Kitty with their studies and delighted, with Jane, to jointly chaperone Mary and Mr. Timmons in the sitting room, freeing Mrs. Bennet of the burdensome obligation.

Mr. Darcy had departed for London immediately upon the announcement of the engagement between himself and Elizabeth, with promises of returning in time for the marriage of Jane to Mr. Bingley. While this seemed hard to Elizabeth, she reluctantly reconciled herself to the separation and assisted, as her health and mother would allow, in the wedding preparations.

"Lizzy."

"Yes, Papa?" Elizabeth's head peered with some trepidation into her father's study. She had attempted to pass the door undetected so as not to excite his temper.

"The post has arrived, with yet *another* letter from Mr. Darcy! It appears that the man is remarkably fond of correspondence, judging from that which arrives daily." He nonchalantly tossed the letter onto the tray for outgoing post, although his indulgent smile revealed his growing approval due to the attentive nature of the man who aspired to be his future son-in-law.

"Thank you," Elizabeth picked the letter
her father had dropped it, her eyes scanning t
her name on its cover, only a second ahead o
that caressed it.

"For a man of so few words in compan
verbose with the pen." Mr. Bennet chuckled. "
seem to encourage all these letters flying bac
cannot be prevailed upon to return a letter at all ... it is a matter of great urgency, and, even then, I wait no less than a full fortnight as a matter of principle!"

Elizabeth wavered in the doorway, clearly eager to read her letter in privacy but loath to break away from a father who was suddenly witty rather than dour.

"You have come to depend on those letters, I do believe," Mr. Bennet observed. "It is a good thing that he is only in town and not off to the war like so many young men are today. I do not know what you would do then!"

"Papa…" Elizabeth smiled charmingly at her father.

"Go. Go and read your letter," he smiled indulgently. "And then perhaps you might be persuaded to rest. You seem not to have recovered fully…"

"Oh!" Mrs. Bennet said from behind Elizabeth. "Another letter from your Mr. Darcy! When is he to return, Lizzy? I have never heard of such a thing as his leaving so soon after your engagement. It is most vexing. His manners are…"

"He had matters to attend to that he could not postpone. He will be here in time to stand up with Mr. Bingley. Do not worry, Mama." Elizabeth smiled reassuringly at her mother as she opened the letter and scanned its contents. "He has called on Aunt and Uncle Gardiner to discuss my stay in London, and he is to help Uncle expand his trade connections! Oh, that will certainly put him in their favor!" She folded the letter against her mother's curious eyes as she moved down the hall toward the stairs. "Excuse me."

"Jane! Jane! He is here!" Kitty suddenly appeared in the hallway. "Where is Jane? Mr. Bingley has come!"

"Well," Mrs. Bennet sniffed at Elizabeth's rebuff before she allowed herself to be pleasantly distracted. "A person could nearly set the clock by Mr. Bingley. It will be no surprise to Jane that he is here, Kitty. Elizabeth, go up to her room and tell her to come down. I myself have no time for social calls and certainly shall not until after the wedding is over." She waved her hands around her head to emphasize how busy she was and turned toward the kitchen.

a." Elizabeth proceeded down the hallway. Hill had a beaming Mr. Bingley into the foyer as Elizabeth the corner to go up the stairs. Elizabeth stopped at the of the stairs in order to extend a brief greeting when the ouette of a taller man filled the entryway behind Mr. Bingley, arkening the foyer.

"I hope you do not mind, said Mr. Bingley with a grin as he gestured toward the man and a woman who had also stepped through the door. "I have brought some friends along today."

Elizabeth curtseyed and offered an uncharacteristically shy smile, lowered lashes and averted gaze. "Your friends are very welcome."

"Very welcome, indeed!" Darcy cried as he closed the distance, stopping short of embracing her.

Elizabeth took a step backward into the dimmer light of the hallway. "Do not doubt me! You *are* very welcome, sir, but I did not know you were coming!"

"Did you not receive my letter?" Darcy looked at the paper in her hand with raised brows.

"It only just arrived. I have not fully read it yet." Elizabeth moved aside, further into the shadows as Jane descended the stairs, and waited, with slight impatience as Jane greeted Mr. Darcy, Georgiana and Mr. Bingley. Elizabeth's eyes did not leave the face of Mr. Darcy—and his only left hers for a brief instant to acknowledge Jane's greeting.

Jane blinked, then smiled knowingly, and suggested that Mr. Bingley and Georgiana might find the comforts of the sitting room to their liking, adding that her sisters would be most delighted to learn of Georgiana's arrival. Elizabeth greeted Georgiana warmly, drawing her into the dimness of the hallway in order to do so. She smiled and nodded when Lydia and Kitty came to claim Miss Darcy, each taking one arm and linking it with her own.

"My sisters are excessively fond of Miss Darcy." Elizabeth said as she watched them escort Georgiana away. "They have missed her these past weeks since you went away."

"And she, them," Darcy replied with a nod, adding softly, "as did I, you."

"Were you able to conclude your business in town?" Elizabeth glanced fleetingly at Darcy and looked away.

"I was." Darcy nodded again.

"I am pleased to hear it." Elizabeth wandered to the foyer table and began straightening the dried lavender, herbs and greenery that Hill had placed in a vase, her back turned on Mr. Darcy in so doing, although the wintery light now fell upon her hair and neck as she fumbled with the arrangement.

"Please turn around," Darcy whispered.

Elizabeth froze at this request and then dropped her hands to her sides. "I was hoping that I would have recovered more fully before your return." From where he stood, Darcy could see that Elizabeth was trembling.

"I wish to look at you," Darcy replied gently. "For a fortnight, although it seemed a year, I have dreamt of your face, your voice and your laughter, keen to return to Hertfordshire and be near you. Do not deny me the sight of that which I have yearned for daily."

Elizabeth nodded and slowly turned. As the light fell across her face, Darcy understood her reluctance. The luster was gone from her complexion, and her eyes were cradled in skin so dark that it appeared bruised. "Oh, Elizabeth," he said softly, "this will not do." He reached for the anxious face before him and cupped her chin in his still-gloved hand, raising it gently upward. "I have brought fresh fruits and vegetables from the hothouses in London. I sent them into your mother's kitchen upon our arrival. I did this to surprise your family with delicacies not usually to be had in winter, but I am exceedingly pleased to know that they will serve to strengthen you … restore you."

Elizabeth raised her eyes to meet his directly and found that they shone with that same kindness and tenderness that she had known before his departure for London. "Thank you," she replied to his expectant gaze and added, "I enjoyed your letters very much, Mr. Darcy."

Darcy's hand fell away from Elizabeth's face, and with a disappointed sort of smile, he removed the gloves from his hands, and handed them to Hill, who had stood quietly by while holding Mr. Darcy's greatcoat and hat. Hill hung them and disappeared, leaving Elizabeth and Darcy alone in the entryway.

"Miss Bennet," Darcy said, one eye squinting slightly. "Would you be so kind as to show me to the parlor?"

"The parlor?" Elizabeth quizzed.

"Yes, I am informed that Longbourn has a parlor."

"Why, yes. It does." Elizabeth blinked and waved her upturned palm toward a doorway. "It is right here."

Darcy looked at her expectantly, so she led the way through the door. The room had been freshly decorated in preparation for the wedding day guests, and Darcy nodded appreciatively as he looked around the room. "This is a fine parlor," He finally said, his eyes scanning the ceiling.

"Mama would be pleased to hear your praise, Mr. Darcy." Elizabeth said, adding, "I am, however, certain it does not rival even the smallest rooms, nay, not even the closets of Pemberley."

"You are wrong," Darcy replied. "Quite wrong."

Elizabeth muttered something unintelligible as she ran her hand along the back of a chair, and Darcy continued. "Bingley personally informed me of the splendors of the Longbourn parlor. Indeed, he was in raptures over it and insisted that I experience the beauty of this room first hand as soon as possible."

Elizabeth looked around her in some disbelief. "The furnishings, sir, are older than I am."

"That well may be, but it has a certain country charm about it. The architecture is sound and versatile too. Look here," he waved toward a recessed area. "Bingley suggested that I would find this part of the room particularly exceptional."

"What? This?" Elizabeth walked to the place Darcy had indicated. "You have been sadly misinformed. There is nothing here but shelves with a few trinkets on them, sir,. nothing exceptional to impress or entertain."

"Ahem, I pray you will forgive me, but I beg to differ on that count," Darcy said with a grin.

"Upon my word, you are teasing me!" Elizabeth frowned slightly and folded her arms across her chest.

"I promise you, madam, I am not. The very spot upon which you stand shall prove to be a great source of delight." Darcy took a step toward her.

"How so, when you vex me with riddles?" Elizabeth's hands shifted to her hips.

"Well, this is a new Elizabeth! Your color has half-returned already!" Darcy observed. "But I do not intend to vex you, not at all."

"Then tell me what it is you find so compelling about this room that to see it, of all the other possibilities, was the first thing you desired on your return to Longbourn!" Elizabeth cried out in frustration.

"It is not exactly the room I desired, my love, but rather the excuse." Darcy said, glancing upward with a sideways tip of his head.

Elizabeth's eyes naturally followed, tipping her head backward to observe, with a small gasp, the mistletoe, hung with a red ribbon directly above her head. Her eyes widened, and then, looking directly at Darcy, she declared with a saucy grin, "Why, Fitzwilliam, you have resorted to trickery!"

"Perhaps." Darcy's face grew serious, and he took another step toward Elizabeth. "Does this trouble you? I do not wish to frighten you…"

"I am not frightened of you." Elizabeth raised her chin and laughed nervously. "I am merely impatient now for you to carry out your scheme, for now we are to the stuff of my dreams."

"Truly? Tell me of your dreams, Elizabeth." Having closed the distance between them, his face was near enough that she could feel the warmth of his breath on her cheek.

"Oh, they are clouded, hazy dreams, inspired, I think, by a sweet interlude on the road some two weeks past. In my dreams, there are a horse, and a dog, and you, of course…," Sudden color rushed to her cheeks. "Am I wanton to you now, dreaming of your kisses as though that is all there is in the world? One cannot help what one dreams…."

Darcy stopped her with a fingertip pressed to her lips. "My dearest, loveliest Elizabeth, I am delighted to discover that you have such dreams, although I assure you they cannot compare to mine. It occurs to me that this is most opportune, for I ascertain that it is now within my power to fulfill your dreams. Shall I do so?"

Elizabeth hesitated. "We are once again upon the very precipice of propriety, Fitzwilliam."

"True. However, we are engaged now, and that cheery sprig above you grants the gods of propriety some leniency. Will you indulge me this once?

Elizabeth nodded sweetly, which small encouragement led Darcy to capture her lips with his own. He held them as though they were a succulent fruit and he was a man parched. Lost in emotions he had grappled with but never faced, it was not until he felt her exhale and draw a new breath that he awoke from the spell cast in that moment. This ignited his passions anew, and he wrapped his arms around her, embracing her with all the longing and desire that had surged from the day he had fallen in love with her. His lips caressed her mouth tenderly and ardently before he reluctantly released her.

She stood before him serenely, eyes closed, head tipped to one side, a faint smile on her lips. Eventually, her eyes fluttered open and she looked at him with shining eyes. "You astonish me!" She said bluntly and added with great urgency, "We must convince my father that six months is far too long. We must!"

"Agreed, but we will do so after Jane's wedding when peace has been restored to the household." Darcy said. "I have brought a present for you, a token." He reached into the pocket of his waistcoat and retrieved a tiny, shining object. "This was my mother's ring, given to her by my grandfather upon her entrance into society." He held out the ring for Elizabeth to see. It was simple, with a few small gemstones set in a pattern of intertwining ivy. "I had it engraved for you." Darcy caught Elizabeth's hand and placed the ring into her palm.

"Oh, oh, oh!" Elizabeth cried out. "It is so beautiful! But I cannot take your mother's ring!"

"It is yours now." Darcy stated. "She would have wanted you to have it."

"But Georgiana!" Elizabeth protested.

"Shall have pieces of her own. Besides, the engraving would be highly inappropriate for a brother to present to a sister."

Elizabeth carefully inspected the inside of the ring, searching for the engraving, which she read aloud. "'Mon cœur est a vous' That is French! Give me a moment...," she pondered briefly and said. "My heart is yours?"

Darcy nodded, took the ring from Elizabeth, and slid it onto her finger. "If we are to endure a season in London before we wed, I wish you to always have this token with you, my sentiments wrapped around your finger to assure you of my love at every moment. My heart is indeed yours, Elizabeth."

&

The next day an express arrived at Longbourn for Mr. Bennet. The household had been assembled in the sitting room discussing the final preparations and wedding day schedule when Hill brought the delivery to Mr. Bennet.

"Who is it from, Mr. Bennet?" Mrs. Bennet attempted to peer over his shoulder.

Mr. Bennet raised the envelope aloft. "Mrs. Bennet, a man must be entitled to read his correspondence in privacy, particularly when it is undoubtedly regarding business affairs which you would find terribly dull compared to this business of marrying off your daughters."

"Yes," agreed Mrs. Bennet crossly, "your business affairs *are* exceedingly dull, and I must believe that you prefer it that way. Not that I blame you, of course, for you are a man, and have not a woman's fear of living in the hedgerows if we do not secure good husbands for the girls."

"You must give up this fantasy of the hedgerows, wife. Bingley will not put you out in the cold, even if Collins would." Mr. Bennet smirked.

"Do not *speak* that man's name in this house!" Mrs. Bennet railed. "Covetous, greedy, insufferable man. He is a hypocrite, that is what he is, and so is that Charlotte Lucas, if you ask me! I always saw through him, and I cannot bear the thought that such a man will someday be master of Longbourn. You must not die, dear; that is the only solution!"

"I think you must invent another plan, my dear. This one is decidedly flawed." Mr. Bennet said as he moved toward the door.

"Do hurry and read your letter, Mr. Bennet, for we will serve tea in half an hour. Mr. Darcy and his sister will be here, and he does seem to prefer your company to mine."

"That is nonsense—he prefers Lizzy's company to that of us all." This, Mr. Bennet said across his shoulder as he quit the room to peruse his letter in the seclusion of his study.

The Bennet household was the site of a merry dinner party that evening. In addition to Mr. Bingley, Mr. Darcy and Georgiana Darcy, the Gardiners had arrived to share in the wedding festivities, as had Colonel Fitzwilliam. Mr. Timmons, at the special request of Mary, had been invited to dinner, so the Gardiner children had eaten in the kitchen and been sent to bed before the dinner hour.

Mrs. Bennet had overtly seated three of her daughters beside the gentlemen whom they were engaged to or being courted by, and Colonel Fitzwilliam was seated between Kitty and Lydia, who were most pleased at this arrangement. In addition, the dark cloud, which had shadowed Mr. Bennet in recent weeks, had lifted, and he proved a remarkably jovial host, to the delight of his family and guests.

"Mrs. Bennet," he addressed his wife as the soup was served, "you have set a fine table this evening. In order that I may pace myself, I must inquire—how many courses are you to subject us to?"

"Pish, Mr. Bennet, you exaggerate! It is only two courses…plus dessert."

"Colonel, you must save room for the dessert." Lydia said as she fluttered her lashes with a coy smile.

"If it will ease your mind, Miss Lydia, I shall gladly guarantee that my appetite will not fail when the time comes to summon it." Colonel Fitzwilliam smiled. "Your mother, I recall, has a reputation when it comes to the confectionary excellence of her table."

"True!" Mr. Bennet interjected. "And she has kept our local merchants in great suspense of late, wondering when she will require more sugar. You are bound to be served something absurdly sweet."

"I am certain it will be wonderful." Mr. Bingley beamed.

"The soup is delicious, Fanny." Mr. Gardiner said to his sister. "What kind is it?"

"It is a soup recipe that has especially belonged to Longbourn house for generations but will die with this generation, for I swear I will not give it to the Collins'!" Mrs. Bennet spoke bitterly.

"Well, my dear, it is my pleasure to inform you that you need not assassinate the recipe after all." Mr. Bennet said mysteriously as all eyes turned to him.

"What a ridiculous notion." Mrs. Bennet said with a humph. "One cannot kill a recipe."

"You mistake me," Mr. Bennet said cheerfully. "What I meant to imply was simply that Longbourn shall not fall to the Collins'."

"What?" Mrs. Bennet cried out. "Whatever can you mean?"

"Be not alarmed. I have not discovered the secrets of immortality." Mr. Bennet smiled mischievously as he reached into a pocket and retrieved a paper with a flourish. He smiled in turn at each family member and guest, enjoying the rapt attention they had fixed on him, and then he unfolded the paper with some ceremony. He positioned his glasses on his nose and silently scanned through what was clearly a letter before he looked back up at his audience.

"I received this letter today from my solicitor in London," he began, giving the paper a shake for emphasis, "and it contains information that is astonishing, yet happy news."

"What news. Mr. Bennet?" Mrs. Bennet prodded. "Do not keep us in suspense!"

"You may recall that I sent an inquiry to my solicitor some weeks ago regarding what would occur in the event of Mr. Collins' demise, for at the time, his health was precarious."

"But. Papa, he is recovering now. His demise is not imminent." Elizabeth said gravely.

"His demise, as it turns out, is not our concern." Mr. Bennet said. "The solicitor, in researching the conditions of the entail along with Mr. Collins' claim to Longbourn, discovered something disturbing."

"Disturbing?" Mr. Gardiner glanced at his wife. "What did he discover?"

"Well, he looked at the Bennet ancestry and posterity for several generations, and he discovered something that I hardly find surprising, considering my own situation." He paused dramatically.

"The Bennet men rarely produce sons. It is true! Many daughters we have spawned, but sons? Sons are rare. It could be said that my very existence is a miracle."

"Perhaps this is the reason for the entail." Mr. Darcy suggested.

"Perhaps." Mr. Bennet acknowledged. "But what is certain, is that Mr. Collins is not the natural offspring of a Bennet or any past master of Longbourn. The solicitor checked the records three times, traveling to personally inspect every related document and record himself. Every fact supports it." At this pronouncement, he stopped speaking and waited for the reactions he knew would come. After nearly every person at the table had made some exclamation, he continued.

"My distant cousin married a woman who was widowed. She brought a son who was but a year old to the marriage. That son was adopted by my cousin and raised as his own son, presented to the world as his own. The deception was on the part of his father in making the claim that his son William was the legal heir should I not sire a son. Of course, had we been closer, such duplicity would not have been possible, but all attempts at so much as an introduction were rebuffed, likely in order to prevent the discovery of his fraud."

"Does Mr. Collins know?" Colonel Fitzwilliam inquired.

"The express rider was on his way to Lucas Lodge after his delivery to me, to notify him of the development. If he did not know before, he knows now." Mr. Bennet replied.

"What is the status of the entail? Who is the heir?" Mrs. Bennet demanded.

"Mr. Collins had renewed the entail; however, since he is not a legal heir, the renewal is invalid. The entail is broken." Mr. Bennet said with a smile. "My daughters may inherit."

"Praise the Lord!" Mrs. Bennet exclaimed. "We are saved, Mr. Bennet! We are saved!"

"Indeed we are." Mr. Bennet smiled at his wife. "Indeed we are."

Chapter Fifty-Five

THE FINAL CHAPTER, A NEW BEGINNING

"Wake up, Lizzy, wake up!" Lydia whispered loudly in her ear. "Mama is to call upon Lady Lucas, and we are to accompany her!" Lydia shook Elizabeth's shoulder. "Make haste! We are to go in fifteen minutes, no more!"

Elizabeth sat up in her bed, peering in the dim light at her sister. "What madness is this, Lydia? We cannot visit at such an hour!"

"It is not madness Lizzy! I do not know all the particulars, but I do know that Mama received a message from Lucas Lodge at dawn, bidding her to come and wait upon Lady Lucas as soon as may be. It is a matter of great urgency—do not subject me to an interrogation for that is all I know. Just rise and dress while I do the same. Certainly all will be revealed before the morning is done. Make haste!" Lydia pressed her hands down on the mattress and shook her sister's bed before she turned and ran from the room, pulling the counterpane off her sister as she did so.

Hill's best efforts could not put breakfast on the sideboard before the carriage came around for the ladies, so they quickly donned their warmest pelisses and mantles, departing without so much as a slice of toast or a sip of tea to begin their day. No sooner had the carriage passed through the gates than Elizabeth demanded an explanation of the outing from her mother.

Mrs. Bennet's lips pressed together and her eyebrows shot up. "Can you not imagine, Miss Lizzy? Lady Lucas has requested our presence the very morning after the news on the entail was delivered to her future son-in-law. His prospects are not so very bright now that Longbourn is no longer his inheritance. I cannot pretend to summon even one tear for that wretched man, Mr. Collins, but I most certainly have sympathy for Lady Lucas. To be forced to endure a connection to such an odious creature as that horrid parson is a sorry, sorry fate indeed. Doubtless they need our consolation."

"But he does have a living, Mama." Elizabeth said quietly. "That at least, is something."

"Ugh!" Lydia burst out. "To be forced to endure the marriage bed with him would be the sorriest fate of all! Poor Charlotte!"

"Lydia!" Elizabeth gasped. "You must not speak of such things!"

"La! Why ever not? The thought of so much as a kiss from that toad causes me to suffer goose flesh in the worst way. He disgusts me!" Lydia shivered.

"Then be grateful that he did not offer for you. Mama was quite enamored of the idea that he would marry one of us—had he offered for you, you well may have been forced to accept." Elizabeth looked at her mother expectantly.

"Now, Lizzy," Mrs. Bennet scolded, "you know that it was only when he was to inherit Longbourn that I thought him suitable. Besides, with Jane nearly wed, and you engaged to be so, Lydia shall become the most beautiful and eligible maiden in all of Hertfordshire. With your Darcy connections and Jane's place in society as Mrs. Bingley, Lydia could come out in a year's time. With her beauty and lively nature, she will undoubtedly attract a fine, rich husband."

"But Lydia is already out in society, Mama." Elizabeth objected, glancing with a frown at her sister, whose eyes gleamed with delight at the turn of the conversation.

"Ooooooo!" Lydia squealed. "And I shall have new gowns in the latest fashions from London—nothing made-over or turned!"

"Of course," Mrs. Bennet nodded as she looked out the window of the carriage. "And Lydia is *not* out, as you well know. Mr. Bennet declared her not to be so and will not allow it until she is at least seventeen." They were approaching Lucas Lodge, and she tsked impatiently at the sight of a large equipage in front of the house. "Who else would call at this hour, and with such horses as those?"

Elizabeth craned her neck to see past her mother. "Mama! That is the de Bourgh crest! Why would Lady Catherine call on the Lucases? What can it mean?"

"She is, after all, Mr. Collins' patroness." Mrs. Bennet reflected. "Perhaps the condescension he goes on about has extended to calling on him here, in Meryton. Could it be that she has come to wish him joy?"

"Upon my word, I do not believe *that* Mama. Lady Catherine would not suffer the expense and hardship of such a journey for so small a purpose. There must be some other reason. Perhaps this has something to do with our own summons here this morning."

The door to the carriage opened before Mrs. Bennet could reply, and the footman handed the Bennet ladies out of the coach. They were ushered into Lucas Lodge with no ceremony and led by the housekeeper to the drawing room, where the Lucases, the de Bourghs and Mr. Collins were already assembled. The sound of raised voices marked their approach, but once the door was opened and the Bennets were announced, silence hung in the air for a long, tense moment.

Elizabeth took in the scene with great curiosity. Lady Lucas sat beside a tea set, as stiff as a piece of stone. Charlotte appeared to have been crying but was now composed. Mr. Collins sat in the corner, his face flushed and his head hanging low—giving the appearance of a schoolboy being punished. Lady Catherine was enthroned in the center of the largest settee in the room, and Miss De Bourgh was seated with her companion on another settee nearby. Anne's face lit with what appeared to be relief when the Bennets entered the room, although she did not speak.

Mrs. Bennet froze in the doorway, as much a statue as her friend Lady Lucas. Lydia looked about the room and, seeing no sign of Mariah, muttered something about finding her friend and unabashedly walked away. Only Elizabeth seemed fully possessed of her wits. She gracefully walked until she stood directly in front of the dowager. She curtsied slightly with an amused smile upon her lips. "Good morning, Lady Catherine. It is indeed an unexpected pleasure to find you here. I hope your travels were pleasant."

Lady Catherine squinted at her. "Travels, Miss Bennet, are never pleasant, least of all in the winter months. If you traveled more, you would not say such things."

"Perhaps you are right." Elizabeth nodded graciously and turned to face Lady Lucas. "We came as quickly as we could. I trust you are well?"

Lady Lucas's eyes grew round and she nodded, casting a nervous look toward Lady Catherine. Mrs. Bennet grew suddenly animated and rushed to the side of her friend. "Yes, yes, we have come. What can we do for you, dearest? What is this matter of great urgency you have encountered, and what must we do to come to your aid?"

This drew a moan from Mr. Collins, a whimper from Charlotte, and a grunt from Lady Catherine. "There is nothing you need do, Mrs. Bennet. I have the situation well in hand now. I am here to retrieve Mr. Collins, whose absence has been most keenly felt by the parishioners at Hunsford. His return is long overdue, and I fear his neglect of his duty cannot be allowed to continue a moment longer."

"He has been ill!" Elizabeth came to his defense. "He could hardly return to Kent in the condition he was in. The journey itself could have killed him, and if it had not, he may well have brought the sickness with him and spread it about the countryside there."

As if to emphasize the seriousness of his condition, Mr. Collins sneezed.

Lady Catherine turned her eye upon him. "It was most irresponsible of you to tarry here. It displeases me that I was forced to intervene and put Anne's health at risk in doing so." She waved her hand toward her daughter. Mr. Collins gulped loudly.

"Your ladyship, it was the apothecary, Mr. Jones, who advised me to stay abed. Indeed, he forbade…"

Lady Catherine turned her head and squinted at Charlotte. "I suppose you nursed him." Charlotte nodded timidly. "Most irregular. The task should have fallen to his relations at the Bennet household." She looked directly at Elizabeth and raised an eyebrow.

"I do not see why that should be." Mrs. Bennet interrupted indignantly. "Elizabeth herself was taken with the fever, and the burden of her care fell to us. Charlotte is engaged to him, and as it turns out, we are not related to Mr. Collins after all, unless you count a relation by marriage, which I do not in this case. In fact…"

"Not related?" Lady Catherine's head pulled back in surprise. "Engaged to Miss Lucas?" A deep frown crossed her features. "Mr. Collins, you have handled your affairs here in Hertfordshire most clumsily, and your failure to notify me at once of these developments is alarming indeed." She scowled and puckered her face, tipping her head slightly before returning the focus of her frightening visage back to Mr. Collins. "Am I to understand that not only have you aligned yourself with a family of not even a small fortune, but that you are not the beneficiary of an entail on the Bennet estate after all?"

Collins shook his head as his face colored and beads of moisture formed on his brow. "I was deceived, your ladyship, by my father, into the belief that I was his natural son. It was discovered—by means not yet clear to me—that my true lineage differs from what I have known all my life and that a grievous wrong has been perpetrated by my parents. My father was always resentful that the lands and manor house at Longbourn had fallen to Mr. Bennet, and he insisted to the very day he passed from this mortal coil that justice would only be served when I ascended to take the place of Master at Longbourn upon Mr. Bennet's death. I am as shocked as you are."

"Have the facts of the claim against you been verified?" Lady Catherine challenged. "Is it certain?"

"The legal papers delivered to me by express courier yesterday are quite clear. My birth record names one John Sutton as my father. There is a death entry for him in the same parish mere weeks after I was born. The registry entry for my mother's marriage to Mr. Collins, the man I believed to be my natural father, was made well after my first year of life had passed. I never knew John Sutton or that I was christened William Sutton as an infant, although the remnant of this identity persists in my full name, which is William Sutton Collins. I was told that 'Sutton' was the surname of a grandfather, which is true enough, but I wonder if this did not make forging the name change on documents a simple task. It is perverse! The elder Mr. Collins treated me as a father ought to treat a son; I never had any reason to doubt that he was my true father, although in retrospect, his disappointment when my sisters were born was perhaps a hint of his motive and desire to produce a legitimate heir to Longbourn, although I never suspected the reason for his melancholy. I proclaim myself to be innocent of any intentional harm to the Bennets, quite the opposite in fact, for I intended to heal the breach through marriage, thus returning the inheritance to the family fold. It was only after I was twice refused that I sought to secure the hand of one who is more amiable by far—*and* in every way better suited to be my wife."

"Humph," sniffed Lady Catherine, her attention once again falling to Charlotte. "Does this lady still accept you, now that your fortunes have fallen? You owe her the chance to back out gracefully, since your situation in life is so decidedly beneath what it was when you offered for her. Can you even afford a marriage settlement now?"

Charlotte sat up straight in her chair and quietly spoke. "Jilt Mr. Collins? I would not do such a thing for all the world! His fortunes may have fallen, true, but the inheritance in question was always subject to the eventual death of Mr. Bennet—an event that will bring great sorrow to my dearest friends, and which I always hoped was many years in the future. My acceptance of Mr. Collins never had anything to do with his ties to Longbourn. He has the living at Hunsford, as you well know, and with the tithes and proceeds from the glebe, we shall have more than sufficient for our needs, regardless of any other income. I am resolved to proceed with the marriage. Nothing material has truly changed."

"Well, that's settled then. Mr. Collins, you are fortunate indeed to have chosen a woman who would not abandon you in the face of misfortune. You should marry as soon as it can be done. All this traveling back and forth will become tiresome ere long, and you cannot afford it." Lady Catherine looked bored and cast her eyes upon Elizabeth. "My business here in Hertfordshire is not yet concluded. There remains the matter of yet another untimely engagement that has transpired in my absence. Miss Bennet, it has come to my attention that you have attached yourself to my nephew. You cannot deny it—the announcement was published in the Morning Post, which you must have known could not escape my notice."

"I can think of no possible reason to deny it, your ladyship." Elizabeth said sweetly. "I am engaged to Mr. Darcy. It is, much to my happiness, a fact."

"It is a lie and an outrage! Mr. Darcy is engaged to *my daughter* through a decades old contract. A retraction of the error must be printed within the week. If it is skillfully worded, no lasting damage will have been done. I will see to the details myself."

"You should confer with your nephew before you publicly contradict him, your ladyship. I know him well enough to judge that he would be most displeased with the interference." Elizabeth pressed her lips together.

"Darcy displeased? He has no right to be so! He ought to have turned to *me* before he became entangled with such a family as this!" Lady Catherine looked scornfully at Mrs. Bennet. "I would have reminded him of his duty, the honor of the Darcy name, the high expectations of society and the debt of gratitude he owes. To fall so profoundly from that which is his birthright is an error I would never have ascribed to my nephew before this! It is plain that you are a Delilah come to ruin him! I shall not stand idly by while his eyes are closed to your true nature!"

"Nevertheless," Elizabeth said resentfully, "you must consult with him before you take any public action in this matter. To fail to do so would be unwise."

"I shall do no such thing! Why must I consult with him? I am as a mother to him, and have every right to act on his behalf!" Lady Catherine sputtered. "More of a mother than his own has been, for he knew her but a few years before she left him, while I have watched over him and seen to his interests in all the many years since that unfortunate day."

"Do not speak ill of Lady Anne!" Elizabeth fumed. "Your nephew has made his choice and his course is set. I shall be his wife, and I look forward with pleasure to the day when I shall be known to the world and to my husband as Mrs. Darcy, wife of Fitzwilliam Darcy, mistress of Pemberley and sister to Georgiana Darcy."

"You will destroy him!" Lady Catherine bellowed. "You are not fit to walk the halls of Pemberley, let alone be the mistress of that grand estate. To think that you would take the name that belonged to my sister, and which has been owed to my very own daughter from birth, is not to be borne! I shall have my nephew declared mad—unfit to govern his own affairs."

"You cannot be serious." Elizabeth laughed, mocking her gently. "Anyone can see that he is the sanest of men. Come, come, Lady Catherine, I do not wish to antagonize you, but I will never allow you to claim any authority over me, even when I am married to your nephew."

"Not over you, perhaps, but I am nearly my nephew's closest relation! It will not stand for him to defy his duty to his family with such an alliance as this! You, a ridiculous country maiden, have the pretension to aspire to a marriage that is far beyond your reach. No, Miss Bennet—this wedding must never happen."

"You know as well as I do that he cannot back out of the commitment now even if he so desired. To do so would bring unthinkable dishonor to your family. Just a moment ago *you* spoke of the importance of preserving that very honor. No, your ladyship, there is nothing to be done. You cannot undo what is already set in motion."

"That is not completely true," Lady Catherine said coldly. "My nephew may not honorably break the engagement, but you have more latitude than he."

"I have not the pleasure of understanding you," Elizabeth said calmly.

"You are clearly a lady of *some* intelligence," Lady Catherine replied. "Surely with such wit, you can ascertain my demand that you break the engagement immediately. Today is not too soon."

"You astonish me!" Elizabeth cried out. "I am not the sort of woman who would trifle with a man in such a manner. What you suggest is abhorrent to my character and to all my feelings."

"Set your feelings aside, child—they serve you ill in this case. You cannot have any idea of the obligations of the position of which you so lightly speak. It is impossible for you to comprehend the workings of the social sphere in which you will be required to circulate. They will reject you before you are even seen in their circle, simply for what you represent. You will be the contempt of the world!"

"This means nothing to me. The acceptance of a society who would reject me without just cause is of no interest to me. I am quite content in the society of Mr. Darcy, his immediate circle of friends and any other thinking persons who will fairly judge the situation for themselves."

"This engagement may well cause him to lose those very friends!" Lady Catherine pointed an accusatory finger at Elizabeth. "They will question his judgment and wonder at the soundness of his mind in making an alliance with one such as you—a wench of no consequence, no fortune, no family name or connections. They will believe that you have drawn him in with your arts and allurements! I am resolved to bring an end to this charade!"

"Your ladyship, I must inform you that although you bluster and insinuate evil against my character, you still have not the power to end anything," Elizabeth said, unperturbed.

"An astute observation, and unfortunately, true. That is why *you*, Miss Bennet, must break the engagement immediately and preserve my nephew's honor in so doing. Although it should not even be a consideration, I am more benevolent than you might suppose and not without sympathy or recognition of your sacrifice. In recompense for any inconvenience you might suffer, I will pay you handsomely to break with him. Tell him that you have made an error and that you cannot in good conscience marry him. Do this, and I will pay sufficient that your family will never want, your properties will once again prosper, your mother and sisters will be clothed in finery, and you will afford fine carriages and always have an abundance of tea and meat on the table. The funds will be paid as an annuity that would keep you in comfort even if you never marry. Name your price, and I will make the arrangements in London tomorrow."

"Elizabeth," Mrs. Bennet whispered beseechingly, "do not answer rashly. Now is not the time for your foolish, impetuous ways. For once, set aside your selfishness and think of your family instead! Consider what she offers. Think what it would mean to all of us. You will have other suitors…"

Elizabeth, ignoring her mother, raised herself to her full stature, and stood before Lady Catherine, her eyes coldly upon her betrothed's aunt. "Lady Catherine, I believe that in such a situation as this, many would be tempted to accept the generous terms you have offered, but I assure you that I am not so inclined. I am not moved by fortune, nor do I waver in the face of intimidation. My courage, madam, always rises against every such attempt, and it is strengthened by the tender feelings I hold for Mr. Darcy and by the anticipation of a joyous life together with him. I do not fear for the comfort of my family—I was raised in the household of a gentleman, and I assure you that Longbourn has sufficient resources to provide an adequate home and income for its dependents for many generations to come. Your wretched attempts to bribe me into rejecting Mr. Darcy are shameful—an act of deceit beneath your station. I shall not repeat them to any soul nor ever mention them again. May God forgive you for your sin, and I shall attempt do the same. Good day. Come, Mama, we must be on our way." Elizabeth bobbed a curtsey and spun on her heel, her mother scrambling out the door behind her.

"Not so hasty, if you please..." Lady Catherine's voice trailed after them, her sentence unfinished as Elizabeth pulled the door closed behind them.

෴

The day of Jane's wedding dawned cold and sunny. Mrs. Bennet was in an uproar from the moment she arose until they finally stood inside the church. Mr. Bennet set aside his bad temper, and Mary looked quite pretty in her new bridesmaid dress, a detail that was not lost on the parson, Mr. Timmons, when the party of Bennets entered the church that day. Kitty and Lydia were both pleased with the fine dresses with trimmings more handsome than any they had previously owned, and many in Meryton were surprised to note that the behavior of the three youngest Bennets was not silly at all on that day.

Elizabeth looked well, her bloom and health seeming to have returned quite suddenly in just a few days. The village gossip was that Mr. Darcy had paid for a city doctor to come to Meryton and cure her, but the Bennets were blissfully unaware of such things, as they were quite engaged in the wedding festivities. Only Elizabeth knew that her rally was the direct effect of the challenge from Lady Catherine.

Mr. Bingley cut a fine figure in a pale green suit, which suited his fair complexion nicely, while Mr. Darcy stood-up with him in a muted dark green ensemble. Jane's dress was a shimmering gown of silver-trimmed white, easily the finest gown anyone in Meryton could recall seeing in their village... at least that is what the Meryton ladies said to Mrs. Bennet.

The simple wedding ceremony was quickly performed. Only those with an observant, watchful eye noted the meaningful, bold glances Mr. Darcy directed toward Elizabeth Bennet during the Bingleys' vows or the rising color in Elizabeth's cheeks due to his silent attentions. The family and close friends who had attended the ceremony were met by a contingent from the village and some of the militia officers outside the church, all there to wish Mr. and Mrs. Bingley joy.

The wedding breakfast that day filled Mrs. Bennet with pride as her guests marveled that she had managed to procure fruits and vegetables out of season for the feast. The bride's cake was a beautiful, pristine white, and several of the guests, perhaps a bit tipsy from the wine, were thrilled to discover a certain alcove in the parlor that merited their attendance.

A number of prominent families from Meryton shared in the wedding breakfast festivities, including Charlotte Lucas and her parents. Notably absent was her fiancée, Mr. Collins, who, although he was widely known to be a relation of the Bennets, was reputed not to be welcome at their house. Few knew that he had been removed from the county two days previous by his patroness, the Right Honourable Lady Catherine de Bourgh. What was known by nearly all was that Charlotte was to marry Mr. Collins, the ceremony to be performed by Mr. Timmons in four weeks' time to allow for reading of the banns.

Kitty had finished packing her trunks before the day of the wedding had arrived, which completed her preparations to depart with Jane and Mr. Bingley on their honeymoon. She had been honored when Jane had invited her. The position of traveling companion to newlyweds was traditionally reserved for the unwed sister closest in age to the bride, but with Elizabeth scheduled to go to London, the fortunate opportunity had fallen to Kitty. The honeymoon party set out in two days' time for a leisurely three-month winter tour of the seaside resorts, including a brief visit to see Caroline and Annabelle Bingley on the Isle of Wight.

The day after the wedding, Mr. Bennet, who had always expected that Mary would remain at home and care for her parents in their old age, was surprised in his study by the approach of Mr. Timmons. The parson had come to seek permission to marry the third eldest of his daughters, a request which Mr. Bennet granted with only slight hesitation. Mrs. Bennet, listening at the keyhole, was obliged to suppress the squeal that threatened to expose her espionage. She raced to the kitchen where she exclaimed to the cook, "It is going exactly as I planned! Mary is to wed the parson! Oh, what distinction she will enjoy! Whoever would have thought that all her spouting of philosophy and verse would come to this? And Mr. Timmons! I do believe he is the most amiable and handsome parson in all of

Hertfordshire! Mary has done well, very well indeed!" Her cries of joy, overheard by everyone in the household, merely elicited indulgent smiles.

The wedding date for Mary and Mr. Timmons was set for six weeks from the day of their engagement. To their credit, Darcy and Elizabeth said nothing of the unfairness of this arrangement when compared to their own six-month engagement stipulated by Mr. Bennet, although the complaint most certainly crossed their minds.

In the days leading up to Jane's wedding, and for the week afterward while the Darcys remained at Netherfield, Lydia spent every spare moment with Georgiana Darcy. Some days, Georgiana was at Longbourn, others, Lydia spent at Netherfield, but the two girls were very nearly inseparable, although Colonel Fitzwilliam, who seemed to take great pleasure in their conversation, sometimes joined them in company. Lydia's liveliness emboldened Georgiana, suppressing the timidity that had overtaken her since the unfortunate incident at Ramsgate. In Lydia, Georgiana discovered bonds of friendship she had never before experienced. Lydia was terribly impressed by Georgiana's accomplishments and begged her tutelage on the piano, drawing and in speaking certain phrases in French—a game reinforced by the colonel's delighted laughter at Lydia's attempts at a French accent. The affinity that developed between the two girls came as a great surprise to those who knew them. Their temperaments were as opposite as two persons could be, and, yet, the combination appeared to bring out the best in both. To Georgiana was added a spark, while Lydia's impetuous and sometimes bawdy behavior was tempered by her desire for Georgiana to think well of her.

By the time the Darcys were bound to return to London, Georgiana had elicited a sworn promise from Lydia that she would join them there for a visit at a time yet to be determined by Darcy and Elizabeth. Until that time, the two promised to correspond faithfully by post.

The two girls dared not yet reveal their plot that in a years' time, when both were seventeen, they would persuade Elizabeth, who would then be Mrs. Darcy, to coordinate their coming out season together in London.

Aunt and Uncle Gardiner had come to Longbourn to attend the wedding of their eldest niece, Jane, with a planned stay of one week with the Bennets before returning to Gracechurch Street with their niece Elizabeth, who was to be their guest for the upcoming London season. During this time, the friendship between Mr. Darcy and

Edward Gardiner flourished, and to his great pleasure, Darcy discovered that Mr. Gardiner was both a sportsman and excellent company—a connection he not only could tolerate but would greatly enjoy.

The day finally came when Aunt and Uncle Gardiner, their four children, Elizabeth, Darcy and Georgiana set out at sunrise for London in a small convoy of carriages, with Darcy on horseback. They had not gone far before Georgiana dozed, laying her head on the shoulder of the woman who would be her sister. Elizabeth gazed out the window of the finely appointed Darcy carriage. The countryside was grey and dreary, with a light skiff of frost and snow trimming the earth and bare trees with a delicate white lace. She sighed at the thought of leaving her beloved home for so many months, although anticipating the upcoming season filled her with a deep longing for the time when she and Darcy would together call Pemberley home.

Pemberley. A shiver of anticipation shook her as she contemplated the upcoming sojourn to that place at Easter. Her pleasure, although grounded in thoughts of finally seeing the place where Darcy had been raised, and where her future as his wife would be spent, was not limited to this alone. No, she took guilty pleasure in knowing that she had diverted both Darcy and Colonel Fitzwilliam from their traditional Easter visit to Rosings Park. Darcy knew nothing of the confrontation his aunt had initiated, but Elizabeth sensed that Lady Catherine was not yet finished with what would be a concerted effort to undermine her place in Darcy's life, with her ultimate goal remaining to prevent their marriage from ever taking place.

As the hours of the journey passed, Elizabeth pondered upon the upcoming months and was filled with thoughts of initiative. She was freshly resolved to emerge from the season triumphant in every way. She would not only find acceptance among those of Mr. Darcy's sphere, but she would win their respect on her own terms. She would use whatever natural aptitudes she possessed and add to them through the cultivation of additional talents she deemed useful and advantageous in her quest. The plan pleased her, for she detested days spent in forced idleness. With no countryside to explore, she was certain to find great diversion in these pursuits. By the time they arrived at the outskirts of London, Elizabeth had devised the structure of her plan and formulated the design whereby she would be able to execute it without early detection, for she dearly hoped to please and surprise Darcy over the course of the upcoming months with ongoing discoveries of intellect and ability on her part. She was determined that he would not only be perceived as having made a wise choice for a bride, but that she might even inspire some envy among his peers on his great fortune in that regard.

Upon arrival at the Gardiner home on Gracechurch Street, Darcy stepped forward to assist his betrothed from the carriage. He expected to find her weary from the long ride but found, instead, the sparkling, intelligent eyes that had first intrigued him so many months ago, dancing with anticipation and excitement.

"Welcome to London, dearest," was all he could think to say as he was once again caught in the spell of her eyes. "Did you have a pleasant trip?"

Finis

ABOUT THE AUTHOR

Diana Oaks is a married mother and grandmother. She resides in Salt Lake City, Utah, where she 'tsks about the yard, putters about the house, and spends far too much time wishing she had a cook, a housekeeper and a maid. Born in the wrong era, the wrong class and the wrong country for such fantasies, she writes about them instead.

Email: Diana.J.Oaks@gmail.com

Blog: SunriseAtPemberley.blogspot.com

Made in the USA
Lexington, KY
25 May 2013